OPINION OF THE COURT

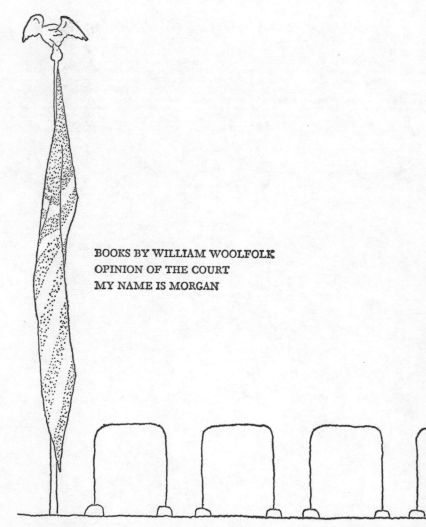

BOOKS BY WILLIAM WOOLFOLK
OPINION OF THE COURT
MY NAME IS MORGAN

William Woolfolk

OPINION OF THE COURT

DOUBLEDAY & COMPANY, INC.
GARDEN CITY, NEW YORK
1966

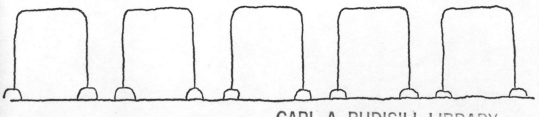

All of the characters in this book
are fictitious, and any resemblance
to actual persons, living or dead,
is purely coincidental.

For D.W.

with all my love

A man should share the action
and passion of his time at peril
of being judged not to have lived.

OLIVER WENDELL HOLMES

1

On October twelfth, his forty-sixth birthday, Paul Lincoln Lowe received a telephone call while he was having breakfast in his home.

Eleanor kept her hand over the mouthpiece. "It's Race Hardman, dear. He sounds upset."

Paul Lowe took the phone. "Hello, Race."

Race Hardman's high voice held an overtone of urgency: "Paul, the Supreme Court has just handed down a decision on that water dispute with Colorado."

"The decision went against us?"

"Six to three. Charles Edmunson wrote the opinion for the Court."

"Well, that means Colorado will go ahead with its hydroelectric project on the South Platte River."

"I'm worried about you, Paul. A thing like this can wreck a promising political career. And you haven't been governor a year yet."

"Eleven months and a week. But I'm not as worried about my political career, Race, as I am about our farmers and ranchers."

Paul Lowe thought of the patient brown men in overalls who tilled the black vegetable humus that lay several feet deep over the farmlands of Nebraska, and the men who tended herds of cattle that fed from its vast grassy plains. They needed water—the water from the South Platte that would now be diverted to the State of Colorado. Unless something were done, and done quickly, Nebraska might well become again the semiarid plain discovered by the first white man. Francisco Vásques de Coronado had needed water for only thirty Spanish horsemen and two Indian guides and did not have to reckon with the Supreme Court of the United States.

"What are you going to do about it, Paul?" Race Hardman asked.

Paul Lowe had thought about his answer a good many times. "Now we'll have to build that dam on the North Platte River. I'll go to see the President."

"When will you be coming to Washington?"

"I'll leave today. This morning. Will you set up an appointment with the President for me?"

"Sure. And can I make a suggestion? Charter a plane and fly it here yourself."

1

"Why?"

"It'll show the voters that you're going all out to remedy the situation."

"I'm not very good at making flamboyant gestures, Race."

"Paul, you've got to point out what a calamity this is for the State of Nebraska. That means you don't start with a routine flight to Washington for a routine meeting with the President. You don't go through ordinary channels; you set out to do battle with the enemy. You charter a plane and fly here wearing all your shining armor."

Paul Lowe chuckled. "All right. I'll do it your way."

"What time is it now?"

"Almost nine-thirty."

"It's ten-thirty here. Look, put it off until tomorrow morning. Then you can make the flight all in one day and I'll have time to alert the dear voters."

"How?"

"I'll put it in as a subhead to the Supreme Court's decision in tomorrow's papers. The headline will read something like this: 'Court Kayos Nebraska in Water Fight,' and then, 'Governor Lowe Flying to Washington for Dramatic Meeting with President.' How does that sound?"

"I can't wait to see how it all turns out," Paul Lowe said.

Balancing aloft between equidistant wings, Paul Lincoln Lowe glanced at the altimeter. Seven thousand two hundred feet. Not so high as Mahomet's coffin but beyond the reach of jurisprudence.

Below him, through the wide picture windows of his Beech Debonair, he made out the winding course of the Platte River—source of his woe. Someone plans a water control project at the boundary of two states and constitutional questions are raised. Hundreds of dry legal pages, ironically called briefs, precede the moment when nine robed men on the Supreme Court of the United States write the fate of a river into history.

Now the Decision was made—and Nebraska had lost.

Paul Lowe scanned his personal chart. He had made a straight course on the map, estimating the wind, working out a compass heading. *Howgozit.* A useful and descriptive name. Actually, the *Howgozit* was a graph that showed the miles flown on a horizontal coordinate and the fuel consumed on a vertical. A slanting black line indicated the planned fuel consumption and a red line showed the actual fuel consumption. In an instant he could read whether the red line of actual performance was better or worse than the black line of planned performance.

If one could graph the course of a life, what would his *Howgozit* say? Forty-six years old and by the usual measurements his red line was better than his black. He was governor of a state that was bounded on the north by South Dakota, on the east by Iowa and a corner of Missouri, on the south by Kansas, by Colorado on the south and west, and by Wyoming on the west. All of this great undulating plain that sloped gradually from the northwest to the southeast was under his personal dominion. Nebrath-ka—land of the shallow water.

2

The plane wing dipped over woods and fields. The river had disappeared. There were no landmarks. No matter where you were at any given point of your life, you needed something to steer by. He had planned this course, crystallized it in his mind's eye, drawn it on a map with small circles around the towns—checkpoints along the way. But nothing was sure, nothing predictable.

Below him, he saw the river Platte again, broad and comforting, rolling eastward to the Missouri. Woods and fields have little meaning to the airborne who must learn to disregard the earth's mere cosmetic, and watch for the pattern of permanent things such as rivers.

Before leaving he had called the Weather Bureau and its complex data replied CAVU—ceiling and visibility unlimited. At the airport he had filed a flight plan—North Platte Airport to National Airport, Washington, D.C. The Civil Aeronautics Administration was now aware that he had taken off, where he was going, and knew all the details of the proposed flight including the type of airplane, identification number and color, route, how much gas carried, estimated time of arrival. . . . He was expected, known; some part of the world was diverting its energies to the problem of him.

At four o'clock he received a Flash Advisory—thunderstorm along the route. He took down new route directions, altered course. Flying requires only the kind of intelligence a good bookkeeper has or a checkout clerk in a supermarket. You have to be accurate. But in a modern wilderness one could hardly get lost. In the most remote places there were lonely houses whose TV antennas pointed in the direction of the nearest city, groping toward the warm centers of life.

Within the hour he was flanking the line of a darkly powerful storm. He was borne upward in a river of air that rushed past, shaping and curving to the plane, a flow that sustained and suspended him in space. In the riveted and welded structure of aluminum, magnesium and alloy steel, he traveled along a highway in space. The plane had inherent stability, a delicious self-control that informed the machine to fly, to balance itself like a rolling ship at sea.

The machine's nerves lay exposed. They kept in touch with themselves, allowing him only to guess at their hidden intricacy. Airspeed indicator, magnetic compass, altimeter, complete engine gauge cluster, manifold pressure indicator, fuel pressure indicator, stall warning light, tachometer, generator switch, throttle control, starter switch, directional gyro, attitude gyro, turn-and-bank indicator, flap control and red and green light indicators, navigator light switch, turn control and elevator positioning, emergency switches, battery and generator, circuit breakers, cabin heat control and clock. The automatic pilot, final rebuke, consisted of two buttons and a small dial that replaced fallible men and kept the plane on altitude and on course.

He was passing to the right of the thunderstorm. Rain poured out of the sky in a black cascade. The doughty plane surged forward through tumulting air. If he flew below the storm he would encounter violent updrafts and downdrafts, heavy rain, hail and a possible lightning strike. So he climbed higher and kept to the right, the best direction to avoid head winds in the northern hemisphere. He looked for greenish or off-colored regions of sky—danger signs. That thin-looking part of the thundercloud might be a channel to safety on the other side but might also lead into a dead end with storm all around and closing in behind. The blackest part of the storm would be safe from lightning but would have dangerous vertical winds.

After a few tense minutes, the turbulence began to ease. He was skirting the storm. Nearing Chicago he tuned in the tower frequency and listened to communications with other aircraft, picking up what he needed to know about runways in use, barometric setting and direction.

At last he called Approach Control.

"Beech Debonair—number 137451, flying four thousand eight hundred feet, heading northwest. Approximately twenty-five miles from the airport. Coming in for landing. Call me back on 1220.3."

He flew into the city from the southeast, coming in over water. On the beam he brought the Debonair down on a long straight-in approach from altitude, holding a speed of one hundred thirty miles per hour and twelve hundred foot per minute descent. The lake front of the city loomed out of drizzle and fog, swelling in size like a picture painted on an expanding balloon. Then the plane was down, lightly, the wheels touching once before they began the run.

He stopped for coffee and a doughnut at the airport lunchroom. He wore a storm jacket over a ribbed heavy brown wool sweater, no tie, and corduroy trousers that bagged slightly at the knee. In the mirror above the counter he saw his reflection. In strange mirrors he always saw a stranger—a rugged-looking face with dry crinkles beginning in the skin, deeper at the eye corners, and shaggy eyebrows.

As the waitress poured fresh coffee into his cup from the large aluminum dispenser he glanced at his watch. Five-twenty. The plane should be gassed up by now, windows cleaned of insects, and ready to go. The last part of his journey to Washington would be in the dark.

At five-thirty the sun went down at his back while he flew up and out of the fading light. He leveled the Debonair off at five thousand feet to plot a course.

A few minutes later he settled back in his contour chair. The *Howgozit* caught his eye. Red line, black line. Would Washington look the same? He had not been there in many years.

There was haze over Baltimore as he began to let down for the airport. He called Approach Control for coverage and came in past the radiating light of the Washington Monument and racing black cars on the Memorial Parkway.

As the Debonair settled onto the runway, Paul Lowe saw sharply again an old never-forgotten vision: the rising formidable canyon rock just before the wing of the P-38 caught and spun him around and dropped him

4

sickeningly into a clearing. He could see that scene almost as clearly as he now saw the dark runway that was leading him to safety in Washington.

"Flight plan is closed," said a reassuring voice from the tower. "Welcome, Governor."

He was crossing the field on foot, carrying his valise, when several reporters came out to meet him.

"Right on time, Governor. How was the flight?"

Without breaking stride, "Fine. Good weather all the way."

"We understand you're in Washington to see the President. Trying to get approval for the North Platte dam."

"Yes, that's true. It's absolutely vital. The people of my state aren't going to have enough water."

"How did you feel about the Supreme Court decision, Governor? Justice Charles Edmunson wrote the opinion."

"I sometimes disagreed with him even when I was his law clerk," Paul Lowe said, smiling.

"Will you try to get the decision reversed?"

"There's no way to do that. The only appeal from the Supreme Court is to God." He put down his valise and waved. At the fence a tall man waved back. Race Hardman was carrying a tailored black overcoat, a bowler hat and light-colored gloves. "I'm sorry I have to break this up, gentlemen. I see my host."

"The Supreme Court's been under heavy fire lately, Governor. A lot of people say its power ought to be curbed. Do you go along with that?"

"No."

"The decision in favor of Colorado didn't change your mind?"

"Why should it? I've lost elections but I didn't lose my belief in the right of the people to vote."

"How about the people in your state? Are they angry?"

"Just thirsty," Paul Lowe said.

Amid the general laughter he picked up his valise and moved toward the fence.

"Hi, Paul," the tall man said.

"Hi, Race. I hope I didn't keep you waiting."

"Right on time. You might have been a scheduled airline." Race Hardman blinked magnified eyes behind thick eyeglasses. "The car is waiting."

"Mr. Hardman," a reporter began.

Race Hardman waved him away. "No questions. I have no comment on anything. Sorry, fellows."

A gunmetal-gray Bentley was at the curb outside the terminal building. The uniformed chauffeur held open the car door, tipped his visored cap, and Paul Lowe seated himself beside Race Hardman in the rear. The chauffeur took Paul Lowe's valise to stow into the trunk compartment.

Paul Lowe noticed Race Hardman staring at his jacket.

"It's all right. I brought a change of clothing."

"Good. Tonight's an important dinner. And tomorrow you have a date with the President."

Paul Lowe smiled. "I understand the President prefers informality."

"Of course he'd say so. He's a politician." The car got under way smoothly and soon they were on the Memorial Parkway that linked the airport with the city three miles away.

"I'm a politician, too, Race."

Race Hardman looked out the car window. "I don't consider you one. You're too intelligent. You don't fit the conception of the political animal—of whatever breed. But every now and again someone like you—for reasons I don't understand—wants to get down in the sandbox and play with the children. And every now and again, by some miracle, someone like you gets elected."

The car moved swiftly along the Potomac, past the waterfowl sanctuary and on to Columbia Island. Ahead was Memorial Bridge with those muscular bronze guardians on horseback. On the left was the Robert E. Lee mansion confronting Abe Lincoln in his memorial across the bridge. Old enemies linked by history—the universal solvent that reduces old feuds, old meanings, to footnotes.

"The way I look at it," Paul Lowe said amiably, "almost everything is politics. It's just the art of getting things done."

"The job you came here to do won't be easy. In fact, it's going to be damn near impossible."

"Do you think so? Why?"

"I don't like to be discouraging, Paul, but I can't see the President granting any federal money to build the North Platte dam. Not this year."

"Lamont Howard worked in the Agriculture Department before he became President. He knows how important this is."

"He's in the White House now, Paul. Things look different when you look around those eighteen acres and say to yourself, I'm the new proprietor."

"He's President of all fifty states. He can't ignore any of them, and I can prove to him how urgent the need is."

"One thing Lamont Howard knows, Paul, is how to weigh pressure."

"What has that got to do with it?"

"On your side what is there? You, a promising new Democratic governor with a bright future that may be ruined by the disaster that's struck your state. And then there's your two Senators, both Republicans. Lamont Howard knows they can't support him in return for anything he does about the North Platte dam. And there's me, with a chain of fourteen newspapers spread over eleven comparatively small Midwestern states, including two in Nebraska. That's about the size of the support for allocating federal money to build the North Platte dam."

"We should have started building that dam at least three years ago."

"But it didn't get started. And this year Lamont Howard is all out for economy. I happen to know he's sent the word out to put the lid on practically all multibillion-dollar public works projects—the kind that need federal money."

"He can't put the lid on what people have got to have."

6

"He can try—within limits. Lamont wants to balance the budget this year. He thinks economy is what most people want and he intends to put on a juggling act to impress them. He has the juggler's faith that he can pull it off."

"I hope you're wrong, Race, but you worry me. Your political instincts are better than mine."

"My instincts aren't political."

"What are they?"

"They're the instincts of every well-bred, upperclass, literate, Groton-and-Harvard educated young man who just happened to inherit twenty million dollars—and a family shield that says to love the people even as yourself."

The high-riding Bentley moved gingerly down a narrow tree-lined street and halted before a fine Georgian house. The Hardman home was one of the best of the hugely overpriced century-old brick houses in the Georgetown area. Somehow, despite all the money spent on it, the house retained individuality and charm.

Race Hardman got out while the chauffeur held the door. Paul Lowe followed.

"Come on in and I'll fix you a drink," Race said.

"I'm more interested in a bath and a change of clothing. What would Brenda say if she saw me like this?"

Race Hardman chuckled. "My wife thinks you're an original. Original people don't have to be correct. That's one of the chief advantages."

Paul Lowe followed him up the short walk to the stairs that led to the porch.

Race Hardman rang the antique bronze clapper on the door. A butler in formal livery answered.

"Mrs. Hardman is upstairs, sir—dressing for dinner."

"And the children?"

"Miss Elaine is having dinner in her room. Miss Juliet is dressing also."

Race Hardman turned to Paul Lowe. "Last chance. You want that drink?"

"That hot bath."

"Can this be the Paul Lowe I knew? All right, I'll show you to your room."

The room was rectangular, comfortable, deep-carpeted. There was a fireplace on the right side, and a deep-looking bed on the left. A reading light whitened the pillow. The coverlet was turned back. Directly ahead as they entered was a dark wooden desk flanked by two ornate hardbacked chairs.

"I thought you'd like this one," Race Hardman said. "It's nearer the staircase and we're just three doors down the hall."

"This is fine."

"Dinner at eight o'clock."

Paul Lowe nodded. When he was alone he tested the bed with one hand

—as springy as it looked. Currier and Ives originals pranced on the walls. He slipped out of his jacket and pulled the brown ribbed sweater over his head.

A discreet knock at the door. The butler entered and put the valise just inside.

"Would you care to have me unpack, sir?"

"No, thanks. I'll handle it."

"Shall I draw your bath?"

"I'll handle that too. Thanks, anyway."

The butler nodded and withdrew. He was a solemn man schooled in lack of expression.

In the steaming solace of his tub, islanded in a room of white tile, Paul Lowe saw mist gather on the mirror of the bathroom cabinet. He stretched out in the oval slightly cramped space and placed his feet firmly against the far end of the tub, enclosing the drain with turned-in toes. The bar of soap squeezed out of his hand and sank to the bottom in the vicinity of his left hip. He made a tentative attempt to recover it, abandoned the search and relaxed. He put his head back, slipping lower into warmth. No wonder the old Romans chose to die in their baths. Red ooze gently swelling from cut wrists. Soapy, slightly green water turning red, redder, reddest. His bony kneecaps protruded like twin Ararats above the flood. Thought floated. He shifted and the soap bar squished under his hip. He found it and began a slow-motion swab of his shoulders, along the extended clavicle, then to the wide chest with its dark and graying hairs floating in the stirred-up bath water.

What was his wife doing, he wondered—right this minute? Allowing for the time differential she would be eating dinner. Her handsome cold face, munching palely. One slightly overlapping tooth pushed out of her lip . . .

His foot accidentally dislodged the rubber stopper. The tub gurgled slowly. Warmth retreated down the slope of his chest to his navel.

Tomorrow he would see the President. This very corporal body would pass the sacred portals.

He stood up out of the dwindling pond. He rubbed himself dry with a rough-textured pale green bathtowel.

He felt ready for anything.

At precisely one minute before eight o'clock, through the windows of the drawing room, a Chrysler Imperial drew up before the Hardman mansion. Mr. and Mrs. Walter Schonberg emerged from cushioned privilege into a hard winter night. There was a biting wind. A deep maroon Cadillac slowly moving into position prodded the Imperial on its regal way. Senator and Mrs. Vance Murdoch and daughter emerged from the Cadillac. Then a black Chevrolet and, chattering and laughing, Peter Daris helped Laura Connell to the brick sidewalk. Laura was lovely, and Peter grayishly young and elegant.

Brenda Hardman was covertly watching through the window in the drawing room. Paul Lowe sensed her pleasure that Peter Daris and Laura

Connell would be among the first arrivals. The opening moments of a party are critical. If too many sober important people arrived together, a party might begin an irretrievable descent into collective weighty self-consciousness. Paul Lowe tugged at his tuxedo. The fit was impeccable but he felt awkward and out of place. No amount of combing could bring his sandy-looking hair into the casual order other men achieved. He cherished a suspicion, founded in full-length mirrors, that his barrel-shaped torso and slightly bowed legs offered a profound natural resistance to formal clothing. In the past ten minutes he had exhausted every possible use for his hands, which now dangled at his sides. He hoped to look more nonchalant than anthropoidal. At his best he sometimes managed to resemble an aging rodeo rider.

Mr. and Mrs. Walter Schonberg were inside the foyer and she was being relieved of her gray Persian. She made last-minute repairs in the gold-framed hall mirror and oh! how lovely, it's the Murdochs! While the ladies exchanged gaiety, the butler referred the gentlemen to a side table on which there was a seating chart of the dining room. Each gentleman was given a miniature white envelope bearing his name and inside the envelope would be a small white card with the name of the lady he would escort to dinner. On the reverse side, Paul Lowe remembered from the days of his youth—his social agony had been greater then—was a diagram of the dining room showing on which side of the table and how far down he would find places for himself and his partner.

Mr. and Mrs. Walter Schonberg entered the drawing room. Race and Brenda Hardman moved forward in greeting—the motion was warmth, was democracy in action. *Where the elite meet to eat*, Paul Lowe thought —the sign had been in a little lunchroom near the University of Nebraska.

Here they came.

Race Hardman said, "Mr. and Mrs. Schonberg, this is our guest of honor, Governor Paul Lowe of Nebraska."

"A great pleasure, Governor," said Mrs. Schonberg. She was a gray-haired lady who tinted her remaining black hairs, wore enormous pearls, and gave mightily to charity. Her blue dress was of a silken material that rustled as she moved.

Walter Schonberg shook hands. Soft but firm grip, befitting a man who had been Ambassador to India and director of three fairly large-sized banking concerns. He was small and rather plump in physical appearance and his shirt front wrinkled a bit at the stomach. He was a power in New York politics.

"I'm glad to see we've got some Democrats out in your part of the country," Schonberg said.

"Always had them. Just don't get them into office too often," Paul Lowe answered, smiling.

Schonberg laughed heartily as he squeezed Paul Lowe's upper bicep with a pudgy hand.

9

"You're doing a great job, Governor. A great job." He moved on toward the bar.

The Murdochs came next; Senator Vance Murdoch was a heavy-bodied, dark-faced man, with large liquid eyes. His wife, Patricia, was a pretty woman, with a triangular white face and the same huge eyes. She had a slender torso, and, Lowe guessed, rather heavy hips and thighs which a flowing gown artfully concealed. Their daughter was about eighteen or nineteen; she had inherited the family eyes, and, unfortunately, the family hips which a pink dress with a bow tied at the side did nothing to conceal. They went through the greetings and introductions. Senator Murdoch was from Indiana, second man on the Judiciary Committee and, more important for Paul Lowe, Chairman of the Committee on Public Works. Lowe gripped Senator Murdoch's hand with warmth, and exerted charm on the distaff Murdochs. They responded gracefully.

Here were Peter Daris and Laura Connell. Peter was the Solicitor General and Laura was the actress-daughter of the Postmaster General. Generals everywhere. In a civilian government why keep military caste titles? Fall in! 'TENSHUN! Paul Lowe's greeting to Peter and Laura was smiling, lacking in formality. Youth has its shibboleths: stuffiness was to be avoided at all cost.

The room was crowding; everyone in Washington observed the unwritten law that you must arrive between eight o'clock and ten minutes after for a formal dinner. Names and faces blurred into each other. Paul Lowe's smile became fixed. A butler circulated with a tray of martinis. He chose one. The bitter sharp taste helped to clear his head. The large drawing room resounded with small talk. No one sat on the chairs or the sofa. Another unwritten rule: small talk must be maintained in a vertical position. Probably on the theory that if anyone approached a comfortable position he would promptly fall asleep.

Brenda Hardman, porcelain beauty, moved from group to group to announce that the dinner hour had arrived. There was a general redistribution of people as the gentlemen sought out the ladies they were to escort. Until this moment they had observed a third unwritten law: do not engage in cocktail conversation with the lady who is to be your partner at dinner. Like the thundering verbotens of the Hebraic, this was founded in good sense. There was hardly enough store of conversation to last through soup and fish.

Paul Lowe drew Brenda Hardman for his partner. As the guest of honor he was seated at her right. Brenda was an exquisite woman, delicately fashioned, with tiny chiseled nose, small full round mouth, glacial complexion. A tiara shimmered fire in her dark hair. Her bare arms, perfectly white and slender, ended in small well-formed hands. On the third finger of her left hand a diamond solitaire caught blue flashes from the chandelier in the dining room.

At the long formal table forty or fifty people were seated. Paul Lowe showed Brenda Hardman to her place at the south end of the table and seated her. Her waist was supple and narrow, her posterior fetching as she sat down.

Sitting beside her, Paul Lowe began the ritual, concentrated conversation with your assigned partner oblivious to everyone else in the room. All the length of the table the others were faithfully performing the sacred social duty. He said to Brenda it was a lovely party and she was a gracious hostess and he was indebted, and Brenda demurred and told him how fond Race Hardman was of him and how pleased they had both been when he became Governor of Nebraska. They discussed his flight to Washington and Brenda thought it was exciting and so different of him always to fly his own plane. (Race was right—she considered him an original.) Brenda Hardman was a pleasant, simple-minded woman beneath her patina of physical elegance and by the time they worked their way through the soup (vichyssoise) and wine (Pouilly Fuissé 1961) he struck dead bottom. At last there came, simultaneously with the arrival of the fish, Brenda's awaited signal to turn the table. He turned to talk to Patricia Murdoch on his left. Patricia's huge eyes held him in liquid suspension while he ate minute forkfuls of the filet of sole amandine. Patricia Murdoch thought it was a lovely party and so many interesting people, people who mattered, and wasn't it a comfort not to have to talk small talk as people did at other parties but to discuss things that really counted? Paul Lowe said yes. Patricia, who kept up with things, remarked on the adverse decision of the Supreme Court and thought it was a shame about his state losing that water (what would she say to the Governor of Colorado? he wondered). Her husband, Senator Vance Murdoch, received stacks of mail, simply stacks, complaining about the Supreme Court because naturally they thought her husband as a member of the Judiciary Committee should do something. But what could he do, except pass on the appointment of the next Supreme Court justice and had he heard whether or not the President had picked anyone to replace Frank Joyce? Paul Lowe said no. There had been some talk, her voice fell to a confidential whisper, that it might be a Negro, that man Clayton, from the Court of Appeals, but she didn't believe it because even from her slight acquaintance with President Lamont Howard she knew he was not a man to stir up controversy. Not that she, personally, had anything against such an appointment but there were certainly a lot of people in Washington who would have strong reservations. Was her husband one of them? Paul Lowe asked. The liquid eyes turned reproachful. Senator Vance Murdoch did not have a prejudiced bone in his body. All that mattered to Vance Murdoch was the man, not the color of his skin. Paul Lowe remarked that Clayton had a very good reputation as a judge. Just the same, Patricia hoped the President would not get such an idea into his head because this was not the time and it was his first appointment to the Court and it might be taken as a sort of precedent. For all that people knew, he might go right on appointing Negroes and we would end up with an all-black Supreme Court, and nobody, not even colored people, would want that to happen. I guess not, Paul Lowe said. The filet amandine was finished. It was almost time to begin the game of swivel. What are you going to do now, Patricia Murdoch asked, about water, I mean? Paul Lowe said, Mrs. Murdoch, something has to be done and as a matter of fact there *is* a project that would solve the problem once and for all. It's before your husband's Senate Committee now and . . . The table turned. Brenda Hardman's regal beauty confronted him, along with saddle of lamb. There was a slight flush in her cheeks. Peter Daris, on her left, had doubtless paid her some compliment. He tried to remember, even as he spoke with Brenda Hardman of other matters, the last time he had brought forth a flush on a beautiful woman's face. He put that thought out of his mind, but not before the familiar sadness. During the salad serving, back with Patricia Murdoch, he managed to work the conversation again to the North Platte dam. Patricia's large eyes glazed with calculated indifference, husband-deferential; she remarked that her husband had told her what a terrible backlog of work was piling up on the Committee for Public Works and it was just a wonder they managed to get through as many things as they did. Heaven knows she simply didn't understand how her husband could work so hard and there couldn't be many men in the Senate who took their responsibilities so seriously. Paul Lowe received his salad plate with doily, knife and fork for dessert, put the knife and fork to each side for later use, and the finger bowl to the left. He locked his eyes in a contest with Patricia Murdoch's mesmerizing glance, feeling the world slipping away while he nodded sympathy. They began on the salad, simple oil and vinegar dressing, and she changed to the problem of schooling. The Murdochs' daughter Ann, it turned out, had just enrolled in the Madeira School and was being assigned an amount of work which in sheer volume and difficulty was apparently surpassed only by her husband's.

There were two more courses and twice more the table turned. Everything went perfectly except for an inadvertent use (it *must* have been inadvertent!) by Walter Schonberg of the finger bowl. He dipped his fingers in it, which no one ever did and Walter doubtless was aware of that, but either it slipped his mind or he was in a mood for social outrage. Brenda Hardman covered diplomatically for him by using the finger bowl in the same way herself and the table returned to its customary decorum. The snail on the thorn and God in his heaven.

At last dinner was over and the ladies, led by Brenda Hardman, went their separate way to the drawing room while the gentlemen, following Race Hardman, went into the library. The library was a long rectangular room with high arched windows at the far end that looked out on a formal Georgian garden. The butler closed the doors behind the last male guest. At the small bar in the corner a bartender was pouring brandy.

Holding the bulging bottom of his brandy goblet in two warming hands, Paul Lowe said to Senator Murdoch, "Off the record, Senator, just what are the chances of getting the appropriation for the North Platte dam out of your committee?"

Senator Murdoch looked slightly startled. He swirled golden fluid in his goblet.

"Hard to say, Governor. We've got a lot of work. But we intend to get around to hearing testimony one day real soon."

"I'm here now," Paul Lowe said. "I can delay my return to Nebraska to suit your convenience."

"Nothing will happen as fast as that," Senator Murdoch said. "I'm afraid you've got to have patience, Governor."

"This is an emergency situation," Paul Lowe said. "You wouldn't counsel patience to any man who just had an artery cut."

Senator Murdoch shook his head. "I don't understand why the Supreme Court took jurisdiction. I agree with Justice Bill Branch in his dissent. He said judges don't know enough about water rights to decide such cases."

"The point is, they did decide. There's no turning back now. And the State of Nebraska badly needs water."

"You can rest assured, Governor, that I'll do everything in my power to help you."

"Does that include holding immediate hearings?"

Senator Murdoch took a sip of brandy. "I'm afraid not."

"The North Platte dam project has been under wraps in your Public Works Committee for some time."

"We plan to take action in the near future."

Paul Lowe persisted: "When?"

"One thing I've learned," Senator Murdoch answered, "is never to make predictions."

The language of politics is prudence. Speak in watchwords: never be committed, don't get into a position from which there is no retreat, advance sideways.

Paul Lowe said, "I came to Washington to get some action. I intend to speak to the President tomorrow. What do you think my chances are?"

"I really can't say. When is your appointment with the President?"

"Eleven o'clock tomorrow."

"The timing might have been better."

"Why do you say that, Senator?"

"Lamont fits people in around a basic schedule. Wednesday is economic advisers. Two hours. Nine to eleven. You're going in right after. He's likely to be budget-minded because he'll be fresh from meeting with his economic advisers."

"What's a good approach to take?"

"Stick to the Supreme Court. It's one of Lamont's favorite peeves. Blame all your troubles on the Court and you'll get sympathy at least."

"Senator, if the President doesn't intervene, would you tell me whether there's any chance of the North Platte project being reported out of your committee at this session?"

"As I say, it's hard to predict."

"Yes or no. I want your answer straight from the shoulder."

Senator Murdoch chose a cigar from a humidor and lit it. Under the rodomontade of the politician there lurked the American's secret admiration for candor, for black and white, yes or no, without shilly-shallying. Ben

Franklin stalking through the frippery and subtlety of the French court, his broadsword clanking against rapiers. A million dollars for defense, not one cent for tribute. You may fire when ready, Gridley. Damn the torpedoes.

Senator Murdoch said, "If you want my honest opinion, I'd have to say the answer is no."

"I appreciate your honesty, Senator."

Paul Lowe managed to sound sincere. Senator Murdoch became very friendly and even compassionate about Paul Lowe's problem, but he offered no further constructive suggestions. A few moments later Senator Murdoch pantomimed welcome to someone at their rear, murmured "excuse me" and politely drifted away.

Race Hardman joined Paul Lowe, having detached himself from a group which included the assistant director of the FBI, an ambassador to Venezuela and the editor of Hardman's Minneapolis newspaper.

"I saw you buttonholing Vance Murdoch. You had a gleam in your eye that meant you were talking about the North Platte."

Paul Lowe said glumly, "It looks as if I'll have to take a bitter message back to the folks at home. Unless the President will do something, I'll have to figure out a way to get the dam built without federal help."

"There isn't another way. A dam will cost more than your state budget can afford."

"I might get the legislature to approve a state bond issue—and a state income tax."

Race Hardman said, "Nebraska is farmers. The per capita income isn't enough to yield a big return."

Paul Lowe shrugged. "Then I'll try to get a corporate tax too."

A slight redness appeared high on Race's cheekbones. "Dangerous socialistic nonsense," he snapped.

"Anything that makes the North Platte dam a reality isn't nonsense, Race. Besides, a corporate tax isn't socialism. A number of states are using it already."

"It's discriminatory," Race Hardman said. "I'm in favor of the North Platte dam too—but I won't stand for fiscal tomfoolery to get it."

"There are two points of view about whether it's tomfoolery, Race."

"Only one is correct."

"Yours?"

"Mine."

Race Hardman's gray eyes blinked behind the powerful eyeglasses. His complexion, as clear and transparent as a child's, was pink. Paul Lowe thought, when you peel the veneer the subsurface is always the same: a man who accepts, fully accepts, his right to be a leader hears a divine signal. How did the story go? William drawing with his brush, and the tutor asks, "What are you drawing, William?"—"God."—"But no one knows what He looks like."—"They will when I am through." Dear sure William.

14

"It's premature for us to argue about it, Race. I haven't seen the President yet."

Race Hardman's high-pitched voice seemed to be coming from a great distance.

"I'm not joking about this, Paul. I've been your supporter for a long time. But if you try to push through a radical program like this, I'll fight you. And when I go into a fight I go in with everything I've got."

Peter Daris came toward them, carrying a cup of coffee. He took a sip and put the cup back on the saucer with a slight rattling. He grinned.

"I'm trying not to drink. Still hung over from the night before. But I couldn't resist sampling the wines at dinner." He turned to Race Hardman. "Your taste in wine is still exquisite, old boy."

Race Hardman resumed his usual posture—slightly hunched, his neck dropping a little forward and seeming to carry his shoulders down.

"I wish I had the stomach for it," Race said. He twisted a ring on his finger, a wide band with heavy intricate carving and inset diamonds. "The doctor limited me to one glass a day."

Through heavy double doors of the library the intermittent strains of music penetrated. The orchestra had begun playing in the ballroom.

"Time we rejoined the ladies," Peter Daris said. He put down his cup of coffee on a table.

Race Hardman turned to Paul Lowe. Protocol order. Guest of honor and host. "Shall we?"

"Of course," Paul Lowe said.

2

"Do you know what they say this room is like?" Martin Gannett asked. He was a silver-haired, good-looking man with even white teeth. He was seated at a long black kneehole desk with papers bulging from a file folder on the right side.

"What?" Paul Lowe asked.

"A doctor's waiting room." Martin Gannett smiled. He was the appointment secretary to the President of the United States.

"I can see what they mean," Paul Lowe said.

The walls of Martin Gannett's large office were painted light gray, and four plain dark leather chairs stood against a wall. Manuscripts and papers were piled on a fairly long wide table. Behind Gannett's desk hung a large framed painting of the UN with all the flags of the member countries.

Seated in the other chairs near Paul Lowe were a representative of the National Fine Arts Commission, a member of the United States Committee for the UN, and the president of a college in Ohio. They were such distinguished-looking gentlemen that no one would suspect they belonged to the second echelon of importance among presidential visitors.

"How much longer?" Paul Lowe asked.

Martin Gannett consulted a schedule sheet marked off in hours and days. Most of the squares were filled in.

"It's hard to say, Governor. Economic advisers were scheduled until eleven, but Mr. Forrester of the Disarmament Commission got in for a last-minute appointment. What time is it now?" He glanced at his watch. "Eleven thirty-six. We're running behind. He has to nominate several hundred postmasters before lunch."

"Will he see me today?"

"Oh, I'm sure he will, Governor. He's been looking forward to it."

A woman staff assistant came to Martin Gannett's desk and he spoke with her for a moment. The telephone rang—a muted pleasant signal. It had been ringing every few seconds.

"A pretty busy doctor's office," Paul Lowe said.

"Everything seems to be backing up." Gannett's voice became a trifle shrill.

A calendar over the manuscript-laden table showed the month of

November. Against a long window, brown drapes reached to the floor, framing a dimensional view of a tall maple tree on the White House grounds.

Waiting upon the President of the United States, Paul Lowe became acutely aware of the passing minutes. Each one seemed to become dislodged and tumble like a boulder slowly down a mountain. Lost, lost in the caverns of time. Then another minute detached and began the same ponderous journey. Opposite him the member of the United States Committee for the UN groped in his briefcase. He looked up, all guilt and apology, as paper rustled noisily. The representative of the National Fine Arts Commission was hunched in his chair in an effort to be inconspicuous. The president of the Ohio college was sitting with his legs too far out into the room, doodling on a pad and smiling to himself.

Martin Gannett was on the telephone again at the desk at the far end of the room. He listened a moment, then hung up. As he walked across the room to Lowe, the appointment secretary's face seemed huge. In a doctor's waiting room that was how the nurse appeared when she finally opened the door to call the next patient. Paul Lowe's scalp and nose began to itch.

"The President will see you now, Governor Lowe."

The others looked at him, with envy, but feeling a little sorry for him too. His time had come. As he followed Gannett, Paul Lowe thought: exactly like a doctor's waiting room.

"I'm sorry you had to wait, Governor," Martin Gannett was saying. "I just couldn't interrupt him when he was with someone from the Disarmament Commission."

Paul Lowe smiled. "We can't endanger the peace of the world."

Martin Gannett was not listening. His perfunctory "Thank you, Governor" was hardly audible. He opened the door to the President's office and stood aside for Paul Lowe to enter.

President Lamont Howard was at his desk, reading a typewritten sheet and marking it with a white-topped pen. He looked up.

"Come right in, Paul."

He stood smiling, and shook hands. In eighteen years Paul Lowe had met Lamont Howard exactly three times, and the longest of these meetings had taken place a year and four months ago when the President had stopped in Lincoln, Nebraska, to make a short speech in which he endorsed the candidacy of his good friend, Paul Lowe.

"It's good to see you, Mr. President," Paul Lowe said. "You're looking well."

Indeed he was. A tall, slightly portly man in a well-tailored blue suit who looked like a *New Yorker* or *Esquire* version of the successful executive. Fifty-four years old, pleasantly lined face, furrowed brow, eyes too small but the lips full and capable of smiling with warmth. Just beneath the point of his jaw, the comfortable wadding of a second chin was visible.

"How are things in Nebraska?" he asked. "Are you making the state safe for Democrats?"

"Trying my best, Mr. President."

The President sat down at his desk and Paul Lowe took a chair nearby. "Smoke?" The cigarette box was carved of smooth and gleaming wood.

"No, thanks."

"Don't indulge?"

"I gave them up three years ago."

"So did I. Doctor's orders. I'm thinking of making some sort of public pronouncement. How do you think the public would react if I mention the danger of smoking in my next State of the Union address?"

"I think it's too early."

"Too many smokers?"

Paul Lowe smiled. "And most of them vote."

The President grinned at a comrade-in-arms. "I'm glad to see you again, Paul."

The green phone on the President's desk buzzed and he picked it up. His way of talking on the telephone was intimate—elbows on the desk, phone receiver firmly in left hand at one ear. His other hand rested against his cheek with the fingers bridged on his forehead. This made an enclosed area in which all his attention seemed devoted to the voice at the other end. He spoke a few seconds, replaced the phone in its cradle and swiveled his chair to confront Lowe.

"What's on your mind, Paul?"

"The thing that's on the minds of most people in my state, Mr. President. The recent Supreme Court decision."

The President's forehead creased into two deep furrows. "I wish you could read the letters I get attacking the Court. Hundreds a week."

"The judges have to hand down some pretty unpopular decisions."

The President's voice firmed with annoyance. "They couldn't get elected to the street-cleaning department in any town in this country. But they don't worry about elections—they're appointed for life. I can't fire them. All I can do is replace one of the justices when he finally decides to retire. Until Frank Joyce quit I thought all nine of them were going to hang on through my whole time in office—just out of spite."

"The point is, Mr. President, that the decision is made. And it's created a serious situation in my state."

The President grunted. "There's a traditional way of settling water disputes between states—first come, first served. Why couldn't the Court have handled it that way? No—they had to stick their chins out and get everybody mad."

"I wish they'd been a little less bold, Mr. President. But I guess we can't change what's happened. So we have to concentrate on what can be done now. And there's only one thing that can help the State of Nebraska."

Lamont Howard sat back in his chair and steepled his fingers. His hands were solid but graceful, medium-length tapering fingers with strength in the wrists. Black hairs grew in profusion around the expandable metal band of his gold wristwatch.

"I know," he said. "The North Platte dam."

"I was at the site a few days ago, Mr. President. I can assure you that the

18

dam is a perfectly feasible project which will more than pay for itself in years to come."

The President smiled at Paul Lowe ingratiatingly. He clearly wanted to impress upon his visitor that there was a private personality behind the public figure. But in truth there was not. Lamont Howard was a totally integrated man for whom the reality of public life was the only reality and he experienced no division between what the job called for and what he was.

"You may be right, Paul. In fact, I *know* you are. But there are fifty projects just like the North Platte dam waiting to be built in other parts of the country. Every blessed one of them is needed and every one will pay off sometime in the future. But how are we going to pay for them now? That's the problem—and I wish I knew the answer to it."

Build them, Paul Lowe thought savagely. The price of everything is not the only measuring value. It does not explain all or cover all. Too much of value cannot be manipulated into the columns of profit and loss. Let us trade paper and gold for bridges, dams, schools, and grade crossings— let us coin silver not into drachmas but into libraries, melt our most precious metals for housing and hospitals; let us be unsentimental and ruthless about paying the costs of a better life.

He said calmly, "Yesterday's Supreme Court decision makes the North Platte an exception. It creates an emergency. There isn't a moment to waste, Mr. President."

"One thing I can tell you," Lamont Howard answered patiently. "We've got more time than money."

Paul Lowe watched the President's face as though it were a map on which his direction could be charted. The President's attitude was tolerant —with a touch of mild contempt. He doesn't like me, Lowe realized. He thinks I'm one of the intellectuals in politics, the dedicated inept amateurs.

"I'm not talking time or money," Paul Lowe said. "I'm talking people —who need water to keep their farms going and their land fit for grazing."

A veil descended over the President's eyes. Paul Lowe realized he had said the wrong thing. He had appealed beyond the practical limits of the problem to a man dedicated to working within those limits.

"Paul, if I were in your shoes I'd probably be saying exactly the same things. But I've got other things to consider."

"I'm aware of that, Mr. President."

"For example, I'm trying to hold down the budget. Congress is laying for me this year. They'll go over every proposed expenditure with a fine tooth comb. Those boys know that the public wants economy."

Paul Lowe brushed back hair from his forehead. His fingertips touched beads of perspiration. The contact with imminent defeat was painful. His nerves were demanding clearer sharper responses, the therapy of a persuasive argument. What? *What?* He could not allow himself to lose. Yet the answers seemed to run away from him. He felt the genuine weight of the President's dilemma and his eyes smarted with the need to resolve it for him.

"If we don't do something for the people of my state, we won't elect any Democrats there for a long time to come, Mr. President."

"I might be able to do something for you next year, Paul." The small eyes twinkled with benevolent wisdom. "It'll be closer to the next gubernatorial election."

Paul Lowe had a flash of anger. "I don't care about that! We need that appropriation from Congress now. No one has a right to play politics with people's lives."

The President answered sharply, "Nobody's playing politics, Paul. I'm talking about the way our government works. These are *facts*."

As Congressman, Assistant Secretary of Agriculture, Secretary of Commerce, Lamont Howard had developed his reverence for facts. His imagination no longer extended beyond the boundaries of the possible. Immersed in reality, he was the essential pragmatist.

"And while we're on the topic," he said, "let me point out one more thing. Every congressman knows what the United States Supreme Court did to the State of Nebraska. A lot of them are pretty critical of the Court. So they won't mind letting public indignation build up against the Court. In Nebraska or anywhere else. Sure as the next snowfall they won't vote for anything to get the Court off a political hook. And they're not going to spend a hundred million dollars for a project that wouldn't be necessary if the Supreme Court hadn't made it necessary."

Lamont Howard's eyes were shrewd and challenging. Obviously he felt that he had weighed a great many issues, had identified and absorbed the essence of a complicated and critical question. He would not be moved to compromise. There was something in his firmness—the elemental sense of power—that suggested it might be dangerous to cross him further.

Paul Lowe said wearily, "I had a report prepared on the benefits that could result from building the North Platte dam. Would you read it? You might change your mind, Mr. President."

The President's tension noticeably relaxed. "Glad to read it, Paul. If you have extra copies, send them to the Secretary of the Interior and to the Chairmen of the Senate and House committees."

"I'll do that, Mr. President."

Subtly agreed upon was the face-saving gesture, the rope thrown across a chasm that would carry no weight.

The time had come to leave. "Well, Mr. President . . ."

Martin Gannett entered the office to hand the President a slip of paper on which the words were printed large enough to be read by Lowe: "YOUR NEXT APPOINTMENT IS WAITING."

The President did not rise. He nodded absently. "I'll be with him in a minute."

With an impatient accusing glance at Paul Lowe, Gannett left. Waiting for a signal to leave, Lowe gazed out the window. On the lawn outside a man with a portable tank on his back was using a hose to spray the winter grass with green coloring.

The President said, "I think you can help me with a problem, Paul."

"What is it, Mr. President?"

The President crumpled the small piece of paper that Gannett had given him and tossed it into the wastebasket.

"I have to make an appointment to the Supreme Court. My first. You worked there, didn't you?"

Paul Lowe nodded. "I was law clerk to Charles Edmunson." It was hardly news to this man with his limitless memory for intimate personal and political facts.

"You knew Frank Joyce, didn't you?" the President asked.

"Frank Joyce and Charles Edmunson were the two giants of the Court when I was there."

"It's going to be hard to replace Joyce. I need somebody with prestige, but I don't want a man who'll go along with the majority. Edmunson's been running the Court, unofficially, for a long time. No Chief Justice ever had the guts to stand up to him. It's time to get a little balance back before the Court takes over functions that belong to other branches of government."

"It's a strong Court, Mr. President. Even its worst critics admit that."

The President smiled remotely—small warming fire in an igloo.

"The main thing I have to do is keep the government running on a smooth keel. The Supreme Court hasn't helped me. Every term they come down with some thumping decision that makes a lot of people angry. And that makes it harder for me to do my job." Lamont Howard swung partly around in his swivel chair. "This is my first chance to bring the Court back closer to my way of thinking. How about Clayton?"

As he asked the question Lamont Howard swung back in his swivel chair to confront Paul Lowe directly.

Paul Lowe asked, "From the Sixth Circuit?"

"He's a good judge. He has good political connections. Fine reputation for integrity and judicial temperament. I worked with him on a couple of commissions and he's got a clear logical mind. No nonsense. He isn't one of these judicial activists who think the Court ought to be making policy instead of just interpreting the Constitution of the United States."

"Whether that's good or bad depends on your point of view."

The President's full lips widened slightly in a semismile. "That means you don't like Clayton. Most members of our party wouldn't like the appointment either." The smile widened. "Except for one thing. He's a Negro. He'd become the first Negro ever appointed to the Supreme Court. I figure that will bind and gag the liberal opposition to him." There was pure delight in the small eyes; they watered with self-appreciation.

"I wouldn't like to see a nominee accepted—or rejected—because of his race."

Lamont Howard's face crinkled into open amusement. "I've got other reasons. Clayton was born in South Dakota. Born and bred in the Midwest. I need someone from that part of the country for geographical balance. And Clayton's a Baptist. There's no Baptist on the Court." He watched keenly for some sign of agreement. "Adds up, doesn't it?"

"You already have my opinion, Mr. President."

The door opened and Martin Gannett entered.

"Mr. President," Gannett said, "your other appointments are stacking up. And Mr. Chisholm has to make a plane."

The President stood up and Paul Lowe rose with him.

"Do you want photographs?" Gannett asked.

"Fine," the President said. "Are they ready?"

"Yes, Mr. President."

Martin Gannett opened the door to the outer hall. Photographers hurried in carrying boxlike cameras. As soon as the floodlights were plugged in they aimed and fired at the President shaking hands with Paul Lowe. The President and Paul Lowe faced the cameras and smiled, clasping hands together. "Look this way, please," "Smile," "Shake hands again, please," "Just one more." As suddenly as the invasion began it was ending; the photographers unplugged the floodlights and got the equipment out of the way.

Paul Lowe emerged from the oval room in the southeast corner of the West Wing executive offices.

Martin Gannett left with him. "This is public visiting hours," he said. "You'd better leave by the east entrance to avoid crowds."

"I didn't intend to stay so long," Paul Lowe said.

Martin Gannett reproachfully wound his watch. His job was to guard the President's hours as though they were crown jewels.

"*He* wouldn't let you get away. Everyone says that."

Paul Lowe indicated a door across from the President's office. He wanted to depart, if possible, on a more friendly note. "What room is that?"

Gannett's tone still carried reproof. "The fish room, Governor."

"What's that?"

"F.D.R. kept his stuffed fish trophies in there. It's been known as the fish room ever since. Except during President Eisenhower's terms, when it was called the staff conference room."

"Republicans have a different idea about the fitness of things, don't they?" Paul Lowe asked with a smile.

Martin Gannett did not reply.

The Bentley pulled away from the White House in the wide curve of Pennsylvania Avenue. The last time Paul Lowe had been in Washington a tall magnolia tree stood south of the President's bedroom. The old tree had been planted by Andrew Jackson and rose loftily to the roof parapet. Now it was topped. President Eisenhower had ordered it topped to remove a nesting place for starlings that disturbed his sleep. Workmen had done it in the dark of night, to avoid complaints from historians.

On the drive they passed Capitol Hill.

"Wait," he told the chauffeur.

The white marble of the Supreme Court building rose in austere grandeur. Every day for a year, as Edmunson's law clerk, he had entered that building. He could retrace every step of the journey.

A hall of echoes . . .

A young redheaded lawyer, nervously turning to the robed justices: "I appeal, Mr. Justice Edmunson, to your well-known sense of fair play. . . ."

Edmunson's deep slow rebuke: "Young man, you are arguing this case before the entire Court."

The young lawyer's widening entreaty: "Then I appeal to all of you who believe in justice."

Edmundson: "You are mistaken in appealing to our belief in justice. We sit here as a court of *law*. . . ."

Somehow Edmunson succeeded in reconciling law and justice. In his magnificent written opinions, Charles Edmunson described heights hidden to the vision of ordinary men, searched for truths on the mountaintops and returned with commandments that benefited and protected those who lived on common ground.

Not a far-reaching conceit. Edmunson himself in a famed decision that upheld the separation of church and state had uttered a biblical thunder: "One does not have to belong to a church to be an upright man. All thoughtful men talk the true language of God. . . ."

Echoes faded. . . .

The driver turned around questioningly.

"All right," Paul Lowe told him. "Drive on."

He looked back once at the marble palace on Capitol Hill, the building which contained a part of his youth and a part of his innocence. One needs perspective. The influence of great men is horizontal, not vertical, extending its reach pervasively only over a brief time. Future generations are born skeptical. Greatness built into the earth will be topped for starlings.

3

On Thursday evening, shortly after seven o'clock, Paul Lowe's single-engined Debonair circled over the Nebraska University grounds. The football stadium slid slowly by with its arching tiers of empty seats, dark rectangle of playing field and vanished hurrahs.

Those buildings with the small planes parked near: the Airplane and Flying School. There, many years ago, he first took a plane alone through the sky, turning at will in supporting ether, free beyond the world. A serene world. In less than two years the skies were aflame with danger and the planes were at war.

Now he was passing over the state agricultural college, letting down for the airport on an assigned flight path. He came around Capitol Beach, fronting the lake that had been formed from an old salt basin. Across the motionless blue water the city's lights glittered wanly. Then the city itself, a patchwork of lights, rose on a gentle swell of prairie from the valley on the west. At closer range, the lamps in homes glowed welcome at windows. The open area of a city park yielded to the state capitol building—beautiful straight tower centrally aloft with a row of trees guarding its base.

He loved this city which had been not too long ago a hamlet of ten stone and log houses on a bare prairie. It had survived grasshoppers and locusts and William Jennings Bryan. The plane turned into the prevailing northwest wind and settled down onto the airport runway.

On the oval concrete apron in front of the hangar, Paul Lowe met reporters who had streamed across the field to meet him.

"Did you have a successful trip to Washington, Governor?" This—from a radio newsman carrying a hand mike with a portable tape recorder on a shoulder strap.

"I had some useful discussions."

"Is it true you called at the White House and spoke to the President?" This—from a reporter on a local newspaper.

"Yes. We talked about the North Platte dam."

"What did the President say? Is there any chance of getting started this year?" This—from a dark woman in a gray tailored suit.

Suddenly conscious of his informal attire—his jacket and ribbed sweater

24

and slightly baggy corduroy trousers—Paul Lowe answered, "The President made it pretty clear there won't be any federal money available for it. But the North Platte dam is still going to be built."

"How?" asked a tall thin young man wearing black-rimmed glasses. "There isn't enough money in the state treasury."

"I'll have more to say about that in a special message to the legislature."

"Doesn't the press have a right to know?" The dark woman reporter was rather tall, an inch or so shorter than himself.

Paul Lowe said, "The press has a right to report news. At the moment there isn't any news to report."

Her attractive face was severely set. "In other words, you're not going to tell us."

"I'm afraid the legislature will have to hear it first."

"Well, Governor, it seems your dramatic," her slight emphasis underlined the word, "flight to Washington didn't do much good. Except for getting your visit some press coverage."

Paul Lowe pushed the silver knob of the hand microphone away from his face and turned to give her a deliberate appraisal. She had a ripe figure, buxom, with a clear complexion and full lips, and while her expression was stern now, there were smiling lines in her full smooth cheeks.

"I'm not quite sure what you mean, young lady."

"If you hadn't flown your private plane cross country, Governor, you'd have avoided all this publicity. You could have taken a scheduled airline. But then everyone in the state wouldn't have known how our Governor was going all out for the North Platte dam."

"What is your name?" Paul Lowe asked sharply.

The answer was lost in a sudden rush of questions from other reporters. He rode choppy currents: no, he did not discuss other state problems with the President. Yes, he talked to other people in Washington. He had some good friends in that city. No—he did not have further comment on the Supreme Court decision. Everything that could be said on that topic had been said. Personal problems—what personal problems could he possibly want to discuss in Washington? Most emphatically no— he was not thinking of accepting a post with the federal government. There was far too big a job to be done in his home state.

Finally, the tall thin reporter ended the impromptu conference. "Thank you, Governor."

"Thank *you*."

In the terminal building Ken Norris was waiting. Ken was a short stocky blond man, with a face slightly pockmarked from acne. He shook hands with Lowe.

"Right on time," Ken Norris said.

As they left the terminal, Paul Lowe saw the reporters entering the building through another door.

"Who is she?" Paul Lowe asked.

"Who?"

"That tall dark girl."

"I don't think I've ever seen her."

"She's a reporter. Thinks my only motive in flying to Washington was to feather my political nest."

Ken Norris led the way through the doors. "Your strength is as the strength of ten," he said. "Everyone knows that. How can they knock Sir Galahad?"

"If Sir Galahad was in politics, he'd have been unhorsed pretty regularly."

Ken Norris' pale eyes were friendly-inquisitive. "She got under your skin. What'd she say?"

"It doesn't matter," Paul Lowe said.

They reached the parking lot and located a powder-blue Pontiac Tempest. Ken opened the door.

"I gather you didn't bowl them over in Washington."

"They treated me like a tenpin. The President suggested something might be done in a year or two. Closer to the next election."

"Good old Lamont Howard. If they ever open up his head they'll find it's stuffed like a ballot box." He held the door open while Paul Lowe got into the car. "To the official residence—or Chilmark?"

"Chilmark. I need to get away from people."

As they drove out of the parking lot, Ken Norris asked, "What now? Are you going to forget the North Platte project?"

"I'm going to send a special message to the legislature. I'll get the money somehow."

"New taxes?"

"Several."

Ken Norris gave a silent whistle. "Old John Marshall was wrong, you know. The power to tax isn't the power to destroy. The power to tax destroys the party that taxes."

The airport fell behind them as Paul Lowe stared out the car window. "I can't walk away from it and pretend the problem doesn't exist, Ken."

"A good politician would. He'd beat his breast and blame Washington for everything."

"Then I'm not a good politician."

Ken Norris sighed. "You were never meant to have two terms as governor, Paul. You're the egghead type that doesn't stay popular."

"What should I do—have a prefrontal lobotomy?"

"Not a bad idea. But with your luck they'd take out your brain and leave you with that goddamned conscience."

Paul Lowe chuckled. "What are you and Sheila doing tonight?"

"Staying home with the twins. Playing canasta until we get tired and fall into bed." Ken Norris smirked.

"You're hopeless."

"I just have an attractively dirty mind. Of course we can postpone our sex life a few hours if you'd like to pay us a visit."

"No, thanks. I really am tired. I've been looking forward to a weekend of rest at Chilmark."

The car bumped across the short unpaved stretch of road to Paul Lowe's country home. The two-story farmhouse with stone facing on the side and white clapboard in front had been his year-round residence until he moved to the governor's mansion. He still used it as a retreat.

As they approached the house, Eleanor Lowe appeared on the glassed-in porch. Ken Norris parked on the semicircular driveway near the rail fence. Geisha, barking loudly, bounded out across the lawn. Paul Lowe got out of the car in time to take the full brunt of his police dog's affection. He wrestled Geisha down and sent her away with a pat on the rump. Geisha barked excitedly, ran around in steadily shortening circles and came to rest with head and shoulders down and paws extended, ready for play.

Eleanor came up, wearing a black coat open over a simple beige wool dress.

She kissed him. "I'm glad you're home, darling."

"I'm glad too."

Ken Norris waved from the car window. "I wish you luck with your political high-diving act, Governor. Just make sure before you jump that there's water in the barrel."

The powder-blue Tempest rocked off down the unpaved road to the highway. Standing on the lawn in front of his home with his arm on his wife's shoulder, Paul Lowe felt like a figure in a photograph, the very image of a settled family man. He thought: all photographs are two dimensional and therefore deceptive. Photo albums perpetuate hypocrisy.

They started toward the porch. Geisha kept bounding away and back to get his attention.

"How was your trip?" Eleanor asked.

"Fine. Good weather both ways."

"Did you see the President?"

"Yes."

Eleanor loved small confirmations of his stature—to her the President's name was like a signature on a check which made the amount valid.

Snowflakes idly turned outside the four-paned view at the rear of the home. In the comfortable living room Eleanor was talking, ". . . and then yesterday after Sheila Norris called, I took the car and went into town to do the shopping. It was a little warmer, I think. There was no snow. I'm a little worried about driving on some of these roads, though. Don't you think we ought to have tire chains? I think I'd feel safer."

She was doing needlepoint—the needle dipped into the colorful square of cloth in the rim, and rose. She seemed to draw comfort from the small physical movement.

". . . and I do think the left rear tire is a little soft, Paul. I wish you'd look at it when you get a chance."

She always thought one of the car tires was about to go flat. It amounted to an obsession. Alone on a deserted road, amid snowdrifts, the car settling slowly onto a wounded haunch while she froze far from help, carbon monoxide within. He had acquired this film of her fear over years, in scattered images, torn strips of acetate.

"Anyhow, when I got back Lucille wasn't feeling well. That back trouble of hers. She's getting too old for housework, poor darling. So I told her she could go home early and at five o'clock I drove her to the bus."

"Why didn't you take her all the way?" Paul Lowe asked.

"She didn't seem to want me to. And the roads are so bad, especially when it's getting dark. And I was worried about that left rear tire."

"Oh, yes," he said.

"I called Mother this morning and we talked for a while."

"How is she?"

"She's fine."

"And Natalie?"

Natalie was her sister, a shy pale frail girl-woman of twenty-nine whose life had been by now almost entirely consumed in Mother's devouring embrace.

"Natalie isn't feeling too well."

"What's the trouble?"

"The same thing. She has such terrible periods. She gets those blinding headaches and feels terrible. She was in bed when I called. The doctor had just left."

There are medicines that can minister but the disease remains royal; it will assert its prerogative. Unviolated thighs, preserved hymen, call for succor until the mind becomes untranquilized. He felt sorry for Natalie. A sweet woman, a slowly fading flower.

Suddenly he wanted to communicate with his wife, to make contact in a crack of noise.

"Eleanor . . ."

Her head lifted.

"About this trip to Washington. I've got a problem on my hands—a big one. I'd like to talk to you about it."

Her greenish-brown eyes flickered with satisfaction as she put down her needlepoint. He told her, briefly and simply, of the Problem, the Importance, the Action, the Response—her mood fluttered aloft, descended with rude force, was plucked up like a hurt butterfly. Then her attention slowly fixed upon the Threat.

"I wish Race Hardman weren't opposed to it. He's a powerful man. He can be a bad enemy."

"The only thing that matters is whether I'm right."

"Well, it does sound a little unfair—this business of putting on special taxes. I don't see what harm it would do to wait. Especially when people like Race Hardman feel so strongly."

She had the feminine instinct for danger, eons old, the terror of darkness where malign shapes wait. Light the fire. Stay in the cave. Guard the children; don't feed them to tigers.

"Suppose *I* feel strongly about it. Shouldn't that count for something?"

"Of course, dear." Placating, affectionate. "But you've done your best, so there's no point in your feeling strongly about it. Is there?"

With child's eye sharpness he saw an old farmhouse, carefully erected stone upon stone, as his father's ancient Plymouth ground up to the door. In the back bedroom was the patient, a pale frightened woman with deep-circled eyes, whose bony hands worked the coverlet as though to assure herself of the reality of touch and feeling. Her white nightgown, its oval neck tied in front with a single looped string, hung on a flattened bony chest.

His father prescribed a pill—something to hollow feeling out of the senses. On the porch as they were leaving, the prosperous farmer stood, in overalls, brawny and solid with a sorrowing face. He told softly how he had built the house, cleared the land, how many cows he had, how rich the crops were on his farmland. All of these things God had given him, but "What have I done for God?" he asked. Therefore he accepted his wife's dying as a settling of an account. A lovely summer's day, bright and full of green life, birds singing, and the stubborn farmer's voice, "What have I done for God?" What arrogance, presuming to bring gifts to his Creator.

But Eleanor seemed to have lost interest in his topic—or rather a more immediate and personal concern seized her.

"This morning I had a letter from Nancy. I almost forgot to tell you."

"What did she say?" he asked.

"Nothing very much. I was hoping she'd be able to visit us at Christmas but she didn't mention a word about it." Her sadness was touching. The empty womb, sprung child; once that flesh had been hers. "Would you like to see her letter?"

"Not just now."

Eleanor's handsome solemn face bent again over the needlepoint, closely intent. Her fingers dipped the needle, drew it.

As they were going upstairs to the bedroom later that evening, Eleanor said, "Whatever you decide about Race Hardman is all right with me. Only be sure you know what you want to do before you go ahead."

"Yes, dear," Paul Lowe said.

Over the weekend he finished a draft of the special message to the legislature. On late Sunday evening he sent the draft to Abe Weisinger for comment. When he heard a ringing at seven-thirty Monday morning he thought it was the alarm clock. As he reached for the clock the telephone rang again. He picked up the receiver to hear Abe Weisinger's amused drawl:

"I hope I woke you up."

"You did." Now the alarm began ringing. "Just a minute." He reached

29

over to turn it off. "See? I could have slept another ten or fifteen seconds. What's on your mind, Abe?"

"I've just read the speech you're going to send to the legislature."

Paul Lowe sat up. "Did you like it?"

"Ver-y interesting. Finest document of its kind I've seen since *Das Kapital*."

Paul Lowe arranged the pillow in place behind him. Eleanor put the covers back, got out of her bed and fumbled into slippers.

He said, "The trouble with you, Abe, is that you're an arch-reactionary Bourbon Democrat with fascistic tendencies and a pronounced bias in favor of J. P. Morgan."

"That's the kind of man you need for speaker of a nonpartisan legislature." Abe Weisinger chuckled.

"Seriously, Abe, you think we've got trouble?"

Abe Weisinger's voice became briskly professional.

"Well, Governor, this is how it looks to me. I can't see the Budget Committee voting for a state income tax and a corporate tax. They might go along with the state bond issue."

"That won't raise enough money."

"Well, we've got a problem. Where are we going to get the votes?"

"I have some suggestions," Paul Lowe said.

"I'm all ears."

"Start with what we need the money for. The North Platte dam project is going to save thousands of people from bankruptcy or eviction from their homes. We've got to reach those people and convince them their vital interests are at stake. Tell them to write, phone, wire—come in person to the capital—and let it be known where they stand. That should swing some votes our way."

"Maybe. Maybe not."

"Then there are the legislators elected from districts that need the North Platte project. Those men can't afford to ignore the well-being of their constituents. Especially if the pressure is really on from folks back home."

"It might pick us up a couple of votes," Abe conceded. "But there's no guarantee."

"Wait, I'm not finished. The North Platte dam will cost a lot of money and that money is going to be spent right here in this state. It's going to create business for subcontractors, engineering firms, suppliers of parts and raw materials. So there's a fairly substantial portion of the business community—that part getting the contracts and orders—that will line up with us. Most of them probably have influence. Particularly if they work through organizations like the Chamber of Commerce, the Shriners, the Rotarians, and all the rest."

Abe Weisinger said, with grudging respect, "It'll take a lot of groundwork. At best it'll be a battle."

"We'll win it. Because we have to."

"Governor, if this is a must it's a must. You can count on me. I've got a few suggestions about the message. I think it would help to soft-pedal the language. Get in all the statistics you can. Drown 'em in figures. Then let's not come straight out with your proposal. Let's just get the authorization to set up a study on how to raise the money. We can send that proposal through the Standing Committee of the legislature. In fact, if we're smart, we'll make it strictly an investigative problem. As a non-controversial measure that could be referred to the legislature by the Reference Committee without public hearings."

Abe Weisinger's response to any problem was to find the gimmick—the tricky technical approach.

"We can't waste time," Paul Lowe said. "I want work to start this spring. Early summer at the very latest."

"It's better to make haste slowly."

"*Festina lente.*"

"What?"

"The Latin. You were quoting the Emperor Augustus, Abe."

"Oh, sure." Abe Weisinger had not gotten used to having a governor who knew Latin. "Well, it's still good advice, Governor."

"Not this time. The lives and futures of too many people are involved. This is a human problem—not merely a legislative problem."

Abe Weisinger assumed a determined optimism. "Well, we've got some punches to throw at them. As long as Race Hardman is around the press won't be entirely against us."

There was a pause while Abe waited for confirmation that did not come.

"Have you discussed this with Race Hardman, Governor?"

"Yes. You may as well know now that he's opposed to it."

"Mildly?"

"I wouldn't say that."

The exhaled breath was eloquent.

"Well, we're going to do the best we can, Governor."

"Send the message back to me with your suggestions and I'll go to work on it right away. I'll pep it up—give it more popular appeal in the final draft."

"It's going to be tough to swing it, Governor. I warn you—if we push too hard they'll push back."

"This is only the first round, Abe. The fight's just starting."

Showered and shaved and dressed he went down to the dining room. The day was bright and clear and cold; icicles clung to the roof of the house and glittered palely through the tall windows. Eleanor was at the breakfast table. While he was having orange juice, he made a phone call to the State Attorney General, Hiram J. Sloane.

"Hiram, can you come to my office at ten o'clock this morning?"

"Any particular reason, Governor?"

"I want to go over some legal points in a message I'm sending to the legislature."

Hiram Sloane said, "You know more about law than I do, Governor. But I'll be glad to help in any way I can."

"This can't have any wrinkles in it, Hiram. I don't want the opposition to find a way out through some technicality in the law."

He drank the last of his orange juice. On the white napery the orange juice pitcher made a vivid sunlit color beside translucent blue-white water glasses and gleaming silver. Paul Lowe lifted the aluminum cover of an elongated platter, exposing slices of crisp dark bacon and two white eggs staring with bulbous yellow eyes. Eleanor poured coffee from a silver carafe to brim his cup blackly.

"I'm being spoiled this morning," Paul Lowe said.

"I thought you might need your strength." Eleanor hovered worriedly nearby. "You're going through with it, aren't you?"

"Yes, dear," he said. "I am."

Eleanor managed to smile. Paul Lowe held out his hand to her and she held it between both of her hands, still smiling.

. . . and before closing I would like to say a personal word to you, the men responsible for making the laws that govern this great state. None of us must forget that we have been given our jobs by the people, and our responsibility is to them. When we ask ourselves if we have performed well, we cannot look for the answer in dusty records or the pages of newspapers or the approval of the wealthy and powerful. We must look out of doors, beyond the Capitol building to the people of the farmlands, the sand hills, the high plains and the Bad Lands. We must find our answers in *their* hopes and fears. We must be sure that the burdens of office never blind us to the kind of state in which our people want to live, the simple purposes they have put us here to fulfill. . . .

Why do we need to raise money to build the North Platte dam? Because the men and women who work on the farms, the men and women who tend cattle that feed on the plains, and countless others who supply the needs of our farmers and ranchers in order to live themselves, have a right to be defended in their homes and in their jobs—not just for today or tomorrow but as far ahead as any of us can see. In trying to fulfill our task, which the people have given us in trust, we must not be appalled at the size of the work to be done, at the amount of sacrifice to be made. In pursuing the greater interest of all our people, we must not be deterred by disappointment. And, above all, we must *never* give up.

Martha Scully, his personal secretary, reported first. She appeared, awkward, sloping-shouldered, in the doorway of his private office. "It was a fine statement, Governor." Her hand, attached to a rather too long arm, brushed a blonde-gray hair from her forehead.

"Thank you, Martha. We'll soon hear what everyone else thinks."

The next report was from Abe Weisinger.

"Good message," Abe said carefully on the telephone. "It got over. On the whole I thought it was well received."

"Has the opposition started to denounce me?"

The answering chuckle was dry. "That comes tomorrow. Right now they're a little stunned. As soon as they gather their forces we'll hear from them."

After lunch, Ken Norris called.

"I heard a radio report on your message on my way back from lunch, Paul. It's getting plenty of publicity."

"Good or bad?"

"All I can say is I was driving back with a client. A banker. We heard it on his car radio. I thought he was going to drive into the nearest telephone pole. He was apoplectic by the time he got back to my office."

"I hope the opposition is limited to bankers."

"It won't be," Ken Norris said cheerfully. "Don't forget that every little cloud has a nuclear lining and this one is likely to blast you right out of the governor's chair. But I want you to know that personally I'm damn glad I voted for you."

"Thank you, Ken. I appreciate that."

"You can always come back and be my law partner. Even *after* you're impeached."

The next telephone call was from Race Hardman. The familiar high-pitched rapid voice was deliberate and measured.

"Paul, I hope you know what you're doing. Your proposed tax program is a socialistic mess. We can't afford it."

"I don't have any alternative, Race. We're entering a dry cycle in this state. The last time it happened we had six or seven dry years and only one wet. We can't get through another dry cycle without the North Platte dam."

"I warned you I was going all out against you on this issue. If I'm not for you, who will be?"

"Even if no one is, I still have to do what I think is right."

From then on the telephone calls increased in frequency. Paul Lowe answered as many as he could in person. There was one in particular. About four-thirty in the afternoon Martha Scully said on the intercom:

"Katherine Prescott on the phone. She wants to talk to you."

"Who is she?"

"A newspaperwoman. Shall I tell her you're not available?"

"I'll talk to her. This is no time to offend members of the press."

He didn't recognize the voice.

"Governor Lowe, this is Katherine Prescott. I'm afraid I owe you an apology."

"Why is that?"

"The way I acted the other day at the airport." And then he knew. "I'm the one who was badgering you about your flight to Washington."

"Oh, yes, I remember."

"I just finished reading your message to the legislature. I liked it very much."

"Why, thank you, Miss Prescott." Her image flashed in his mind, embodying the voice which had a darker color than he remembered.

"In fact, it's made me change my opinion of you."

33

"For the better?"

She laughed. "Distinctly."

He suddenly remembered the byline in the Lincoln *Sentinel*. *View of the Man in the News* by Katherine Prescott.

"Incidentally, Miss Prescott, I've seen your column in the *Sentinel*. I enjoy it."

"Thank you. It's one of my chores. I also contribute to the *Washington Insider* column. It appears twice a week in all of Mr. Hardman's newspapers."

"I've seen that too."

She hesitated, then sighed. "I'll tell you off the record, Governor, that editorials in the Lincoln *Sentinel* and Omaha *Bulletin* tomorrow will attack your message to the legislature. In fact, you'll be raked over the coals backwards."

"It's all part of politics, Miss Prescott."

"Perhaps it will help you to remember this. They wouldn't be so violent if they weren't afraid you might win."

"Thank you very much, Miss Prescott."

As he hung up the telephone he was smiling. What she had said was exactly what he needed to hear. *They were afraid he might win.* A keen sense of combat thrilled like a live wire in his blood.

Nothing could be achieved without effort. But he was prepared to make the effort. As soon as practicable he would begin. He would go from Chadron to Scottsbluff, from Scottsbluff to Sidney, to Grand Island and McCook and Holdress, past the site of Winter Quarters where Mormons died for their faith astride the historical routes of the Oregon and California Trail, down the swift Nebraska and along the route of the Republican, from one end of the state to the other, from the tall Buttes in their rocky splendor to the long bare land where a parched wind blew desolation. He would talk to many many people. Out of his journey, out of the travail of words, would arise a triumphant fact: three hundred feet high, holding twenty million cubic tons of water—channeling it through canals to dried-out land, harnessing its propulsive force to giant turbines. The North Platte dam would be his creation.

Paul Lincoln Lowe, in a quiet office, swiveled his chair about: arrogance, arrogance, he warned himself.

4

At seven-forty of a drizzly January morning, Paul Lowe took off from Lincoln Airport in a chartered airplane on the beginning of a long and intensive speechmaking tour.

It was an exhausting program. Eleanor pleaded with him to make it less strenuous.

"I made a promise and I intend to keep it," he told her.

Less than two weeks before he left on his journey a bill providing for the tax moneys needed to build the North Platte dam had been drafted along lines suggested in his message to the legislature and had been jointly sponsored by two distinguished legislators, Phil Kada and Bill Sutherland. Prospects for the bill's passage were dim unless there was a groundswell of support from the citizenry.

"You will win, Governor," Martha Scully told him. "They don't have the arguments to stand up to you. If you fight hard for it, you'll win."

He went first to the larger cities. In the evening he spoke indoors in public halls. At lunchtime and at five o'clock closing he waited at factory gates or parking lots. As the workers gathered around, his local volunteer assistants—mostly pretty young girls—passed out free hot coffee and doughnuts. His audiences were friendly and curious but when he tried to emphasize the importance of the mission on which he had come they usually began to chaff him good-humoredly. They had read in their newspapers that his scheme was impractical.

So they listened, went home, and did not write or telephone or wire their representatives. Nothing happened. For the most part, people simply did not seem to care. In each new city reporters arrived for the press conference primed with difficult and often hostile questions. Paul Lowe would say hello, shake hands all around, and answer their objections. When the conference was over the reporters would sometimes give him a round of applause. But the next day the stories that appeared in the newspapers were uniformly unfavorable.

A newspaper sampling across the state showed the voters were against the Kada-Sutherland bill. Martha Scully, who saved the press clippings, wrote to him "the press is two hundred percent against you."

In Osceola his plane had engine trouble and he stayed over for the night. The Lieutenant Governor, Henry Wellman, Speaker Abe Weisinger, and the Chairman of the Committee on Committees, Judson Bell, met him there for luncheon the next day. These three gentlemen constituted the Reference Committee that would decide whether the Kada-Sutherland bill should be passed on to a Standing Committee.

Paul Lowe told them forcefully, "The legislature has got to hold public hearings. I want a date set far enough in advance, and enough publicity. I want the public to show up and make its voice heard."

"Are you sure you'll like what the public has to say?" Abe Weisinger asked. "People believe what they read—not what you tell them. In cold print a fact looks like a fact. There's nothing you can say that can match it."

Abe Weisinger's broadshouldered corpulent body remained massively still during the tongue-lashing Paul Lowe gave him. His small brown eyes retreated into folds of flesh. Later, Paul Lowe apologized.

"My nerves are all on the surface of my skin, Abe," Lowe told him. "I haven't been sleeping well."

"You need a rest, Governor," Abe said. "The pace you're keeping could kill a man."

His warmest reception was in North Platte. The town's school children were given the day off and the main street was crowded with children waving banners and placards. The motorcade from the airport to the city hall where Paul Lowe was to speak was a stampede in slow motion—crowds kept breaking through the police ranks to reach his car and shake his hand. At the hall the applause started while he was backstage and built to a crescendo when he came out, in his somewhat dusty blue suit, walking with a swift forward lunging and slightly bowlegged stride.

"My fellow citizens," he began, and for the first time the formalities dropped away and he found himself talking freely and frankly to the people. But toward the end there were long pauses; he could not group sentences properly from his scribbled notes or collect and hold a sustained thought. No one seemed to notice. When he left the crowds were jammed in around his car and he stood up and waved to them and gratefully heard their cheers like cooling rain on his face. But there was a great pressure inside his head and an engine raced somewhere inside his body at a tempo that threatened to shake him apart. He was bitterly tired.

In Grand Island he spoke at a businessman's luncheon but the motorcade afterward moved through scattered and unenthusiastic crowds. It was Saturday and there was no school for children to be set free from, and therefore no children. In North Platte (how long ago?) had the children turned out to cheer him or their unexpected holiday?

That night fragments of speeches ran over and over in his brain until the words became nonsense and all the paragraphs were twisted. German and Latin crept in. *Qui desiderat pacem praeparet bellum.* . . . *Wo du singen horst dort last sich ruhig.* . . . *Domum, domum, dulce domum.* Old phrases remembered from schoolbooks. In the middle of the night he got up, struck by a brilliant inspiration for a quotation, and scribbled it down. He awoke in the morning to find gibberish.

As the tour went on what became apparent was that President Lamont Howard had been uncannily attuned to the public mood. This was indeed a year for economy—at least in Nebraska. Still Paul Lowe kept fighting. He flew back to Lincoln to help Bill Sutherland, one of the bill's co-sponsors, prepare and submit to the Standing Committee a statement setting forth the reason for the bill and the purpose to be accomplished thereby.

"This ought to help," Bill Sutherland said, gathering the scraps of notes together with pride. "It's a powerful aggressive statement."

Paul Lowe spent that night in his own home, tossing restlessly. He kept Eleanor awake and she pleaded with him not to set forth on his tour again. But he had no choice. The bill had been printed and copies furnished to members of the legislature. A brief digest was being carried in newspapers which also announced the date of public hearings. Now, if ever, was the time for the populace to make known its sovereign irresistible will. This was the crisis.

In a hotel in Madison the next afternoon he spoke at a Women's Tea Dance. All the women came up to shake his hand and he told them that theirs was a lovely city made lovelier by the most beautiful women west of the Mississippi. "East of the Mississippi, as we all know," he said, "the country is inhabited by Indians." The women laughed and seemed to like him. He lay down in a hotel room for an hour's nap and thought of whether any great lovers of history would have made successful politicians. Imagine Casanova for Mayor or Don Juan for alderman? How about Cellini for Congress?

At nine-thirty that evening he rose from a canvas chair in a tent in Ainsworth to tell four hundred listeners at a religious rally that "God did not intend for man to have either brains or money and not spend them for his salvation. If we do not build the North Platte dam, we will have ignored the wisdom of the adage that 'God helps those who help themselves.'" There were shouts but he could not tell whether they signified approval or dissent. He was blind with fatigue. That night, in a fly-ridden hotel room, he sat with a bottle of bourbon at his right hand and worked on his next speech. His throat was raw and inflamed. His headache was murderous. But the public hearings were to begin in the morning and he was working desperately against a racing clock.

The hearings in the State Legislature were a disaster. Five days notice had been given and that was more than enough for enemies of the bill to rouse and present themselves. The lineup of witnesses waiting to testify against the proposed taxation seemed endless. They ranged from the usual cranks to the usual experts.

Paul Lowe appeared before the committee at his own request. His voice was hoarse: "My cause is the welfare of Nebraska's people—and that cannot be totaled in dollars and cents. William Jennings Bryan, the Great Commoner, proclaimed that mankind would not be crucified on a cross of gold. In our day man—the good people of this state—is more likely to be crucified by thirst and poverty in a waterless desert." He did not like to quote Bryan, but after all Bryan was a Democrat and his name still rang echoes in parts of Nebraska—and in some hearts in the State Legislature. He was beyond scruple in the matter of an appeal *ad hominem*. He felt like a man in the center of a vortex and the walls were whirling him in.

On the day preceding the final vote Paul Lowe slept only a few hours. During the long afternoon while the votes were being taken, first on the amendments and then on the bill as a whole, he stayed close to the telephone to get news directly from the floor of the legislature.

The final vote was anticlimactic. Paul Lowe had been sure what the result would be, but he was surprised at the size of his defeat. Only fourteen legislators voted for the bill, thirty-one were opposed, and seven were not present or abstained.

When the voting was all over he put on his hat and coat and went home to Chilmark.

He lay down on the sofa in the living room at five o'clock and awoke in darkness to the telephone ringing. As he picked it up, Eleanor answered an extension in another room. He said "hello" simultaneously with her before an almost-familiar woman's voice said, "Governor Lowe, is that you? It's Katherine Prescott."

Paul Lowe said, "It's all right, Eleanor. I'll take it."

Eleanor's extension clicked off.

"I'm sorry to bother you at home, Governor," Katherine Prescott said. "I was in the visitors' gallery today and saw what happened. It was terrible. I wish I could help in some way, and perhaps I can. Would you sit for a typewriter portrait? I promise it'll be favorable. We can give another hearing to your reasons for wanting the North Platte dam. I know it's a little late and can't help now, but next time around it might be useful."

"Will Race Hardman let you put anything in print that goes against his own policy?"

Katherine Prescott said gently, "He's won, Governor. He can afford to be magnanimous in victory. And he really does admire you, you know. He thinks you're an exceptional man—for a politician. Can you spare any time on Thursday for the interview?"

Paul Lowe said, "What's a good time for you, Miss Prescott?"

"Any time you say."

"Eleven A.M.? In my office."

"I'll be there."

When he got up from the sofa he saw Eleanor in the entrance to the kitchen. She was wearing an apron.

"Who was that?" she asked.

He said, "A newspaperwoman who works for Race Hardman. She wants to do a column about me."

Eleanor said, "Dinner will be ready in a few minutes. I tried to let you sleep as long as I could, dear."

"I feel much better," Paul Lowe said.

38

On Thursday morning Paul Lowe had an unexpected visitor. Martha Scully announced on the intercom at ten forty-five: "Senator Vance Murdoch of Indiana is waiting outside, Governor. He has no appointment."

"Send him in right away, Martha."

Martha Scully sighed. She was in charge of his appointment schedule and during an average day he had conferences approximately every thirty minutes with a little leeway between to allow for answering telephone calls. Whenever he added anything to this schedule the logistics became complicated and Martha Scully's ingenuity was strained to the breaking point.

Paul Lowe crossed his office to meet Vance Murdoch at the door.

"This is a very pleasant surprise," he said.

They shook hands. Senator Murdoch moved into the office and sank his heavy body into a deep leather armchair facing Lowe's desk.

"You're probably wondering right now what's behind my coming here," Senator Murdoch said.

Pseudo-directness, Paul Lowe thought, the artful substitute for plain talk; the openness of manner that opaques purpose.

Paul Lowe sat down behind his desk. "You'll tell me in your own good time, Vance. Meanwhile, it's a pleasure to see you again."

"How much time have I got, Paul?"

"I have a newspaper interview scheduled at eleven. I can put it off a while."

"What I want to talk about won't take long. Paul, I had a very interesting talk with the President the other day. You may be the man to solve a big problem."

"What sort of problem?"

"Did the President speak to you about appointing Clayton to the high court?"

"Yes."

"What do you think of the appointment?"

"Clayton's a good judge. But I told the President I didn't want to see him on the highest court in our land."

"That's exactly how I feel," Senator Murdoch said. "Lamont Howard doesn't have to take his hat off to anybody as a politician. But sometimes he gets carried away with his own cleverness. That's the only way I can explain his wanting to appoint a Negro."

"I think we have different reasons for opposing the nomination, Senator."

"Sure," Senator Murdoch said absently. "Anyhow I told Lamont that this idea of his was a clinker. Naturally he was interested in what I thought since I'm on the Judiciary Committee and I'll have a lot to say about who gets confirmed." Senator Murdoch lowered his gaze. "Lamont finally agreed that the time isn't ripe for Clayton. Maybe he can be the next appointment after this one. Old Edmunson can't go on forever and we'll probably need someone to replace him in the next year or so. But that still leaves us with the problem of who can take over the seat Frank Joyce left vacant when he retired."

"Who does the President have in mind?"

"It's quite a problem. I've been trying to help Lamont work it out. We started with a long list and whittled it down. Then we whittled it some more. Finally Lamont asked me to dinner and we went over the names we had left. Then he commissioned me to find out how you'd feel about taking the appointment."

Vance Murdoch tried to make the final sentence sound as casual as the accounting of preceding events, but a subtle alteration in tone and emphasis betrayed him.

Paul Lowe stared at him. *"Me?"*

Senator Murdoch was amused. "I figured you might be surprised. But it makes sense. You fit the bill, Paul."

"How?"

"Right section of the country, right politics, right religion. The Court's got two Catholics—Gabriel Hart and Edward McCann—and one Jew, Waldo Shuler. That's enough of the minorities."

Paul Lowe was holding his chair arm tightly. "I don't have enough legal experience. I'm a country lawyer."

"You ran for attorney general of the state."

"And got licked."

Senator Murdoch shrugged. "Law training isn't the most important qualification. The Court needs men with broad experience. Experience in administration. Experience in the world."

"I don't have much of that, Senator. I've spent most of my life here in Nebraska."

"Served in the Army Air Corps, didn't you? Burma theater. You got to see how the other half of the world lives. And you worked in Washington as a law clerk to Charles Edmunson."

"One year."

"Edmunson says you're the best law clerk he ever had."

"That *is* a compliment. But I'd hardly call it judicial experience for becoming a Supreme Court justice."

"Only two of our current justices have ever been judges. If we picked only men who'd served as judges to be on the high court, we'd have missed some of our greatest justices. John Jay and John Marshall, Harlan Stone and Felix Frankfurter and Charles Evans Hughes. As Edmunson's law clerk you got a real inside view of how the Court operates."

"I've never dealt with constitutional law in my private practice."

"Who has? The Chief Justice, John Hampton, was a governor when he got appointed. He wasn't a constitutional lawyer. But he's worked out pretty well, hasn't he?"

Paul Lowe said, "There must be a hundred men better qualified to be a justice of the United States Supreme Court."

"Don't sell yourself short, Paul. You made a good reputation as a lawyer

—and you've done a good job as governor. We've had our eye on you for some time. And you've got powerful friends in the right quarter."

"That's news to me."

"Race Hardman thinks a lot of you. He was among the first to mention you for the appointment. He's even been to see the President about it. And Race Hardman swings a lot of weight."

"Race Hardman," Paul Lowe answered absently. It must have begun the night of the party in Hardman's home. The moment he told Race Hardman that he would try to get the North Platte dam built, the battle had been joined. But from the first clash Race must have been looking beyond the moment of triumph. Next year there might be another battle —the public temper might be different. Race Hardman might lose—and he couldn't trust Paul Lowe as governor of a state where he owned so much taxable property.

"Race thinks a lot of you," Senator Murdoch was saying. "You're doing a wonderful job as governor but you can't stay put here if you've got the stuff to go further. You owe a debt to the people of the whole United States, not just one part. You have to give them everything you've got. Just like we all do—or try to."

"I've been happy here," Paul Lowe said gently. "I'm not sure I'd like to be . . . kicked upstairs."

"Nobody's kicking you, Paul."

It's happened before, Senator, Paul Lowe thought. Harlan Stone was kicked upstairs to the Supreme Court because he did his job as Attorney General in a way that made things uncomfortable for some big corporations. And that's why Teddy Roosevelt was kicked up from Governor of New York to the Vice-Presidency. This gentle way of getting rid of someone was invented by Americans—if you can't fire a man, promote him.

Paul Lowe sat back from the desk. "Are you seriously offering me the nomination, Senator?"

"I can't do that, Paul. It's up to the President. I'm just supposed to sound you out to make sure you won't refuse if it's offered."

"I'll have to think it over."

"Fine." Senator Murdoch stood up. "One more thing, Paul. This mustn't go any further until you've made up your mind. The next word has to be from the President. Lamont is touchy about things like that."

"I understand. Thanks for coming to see me, Vance."

"Always a pleasure, Paul. Always a pleasure. Give my best to Eleanor."

"My best to Patricia. And your lovely daughter."

Paul Lowe opened the door. Senator Murdoch said, "If everything works out and you come to live in Washington, we hope to see a lot more of you."

Vance Murdoch went out through the anteroom. Martha Scully was hard at work at her desk and beyond her Katherine Prescott was seated in a chair, leafing through the pages of a magazine.

"Miss Prescott?"

She looked up from the magazine and smiled.

41

"Won't you come in?"

In his office she took the chair that Senator Murdoch had recently vacated. He noted that her figure was almost heavy, but with a small waist which made the total effect curvesome rather than plump.

"Wasn't that Senator Vance Murdoch who left your office?" she asked.

"Yes, it was."

"I've seen him in Washington. On the Judiciary Committee, isn't he?" There was a steadiness in her hazel eyes that asked a further question.

Paul Lowe countered, "If you're trying to read something into his visit, Miss Prescott, I merely met him on my last trip to Washington and invited him to stop by and see me when he could."

She nodded, skeptically, and they quickly got down to the reason for the interview. She balanced a steno pad on her knee and her pencil seemed to fly over the lined pages. Her green wool dress had pulled back slightly from the rounded sheen of a stockinged leg.

Paul Lowe enumerated for her the reasons he thought the North Platte dam was vital to the future of Nebraska. Katherine Prescott's pencil kept time with him, then stopped near the bottom of a page. She flipped the page over.

"Governor, my column is supposed to deal with interesting viewpoints of the man in the news." She tapped the steno book. "I'd better try to surround this material with some of your other opinions."

"You can ask questions and I'll try to come up with answers."

"All right. What was your reaction to the Supreme Court's decision?"

"The one affecting our rights in the South Platte River?"

"Yes."

"As governor of Nebraska there's only one way I could feel."

"And if you were not governor of Nebraska?"

"Hard to say. The Court did flout the traditional method of apportioning water rights. But Justice Edmunson had strong arguments. And someone had to make a decision—no matter how difficult or painful."

"You worked for Justice Edmunson as his law clerk. What was your opinion of him?"

"The same as most people's. A great man."

Katherine Prescott's light-colored eyes seemed to become warmer and more brilliant. "Yes, he is. I particularly admire the way he treats sacred cows as though they were ordinary heifers."

Paul Lowe felt the tug of perverse contrariness. "Well, there's no reason he couldn't pay a little more attention to precedent." She was looking at him, puzzled, and he plunged on: "A judge can't ignore what's been built up over centuries. You have to compare the experience of past and present —and make progress by moving the line forward between what's permitted and what's forbidden."

"Is that what you would do on the Court?"

He smiled. "I can't answer a hypothetical question."

"Governor, I don't believe it is a hypothetical question."

42

More than steadiness behind the hazel eyes now. She was not a woman to be underestimated.

Paul Lowe asked carefully, "What leads you to say that, Miss Prescott?"

"Oh, a number of things."

"Such as?"

"An item that appeared in the *Washington Insider* column. It mentioned a rumor in the capital that a Midwestern political figure would be appointed to a high judicial post. I didn't write the item and neither did any of the other regular contributors. Then I found out it had come in directly on the teletype from Race Hardman's office."

"That doesn't sound very significant to me."

"It didn't to me either—until I saw Senator Murdoch in your office. I'm quite sure that as he left I heard him say something about your living in Washington. And he is the second-ranking man on the Judiciary Committee and a good friend of the President. And there has been a vacancy on the Supreme Court ever since Frank Joyce retired."

"You're a good reporter, Miss Prescott. But you don't really expect me to confirm or deny this kind of speculation, do you?"

"Governor, would it help if I promised that anything you say is strictly off the record?"

There was no reason for him to trust her—but he needed someone to talk to. If this was being naïve, he had a compulsion to be.

"You won't publish anything unless I tell you?"

She held up three fingers. "Scout's honor."

"There isn't much of interest to tell," Paul Lowe said. "Senator Murdoch didn't offer me the nomination. He only came to find out if I'd accept if it were offered."

"What did you tell him?"

"That I'd let him know tomorrow morning."

"What will your decision be?"

He had not confronted that. "I think my answer is going to be no," he said.

"Why?"

"Several reasons. I have an important job to do in this state—a job I was elected to do."

"You're being offered a much more important job."

"Secondly, I honestly don't believe I have the qualifications."

"Apparently the President thinks you have."

Paul Lowe returned slowly to his desk and sat down. "He uses a different standard of values. It's important that I come from the Midwest, for example, that I'm a Protestant, and that I have no important political enemies outside the state."

"Other men fit that description. He chose you."

He became very still. He did not know exactly when he decided to tell her, or why he did, except out of sheer turmoil of mind.

"If you want the truth, I'm scared."

"That the job is too big for you?"

He nodded. "When I was Edmunson's law clerk, one Supreme Court justice nearly had a nervous breakdown. The work was too much for him."

"I can't imagine that happening to you."

Paul Lowe made no reply. The intercom buzzed but he paid no attention. It was curious but during the silence he felt as though they were talking with no words audible. With aimless curiosity he watched her. Her hand lay loosely outstretched on her lap. Her shoe dangled partly off her stockinged foot.

He had to refer to an obscurely felt loyalty. "I want to talk to my wife first. Find out what she thinks."

"She'll approve. Almost any woman would."

"Yes, I suppose so." Strange—he no longer felt that Eleanor's approval was important. He had been able to say what he really felt to this woman, this stranger.

Katherine Prescott rose. "I've taken up enough of your time, Governor." She extended her hand. "May I wish you luck in whatever you decide to do?"

"Thank you."

Her handclasp was firm but soft.

She said, "You won't need luck, though. You'll succeed. Some men are like that."

Paul Lowe said, "I think somehow you've gotten the wrong impression about me."

"I think somehow I haven't." She put the steno pad into her large handbag. "I hope you'll like my article when it's written."

"I'll look forward to it."

When the door closed behind her, Paul Lowe glanced at himself in the long wall mirror opposite. There, in three-quarters length, stood a replica of himself. He pushed out his chest. In the mirror he saw himself clothed in black robes and majesty, judiciously graying.

When he was alone, he was subject to this sort of foolishness.

"If you've made up your mind," Eleanor said, "why not call Senator Murdoch right away? I don't see any point in making him wait."

She tilted the small watering can over the African violets in the white flowerpot. It occurred to him that her liking for flowers was so invariable, so patterned, that it was really an attempt to introduce some sort of order into her world, to give her environment a needed symmetry.

"I promised to tell him tomorrow," Paul Lowe said. "I can afford to sleep on it."

"You can't turn it down. It's too big an opportunity. This could be a turning point in your life."

"In one way or another, everything is."

"I suppose it's up to you. It's no use my saying anything or making any suggestions."

44

The large window reflected her glasslike movement with the watering can.

He called Senator Murdoch that evening.

"Vance—this is Paul Lowe."

"Good evening, Paul."

"I decided not to wait until morning to call you. I've talked it over with my wife and she's in favor of my accepting the nomination if it's offered to me. If the President wants me, I'm his man."

"I think you've made the right decision, Paul. The President will be pleased. I'll report to him right away."

In the morning while Paul Lowe was showering, he heard the thin ringing of the telephone through the rush of water. His hand stopped a bar of soap against his chest. A few moments later footsteps hurried to the bathroom door.

"Paul, Paul, come quickly! It's the President. Calling from the White House."

"Tell him I'll be right there."

"But it's the President!"

"No matter who it is, I'm full of soap."

He rinsed hurriedly, grabbed a towel and wrapped it around his midriff. He ran in bare feet, damp-dry, dry-damp, damp-smudge prints behind him in the wood flooring.

"Governor Lowe? I'll put President Howard on now."

Lamont Howard's twang, "Got you out of bed, did I?"

"Not quite. I was taking a shower, Mr. President."

A drawling amusement in the voice: "I forgot the hour's time difference between here and Nebraska. But you'll have to get used to getting up bright and early if you're going to be a justice of the Supreme Court."

There was a barely audible gasp of breath on the line that meant Eleanor was listening in.

"That decision is up to you, Mr. President."

"That's why I'm calling. I heard from Vance Murdoch a few minutes ago. I've got a form right here in front of me—for nominating a Supreme Court justice. I'm going to fill in your name and send it to the Senate today. I don't expect any trouble getting you confirmed. Of course you'll have to come to Washington for the hearing."

"When do you think that will be?"

"Probably a couple of days."

"I'll be there, Mr. President."

"Fine. Now I want to ask a favor: don't mention this to anyone. I don't want the news to leak out before the newspaper boys are informed. That way nobody's feelings get hurt."

"Whatever you say, Mr. President."

"Congratulations . . . Mr. Justice Lowe."

The receiver made a clicking sound. Paul Lowe put down the instrument. Her heels clicking toward him on the flooring were like excited exclamations.

Paul Lowe held out his arms as his wife burst into the bedroom to greet him.

Newsweek, January 19th:

The Senate's press gallery was full when at a few minutes past noon a messenger arrived from the White House to give the list of new appointments to the Clerk.

The Clerk intoned, "A message from the President of the United States."

In the wide room perhaps thirty Senators were at their desks. There was a sudden tensing. The press section and the public galleries hushed.

The Clerk said, "Paul Lincoln Lowe to be Associate Justice of the Supreme Court of the United States."

A moment later as other Senators quickly filed in to the chamber, Senator Vance Murdoch of Indiana rose to ask for immediate consideration of the nomination by the Senate. On a motion from Senator Binder of Tennessee, however, the appointment was referred to the Judiciary Committee for further consideration.

If confirmed, Governor Paul Lowe will fill the vacancy created by the retirement of Mr. Justice Frank Joyce.

Now all Washington is asking: what sort of man *is* Paul Lincoln Lowe?

"If they want to know what sort of man you are," Martha Scully asked, "why don't they come to me?"

She stood over the desk as Paul Lowe finished reading the report in *Newsweek.* On the desk nearby were stacked *Time* magazine, *The New York Times,* the Washington *Post,* the St. Louis *Post-Dispatch,* the Chicago *Tribune,* and several other newspapers and magazines.

"None of the stories really tells what sort of man you are," Martha added firmly. "I wish you'd grant some of the requests for interviews that are piling up. Then they could do a better job of telling people what you're like."

"I haven't time for interviews, Martha. I've got to wrap up matters here before I leave for Washington. Is Wellman here?"

"He came in five minutes ago, Governor," Martha said. "But you'd do yourself more good if you talked with the newspaper people. I've been barraged with phone calls and telegrams and . . ."

"If my appointment goes through," Paul Lowe said patiently, "Henry Wellman will be the next governor of the state. It's my job to bring him up to the minute."

Martha sighed. "Henry Wellman as governor. It'll be quite a comedown." She started for the door.

"Martha," he said.

"Yes, Governor?"

"If I'm confirmed I'm going to need a staff. I have to start with a secretary."

Martha Scully waited, angularly tense.

"I'm not sure whether you'll like Washington. But I wish you would come with me."

Martha's wide thin mouth trembled. "You know I'll come, Governor. After seventeen years, I can't leave you to fend for yourself."

Lowe slouched back in his swivel chair. "I'll need law clerks too. A lot of young men would like the job but I want the right pair. And I don't have time to look around."

"Have you talked with Mr. Norris, Governor?"

"Ken?"

"He's your best friend, and a good lawyer. I'm sure he'd be glad to help you find the right people."

"A good suggestion, Martha. When I'm through with the Lieutenant Governor, put through a call to Ken Norris for me."

She left with a quick and carefree step.

The door opened a moment later and a small man entered who seemed all awink with expectancy. His eyes glinted under wrinkled brows and there was nervous impatience in the very articulation of his body. Henry Wellman—on the eve of his greatness.

"Henry, I hope you've got a couple of hours," Lowe said. "We have a lot to go over."

"I'm at your disposal, Governor," Henry Wellman said.

Paul Lowe carefully went over the accumulated mass of state papers, proposed legislation, bills waiting to be signed, invitations to be accepted or refused, projects pending and the power arrayed behind each. Wellman's questions were laconic; his eyes observant. Paul Lowe felt that not only his answers but his method of answering was under scrutiny. Henry Wellman was visibly changing his image, pouring himself like hot wax into a mold.

"Now for the most important thing," Lowe said finally. "The one I wish I had been able to see through to the finish. I suffered a defeat on raising money for the North Platte. This is the most important piece of legislation I'm bequeathing to you, Henry. When you succeed in raising the money for it, it will be the biggest accomplishment of your administration."

Henry Wellman shifted in his chair and grimaced, squeezing his pointed face together like the collapsible features of a rubber doll.

"I believe in going at these controversial questions with patience." Rabbit smile. "Everyone has his way of working, Governor. You're a more dynamic type than I am." A keen knife of resentment slicked through the words. "I have to work things out thoroughly in my own mind before I take action." The usurper "I"—he was already in office.

"Of course. I'm only emphasizing the vital importance of this problem."

"I appreciate that, Governor. And you can count on me to do my best."

"My best"—ambiguous words under which men escape their responsibilities. Omnibus words freighted with enough meanings to satisfy the weakest and the strongest. Paul Lowe had a photo flash of Henry Wellman, with pinched face and worried air, peering over an edge of Race Hardman's capacious pocket.

"Henry," Paul Lowe said, "I'm going to count on it because I'd hate to leave this job in the hands of a man who wouldn't give it everything."

"I certainly will, Governor."

They shook hands. Henry Wellman's handclasp was firm and assured: the practiced grasp of one who had schooled himself in the lesser signs of character. His gaze was straightforward also, disconcerting, steadfast honest stare.

"Governor, you're going to be a hard man to replace in this job. If I can do half as well as you've done, I'll be satisfied."

"I want you to make a fine record, Henry. That's my wish for you."

Henry Wellman was touched but wary, responding to the wish but guarding against the admonition. He departed in an atmosphere of warmth. When the door closed, Paul Lowe felt oppressed. He sat in his chair with his hands on his knees and stared without seeing at the small figures in the carpet until vision faded in the replication of detail tracing itself through the fiber. In this way the Buddhists gathered before an altar and repeated "*Amida, Amida . . .*" until they lost all consciousness of self. One could dip the self into a bottomless pool of monotony and meaninglessness until the soul was quiet.

Somehow the secrets of the East never worked for him. The task unfinished still loomed larger than his powers.

He searched his mind for some kind of reassurance . . .

Edmunson was famed for his dissents—"The voice of liberty speaks in the accents of a minority," he had said—but few realized that Charles Edmunson had written over four hundred opinions for the majority of the Court. Only fifty or so in dissent. Yet those fifty had made his reputation as an idealist, a humanist. It had been chastening to work with him, to watch the painstaking movement of his mind toward those concepts now accepted as a part of the fundamental law. Edmunson did not reason from a fixed or unmalleable theory; he rested his faith in the power of the human intellect to discover truth. "Do not live in a closed universe but in one expanding outward to meet new experiences, new data, new revelations. We must stretch the past to fit the size of the future."

That was Charles Edmunson. Men like Edmunson were great because they could express a vision of the world that was original yet self-consistent. "Let us all labor to lift the quota of reason that operates in human affairs." A lofty ambition—Edmunson could reach for such a serene and magnificent goal because he was a hero of a kind before Nietzsche, before Dostoevski, unable to conceive self-doubt. Lesser men, Paul Lowe thought, are racked with self-suspicion. The spears we gather into our breasts are of our own making.

But the fever of his uncertainty was beginning to subside. Four hundred opinions written for the Court and only fifty in dissent—and that

48

was Charles Edmunson. The other eight justices were not natural enemies. In most instances he could agree with them. And he would have Edmunson for a guide. How wonderful to know someone *knew*.

One might call Edmunson a poet—"Between two worlds that may otherwise spin to destruction, the law inserts the power of its gravity." He wrote poetry compact, austere, Olympian, that somehow contained hard dimensional experience.

Paul Lowe shook his head dubiously. *Restrain poetical flights.* Memorize the content of the jars that hold political and economic and legal wisdom. For a time at least he must cease all other forms of reading. He must read law.

Thank God for Edmunson, he thought.

5

"Dear Mr. Justice To Be"—Ken Norris wrote—"On the eve of your confirmation I would like to assure you that you are as fitted for the job as any man can be who has had absolutely no training or experience and lacks the proper judicial temperament. There is little danger of your carrying the high degree of legal scholarship to the Court which in earlier days was brought by Holmes and Cardozo and Brandeis. So all of us who know you surrender you to the unparalleled tasks that lie ahead with confidence that you will return the law to the strong and simple faith of our Founders, bring back the horse and buggy, and assist the hoodlums masquerading as corporation presidents in the marvelous and diversified ways they have discovered to rob our country blind."

There was a postscript: "I have asked my own law clerk, Jack Broderick, if he would like to go to Washington to teach you the fundamentals of constitutional law—as your clerk. Jack is very bright—number-two man in his class at Yale—and a hard worker who loves to dig for facts more than a pig does for truffles. If you want him, he's yours. I'll send him along postpaid as soon as I get word of your confirmation."

Paul Lowe held the letter in a pocket of his robe between two fingers of his hand. His smile slowly faded as he stared out the hotel window at a tree-lined street. Yellow morning light streamed past white curtains into the room.

"Aren't you going to eat your breakfast?" Eleanor asked.

"In a minute."

"Please stop worrying, Paul. It's going to be all right."

"I wish it were over with, that's all. It's the waiting. We've been in Washington two days and they keep postponing the hearing. Who are these other people they're talking to?"

"Nobody important. Senator Murdoch explained that. But they have to listen to any witnesses who want to testify. Your turn will come."

He left the window and sat opposite her on the deep-cushioned chair. The table's white linen was immaculate. Cutlery gleamed and a discreet flame burned below the container that had kept the food warm. Breakfast waited on Wedgwood plates. Eleanor wore a light blue robe over her white nightgown. Curlers were in her hair—iron braids amid the brown.

How much gray without color rinse? Still, she was a handsome woman. He inserted his finger through the hole in the top of a round metal cover and looked in at the wedge of ham that turned up pink-brown edges toward him. On a plate nearby the sunlight retoasted the toast with golden color.

"I don't like being cooped up," he said. "All we've done since we came here is stay in this hotel room."

"Why don't you go for a walk?"

"How can I? The phone might ring."

"Fifteen minutes won't matter one way or the other."

"A fifteen-minute walk won't help. I have to get out for a while. I'd like to go for a long hike."

"Where would you go?"

"I don't know."

"Then you may as well relax and have your breakfast."

Even when what she communicated was not specifically helpful, Eleanor had a calming effect, because she enabled him to glimpse her simple ordered world and momentarily accept its values. If nothing else, eat breakfast. If housebound, go for a walk. For every problem there was waiting a neatly wrapped solution.

They finished breakfast in silence.

"Why don't you go down and see if there's mail?" she suggested.

One of her favorite solutions was to occupy time. Time, when occupied, left no space for problems. It was as good an answer as any. The difference between simple and sophisticated minds is that sophisticated minds take longer to arrive at the same answers—and then don't trust them.

At the hotel desk, the short bespectacled clerk was deferential.

"Yes, Governor Lowe. There are several letters. I was just about to send them up to your room."

"I'll look at them here."

He sat in the lobby and opened the mail that Martha Scully had forwarded. Letters of congratulation—adulatory, warm, some sincere. All made him uneasy. Ken Norris understood that the way to banish doubt is to exaggerate it, not pretend there is no reason for it. These letter writers saw him as a hero leading a parade down an avenue of triumph—bemedaled, stiffblooded. A quaking heart pulsed behind the medals.

A smaller envelope appeared among large white official envelopes, lightweight and light blue, addressed in a graceful hand in darker blue ink. In the upper left-hand corner was a name: *Katherine Prescott*. Her address followed.

His fingers felt for the edge of the letter within and carefully ripped down the envelope. A clipping fell out together with a note handwritten on folded light blue stationery.

Dear Governor:
Enclosed is my column about you that appeared in the Lincoln *Sentinel*. Race Hardman called today and said he liked it! In fact, he now thinks

51

we should do a six-part series on Nebraska's contribution to the Supreme Court—which means you. By the time this reaches you, you should be settled into your judicial robes [Lowe winced] and ready to think about your place in posterity. I would like to do the series about you but I would need more than the usual biographical data. By now everyone knows that. I would need more intimate detail—a closeup look at what has been seen so far through a telescope.

All this doubtless interests you hardly at all—but would be a marvelous break for me if I can do it. If you can spare the time for a few auto-biographical sittings, I will come to Washington at your convenience. And be most grateful . . .

She signed her name with an arching graceful stroke. He turned the page.

P.S. While you're in Washington, I think it might be helpful for you to meet Tom Jeffreys. He's with a television network, bright and knowl-edgeable, and a very good friend of mine. He can fill you in on things you might need to know. I've written him and he will call.

He glanced through the clippings. The column based on their interview was interestingly written in a discursive chatty fashion.

He read her letter again and found that he was listening to the words as she would speak them. Her voice held her picture in his memory. Through the lobby doors intermittently streamed prosperous-looking men and women in the wake of bellboys carrying luggage.

"Governor Lowe?" He looked up. A young bellboy in a red suit with prominent brass buttons hovered near him.

"Yes."

"Phone call for you, Governor. You can take it in the lobby."

He followed the boy across the lobby to a bank of yellow phones stationed on a shelf. He picked up the indicated one.

"Governor Lowe speaking."

"Just a moment." The operator's voice was quickly succeeded by the voice of Senator Vance Murdoch.

"Paul? Can you get over here to the Judiciary Committee at about eleven o'clock?"

Paul Lowe glanced at his watch. "That gives me an hour. Plenty of time."

"Good. See you then."

He could not resist. "How does it look, Vance?"

Senator Murdoch sounded a bit tired. "Not as good as I hoped. We've had a few witnesses who seem to be working off personal grudges. But I hope you'll have the answers."

"Is that all you're going to tell me?"

"It's all I'm supposed to. Better if you don't come over-prepared. There's only two pieces of advice I'll give you. Don't lose your temper no matter what. And keep an eye on George Walsh."

"The Senator from Virginia?"

"He's been sharpening a few shafts for you. You'll have to get by him to get the nomination." Senator Murdoch sounded worried.

"I'll be there at eleven o'clock," Paul Lowe said.

As he made the turn down the wing of a corridor that led to the entrance of the Committee Room, Paul Lowe walked rapidly with a slightly lunging stride. Massed near the entrance were reporters, television cameramen and press photographers. Fragments of questions reached him, quick-flaring, gone as swiftly as the flash of bulbs. He moved through floodlights, bathed in artificial glare until he entered the doorway. At the committee table the Senators were seated in a formidable phalanx, raised a few feet above floor level. At the press tables nearby every chair was taken. Some reporters were already scribbling notes but most were lounging back with chairs half turned to observe new arrivals. The clock on the wall read one minute before eleven.

A policeman on duty at the door nodded, "Good morning, Governor." A committee clerk moved quickly forward, threading his way past the press tables in the room.

"Will you come this way, Governor?"

Paul Lowe followed him to the witness table, and the clerk pulled a chair out for him. High windows on the east side showed the sky—gray with long ragged streamers of cloud.

The room *bustled*. "Governor, will you let us have a couple of pictures?" "Stand right there, please. Now move over and let's have one with Senator Murdoch." "Mr. Chairman . . . Senator Sherman . . . will you step over here?" He was breathless, caught in a whirl of people and apparatus, trailing wires, microphones, whirring cameras, *"Will you get off the goddamn cable, please?"*

"Governor! A moment!"

He was standing between Vance Murdoch of Indiana and the chairman, Carl Sherman of Ohio, and they were all smiling into cameras. Then they were shaking hands. A photographer pushed through, puffing slightly, taking quick shots with his Rolleiflex. Other Senators edged forward to the center of the scene, a bit nervy, but politicians are born with brass skins. Arm in arm. Usual blather . . . That's George Walsh—tall thin sour-looking man standing on the edge of the crowd with a slightly superior smile. The fact he did not try to join in the picture-taking stamped him an enemy.

"Are we ready?" Senator Sherman asked. He was back at the center of the committee table.

Paul Lowe said, "I'm at your disposal, Mr. Chairman."

The clerk came forward with a leather covered Bible.

"Do you solemnly swear," Carl Sherman intoned, "that the testimony you give before this Judiciary Committee will be the truth, the whole truth, and nothing but the truth?"

"I do," Paul Lowe answered.

Carl Sherman looked to the right end of the committee table and then to the left to be sure all members were present. Photographers found places along the side walls of the room; reporters turned their chairs forward to face the committee. Paul Lowe took his place at the small witness table. He brushed back his sandy hair and waited.

"This hearing of the Senate Committee on the Judiciary," Senator Sherman announced in a clear resonant tone, "is being held to consider the nomination of Paul Lincoln Lowe as an Associate Justice of the Supreme Court of the United States. On this third day of the hearing, we are privileged to have before us the nominee himself, the distinguished governor of the State of Nebraska." Carl Sherman made a slight inclination of his head to where the Senator from Nebraska, Harold Campbell, was seated. Then his gaze returned to Paul Lowe. "Governor Lowe, we are happy to have you with us today to answer our questions. We know you understand that the purpose of this investigation is to carry out a constitutional function fully and fairly. There is nothing of any personal nature meant or implied in any questions you will be asked."

In the momentary silence, Paul Lowe heard the whirring of television cameras.

"Senator," he answered slowly, "I think the character of every public servant must always be open to public scrutiny. I am fully prepared to answer any questions."

He wished his voice had less of the twanging sound of his Western origin. It seemed inadequate to the formality of this moment.

"Would you care to make any public statement before we begin?" Senator Sherman asked.

"No, Mr. Chairman."

"Very well, then," Carl Sherman said, "I think we should begin questioning in our customary fashion. Senator Murdoch?"

Senator Murdoch's large bulk leaned forward slightly in his chair. "Governor Lowe, would you tell this committee your legal training and experience? Whatever you think qualifies you for appointment to the Supreme Court."

Paul Lowe said, "Well, Senator, I have been for many years a practicing attorney. I am a graduate of Yale Law School, in 1947. I am also qualified to practice before the Supreme Court."

"Is it true," Senator Murdoch asked, "that you also served as a law clerk on the Court?"

"Yes, Senator. In 1948 I served as law clerk to Associate Justice Charles Edmunson."

Vance Murdoch nodded approvingly. On the other side of the committee table there was a restless stir from George Walsh.

"How many years have you actually been engaged in the practice of law?" Senator Murdoch asked.

"Well, I set up an office in 1949 and continued in the private practice of law until I retired in order to accept the Democratic nomination for governor in my state."

54

"Is it true, Governor, that in those years of private practice you became one of the leading attorneys in your state?"

"I don't think I'm the proper person to comment on that, Senator."

"We all appreciate your reticence, Governor," Senator Murdoch said. He held up several sheets of paper. "But I would like to put into the record a brief summary of opinions from bar associations, prominent persons, and nonpartisan groups who have studied your commendable career at the bar. Is there any objection?"

"How long is it, Senator?" Carl Sherman asked with a trace of weariness.

"Approximately eight pages."

"And it consists mainly of tributes to the good character and high ability of the nominee?"

Senator Murdoch nodded. "In addition, there are two pages listing prominent corporations which have employed the noteworthy legal talents of Governor Lowe before he was elected to his present high office."

"I don't see any objection, Senator," Carl Sherman glanced at his colleagues seated at the table, "to having this material entered in the record. But it will save valuable time for the committee if we obtain consent to have this valuable document entered *without* being read."

There was relieved assent along the length of the committee table and a small murmur of amusement from the press and the audience.

Senator Murdoch handed down the sheaf of papers to the recording clerk, who placed it alongside his stenotype machine.

"Do you have any further questions to ask the nominee?" Carl Sherman asked.

"Yes," Senator Murdoch said. "I would like to know whether he was ever selected to run for any political office before he was nominated for governor."

Carl Sherman rubbed a hand over his balding head and smiled at Paul Lowe.

"I'm sure the Governor can fill us in on that."

Paul Lowe said, "In the year 1952 I was nominated for attorney general. I was very roundly defeated."

The large room warmed with laughter. Senator Campbell of Nebraska turned approvingly to speak to Senator Dunbar of New Jersey on his left.

Senator Murdoch waited for the laughter to subside before he added: "Isn't it true that the post of state attorney general is the most responsible legal position in the power of your state to confer on any man?"

"Yes, sir," Paul Lowe said. "Perhaps that is why the people chose not to confer it on me. But I flatter myself that the decision was taken out of my hands by the fact that 1952 was the year Dwight D. Eisenhower headed the Republican national ticket. It was not a good year to run for political office on the opposing political ticket."

He was at ease—responsive to the audience behind him and to the Senate committee members before him.

"Were you nominated for any other high political office?" Senator Murdoch prompted.

55

"Yes, Senator. I was nominated for lieutenant governor in 1956. With my usual exquisite timing, that was when Dwight D. Eisenhower ran again—this time for re-election."

The responses came from the audience, the members of the press and the committee members as easily as though he pushed a button that called for simulated laughter. Here he was as he would appear on a television news screen. A forty-six year old, rough-cut farm boy with untidy sandy hair and skin rather grizzled and on closer view a little pockmarked, sliding down in his seat as was his custom. Head well shaped with large ears that lay close to his head, fierce-looking shaggy brows, and deep sun-graven wrinkles at the eyecorners. Not too bad-looking in the rugged way that most Americans were trained to consider as trustworthy because it reminded them of open land and venturing pioneer spirits who went trustworthily to slaughter Indians and drive them from their land and establish rude prairie towns where a man could drink himself insensible and consort with cheap women and gamble his money away and shoot other men over a chamois bag of gold, sleep in the open with pine needles for a pillow and stars above and be kind to his horse. What could be wrong with a man like that?

Senator Murdoch said, "After that, did you return to the private practice of the law?"

"It began to strike me, Senator, that that was the sovereign wish of the people."

Senator Murdoch cut quickly through resurgent amusement. "Fortunately, the people of Nebraska later changed their minds and elected you governor of their great state. It seems to me, Governor, that their last decision was the mature and wise one." Vance Murdoch's large eyes glowed with pleasure at his own grace. "I have no further questions for the distinguished witness."

"Senator Campbell," Carl Sherman said.

Senator Campbell inclined his pale, haggard-looking face forward, blinking in the strong lights:

"There is one point I'd like to be reassured about by the governor of my home state. The Supreme Court has been criticized for making laws rather than interpreting them. I'd like to hear your opinion on that subject, Governor."

"It seems perfectly clear that our Constitution vests the power to make law with Congress, not with the Supreme Court," Paul Lowe said. "I think a major task of the Court is to obey the Constitution as well as to interpret it."

"Do you think the Supreme Court should bring about major changes in this country by suddenly discovering new things the Constitution is supposed to mean?"

"I think the major instrument for social change in this country is the Congress. I am perfectly willing to leave that job to the wisdom of the Congress."

Senator Campbell smiled. "Thank you, Governor. That's all." He sat back and then suddenly leaned forward to speak into the microphone on the table before him. "I just want to add that even though I'm from the opposite party, I think the people of Nebraska have had a devoted public servant in Governor Lowe."

Senator Murdoch beamed. At the first hint of applause starting, Carl Sherman's gavel came down.

"Senator Sprigh," he announced.

Senator Sprigh said, "I want it clearly understood that I certainly do not intend to cast reflection upon Governor Lowe's wartime service and honorable record. He is entitled to wear the Air Medal Cross, the Purple Heart, and the Distinguished Flying Cross. He served four years in the Army Air Force and received an honorable discharge. He was wounded in action in the Burma theater of operations. But I would like to inquire a little more closely into this part of Governor Lowe's life, because of certain questions raised by other testimony we have heard."

Vance Murdoch snapped, "I don't put any stock in testimony obviously motivated by prejudice."

The gavel tapped lightly again in warning, and Senator Murdoch fell silent.

Senator Sprigh said, "I would like to ask if you know a man named Oliver Owens."

Ah, that was it.

"Yes, I do, Senator," Paul Lowe said. "I flew with him in the Burma theater."

"On March seventh, 1943, were you on a mission with Oliver Owens?"

"I was."

"And were you both shot down by enemy ground fire?"

"That is approximately what happened."

"What *exactly* happened, Governor? We've already heard Mr. Owens' version of what occurred."

"Captain Owens and I were both serving as fighter pilots with the Tenth Air Force under Major General Bissell . . ."

"Don't you mean the Fourteenth Air Force, Governor?"

"No, sir. On March seventh, it was still the Tenth Air Force. Three days later, on March tenth, our unit was merged into a separate United States Air Force called the Fourteenth, including the China Air Task Force under the command of Brigadier General Claire Chennault. On that date, however, neither Captain Owens nor myself was active."

"You had been shot down?"

"That is correct, Senator."

"Will you describe, briefly, how that happened?"

"On March seventh we were flying escort protection for heavy bombers that were attacking a Japanese airdrome. We were jumped by thirty Japanese fighters. In the battle that followed, Captain Owens and I became separated from the rest of the group. His plane was damaged. I flew escort with him until he was forced to make a landing in mountainous terrain. I was about to mark the position and leave when two Jap Zeros appeared above him. I stayed to keep them off and destroyed the planes. By that time I was too low on fuel. In attempting an emergency landing near Owens' plane, I crashed."

"What happened then, Governor?"

"Friendly Burmese natives took us down to their village, and treated our injuries. Later they helped us to return to our base."

"How long were you with these natives before you returned to your own people?"

"Almost five weeks."

"During that time you became very close with these natives, did you not?"

"I was very grateful to them for having saved my life."

"Was there anyone in particular you were most friendly with, Governor?"

"With the family of Chung-jin. I lived in his house."

Thatched hut with a large open room and the small sleeping chambers. He was lying on a bamboo matting, his leg in wooden splints, and Miat was bringing him an earthenware mug. The mug was cold and wet and the strong brew was hot and salty.

"Chung-jin was the leader of the group who rescued you and pilot Owens?"

"Yes, Senator."

"How many were there in Chung-jin's family, Governor?"

"Himself, his wife, and daughter."

"How old was his daughter?"

"Miat was seventeen."

"Is it true, Governor, that the girl Miat was very much attracted to you?"

Slender and beautiful figure in lissome cotton with small budding breasts. Solemn tan face. Bad teeth. A scar on her leg where it had been slashed for the snakebite.

"I was friendly with all of Chung-jin's family. I liked them all very much."

"Is it true that you went through a form of marriage ceremony with the girl Miat?"

How Miat would laugh—her broken teeth showing broadly.

"It most certainly is not true, Senator."

"You are aware, Governor, that you are testifying under oath?"

"I am perfectly aware of that, Senator."

Senator Sprigh seemed satisfied.

Carl Sherman asked, "Is that all, Senator?"

"Yes, Mr. Chairman," Sprigh said.

Senator Murdoch leaned forward to speak clearly into the microphone before him. "I'm glad this is on the record. I hope it will dismiss once and for all what I believe has been malicious testimony before this committee."

"Senator Dunbar," Carl Sherman announced.

Senator Dunbar of New Jersey looked over the top of his gray-rimmed glasses inquisitively.

"Governor, do you know what sort of beliefs were held by Chung-jin and his family?"

"I'm not quite sure what you mean, Senator."

"Political beliefs—religious beliefs."

Wizened wise and grinning old man, muscular thin body seated with arms akimbo—how do you say to that, Master?

"Chung-jin had no politics as far as I was able to discover. He was a Taoist."

"Were you in sympathy with Chung-jin's religious beliefs?"

"I am in sympathy with any man's religious belief if it is sincere."

There was a small scattering of applause. Carl Sherman lifted his gavel threateningly. Sound died.

"Did you have long discussions with Chung-jin about what Taoism meant—its possible value to those of us in the Western world?"

"I believe I did, yes, Senator."

"Do you believe Christians have something to learn from the teachings of Tao, Governor Lowe?"

"I believe all men have a great deal to learn from each other. What's necessary is that we keep our minds open to hear what the other person has to say."

Again a small riffle of applause, which Senator Carl Sherman scowled into silence. Down the length of the committee table some shifting of position occurred. Senator Murdoch's heavy dark face became a trifle solemn. Senator George Walsh pursed his underlip thoughtfully.

"Would you call Taoism a native American philosophy, Governor?" Senator Dunbar asked.

"Obviously not."

"Would you call it an alien philosophy?"

That word has been abused, Senator, Paul Lowe thought. Nothing should be alien to an inquisitive mind.

Paul Lowe said, "I can't believe that we in the United States have a monopoly on all the wisdom accumulated by man over the centuries. A philosophy is not necessarily wrong because it is alien. Other nations and other cultures have also learned from their experience and it would be shortsighted and foolish of us to refuse to hear what they have learned."

"Would you include the political theories of, say, Russia in that category, Governor?"

"I believe we can learn from the wise men of any country—even those we might consider our enemies."

A note of incredulity entered Senator Dunbar's voice: "You think America has a good deal to learn from Karl Marx or Lenin?"

"I would also say the Russians have a great deal to learn from Thomas Jefferson and Abraham Lincoln."

"Do I understand, Governor, that you would put Marx and Lenin on the same level as Jefferson and Lincoln?"

"In the sense that all have made contributions to human thought."

Senator Dunbar's long face seemed drawn longer by vertical cheek lines. He said gravely, "I have no further questions to ask this witness."

Carl Sherman looked vacantly about the room at a level above the heads of the audience.

"Senator Kiley?"

Senator Kiley of Arizona placed his hands together on the committee table. His head was considerably lower than any of his fellows, and his deeply tanned prunelike face was serious.

"I would like to know, Governor, what is your present religious affiliation?"

"I am a Unitarian."

"Has that always been your religious affiliation?"

"No. I was born a Methodist."

"I suppose you changed because you found the Unitarian belief more in accord with your views. Isn't the Unitarian religion generally considered the most liberal of the Protestant sects?"

"I don't believe that word can properly be applied to religion."

"Let me be specific. The Unitarians don't believe in any of the Sacraments?"

"No, Senator."

"And they don't believe in the divinity of Jesus Christ?"

"We believe Jesus Christ was a great, great human being. One of the greatest men who ever lived. And an inspiring spiritual leader."

"But you would say the same thing about Mohammed, wouldn't you? Or Buddha?"

"How those men rank as spiritual leaders depends on personal opinion and that probably varies a great deal from one person to another."

"They were spiritual leaders too, weren't they?"

"Yes, Senator."

Senator Kiley nodded absently, hardly listening.

"Thank you, Governor Lowe. That's all."

The air seemed to have grown warm. The whirring of cameras was as distracting as the buzzing of a legion of persistent flies.

Carl Sherman said, "The Chair recognizes Senator Vance Murdoch for the purpose of making a motion."

Senator Murdoch said, "It is now noon, I move that this committee adjourn for one hour for lunch."

"I second the motion," Senator Sprigh said promptly.

"As there is no objection the committee stands in recess," Senator Sherman said, tapping his gavel. "We will reconvene in this room at exactly 1 P.M."

Carl Sherman and several other Senators pushed back their chairs and got up. Senators Dunbar and Campbell turned sidewise to each other, talking earnestly. Senators Lipscomb and Rockwell went over to Carl Sherman and after a few words behind the chairs, left the dais together. At his place Senator Dunbar, still seated, was gathering papers and stuffing them into an attaché case. Senator Kiley stood up to his entire five-foot three-inch height. When Paul Lowe looked toward him Kiley looked away and abruptly left the dais.

Reporters were thronging about Paul Lowe. From the center of the crowd he glimpsed Senator Murdoch starting to leave. Murdoch looked toward him once, managed a smile and a deprecatory shrug of his shoulders before moving on.

Paul Lowe started down the aisle, past the press tables, fending off reporters' questions as he went. Photographers closed around him and flashbulbs began popping. Before he reached the door a tall lanky man in a loose-fitting gray suit stepped forward.

"Governor Lowe." He offered his right hand in greeting, holding Paul Lowe's elbow with his left hand, moving with him toward the door in a maneuver that blocked off pursuers. "My name is Jeffreys. A mutual friend asked me to look you up."

They went through the door together and, following the tall man's lead, Paul Lowe found a passageway through the group of reporters and photographers waiting outside the Caucus Room. The tall man moved with assurance and seemed to know most of the reporters. A brief word here and there helped clear the way. Soon they were before the elevator door.

The tall lanky man smiled. He had a good set of slightly yellow teeth that curved sharply inward at both sides of his mouth. His face was lean, handsome, sharply boned, chiseled with no excess flesh. His nose was thin and long, his mouth wide, the skin at his jaw seemed barely to stretch around the sharp angle.

He said, "I'm with CBS and a good friend of Katherine Prescott. She wrote me about you, Governor."

"Oh, yes. Tom Jeffreys."

The elevator came and as they got in several reporters seemed about to enter. Tom Jeffreys held up his hand. As the reporters hesitated the door closed.

"What's your mysterious power?" Paul Lowe asked.

"Simple. They aren't getting anywhere asking you questions. They think I might, and if I do I have to share it with them. We'll figure out a bone to throw them before we get back."

"Where are we going?"

"There's a good coffee shop across the way. A block or two. It's so crowded we can talk with comparative privacy because everyone else will be talking and paying no attention to us."

"I'd rather go someplace quiet."

"There is no such place in Washington at lunch hour, Governor. The fancy places take too long and there'll be too many people watching us. Leave it to me. Katherine put you in my care."

They emerged from the new Senate Office Building and went rapidly past several groups of visiting tourists, who turned to stare after them—the long man with his rapid long stride, and the somewhat shorter man with slightly bowed legs and rolling lunging walk.

"Who are they?" asked a lady wearing a fruited hat.

"They're no one," said her companion.

Paul Lowe and Tom Jeffreys smiled at each other.

"*Lèse-majesté?*" Jeffreys suggested.

"She happens to be right."

"I suppose you think they gave you a hard time this morning, Governor?"

"That impression did cross my mind."

"I've sat through a score of these committee hearings—Foreign Relations, Judiciary, Interior, and Commerce. About half are strictly routine. The other half can get interesting—especially when it's an important nomination like one for the Supreme Court."

"They seem to have done their homework about my past."

"That Chung-jin stuff came from a single witness. Oliver Owens. They had him for three hours before the committee yesterday."

"I gathered as much."

"He was obviously doing a smear job. Would you care to tell me why he's out to get you?"

"It's an old feud—but I'm afraid it's strictly one-sided. He started writing letters to me when I was law clerk to Justice Edmunson. He hated Charles Edmunson—accused him of being a Communist—and kept urging me to either quit or do something about him. When I explained that I was rather proud to be working for Edmunson, Owens decided I was a Red too."

"Under cross-examination this morning, Owens admitted he was a founder of several super-patriotic groups."

"I remember one. Something called Sons of the Federalist United States. When I ran for attorney general, Oliver Owens circulated the whole State of Nebraska with pamphlets bearing that imprint."

They stopped across the street from a small coffee shop.

"That's the place, Governor. Okay?"

"Okay," Paul Lowe told him.

As they crossed the street together, Tom Jeffreys said, "I'm afraid the worst is still to come. When you go back for the afternoon session, George Walsh of Virginia takes over. You've been treated lightly on the political issue so far. Walsh will go after that heavily."

"Why is he so opposed to my nomination?"

"He's an admirer of Justice Waldo Shuler. He wants someone appointed who'll line up with Shuler on the Court. Let's find a table, Governor."

They entered a large room swarming with activity. In crowded jumble and noise they searched until Tom Jeffreys found a space. It was a small empty booth squeezed in from a narrow aisle in which people formed a jostling double channel of movement. Above the din rose the steady sharp ring of the cash register. An occasional voice, finding an unused frequency in the general babble, cut through audibly, "and then he told me, if you don't want to, then *say* so, and I said, I'm *saying* so, buster . . ."

There was no service. Paul Lowe told Tom Jeffreys what he wanted to eat and kept their booth table while Jeffreys went to get it. In a few minutes Jeffreys returned through the milling throng. Because he was taller than anyone around him, he looked as though he were descending a flight of stairs. He was carrying aloft a tray with two bowls of Yankee bean soup and crackers, one swiss cheese and one sliced sardine sandwich, and coffee. He tacked across the double channel of people like a graceful high-rigged sailing ship and by a quick artful maneuver reached the table and deposited the tray.

Paul Lowe started to get up. Jeffreys said, "Don't," and with what seemed a single sinuous movement stepped across Paul Lowe's lap, drew his other leg cranelike up behind him and slithered down onto the yellow vinyl banquette.

"An impressive bit of acrobatics," Lowe commented.

"Anybody in Washington who pays less than a dollar for lunch can match me," Tom Jeffreys said. "Of course I can afford better. I do it to keep in condition."

The Yankee bean soup was delicious. They talked very little, recognizing the hopelessness of competing against the uproar. They finished the soup. Paul Lowe took the swiss cheese sandwich. Jeffreys peeled the top slice of bread from his sardines and bit into the squashed brown and silver paste.

"Would you like my guess on how things stand right now on the Judiciary Committee?" he asked.

"Sure," Paul Lowe said.

"Five votes against you. Walsh, Dunbar, Lipscomb, Kiley and Margrave. Two or three votes for—including Murdoch, Sherman and Campbell. The rest are waiting to see how you come off in the afternoon session against Walsh."

"Well, wish me luck."

"I do, Governor. I'm a liberal both by instinct and by racial inheritance. My grandfather was a Wobblie." He lifted a crooked elbow and raised his hand. "If my right hand offend thee, oh F.D.R., may it wither. Most people in communications feel the same way. But our bosses are all Republicans so we never can say what we really think. I ask you, is that democracy?"

"Katherine Prescott said you're a TV commentator." Paul Lowe had been waiting to bring her name into the conversation.

"That's right. Katherine and I are old buddies. I knew her before her husband."

Holding his forearm close to his chest in the cramped quarters, Paul Lowe sipped his coffee. "I didn't know she was married."

"Married and divorced. I could have told her he was no good. If memory serves me, I did tell her. But she wouldn't listen. She only stayed with him as long as she did because she's capable of fantastic loyalty. She made up her mind his drinking didn't matter, his bullying didn't matter and his vulgarity didn't matter."

"He sounds fascinating."

"Oddly enough, he was. A writer, of sorts, for magazines. Hairy-chested fiction. One of the Jack London *cum* Hemingway writers who know how to make physical danger sound exciting. He'd had his fill of it in real life. Iwo Jima. Twice decorated. Three times wounded. He liked to get drunk in bars and beat up fellows who'd been rejected in the draft. He occasionally beat up on Katherine too."

Paul Lowe felt small muscles tighten at the corners of his mouth. "You mean he struck her?" The question rang with an odd sort of Victorian prudishness. You, sir, are a cad.

"Katherine never talked about it. But I'm pretty sure. She sported occasional bruises. If I know Katherine, she's the type who would fight back. Pots and pans flying. It's a wonder she didn't brain Timmy. Her aim is terrible."

"Who is Timmy?" Paul Lowe inquired.

"Katherine's son. He's six now. A very nice lad but shy and bookish and retiring. Needs a man around the house." Tom Jeffreys turned to look at him with a pleasant directness. "You don't really know Katherine very well, do you?"

"I'm afraid not. She came to interview me. Now she wants to do a series of articles for Hardman's newspapers. *If* my appointment is confirmed."

"Katherine's a good writer. Impulsive, fresh, discerning. Her real metier is short pieces. I don't believe she can organize her mind well enough to do anything else."

"As a new justice I'll be pretty busy," Paul Lowe said. "I don't know if I'll be able to spare time for any long interviews." Suddenly he was sure he would not.

"Then just tell her so. She'll understand." Tom Jeffreys swallowed the last of his sardine sandwich, his adam's apple working visibly in his long corded throat. He reached for the check but Paul Lowe lifted it off the tray first.

"It may be a while before I can get around to answering all my correspondence," Paul Lowe said. "If you talk to Miss Prescott, will you thank her for taking such an interest? And, incidentally, for recommending you as my guardian."

Tom Jeffreys smiled. "A pleasure. How would you like to come to a wedding?"

"Who's getting married?"

"Didn't Katherine tell you? If everything progresses at a satisfactory rate, we'll be married this time next year. It would have happened already if not for the damn geography. Me in Washington—her on the godforsaken prairie . . . Sorry, Governor. I forgot it's your home state."

Paul Lowe was hardly listening. Somewhere in the middle of what Tom Jeffreys was saying his mind had tuned him out—and the rest was interfering static. He put the cup down carefully into the center of the raised saucer rim.

"She seems to be a very lovely girl," he said. "I'm sure you'll be very happy."

64

Senator Carl Sherman said, "If at this time the witness would like to exercise his prerogative to make a statement, we will be glad to hear it before we proceed with the questioning."

Paul Lowe answered, "I have no statement, Senator."

"Very well then. Senator Walsh?"

The large room became electrically quiet. The senior Senator from Virginia rubbed a thumb and forefinger over gaunt cheeks, hardly seeming to be aware his name had been called. He looked off broodingly into a part of the room somewhere to the left of Paul Lowe. When he spoke his voice was deep pitched but so low that at first the words were hardly audible.

"Governor Lowe, when you assumed office, you took an oath of fealty to the United States of America, did you not?"

"Yes."

"You swore to uphold the ideals of this republic and to safeguard us against enemies from within and without. Is that correct?"

"It is."

"Do you feel you have lived up to that oath?"

"I most certainly do."

"I ask because there has been testimony here which would tend to indicate the opposite—if it were believed. But we are not here to collect statements for and against you. We are here to get at facts—facts to help us determine your fitness to sit on the highest court in this land. I would like now to proceed to discuss the facts. Have you, Governor Lowe, ever been a member of any subversive group?"

"I have not."

"You understand the meaning of that term, do you not?"

"I believe I do."

"By subversive I mean an organization working in any way to undermine American ideals or change or overthrow venerated American institutions. Would you agree with that definition, Governor?"

"Within limits."

"What limits, Governor?"

"People may have different ideas about what constitutes constructive change. Our institutions have been changing since they were first formed— and I hope they will continue to."

"Would you knowingly join an organization which was dedicated to subverting our American institutions?"

"I think men may honestly differ as to what certain organizations represent. I don't believe a John Bircher would agree that he was a member of a subversive organization, but there are those who would say he was. The same applies to other organizations with political aims."

"How about the League for Legislative Action?"

"There are people in this country who might say that organization was subversive."

"Do you think it is?"

"I do not."

"Do you subscribe to their principles?"

"I agree with some—disagree with others."

"Would you consider joining such an organization?"

Paul Lowe answered slowly. "I was invited to join and did not. But that was not because of any disagreement over basic principles. I was simply too busy to join still another organization to which I could give nothing but the use of my name. However, there are many distinguished Americans who do belong to the organization and with whom I would in ordinary circumstances willingly be associated."

Senator Walsh's brilliant beady eyes seemed to gather incredulity.

"*Willingly* associated?"

"That is what I said, Senator," Paul Lowe said firmly.

"Well, we're learning something about each other, aren't we, Governor Lowe? That's all to the good." Senator Walsh steepled his fingers with both index fingers joining beneath the tip of his nose. "Is your feeling of—shall we call it fraternal friendliness—for the League for Legislative Action based on the fact that this organization supported you in your recent campaign for governor?"

"It is not. I was grateful for their support, however."

"You do not feel obligated to repay them in any way for supporting you?"

"No, Senator."

"In the event that a legal decision involving the League or any other leftist group which supported you should come up for decision before the Supreme Court of the United States, could you make an honest judgment based upon the merits of the case?"

"I take exception to your designation of the League as a leftist group. The answer to the question you asked is yes."

"Would you call the Everyman's Legal Guild a leftist group, Governor?" Walsh asked sharply.

"It is not a term I would be likely to use."

The Southern drawl became pronounced. "Would you call it extremist?"

"You may use any adjective you wish, Senator. That's your privilege."

"Why, I thank you, Governor," Senator Walsh said with exaggerated courtesy and a bleak smile. "I have a feeling that you do not go along with me on my choice of adjectives."

"We have a right to differ with each other, Senator."

"Indeed we do. All I want to accomplish here and now, Governor, is to set forth the principles on which we do most decidedly differ. Let me try to close in on that. Would you join the Everyman's Legal Guild if membership was offered to you?"

"Probably not."

"Would you explain to this committee why not?"

"I don't feel I have enough in common with their principles."

"Yet you accepted their support in the recent campaign, Governor?"

"I don't adopt the principles of every person and every organization that supports me, Senator Walsh. Do you?"

Paul Lowe's challenging question lay like a black wire tossed over to the Senator, carrying a charge of enmity.

Senator Walsh's reply fairly crackled. "We are investigating your qualifications, Governor Lowe, not mine. I am not a nominee for the highest court in this land. You are. Now, would you describe the Everyman's Legal Guild as being to the right of your beliefs—or to the left?"

"That would be oversimplification, Senator. As with the League for Legislative Action, there are some things they stand for that I approve of—and some that I don't."

"Are you aware that this organization was named by the Attorney General of the United States as a subversive organization?"

"That action was later challenged in the courts, Senator. The Attorney General was forced to withdraw that designation."

"It's in the record, sir. Surely you don't believe the Attorney General was actuated by malice when he listed the Everyman's Legal Guild as subversive, do you?"

"I simply believe he was mistaken. And the courts agreed."

"Governor Lowe," Walsh's voice cut with heavy emphasis across the room, "do you know a man named Kenneth Norris?"

"My former law partner. And my very good friend."

"Your very good friend," Senator Walsh repeated with lingering relish. "Are you aware that Kenneth Norris is a director of the aforementioned Everyman's Legal Guild?"

"Yes, I am aware of it."

"Yet Kenneth Norris remains your very good friend?"

"I hope so, Senator."

"You hope so." Senator Walsh's deep voice hung enraptured over the syllables. "Do you know that the Everyman's Legal Guild recently appointed one of its members to defend a couple accused of breaking a law against mixed marriage? The man was white and the woman was a Negress."

"Yes. I read about that."

"Do you approve of marriage between the races, Governor?"

"The point at issue would seem to be whether I approved of the law, Senator."

"All right, let's have the answer your way. Do you approve of a law that keeps black people from marrying white people in this country?"

"The law was tested in the Supreme Court, Senator. As I recall, it was declared void."

"That is not a responsive answer."

"I don't believe it is proper for a nominee to the Court to pass judgment on any of its decisions, Senator. That issue, or one closely akin to it, might again be raised. It would therefore not be proper to answer questions which commit me in advance in a case that I haven't heard. I'm sure you will agree with my position in this, Senator."

Senator Vance Murdoch smiled widely. The background noise from the audience became lighter in substance and took on a bubbling quality.

67

Senator Walsh's face darkened. "The decision of the Supreme Court to which you refer was rendered by Associate Justice Charles Edmunson—and it was a five-to-four decision. You were close to Justice Edmunson at one time, were you not?"

"I was his law clerk, Senator, a number of years ago."

"You worked closely enough with him to become infected with his opinions."

Paul Lowe leaned forward. "Did you say 'affected' or 'infected,' Senator?"

"Do you have trouble with your hearing, Governor? I said 'infected.'"

"I thought you did—but could scarcely believe it. I never knew superior mental qualities could be acquired by contagion. I'm delighted to hear it."

Most members of the committee joined in the laughter. At a glance from George Walsh, the chairman, Carl Sherman, banged his gavel. The room subsided.

"What we are after here, sir," Senator Walsh's deep growl was like preliminary low thunder, "is to discover whether we should permit a slavish disciple—a mere vassal—of Justice Edmunson to sit upon the Supreme Court. Whatever Edmunson's abilities, sir—and there is dispute about that, a good deal of dispute—the Constitution does not allow any justice to cast two votes instead of one. Some of us here are afraid that is what might occur if you are allowed to sit with your acknowledged master on the Supreme Court of this United States."

"I can safely reassure you on that point, Senator. I never have any difficulty in making up my own mind on a subject—once I know the facts."

"How will you judge the facts, sir?" Senator Walsh asked in a rising rhetorical tone. "Do you consider yourself to have the necessary training in constitutional law?"

"I make no pretense of being an authority on the Constitution," Paul Lowe said. "Although I have studied and practiced law for a good many years, I have only come incidentally upon the field of constitutional law. As a practicing lawyer I have had some occasion to advise on constitutional questions and on rare instances to argue a case involving such questions. But that is far from making me an expert."

"Don't you think your admitted ignorance in this field disqualifies you from consideration as an associate justice?"

"No, Senator. Oliver Wendell Holmes was not really well trained in constitutional law. But he always said that when in doubt he could read the Constitution itself. I suppose I can do the same thing."

"Any of us can read it, Governor. But are we fit to interpret it? This is the question. We have a great judicial scholar on the Constitution in Associate Justice Waldo Shuler but he shouldn't be allowed to carry the heavy burden alone. He needs men capable of helping him in the immense task of safeguarding our precious Constitution."

"There are eight other justices—seven now sitting—who share the same heavy responsibilities. Are you suggesting, Senator Walsh, that they are not fit to do their jobs?"

"I personally do not think any man should sit on our high court who has not had at least seven years of previous judicial experience. You have no such experience at all, sir."

"You are entitled to your own standards of determining the fitness of a particular nominee. But if that standard of judicial experience were used some of the most distinguished Supreme Court justices would have been barred."

"And that might have been a good thing for this republic. A very good thing indeed."

"I don't agree, Senator, that this nation or any other nation is so rich in human resources that we can afford to lose any part of them. In that sense to have barred those men from service would have been a very bad thing for this republic. However, if you feel strongly on this point, you can always propose a law to that effect. If enough of your colleagues agree with you that will become a necessary qualification for the confirmation of justices to the Supreme Court. Until there is such a law, however, I don't think you should try to impose that standard on your fellow Senators."

"No one's trying to impose anything!" George Walsh retorted angrily. "I'm just trying to find out what sort of person you are, Governor. And I must say that I've found out all I need to know. All I need to know."

Senator Walsh tugged angrily at his black string tie.

"Do you have further questions for the witness?" Carl Sherman asked.

Senator George Walsh shook his head. His eyes glared out of a saturnine countenance.

"No questions," he said.

Senator Sherman's glance passed him over.

"Senator Rockwell?"

In the moment before interrogation began from a new quarter, Paul Lowe turned in his chair, stretching his neck muscles slightly. By chance his gaze met that of Tom Jeffreys at the press table. Tom Jeffreys was grinning, holding up both hands to form an O with the index fingers and thumbs. Beside him, a small round gray man nodded and winked. Paul Lowe recognized Teddy Strong, editorial writer for *The New York Times*.

As he turned his attention back to the committee table to face the next inquisitor, he thought: at least the press is sure I'm in.

6

Paul Lowe held the Washington *Post*, folded like an accordion, while he finished reading the account of his appearance before the Judiciary Committee. He was seated near a window in his hotel room. He turned to an appraisal from the American Bar Association of his nomination to the Federal Judiciary.

"Well qualified" was the report, which went on to say, "under ordinary circumstances we might hesitate to give our endorsement to a man of Governor Lowe's comparative youth and lack of judicial experience, but his high moral principle, his adherence to the highest standards of constitutional government and his demonstrated capacities as a lawyer and a state executive, should make him a fine addition to the Supreme Court of the United States."

Nevertheless, Paul Lowe noted wryly, the assessment had been "well qualified" and not the customary "exceptionally well qualified." The distinguished members of the American Bar Association had not thrown their hats in the air.

When the telephone rang, Eleanor answered.

"Someone named Tom Jeffreys wants to speak to you."

Jeffreys was laconic: "The Judiciary Committee just had its executive session. They voted fourteen to five to send your nomination to the Senate for final approval."

"That is good news. Thanks for calling."

"George Walsh will fight you down to the wire but it's a sure thing now, Governor. Or maybe I'd better start calling you Mr. Justice."

When Paul Lowe put back the telephone Eleanor was watching him.

"The committee approved," he told her. "Now it's gone to the Senate. It looks as though I'll be confirmed."

"Oh, Paul, that's wonderful." Briskly, her thoughts moved on: "I suppose we should find ourselves a place to live in Washington. We can't stay any longer in this hotel room. It's too expensive, and there's no place to turn around."

"I'm jittery. A curious combination of nervous and numb. So I can't stay in. Would you like to start apartment hunting this afternoon?"

"I'd love it!"

The agent, a blonde woman about forty-five, large build, large bosom, large mouth, put a key into the rust-colored door. "I'm sure you'll like this one. It's just made to order for you!"

There were four rooms—one large-sized living room, a large-sized study connected to it with sliding doors, and a small bedroom and a tiny, tiny kitchen. Eleanor looked about the kitchen with dismay. As she turned she bumped into the blonde woman agent in the constricted space between the cabinets and the oven and refrigerator.

"I don't know," she said dubiously.

Paul Lowe drew a deep breath. "Well, I do," he said.

The agent was a stout slow-moving man whose jowls shook sadly as he took them on the rounds of apartments he had to show.

"It's a lovely location," he said. "You can't do better than Georgetown. All the best people live here. Including three members of the present Supreme Court."

It was already in the morning newspapers. SENATE APPROVES PAUL LOWE 81–16.

Lowe looked around the old spacious apartment, with its high ceilings, fireplace in the living room, and the small brick garden in back. There were two dark bedrooms but the kitchen was long, angling sharply off to the right into a lot of cabinet space.

"It isn't bad," he said. "How much?"

"They're asking seven-fifty a month. I can get it for seven."

"That's too much."

"How about six-fifty?"

"I don't know," Paul Lowe said dubiously.

"Well, I do," Eleanor said.

The agent was a genial man of medium height and thinning hair who took the attitude of criticizing his wares before anyone else could do it.

"I don't believe this place is suitable," he said. "It's really a two-family house. The owners occupy the top apartment during four or five winter months. You have to pay for heating yourself and it can get pretty cold here in Washington sometimes. Of course, there is a fireplace but I'm not sure it's in good working order. . . . The real trouble is, the people who built it couldn't make up their minds if they wanted a city or a country place."

They went through the spacious living room, the antique kitchen with its polished wood cabinets, the huge master bedroom and the slightly smaller guest bedroom, and came to the library. Bookcases lined the lower walls. The room was quiet and the light was good. On two sides were tall windows and on the rear a French door opened into a pleasant unbricked garden.

"We'll take it," Paul Lowe said.

"You didn't ask how much," Eleanor said.

"I know," Paul Lowe said.

That night they returned, with the key the genial agent had given them (on receipt of their deposit for the first month's rent and an additional two months' security) and in darkness they stood together. Paul Lowe put his arm about Eleanor in the library room with its vacant bookcases. There was misty light from the very top of a street lamp beyond the garden and reflected light from the rear windows of the house adjoining. He felt her slimness beneath the cross of his arm, the delicate shoulder-blade arching bone and his fingers touching the soft flesh on her upper shoulder. In shadow he could make out the profile unchanged with years, aging lines hidden in the blessed dark.

—Come on, Paul, show us your picture. You have to sooner or later.

—Not me. I said I wouldn't and I won't. Jim Hegan isn't going to show his picture either.

—Jim already showed us. What's the matter with you? We saw you in your bathing suit. The picture won't be any different.

—Nope.

—You're not going to? Really not?

—Nope.

—I know why, Sally Hanes said. Everyone knows why—she said to the others—it's his skinny legs.

—We know all about them, Paul. We saw them when you went swimming at the picnic.

—It isn't that at all, he said.

Sally touched colored braid in her cornsilk hair.

—It's the skinny legs, that's what it is all right.

Thirty-two years had not taken away the sting nor filled the hollow in his stomach that he felt in that school courtyard. A tall brick wall against which they played handball, the round circle of the basketball hoop inset in a twelve-foot-tall paddle of wood and the silver-painted metal gates beyond. Absolutely no place in the world that he could run. On the fringes of the group passing was the one whose presence hurt most. Eleanor Olson. Walking with Sal Putanto she had the eager almost frantic look of trying to find something to talk about to interest him while Sal glowered handsomely, darkly, thick black brows drawing slightly together in the way that girls went mad over.

Eleanor's voice trilling:

—and he won't show the picture they took of him at the class picnic. Isn't that too silly? Isn't it, Sal?

—Who cares? Sal answered.

—They all know it's because he's too skinny in a bathing suit. He is. Those arms and legs and . . .

Trilling on. One arm looped through Sal Putanto's arm who was seemingly unaware of her hanging to him and keeping his interest alive with incessant talk.

In the dark library of their new Washington home, his arm comfortingly about her, Paul Lincoln Lowe (aged forty-six), said:

72

"I feel sad about leaving our home in Lincoln. I wonder if we can be happy here. New places always mean new friends, new experiences. . . ."

She put her head against his shoulder. "I wish Nancy were with us. I miss her."

"We can't hold on to children forever, dear," he said. Nothing was better solace for Eleanor than a cliché. It went down as effortlessly as mineral oil—a bland capsule carrying a dose of moving wisdom.

"In her last letter she said she would be here for your first day on the Court. She wouldn't miss that. Imagine what a thrill it must be—to have her father on the Supreme Court."

Looked at in Eleanor's special way all greatness could be measured as social prestige. History itself was an immense banquet table set in protocol order. Though they would sit at the foot of the table near the kitchen (in the space reserved for a new justice of the United States Supreme Court) the seat afforded a view of the resplendence. George and Mrs. Martha Washington having a word with Abraham Lincoln, and over there Andrew Jackson nodding in agreement with Woodrow Wilson while Franklin D. Roosevelt exchanged pleasantries with Oliver Wendell Holmes.

"I'm proud of you, darling," Eleanor said. He sensed her head turn and bent to kiss her in the darkness.

She had been Helen of Troy in the high school senior play. He, with thin arms and legs, was Doctor Faustus. *Ah, Helen . . . Her lips suck forth my soul.* He waited through interminable Marlowe for the moment. When he touched her lips he would willingly have lingered. Faustus was no fool. What price a mere human soul for unendurable bliss?

Afterward, he got the congratulations of the faculty, the principal, his classmates. They had sensed some love for poetry in his reading. Eleanor, all agreed, was beautiful but they reserved comment on her reading of the mighty Marlowe lines. . . . She *had* been beautiful. What spirit would not be struck like tinder to fire by her loveliness?

—I thought you were just great, Eleanor.

—It's nice of you to say so, Paul.

—The thing is, you really look like Helen of Troy.

She laughed.

—Now, Paul, don't exaggerate.

It was shattering when she laughed. He could have lost himself in her, drowned gladly. Full fathom five Paul Lowe lies and these are pearls that were his eyes.

—My mother is having a dinner for the cast after the performance for the parents on Friday. Will you come, Paul?

—I sure will.

Friday was eons away, light years distant, a day like a star in some never-to-be-reached nebula.

When Friday's dinner party came the sheer magnificence of its Fridayness made him masterful. He was Faustus in flame, impassioned, Mephistopheles-ridden. *Oh, I'll leap up to my God. Who pulls me down?* . . . *Come, Helen, come, give me my soul again.* . . . *Ah, Mephistopheles!*

At dinner in her mother's home, with the other members of the cast, he was seated directly opposite the face that launched a thousand ships. Her home bore the clear traces of shabby genteel poverty but when she talked to him, he existed in a rare dimension she inhabited. Once her hand touched the back of his hand, stayed briefly. The spot burned.

—This pot roast is delicious. Your mother's a wonderful cook, Eleanor.

—Yes, isn't she?

Her mother was a human weapon forged in corseted steel. Her figure protruded at the bosom, retreated toward the rear, swung forward again in the pelvic region. Her coarse face bore some trace of vanished good looks and her manner was that of a Colonel in the Light Infantry.

—Eleanor, come here. You serve the dessert.

He watched covertly as Eleanor spooned out a coconut concoction with ice cream smothered helplessly beneath it. As she bent over the table her pink dress drew tight across well-formed breasts. Some boy must have touched them. Sal Putanto certainly. The palms of his hands tingled.

There were two classes of girls in school as there were two classes of boys: those who did and those who didn't. Their worlds were separate and apart and the non-doers regarded the others with hostility, disdain and envy. He would search their sinful faces for the vile secret, willing not to believe. It seemed to him the experience must leave its mark somewhere. In the ordinary course of human affairs they were as Lazarus returned from the dead; they knew strange forbidden things.

Leaving the house now, lined up Indian file, the guests ran the gauntlet of gratitude to the door:

—I had a wonderful time, Mrs. Olson. And that was a wonderful dinner.

—Thank you for coming, Paul.

Eleanor's hand lightly in his like a fragrance:

—Goodbye, Paul. I guess I won't see you now until graduation.

They shared only a Wednesday class in English literature, and there would be no more Wednesday afternoon classes. Sudden desperation seized him.

—I'd like to call you. May I?

Perfect brows lifted in surprise—and the pleasure of an unexpected conquest.

—Of course, Paul.

He took her to a movie on Tuesday night and brought her kissless home. Thursday was Graduation Day. Through the ceremony he kept an eye on her whereabouts, peering above heads in the crowded auditorium. There was a long intimate moment when her name was called and she made the slow public walk to the stage to get her diploma. His eyes followed gently swaying hips the whole journey. . . . Afterward he was part of a group that went to a nearby coffee shop to celebrate. Sal Putanto was there. Eleanor stayed close to Sal, her chair beside his at the table. Sal's arm negligently rested upon her knee. Once she saw Paul watching and returned his gaze with challenging insolence. *O perjured woman! Thou dost stone my heart. . . . Think on thy sins!* She put her cheek next to Sal's. Sal pulled away impatiently. He was discussing the respective abilities of Pie Traynor and Stan Hack at third base. Paul joined in on Sal's side. Pie Traynor by all odds.

Sal Putanto grinned; for a moment Paul felt Sal liked him better than he did Eleanor. Then Sal turned, took Eleanor's face in the palm of one hand and kissed her, held her and worked his mouth on hers. She made no move to escape. When he released her she said "Oh, Sal" in a voice not quite reproving.

He let a week go by before he called her. She was busy. She was busy the next evening also.

He nursed rancor. He stayed indoors and brooded. His mother brought him chicken okra soup and he munched dry crackers and stared out the window of his room at scenes of desolation.

Jim Hegan had taken pictures of the school play and came to show them. Paul was delighted, won away from the brink. Like so many who do acts of charity, Jim Hegan worked more wonders than he knew. He gave Paul an excuse to call Eleanor.

—Hi, this is Paul. Did Jim Hegan show you the photos he took of the school play?

—No, he hasn't been here yet.

—You look great. I'm going to order a dozen prints for myself. Are you going to order any?

—I don't know. Mother wouldn't want me to spend the money.

Eleanor's father, a mild sweet bald man, had worked in the department of mail and telephone inquiries at a stock brokerage concern until his death the previous year. They were rather poor. Paul liked that. Poverty made her accessible.

—I'll get them for you.

—I couldn't let you do that.

—I want to. There's a couple of especially good shots of you.

He carried the day—and the snapshots to Eleanor. Eleanor greeted him at the door. She was alone. Her mother worked as a beautician in a local beauty parlor.

They sat on a sofa in the living room of her home and looked through the snapshots. Soon she was gay and smiling. She exclaimed with delight at one photo in particular which showed her with Paul. His face was hidden but hers was clear and radiant in the direct path of the spotlight.

She offered him milk and a chocolate cupcake. They talked. She was not going to college but hoped to get a job as a salesclerk in the local department store. He had already been accepted at the University. With every moment the terrible unbalance of forces was changing. He was emerging from a chrysalis of unworthiness. In some ways he was her equal. All things considered, she could do worse. He did not expect love, it was obvious that she alone had magic chemistry, but he was qualified to adore her. More than qualified. In time she might come to take pride in his achievements and he would perform prodigies for her favor.

He gathered up his courage and crashed it through iron gates.

"What is Sal going to do?"

Her slightly sallow skin flushed with sadness.

"He's going away. To Chicago. He's got some sort of job there."

"For the summer?"

"I don't think so. It's with a meat-packing firm. If he makes good, I think he'll stay there."

Sal Putanto was an unutterable fool. As though money fame or the wide wide world could matter beside Eleanor. *Oh, tell me what the vintner buys one half so precious as the stuff he sells.* Sal had sold his birthright, his Eleanor, and thereby closed himself into dark futureless caverns. And he had bequeathed to Paul this most precious inheritance.

—I thought if you weren't doing anything Saturday, Eleanor, you might like to go to the ball game. Lincoln is playing Council Bluffs.

—I don't know. I'm not too interested in baseball.

That would have been news to Sal Putanto, who had taken her to a baseball game every weekend.

—Neither am I, to tell the truth. How about taking in a movie? It's a Cary Grant picture this week.

Her face lighted.

—I read the review. It sounds wonderful. I'd love to, Paul.

On Saturday evening he called for her. A light rain had begun to fall. They ran to the bus. He took off his jacket and held it around her as they ran. In the bus, breathless, he paid the driver. Rain splashed heavily against the bus windows as they went to their seat.

—Who would have thought it this morning? she asked.

—You know what they say. If you don't like the weather just wait a minute and it'll change.

She laughed as though he had delivered himself of an original witticism. Encouraged, he put his arm on the back of her seat in the bus.

In the intimate dark of the movie theater he caught fire with resolve. She was intent on the screen, her mouth slightly parted. Cary Grant was debonair in a room with Katharine Hepburn and Edward Everett Horton. Their images swam together in a blur. Sphincter muscles urged him on, nerve ends tugged at his arm muscles, his will impelled him. Still he hesitated in a paralyzed suspension. Alternating currents of fear and desire chilled and warmed him.

Finally he moved. All to be lost, all gained in one instant. She sensed him, turned, and her beauty burst upon him like a symphonic poem. At the swelling chorus his heart stifled him with its pounding and their lips met.

Actually, it was a little disappointing.

They parted and he moved close and put his arm about her possessively. She returned her attention to the screen. Cary Grant was being debonair with Katharine Hepburn on board a transatlantic liner.

He kissed her twice more before the movie ended. Then he brought her home and kissed her again. He suggested seeing her during the week and she agreed, and he went home in a mood of surly Byron, masterful and sure. He slept restlessly and by morning could hardly believe what had

76

happened. On the film of memory he played their kisses again and again. In retrospect rapture became greater and he could hardly wait to try again.

When she opened the door that evening she was wearing a frilly dress with straps over her shoulders and a round neckline that showed her white chest almost to cleavage. The rounds of her breasts were outlined in halfmoons. His thoughts churned lustfully while he made conversation with her mother. He saw himself through her mother's eyes, accepted her type-casting of him as the thin intellectual type, filled in the outline of himself with remarks about the University and his future career either as a scientific farmer or a lawyer. He explained why he did not think he would follow in the footsteps of his father, who was a doctor, and approved Eleanor's taking a job because there was much to be learned in the practical world, perhaps more than in the universities. He left the clear impression that the chief reason he was going to the University was that affluence made his choice inescapable.

They left surrounded with Mother's approval. This time he kissed Eleanor in the bus (she demurred slightly because of her makeup) and later on the dance floor he kept his lips close to her ear and whispered poetry. Eleanor, like many pretty girls, had a deep appreciation of romantic poetry provided the focal point was herself. He held her close. Occasionally she hummed snatches of a song the orchestra was playing. *You are the promised breath of springtime. . . .*

At midnight, as the dance ended, they decided to walk home. When they reached a park he directed her into it. They sat on a bench. The night was soft and the air intoxicating. She became dreamy and put her head back to look up at the stars. He bent over her and kissed her. She stirred resentfully and then didn't. He was lifted above himself with masculine power. He began to kiss her with meaning. Her slightly protruding tooth clicked against his teeth. He moved his hand over her shoulder and down to her breast.

She sat up instantly.

—No, she said.

—What's the matter?

—I don't like you to do that.

—It isn't all that important, he said sullenly.

—I just don't like it, that's all.

After a moment she was pacified and they resumed their embrace. By accident when his arm went about her his fingers touched the side of her breast. She pulled back a little but said nothing. A matter of time, he thought.

The next day when he called for a date Eleanor said she couldn't because her older sister Natalie was in town for a visit. He could not afford to wait. He was in the rhythm of his desire.

—That's wonderful. Why don't I take you and your sister to dinner? As a matter of fact, your mother can come too if she likes.

—Paul, that would be so expensive.

—It's all right. I want to.

They went to the Tavern and he bought a champagne cocktail for her mother. That formidable woman became giggly. Natalie, the wispy sister, had a faint touch of color in her wan cheeks. Eleanor gave him melting looks all through dinner. He ordered without stint. (He had borrowed ten dollars from his mother and added his own savings to it.) He took everyone home in a taxi.

Her mother fawned upon him.

—I had the most wonderful time, Paul. I don't remember when I had such a wonderful time.

—So did I, Natalie said.

In the living room of her home Eleanor looked at him with gratitude. Her mother gave Natalie a glance.

—I'm tired, she said. If you'll excuse me I'll go right up to bed. If you two get hungry—she said to Eleanor—there's cake in the icebox.

They departed the living room like a defeated army retiring in good order, leaving its wounded upon the field to be taken by the victor.

Paul and Eleanor waited until the sounds of retiring faded away in the flushing of the toilet. Doors gently closed. On the sofa they were quickly in each other's arms. Her breath was warm, her eyes greenish in color, lambent as a cat's in semidarkness. When he took her into his arms he put his hand confidently on the swell of her bosom. Only the slight hiss of indrawn breath told him she was aware. He kneaded soft flesh with his fingers.

Actually, it was a little disappointing.

—I've never let anyone do this before, she said.

He was sure she was lying.

—Do you want me to stop doing it?

—No, she said.

He didn't try to go further. Later, when they walked to the door he had his arm about her waist and she rested her head on his shoulder. She liked him all right. Probably more than he liked her.

—When will I see you? she asked.

—I'll call you.

He waited two days to assert his new mastery and then called. They went to Jim Hegan's house and played cards with Jim and his sister Dorothy.

They stopped in the park again on the way to her home. She was eager when he touched and fondled her. He put his hand beneath her dress.

—Oh, Paul. I'm frightened.

—There's nothing to be frightened of.

—Please, she said. Please stop.

He persisted until she broke away. He was annoyed.

—Well, if that's the way you feel, he said.

—I told you to stop, she said accusingly.

They returned to her house in sulky silence. So it was to be a contest of wills. He would make her aware who was master. Cold determination filled him. He would persevere to the end and she would yield.

—Well, good night, she said at the door.

—Goodbye, he said firmly.

He turned and left her without further word or embrace. She called him. He hurried on without turning. She called again with panic in her tone. Her high heels clattered after him.

—Paul!

He kept on.

—Paul, please!

He heard the choke of surrender in her voice.

He stopped then.

She came into his arms, like Niobe, all tears.

—Paul, what's the matter? Where were you going?

She turned a blank face upward.

—I wasn't going to see you again, was I?

—You made the conditions, he said cruelly. Not I.

She began to cry.

—Oh, Paul.

He walked slowly back to her house with his arms about her. She was trembling.

—I didn't realize how much I cared until I saw you going away, she said.

They entered the living room of her home. There was only a small dim light in the foyer. She put her fingers to her lips, cautioning, as she took him into the kitchen. The kitchen was farthest removed from her mother's bedroom. They sat in wooden chairs alongside each other and after one kiss he heard her whisper.

—It's unbuttoned.

He didn't know when she had done it but he was sorry for not having noticed. He slipped his hand in, expecting her bra, but his fingers went beneath the bra to touch warm flesh. He felt a stiff nipple against his palm. My god. Is it possible? She might yield all the way.

He wasn't ready. The prospect overwhelmed him. Passion ebbed quickly like a tide away from a pier post. But he persevered in the motions. His hand stroked her thigh, felt her garter and then smooth leg above the stocking. He placed his palm on her supple abdomen and then moved down two fingers to touch her *there*. Her mouth opened mimicking the reply of her vagina. Her kisses became moistly soft and welcoming.

Somehow they were on their feet and crossing toward the porcelain-top table. He helped her up onto it. Her eyes were half closed, unfocused with terrible tenderness. She took off her panty girdle and rolled down her stockings. As he watched her a swift resurgence of desire shook him. He zipped down his trousers. There was proof he was ready. She took off filmy black panties and partly opened her thighs. She edged forward over the white porcelain. Straight level power of red flesh aimed toward her. He guided it with his fingers. She put her hands on his shoulders and held. At the first touch a convulsion gripped him irresistibly. He fought against it, then with rude urgency drove himself forward. She gave a cry

79

and then as his whole body seemed to heave in spasm he was aware he was in her. Her mouth hung slack and her head twisted to one side and her eyes closed. She made noises in her throat. Her fingers bit deep into the shirt at his back. He felt himself curling away and dying as she urged her hips forward to hold him tighter in place.

—Paul, she said. Oh, Paul.

It was not at all disappointing.

They stood together in the dark library of the new home in Washington.

"Well, not much sense in staying here," Paul Lowe said. "There isn't even any furniture."

"I know where everything will go," Eleanor said. "We can use most of the things from our home. I have to go back for a few days to pick out what I want to go on the van."

"Any time," Paul Lowe said.

They came out onto the quiet street. The dark house loomed behind them with closed windows and solidly shut door. Paul Lowe experienced a moment's misgivings. Had they made the right decision? He glanced at his watch. Nancy had said she might arrive any time after ten o'clock. It was now a quarter to ten.

As they arrived at the hotel a long gray Chrysler stopped at the curb in front of the entrance. Arthur Montgomery got out. A moment later Paul Lowe made out Nancy within the car.

"They're here," he told Eleanor.

Arthur Montgomery was talking to the doorman, but he saw them coming and opened the car door for Nancy.

Nancy wore a plum-colored suit. Her blonde hair was piled high on her head, and she wore beige gloves and beige lizard shoes. She waved, smiling, and Paul Lowe was struck again by what a beautiful young woman his daughter was.

Eleanor and Nancy hugged each other. Paul Lowe shook hands with his son-in-law. Arthur Montgomery had curly light brown hair, bright blue eyes, and a broken nose acquired from his playing days on the University of Missouri football team. He was several inches taller than Paul Lowe and gave the impression of having been poured into a block of cement. He had very wide massive shoulders and a deep chest and his legs seemed planted firmly in the sidewalk.

"How was your trip?" Paul Lowe asked.

"Fine. Just fine. Didn't have a bit of trouble."

Paul Lowe opened his arms to Nancy. As she came into his embrace, the subtle rich scent of her perfume reminded him that she was a grown woman. Nancy, whose bare bottom had been turned upward in the snapshot they took in the park the afternoon he changed her diapers. Nancy, whose first steps had been luckily recorded with the home movie camera the day she suddenly took it into her head to venture off alone. A reeling rocking journey it had been, punctuated by falls, until she reached the safety of an upholstered chair with smiling assurance of her newfound powers. That was the beginning, Paul Lowe thought, the ability to walk alone. We go separate paths from that instant.

"You're looking beautiful," Paul Lowe said.

"Thanks, Dad. You're holding together pretty well yourself."

This lovely woman with delicately ointmented face, carefully blue-shadowed eyelids, rouged lips; a name plus a voice cut out of the texture of the universe in a certain pattern, equipped with a history and a necessary personal relationship. Nancy. Daughter.

"Are you hungry? Have you had anything to eat?" Paul Lowe asked.

"We had dinner in Wilmington. Arthur had to meet a client." She added in an offhand tone, "You know Arthur."

"Well, would you like a drink?"

"Sounds interesting. Where?"

"I thought the cocktail lounge. Will you be staying here at the hotel?"

"No, we're staying with friends. Someone from the company. They invited us and Arthur thought it might be a good idea." She had a way of underlining Arthur's name in a sentence.

"The Nordstroms have a lovely home in Georgetown," Arthur said. "Incidentally, they'd be honored if you'd have dinner with them tomorrow night."

"I'm not sure I can make it," Paul Lowe said. "The swearing-in takes place the next morning and I expect a delegation from my home state to arrive the night before. If they do, I may get involved."

"Well, if you don't have other plans, it would be fine with the Nordstroms if you showed up."

Nancy said acidly, "They don't get too many Supreme Court justices to dinner. This man is Arthur's direct superior at the company."

"It was nice of him to invite me," Paul Lowe said.

"He's a dreadful bore."

Arthur said, "Nancy, that isn't fair. You like the Nordstroms as well as I do."

"Exactly as well as you do, darling."

Eleanor's gaze met Paul Lowe's imploringly.

"How about that drink?" Paul Lowe took his daughter's arm. "As I remember, it used to be champagne."

"Still is."

"That's my girl. Expensive."

"Compensations," Nancy said as they entered the hotel arm in arm. Arthur delayed long enough to tip the doorman before he followed with Eleanor.

In the dim cocktail lounge they found a group of comfortable chairs placed around a low polished black wood table. Paul Lowe ordered drinks: champagne cocktail, whiskey sour, extra-dry Tanqueray martini, Jack Daniels on the rocks.

Arthur told about his latest building project, a shopping plaza in Wilmington complete with supermarket, stores, motion picture theater, and bank.

"We've just broken ground," he said earnestly, "and over ninety percent of the space is already leased. Most of them have taken ten-year leases or longer."

"Imagine that," Nancy murmured into her champagne glass.

"I think we're going to have it completed two months ahead of our schedule," Arthur said. As he explained the details of construction, muscles worked in his chest and shoulders—he was born to labor, barechested, lifting and heaving in the noonday sun. He worked at one remove from his real love.

Nancy blew out smoke from a cigarette in a long ivory holder. "Arthur thinks it's fascinating to pile one brick on top of another."

Arthur gave a self-conscious laugh. "I guess I've been talking too much."

"It's been very interesting," Eleanor said.

"Very," Nancy said.

Arthur Montgomery drained his martini. "You just don't happen to care about business," he told Nancy.

Nancy said, "Do you think we could have another drink?"

Paul Lowe signaled the waiter.

Arthur said, "You don't understand business."

"It isn't hard, darling. You make something and then sell it to somebody. Then you start all over again making something."

"You don't have to like what I do," Arthur answered, "but you don't have to make fun of it either."

Nancy's long lashes fluttered. "Darling, I admire you. You have beaver blood. Always busy busy busy at something."

Eleanor said, "Arthur has gone a long way ahead in his profession."

Nancy tapped the cigarette with her index finger—the nail long and gleaming—until the ash dropped obediently into a curved dark ceramic tray.

The waiter came to serve the new round of drinks. Arthur brooded over the knuckles of a clenched fist until the waiter left.

As he started to speak, Nancy interrupted.

"Look at this!" She picked up the deeply curved ashtray of heavy dark glass. "They're getting more artistically obscene in luxury hotels all the time."

Neither Paul Lowe nor Arthur fell into the trap.

Eleanor did. "I don't understand what you mean."

"Look at it, Mother. For heaven's sake, it's shaped just like a vagina."

"Now, Nancy," Eleanor rebuked her. Her authority over Nancy had long since vanished but she still spoke with the reflex of motherhood.

Nancy held the ashtray on the flat of her palm and extended it toward the light of the antique lantern lamp on the wall.

"It's beautifully done," Nancy said admiringly. Without turning she said to Arthur, "Don't you think so?"

"It's just an ashtray," Arthur said with annoyance.

"Is that really all you see?"

"Yes."

Nancy turned to Paul Lowe.

"That's why my husband is a builder and not an architect. No imagination."

"Maybe you have too much imagination," Paul Lowe said.

"It *is* a vagina. They must have done it as some sort of joke."

"I doubt that," Arthur said.

"Do you?" Nancy asked. She put the ashtray down gently on polished wood. "Do you really?" She turned her head to examine it with quizzical delight.

"All I know is that's a pretty stupid topic," Arthur said with anger.

Nancy said to Paul Lowe, "Can you imagine? I married a puritan. Your very own precious daughter."

"Don't you really think we've had enough of this?" Paul Lowe asked.

"I don't understand why you take his side, Dad."

"I agree with Arthur that this is an embarrassing discussion. Of course, I realize that's exactly why you're persisting with it."

Nancy lifted her glass and drank half the champagne. "Everyone likes Arthur," she said, putting the glass down. "That's his whole stock in trade. If one more person comes up to me and says how sweet Arthur is I think I'll shoot myself."

"I think my watch has stopped," Arthur Montgomery said to Paul Lowe. "Do you have the right time?"

"Eleven o'clock. Just thirty-six hours from now I'll be getting sworn in to my new job."

Arthur brightened at the promised shift in the conversation.

"I wouldn't miss that for anything in the world. How do you feel about it? Excited?"

"I'm a little nervous," Paul Lowe confessed.

Nancy brought her empty champagne glass forward to touch the rim gently against Arthur's nose.

"I'll have more champagne, Arthur. We can afford it, can't we?"

"You can have anything you want," Arthur replied shortly. He gestured to the waiter.

A bellboy made the rounds of the tables in the hotel lounge. As he came near his voice was audible.

"Telephone call for Mr. Arthur Montgomery."

"Over here," Arthur said.

"My God," Nancy said. "Why did you tell them you could be reached at the hotel?"

"I left the Nordstroms' phone number too," Arthur began, rising from his chair.

"What a damn fool thing to do."

Arthur turned to Paul Lowe and Eleanor. "I'm sorry. I won't be long. Excuse me."

"Of course," Paul Lowe said.

Arthur followed the bellhop out of the lounge.

Eleanor said sternly, "You really treat him very badly, Nancy. Arthur is a sensitive man. I don't know why he puts up with it."

"He says it's because he's in love with me." Nancy took the burned-out cigarette from her holder and ground it out in the ashtray. "But that isn't really it. Arthur just puts up with things, that's all. It's one of his accomplishments."

"You might stop testing him," Paul Lowe said.

Nancy gave her cigarette an unnecessarily hard turn in the ashtray. "I can't stand the way he just sits there. You'd think he would hit back once in a while."

"He's a fine man," Eleanor said. "You shouldn't take advantage of the fact that he's a gentleman."

"Oh, leave me alone, Mother!"

Eleanor said, "Give yourself a chance to be happy with him."

Nancy turned to her father. "She means I should act toward Arthur the way she does toward you. Shall I have blind faith in him? Shall I be blindly adoring? Do you think *he'd* like to be simpered over?"

Eleanor said indignantly, "Nancy!"

"That was uncalled for," Paul Lowe said.

"I'm sorry. I know I'm being a bitch. But I can't help myself. When you're miserable you can't help making other people a little unhappy too." She shrugged. "I'm under analysis. What more can I do?"

"Are you really seeing a psychiatrist?" Eleanor asked.

"Yes, Mother," Nancy answered. "I am really seeing a psychiatrist."

"But you're not sick in that way."

"You could get another point of view on the subject. Ask Arthur. Ask my analyst. I'm seeing him four times a week and he hasn't made me feel any better. Do I seem better to you?"

Eleanor gave Nancy a look that was kind and sympathetic and stricken.

Paul Lowe said, "Is there anything we can do?"

"According to my analyst you've already done quite enough. It's always the parents' fault. That's what's so wonderful about analysis. I don't have to feel responsible for the fact I'm a bitch. You two did it."

"I don't mind what you say about me," Eleanor answered in a hurt tone. "But how can you talk this way about your father? You ought to be ashamed."

Nancy asked, "Should I be ashamed of talking that way about you, Father?"

"If that's how you feel, you have a right to say so, Nancy."

"Of course she doesn't," Eleanor said. "How could she feel that way after all you've done for her?"

"What about you, Mother? Haven't *you* done anything for me? Or do you only follow around after Dad like a pilot fish after a whale?"

Eleanor's rather narrow eyes opened in a way she had of keeping off tears.

Paul Lowe said, "You've had too much to drink, Nancy. You're saying things you don't mean. I think you owe an apology to your mother."

Nancy said, "I didn't mean to hurt you, Mother. I'm sorry if I did."

"I know you didn't mean to, dear."

Nancy turned to Paul Lowe. "Is that better?"

"I'm not your enemy, you know, Nancy."

"I know that. You and I . . . we're too much alike. Cut from the same cloth."

Paul Lowe's throat tightened. "I hope we are."

"I learned everything I know from you. Surprised? That's why I can afford to hurt Arthur—because he can't possibly hurt me. He can't even reach me. Like you and Mother, isn't it? It's the same way."

"It's possible you're only projecting your own emotional state, Nancy."

Nancy stared at him.

"No, it's perfectly true. *Nobody* can reach you. Not Mother or me or anyone. You cover that up better than I do because you're smoother. Older and smarter—and I'm unhappier. I don't have a career to fill in empty places. But you don't honestly *care* about anyone—do you?"

Deepening his apprehension of her, discerning her boundaries, Nancy, daughter, became a clearer zone of consciousness. He was able to take her out of a boundless realm in which he was not able to describe anything about her with certainty. Now he could say of her: she can be frank, she can be subtle, she can be cruel.

He moved his lips. "I don't think that's true."

"I wish I believed you thought so," Nancy said. She looked away. "Well, here comes the hero of the hour."

Arthur Montgomery wended his way toward them.

Paul Lowe felt a sudden surprising contact and, looking down, found Eleanor's fingers groping into his own. He squeezed her hand. There *was* a sense of commingling warmth, palm against palm.

7

He stood before the huge marble palace that was the Supreme Court building and looked up at the words carved high on the west façade: *EQUAL JUSTICE UNDER LAW*. The flag on the rear of the roof was sinuously flapping red, white and blue in a stiff morning breeze.

A stray piece of paper blew across the broad marble steps as he mounted toward the massive double row of Corinthian columns.

He went briskly up to the public entrance. Within the high vaulted lobby two policemen were on guard beside the red velvet rope that guarded the Court's chamber. He smiled, turned right, and hurried down the corridor past the Marshal's office.

When he entered the office assigned to him, a young man was standing on a chair removing a framed picture from the wall. He turned as Paul came in.

"Oh, I'm sorry." Quickly he put the picture back on its hook and stepped down from the chair.

"I'm Bill Tobin," he said.

"Oh, yes. Justice Frank Joyce's law clerk."

Bill Tobin was a medium-sized, pale-looking young man with a high forehead.

"I'm Paul Lowe."

"I recognized you right away, sir. I thought I'd stick around to see if there was anything I could do to help."

"I appreciate that."

Paul Lowe glanced about the large room. Gray steel filing cabinets were joined along one wall. Near the large desk between two long windows was a light blue electric typewriter on a small table. There were waxy-leaved red and green begonias in boxes on the window sill. The rug was dark brown, thick but slightly worn. Lowe wondered if it were the same rug that was here when he had been a young man and law clerk to Charles Edmunson. Probably not, but everything in this room except for the electric typewriter looked the same as before. Justice Frank Joyce was a man of simple, unchanging habits.

Bill Tobin said, "Mr. Justice Joyce asked to be remembered."

"Did he really? I didn't think he'd remember me."

"He has no trouble with things like that," Tobin answered defensively. "Nothing wrong with the way his mind works. It's just his heart—and his age, you know."

Paul Lowe nodded. "He's always been an extraordinary man."

"Yes." Bill Tobin was carefully appraising Lowe. "I'm sixty years younger but I could never understand how he did it. The amount of work he did was backbreaking."

"I know what you mean. I felt the same way when I clerked for Edmunson. It was a great privilege, and it does teach humility."

"It certainly does, sir." Bill Tobin's glance traveled about the main office with tender familiarity. "Would you care to see the other offices?"

"Yes."

Bill Tobin took him first to the room that he had shared with Joyce's other law clerk. The room was surrounded on three sides by shelves of law books. In the center were two large desks at which the clerks worked. There were typewriter stands beside each desk, with the typewriters shrouded in gray covers. Every available space, including the six-foot-long narrow table on the right side of the room, was covered with neat piles of papers. These would be the cert petitions—the briefs asking the Court to hear cases. The law clerks' duty was to go through the tremendous accumulation of petitions for certiorari and somehow reduce it to workable proportions. A law clerk could not pass upon the worth of petitions nor could he eliminate or assign priorities. All he could do was condense the facts, distill points of law, cite authorities to better enable the justice to pass upon each petition.

Paul Lowe saw all this with partly averted face. How neatly, quickly, with what admirable certainty men like Frank Joyce disposed of such minor problems.

"This is where Lionel Trask and I worked," Bill Tobin said softly.

"In my day there was only one law clerk."

"Things have changed, Mr. Lowe." Bill Tobin did not make the mistake of addressing Lowe as Mr. Justice. "Even Justice Edmunson uses two clerks now. The work keeps getting harder." He shook his head. "As it is, I don't know how any of the justices manage to keep up with it."

Paul Lowe winced inwardly. "I may be wondering the same thing all too soon."

Bill Tobin led the way toward Frank Joyce's office. Each of the nine Supreme Court justices' offices had certain features in common: a handsome fireplace framed in dark polished wood, a large desk, and walls inset with bookshelves. But most of the furniture was chosen according to individual taste, as were the decorations, and therefore in ways too subtle for definition the character and personality of each man was revealed. On either side of a black phone on Frank Joyce's desk were tidy stacks of papers awaiting an action that now would never be taken by him. Here were problems that would now never be resolved by a mind quite so meticulous in detail, so impeccable in its use of the law. A clearly printed calendar in a plastic frame stood on the functional green blotter. Other papers lay asymmetrical but orderly on the desk; some were carefully piled in a manuscript box. A square glass paperweight held down the papers in the box. There was a printed quotation in a small wooden frame: *The man himself is part of the decision he makes.*

Near the center of the desk a freeform pipe lay casually across a brief Joyce must have been reading at the moment illness struck him down. On a lower shelf of the bookcase just behind the deep-ribbed upholstered red leather chair was a photograph of a young man in uniform—Joyce's son, killed in the Battle of the Bulge. Nearby was a humidor that contained Joyce's pipe tobacco, and beside that a silver-framed picture of his wife as she had looked in 1911, the year after they were married. Frank Joyce had once shown Paul Lowe that picture with evident pride in the good-looking, dark-featured, masterful woman who stared out of the frame. In the oil portrait above the fireplace she appeared more gently beautiful—an open book spread on her lap, her gown flowing, a moderating vase of flowers on the table beside her. Below her portrait an antique clock kept time, the pendulum counting out the hours since she had vanished from Frank Joyce's world.

On the day after her funeral Frank Joyce had come as usual to the office, looking a bit more shrunken, his thin lips drawn even tighter. He had spent the day working on his opinion in the case of a sailor who suffered an injury swabbing the deck of a ship in dock. The sailor claimed the vessel unseaworthy because of the way her cargo had been stored. Joyce's written opinion, upholding the right of the sailor to compensation, had been as always tidy, logical, complete, every issue confronted, mastered and restored in the proper place. Frank Joyce never slighted a legal difficulty, never failed to ask himself the crucial questions—or answer them.

"I've tried to keep everything the way it was when he left," Bill Tobin said. "There didn't seem much point in changing anything until his successor was appointed."

"I'm glad you didn't," Paul Lowe said.

Bill Tobin glanced at him briefly.

"On the day he was stricken he was working—I even left the brief right there." Tobin continued in a strained voice, "I came in and found him slumped on his desk. He had just time to take off his glasses—they were in his hand."

"It must have been a terrible shock for you."

The young man's lips moved before the words came. "I haven't gotten over it yet."

Paul Lowe wondered how much more the young man might have said if there were a better language to express hidden emotion. He said kindly, "Well, I suppose I'd better get busy. I don't have too much time."

"Yes, sir," Bill Tobin said.

"Would it be too much trouble for you to help me go over some of the work Mr. Justice Joyce left behind?"

"No, sir," Bill Tobin said.

He showed Paul Lowe the first draft of an opinion. Frank Joyce had typewritten it. The pages were single spaced and black with too heavily inked letters, strikeovers, and scribbling in small spidery handwriting.

"He had turned it over to me that morning to check on the authorities and fill in the citations," Bill Tobin explained.

Glancing at the typewritten pages, Paul Lowe picked up an occasional pungent phrase that was almost like hearing Joyce's voice: "An obsolete morality is a gradual stain spreading among ruins" . . . "We cannot pick daisies on the fields of Armageddon." A more precise and elegant diction than Edmunson's, more exquisite, although not so grand or masterful. Joyce and Edmunson had been a mighty pair—Vikings in black robes, charting unexplored continents of law. Now Frank Joyce was gone and Edmunson was left to carry on alone.

Bill Tobin showed the notes he had written in comment on Joyce's opinion. As Paul Lowe scanned the pages he managed to obtain a clear impression. Tobin was an excellent law clerk—capable of arguing, pleading, cajoling, imagining new hypotheses, even indulging in occasional sarcasm. He was not inhibited by his hero worship. In the completed result there would be evidences of a constructively critical other mind.

Paul Lowe asked casually, "What are your plans now that Frank Joyce has retired?"

Bill Tobin shrugged. "I'll stay until you take over, Mr. Lowe. Then I'll probably go to work for the government."

"Have you been offered a job?"

"Yes—Mr. Justice Joyce took care of that, while he was in the hospital. He insisted on writing a letter of reference. When I showed Mr. Daris the letter . . . well, he offered me a job."

"Peter Daris?"

"Yes, sir. The Solicitor General himself."

"Have you told him you'd accept?"

"Nothing final."

Paul Lowe met Tobin's eyes. "How would you like to go right on working here?"

"For you?"

"I've got one law clerk on his way. A young man named Jack Broderick who worked for my former law partner. But I can use someone with your experience."

Bill Tobin's pale face stayed expressionless. "Lionel Trask is the senior clerk. I've only been here a few months."

"I think we might get along well together."

"Come to think of it, I don't know whether Lionel would accept. He wants to go into private practice."

Paul Lowe smiled. "Well, then . . . ?"

"I'd like to think it over, sir, if I may."

"I won't make any further commitments until I hear from you."

Bill Tobin glanced at the antique clock on the fireplace. "It's a quarter to ten."

"All right. No use putting it off any longer."

In the outside office Paul Lowe found the cardboard package he had left there, broke the strings, and took out a black silk robe.

"My friend Ken Norris bought it for me," he told Bill Tobin. "He's the man I told you about. My former law partner."

"It's a good-looking robe, sir."

"It's not the robe I have to fill," Paul Lowe said soberly. "It's the shoes."

Bill Tobin abruptly held out his hand.

"You'll do fine, Mr. Lowe."

Paul Lowe went down the marble corridor to the judges' private conference room. He hesitated before opening the door. Then he grasped the knob firmly, turned it, and went in.

In a large rectangular room at a long table beneath a heavy crystal chandelier seven of the justices were waiting. They were gathered in two groups. Their white faces seemed to turn toward him and focus like so many magnifying mirrors reflecting an intense glare. Then reason returned—the faces became men, and the men were smiling.

Paul Lowe shook hands with each justice. Andrew Cutler, slightly forbidding man, high forehead, cold steady eyes hemmed in by small pouches; Gabriel Hart, round faced, heavy browed, balding, a homely, dumpy man; Henry Merriam, disdainfully good-looking with his gray eyebrows and large leonine silver-gray head; Bill Branch, jowly, kindly smiling with prominent roughly formed nose and tiny red vein lines on his cheeks; young-looking Edward McCann, pleasant face, square black eyeglasses below a fine curling head of reddish hair; Chief Justice John Hampton, square faced, square jawed, black-gray brows beneath black-gray hair. Then a tight firm handclasp that was Waldo Shuler, brisk, energetic, short of stature—face with definite bone structure, sharp downward-angling nose, small dimples at the mouth corners. Paul Lowe finished the round of shaking hands.

Then the door to the conference room opened and closed behind the last of the justices to arrive.

"Good to have you back, Paul."

He could never mistake that voice: sonorous, penetrating. But there was something new, a slightly offkey tremor in an organ.

"Mr. Justice Edmunson," Paul Lowe said warmly.

The regally tall erect figure was exactly as he remembered. But the long face with the large prominent ears and aquiline nose looked older; time had sagged it a little and below the eyes there was mottled redness. But the massive jaw was the same and the mouth with the long full underlip, and the upward-lifted straggly white eyebrows that reached toward bushy white hair at the temples. Edmunson's dark blue eyes, in down-turned lids of flesh, had unnaturally large pupils that looked out with such immense gravity and wisdom one *felt* the weight of the glance. His hand was big, the long fingers curling almost around Paul Lowe's wrist when they shook hands.

"We'll be working together again," Edmunson said.

90

Paul Lowe answered, "Only this time I can vote."

Edmunson's amused rumble filled his deep chest. "That's what you always wanted, isn't it? Some way to back up your convictions."

Chief Justice John Hampton said, "We only have a few minutes, Mr. Lowe. We thought it better to administer the oath here."

"I'm ready any time you are."

The justices, at a signal from Chief Justice Hampton, took their places at the conference table. John Hampton remained with Paul Lowe. He indicated a cloth-covered Bible on the table and Paul Lowe put his left hand on it, raising his right hand.

"Will you repeat the words after me? . . . I, Paul Lincoln Lowe . . ."

"I, Paul Lincoln Lowe . . ."

". . . do solemnly swear that I will support and defend . . ."

". . . do solemnly swear that I will support and defend . . ."

". . . the Constitution of the United States against all enemies foreign and domestic . . ."

". . . the Constitution of the United States against all enemies foreign and domestic . . ."

Under his right hand the cloth binding of the Bible was granular and rough. He faithfully echoed the words in a solemn room in the east corner of the Supreme Court building. I, Paul Lincoln Lowe, in a room where every chair around the black oblong table had held the physical presence of men whose words had become the living law of the land. Felix Frankfurter had sat here. *As Judges we are neither Jew nor Gentile, neither Catholic nor agnostic—*

". . . that I will bear true faith and allegiance to the same . . ."

". . . that I will bear true faith and allegiance to the same . . ."

". . . that I take this obligation freely . . ."

". . . that I take this obligation freely . . ."

". . . and that I will faithfully and impartially discharge the duties incumbent upon me as Associate Justice of the Supreme Court of the United States . . ."

". . . that I will faithfully and impartially discharge the duties incumbent upon me . . ." From Chief Justice John Jay to Chief Justice John Hampton nearly two centuries had passed. In all that time less than a hundred men had repeated an oath that had changed in language but never in meaning.

". . . as an Associate Justice of the Supreme Court of the United States . . ."

Chief Justice Hampton coolly going on: ". . . according to the best of my abilities and understanding, agreeable to the Constitution and the laws of the United States . . ."

". . . according to the best of my abilities and understanding, agreeable to the Constitution and the laws of the United States . . ."

The Law is a ass, a idiot. Bumble, how little you know. The law is sometimes an ass, but Jesus rode one on his way to Salvation. *I think it not improbable that man, like the grub that prepares a chamber for the winged thing it has never seen but is to be—that man may have cosmic destinies he does not understand.* In Oliver Wendell Holmes' hands the law was philosophy and literature. There are more kinds of poetry in heaven and earth, Charles Dickens, than your Bumble dreamed of.

". . . so help me God."

". . . so help me God."

In the robing room, Sam Davids, the Negro attendant, stood beside an open locker near the end of the line of oak paneled lockers. Each locker had a silver nameplate on it.

Sam Davids smiled. "Good morning, Mr. Justice."

Mr. Justice.

Davids had been the attendant for almost thirty years. He was a serious-looking tall man with very close-cropped gray hair. Old in the job even when Paul Lowe was a law clerk.

"Good to see you, Sam."

Sam Davids indicated the open locker. A silver plate bore the name *Mr. Justice Paul Lowe.*

"May I help you with your robe, Mr Justice?"

Paul Lowe nodded. At the moment he did not trust himself to speak.

Robed and silent, the nine justices filed across the private corridor to where tall maroon drapes curtained off the courtroom. Chief Justice Hampton signaled. A buzzer sounded from beyond the drapery. That would be the Marshal. Then the bang of a gavel and the Marshal's clear ringing voice:

"The Honorable, the Chief Justice, and the Associate Justices of the Supereme Court of the United States."

The heavy maroon drapery parted in three places and by threes the nine robed men entered the high-ceilinged chamber in the order of seniority. In the courtroom the spectators were standing. As the justices moved toward the bench, soberly dressed page boys waited to pull out their chairs. Not long ago the page boys had worn blue knickerbockers, blue jackets and black stockings, but their colorful costumes had changed to ordinary dark colored suits. One by one, like musical instruments in a fugue, the old ceremonies were departing.

Paul Lowe went to his left behind the long mahogany bench and stopped at the last place on the platform behind the highbacked leather swivel chair he had chosen only the day before from a stock the Marshal kept in the basement.

Robert Perry, the Marshal, banged his gavel.

"Oyez! Oyez! Oyez! All persons having business before the Honorable, the Supreme Court of the United States, are invited to draw near and give their attention, for the Court is now sitting. God save the United States and this honorable Court. Please be seated."

The justices took their seats. Chief Justice Hampton said: "I announce with deep regret the retirement of Mr. Justice Frank Joyce who has served this Court with very great distinction for thirty-two years. He has made a contribution to the law of this land, and to this Court, which few men will ever equal and probably none will surpass. It has been a privilege, deeply felt by all of us here, to have served with him and to have benefited from his wisdom, his comradeship, his zealous devotion to arduous labors. I will not attempt to fully express our feelings which have already been set forth in a letter to him. That letter, together with his response, will be recorded in the Minutes of the Court."

Chief Justice Hampton paused and in the crowded courtroom there was a momentary stirring.

He went on: "We are fortunate, however, that a successor to Mr. Justice Joyce has now been appointed by the President of the United States and duly confirmed by the Senate. Paul Lincoln Lowe took the constitutional oath of office a few minutes ago in a private ceremony with the other justices of the Court as witnesses. The Clerk of the Court will now read Mr. Justice Lowe's commission and administer the judicial oath."

At a nod from John Hampton, Paul Lowe rose and walked over to a small table at the far right of the bench. The Court Clerk, Gordon Doughty, a thin narrow-shouldered man with scanty gray hair, held a Bible out to Lowe.

Facing the Clerk and the audience, with his hand on the Bible, Paul Lowe half listened to the archaic words of the commission being read. His glance took in a part of the courtroom and the spectators. In the reserved section Eleanor and Nancy and Arthur Montgomery were seated, very erect, very attentive. Eleanor's hand was clutching a handkerchief tightly near her chest.

In the public section were Race Hardman and the contingent from Nebraska—Ken Norris, Henry Wellman, now governor, and Phil Kada, Hiram Sloane and Abe Weisinger. Martha Scully was seated behind Bill Sutherland, her body rigid with a nervousness that was apparent even from where Paul Lowe stood.

Every seat in the courtroom was filled. Members of the Senate were present—he identified Senators Murdoch, Campbell, Sherman, Sprigh, Margrave. Seated prominently up front were Phil Keenan the Attorney General and Peter Daris the Solicitor General. Those two gentlemen often argued cases before the Court and their presence was an act of public relations as well as a tribute to a new justice.

Gordon Doughty finished reading the commission. He began to administer the oath. Paul Lowe raised his right hand and with his left hand on the Bible repeated in a firm voice:

"I, Paul Lincoln Lowe, do solemnly swear . . ."

Out of the blur of faces in the public section, he saw, as sharp as in a developing print, Katherine Prescott with another face clear beside hers. Tom Jeffreys. Their seated intimacy islanded them apart. For Paul Lowe the two became a center of interest which disturbed the unitary solemn occasion. He had to force his attention back to what was taking place in these awesome surroundings. The splendor was Byzantine—as though there could be dignity in marble, meaning in ceremony, wisdom in ritual.

93

Was there? Did men respond to enhanced power, sacramented by tradition, hallowed in styles of architecture?

". . . so help me God."

The Marshal escorted him behind the raised marble platform to his seat at the far left of the bench. As Paul Lowe sat down, his nearest neighbor, Justice McCann, reached over to shake his hand.

There was a good deal of handshaking, Paul Lowe thought.

Before they could begin hearing oral argument, there were new lawyers to be presented for admission to the Court. This morning there were thirty-five new admissions. The ceremony was simple. The name of the lawyer was called and as he stepped forward his sponsor, an established member, moved for his admission. "May it please the Court, I am satisfied that—————possesses the necessary qualifications."

Paul Lowe watched each lawyer step forward. Few of these men would ever argue a case before the Supreme Court, but for their twenty-five-dollar fee they would get a handsome engraved certificate that they could frame and hang in their offices to impress clients.

Chief Justice Hampton, at the conclusion of each brief introduction, made an unvarying speech that lasted all of seven seconds. "Mr. ——— ———, we are very pleased to welcome you to the bar of this Court." Let's see now. Approximately fifteen hundred new admissions each year. Multiply that by seven seconds . . . no, allow time for the sponsor to make his introduction and for the new candidate to walk to the bench. Let's say a total of two minutes for each candidate. That works out to more than three weeks of the Court's precious working time. Paul Lowe kept an alert look on his face while he privately ruminated mathematics.

At last the admissions ceremony dragged to a close.

A few minutes later the first case of the day was called. It was a routine matter of interest to no one except the contending parties and their lawyers. For this case, one hour had been scheduled to hear the oral argument; each side was allotted half an hour. Little enough time. Each attorney was under pressure to be concise, to deal only with high points, to remember that often the soul of an argument is saved by its brevity.

Paul Lowe sat, fascinated, while the opposing lawyers debated whether a domestic court had the power to freeze defendant's bank account in a foreign branch of a New York bank pending the outcome of a tax case.

Occasionally a justice interrupted to ask a question. As the arguments proceeded, Paul Lowe concluded that in this instance the domestic court did not have the power it had taken upon itself. Still, he hesitated to ask a question that might reveal the trend of his thinking. Toward the end of the hour he was relieved when questions from the bench by Justices Hampton, Edmunson and Merriam indicated that they all inclined toward his own position.

A red light glowed on the lectern while counsel for the State was still arguing the case. His allotted time had expired. He promptly nodded, thanked the Court and stepped down. With Chief Justice Hampton presiding, few tried to overstay their time. Hampton brooked no nonsense.

He was the most peremptory Chief Justice since Charles Evans Hughes, who reportedly once cut off an attorney's argument in the middle of the word *if*.

The next case involved a conviction for fraud. The meaning of the statute involved seemed plain but as Mr. Dooley said: "A statute that reads like a stone wall to a layman can become in the hands of a lawyer a triumphal arch." Argument dwelt upon the shadow of the reflection of a nuance of meaning. Split hairs gathered.

This first day on the Court began to seem endless. From now on, Paul Lowe thought, until the summer recess began, the Court would be on a regular schedule. Two weeks of hearing arguments followed by two weeks of recess, from ten o'clock in the morning until noon and then from twelve-thirty to two-thirty on the first four days of the week. Then the conference day on Friday. And this represented only the work done in public view. The huge bulk of the Court's labor, the hidden part of the iceberg, was unseen—the vast amount of reading, discussion, reflection, during early morning, late afternoon, evenings, and all day long during the weeks when the Court was not sitting.

Over three thousand cases a year reached this marble palace on Capitol Hill. In each case Paul Lowe would have to cast his vote at least once. If the Court agreed to hear arguments there were hundreds of pages of briefs to read in addition to supplementary records. Then there were the arguments to be heard, the debates and the voting in conference before one justice would be assigned to write an opinion to be circulated and read by all the other justices, commented upon, revised, recirculated. Other justices might write dissenting or concurring opinions.

It loomed as an endless job, a job that would never be done.

At two-thirty the Court adjourned for the day. Paul Lowe returned to his office and worked for another hour. Then he left for his hotel where he showered and changed clothes to attend a reception in his honor at Race Hardman's home. He arrived there with Eleanor a few minutes after five o'clock.

Most of Paul Lowe's friends were there and he accepted their congratulations. The joking was self-conscious, the reminiscences starchy.

At the midway point, when the party scattered into constantly shifting and mingling groups, Paul Lowe was briefly alone with Katherine Prescott and Tom Jeffreys.

"You seemed at ease on the bench today," Katherine Prescott said.

"I was stupefied. I kept going over in my head all the work to be done."

"Does it worry you?"

"I just have an overwhelming feeling that I can't handle it."

"You'll get used to it," Tom Jeffreys said.

"I don't have much choice. It's too late to back out now. What would everyone think if I resigned after my first day?"

Katherine Prescott said, "I wish you'd give some further thought to letting me write that newspaper series about you."

"I'd better wait until I get settled into the job. If I ever do."

A new voice cut in: "The way I see it, it won't be just a personality piece."

Paul Lowe turned to find Race Hardman standing almost at his elbow.

"It'll help people to understand the problems that confront the Court," Race added.

"Race, I still don't understand the problems myself."

"It won't take long. As soon as possible, I want you to sit down with Katherine and get this series under way. We can't afford to delay. Right now you're news, Paul—and in a couple of months you won't be."

Race Hardman waved to someone and moved on.

"*Sic transit gloria mundi*," Paul Lowe said.

"Race thinks anyone who isn't newsworthy is practically dead," Katherine Prescott said.

It occurred to Paul Lowe that she seemed to favor tailored suits; the one she was wearing had dull brass buttons and fit her full figure with snug flattery.

"Is it out of order for me to say that you're looking very lovely?" he asked.

She smiled. "Is that a final ruling of the Court?"

"Well, if you'd like to petition for a rehearing . . ."

"I think I'd better get you out of his jurisdiction," Tom Jeffreys said.

Instead Tom Jeffreys himself was claimed—by a Congressman who was annoyed by a television show on public affairs that had slighted his favorite legislative project.

Alone with Katherine Prescott, in the middle of the surrounding hubbub of conversation, Paul Lowe was oddly ill at ease.

"Do you plan to be very active in Washington's so-called cultural life?" she asked.

"I really haven't given it any thought."

"There is a highly vocal minority who think Washington is a cultural center. I suppose there are concerts and a smattering of legitimate theater, and a justifiably famous art museum. But I wouldn't rank this town with either New York or San Francisco."

"I'll go along on New York. But I'd be inclined to give Washington second place over San Francisco. However, I won't be spending much time attending the sort of affairs you describe. Most theater is out of my line, and I tend to prefer music on a hi-fi set where I can turn on what I like when I want to hear it. As for paintings, I'm a bad case of arrested development. I stopped somewhere around Renoir and the Ash Can school."

"You ought to look at some newer things. They've got their points."

"You're probably right." Paul Lowe had begun to relax with the discovery that they could make innocuous conversation, so he yielded to a more personal curiosity. "How often do you get to Washington?"

"Oh, three or four times a year usually. I'm supposed to spell the regulars on the *Washington Insider* column. Whenever someone needs a vacation, or the work starts piling up, I'm thrown into the breach."

Eleanor came over to them. While Paul Lowe made the introductions, she looked directly at Katherine Prescott.

"Oh, yes," Eleanor said, "the newspaperwoman."

Katherine smiled. "That's right."

Tom Jeffreys returned to get Katherine, and a moment later they drifted away to join a group that included Governor Henry Wellman and Race Hardman.

"An interesting woman," Paul Lowe said.

Eleanor said, "She could be pretty if she'd lose weight."

At nine o'clock that evening, Paul Lowe and Eleanor went to dinner at the Bit and Bridle Club with Nancy and Arthur.

They had just finished their cocktails when it became obvious that Nancy was in one of her troublemaking moods. It began while Arthur was studying the large varnished menu.

"What's the matter?" Nancy asked. "Can't you make up your mind?"

"Everything has calories in it. I'm supposed to be dieting."

"Try the seafood."

"Well, the oysters Rockefeller look good."

"My God," Nancy said. "You're not worrying about your virility, are you? Let me assure everyone present at this table that virility is not Arthur's problem."

"All right, Nancy." Arthur had color in his cheeks.

The waiter came to the table and Paul Lowe began to give him their orders.

"No, that certainly is not Arthur's problem," Nancy said. "I don't say he doesn't have other problems, though. I only say virility is certainly not one of them."

Arthur said under his breath, "Cut it out."

"If anything, it's usually a question of too much . . ."

"Nancy!"

". . . and much too soon."

Arthur was holding the menu and not looking at it. His face was dark with anger.

Paul Lowe said sharply, "Nancy, it's been a long tiring day. I would appreciate a quiet dinner."

"All right, Dad. This is your Big Day. You're in control. What would you like to talk about?"

"Well, we might begin by letting Arthur tell the waiter what he'd like for dinner."

"That's a marvelous idea. Aren't you fascinated by the way Arthur is hiding behind the menu? Do you think he's ashamed? Do you know of anything Arthur has to be ashamed of?"

Arthur put down the menu with an inaudible muffled exclamation. "You're spoiling for a fight, Nancy. If you don't look out you're going to get one."

"Oh, my. You're *really* angry. Well, it might do you a world of good to work off steam. That might be exactly what you need."

The waiter said, "Shall I return later for the gentleman's order?"

Arthur, simmering, did not answer.

Paul Lowe said, "It might be a good idea."

The waiter nodded discreetly and left.

Without looking at anyone at the table, Arthur said quickly, "Excuse me," and dropped his napkin beside his plate. Then he pushed back his chair and got up and left the table.

"Where do you think you're going?" Nancy asked.

Without turning, Arthur strode away from the table. The waiter, a short distance away, watched with a polite interest.

"Arthur!" Nancy called, staring after him.

"He's leaving. Now you've done it," Eleanor said. "You've succeeded in making a scene."

Nancy turned to Paul Lowe.

"Go after him, will you? Find out what he thinks he's doing."

"Why don't you, Nancy?"

"Did you ever see anything so rude?" She looked toward the front of the restaurant but Arthur had disappeared behind the partition wall. "We've already checked out of the Nordstroms'. He wouldn't go back there." Nancy touched Paul Lowe's arm. "Please. Talk to him."

Arthur was in the checkroom giving a tab to the girl attendant.

Arthur said, "It's no use. I can't stand it when she's in one of these moods. She's impossible."

"Do you think it will help matters if you walk out?"

"It can't hurt. I've tried everything else."

"Where will you go?"

"I don't know. I'll probably check into a hotel. I've got all the baggage in the trunk of the car. Nancy's things, too, dammit. She'll need them. Can I call you later?"

He nodded. "We'll be at our hotel."

"All right."

The girl attendant returned with Arthur's coat and hat. She helped him to get into his coat and he gave her a coin.

He went with Arthur to the door of the restaurant.

"I'm sorry this had to happen," Arthur said. "I know it's spoiled your evening."

"Arthur, if you come back with me now we'll try to thrash this out with Nancy. I think she's starting to feel sorry already."

"No, she isn't. She's wanted this to happen. But I guess she never believed it would. She thought she could humiliate me forever and I would never do anything. But she's finally pushed me over the brink. It's what she wanted only not exactly *when* she wanted it. I'll call you at the hotel, sir. Before midnight."

"You may find her in a much different mood."

Arthur put out his hand. "Anyhow, I wish you luck in your new job.

I really am sorry this happened tonight of all nights. But it was bound to happen sometime. Good night."

"It's nothing permanent, Arthur. I know that."

"That's up to Nancy," Arthur flung back. He went out onto the street.

Paul Lowe returned slowly to the dining room. Eleanor and Nancy were leaning toward each other across the table. Nancy was smiling an in-control, superior, slightly disdainful smile. Eleanor's face was flushed and her body strained forward as though to give further thrust to her words.

". . . I don't know what's come over you but if you expect to hold on to your husband you're going to have to stop belittling him."

Nancy turned to Paul Lowe as he sat down.

"Mother has been reading me a lecture on how to have a happy and successful marriage. Or an unhappy but successful marriage."

"Arthur left. He wouldn't say where he was going."

"You don't know Arthur as well as I do. Right now he knows he's made an awful fool of himself. In a couple of hours he'll be saying it was all his fault."

"I'm only trying to warn you, Nancy. There is a limit to everything. I wouldn't push Arthur any further than you already have."

"What will he do—divorce me? Or take up residence in a local brothel?" A tic worked spasmodically in her throat. "That might not be such a bad idea. Let some other women take over for a spell. I'm tired of being a living human receptacle. It might be good for Arthur. Some synthetic passion might restore his bruised male ego."

Eleanor's teeth set together so firmly her face appeared sunken. She said in a clenched voice, "I can't believe you're my daughter when you talk like that."

"Sometimes I do wish Dad had picked a mother for me who was more my type."

An exclamation was wrung from Eleanor like a gasp. She stood up suddenly.

"It's up to you to do something with her, Paul . . . I can't." Eleanor began making her way among the tables to a door marked *Mademoiselle*.

Paul Lowe rolled a water glass on its thin stem. "If I leave now, Nancy, you could claim a full sweep."

"But you won't, will you?" Nancy's face was turned away.

"No." He stopped turning the glass. "Can you tell me what your real problem is?"

"Does it have to be my problem? Couldn't it be Arthur's?"

"Any other man would have walked out a long time ago."

"I'm a bitch, is that what you mean?"

"I'd like to hear your side of the story."

"I don't have one." She had become very pale. "It's true, Dad. I *am* a bitch. First class, chromium plated. But I can't suffer fools gladly. Arthur is a fool. Mother is a fool. There's the whole thing in a nutshell."

"What are you going to do now, Nancy?"

"I don't know. I don't know."

"Would you prefer not to talk about it?"

She shook her head, smiling tightly, with glistening eyes. "When I was a little girl you were my God. When I read about Him in the Bible it was your face I saw. *You* clothed the neck of the horse with thunder. I wish I could be a little afraid of Arthur. Then I wouldn't mind so much feeling sorry for him."

"He's in love with you."

"He thinks he is. All his animal drive has to go somewhere and wherever it goes he has to believe love goes along with it."

"Don't you care for him at all?"

Her loveliness had a glacial subsurface as though her skin were stretched and formed on a mold that itself lacked expression.

"I suppose I hate him a little. That's a form of caring, isn't it?"

"You must have been in love with him once."

The answer came with intense low force. "Because I gave him visiting rights in my bed? Sure I hoped it would be fun. I didn't know any better. And I was curious to know what it would be like to have that much man inside me."

Her strictness of detail in intimate matters was part of her need to shock him.

"If that was all you wanted, your marriage would have ended some time ago."

With a quick shallow breath she went beyond: "I don't want him to put his hands on me ever again. I can't bear to have him touch me!"

The words were summoned out of her by some suddenly tapped emotion.

The waiter came to the table with a silver cart and began putting platters down—kidneys with wild rice, a rich-looking beef *bourguignon* with irregular chunks of meat awash in dark wine gravy, and a filet of sole amandine with the flat white skinned fish neatly browned on top and flaked with shaved nuts.

Nancy did not speak again until the waiter had gone.

"I'm sorry, Dad. I didn't mean to get so worked up about it."

"That's all right."

"You don't know what it's been like this past year." She did not look at him as she spoke. "Every time he comes near me I flinch. He can barely start making love before it's over. And there I am. He goes to sleep and there I am, staring into the darkness and wishing to Christ I were somewhere, anywhere else."

There was no catharsis for her in this literal recounting of a private agony. Yet he had no choice but to listen. Confidence builds confidence. He had to help her construct the bridge so other thoughts would pass over freely from her mind.

"It can't be a very serious problem," Paul Lowe said. "Has he been to see a doctor?"

"You know Arthur. Can you imagine him going? About a thing like that? Besides, Arthur has convinced himself that it's my fault."

"Are you quite sure it isn't?"

"I'm probably unresponsive. But I can't help it. It's like going to bed with a boy—a strong boy, an eager boy. What makes it worse is that he's always ready. Try, try again. Every night. Every damned blessed night."

He remembered a night after Nancy's fifteenth birthday when he suspected what she had been doing by herself in the bedroom and he sat on the side of her bed and talked to her about normal sex and abnormal sex, legitimate and illegitimate desires. She had listened carefully, her long blonde hair down on her cheeks, sitting up with her hands clasped about her knees, embarrassed by what they were discussing but soberly adult with pride that they were discussing it freely, frankly (*almost* frankly) without artificial barriers of modesty or inhibition. She had the complete trusting wonder of an ignorant savage afflicted with an unknown ailment, taking the advice of her witch doctor. If the nostrums no longer worked that was because not only the patient but the doctor had to believe in the efficacy of his magic.

Nancy asked abruptly, "Do you think it's a crime to make love to someone else when you're married?"

"The answer depends upon the circumstances."

"You've done it, haven't you? Or would you rather not admit it? I don't mind admitting I've had affairs. Several. Do you know what I've discovered?"

"No—and I'd prefer not to hear any more about it."

Her voice contracted and grew harder. "I discovered that the trouble isn't Arthur. In fact, Arthur should get credit because I didn't destroy his manhood—just made him impetuous. Believe it or not, the others became impotent. After a while they simply couldn't do anything. Isn't that a laugh? I froze them out."

"Do you get pleasure in talking about these things, Nancy? Why don't you discuss them with your psychiatrist?"

"One man told me that when he was inside me he felt that I was somewhere far away, laughing at him. And it was mostly true. In fact, he was wrong in only one particular." She faltered for an instant: "I wasn't laughing. You can't really laugh at people you hate." She bowed her head. "I'm going to have Arthur's baby. That's what's so awful."

For a moment his thoughts were confused. She was fifteen with long blonde hair against her cheek—how could she have a man's child?

"Have you told Arthur you're pregnant?"

"No."

"Are you sure," he asked. "How long is it?"

She did not look up. "Six weeks. I'm sure. I don't want to be pregnant. I can't be a mother." Her face tightened across her skull as her beauty sharpened. "The baby isn't going to be born. I'm going to get rid of it."

"You don't mean that." A heavy sensation contradicted him: she did.

"Dad, I hope we're not going to make the standard speech about the sacredness of life. At this moment my baby is about the size of a half dollar—has no feelings, no consciousness. When it ceases to exist it won't even know it did."

"You'll know," Paul Lowe said gently.

She blinked. "And I'll be glad. Think of the agony I'll spare another innocent human."

"You're being dishonest now."

Her assurance drained dry. "All right. But I'm being honest when I say I don't love Arthur and I won't have his child." Brilliant green eyes turned slightly opaque. "I've already talked to my psychiatrist. He'll find one more psychiatrist to say I'm not emotionally fit to have a child. That's all I need. Then I can have the abortion under the best possible circumstances. In a hospital with no more danger than pulling a tooth, as they say."

The door in the rear of the dining room opened and Eleanor came out, looking anxiously in their direction.

"I don't think Arthur will ever consent to it."

"He won't know anything about it. Not until it's too late."

Eleanor was making progress through the room toward them. It was then Paul Lowe made his decision. There are rules which govern conduct, rules which he had consciously learned and come to accept.

He said, "Don't tell your mother anything about this. But I want your promise that you'll tell Arthur you're going to have a baby. And that you're planning to have an abortion."

"Why should I tell him anything like that?"

"If you won't, I'll tell him myself."

Nothing else to do. To do otherwise would be to confess ignorance of the rules or a failure to seek out what they were.

Her eyes widened. "I'd never forgive you. You wouldn't do it." She partly lifted her hand to fend off the thought—then let her hand fall. "It would be a betrayal."

Paul Lowe went on firmly, "When Arthur calls the hotel tonight, you'll tell him everything. And when he leaves Washington in the morning, I want you to leave with him."

"What do you hope to accomplish by this?"

"If you tell Arthur what you're planning to do, he won't allow you to do it. And he can stop you. The law is on his side."

"I don't believe you're capable of acting like this. My own father."

"Here comes your mother, Nancy. What's your answer?"

Her lips tightened. She stared at him and, just before Eleanor reached the table, she gave a small quick nod.

Eleanor said, "Well, I must say the atmosphere seems friendlier here than when I left. Did you two have a nice long talk?"

"I think we understand each other," Paul Lowe said.

"All too well," Nancy said.

He caught the note of finality. He had committed the unforgivable—stepped out of his role as father, protector. She would never never accept that he meant it for her good.

The waiter came with the check. As he paid, he looked up for an instant and exchanged a glance with Nancy. He regarded her through a veil of kindness, with compassion that caused a puzzled reaction beneath her hostility.

There was really nothing so strange about what he was doing. She should not be surprised. He understood her well. He had lived her torment. She was suffering because she had learned it was not enough to be loved—that one must love. But she would make her adjustment to it.

She was young.

8

"Let us begin," Chief Justice John Hampton said at precisely ten o'clock Friday morning.

In the conference room Paul Lowe took out the assignment sheet which listed those cases ready to be discussed.

This room, situated directly opposite the courtroom and adjoining the Chief Justice's suite of offices and the robing room, was truly the heart of the Supreme Court building. In a sense this area was the center stage and all the rest was a sideshow.

In the middle of the room stood the dominating presence of the conference table. The center of the table was covered in green felt with a narrow wooden rim enclosing it so the appearance was almost that of a very long billiard table. At one end of the room was a large fireplace with a portrait of John Marshall solemnly glowering above it.

At his seat at the conference table Paul Lowe felt himself in the center of things. There was an attraction about being at the center, performing important service, that was both irresistibly appealing—and breathtaking in its potential dangers.

His gaze wandered to the books in the shelves that lined the walls from floor to ceiling. What he decided this day with his colleagues would eventually be included in one of those volumes. What he said, what was spoken by the others, would go far toward making decisions that, by rule of precedent, would become a part of countless other decisions to be made in future by the Court.

Paul Lowe shook his head. He dared not venture too far into such intimidating thoughts.

At the conference they took up first the appeals and the petitions for certiorari. The order of discussion was always the same. Chief Justice Hampton stated the pertinent facts and gave his own opinion. Then Charles Edmunson, as the senior justice, continued the discussion before yielding to the next senior justice, and so the argument led down the table.

Paul Lowe was impressed with the way Chief Justice Hampton presided at the conference. Hampton had a rare ability to state facts succinctly and to identify the question to be decided. They briskly disposed of the few appeals on the conference list and began with the applications for writs of certiorari. Those on the Appellate Docket were handled first.

Paul Lowe occasionally got up from the conference table to deliver a memo to a page waiting outside or later to accept the material which returned in due course—a law book, a needed citation, or the briefs in a related case.

As the junior justice, doorkeeping was his chore and he maintained the only contact with the outside world. No one was allowed to enter the room once the messengers had placed the carts with the petitions for certiorari and other briefs and papers behind each justice's chair. No law clerk, no clerk of the Court, no government official, no secretary or messenger or page boy was permitted to enter the sacrosanct portals.

The secrecy of the conference room was kept absolute.

Just before one-thirty, he glanced covertly at his watch. They had considered all the petitions for certiorari on the Appellate Docket and only a few paupers' applications remained on the Miscellaneous Docket. These were from petitioners—many from convicts in prison—who could not afford the costs of a regular petition. The petitions were often without any legal grounds at all.

At two o'clock, they recessed for half an hour and with the other justices Paul Lowe went up in the elevator to the private dining room on the second floor.

Edward McCann fell into step beside him.

"Well, how do you like your first few days on the Court?"

"It's interesting. Different from being in the Governor's chair."

"In what way?"

"Quieter—and a lot harder. I thought my experience as a law clerk had prepared me for the work to be done. But it hasn't."

"It's gotten worse," McCann said soberly. "Somebody once figured out that the average weekly conference dealt with a hundred different items. That works out to about thirty seconds apiece for each judge to speak his mind. We'd never keep up at all if we didn't have a Chief like Hampton."

"He's very efficient."

"None better. As you noticed, his first statement of a case is often the last. That's a big timesaver. And whenever he can see there's a unanimous or near-unanimous agreement on a question he uses that brusque manner to discourage further comment."

"Being Chief Justice is a difficult job."

"I could never do it."

Paul Lowe shook his head. "I'm not sure right now that I can handle the job I've got."

"Do you get that feeling too?"

"You mean you have it?" Paul Lowe asked with surprise.

As they entered the dining room Edward McCann answered, "I live with it, sleeping and waking. You know when it's worst? Every time I sit down to write an opinion. That's when it comes over me that my pen is really a chisel and I'm carving words on stone—and I'm the only one who happens to be writing nonsense limericks."

"How long does it take to master this job?"

"Don't ask me. I've been here five years and I don't think I'm even close to it."

"Thanks for the encouragement," Paul Lowe said wryly.

He sat down at the luncheon table. That morning he had marked the menu sent up by the cafeteria and now the lunch he had ordered was waiting: broiled pork chops and mashed potatoes. Down the table from him Charles Edmunson was dining on fruit salad and cottage cheese.

The atmosphere at the dining table was informal and cheerful. Chief Justice Hampton, laughing heartily with Henry Merriam at a cartoon in the Washington *Post*, did not seem to be the same man who, stern of eye and commanding of appearance, had dominated the conference table.

Waldo Shuler and Bill Branch were exchanging gossip about the members of a prominent Washington law firm. Gabriel Hart was relating an interminable anecdote about hunting to Andrew Cutler who was only half listening. Charles Edmunson ate in silence, alone, brooding on some thought that no one wished to interrupt.

Paul Lowe engaged Edward McCann in conversation which turned to the Washington Senators' prospects (dismal) for the coming baseball season.

"Who do you think will win the pennant in the American League?" Paul Lowe asked.

"The safe answer is the Yankees."

"I don't know. The last couple of seasons it's begun to look as though we're entering a new era. The Yankees are acting like just another ball club."

"Don't bet on it," McCann said gloomily. "They'll be back winning everything in sight. The prescription for a long happy life is—be a Yankee rooter. I'm raising my children that way. Why should they grow up frustrated and bitter like me?"

"Have you thought of trying to break up the Yankees under the antitrust laws?"

"It's a good thought," McCann said, brightening. "We can get four votes to grant the certiorari."

"Do you think the Chief would go along?"

"Hampton?"

"He strikes me as a Yankee fan."

"It so happens you're right. But how did you know?"

"Yankee fans are a type. I can spot them by now. They're the ones in charge of a situation and they generally end up on the winning side."

"I hope they find out someday how the rest of the world lives." McCann sighed. "I haven't been to a ball game in almost five years. The last game I saw was just after I was appointed. The Senators won and I missed the home run that decided the game because I was busy signing autographs."

Chief Justice Hampton announced, "Brethren, the time has come."

They rose from the luncheon table. The tall figure of Charles Edmunson towered over Waldo Shuler standing beside him.

"I've got two bucks on you in the office pool," McCann said to Paul Lowe. "I'm betting you wind up on Edmunson's side."

"On his side?"

"In Kenton versus Farraday. How you vote on that case will register just as it would on a lie detector. That one will give us the first solid clue as to how you'll line up—with Edmunson or Waldo Shuler. Anyhow, everyone has agreed to pay up on the way you vote in that one."

"Who's betting?"

"Oh, most of the secretaries and law clerks. Some people from the Court Clerk's office. The two guards at the public entrance wanted in on this one."

"And you think I'll vote with the Old Man. Why?"

"A couple of reasons. You were his law clerk years ago, so you probably caught a bad case of hero worship from which you haven't recovered."

"What's the other reason?"

Edward McCann's expression sobered. "Because I want it so badly to happen, I guess. There used to be only Waldo Shuler, Andrew Cutler, and Gabriel Hart on the other side. The Three Musketeers. Then Bill Branch became a swing man—and lately I think he's tending more to their side. Actually, Kenton versus Farraday will be a lie-detector case for Bill Branch too. If he votes against the Old Man, I'm going to write him off as a liberal who deserted. That makes the lineup four to four. Now you're coming up to bat in Joyce's place—and it's the last half of the ninth inning."

"Kenton versus Farraday, eh?" Paul Lowe asked. "I'll be watching for it."

"Keep your eye on Waldo Shuler's curve ball," McCann cautioned. "It's sneaky."

The oak-paneled conference room was gloomy in afternoon light. The view from the windows overlooking the street and homes was uninspiring.

"Shades of the prison-house close upon the growing boy," Edward McCann said.

Paul Lowe smiled. "So you read Wordsworth?"

McCann winked. "How would you know—if you didn't? I'll keep your secret if you keep mine."

As soon as all the justices were seated Chief Justice Hampton called the conference to order. Work began with a rhythm that showed no sign of having been interrupted. They went rapidly through the remaining cert petitions on the Miscellaneous Docket, granted three paupers' applications which were then transferred to the Appellate Docket, and turned down two petitions for a rehearing.

Chief Justice Hampton said, "We will now consider Kenton versus Farraday."

In his concise way the Chief Justice set forth the facts:

"William Kenton is a Civil Service employee who had a hearing before the Civil Service Commission on a charge of moral misconduct. The moral misconduct of which he was accused was homosexuality. At his hearing before the Commission there were several affidavits presented which supported the accusation of William Kenton's homosexual activities. He was then discharged. Later, he took his case to the courts, which have upheld the right of the Civil Service Commission to discharge him. Are there any questions?"

The Chief Justice glanced separately at each justice with eyes that seemed to pierce like a knifethrust.

"Very well then. William Kenton's appeal to this Court is based on the fact that he did not have a chance to confront his accusers. He was unable to cross-examine them. The question to be decided is whether the denial of William Kenton's right to confront his accusers is an offense to the principle of due process of law. Also, we shall have to decide to what extent the principle of due process is necessarily involved in an administrative hearing of this kind. We shall have to bear in mind that a hearing before a Civil Service Commission is not a trial—and that being found guilty does not carry with it a criminal penalty. The hearing deals only with a man's right to employment."

Chief Justice Hampton paused and took a sip of water from a glass on the table. He adjusted his eyeglasses as he cited several previous decisions by the Court.

"These considerations lead me to believe that relief should be granted to William Kenton and his case remanded for a fuller hearing," he concluded.

As the Chief Justice turned to Charles Edmunson seated beside him at the same end of the conference table, his manner became almost deferential.

Edmunson's large hands were folded together on the table. He spoke slowly, examining each phrase before uttering it: "William Kenton presumably performed his duties responsibly for twenty-one years preceding his discharge. During that time no questions were raised as to his intellectual or moral fitness to hold his position. After twenty-one years, allegations about him are made in affidavits—and as a result he is discharged. At the hearing William Kenton's accusers were not present. He had no opportunity to cross-examine them on the charges contained in their affidavits. This right to confront and question is a deeply rooted principle of criminal law, guaranteed by our Constitution. I would therefore agree with the Chief Justice that William Kenton's case should be remanded for a further hearing."

Edmunson's chin sank lower into his collar to signify that he had ended.

Chief Justice Hampton said, "Mr. Justice Shuler?"

Waldo Shuler's thin high voice cut into the silence of the room like a whining electric fan.

"I think some important points have been overlooked by both the Chief Justice and Mr. Justice Edmunson. First, at the hearing William Kenton did not request that the witnesses against him be brought in—or that he be allowed to cross-examine them. This important issue should have been raised then, not as an afterthought by his lawyer some weeks or months later. Second, even if the issue had been raised, the Civil Service Commission could not have complied with the request. And for a very good reason. The Civil Service Commission doesn't have the right to subpoena witnesses." Waldo Shuler looked about him with satisfaction. Edward McCann seemed about to say something but changed his mind.

Waldo Shuler went on: "It is perfectly clear from a reading of their regulations. I suppose no one but myself has taken the trouble to read them—so let me tell you what they say. 'An accused, or his representative, must make his own arrangements for witnesses to appear.' Now that seems clear enough, doesn't it?"

Edward McCann said indignantly, "I don't see how the regulations of a Civil Service Commission can take precedence over the Constitution of the United States. What the regulations say hardly matters if they deny a man a full and proper hearing."

Chief Justice Hampton said sharply, "Mr. Justice Shuler still has the floor."

"Thank you, Chief," Waldo Shuler said. He continued imperturbably, "William Kenton was certainly aware of the regulations. He was a Civil Service employee for enough years to be aware. He was notified well in advance of the hearing what the charges were, and he had plenty of opportunity to arrange for the witnesses to appear. He failed to make such arrangements."

Edward McCann shook his head, muttering. "A technical point, a technical point," in too low a tone for it to be considered a further interruption.

It was not a technical point at all, Paul Lowe thought. But Waldo Shuler was deliberately overlooking the fact that William Kenton did not have a lawyer present at his hearing and so probably was not thoroughly conversant with all his rights. That had been a most regrettable omission on William Kenton's part.

"I now come to the crux of the matter," Waldo Shuler said, "which is simply that the Civil Service Commission has an indisputable right to hold hearings and to discharge employees. The grounds on which William Kenton was discharged—homosexuality—are certainly sufficient to justify his discharge. If in the opinion of the Commission he was morally unfit, or a potential danger to the proper carrying out of a government function, the Commission had no choice except to discharge him. To have done anything else would have been simple dereliction of duty on their part."

Waldo Shuler glanced at the other justices and smiled a quick fugitive smile.

"Mr. Justice Andrew Cutler," intoned the Chief Justice.

Andrew Cutler said gravely, "I agree with Mr. Justice Waldo Shuler. In my view the case for upholding the verdict of the Civil Service Commission, and of the lower courts who reviewed that verdict, has great force."

"Mr. Justice Gabriel Hart," the Chief Justice said.

"I will pass at this time," Gabriel Hart said in a whispery voice.

"Mr. Justice William Branch."

Bill Branch rubbed his veiny nose with his forefinger. "First off, somebody ought to point out that a Civil Service Commission hearing can't be treated in exactly the same way as a trial. They're two different things entirely. What you're really talking about is the right under the Sixth Amendment to confront witnesses. That's what everyone is bleating about here. And that can't be invoked in this case."

"Why not?" demanded Edward McCann. "I don't follow that reasoning at all."

Bill Branch said, "It's simple enough. The Sixth Amendment applies only in criminal prosecutions. No crime has been committed here and there's no criminal penalty. All that happened is a man lost his job. He didn't go to prison. If he had a trial, when he was found guilty there'd have been some sort of sentence passed, wouldn't there?"

Edward McCann ran blunt fingers through thick red hair. "If you're trying to make a distinction based on . . ."

Chief Justice Hampton said coolly, "Have you finished with your discussion of the case, Mr. Justice Branch?"

Bill Branch grinned. "I'd like to hear what my colleague McCann here has got to say for himself."

"Mr. Justice McCann," said the Chief Justice.

Edward McCann spoke in an annoyed tone, "I've got a lot to say about some of the arguments we've been forced to listen to so far. They're nit-picking—and now it's gotten to where nits are riding on the backs of other nits. Did William Kenton request witnesses to appear *at* his hearing or *after* his hearing? What's the difference? It's either his right to confront witnesses or it isn't his right. *When* he asked for his rights hardly matters a damn except to the kind of legal mind that's still trying to count how many angels can sit on the head of a pin. Then along comes Bill Branch to say it isn't a trial so William Kenton didn't even have any constitutional rights. Well, when the issues at stake are as serious as in this case it doesn't make a hell of a lot of difference whether you call it a hearing or a trial or the Spanish Inquisition."

"As far as I can determine," Chief Justice Hampton said dryly, "Torquemada is not sitting on the Civil Service Commission."

There was a ripple of amusement along the table. Waldo Shuler gave a short barking laugh.

Edward McCann said doggedly, "The question is what sort of penalty did William Kenton pay for being found guilty? He lost his job—the only job he is trained to do. And that isn't all. He lost his reputation too. He's branded as clearly as a branding iron could have done. *Homosexual!* They put that kind of stigma on a man—and who will dare say what happened to him isn't serious? How much more penal can any criminal court get? That's what I'd like to know."

McCann bristled with challenge. His fellow justices said nothing, until Chief Justice Hampton spoke.

"Mr. Justice Merriam," he said.

Henry Merriam smiled ingratiatingly. "There's been a lot of heat on this question. It appears to me that there's something to be said on every side. I agree that William Kenton should have raised the issue of getting witnesses to appear at the hearing—and not some time afterward. Mr. Justice Shuler contributed an important bit of information when he told us that the Civil Service Commission would not have been able to subpoena witnesses if witnesses had been asked for. That leaves no doubt in my mind that it was up to William Kenton, at the proper time, to arrange for those witnesses to appear and to be questioned by him or by his legal representative. I would also be inclined to support the general proposition that the Civil Service Commission should have the right to hold hearings and to discharge employees who can't do their jobs, or who constitute a menace to the proper functioning of our government for other reasons. If the Commission can't do that, we might as well take away their right to hold hearings altogether."

As Henry Merriam's mellifluous voice went on, soothing as music at cocktail time, Paul Lowe wondered where the argument was going to come out. Merriam was a consistent supporter of Charles Edmunson on the Court. Would this mark some sort of break with Merriam's previous record? Or was there a further station to be reached in his argument, some point which would expand to include the opposing point of view within his conclusions?

"However," Henry Merriam said, "I am afraid I cannot ignore the argument which Mr. Justice McCann has made with his customary fervor." Merriam offered Edward McCann a flashing and ironic smile. "Even if the hearing was *not* a trial, the penalties inflicted were certainly equal to those which might have been inflicted in a trial. And because that is so, William Kenton should be entitled to the same safeguards which are granted to defendants in a criminal trial. Among those safeguards, as Mr. Justice Edmunson so well said—deeply rooted in our criminal law and guaranteed by our Constitution—is the right to confront and to cross-examine an accuser."

Everyone was so lulled by Henry Merriam's voice, by his willingness to bring conflicting chords of argument into pleasing harmony, that no one was aware when his discussion of the case was over.

Chief Justice Hampton was first to recover.

"Mr. Justice Lowe," he said.

Paul Lowe said, "In my view, when a man's career, when his whole future is at stake, there can be nothing more crucial for him than the hearing which decides his fate. Therefore the guarantees of due process in the Fifth Amendment must protect him as fully as they protect the accused criminal."

Waldo Shuler broke in, "This question has been decided previously by the Court. May I remind the junior justice of Reese versus Campbell?"

Paul Lowe said, "No matter what has been previously said on the question, it seems to me that a man should not be condemned without the safeguards of a trial."

"You're using an emotionally colored word to make a point. 'Condemned'! What does that mean? He lost his job. There are other jobs. He could go out and get one."

Paul Lowe felt blood rise warmly to his face. "If he's discharged for immoral conduct, there aren't too many places he can go. Our society doesn't approve of homosexuals. In many states homosexuality is itself a crime. William Kenton lost not only a job but an entire character, an entire reputation."

"Perhaps he deserves to lose it. You might at least weigh the possibility that he's guilty."

"I have weighed it. Whether he's guilty or not, he deserves his day in court. He deserves to see the men who are destroying him—and to cross-examine them. That seems to me to be the real issue here."

Waldo Shuler snapped, "That issue didn't even occur to William Kenton until after he had been fired. He waited until he had his hearing and lost before he started crying foul."

Charles Edmunson turned to Waldo Shuler with slow gravity.

"Waldo, this can't be considered a game in which the petitioner's constitutional rights are gambled on the spin of a wheel. It's much too important for that. If you would care to cite authorities, this Court has held in previous cases that the Government *must* call as witnesses all informants. That decision—I believe it was Vitarelli—should control this one. It is not pertinent that the petitioner did not demand his rights at the time of the hearing. He demanded it—or his representative did—in court later. That was sufficient to raise the issue. We cannot tie our constitutional guarantees to a calendar or count them lost by a clock. When human rights are involved, the question is too precious to us all."

Waldo Shuler said sharply, "I don't agree that the failure to raise the issue at the proper time is a mere technicality."

Chief Justice Hampton glanced around the table. "Does anyone have anything more to contribute to this discussion? If not I suggest we vote." He paused to assure himself there was no opposition to the suggestion. "Justice Lowe?"

As the junior justice, Paul Lowe spoke last in the order of discussion, but he was the first to vote, on the sound theory that as the newest member he was most likely to be influenced by the votes of his elders on the Court.

He felt the attention of the others turn toward him. This preliminary vote would be tentative. It would determine the majority so the Chief could assign a justice to write an opinion for the Court. But any other justice would be free to write his own concurring or dissenting opinion. All the written opinions would then be circulated to other justices and when all the arguments were fully weighed some votes might change. There might even be further discussions at later conferences before the final opinion of the Court was handed down. Nevertheless, this was the first time Paul Lowe would help to decide an issue in which a sharp

112

controversy had arisen, and the way he voted would begin to classify his position as a justice. It's a lie detector all right, he thought.

He said, "I vote to reverse the lower court and send the case back for a full hearing."

Waldo Shuler frowned and tapped his pencil eraser on the table. Edward McCann grinned broadly. Charles Edmunson did not react. His large eyes appeared to be half closed behind heavy lids.

Henry Merriam and Edward McCann also voted to reverse. Bill Branch, Gabriel Hart and Andrew Cutler voted to uphold the lower court. That made a tie three to three. Waldo Shuler's vote broke the tie, and Charles Edmunson's restored it.

Chief Justice Hampton sat back from the table. He looked slightly down while he took a few seconds to deliberate.

Then he said, "I vote to reverse. William Kenton should be given another hearing. That becomes the majority opinion of the Court, as of now."

Paul Lowe unlocked the hinge on the flyleaf of his large docket book and opened it to record the result. Five to four. His vote had been decisive and he had cast it with Edmunson.

Chief Justice Hampton was already announcing, "We will now consider the case of Roubicek versus Municipal Bus Company."

It was a little past four o'clock in the afternoon. The process of determining his position on the Court was already well under way.

Outside the two-story house on Volta Place in Georgetown, two workmen struggled to move a paisley sofa from a huge van. They got the sofa down from the van platform and there it went, over the curb and up the sidewalk to the entrance of the house.

"Do they know where everything is supposed to go?" Ken Norris asked. "If they just pile it in you'll be living in one of the nicest furniture warehouses in town."

"Eleanor brought the floor plans back to Lincoln with her. She gave it to the movers with the position of all the furniture marked."

"Thank God you have an efficient wife. You couldn't keep a telephone booth in order if you had a maid who came in twice a day."

Paul Lowe was watching the rolled-up living room rug follow the path taken by the sofa. Its flowered design was visible in stitching on the rug's reverse side. "Things might go faster if I gave them a hand," he said.

"I can see it in the society columns, tomorrow," Ken Norris said. "'As Mr. Justice Paul Lincoln Lowe of the United States Supreme Court was hauling a bidet up the steps of his new Georgetown residence . . .'"

"We don't own a bidet."

"It's a damn civilized custom. Sheila brought two back from our last trip to Paris. Now she tells me she couldn't get along without them."

"*Both* of them?"

"I've got twins, remember? Girls."

"Aged eight."

"You're never too young to break in a bidet."

"The hell with the society columns," Paul Lowe announced. "I'm going to help."

"Why am I always around at a time like this?" Ken Norris asked plaintively.

Paul Lowe carried in the heavy glass top of a coffee table while Ken Norris carried four small engravings lying on the huge print of the Adoration of the Magi. On the way out, they flattened against a wall to let the moving men go by with a Louis XV desk.

As the gracefully curved legs scraped past, Ken Norris held his breath. He let his breath out as the bulk of the desk went by him.

He asked, "Have you decided what you're going to do with Geisha?"

"I guess Eleanor will bring Geisha with her when she comes back."

"That dog won't be happy in Washington. She needs wide open spaces to romp in. Besides, she's a neurotic animal who needs affection all the time. I have this on very reliable authority."

"Whose?"

"My twins. They've fallen in love with her."

"I see. What you're trying to say is that you'd like to keep Geisha."

"A sort of permanent boarding arrangement. You can have visiting rights. And there's summers."

"I don't know how Eleanor will feel about it."

"Sheila is working on her at that end, and so are the twins. It's a pincer movement."

"I'll talk it over with Eleanor when she gets here next week."

Ken Norris nodded with satisfaction. "Good enough."

They started toward the front door through a maze of furniture.

"How are things going on the Court?" Ken Norris asked. "Have you been assigned an opinion yet?"

Paul Lowe nodded. "I got my first assignment after the conference on Friday."

"Congratulations. Anything interesting?"

"It involves broadcasting music to people who are traveling to work on a municipal bus. The broadcasts are mostly for entertainment but they also carry advertising commercials to defray the cost."

"Ah," Ken Norris said. "A right-of-privacy case. How about the right of some people *not* to listen if they don't want to? Isn't that what it's about?"

"Something like that."

They were out on the sidewalk again. Paul Lowe indicated a huge barrel loaded with china and glassware.

"We'll take that next."

He tilted the barrel carefully onto its rim and with Ken's help began rolling it carefully toward the entrance of the house. Ken made grunting noises. Before they reached the steps he called for a halt.

"I'm not in very good condition. Let's leave this for the moving men."

"Nonsense. It's just the sort of exercise you need."

114

"Slave driver. I demand a minute to rest." Ken Norris leaned against the side of the barrel. "What did Edmunson say?"

"About what?"

"That bus broadcasting case. I bet I know which side he was on."

"I've told you all I'm going to."

"Just between friends. I won't pass it on."

Paul Lowe shrugged. "Edmunson thinks the right of broadcasting in such conditions—to a captive audience—*is* an invasion of privacy. He said it goes beyond the ordinary risks of travel—as he put it 'beyond the noise or jostling of a crowd or the babbling of tongues.'"

"I knew it," Ken Norris said happily. "It ought to be a cinch for you to write this opinion. Just borrow Edmunson's arguments, add a few supplemental authorities and present the whole thing in a slightly different order."

"This might come as a surprise," Paul Lowe said, "but I do have a mind of my own."

"You can't improve on Edmunson. What he says is usually the last word. Why fight it?"

As Edmunson's law clerk, Paul Lowe had often marveled at the great man's ability to go absolutely straight to the heart of a matter, clearing a way through a jungle of law and a wilderness of logic. Ken Norris' suggestion was tempting: let Edmunson point the way out of confusion, let him show how to avoid blind alleys that led nowhere. He remembered how, at the conference table, Edmunson had dealt serenely with Waldo Shuler's forceful argument that the right of privacy of people who did not want to listen had to be limited by the rights of the majority riding in the bus. Yes, it would be easy to adopt and expand Edmunson's approach.

Then he remembered Friday evening when the memo from Chief Justice Hampton had arrived at his hotel. The memo listed all the assignments to write opinions on cases that had been discussed in conference earlier that day. A notation opposite the *Roubicek versus Municipal Bus Company* had registered with a small electric shock. *Opinion assigned to Mr. Justice Paul Lowe.*

"I'm going to do this one my way," he told Ken Norris.

"Have you started work on it?"

He nodded. "Last night. It's coming along. I hope to finish a first draft this week while the Court's in recess."

"Well, good luck," Ken said. "But I still think you ought to play it safe and follow Edmunson. What can you lose by borrowing from the best?"

He smiled. "He's a great man. But he isn't the Second Coming. . . . And *you've* stalled long enough. Let's get this barrel inside the house."

They maneuvered the heavy barrel up the steps and inside the foyer. As they emerged, Ken Norris wiped the back of his neck with his handkerchief.

Another furniture van rumbled up the street and pulled to a grumbling heavy laden halt behind the first van.

"That yours?" Ken asked.

"Yep. And everything in it has to be moved in tonight. We've got our work cut out for us."

Ken Norris said weakly, "I went to law school to get out of doing hard manual labor. I don't know where everything went wrong."

At ten o'clock Wednesday evening Paul Lowe recalled his conversation with Ken Norris. He was working alone in his hotel room, revising the draft of his opinion in the bus broadcasting case.

His pen stopped. He had repeated almost word for word what Edmunson had said in the conference room. He crossed it out with savage back and forth brushes of the pen.

He began to read again.

If we allow broadcasting to be used in this way today, for entertainment, who will prevent it from being used tomorrow for political reasons?

Damn. A direct quote of Edmunson. He read quickly ahead through the rest of the page.

We would open a Pandora's box of troubles. In the future this Court would have to pass on hundreds of cases in which we would be forced to establish an ever narrower and narrower line between what is entertainment and what is propaganda. Let us suppose someone should decide to broadcast only operatic music. Would that not be an attempt to influence the taste of passengers who prefer rock and roll or musical comedy ballads? If this were done over a radio or a television set, each member of the audience would exercise his right to tune out, but how could anyone on the bus make known his objections?

Some of the language had changed but the arguments were all Edmunson's. What was the matter with him? Wasn't he capable of thinking for himself?

He marked a place for his clerk to insert a citation. Then he got up and moved restlessly about the small hotel room. The island of brilliant light at his desk both summoned and repelled.

He sat down at the desk again.

If you force a man to listen to one thing, you can force him to listen to another. Today it is music. Tomorrow it might be propaganda—inoffensive and unobjectionable at first—perhaps a speech favoring Americanism or attending church on Sundays. Once we allow our privacy to be invaded our privacy is no more. And the right of privacy must include the right to pick and choose from competing programs of music or from competing philosophies or religions.

If he were writing a literary work, it would be clear plagiarism. Ludicrous. He might as well be Edmunson's stenographer. The whole argument proved only that he had total recall. He remembered with nostalgia his bravado with Ken Norris. So short a time ago he had not discovered the depths of his self-deception.

The telephone on his desk gave a hesitant buzz. He picked it up impatiently.

"Hello!"

"Mr. Justice Lowe?" He recognized her voice at once. "This is Katherine Prescott. I'm sorry to call at this hour but I tried your office several times earlier in the day and you weren't taking any calls."

"I'm sorry—did you leave a message?"

"There was no place for you to have reached me. I wonder . . . is it possible to set up an appointment with you?"

"What about?"

"Orders from Race Hardman, to start this series about you. I thought, if we could talk—I promise I won't take much of your time."

Odd—he had been writing an opinion on privacy at the very moment his privacy was shattered. Since the invention of the telephone no one has been completely alone. The telephone is an all-purpose intruder.

"These are busy days for me, Miss Prescott. I'm sure you understand."

"Just half an hour for a preliminary talk. Any time and anywhere you say."

The last line he had written blurred in strong light. He rubbed his eyes and turned out the desk lamp. Light vanished in a long white flame stretched by the effect of rubbing the image into his retina; at his feet a red speck slowly faded. He was tired.

"How about eleven o'clock?" he asked on a sudden impulse.

Her voice lilted with surprise. "Tonight?"

"I can meet you in the hotel lounge for a drink."

"If you mean that—this is really very good of you. You're a very nice man."

"Eleven o'clock," Paul Lowe repeated.

He replaced the white phone, stood up and stretched. The mantel clock read twenty-three minutes to eleven. He fingered the beard stubble on his cheeks. He needed a shave. He could barely be ready in time.

She wore a dark coat with a white fur collar that framed her round vivid face. The coat was slightly open and a wide belt hung down.

Paul Lowe moved over on the leather banquette and stood up to greet her.

"May I take your coat?"

"Thank you."

He helped her off with it. On the back of her neck a few stray hairs were wispy, almost transparent. A very thin copper-colored chain rested lightly on her skin above the oval neckline of her dress.

"What can I get you to drink?"

"What are you having?"

"The usual Jack Daniels on the rocks."

"I'd like a Canadian Club manhattan."

She sat on the banquette beside him. Her black dress was loose but somehow clinging.

"I really hate to be persistent about this," she said. "But I propose and Race Hardman disposes. He thinks there is a lot of native pride about a native Nebraskan being appointed to the Supreme Court. I do think he's right about that." She took out a pack of cigarettes, chose one, and Paul Lowe lit it for her, watching the match flame eat into the tip.

"I don't know what I can tell you about myself," he said. "Everything of any possible interest is on the record."

"I don't believe that."

"I'm afraid it's true."

"I'll take my chances. All I want are the facts, sir." She laughed. "I'll fit into any niche or cranny of your day. This is rather important to me. Race Hardman held out a promise of a promotion if I do the kind of series he wants."

"What sort of promotion?"

"I'll become the regular staff girl in Washington for the *Insider* column."

He smiled. "I'd be a scoundrel to stand in the way. But I don't know how much time I'll be able to give you. This new job of mine is going to demand everything I can give it."

"You sound faintly discouraged."

"I've just had a discouraging experience. I've been trying to write my first opinion."

"Is there a special problem?"

"I'm afraid my special problem is Charles Edmunson."

"I rather thought you'd both be on the same side."

"That isn't what I meant. I used to be his law clerk, you know, and I'm afraid the hero worshiping has carried over. Once Edmunson has stated an argument I can't seem to get over or around it to say anything of my own."

"I can see where that might happen—at first. Until you get more confidence in how you really think and feel about things."

There was a quality in her that invited confidence—more than curiosity, more than personal warmth—it was a sharing of her vitality, a linking of her sympathy and attention and energy with the task to be done. He had no intention of doing it, but he told her about the bus broadcasting case.

She asked, "How do you feel about that kind of broadcasting? Is it right or wrong?"

"I have an objection to it that's practically visceral."

"Why?"

"For me it's part of the struggle of the individual against the mass-man. Hmm. I didn't intend to sound quite so portentous. But I think you know what I mean."

"Yes. I don't think you like a society that really believes it can buy people at a dollar a thousand."

"That's about it. Everything seems to be conspiring to herd people together these days."

"That leaves only one question. Does the Court have a right to decide this?"

"Well, yes. There's some argument about it but I think it's the Court's job to mediate between the rights of an individual and the power of the state. That's what it basically comes down to."

She nodded a little. "I didn't realize it was that important."

"You mustn't think that this particular issue is trivial just because the messages that are being broadcast are trivial. The question goes right to the heart of an individual's place in a democracy. As you said, some people will reckon a thousand men at only a dollar's worth. But a single man is still priceless. He *can't* be forced to become a part of a guaranteed audience."

"It's hard to imagine anyone arguing that he should be. Doesn't Waldo Shuler feel the same way?"

"Personally, yes. But as a judge he doesn't agree that the people on that bus can be rescued from captivity by the Constitution of the United States. For Waldo Shuler the question to be answered is not 'Do we approve of this?' but 'Does the Constitution forbid it?' and besides, he doesn't think the right of privacy of the minority is clear-cut. At the very least he says it's limited by the rights of the majority. A survey shows that most of the bus passengers like the broadcasts and want them to continue. Therefore he believes there isn't an issue."

"But what are people supposed to do who don't want to listen and can't help themselves?"

"Waldo Shuler says they *can* help themselves."

"I don't see how."

"For one thing, they can complain to the advertisers and refuse to buy their products. Or they can appeal to the legislature or to the transit commission. They might even refuse to ride the buses."

"Oh, dear. That sounds convincing."

"I think he leaves out something."

"What?"

"The relationship between the bus company and the passengers isn't *voluntary*. They're forced to ride—and therefore forced to listen. Ordinary people can't afford to take taxis to work every day, or keep a car, or move to another neighborhood just to avoid something they find annoying."

"But there are a lot of other annoyances incidental to living or traveling around in a city. What makes this one different?"

"The fact that it isn't *incidental*. It's deliberate. It's aimed at intrusion and at no other purpose. A man has a right to enjoy his own solitude and mental faculties. He should be protected in that right against any group that tries to invade it for their profit. What we're talking about, you see, is nothing less than freedom of the mind. That's the first essential of freedom—the right to choose what we will make of our freedom."

Paul Lowe became aware that he had been talking eagerly, carried away as he sometimes was by the passion of his own thoughts. He broke off, embarrassed.

"I get wound up sometimes," he said. "I'm sorry."

She was staring at him. A faint scent of perfume reached him, sweet and delicately penetrating. Very feminine. Eleanor rarely used perfume.

"I think it was wonderful," she said. "Were those all Edmunson's arguments?"

He tried to remember what he had said these past few minutes.

"No, they weren't. Edmunson took a somewhat different line."

"Then why not write just what you told me?"

"I wasn't making a legal argument. I was just saying how I felt about it."

"Isn't that important?"

"There has to be a central idea to develop."

"I liked the way you put it. There's little enough privacy in people's lives so the remainder ought to be even more precious. Isn't that it?"

"The legal jargon would be different."

"But what you're really saying is that a human being in a crowd is no less a human being. You're against his being treated as a commodity or a target. If the law doesn't say that, then the law ought to be changed."

He fixed his gaze on the entrance door to the cocktail lounge across the way. Obediently the door swung open and a couple entered. If you concentrated your attention on any closed door long enough it opened and showed the way out. He had believed that as a child and while he had since been deceived by doors he had never been deceived by those blocked passageways in the mind that read *No Exit*. There was always, always a way out. She had helped him to find it.

"Can I buy you another drink?"

"I don't know if I can handle it." She drained the last of her cocktail and wrinkled her nose. "I love the taste, though. So I'll take a chance. 'Social life and glee sit down and are transmogrified into debauchery.' That's Robert Burns."

"You don't have that quote exactly right."

"How does it go?"

"'See social life and glee sit down, all joyous and unthinking, till quite transmogrified they're grown to debauchery and drinking.'"

"How did you know that?"

"In college, poetry was one of my favorite subjects—along with history and philosophy."

"I feel as though I should be taking notes. Has our interview started?"

Paul Lowe signaled to the waiter. He shrugged. "If you want it to," he said.

An hour later Paul Lowe was telling her about a book he had tried to write about his experiences as a pilot. "I wanted to try to tell a little of what flying has taught me and meant to me."

"What happened to the book?" she asked.

"I showed a few chapters I'd done to a friend who's a good writer. He didn't think much of it. He said it was like Ring Lardner's description of someone who jumped on a horse and rode off in all directions. So I donated it to the wastebasket."

Suddenly she touched her forehead. "I feel awfully warm. Have they turned off the airconditioning?"

"It wasn't on. They don't need it."

"It must be the liquor. I feel giddy. I *have* gone over my quota. I'd better call a halt while I still can make sense out of these notes."

Paul Lowe paid the check and they left the hotel lounge. The street was dark and deserted.

"I'll get you a cab," he said.

"I'd rather walk if you don't mind. I did have a queer feeling back there—as though I were going to pass out. It doesn't take much. I used to drink daiquiris and I really think rum must take longer to act on me."

"I wouldn't be a bit surprised."

"I'm not very sophisticated, am I?"

"I don't like sophisticated people. I'm a small-town boy myself."

"I'm a big city girl—by inclination. I'm stifled in small towns."

"Why?"

"I don't have anything to say to anybody. It's been that way ever since high school. When I went to dances I had two problems—I was the tall girl and the one who didn't know how to talk to boys."

"You've gotten over that."

"Only to a degree. I can talk to some men. Not all. That's another thing. When I find a man I can talk to I usually talk too much. Mother always said I should slow up and let men have their say."

"You spent most of this evening listening."

"I can't remember when I've enjoyed it more." She stopped and held out her hand. "You've been wonderful to give me so much of your time. I appreciate it. But enough is enough. I can find my own cab."

He said, "Washington isn't a very good city to walk alone in. Except for Georgetown and Capitol Hill the distances are too long and the streets too monotonous. You need someone to walk with you."

"Well, if you really mean it."

"I do."

They turned onto Connecticut Avenue.

"This was like a Parisian boulevard when I was here years ago," he said. "Now it's all closed in with glass buildings."

"At least you see the sky. That isn't true in most big cities. There's some sort of regulation in Washington, isn't there?"

"Yes. They can't build anything more than twelve stories high."

"Why is that?"

A cab halted briefly at the corner ahead of them, let someone out, and then raced across the avenue. She did not appear to notice.

He said, "They're afraid the new construction might dwarf the federal buildings. Washingtonians are pretty proud of that monumental skyline."

"I like it too. But I get a feeling sometimes that the whole city is a marble graveyard and our national monuments are the tombstones."

Another empty cab went down the avenue. This time, he was sure she had seen it. When she said nothing he experienced a queer sense of elation.

"By the way," he said, "I like your friend."

"Tom Jeffreys?"

"That's the one." He asked casually, "Is it true you're going to marry him?"

"Did he tell you that?"

"Something to that effect."

"No, it isn't true," she said slowly. "He's asked me, but I haven't said yes. I've already made one mistake. I'm not terribly anxious to make another." She glanced up at him. "Did Tom tell you I've been married? I have a son six years old."

"I have a daughter. Twenty-two—and married."

In his hotel last week he had put Nancy on the telephone when Arthur called. Yes, it's true, Nancy had said, I am pregnant but I don't see how that changes anything. I won't let it. I'm not going to have this child, Arthur, and you might just as well get used to that. You're not going to talk me into it either.

Katherine Prescott said, "It must be hard when children grow up and go away. They become such a part of you."

"It's something you have to be ready for."

"I can't imagine what life will be like without Timmy. I'm grateful that his father didn't want custody rights. I couldn't bear not to have him with me."

"Where is he now?"

"Timmy? At my father's home in Lincoln. That's the penalty I pay for being a working woman. But I hope to see him this weekend." She gave him a worried glance. "Unless, of course, you have free time over the weekend for our next interview. That takes precedence over everything for the moment."

"I would never interfere with your family life."

"First things first. If I have to wait another week to see Timmy we'll both muddle through. After all, everything I'm trying to do is for him. If I get that promotion I'll be able to settle down with him in Washington."

Her voice was low, vibrant, full of youth. She was about thirty, he decided, but in most moods she appeared younger.

"You keep your date with Timmy. We'll find some time during the following week."

"You really are a nice man. You have a quality I don't see in many men these days. You're considerate. You're kind." Her directness was almost naïve, but was a part of the enthusiasm which apparently swept over her in tides.

"I just want to see you come to live in Washington," he answered with a smile.

"Well, Mr. Justice Lowe, you may make it possible."

"Try Paul."

"Oh, I couldn't."

"Why not?"

"Can't I settle for Mr. Lowe? That isn't quite so formal—or so familiar."

"I prefer Paul. I may even have to insist."

"I don't think I can get used to it."

"You have to promise to try."

"All right," she said. A friendly glint hovered in her eyes.

After he put her into a cab, he went back to the hotel. But he was out of sympathy with his work. He picked up a book to read—a novel which briefly interested him because of its setting in the high Himalayas—but the words were bare sticks on a blank page. It might as well have been written in hieroglyphics. The whole idea of a story about two people seemed absurd. What did it matter if the disturbed and rootless Eurasian adventurer ever got into bed with the subtle sensuous American girl? Or whether they returned to America or settled down in China to add to the population? In the year 2000 one out of every two people in the world would be Chinese. Nothing could be done about that great sea swell of life rising like plankton from the depths. Against it no politics or economics, no theories, could stand. What could one person do? Armed with the power of a state, what? Preach democracy? respect for constitutional law? the liberties of the individual? It was clearer now than at other times what a ridiculous enterprise he and others like him were engaged in. More practical than writing books or preaching doctrine would be to send a vast armada of planes carrying contraceptives, dropping their loads everywhere throughout the prolific spawning land. Billions of pills. Trojans for China. Against the Yellow Peril pit the valiant ladies of the Birth Control Association.

Far below his hotel window, cars crawled up the avenue in the direction of the bridges across the Potomac into Arlington county. To warm beds and safe coupling. Sound the alarm! A billion Chinese babies are on the way. Do battle in pride of loins.

He saw through himself. It was guilt that exerted this peculiar power to turn his thoughts to evasive generalities. A tall dark-haired female presence stayed with him in the room, her scent in the air.

He was trapped inside his body—a clanking robot machine—and from time to time his brain could not locate the gears that controlled it. He began to undress in his room high above street level yet eight floors underneath the roof. He felt suspended between groundling lust and stratospheric seduction.

She had left her phone number. He would call.

9

In his office Paul Lowe was reading a brown-covered pamphlet on bankruptcy proceedings. A lawsuit had been brought by the Securities and Exchange Commission against a company in which there had been a clear misappropriation of funds. How much simpler it was in Julius Caesar's day, when there was mainly the *societas unius re*—a contract to administer one thing jointly.

The pamphlet in his hands was as heavy as a quality paperback book and there was still another pamphlet of the same size to be got through on this one case. He was discovering that the job was an open-end funnel into which an infinite amount of work could be poured. The required reading alone demanded a good part of his day. Then he had to spend four and a half hours a day in Court, Fridays in conference, and endless hours thrashing out problems with his law clerks or trying to catch up on the background of other Court decisions. In addition, there was the outside reading in daily newspapers, history books, literature, which kept him in touch with the world and with the climate of ideas in which his decisions had to be reached. And he had to find time for considered mature reflection and a proper interchange of ideas with the other justices.

How did the others manage to do it? They earned their thirty-nine thousand dollars a year—any of them could have earned more with less effort in the private practice of law.

When he looked up from his reading again, Bill Tobin was in the doorway.

"What is it, Bill?"

"The figures you asked for about our national dams. In connection with the North Platte."

"Oh, yes. Put them on my desk."

Henry Wellman, now governor, had asked him to help in securing federal funds to build the dam. Governor Wellman had weighed practical alternatives on a balanced scale and decided against trying to raise money through new taxes. Now he was using all the avenues of approach to get money out of Washington. He had enlisted Paul Lowe's help. Paul Lowe had agreed to do what he could for a project that he was so convinced was vital to the people of Nebraska.

Bill Tobin came forward to deposit a thin sheaf of papers. "And there's a young lady waiting in the outer office. She's been there half an hour."

"Where's Martha Scully?"

"She went home, sir."

"What time is it?" He glanced at his watch. Past six o'clock. Where had the day gone?

Suddenly he remembered who was waiting.

Katherine Prescott was wearing a light blue silk dress—the first time he had seen her in so enticingly feminine an outfit. A soft loose fold of material draped in a semicircle across her chest and shoulders. Her hair was done in a new way, swept up over her ears. She had put her coat over the chair beside her.

"I'm terribly sorry," he said. "I almost forgot about our appointment. I've been working."

"I haven't been waiting long. Is it all right now or shall I come back some other time?"

"Of course not," he said. "Come right in."

In his office he moved a chair into position for her beside his desk. She took a stenographer's pad and pencil from her leather portfolio.

"Does it bother you if I take notes?"

"Not at all."

The long evening stretching ahead carried an undefined excitement secreted like an essence within its hours.

"Where did we leave off?" he asked.

"You were telling me about a book you wanted to write on your flying experiences."

"I never did write it, though."

"Perhaps you'd like to tell me some things that would have gone into the book."

"Shall I begin with when I learned to fly—or with the war?"

"You flew combat in the war, didn't you?"

"Yes. A P-38 in the China-Burma theater. Perhaps you'd like to know about the time I was shot down."

Her pencil paused expectantly on the pad. She looked up at him. "That sounds exciting."

He was thinking: after an hour or so I will interrupt and inquire whether she has any plans for dinner. As he began to tell her about his forced landing in the mountains and the long trek to freedom afterward, he realized that he was using the materials of his life to deliberately intrigue her. He kept the account bare, letting the facts supply their own color and thereby suggest more than he could say. She was fascinated, as women are so often by danger. He wondered: do they enjoy living vicariously as men, or is it some other feeling? Do women admire courage and despise cowards more than men do, because men can understand and forgive another man's fear? Women must equate cowardice with betrayal—with the abandonment of the ancient role as protector.

He noticed something odd: he made only a perfunctory remark or two about his marriage. He tested this discovery, brought his narrative swiftly to the end of the war in order to mention the beginning of his career at law and how Eleanor worked to help support him in law school. Her pencil moved obediently, taking notes, but he could not pursue the topic. Was his marriage something he really would rather not discuss with her?

Katherine Prescott sat in the large chair with one leg drawn up beneath her, an attitude that emphasized the feminine curve of her body. Her arm, bare below the swing of blue silk, was plump and white.

At a few minutes before seven o'clock the telephone rang far away in the outside office. Then the buzzer signaled him.

Bill Tobin said, "It's your daughter, Mr. Justice."

Paul Lowe pushed the button to switch off the intercom. "Will you excuse me?" he asked Katherine Prescott.

"Of course." She rose quickly and returned to the outer office. As soon as the door closed, he picked up the telephone.

"Nancy."

"Hello, Dad."

Her voice was toneless; it told him nothing.

"I've been trying to reach you," he said. "There hasn't been anyone at the apartment."

"Arthur is spending most of his time down near Baltimore on some new construction project."

"Where have you been?"

"Staying with a friend. I went back to the apartment to get some of my things. That's when I found your message—the one you left with the building superintendent."

He cleared his throat. "Aren't you living with Arthur?"

"I moved out the day after we got back."

"I'm sorry to hear that, Nancy."

"Are you?" she asked uninterestedly.

"I've been hoping you'd reach some sort of understanding."

"I rather thought Arthur must have gotten in touch with you."

"Nothing like that. I haven't spoken to him. But we both have your interests at heart, Nancy. We want to keep you from making the kind of mistake that could ruin your life."

"Oh, now really. If you keep on that way, I'll hang up."

He conjured up a picture of Nancy at this moment—her face carefully made up, rouged lips, wearing tight slacks, a long-sleeved silk blouse and slim golden slippers. He identified the image. Barbara Stanwyck in some of those old movies when she played the beautiful but cold *femme fatale*.

"I can't talk to you when you're this way, Nancy."

"Dad, let's avoid the more stinking kinds of hypocrisy, shall we? I've been through all this with Arthur. God knows he's done everything he can to mess things up. He scared my pyschiatrist by threatening to drag him into court on a charge of criminal abortion and get him blacklisted from his profession. So now the psychiatrist won't arrange the operation for me."

126

"You can't blame Arthur for wanting his child to be born."

Her voice was dipped in irony. "You know what that damn fool told me? He said having a baby is exactly what I need—that I should learn to worry about someone else for a change. Arthur actually believes a baby will hold our marriage together." She paused, then: "Oh, what's the point? I really wanted to give you a piece of good news. I've been thinking things over and I've decided to compromise with Arthur."

"What sort of compromise?"

"Well, this is what I'm willing to do. If the baby is so important to Arthur, all right, I'll give him his baby. But he can't have me too."

"You mean you'll get a divorce?"

"I won't stay married to him and be a mother to some biological accident that I'd much rather see as a specimen in a jar."

She wanted to shock him, and she did.

"If you really feel that strongly, Nancy, there are other ways to arrange for an abortion."

"I've tried the pills and the quack remedies. They haven't worked and I'm not going to go to some butcher. I'm scared. If I can't have a legal abortion I don't want to take a chance the other way."

"That's a wise decision at any rate."

"But I will risk it—unless Arthur agrees to my terms. I want a divorce with a big fat property settlement and everything agreed to in writing, with my lawyer."

A quick cobra-image of his daughter coiled to strike. Even if the picture was unfair there was imagined truth in it—and fear.

"Have you told this to Arthur?"

"I tried, but he won't listen. He's either hoping I'll come to my senses —or he wants to stall long enough so it'll be too late for me to do anything about the baby. You'd better convince him that I mean it, Dad."

"I don't know how I can do that."

"I'm not going to wait any longer. I have a friend who says she can arrange for the whole thing to be done this weekend. And that's what will happen unless Arthur agrees to everything. I'll give you the address of the job he's working on. Will you talk to him?"

"Nancy . . ."

"If Arthur won't take my offer, he won't have his baby and he won't have me either."

There was a long silence.

"I'll talk to Arthur," Paul Lowe said finally.

When the phone conversation ended, he was shaking with barely controlled anger. He wanted to break open the seal of the past and take out forgotten opportunities. He never should have left so much of Nancy's upbringing to her mother. When as a child she had needed discipline, Eleanor was too negative—she disciplined by indirection.

After a moment he regained control. He reached across to the intercom.

"Bill, would you ask Miss Prescott to come in now?"

They dined at a country inn twenty miles outside Washington in a lovely rambling white farmhouse atop a hill with wide lawns, old tall trees. Inside, in a large main room the tables were placed in quiet separate elegance. Long slender red candles glowed in the center of suspended copper baskets filled with trailing philodendron. In the flame of candles and the shimmering light of shaded wall brackets, everything seemed to shine with subtle flickering radiance.

When he had invited her to dinner there had been no maidenly demurral; she had only asked to go home and change. At eight o'clock he had picked her up in front of an apartment house on Corcoran Street. She had changed into an evening wrap over a black dress cut low in front. Her full bosom was perfectly white and richly textured. She wore long earrings, black and white, and her dress repeated the pattern in barely distinguishable tones. When she took off the evening wrap in the restaurant, he saw that a narrow shoulder strap crossed the white expanse of her shoulders.

Midway through dinner she said suddenly, "This is going against all logic. I'm having a wonderful time. Yet this is supposed to be my unlucky day."

"Why unlucky?"

"It's March seventh. March is the third month of the year and three and seven make ten."

"What's wrong with that?"

He gave her a look of such total bafflement that she broke into laughter.

"I have a fetish," she confessed. "The number five. Five is my bad luck number."

"So ten is bad luck because there are two fives in it."

"You're catching on."

"The number five apparently spreads its malign influence through all sorts of combinations."

She was laughing with him, at the ridiculousness of it. "I don't expect anything good in the year 1967 because all the digits add up to twenty-three."

"And two and three make five. It is perfectly logical," Paul Lowe agreed. He held up his glass to clink hers. He was unusually relaxed in the company of this very attractive woman. She knew he admired her. He was curiously unselfconscious about showing his admiration. He had never seen anyone so fascinating, nor it seemed to him had he met anyone with so much essential vitality. Élan bubbled in her, an endless supply of ever renewable gaiety. And the two cocktails before dinner had made her unusually talkative.

"How do you feel about palmistry?" he asked her.

"It's just a shade too ridiculous. And besides I had an unfortunate experience."

"Really?"

"Well, it happened shortly after a series of family tragedies—too sordid to tell. But they involved things like my brother being sent to prison for mail fraud . . ." (her casual confidences were breathtaking!) ". . . and my having separated from a husband who was both a drunk and a bully. I had no job, no money, no prospects and a one-year-old child to support. Someone took me to dinner at a restaurant where there was a woman who was famous for being able to read palms. She came by our table and offered to read mine, and I let her. She only took a moment's glance, then she pushed my hand away. And you know what she said?"

"What?"

"'Go, my child. Go and live some more.'" She made an expressive gesture, mimicking the haughty dismissal of the lady palm reader. Then she added, "I was twenty-six. If I'd done any more living up to that moment I think I'd have killed myself."

"We've covered numerology and palmistry," Paul Lowe observed. "How do you stand on astrology?"

"I believe in it absolutely. For instance, I'm Gemini. Very warm. Very outgoing. Love people. Easily taken advantage of."

"Does that apply to all Gemini?"

She shrugged. "I suppose there are exceptions. What month were you born in?"

"October."

"October what?"

"Twelfth."

"Libra. You're creative, stubborn, brilliant, logical, and difficult. Essentially kindhearted but temperamental."

"You're improvising."

She nodded, smiling. "That's the secret. It gives you a place to jump off from and then intuition takes over."

"Is that what your intuition tells you about me?"

"It tells me other things."

"What?"

"I might flatter your ego."

"Now you certainly have to tell me."

She stared at him and her forehead wrinkled with appraisal. "Well, to begin with, you're the sort of person who can't be read all at once."

"I can't?"

She continued staring as though she were reading a very fine print. "There are sharp angles and turnings in you. A sort of maze going off into nobody knows where. It's very attractive and in a way very forbidding. A number of people probably like you, but you never quite let yourself get close to them."

"That's pretty perceptive." Suddenly he wanted to close off this avenue of discussion.

"It's all more involved because you're so open and friendly at first glance—so Western and suntanned and amiable. But the sunlight never goes into you or finds the dark places that are hidden from the light."

"Your intuition is working overtime." He was not at all sure he liked himself in her description.

"I'd like to do more. I'd like to try to guess at what you really want."

"Go ahead," he said resignedly.

"It's the best way of measuring people, you know. What *do* they want? The solid life—family, home, dog, steady job, pension and plot under the yew tree in the churchyard of their choice? Or the colored balloons— pliant women, penthouse apartment, foreign car, high-bracket income with deductions for social insecurity, and a big marble mausoleum. You don't fit into either of those categories. You're too dissatisfied and restless to have fixed goals. Everything is a way station with you."

He was beginning to slightly resent her too fluent assurance, her free-flowing impressionistic evaluation of him, her genuine ability to divine, which was shrouded by too quick conclusions and struck toward truth at a downward slant like a tunnel into a mine. It took him a moment to find a suitable compromise between good-natured acceptance and a resistance he wanted to express.

"You're a very bright woman. But I'll bet an awful lot of men hearing that description would stand up and say, 'By God, she's talking about me.'"

She flushed. "I have a sudden terrible feeling that Mother was right."

"What's that?"

"With some men I talk too much."

"Not at all."

Her hazel eyes were direct and disconcerting. "You're being polite so I know it is true. Well, now that I've almost spoiled it, I would like to say that you bought me a very good dinner, sir. I loved the beef Stroganoff. If I promise not to say another word, will we go somewhere where *you* can talk? I've been ignoring my duties as a newspaperwoman."

"I'd prefer you to keep right on ignoring them for a while longer." He signaled to the waiter. "Do you mind? We can arrange another interview later. I'd like us both to enjoy the rest of this evening."

Her reply, one second delayed, said perhaps more than she intended: "I'd like that very much."

She waited in the foyer of the inn while he went to the parking lot for his Chrysler. He pulled the car up in front of the doorway and as she came toward him, turning aside to pass the hedge to the tiny concrete walk, he was struck again by her stunning figure in profile. As she came close, he decided that it was her clear bright complexion that lifted a pleasant attractive face into quite real beauty. Her legs were straight and well shaped and she walked in high heels without forward leaning tilt or totter. Quite suddenly, in the unfathomable way in which desire permeates other emotions, his last trace of resentment vanished. He felt something important would happen to them.

On the drive back toward Washington, speeding in the darkness along River Road past the Kenwood Country Club, they listened to the radio. A bar of light from the radio channel made small tan-white illumination in the car's interior.

"Do you keep a personal diary?" she asked.

130

"I haven't for a long time. As a matter of fact I did it only one year, when I was in the Air Corps. Everything happening to me seemed historic at the time. I was sure I was going to be killed in action, and I had visions of everything I wrote being published posthumously. Young Man's Odyssey or something of the sort. Then I learned three of my fellow cadets were keeping the same kind of journal. I decided posterity could get along without my little contribution."

She said, "You should have kept one anyway. But of course it would have had to be in code. Or it would be like Pepys or Da Vinci."

He said, "Pepys and Da Vinci both used a code in their personal diaries. Pepys invented his own, as I recall, and Da Vinci did mirror writing."

"That's what I mean," she said. "Yours would have to be a good code or it would end up like them. With the whole world knowing."

"Oh." He was beginning to get the hang of how her thinking progressed. What appeared to be a series of digressions were really loosely connected flashes of insight, a stenographic leaping from symbol to symbol. He asked, "What makes you think I've got something to hide?"

"That's one of the safe intuitions. Everyone has something to hide."

"I guess you're right. There's a story about a practical joker who sent out telegrams to the ten most respectable men in his community: 'Get out of town. Everything is known.' By the next morning nine of them had packed up and gone."

"And the tenth man?" she said. "My guess is he was a good bluffer. Or a masochist who wanted to stay to be punished for his guilt."

"Are you really cynical? I don't believe you could be."

"I don't think I am. I like people but I don't have illusions about them. Knowing what sort of person I am I'm vain enough to think most people can't be much better. A teacher told me once to get rid of my inhibitions by sitting down and writing on a sheet of paper everything I've done that I was most ashamed of, then leaving it where everyone could read it. I didn't dare. Would you?"

"No, I wouldn't."

She answered, laughing, "You see? It proves what I was saying. Write it in code. A good unbreakable code. And on your deathbed burn it."

The apartment house on Corcoran Street was an older building that was still standing amid the reconstruction going on in the neighborhood. The small lobby had a locked front door which she opened with her key.

"Would you care to come up for a drink?" she asked.

"I'd love to."

They entered an old-fashioned elevator hardly big enough for them both. They creaked upward.

"I hope you don't mind litter," she said. "Housekeeping is not my strongest point. And this isn't even my apartment."

"Whose is it?"

"A friend of Tom Jeffreys who's in Cambodia or someplace. It's empty for a few months and Tom had the key. He said his friend wouldn't mind and I could stay free as long as I liked."

"Not a bad deal." The creaking stopped, and the gate disconnected slightly at the third floor. He pushed it open the rest of the way.

Inside the apartment, she turned on the light and took off her hat and coat and fussed a moment with her hair before a mirror in the tiny foyer. He had a chance to look around. She did not belong in these obviously masculine surroundings. The small dark kitchen had a faintly deserted look. The rumpled living room had a dark wine-colored sofa with plump cushions and a soft back, two occasional chairs on either side of a table with a cigarette humidor, and a somewhat taupe-colored rug that had seen better days. Near the sofa the rug was badly frayed. Along one wall was a long bookcase which seemed to feature books on foreign affairs, personal accounts of travel, autobiographies of diplomats, generals and their confidants, and several novels and non-fiction books dealing with World War II, Korea, and Southeast Asia.

Katherine went to a bar table at a wall.

"I can offer Canadian Club, vodka, gin or bourbon. But as I remember it's bourbon."

"It's bourbon," he said.

"With anything?"

"No. I'm not a hard drinker, but I favor hard liquor."

Drinks in hand, they settled down to conversation on the sofa. She occupied the farthest corner from him. During the next twenty minutes the large ashtray on the coffee table in front of her filled with cigarette butts. She finished a pack and started another, in the absent-minded fashion of one performing a strictly mechanical function. As she lit a fresh cigarette she noticed him watching.

She said, "Every time there's a new report from the Surgeon General I get scared out of my wits. But there's no help for me. I've made up my mind to enjoy my few remaining years."

"I had the same problem once with drinking," Paul Lowe said. "A doctor told me I was getting too heavy and put me on a strict diet. Its total calories didn't even cover the alcohol I drank. If I drank I couldn't have anything to eat. I stayed with it for a week or so before I cracked. I know how it is."

"You're not heavy."

"Heavy enough. When the scale hits one seventy I start to panic. Right now I've got three pounds to go and just the thought of it makes me nervous . . . So I'll have another drink."

She said, "You know, I think I will call you Paul."

"You've been doing it all evening."

"But I haven't been *thinking* of you that way."

"I'm glad you do now. It means we're making progress."

He was waging calculated war. Ever since she had suggested a drink in her apartment he had been aware of the possibilities. He was acutely aware now.

"Isn't she depressing?" Katherine asked.

"Who?"

He followed her gaze to the mournful Modigliani on the wall, a portrait of a long, emaciated girl who gaped silently, almond eyes wide with shock.

"Powerful," he said, "and depressing."

What scenes those painted eyes must have witnessed in a bachelor's apartment. Dinner with champagne and sweet talk, the necessary preliminaries to seduction, then the sparring on the sofa. Above the crumpled pillow, in the white painted face the mouth was like a red bruise.

He got up to freshen his drink.

"Would you like me to mix you a manhattan?" he asked.

"No," she said. "Thanks."

On a bookshelf was a four-volume history of the Civil War. Fat books, solid enough to contain the record of pain and suffering and bloodshed. His grandfather had come across the Western trail to settle in Nebraska territory and had become one of those who volunteered to fight for the Union. Grandpa had been in Nebraska when the state was accepted into the Union—just about a century ago.

He returned to the sofa carrying his drink.

"Looking at those Civil War books," he said, "it occurred to me that if I had stayed as governor of Nebraska I would have presided over the Centennial celebration."

"Are you sorry to have missed it?"

"A little."

She said, "Men always seem to care more about historical events than women do. We live more in the present tense."

He sat down close to her on the sofa. Listening, he could pick up a rhythmic pulsing in his blood. He moved toward her. She looked up, saw him nearing and—did she start to get up? He embraced her clumsily while she said "please, no" and at the same time stubbed out her half-smoked cigarette on an ashtray. She turned her face away so his kiss only touched her cheek and a corner of her mouth. Her resistance excited him strongly. He forced her face toward him and his lips touched her full soft mouth. He felt the minute tremble of her back muscles. He was boldly sure of her surrender. They had passed the difficult transition from the first kiss to acceptance of what would follow. A kind of ectoplasmic agreement seemed to him to have met and mingled over their heads.

Suddenly to his surprise they were parted. She reached for her cigarette, saw it was unlit and tossed it down. She picked up the pack of cigarettes, took one and tamped it against the pack.

"I'm sorry," he said, not knowing what else to say.

She tried to smile. "It's silly of me. I know it."

He struck a match. The acrid cutting smell of burning smoke dispelled air humid with emotion.

"What's the matter?" he asked.

She shook her head and puffed on the cigarette. She did not utter a sound. She pursed her lips and let smoke dribble out bluely.

"Obviously I've done something wrong," he said.

"It isn't your fault. When you asked me to dinner tonight I had to expect something like this. A woman has to expect anything. But I could have prevented it. Instead I asked you up for a drink. Most men consider that an invitation."

"But you didn't mean it to be."

She shook her head. "Ever since I left my husband four years ago, I've spent a good deal of time avoiding cheap little one-night stands."

"Is that what you think this is?"

"Isn't it? It fits so perfectly. Wife's away, so take a strange girl out for the evening—and back to her apartment."

The generalized description caught him in its net. He rebelled against it. "I can't believe this was all my idea."

"I'm not excusing myself."

"And you're certainly not going to tell me there hasn't been anyone at all since your husband."

She answered coolly, "I don't have to tell you anything, do I?"

What she's really asking is: do you *care?* Do you? *Do you?* They all want the bloody nail to hang a man's scalp on.

"What you're really looking for is to be assured that this isn't some passing affair."

"I just don't want this sort of thing," she said. "I'm too old to be struggling with a man on a sofa."

She had used the wrong word—"struggling" brought back amateurish, diffident, awkward encounters of youth. This evening bore unfortunate resemblances.

His pride quickened. "Perhaps I'd better go."

Actually, it was frustrating to have the night end in nothing. He kept hoping she would relent and ask him to stay. All he needed was a small sign, a mere hesitation.

As he took his hat and coat from the closet, she said, "I'm afraid I've ruined things for us—and that I won't see you again."

A dull prompting held him—he recalled the soft rich bold caress of her mouth. He might persuade her yet. But the thought of the effort involved to renew their intimacy weakened him: resolve flowed out through knees, arms.

"We have to see each other. We still have my life story to get through," he answered, smiling. "But I imagine, all things considered, we should meet in my office from now on." He was gaining control of the situation. The act of confession would purge him, ready him to accept guilt. "I've been acting like a fool. I hope you're not angry—and that you will forgive me."

"You mustn't say that. You really mustn't."

"You're a lovely woman. Despite what you probably think, I've enjoyed this evening very much."

As he put on his coat the episode began to seem amusing. She tried to help him with his coat but he managed without her. He was moving with assurance while she was suspended in a corresponding hesitancy, her hands up to assist him. She lowered her hands, weightless.

He smiled and felt his face crinkling.

In the doorway as he left, she was standing close. By shifting the weight of her body to one leg and leaning her head slightly backward she fell into a vulnerable position. The light from the hallway unmasked her face from shadow.

He made an abrupt downward movement and brushed her lips with his. "Good night."

"Good night," she said.

As he waited for the elevator she kept the door open and rested one hand on the jamb. He gave a farewell lift of his hand. The elevator came and he opened the gate to enter.

When he looked back, the apartment door had shut. She had gone back into her room.

Abruptly he was shaken by a realization of how passionately he had wanted to stay.

There was a sign on the blacktop road leading beyond the small town of Brazierville.

GOLDENGROVE—A MODERN RESIDENTIAL COMMUNITY IS COMING SOON!

The signs of construction activity multiplied rapidly. Long narrow trenches, and yellow painted barriers where men worked installing gas mains—a steamroller flattening asphalt into place on a section of the road. A large dump truck loaded with gravel and tree stumps and boulders. Paul Lowe's car was blocked for a few minutes while that truck maneuvered a turn on the narrow roadway.

He drove through a wire gate with a CAUTION! PROCEED SLOWLY! sign on it, and stopped the car in front of a construction shack.

Arthur Montgomery emerged from the shack. He was wearing a checked shirt open at the collar, dungaree trousers, and dust-covered work boots.

Paul Lowe waved and got out of the car. Arthur came forward to shake hands.

"I hope you found the place with no trouble," Arthur said.

"You gave pretty good directions."

"Sorry I couldn't get away to meet you. We're having some problems here. On these big projects there's always something going wrong and somebody pushing a panic button."

They went into the shack. On a wooden makeshift table were diagrams and blueprints and work charts. Several bottles of Coca-Cola were in a bucket half filled with water and partly dissolved ice cubes.

"Would you like a Coke?" Arthur asked.

"No, thanks. I don't want to take too much of your time, Arthur. But I would like to talk to you alone."

A workman entered, a dark-faced sweating man, to put a piece of canvas down on a gray wooden bench. He opened the canvas to show a heaped mound of earth.

"Look what we've run into on sites sixteen and eighteen," he said.

Arthur picked up a handful of the dirt in his fingers. "Hard compacted

135

loam with gravel and small stones. Didn't any of this show up in the test pits?"

"Sure as hell didn't."

"Well, no use crying about it." Arthur let the dirt sieve back in lumps through his fingers. "We can't loose this with shovels or regular power equipment. Dig it up with the back hoe or dipper stick."

"If we put that stuff into the excavations, it'll have to dig itself a ramp to get out again."

"There's nothing else to do, is there?" Arthur Montgomery asked. "You got any better suggestions?"

"No, sir," the workman said.

When he left, Arthur said testily, "Some of these men get pleasure out of reporting trouble. They like to pretend there isn't any answer."

"Are you superintending the whole job?"

Arthur said with a touch of pride, "Eighty private homes—three to five bedrooms. And we're really starting from scratch. This was nothing here but a forest. Even had to make our own access roads. The city sewer system wasn't in yet. They're coming in next week—almost two months behind schedule. I was about ready to start putting in septic tanks."

Arthur was a good project manager, Paul Lowe decided. He had the strong definite personality that was needed to organize and guide and deal with all types of men and command their respect. He was a man's man, forceful and direct and uncomplicated.

Arthur sat back against the edge of the work table and sipped moodily at a Coke.

"What did you want to talk about? We're about as private here as we can get. I suppose it has to do with Nancy."

"It's no secret that she's emotionally disturbed, Arthur. I didn't take her seriously when she first said she wasn't going to have the baby. But I believe she means it now."

Arthur put his Coke bottle down on the table with a small clattering impact.

"I told her damn psychiatrist what I'll do if he arranges any sort of an operation. I'll ruin him." His hand clenched slowly around the bottle. "I will. I swear it." Knotted muscles formed at the corners of Arthur's jaw as though what he wanted to say required an extra physical exertion. "She's got to understand that she's my wife, and she's got to have my child."

"It's not too hard to block a legal abortion. But there are other ways."

Arthur did not meet Paul Lowe's gaze. "Nancy has always been afraid of physical pain. She's pretty much of a coward about it. And she'd worry about consequences."

"What will happen if you succeed in forcing her to have the baby? She may hate you for the rest of her life."

Arthur's thick neck set deeper into his shoulders, immovably positioned.

"The way I look at it, this is the last chance for our marriage anyhow. I've tried everything I can think of and it doesn't work. She doesn't care. The only person she even talks to is a woman named Tessie Samuels. Tessie's her buddy. They're always talking to each other on the phone or meeting for lunch. I wouldn't be surprised if Tessie Samuels put her up to this whole idea of having an abortion."

"Why would she?"

"She hates men and she's always making fun of things like family—or any kind of morality. She thinks she's liberated because she doesn't believe in anything. Now she's got Nancy thinking like her too."

Through the open doorway to the construction shack Paul Lowe watched a lifting crane. It was a big machine—a twenty-ton crane by the look of it—and its boom lowered a dragline bucket to strip a dish-shaped excavation on a gently sloping hillside.

He said slowly, "Nancy asked me to tell you she's willing to have the baby, provided you'll give her a divorce after the child is born."

Arthur sat farther back against the table, his hand clutching the edges. His head was bowed and the rocklike body seemed to be cleft by the power of suppressed emotion.

"She said that?" he asked.

"Otherwise she'll have an illegal abortion. She says it's been all arranged. I don't know of any way to stop her, Arthur."

Arthur moved out of his set position. "What do you think I should do? Do you think she'll go through with it if I say no to the divorce?"

"I can't be sure, Arthur. But when Nancy is determined she'll usually do anything."

Arthur nodded. "All I know is, she's *got* to have the baby. It may be all there is to show for our marriage; but at least it'll be something. The other way—there's nothing." He seemed to be staring off in space. He ran a hard-fleshed hand through curly brown hair. "The crazy thing is, sir, I love her. I'd do almost anything to keep her."

Paul Lowe could not bear to look at his suffering. When the telephone shrilled he welcomed the interruption. Arthur spoke a few moments in clipped angry tones, then slammed down the receiver.

"Another problem," he said. "I'll be right back."

While Arthur was gone, Paul Lowe looked around the small shack. On the wall was a long white printed sheet with inked entries in handwriting. It was the daily log of the construction job, listing the report number, the inspection date, the percentage of the job completed as of the entry date, the estimated completion date, the location and name of the job, the phone numbers of subcontractors. Different lines bore notations about progress being made on the exteriors, walls, lintels and sashes, partition walls, roof beams, sheathing, coping, gutters, leaders splash pads, on the hardware, the ceilings, plastering, heating system, electricity and plumbing, the fuel system, water system, pumps, tanks, piping.

Everything in its place, ordered, assembled, noted, provided for. But the foundations, once built, cannot be altered. If they are adequate the rest will remain stable. If not, a differential settlement sets in and over the years will cause a general racking of the superstructure.

Arthur came back. "I'm sorry, sir. We won't be interrupted again."

"I don't know if there's much more to say, Arthur. The decision is really up to you."

Arthur cleared his throat. Paul Lowe looked at him.

"I suppose you've already tried to talk to her, sir."

"Yes. She won't listen to me."

"Then she won't listen to anybody." Arthur pushed his knuckles in the side of his broken nose—the gesture of a child who does not want to cry. "If it were different, if she were sick in a hospital and I had to choose between her and the baby, I wouldn't hesitate for a minute. I'd choose her. But I just can't let her murder our baby in cold blood."

"Shall I give her that answer?"

Arthur blinked; then his chin lifted. "Yes," he said. "If she wants a divorce that much, she can have it."

On his way out of the construction area, Paul Lowe drove past a diesel-driven power shovel. In the cab, the operator pulled the gears and the tractor mounting moved slowly away on crawler type treds from a row of juniper trees at the edge of an excavation. The trees were guarded by mounds of dirt heaped around their trunks to keep construction equipment from coming too close or damaging them.

In the midst of our created desolation, we do try to save something. Some legacy of life, some hope for a future—some small surviving testament of a beauty in which we cannot help believing even as we destroy it.

10

"Judging from the way you look," Paul Lowe said, "this is bad news. So we might as well get it over with."

He lounged in his chair with assumed casualness, twiddling a pencil between his fingers. Across the desk from him in two chairs Bill Tobin and Jack Broderick sat tensely. They were holding printed drafts of an opinion together with notes of comment from the other justices. The opinion, which Lowe had circulated to the other justices, dealt with a negligence case under the Federal Employees Act.

"Some of the comments are pretty harsh," Bill Tobin said quietly. "I really think they went a little overboard. Or something about this one struck them the wrong way."

Jack Broderick said, "The main thrust of criticism seems to be directed at the way the arguments were presented more than at the arguments themselves."

"That's small comfort," Paul Lowe observed. "I didn't invent the arguments but I did try to hang them together."

He did not want these young men to know the extent of his shock at the discovery that his brethren on the Court disapproved of what he had done. As far as he could recall he had followed precisely from one point of law to the other and at each step had made sure that he was supported by previous decision of the Court. What had gone wrong?

"We have six comments so far." Jack Broderick adjusted rather over-sized dark-rimmed eyeglasses on his thin face. "Is there any particular order in which you'd like to hear them?"

"Who are the six?"

Broderick checked the sheets he was holding, then the ones Bill Tobin had.

"The Chief Justice and Justices Merriam, Branch, Cutler, Hart and McCann."

Paul Lowe held the pencil as a balancing scale. "Let's see. Justices Cutler and Hart were in opposition. We might as well hear what they've got to say first."

Jack Broderick nodded to Bill Tobin, who picked up the topmost proof on his lap.

"This is from Mr. Justice Gabriel Hart," Tobin said.

Gabriel Hart—stickler for *stare decisis*—would want to be certain of a continuity with the past. Hart approached every problem dragging his precedents behind him. A law always seemed better to him if it had originally been passed by the thirteen colonies.

"I'm ready for anything," Paul Lowe said. "Go ahead."

Bill Tobin read, "'This opinion reminds me of something that was said about Charles Evans Hughes when he upheld the invalidation of contract clauses requiring repayment in gold. His opinion was compared to a train going through the Rocky Mountains; you could tell where it had been and where it was going until it entered a tunnel and then everything went black.'"

Jack Broderick's smile had a certain quality that indicated approval of Gabriel Hart's sentiments.

Noting the displeasure in Paul Lowe's expression, Jack Broderick quickly busied himself looking through the proofs he held.

"I have Mr. Justice Cutler's comment right here."

"I hope it isn't very long."

"No, sir."

"Good."

Andrew Cutler was a distinguished colleague, and in earlier days a formidable lawyer who excelled in constitutional law. But he was a painstaking perfectionist, a man who could be relied upon to thoroughly explore terrain already mapped and staked out by others. Furthermore, he belonged in the opposite camp, and there was no reason why he should approve of Paul Lowe's efforts.

Jack Broderick said, "Mr. Justice Cutler says, 'This entire argument was wrongly conceived and carried the majority of the Court only because of the verbal dexterity of its proponents at the conference table. In writing, the essential hollowness of the central thesis is fully displayed and will doubtless result in a reversal of the preliminary vote.'"

"Let's hope he's wrong about that," Paul Lowe said mildly.

Had he really done so badly? He was willing to grant that this opinion, which dealt with a controversy of no very great import, was neither notable nor eloquent. But when he had finished it, he believed that it fulfilled the first purpose of an opinion—to explain to lower-court judges and to lawyers everywhere the reasoning by which the Supreme Court had arrived at its decision. Nothing was more crucial in the long run than to accomplish this simple-seeming task. For all its vaunted power, the Supreme Court's only real hope for compliance in the lower courts rested in its ability to convince other judges by clear and forceful reasoning to accept its guidance in the development of law.

"So much for the justices who were against," Paul Lowe said. "Let's move on to the ones who voted with me in conference. What has Justice Branch to say?"

Bill Tobin lowered his voice solemnly as he read, "'You disposed of the jurisdictional questions but I don't think you came to grips with previous Court decisions on this issue. As a result, the whole thing rises like a mirage out of an empty desert.' "

The trouble is, Paul Lowe was thinking, that we work so much alone. We function as nine separate courts, each with different backgrounds, moral and legal precepts, economic beliefs. In this contented isolation, a man can easily be unaware of how he is regarded by his own colleagues. Was he listening to the first peals of thunder from what had been a slow-gathering storm?

He put that disturbing thought behind him and asked "Who's next?"

Jack Broderick picked up a printed document to read the handwriting scribbled on it. "Mr. Justice Merriam says, 'There's a feeling of over-all glibness about this. The chute to judicial damnation is greased with wit and this particular brand of well-turned casuistry.' "

Paul Lowe winced. "Let's have the next one."

Broderick read, " 'I do think some parts are well expressed but I also feel that the hard part of the argument is shirked.' That's Mr. Justice McCann."

In some ways the most unkindest cut of all, Paul Lowe reflected. Edward McCann was the justice on the Court who was closest to him in political and judicial philosophy, and he usually went out of his way to praise. But in this brief comment there was undeniable exasperation. "The hard part of the argument is shirked!" *Et tu, Brute.*

Bill Tobin said, "The last one is from the Chief Justice."

Paul Lowe said wearily, "Read it."

" 'This can probably be fixed but will require a good deal of hard re-thinking.' " Bill Tobin hesitated, then continued to read, " 'These qualities seem to be missing in your work of late, Paul.' "

That verdict had the cool clean cutting edge of a guillotine. Headless, Paul Lowe accepted it. From the tone of these comments it was inescapably clear that he was failing to meet the standard of accomplishment required from a justice of the Supreme Court. More was demanded of him. What? It occurred to him that he might have discovered this painful inadequacy even sooner if he had not made an auspicious debut with the opinion he wrote on the bus broadcasting case. That first success gave him an impetus which carried him smoothly over the initial few weeks.

He said, "The only two we haven't heard from are Mr. Justice Shuler and Mr. Justice Edmunson."

Bill Tobin answered, "I understand Mr. Justice Shuler is writing a dissent. I heard it from George Benjamin, his law clerk. I'm pretty close to him."

"Justice Shuler will do a very, very thorough job," Paul Lowe said.

"Yes, sir," Bill Tobin said soberly. "From the number of books I've seen being wheeled into his office from the library, Mr. Justice Shuler will go into the question with his usual . . . uh . . . zeal."

"And some votes might switch—as Justice Cutler predicted." Paul Lowe said wryly, "I could end up unintentionally writing a dissent . . . instead of the opinion for the Court."

"I don't believe that will happen, sir."

"Do you have any idea when Mr. Justice Edmunson will make his comment?"

"No, sir, I don't."

Jack Broderick said, "They say Mr. Justice Edmunson used to be prompt about things like that. But he's been taking a lot of time lately."

Probably looking for an easy way to let me down, Paul Lowe thought. He moved his pencil crosswise on the blotter. Some years ago he had sat where those two young law clerks were now sitting and argued with Edmunson about some of the great man's written opinions. Imagine! The careless presumption of youth.

He sensed the disappointment of his two young law clerks. They had worked hard on this opinion; Jack Broderick had researched it thoroughly while Bill Tobin had suggested valuable changes in the order of argument. They must feel that a joint enterprise had failed.

But the final responsibility was his alone. His two law clerks—though top of their class and on the law review in their respective universities—could only bring to bear the weight of inexperience. Some outsiders thought that the law clerks, because they did all the reading on certs and the opposing responses, became a sort of junior Supreme Court. It wasn't so. They performed valuable chores by winnowing through an immense mass of material, reducing it to memorandum form, and doing endless research. But their most important function was as a sounding board, someone to talk to, try out ideas on, argue with.

"Well, I guess that's all for the moment," Paul Lowe said. "I'll call you when I need your help on revising."

After the clerks left, he glanced through his written opinion which ran to a dozen pages. It had been set in type in the print shop in the basement of the Supreme Court building and each proof had been numbered so no copy would go astray. This proof bore Henry Merriam's handwritten comment clearly along the first-page margin, "There's a feeling of over-all glibness about this." Beneath his courtly southern-gentleman exterior Henry Merriam was a penetrating man. So are they all—all penetrating men Even prolix timorous Gabriel Hart had found a true difficulty—the argument went smoothly for a while and then jarred into abrupt discontinuity. "Everything went black." McCann's observation was truest: "I do feel that the hard part of the argument is shirked."

He had not measured up to the intellectual and logical demands of his subject matter. His argument both obscured and revealed and he sometimes discovered more devious and damnable ways for words to hide meaning than to tell it. Glibness was his curse.

Nothing to do, Paul Lowe thought, except try try again. Somewhere in the confusing web there lurked a real spider and he must somehow uncover the elusive little creature.

It was now four o'clock. Eleanor's plane was due in the airport at half past eleven. He could have dinner here in the office and work straight through until he had to leave to meet Eleanor.

He put the printed proof before him and with pen in hand began to cut away adipose tissue. Whole sections sloughed away all too easily. He foresaw that nearly half of what he had written would vanish in this first surgical separation of bones and fat.

But would the patient survive?

Eleanor's plane was ten minutes late. From the upstairs waiting room at the terminal he saw the giant jet swoop in, a misty gray shape with red and green lights blinking. The jet's wheels touched down racing past ridiculously small planes that were like an audience of sparrows gathered to watch a condor.

A voice, hoarsely distinguishable, came over the loudspeaker:

"Flight 774 has just landed. Passengers will disembark at gate five."

Waiting at the gate he glimpsed her on the walkway, deep in the crowd. In a moment she waved, began to hurry, and finally arrived breathless in his arms.

"Oh, Paul, Paul. It's so *good* to see you!"

"It's good to see you too, dear." Her brown hair was dry as it brushed his cheek and her body in his arms was familiar.

"Did you miss me?" she asked.

"Of course I missed you." His voice assured him. "Of course—of course I missed you."

She put her hand in his. "Let's get my luggage. I have so much I want to tell you."

They started through the airport following signs and arrows toward the baggage room.

"Mother and Natalie send their love. They saw me off at the airport today."

"How are they?"

"Mother is fine. Natalie isn't feeling too well."

"I'm sorry to hear that."

"Her usual trouble. It's always something, but never anything serious. I'm beginning to think Natalie will outlive us all."

They arrived in the brightly lit rotunda where an automated belt was circling with luggage.

"The house is definitely sold," Eleanor said. "I wasn't sure until the last minute when I got a check for the down payment. That Mr. Bartlett just couldn't make up his mind. Last week I gave him a deadline and he finally wrote a check for ten percent of the purchase price. The agent said I don't have to refund it if the sale isn't completed."

Half listening, Paul Lowe watched steadily revolving luggage seeking its owners. The large blue valise came into view.

"There's one." He sidled into the crowd and seized the valise.

He staggered to Eleanor with his trophy.

"What have you got in here—the Seventh Regiment of artillery?"

Eleanor laughed. "Just some things we can use in our new house.

Mother and Natalie divided up the last of the furniture. A few pieces that weren't worth putting into the moving van."

Twin tan suitcases came gliding like well-matched palomino mares riding in tandem on the moving belt. Paul Lowe snatched them, one in each hand. Eleanor signaled a passing redcap who put the suitcases on his wheeled cart and hefted the heavy blue valise on beside them.

"Taxi, sir?"

"Yes, please," Paul Lowe said.

Eleanor put her arm around his waist as they followed the redcap.

"I didn't bring the car," he told her. "It would have meant keeping Jonathan Carter up till all hours, and I was too tired to drive myself."

"I'd as soon go home in a taxi."

"Home is still the hotel, you know. All the furniture is moved into the new house but as far as I'm concerned it's only a place to visit. In its present condition I wouldn't want to live there."

She rested her cheek briefly against the lapel of his coat. "You'll see, I'll have it ready for us in a few days. We'll be living there before you know it."

"You'll need a magic wand," he said.

They passed the electric-eye circuit and glass doors opened ahead.

"I've almost been afraid to ask you," she said. "Is there anything new with Nancy and Arthur?"

"Well, yes."

She searched his face. "Bad news?"

She listened attentively in the taxi going to the hotel while he told her about Nancy's last phone call and his visit with Arthur. Her gray-gloved hands clasped and unclasped. Finally with slack fingers she picked a loose black thread in her dark gray coat.

"I can't understand what Nancy is thinking of," she said worriedly. "Arthur is a fine man. Why does she want a divorce? And an abortion is such a terrible thing. Why would she even consider having one if she doesn't need to?"

Full of memory, her eyes met his.

It had been different with them. They had not been married. Riding in the bus—the grainy leather grip came back to him—she had told him she was six days overdue. He was anxious but not really alarmed. Until the first pregnancy a man is never sure of his power. The same with the first coupling. All the textbooks say don't worry, true impotency is rare, but every man knows himself to be rare and therefore rare things will happen to him. Once he proves himself there is a new question to answer. Fatherhood? A possibility reserved for older men, *hombres on serio*. A father at his age? Only twenty. He was not, could not be a father. How could there already be a double of himself? What does a casual moment, sudden heat, have within it that implies such terrible responsibility?

—I don't know why I haven't come round but I just haven't, she said. There's nothing to worry about, is there?

144

Desire for truth or a desire to inflict pain with the heavy cudgel of truth?—I don't know, Eleanor. There might be. That last time . . . I should have known better.

His words speared her; her body shook.—It's my fault. It *was* the perfect time for it to happen.

The worst time, he thought bitterly. Over the preceding few months he had been making ineffectual attempts to break off their relationship. After all, they had been going together for nearly three years. They had to break off now or it would end in marriage. And he was working hard in college and had just discovered a new passion: he had to pay for one lesson a week at the Lincoln Flying School. Added to the cost of college tuition it really wasn't fair to his mother or his brother William who was married and had expenses of his own. To help pay for it, he had taken a part time job in the college library and there simply wasn't money for dates. Marriage was out of the question until he was able to earn a living. Besides, one or two other girls had caught his eye, more his type really, smarter than Eleanor, more aware of the world. They knew things he knew little about. Music, for example. A girl in his class in Music Appreciation followed the music on a score while the phonograph played or the professor picked out themes on a piano. She was pretty, she had dark eyes and long plaited hair and he admired her sensuous face bent over the musical markings in the wide-open book on her lap.

He took Eleanor home on the evening she told him she was overdue. In a mood of recklessness he made love to her. Later, while he was lying on the sofa in the dark room, she came out of the bathroom with good news. She thought she had come round. He was so grateful he almost convinced himself he loved her. He held her while she laughed and cried in his arms.

The next morning Eleanor had no sign of a period. The staining had been brought on by their lovemaking under conditions of anxiety and tension. After worrying a few more days she finally went to a doctor. The wait for the test results was tormenting. He kept in constant touch with her, partly to find out as soon as she knew, partly to check on how she was bearing up, partly to prove he was not deserting her in her need.

When she called the doctor from a public pay phone in a drugstore, he was standing nearby. What the doctor said to her was all too plain from the way she grew white and turned away from him toward the inside wall of the phone booth. When she turned back, still with the phone at her ear, her eyes were brimming. She shook her head. A tremulous smile wavered on her lips, wistful, sad, hurt and brave.

He became sodden with loss of hope. When she left the booth he put his arm about her and they walked to the park and sat on a bench.

—We could get married, he said.

—That would mean you'd have to drop out of school, she said.

—It can't be helped.

—I won't let you ruin your career.

145

Both of them were reluctant to discuss the alternative. Each knew the other was thinking of it.

Finally she said—I don't have to go through with it.

—I can't ask you to do a thing like that.

—It isn't dangerous. Not if it's done by a doctor.

—I know it isn't dangerous, he said.

—I don't see what else there is to do.

—There are ways. I mean, without having an operation.

—I know. But they don't work, usually.

—Why don't we wait and see?

After two weeks the home remedies were not working. But she would not go to her family doctor. The year before, Paul, frightened by hearing of an acquaintance in college who had come down with gonorrhea, had gone to a strange doctor, just walked in off the street, to be examined for a rash near his genitals. He was given a test for venereal disease and the results were negative because there had been no woman except Eleanor. Nevertheless he was relieved to hear it. The doctor, a nervous furtive little man, now occurred to Paul as a good possibility.

When he took Eleanor there, she insisted on wearing a wedding ring. He bought the ring for her at a pawnshop and perhaps the doctor really believed they were married for he told them with a benign and avuncular air to have their baby. He assured them they would never regret it. He mentioned that he had three children of his own. Paul pleaded that they had a critical money problem and Eleanor added that their parents had not approved of their marriage because of religious differences and had only consented because they had promised not to have children right away. She had devised this rather complicated little fiction on her own. The doctor sailed benignly through all and answered that families have a way of understanding these things and that when a child is born grandparents react in just the way you might expect. He would absolutely and without any reservation advise them to have the baby and not worry about consequences.

Soon they were out on the street with nothing solved. She tried more hot baths and more doses of ergot. Finally she went to a nurse who worked inside for a while trying to dislodge the stubborn child.

The crucial time rushed toward them—beyond three months no abortion was possible because of the risks.

The girl in his music class saw him crossing the campus one morning.

—What's wrong, Paul? You look worried.

He took the girl to a coffee shop because he felt a need for her companionship, but he was unnaturally morose and uncommunicative. She must have been puzzled. In truth, he felt so cut off from anyone by the enormous weight of his problem that he could not help being surly and unfriendly. He was attracted to this girl but could not see his situation as fraught with possibilities for dating other women.

If I ever get out of this, he kept thinking, like a refrain, even while studying or having dinner with his mother or visiting his older brother William and his wife in their small new home. He was totally preoccupied with the trouble, and at the same time very sorry for Eleanor. She had to live at home with her fearful tomahawk of a mother. Imagination simply could not stretch to what her mother would do if she ever found out. He teased himself with masochistic daydreams of the scene but all the while knew that nothing he could envision would match the cataclysmic event.

Finally their persistent discreet inquiries turned up the name of a doctor and arrangements were made cryptically by phone. At the appointed day and hour he took Eleanor there in a taxi. He had seventy-five dollars in cash in his pocket. She was composed but silent.

He sat in a dark and musty parlor of the doctor's home reading *New Yorker* cartoons with unseeing eyes. It was forever before he was told he could see her. He entered the room too early. The nurse was taking Eleanor to a cot to rest. Eleanor was naked and clutching a white pad to her pubic area. He looked away until she was lying under a sheet.

In the room alone with her he brought up a wooden chair beside the cot. All he could think of was to hold her hand. He sat there holding her hand. Occasionally they looked at each other.

—Do you love me? she asked.

—You know I do.

—It's going to be all right now.

—Yes, he said.

She tried to smile but the smile wobbled off.

—It was terrible. It was worse than I thought.

—Try not to talk about it. I love you.

—The doctor told me (she said weakly) he never would have done it for seventy-five dollars if he knew it would be so difficult. I have a little tumor he had to go around.

—A little tumor?

—It's nothing. Only (tears came to her eyes) it made the operation more difficult.

—You're safe now. It's over.

—The doctor kept cursing all during the operation. He was very angry about the tumor.

—Try to rest now.

—How long can I stay here?

—I'll ask the doctor. You rest.

After half an hour the doctor said she could go home. The doctor was a plump bald man who wore a white smock. He shook hands with Paul, told him he was a very nice young man, and said he hoped he and Eleanor would get married and be very happy together. Then he hurried back to his operating room where another patient was waiting.

Her mother had taken Natalie to the movies and thought that Eleanor was out on a date with Paul. As soon as they got to her home, Eleanor lay down with an ice bag on her abdomen.

Her mother and sister came home at shortly past eleven o'clock. Eleanor tried to pass off her ailment as a slight attack of appendicitis, which she occasionally suffered from, but both her mother and sister, in varying degrees, began to fuss. Her mother kept saying that they should call the family doctor. Natalie, wraithlike, anguished, brought her sister a large glass of milk and kept asking if the pain was very severe. Eleanor said no, she was feeling much better. But she had to keep the ice bag on, and finally her mother said she would get the doctor to pay a house call.

Eleanor gave Paul a mute signal of distress.

—It's nearly midnight, he said. I don't think we ought to bother the doctor now. Not about anything like this.

—Suppose she's having a real appendicitis, her mother asked.

—She isn't. She doesn't have the other symptoms.

—What are they?

—Like nausea. Do you have nausea? he asked Eleanor.

—No, she said.

—You see? Paul said to her mother.

The leverage of his superior knowledge gave them a respite. Natalie flitted off to fill the ice bag with ice cubes. At one o'clock in the morning her mother started for the telephone again to call the doctor. Eleanor's manner became agitated. If the family doctor came, he would discover everything.

—You can't just call a doctor at this hour of the morning, Paul said.

—I'm not going to let my daughter lie there in pain.

Her mother had a flushed countenance and her anger with Paul emerged clearly. Her glance traveled from Eleanor lying on the living room sofa to Paul. Apparently she had begun to suspect she was not being told the whole truth.

—I'm much better, Mother. Really I am.

—Do you want another ice bag?

—No. I don't need it any more.

To prove she meant it, Eleanor risked taking the ice bag off. That persuaded her mother a doctor wasn't necessary. The crisis passed.

In the morning Eleanor felt much better. The next day she went back to her job as a cashier in a department store. There was no aftermath except that the next time Paul had dinner at their home her mother brought out a bottle of wine and poured glasses all around and drank to the year ahead in which they would become man and wife.

They were not married until Paul finished college and was about to enter the Air Force. But if he had to choose the time when the decision to marry was taken, he would have chosen the night of the abortion. That crucial event changed the direction of his life. It ended the slow drift toward an inevitable breakup. That was the crossroads. On that evening he began a fortuitous journey along a path he might never have traveled. There are moments when fate overtakes us and we must follow along in its footsteps. Many times since, he had hesitated at a place where several roads opened before him. How slight was the prompting that made him take either this road or the other, how trivial the chance by which the direction of his life was determined. When the first step is taken all the might-have-beens vanish as though they never existed and become part of a measureless wasteland.

Where now was the darkhaired lovely girl who read music and sat with him that day in the coffee shop?

In front of the hotel while the doorman got out the luggage, Paul Lowe paid the taxi driver. He went into the hotel lobby with Eleanor. In all these years they had never descended into the pit where so many married couples floundered. He had never known despair, only absence of hope—and that was a different matter.

"I'm going to talk to Nancy," Eleanor was saying. "After all, there are some things it's easier for women to discuss. I might bring her to her senses."

"By all means talk to her, dear," he said.

They rode up in a swiftly silent elevator with the bellboy and their luggage. He had gone up with Katherine Prescott in a small creaking elevator to her apartment. Now she was another might-have-been, dim as a dream remembered, a dwindling voice that had summoned him beyond the horizons of his world.

The bellboy opened the door to their room with his key. When he had gone, Eleanor took off her hat and fluffed out her hair. Her coat was lying over a chair. The large blue valise and the twin tan suitcases stood near the closet—back from their wanderings.

"Have you missed me really?" she asked. "As much as I've missed you?"

11

Looking out the window of his hotel room, he saw the blue Chrysler pull in to the curb in front of the entrance. The sky was gray and he guessed that it would rain. His skin was sensitive to an impending change in barometric pressure.

At the door of the room he kissed Eleanor goodbye.

She said, "Have a good day, dear. What time do you think you'll be home tonight?"

"Hard to tell. I'll call you."

He had slept badly—disturbed by a dream he could not recall. Usually he could remember a dream if he tried to the first moment he awoke, but this morning he had waited too long before making the attempt. Nearly everything had gone. But he knew that the dream had something to do with death.

On the drive to the Supreme Court, he began to read but he could not pay attention to the pages of the brief. Finally he stopped reading and gazed through the car window at the sidewalks and people apparently walking backward.

His attention sharpened. He felt obscurely compelled to look more closely and to see something that called to him.

Then his breath caught with painful suddenness.

Right there before his incredulous gaze, his brother William was going down the avenue. William had died eleven years before, swiftly without forewarning, in a rainslick veering of his car off the highway. Yet here he now was, walking casually along the sidewalk, his slim figure erect, the graying black hair thinning on the top and growing down the narrow deep valley of his neck, the Indian mahogany face aquiline and alert.

Now Paul Lowe knew that his dream had been of his older brother, and he had cautioned himself, as people sometimes do in dreams, against believing William was alive. As he kept staring out the car window, he had to resist the impulse to roll down the window and shout to the continuing apparition. He almost expected his brother to answer and then another miracle would happen—they would be young and carefree, living on Vancour Street in Lincoln, Nebraska. His brother would be wearing the white wool ribbed sweater with the letter L he had won for starring on the high school baseball team.

The apparition of William stopped at the street corner and bought a newspaper. Even before Paul Lowe saw the full face he knew that the man on the street corner who rolled up the newspaper and tucked it under his arm was not William. The insignificant detail had snapped the thread of his illusion. William was indeed dead. As the car pulled abreast of the man he had thought was his brother he saw only a superficial resemblance. Yet in a submargin of consciousness he was chilled with fear.

I accept the fate we share, William, even while I struggle to escape from it.

That morning while he was working at the desk in his office, Martha Scully called him on the intercom:

"Mr. Justice Shuler would like a word with you."

"Is he here?"

"Yes."

"Ask him to come in, please."

Waldo Shuler's short figure moved briskly into the office. He came over to the desk to shake hands. Paul Lowe indicated a black leather armchair near his desk.

"No, I don't want to sit down," Waldo Shuler said. "I prefer to walk when I'm talking. I hope it doesn't make you nervous."

"Not at all."

"It drives my wife crazy. She says I could wear out a carpet every year. I tell her that we do so much sitting on the Court I have to avoid sitting down when I can."

Waldo Shuler was married to a worshipful woman, a former beauty now grown quite corpulent. Paul Lowe had seen her photograph as a young woman in Shuler's office, and had been surprised when he met her in person one afternoon. She was fifty pounds heavier than in the photograph. She had in tow the Shulers' one child, a very thin girl of about fifteen.

Waldo Shuler stopped his pacing to confront Paul Lowe across his desk.

"I've just read your opinion in the negligence case."

"The one I revised?"

Now why had he said that? To remind Waldo Shuler how hard he had worked on this opinion and thereby crave indulgence? He was reacting to a foreseen challenge.

"I didn't comment on the first draft," Waldo Shuler said. "I figured you'd get enough lumps without my having to add any. But I have something to say about this one, and I thought I'd tell you in person."

"Isn't my revision any better?"

"Better than the first time. But still not good enough, Paul. I think you fluffed it."

Paul Lowe sat back in his chair. "What's the trouble with it?"

"It's not just that we disagree. You have a right to be wrong." Waldo

Shuler smiled his quick, quickly gone smile. "I hope you won't resent this, Paul. I frankly don't believe you're doing your best."

"I'm certainly trying to."

"I don't believe that either."

"It may be that you have too high an opinion of my abilities."

"Nonsense!" Waldo Shuler got up quickly and resumed pacing. "I saw what you could do with your very first opinion in the bus broadcasting case. You were wrong then too, but your opinion had fine things in it. It proved you had the tools—the right tools. You put a thought clearly into a few words and didn't waste time beating around a legal bush. Your writing and your thinking had strength and simplicity."

"I could have been lucky, you know."

"Sure you were lucky. You got hold of an issue you cared about. But even so I was impressed. I didn't believe anyone could get the hang of writing a good opinion that quickly."

"Apparently I didn't get the hang of it."

"That's nothing to be ashamed of. There are fuddy-duddies on this Court—naming no names—who still haven't learned how. The only way they ever get to a point is by surrounding it and then closing in, like Indians attacking a covered wagon. Their writing belongs in the Gutzon Borglum category."

"The what?"

Shuler smiled. "A phrase I borrowed from Frank Joyce. He divided the writing styles of the Court members into three basic categories: the Gutzon Borglum—where the argument is hacked away at until some sort of shape begins to emerge; the Jackson Pollock—where a lot seems to be going on but very little makes any sense; and the Mona Lisa—where everything is clear and ordered and beautiful, but what does that little smile mean?"

Paul Lowe began to feel better. "I know writing an opinion is an art. And it's one I haven't mastered yet."

Waldo Shuler paced the room more quickly, a few steps to the fireplace and a few steps back—nervously, nervously restless.

"It isn't an art," he said. "It's plain slogging hard work. Do you know anything about how Justice Brandeis worked?"

"No."

"Louis Brandeis was the greatest justice who ever sat on this Court. He backed up every opinion he wrote with facts. Mountains and mountains of facts. He read everything on a subject and used it to give a solid underpinning to the law. And he worked hard. I once saw Brandeis' personal papers. They included the thirty-fourth draft of one of his opinions. *Printed* draft. The thirty-fourth! How many did you write of this one?"

"I sent the third draft to the printer."

"Okay!" Waldo Shuler nodded vigorously, straight up, straight down. "You've got thirty-one to go before you catch Brandeis. Don't be discouraged. Learn everything there is to know about it. Then go ahead and do the job."

"The last time I looked there were only twenty-four hours in a day. How do you manage?"

Waldo Shuler answered crisply, "I don't sleep. I haven't been able to sleep since I was twelve years old. You want to be a good judge? Cultivate insomnia."

"I'll see what I can do about that." Paul Lowe smiled. "I appreciate your coming here, Waldo."

"Do you play chess?"

"Well . . . yes."

Waldo Shuler looked hopeful. "How well?"

"I played occasionally with Edmunson when I was his law clerk."

"Who won?"

"I'm afraid he did."

Waldo Shuler snorted. "The old hippopotamus hasn't beaten me in six years. Oh, well, if you're in a mood to be thoroughly trounced sometime, let me know."

"I will," Paul Lowe said, amused.

The magnetic presence of Waldo Shuler departed. A few minutes later, while working at his desk, Paul Lowe discovered to his surprise that he was still smiling. It was easy to disagree with Waldo Shuler but it was very hard to dislike him.

That evening in his hotel room Paul Lowe took clothes off the closet hangers to put on the bed. They would move into their new home on Volta Place the day after tomorrow. In some mysterious fashion, Eleanor had gotten the house ready for occupancy.

Across the room Eleanor was talking to Nancy on the telephone. She had already run the gamut of her emotional appeals, from parental superiority to helpless tears—the final confession of inadequacy.

Now she was positioned somewhere between the two extremes—no longer patronizing, no longer imploring.

"Nancy, dear, it's your life, and I can't tell you what to do with it. What I *can* tell you is that Arthur is a wonderful man and he's tried to make you a good husband. You're not going to find anyone like him so quickly. . . ."

Paul Lowe put his black Burberry coat carefully on the bed where it collapsed into limp shapelessness. He wondered: why do people with a talent for organizing things usually have no capacity for dealing with people?

Eleanor was saying, "It's easy to give up on a marriage. It takes more courage to fight for it and make your own happiness."

Was there a sort of physical law? The ability to control inert matter displaces its own weight in the ability to control a relationship with living humans. The quantum theory of personality.

Eleanor said in a hurt tone, "Oh, I know it sounds silly to you, but it's true. If you lose Arthur you could very well end up marrying someone who isn't right for you at all."

A feminine cry, by romance out of loneliness. One day you will turn a windy corner and Mr. Right will be waiting in a belted trench coat with turned-up collar and smoldering dark eyes. The trouble is, no one stays very long on windy corners and when you take him home to a quiet airless room he will become asthmatic and cough sputum in the mornings.

"You must realize, Nancy, that your father and I are concerned about your welfare. We want to see you happy with Arthur and your baby. . . . No, wait! I won't say another word. I'll let you talk to your fath . . ."

Eleanor broke off in mid-sentence, surprised by the telephone's sudden rebuke.

"She hung up!"

"This isn't the time to reason with her, dear."

Eleanor replaced the receiver and sighed. "The poor girl. I wish there were something we could do for her."

"Better leave her alone until she's in a mood to talk."

"Of course you're right, dear. Time is working on our side."

Time, my dear, is destroying us—bringing us closer to ultimate unawareness, the final uncaring which is called death.

"Shall I empty the bureau drawers?" he asked.

She was cheered by the prospect of dealing with more manageable problems.

"Yes, you do that. Put everything in piles on the bed. I'll pack it later. I'm going downstairs now to settle our monthly bill. I have to give going away tips in the dining room to the headwaiter and the cook. Did you take care of Lorna?"

Lorna was their favorite waitress, who had served most of their meals in the hotel.

"I gave her an envelope with twenty dollars."

"That's fine. She must have been pleased. I think I'll give the others the same thing."

"All right, dear. Whatever you think."

She was gone about ten minutes. He was replacing the last emptied bureau drawer with a jiggle and a rattle of wood when the door opened and she came in, holding an envelope in her hand.

"This was just delivered at the desk by Mr. Justice Edmunson's messenger."

He opened the envelope. Inside was a note in familiar bold handwriting:

Paul:

Just finished reading your revised draft in the negligence case under the Federal Employers Liability Act. Rather than sum up my reactions in a note, I thought we should get together. I've been anxious to do that anyhow. Will you have dinner with me any night this week?

It was signed CE in a large untidy scrawl.

He showed the note to Eleanor.

"What should I do?"

154

"You can go tomorrow night," she suggested.

"That's just before moving day. Won't you need me to lend a hand?"

"There isn't much left to do."

"Edmunson doesn't mention it, but I'm sure you're included in the invitation."

"You'll talk law all night. I'd rather stay home and put the linens and silver in order. I haven't enough time to get to that sort of thing. And I really don't mind missing a dinner at Mr. Justice Edmunson's. From what you've told me it's likely to be carrot and celery sandwiches."

Her gift—a minor one—for dry commentary occasionally surprised him. Impulsively, he put his arm about her shoulders.

She smiled up at him. "Won't you have to send an answer?"

"Yes, but I'll give it to him myself."

He picked up the telephone.

Charles Edmunson lived in a large comfortable house on R Street, Northwest, that had been his home throughout his thirty-two years of service on the Supreme Court. As the Chrysler stopped before the door, Paul Lowe recaptured the excitement, the awe, the overwhelming sense of strangeness he had felt when he first visited here as Edmunson's law clerk.

"What time shall I call for you, Mr. Justice?" Jonathan Carter asked.

"Never mind, Jonathan. I don't know when I'll be leaving. I'll take a taxi home."

He went up the short walk to the two-story frame house as though he were treading a path into history—and would soon knock on a door that might be answered by George Washington or John Marshall.

The antique bronze clapper on the door fell with a hollow sound.

Martin Hyde answered the door. He was Charles Edmunson's messenger and man-of-all-work, a medium-sized man with a smooth high brown forehead and a gentle manner.

"Mr. Justice Lowe, you're expected. Mr. Justice Edmunson is in the library. Dinner will be served in half an hour."

"Thank you, Martin."

There was piano music playing on the hi-fi as he entered the library. He could not identify the composer but he guessed it was Mozart. In his youth Edmunson had been an accomplished pianist and his love for music had never lessened.

The library was an old-fashioned room with a high ceiling and bookcases on every available wall. In one bookcase the hi-fi must have been concealed. Pale lemon-colored curtains were drawn back from two windows in the middle of the far wall, directly facing the door.

In front of the second window on the right, behind a massive and somewhat battered desk, Charles Edmunson was working by the hard white glare of a desk lamp. He wore a green eyeshade and papers were scattered on the desk before him.

"Paul! It's good to see you."

As he stood up to his full six foot four inches he towered out of the light at the desk into the dimness of the room.

"It's good to see you, sir."

In shirtsleeves Charles Edmunson's powerful torso seemed a bit gaunt and sunken. Brown suspenders crossed his stooped shoulders.

"Would you care for a drink before dinner, Paul?"

"Only if you're having one."

Edmunson smiled; his teeth were strong-looking but had long since turned yellow.

"I only allow myself a brandy after dinner . . . I didn't realize it was so late. Is it really seven o'clock?"

As though in answer the small gold pendulum clock on a bookshelf softly chimed.

"It is," Edmunson said with a smile. "You're prompt as always, Paul." He indicated the papers on his desk. "I lost track of time working on this opinion."

Everything in the room was becoming familiar again to Paul Lowe. There had been very few changes in the years since he had sat here, working, talking, playing chess with the great man. Even the opened book on the lamp table beside the capacious upholstered chair was exactly as he remembered. He glanced at the title of this one. Kierkegaard's *Either/Or*.

"I see you haven't lost your interest in philosophy."

"Never will. I inherited it from my father. I've often wondered, if Peter Edmunson hadn't been in that field, would I have chosen it? Instead I rebelled and chose law. We have to make our own way in the world, eh Paul?" He picked up the volume of Kierkegaard, looked at the page, and inserted a leather bookmark before he returned it to the shelf.

"That reminds me. There was something I wanted to read to you, Paul. I put it aside especially. Now, what has Martin done with my papers?"

Edmunson often forgot where he had put certain papers and always made quick heated accusations about someone mislaying them. Paul Lowe watched with patient amusement while Edmunson continued his search. Edmunson loved to read favorite passages aloud. He would slap his leg with enthusiasm as he read a passage for the second, third, even fourth time. Small memories crowded back into Paul Lowe's mind—minor details that established Charles Edmunson's humanity.

In a moment Edmunson found the passage he was searching for. Unpredictably—how varied his tastes!—it was a passage from a Peter De Vries novel. It had something to do with there being an answer to the riddle of the universe, just as there is a combination to a safe, but in trying to find it we discover that the combination is locked up inside the safe. Edmunson read the passage twice, with delight quivering in his deep voice.

At precisely seven-thirty Martin Hyde opened the sliding doors to the library.

156

"Dinner is served."

Edmunson rubbed his hands together with anticipation. "Good. I'm hungry as a bear."

He put on a rough tweed jacket to go into the dining room. Its shapeless bulk suited him well. Charles Edmunson needed the touch of informality to keep him from appearing too formidable.

Dinner was, as always in this household, a meager and depressing affair. It consisted of a plate of vegetable soup and a cottage cheese and fruit salad. Edmunson ate with measured satisfaction, chewing slowly. He had not eaten meat since he was a young man, out of conviction that a vegetarian diet was better for his health and an indignation that time had not dulled: a boyhood comrade, two years older than Edmunson, had fought in the Spanish-American War and had died from the spoiled horsemeat served to soldiers.

During dinner they gossiped about their colleagues on the Supreme Court bench. Edmunson had definite and deep convictions about his associates—during his long service there had been many—and he encapsuled the way he felt in a few words.

On Bill Branch: "A big rawboned boy who never grew up. Not terribly gifted but terribly sincere. People trust him. A man can sell integrity as readily as talent."

On Gabriel Hart: "A bookworm. Any hour of the day or night you find him wriggling in the pages of dusty lawbooks, or burrowing into old records. He is dismayed that none of us rely on precedent quite as much as he does. He distrusts new thoughts."

On Waldo Shuler: "He has a creative spark. Say what you will about his conservatism, he uses that immense learning of his in a creative way. He tries to recreate the past. Like Sisyphus he is forever trying to push the rock back up the hill—but that's better than Andrew Cutler and his like who are busy nostalgically mapping the place where the rock used to be."

Listening to the deep and deliberate voice, a faint echo of Southern accent still audible beneath careful inflections, Paul Lowe felt the impact of Edmunson's magisterial manner.

After dinner they returned to the library and Edmunson rummaged through a drawer in his desk, muttering vague imprecations about Martin Hyde's carelessness, before he discovered several manila envelopes he was looking for.

Edmunson hefted the envelopes in his large hand. "Waldo sent these for me to read in connection with an opinion I'm writing."

"What are they?"

"Pamphlets and studies and monographs having to do with the history of the Civil Service, its relations with employees, the rights and duties of government as employer, and the Lord alone knows what else."

"Waldo goes thoroughly into a subject."

"I suppose he hopes that if we all tread the same agonized road to Calvary we'll share in his glory."

Paul Lowe told him of his meeting with Waldo Shuler. "He strongly recommended that I go to more trouble to collect all the facts and figures before sitting down to write an opinion."

Edmunson put the manila envelopes back on his desk. "Waldo puts too much faith in the minutiae of learning. Statistics are outmoded almost as soon as they're compiled. You can't put statistics to work supporting the law because the figures always change."

"It seems pretty obvious, though, that I need to put something else into the work I've been doing lately."

"Don't be too harsh on yourself, Paul."

Edmunson sat down behind his desk and put on the green eyeshade. He reached forward to turn on the reading lamp.

"Shall we look at your opinion now?"

They went over the printed pages line by line. Edmunson had a fine craftsman's concern for organization and coherence. Midway, he indicated a place in which the argument veered away from a difficulty ("like a horse shying at a stone," Edmunson remarked) and later pointed out several places where the arguments were merely catalogued without anticipating and answering what the response might be. ("What the opposition may reply has to be included, Paul . . . every true statement contains within itself its vanquished opposite.") As they reached the last page, Edmunson remarked that the principle involved in this case seemed to him to be whether the negligence laws were any longer adequate to meet the social obligations of a modern, highly industrialized society.

"That principle is what's important, Paul—not the facts. The *principle*. If the law is going to serve society it has to follow a fixed star. What we have to do is think through to the principles the Constitution stands for, lay them down alongside the present problem, and judge what should be done."

Edmunson made the solution to the problem seem easy perhaps because answers appeared to him with unusual clarity on that rarefied height where his mind moved. But what his advice amounted to was simply: if the law is not adequate, stretch the law to provide a solution. Waldo Shuler would say that it was the duty of the legislature to pass a new law.

In the intimacy of working on this opinion with Edmunson Paul Lowe had lost some of the timidity that was inspired by awe. He stirred with challenge.

"It sounds simple enough," he said. "But how can we tell what the right principles are?"

"It isn't entirely guesswork, Paul. The Constitution is our guide. It's a permanent symbol—standing above and beyond the battle. At the same time it's a living document—it has to grow. We must keep it on the side of progress without breaking faith with the men who framed it."

"That's where it gets difficult, to keep faith with the past and still move ahead into the future."

Edmunson smiled a bit wearily. "I suppose that's why it's useful to have an ancient like myself on the Court. I give the illusion of a continuity with the ideals of the past, which helps to justify the work I do in the present."

"You could justify your approach on other grounds. The oldest known judges excelled in the use of so-called *fictions*. And *fictions* were nothing but rulings that concealed the fact that a law was being changed . . . while keeping the letter of the law the same."

"I don't look at it that way, Paul. For me the job is still to uncover the right principle. It seems to me that at the center of every real problem lies some enduring abstraction. Find what it is and you have the solution."

The Old Man, Paul Lowe thought, was a hero to young lawyers because he believed in keeping vitality in the laws even at the cost of breaking entirely new ground. That bold concept appealed to the young. But Edmunson himself did not think of his work in those terms. He thought he searched the mountain tops for immutable truths which he then brought down to the valley of doubt in which other men lived.

"I don't think I'll ever see to the heart of a problem as clearly as you can," Paul Lowe said.

"Paul, the day will come when you'll be setting me right."

"I doubt that very much."

"But it will. Remember the story of the dispute between two learned rabbis over a technical problem in interpreting the law? When the first rabbi exhausted all his arguments he cried out in desperation, 'If the law agrees with me, let this tree prove it.' Whereupon the tree leapt out of its place and settled some distance away. The other rabbi calmly answered, 'A tree is not capable of giving proof.' Thereupon the first rabbi said, 'If the law agrees with me, let the walls of this house prove it.' Instantly the walls began to collapse inward. The second rabbi said angrily, 'When scholars are in a legal argument, what right have walls to interfere?' Out of respect for him the walls did not collapse but remained standing although inclined. Finally the first rabbi called out in a commanding voice, 'If the law agrees with me, let it be proved from Heaven!' And thereupon a Heavenly voice spoke out of thunder, 'Why do you continue to dispute since I have given proof that the law agrees with the first rabbi?' For a space the second rabbi sat silent. Then he rose from his seat to shout, 'The law is not given to us from Heaven. The law was given to us on Mount Sinai! I will pay no attention to a Heavenly Voice!' Whereupon the thunder pealed and the Heavenly Voice cried joyfully, 'My son has defeated me! My son has defeated me!'"

"I like the story," Paul Lowe said, "but I'm not convinced. I guess I still think the law agrees with you."

"You'll change your mind—when you acquire a little more confidence. Then you'll want to go your own way. In the meantime, it does no harm to be somewhat diffident about your powers. Only the better judges are ridden by self-doubt. Inferior ones are satisfied with the work they do."

"If self-doubt is a criterion, I should have a great future ahead of me."

Edmunson rumbled laughter. "You have, Paul, you have. What you need to do is find the right way for you, the individual way to attack a problem."

"I wish I could shut my eyes and open them to a steady inner light. The way you can."

Edmunson shook his head slightly. "It's never that easy, Paul. In fact, the work seems to get more difficult all the time. I used to turn out about thirty opinions a year. This year I don't expect to do more than fifteen or sixteen." He turned off the reading lamp and rubbed his eyes. "The years levy a tax we all have to pay. I hope Someone's collecting and using the revenue to help newcomers."

"A promising sign," Paul Lowe said, "your talking about Someone up there. You used to be convinced there was no one."

The deep eyes twinkled with amusement. "Only speculating, Paul. Only speculating. I will admit, like a good judge, that the possibility exists of error on my part." Edmunson sat back in his chair. "When I'm gone, I don't expect any idea of mine to long survive me. But I have a kind of faith that someone will carry on. I hope there will be those who believe, as I do, that the law can be a third force in the world, neither a servant of a class nor of a political conviction, but a standard of what is just and fair. If enough people adhere to that standard, if we persuade them to, perhaps together we will be strong enough to maintain ourselves between the two juggernauts that are racing toward mortal collision. Perhaps we will be able to judge actions not by whether they favor one side of a controversy or another but by whether they satisfy a moral consensus embodied in what we call the law."

"But the law itself is an institution made by men. Like governments. Like morality."

"Of course it is, Paul. But it's the best measuring rod we have. We must keep improving it, enforcing stricter ideals of accuracy upon it, because we have nothing better to offer. When the day comes that we can live together in the world with men whose character and opinions we despise, when we can judge an event not by whether it does us good or harm, but by whether it is fair—whether the law would approve of it—then we will have moved a step nearer to the kind of rational and self-governing society that is fit to survive." Edmunson removed his eyeshade and got up from the desk. "I have great hopes, Paul. We who put our faith in the law seem to be transient creatures now—half beached on the shore, neither of the land nor of the sea. Destined to perish in the first hour of Armageddon. But it's possible, just barely possible, that one day we will evolve into the dominant kind."

Paul Lowe listened in the familiar mesmerized trance of agreement which Charles Edmunson so often evoked in him. He believed all that Edmunson said, yet what he said summoned up an anxiety that dwelt close below the surface. When the Old Man retired or died—one or the other could not be too long away—who would lead the Court in pushing out the boundaries of freedom? Who would say how far those boundaries should go? A strong man was needed even to hold the Court on its present course. Lately, the trend had been away from it. And if the President appointed a justice in Edmunson's place who shared Waldo Shuler's philosophy, the balance of the Court would be altered for a long time, possibly twenty years. Important years in America's history, Paul Lowe thought. When we face powerful enemies abroad, there is tremendous pressure at home against hard-won liberties. Some leaders cry to save the system. It is like an airplane going down. Everything, everything must be jettisoned to keep the plane in the air.

To his surprise he found Charles Edmunson watching him intently.

The resonant voice spoke with force and conviction: "You'll be a fine judge, Paul. I hope you'll take over for me when I'm gone . . . and do a better job. It's in the nature of things that a man aspire to have his work surpassed by those who come after him. It's the only way we can make progress."

Something about this praise both pleased and alarmed Paul Lowe. He was glad when qualities were discerned in himself that he was not aware of, but at the same time there was an *expectation* . . . a kind of awaiting a result as though the one who praised had combined certain prescribed chemicals and now demanded the promised chemical reaction.

"Well," he said, "right now I'll settle just to learn to do my job."

As he was leaving, Paul Lowe noticed on the wall of Edmunson's library a large square of embroidery framed in a light wood. After a moment he separated the colors to read *If the law cannot be found, it must be made.*

"Whose saying?" he asked.

Edmunson looked at the embroidered motto with a smile. "Mine, I'm afraid. I don't entirely agree with it. I would never have gone that far— except I had to give something to my wife to prevent her from embroidering some ghastly sentiment like *God Bless Our Happy Home.*"

Just outside the library, Edmunson paused at a side table to hand him a framed photograph. In the small rectangle of fabric the photograph showed Edmunson wearing his World War I uniform as a major and his tiny bride standing behind him in her wedding gown.

Edmunson said, "There was no malice in her. She liked the world—as much as she understood of it."

A small layer of dust was on the fabric frame. Paul Lowe brushed it off before returning it to the side table.

Edmunson said, "I know I don't seem very moved by her passing yet it was only three years ago. The truth is, Paul, one gets used to deprivation as one grows older. As we retreat from life we look back through the wrong end of a telescope until everything that was once alive becomes distant and unreal."

Paul Lowe shivered. He felt a slight chill in the air.

They went slowly to the door, each occupied in his own thoughts.

Edmunson's deep voice lost a bit of its resonance. "Old people outlive their time, I think. Everyone becomes impatient for them to step out of life into a perspective that has meaning—as a beloved grandparent, the honored representative of a vanished order—or even just a grave to visit on a pleasant Sunday afternoon."

"No one feels that way about you. You still have too many important contributions to make."

"Oh, in due course, Paul, I may become a bookend—a fine bronze figure in a bookcase. I hope they won't put me to holding up some sexy historical novel." Edmunson reacted briefly to Paul Lowe's laughter, then his mood darkened. "It doesn't matter. In the long view anything that anyone does has only a limited value in a limited universe. It really doesn't matter at all."

Paul Lowe watched him uneasily. Edmunson seemed tired.

"I want to thank you for this evening," Paul Lowe said. "It's been like old times."

Martin Hyde hovered solicitously near.

"I'd better say good night now, sir," Paul Lowe said. "It's getting late."

"Only twenty minutes to ten. My eyes are almost as good as ever, Paul—it's my hearing that seems to be going. One by one the senses depart like musical instruments in a fugue." Edmunson sighed deeply. "Toward the end Joyce was slipping a little. I had to rebuke him several times for shoddy thinking. Frank Joyce! As finely honed an intellect as I've known. You have to know when to quit. This may be my last year. Did I tell you that before, Paul?"

Paul Lowe was surprised at the straying of the old man's memory.

"You'll go on for a long time yet, sir."

"No, I don't trust my own powers. I seem to think for a while in good fashion and then . . . then it slips. I try to conserve my strength though. I'm in bed every evening at ten o'clock."

Martin Hyde opened the front door.

Edmunson said slowly, "Paul, if I'd had children I would have wanted a son like you."

In the doorway Martin waited.

"My wife liked you, too. Do you remember the good times we had?"

"I'll never forget them, sir."

"Never is a long time. A long long time." Edmunson turned. "I am tired, Paul. I'll go along to bed. Martin will see you out. Good night."

A few moments later Paul Lowe was on the street, looking back at the old house. A light on the second floor winked out. All was dark and still except for barely stirring curtains at the windows.

On the floor level there were signs of life—Martin Hyde crossed before a window as he entered the library and then appeared again to draw the curtain. A cat leaped to a window sill and crouched sinuously with its head between its shoulder haunches, listening, then silently leaped down behind the shrubbery.

There were no taxis on this quiet street. He walked to the corner. A slight mist in the air stung his eyes. His sensations were as unique to himself as his thoughts—all part of the closed circle of himself—and this evening had been a disturbing experience for him. At the quiet center, the innermost nucleus, what was there? A flicker of joy in a transient moment —or silence only?

He turned the corner and made a deliberate effort to listen. His thoughts had merely shut out the noise of the world. Cars honked, and there were voices.

12

On every hand the city of Washington was displaying its April finery to the invaders. Spring and the cherry blossoms had arrived together to the delight of the festival sponsors.

Sightseers were everywhere, decamping with cameras and travel guides from planes and trains and buses and private automobiles. The parklike areas bordering the Potomac were crowded with tourists admiring cherry blossoms, low-growing violet-blue ageratum, pink begonias, gold belled daffodils and beds of long-stemmed white and blood-red tulips. While camera shutters clicked, the tourists posed near mimosas that were waving graceful fans and peered from the lacework foliage of weeping willow trees and leaned against the trunks of sycamores that were spotted like giraffes in mottled white and green and brown. Over their heads large white blossoming honey locust trees were abuzz with bees seeking its nectar amid thorns.

Hotel lobbies were crowded and public buildings flowed with entering and exiting multitudes. The faithful plodded accustomed ways to the Lincoln and Jefferson memorials, the White House, the Smithsonian museum. They watched a sharpshooting agent at the Federal Bureau of Investigation send tracer bullets cutting through lifesized targets on the practice range. At the Bureau of Engraving and Printing they were fascinated as some of the ten billion dollars in currency produced each year rolled unattainably past their eyes. At the National Archives they stared curiously at the Declaration of Independence, the Constitution and the Bill of Rights in their helium-filled cases under specially tinted laminated glass.

En route to the Supreme Court building, Paul Lowe stared out the car window, faintly hypnotized by so much bustle amid so much beauty. Then the car descended a ramp into the dark caverns of the underground garage beneath the marble halls of the Supreme Court and into an echoing quiet surrounded by concrete and plaster, odors of gasoline and exhaust fumes.

Paul Lowe got out of the car. On the twelfth day of the month of April, being a Monday, and in the thirty-fifth day of the Lenten feast, the virgin moon being in her first quarter, Paul Lincoln Lowe said to Jonathan Carter:

"Thank you, Jonathan."

He waited for the elevator that would take him up to the second floor and the halls of law where he and his brethren would continue the attempt to split controversy like an amoeba and choose the better part.

His office was a few steps down the corridor.

"Good morning, Martha."

Martha Scully was still wearing her coat. She was taking off her hat—a formidable contraption that projected like a cannon from her head.

"Good morning, Mr. Justice. I'll bring the mail in right away."

The mail was routine; only two letters interested him. One was from Ken Norris who had become a regular correspondent. Every Monday brought his letter of comment on the previous week's decisions.

Today Ken wrote with rancorous amusement about Gabriel Hart. This past Monday Gabriel Hart had delivered orally, at tedious length, an opinion from the bench. Gabriel had insisted on reading every word, including footnotes, and had made many verbal insertions and digressions to cover points that he had not chosen to put in the written opinion. It had been, Paul Lowe recalled ruefully, a difficult hour. When Gabriel had finally plowed through to the end there were audible sighs of relief in the courtroom.

An account of that morning's monotony had somehow reached Ken Norris in far off Omaha. Ken now wrote: "Gabriel Hart's performance has raised the interesting possibility of government by asphyxiation. By wrapping inanity in chloroform he may have discovered a way to stupefy the lower courts into accepting it."

Ken's certitudes, the necessary basis for his sarcasm, caused Paul Lowe to smile. Ken did not give Gabriel Hart his due. In that opinion, Gabriel had come down through the fog of words to touch solid ground. He had been speaking for a unanimous Court and although it was certainly not an impressive or scintillating performance the social end achieved would be good.

Paul Lowe made a mental note to remind Ken that his zeal for the achievement of social goals should include some tolerance for boredom.

The second letter arrived in a large brown manila envelope. He opened it and took out stapled proofs of the articles Katherine Prescott had written about him for the Lincoln *Sentinel* and other Race Hardman newspapers.

A short note was appended: "I hope this meets with your approval. Do let me know." It was signed "Katherine Prescott."

They had met for interviews a few times since that unfortunate (he could think of it in no other way) evening at her apartment. Their first meeting, a Saturday lunch, was awkward. They pretended amusement at the stilted conversation, but the amusement was forced and the conversation remained stilted. On two subsequent short meetings in his office while the Court was in recess, and during a long session in his office on an evening before he left to dress for a formal dinner, they had completed

164

the interviews. In retrospect what struck him most about their meetings was what had been lost, a spark from a mutual magnetic field—now extinguished.

On impulse he picked up the note to sniff it. No perfume. He opened the staples to glance through the newspaper articles. She had made artful use of the information gathered in their interviews, weaving new and familiar material together in a way that made the articles seem informed and knowledgeable. Her writing style was clear and simple—none of the quick darts of intelligence, the hop skip and leap which somehow vaulted over logical sequence to make its own logic.

He put the clippings aside to attack his other mail. When he looked up Bill Tobin was in the doorway. He might have been there for some time.

"Come in, Bill." Paul Lowe took off his horn-rimmed reading glasses and put them on the pile of opened letters.

Bill Tobin held a stack of printed opinions.

"What's that?"

"Some reactions to your opinion in the Hutchens case." Bill Tobin smiled widely. "It met with the approval of your associates, Mr. Justice."

The opinion dealt with a case arising under the antitrust laws. Certain television program distributors had been trying to compel individual stations to purchase an entire package of films in order to acquire the better, more popular programs. Condemning the practice, Paul Lowe had pointed out that this would force a small, local television station to purchase worthless programming properties along with the relatively few good ones. His conclusion was that this practice violated section one of the Sherman Act, the nation's basic antitrust law, and therefore should be prohibited.

"What are the comments?" Paul Lowe said.

Bill Tobin sat at the edge of his desk to read the notes on each copy: "'A persuasive bit of reasoning'—that's Justice Merriam. 'Good logic and good law'—that's the Chief Justice. 'A useful sound job in every respect; a model of plain writing and straight thinking'—that's Justice McCann."

"Any dissenters?"

"We've had no word yet from Justice Cutler or Justice Hart. But Justice Waldo Shuler sent back his copy: 'A strong and clear statement of your position. However, I began reading with doubts, and am left doubting.'"

"I didn't think I could win Waldo over."

Bill Tobin said, "Justice Edmunson says, 'Another example of the fine work you've been doing recently.'" He put down the proofs he was holding. "Well, sir, you seem to have passed muster with your colleagues. I don't believe anyone else could have made such progress in this amount of time."

"Thank you, Bill. It's a relief to find out that I can learn from my mistakes."

Bill Tobin gathered up the proofs. "Justice Cutler is writing a dissent. I understand Justice Shuler and Justice Hart will go along with him rather than write separate dissents."

"I don't think we should expect unanimity on a controversial issue like this one."

"No, sir," Bill Tobin said promptly. "Not as long as there are nine strong-minded individualists on the Court."

Paul Lowe sighed. "Secretly, I suppose I'm glad. *Sic semper tyrannis* —even the tyranny of intellect. If that Angel came down and wrote with a pen of fire, I'd like someone, somewhere, to stand up and say 'I doubt it.'"

Bill Tobin said dryly, "My guess is it would be Justice Andrew Cutler."

Paul Lowe grinned. "You could be right."

In the robing room, while Sam Davids was helping Paul Lowe into his robe, Justice Andrew Cutler drifted over.

Andrew Cutler was a tall spare man who appeared thin in a business suit but formidable in his black judicial robes.

"I'm writing a dissent on that Hutchens case. I think you're all wrong, Paul. But unlike some of the grandstanders around here you don't put in a lot of useless documentation to bolster up an invalid argument. Yours was a direct, straightforward statement—and within its limits well reasoned."

"Thank you, Andrew."

"Someday I hope you'll get around to doing some hard thinking about the wider meanings of what you say."

It is sometimes, Paul Lowe thought, a great advantage to have no sense of humor. Andrew Cutler's conspicuous lack of that quality enabled him to wax pontifical without any embarrassment.

"I don't suppose we'll ever convince each other," Paul Lowe said.

"Time will tell," Andrew Cutler said. "I never doubt that mistakes will be put right in the long run. We're going to witness one mistake corrected in the very near future."

"Which one is that?"

"The decision Edmunson wrote at the end of last year's session. Looks pretty certain now we'll grant a rehearing."

"Are you talking about the New Jersey school board case?" Paul Lowe stopped in the doorway.

Cutler nodded. "That's the one. Waldo dissented at the time. A brilliant job—but he only carried Gabriel Hart and myself. Now the Chief and Bill Branch have had time to reconsider and they've seen where they made their mistake."

"I don't believe they did make a mistake."

Andrew Cutler's austere look was heightened by the fixity of gray eyes beneath a high forehead.

"You can't defend Edmunson's opinion in that case. It was one of the worst things he's ever done. No real lawyer could have respect for it."

"I wasn't on the Court at the time it was written. But I do agree with his basic position."

Andrew Cutler shook his head. "It displayed a genuine softness of intellect, and sentimentality has no place in the law. It was the sort of thing that has made Edmunson the people's darling—but in time history will expose what he has done."

Andrew Cutler was certain that he was on the side of history in the same way that, as a devout churchgoer, he believed himself to enjoy a special and privileged relationship with God.

"We may have to wait to hear from history," Paul Lowe said. "In the meantime I'm strongly opposed to a rehearing being granted."

He hurried across the corridor with Andrew Cutler, and they took their places behind the maroon curtain just as the guard banged and the Marshal began his announcement on the other side of the curtain.

"The Honorable, the Chief Justice, and the Associate Justices of the Supreme Court of the United States."

Shortly after two-thirty when Court adjourned, Paul Lowe went back to his office. He pushed the intercom lever to talk to Bill Tobin.

"Bill, will you bring in the briefs and records in the New Jersey school board case?"

"MacDonough versus the Board of Education? Yes, Mr. Justice."

A few moments later Bill Tobin entered carrying a stack of different-colored paperbound briefs and a volume of the most recent decisions of the Court.

Paul Lowe turned to the indicated page.

"Do you remember anything about this case, Bill?"

"Yes, sir. It was one of the first important tests of *de facto* segregation in the schools. I had just come to work here. Mr. Justice Edmunson wrote the opinion of the Court."

"Mr. Justice Joyce voted with him?"

"Yes, sir." Bill Tobin hesitated slightly.

"Did he have reservations about it?"

"Well, sir, Mr. Justice Joyce didn't think that the completed opinion was worthy of Mr. Justice Edmunson. He even considered writing a concurring opinion but then decided not to."

"Did he mention what he found wrong with Justice Edmunson's opinion?"

"Yes, sir. He thought it was rambling, disjointed and discursive. Of course that wasn't entirely Mr. Justice Edmunson's fault. He had to make compromises to keep the majority with him. Mr. Justice Branch, in particular. As a result, he partly begged the question—at least that's what Mr. Justice Joyce thought at the time."

"I see. Thank you, Bill."

Paul Lowe read through the factual summary in the petitioner's brief. A New Jersey School Board, attempting to comply with the mandate that the schools be desegregated "with all deliberate speed," had ordered the transfer of some white students to a school in a Negro neighborhood. This action promptly drew protests from parents annoyed at having to shift their children from schools close by in their own neighborhood. One white family, the MacDonoughs, brought suit in the Federal District

Court to prevent the Board from carrying out the plan. The District Court upheld the action of the school board, as did the Court of Appeals.

Then Paul Lowe turned to Edmunson's opinion in the official reports. He read through the pages with sinking dismay. The opinion was more inconclusive even than he feared. Edmunson rambled through the history of previous segregation decisions with what seemed a cavalier disregard for logical order of argument. More important, his entire opinion lacked the lofty philosophic line—that irresistible appeal that Charles Edmunson was able to make to an immutable wisdom handed down by the sages.

What had caused the great man's hand to falter? He could not put the entire blame on Edmunson's need to compromise in order to hold the Court behind him. There were scattered and unrelated arguments, uncoordinated ideas, reasoning based on mere surmise.

Paul Lowe stopped reading and took off his glasses, dangling them. Finally he called Bill Tobin on the intercom and asked him to come in.

"Have you read it, sir?" Bill Tobin asked as soon as he entered the office.

"Yes. I have."

"What do you think, sir?"

"I'm afraid everything Frank Joyce thought about this particular opinion is true. It's the poorest I've ever read by Justice Edmunson."

"Even Homer nods, sir."

"Homer wasn't up against a rehearing on whether the *Iliad* and *Odyssey* should be allowed to stand as written."

Bill Tobin was puzzled. "I don't understand why there should be a rehearing. Not even the lawyers who file petitions expect them to be granted. It's just a way of blowing off steam and showing their clients they've done everything humanly possible."

"This opinion is highly vulnerable. It begs a number of questions that do require answers. That might be enough to convince Bill Branch and the Chief to vote for a petition for rehearing."

"But, sir, they wouldn't have to vote for such an unusual procedure to accomplish that. They could wait for a new test case to make their own position clear."

"Not on a segregation issue. That's the most urgent problem the Court has to deal with. Don't forget that each decision that goes into the record affects the result in dozens of other cases waiting to be heard. If there's doubt about why a decision was made, that doubt should be resolved with the least possible delay." A thought had been germinating in Paul Lowe's mind and suddenly grew into words. "That's exactly what Waldo Shuler is counting on."

"Mr. Justice Shuler? What's he got to do with it?"

"He's a brilliant tactician. And I'll bet *he's* behind this move to grant a rehearing." Paul Lowe's certainty was mounting. "It has all the earmarks of a plan conceived by Shuler. Aimed directly at a vulnerable point— all the angles thoroughly explored—and no matter what happens at the rehearing Shuler's side can't possibly lose by it."

168

"I'm sorry, sir. Apparently I'm not following you."

"This is a maneuver calculated by Waldo Shuler as part of his campaign to win control of this Court."

"How could he do that, sir? Even if the petition is granted, the rehearing probably wouldn't change the original decision. The vote would go the same way."

"I don't think it would, Bill." Sudden restlessness forced Paul Lowe to get up and pace the area behind his desk. Like Waldo Shuler himself—back and forth as though movement itself would ignite ideas. "Don't forget, Bill, there's a sort of ideological backlash taking place in this country. Some people who favored civil rights in the beginning have started to wonder if limits shouldn't be put to it. Or they've begun to think that the pace we're moving at is too fast so a little slowing down wouldn't be out of order. 'With all deliberate speed'—that's how it read in the Supreme Court's decision. I wouldn't be surprised if men like Bill Branch or the Chief Justice—possibly even Henry Merriam—are susceptible to the argument that progress should now be made more slowly."

Bill Tobin was shaken. "There's at least a good possibility that the result would be the same."

"That's where Waldo Shuler's tactics insure his side against defeat! Suppose the rehearing is held, and the vote is the same. The New Jersey School Board's plan is once more upheld. But meanwhile one of Edmunson's weakest efforts is subjected to a fresh unsparing scrutiny. At Edmunson's peak, that would have been a humiliating experience for him. If it happens now—with retirement possibly a year or two away—it might convince him that the time had already come to quit."

"Then this petition for a rehearing has to be denied."

Paul Lowe stopped his pacing. He said crisply, "Bill, I want you to make a summary of the main points in Edmunson's opinion. Use them as topic sentences and arrange the material under those headings. This will show us where the argument becomes redundant or the logic fumbles."

Bill Tobin settled back bewildered. "Why, sir? We can't change it. It's too late for that."

"Edmunson had to work with certain data and failed to follow the implications through. We'll do that for him."

"What's the use of it, sir? We can't revise an opinion that's already in the record."

"We'll use the revision as a memo to circulate among the other justices."

Bill's youthful face lit with eagerness. "You mean it might convince some of the justices—the ones who are wavering—that there's really no need to grant the petition for a rehearing. It'll prove the law is sound and they can afford to wait for another test case to establish more forcefully why it is."

"Exactly. What do you think, Bill?"

"It might work, sir."

"It'll mean a lot of overtime hours, Bill. I can't take you off your regular chores."

"I don't mind, sir. Not for a thing like this."

"All right, then. Let's get started."

Bill Tobin got up so quickly he almost stumbled. At the door he said, "Thank you, Mr. Justice."

"Don't spare the scissors and paste," Paul Lowe said.

He leaned back in his swivel chair. His fingertips felt clammy against the skin of his forehead. When the opinion was revised, before showing it to the other justices, he must show it to Edmunson. To tamper with an Edmunson opinion—even the weakest—passed the limits of impertinence. He would have to be sure he was right. Perhaps there was a grasp beneath the surface argument that he had missed, a kernel of hidden truth within the shell.

If so, his mistake would provoke Edmunson to wrath—and the great man's wrath was volcanic. Paul Lowe had seen the unwary blasted and shriveled by the anger that roared about them. The pure explosive display of energy at such times could be frightening.

He picked up the volume of official reports that contained Charles Edmunson's published opinion. He had better read it again before making impious war on heaven.

On Saturday morning the revised opinion was in type. Before sending it to any of the other justices, Paul Lowe sought out Edmunson in his office.

Edmunson was behind his desk with a book in his lap, the magnificent large head sunk forward.

Paul Lowe rapped slightly on the door but there was no response. He ventured a moderately loud, "I beg your pardon!"

Edmunson's head lifted. He fingered his massive jaw a bit uncertainly before the dark blue eyes came slowly into focus.

"Oh, it's you, Paul. I'm afraid I dozed off." The deep voice grumbled. "Small wonder. I was reading something of Gabriel Hart's."

"Do you have time to talk?"

"Of course. Of course." Edmunson indicated the chair beside his desk. "What's on your mind this morning?"

"The New Jersey School Board case."

"MacDonough versus the Board of Education. What about it?"

"You know that there has been a petition for a rehearing."

"Yes. I expect there'll be a routine denial."

"I've been sounding out some of the others," Paul Lowe said carefully. "There's a strong probability that this petition will be granted."

"Where have you been getting this information?"

"From Andrew Cutler. He says Bill Branch and the Chief will definitely vote to grant the petition for a rehearing."

Edmunson considered this with head slightly lowered. He looked up to ask, "How do you account for their change of mind?"

"I'm afraid your opinion is partly to blame. It didn't meet the issue head-on."

"Indeed? Why not?"

"All you said in effect was that the school board's action was proper because it meant well—meant to abide by the Segregation Cases. You didn't touch on the guarantees of personal liberty, or of freedom not to associate, or whether the Constitution can be used to compel white children to go to a Negro school to carry out an abstract concept of racial equality. Those were the questions raised by the MacDonough family when they brought their suit against the school board."

"In other words," Edmunson answered slowly, "you think I begged all the important questions."

"It doesn't happen often. But it did this time."

"You contend that instead of explaining why, I merely said a thing is so because it is so. Is that what you're trying to tell me?"

Edmunson's query was pitched at a dead level that made it hard for Paul Lowe to determine whether this was a challenge, whether the old man was preparing with subtle patience to unleash a thunderbolt.

He had gone too far for retreat. "You simplified the statement to a set of propositions that simply won't command agreement," he said.

Edmunson pondered this in silence with his shoulder pulled back—the gesture meant he was feeling stiffness from the bullet lodged somewhere beneath his shoulder blade, a souvenir of his service in the First World War.

"You really think I did that shoddy a job?" The long shaggy head remained perfectly still for a moment, then moved affirmatively. "I never was satisfied with that particular piece of work."

Paul Lowe handed over the printed sheets. "I'd like you to read this. It's a revised version."

Edmunson stared at the papers in his hand. "What possible good can it do?"

"I want your permission to circulate this to the other justices. It may influence their voting on the petition for rehearing."

"Do you really think it will?"

"It's worth the chance."

Edmunson's large pupils almost twinkled. "I used to play lacrosse when I was a young man. One of our rules was—if you can't knock it out of their hand, give them a good bash on the head. This is meant to do something like that."

"I suppose so."

"Let me read it, Paul. That rule I mentioned makes for good lacrosse but might be poor judicial politics."

An hour later, while Paul Lowe was at work reading an opinion by Henry Merriam in a patent case, the telephone rang at his desk.

"Paul? Charles Edmunson. I've just gone over your revised draft of my opinion."

Courage began to ebb out through the pores of his skin. "I've been thinking about it, sir," he said. "I only meant to make suggestions. It was bold of me to put them in concrete form and I wouldn't have done it except I hoped to save time and . . ."

"Will you stop rattling so I can say what I think?"

"Yes, sir."

"You didn't put strongly enough the point that the State of New Jersey needed a more or less free hand—within constitutional limits—to carry out desegregation in any way it could. If that point were emphasized it might help to persuade a justice who doesn't like too much interference with the power of state legislatures."

"You're right about that."

"There's one place where I found your reasoning inconsistent. You rely on the Fourteenth Amendment's ban against using race or color as a ground of classification. But how about the Fourteenth Amendment's impact on measures meant to reduce *de facto* segregation in schools? It works both ways, doesn't it? And if not, why not?"

"I see what you mean. I should have covered that."

"And you certainly should have pointed out that a contrary decision in this case—a failure to uphold New Jersey's law—would have threatened the essentials of all previous segregation decisions."

Paul Lowe's spirits were sinking like mercury in a barometer.

"Anything else, sir?" he asked faintly.

"There are instances in which I prefer my own phrases when they were equivalent. I think you might keep in mind that there's no need to change language when there is no change in meaning."

"I didn't realize I'd done that. I will admit, sir, that this was just an immature attempt to . . ."

Edmunson's deep voice became lighter. "Over all, however, I am highly pleased."

"What?"

"I want to thank you for the trouble you have taken. Even as it now stands, this opinion is nothing to be ashamed of. I'd be proud to have written it this way."

Paul Lowe was incredulous. "You won't object if I circulate it to the others?"

"It would be a crime not to, Paul, after the fine work you've done."

He should have known. Edmunson would never allow ego to interfere with his judgment.

He shut his eyes for a moment. "Thank you, sir. Thank you very, very much."

"Oh, and one other thing."

"Yes, sir?"

"You're not my law clerk any more, Paul. You're my associate. I wish you'd stop calling me 'sir.' My name is Charles."

"Yes, sir," Paul Lowe said.

There was no way to discover whether the revised opinion written for the private examination of other justices had any perceptible effect.

Chief Justice Hampton sent a surprised note to Paul Lowe. "This revised opinion of a case already in the record has been worth perusing. But how do you find time for these extracurricular excursions?"

There was a mildly amused note from Henry Merriam. "This may open a whole new field for ambitious legal writers—the rewriting of already existing opinions."

A short sentence was Waldo Shuler's reply, "Interesting but I couldn't disagree with the conclusion any more than I did when it was first handed down."

Andrew Cutler's comment was the longest and most acidulous: "This is an example of how principle, under pressure from practical considerations, will degenerate into sloganeering. The people of this country are not going to sell their integrity for a mess of socialistic pottage. They are becoming frightened of the kind of thinking shown in this revision, as well as in its parent opinion, and I won't be at all surprised if their fears start to show up in the results from the polling booths."

Andrew Cutler's interest in the political aspects of the problem derived from his own ambitions in that direction. At the previous Republican National Convention his name had been mentioned as a candidate for the Vice-Presidency. His qualifications as a distinguished public figure, leading conservative, Presbyterian, aide to Eisenhower in World War II, provided him with a background that no one could cavil at. He had no enemies—and so he clung to his hope that when the moment arrived, as it does periodically in American politics, for warring factions to be placated by the choice of a neutral figure for high office, he would be discovered standing the high ground beneath his blank flag.

No other justice returned a comment. There was too much current pressing business to comment on an opinion that would never enter the public record. The justices read it, and kept their thoughts to themselves.

The real test of whether his effort had been worthwhile would come, as Paul Lowe had known all along, at the weekly conference.

At the Friday conference shortly before noon Chief Justice John Hampton called for a vote on a petition for a rehearing in the case of *MacDonough vs. the Board of Education*. As junior justice, Paul Lowe was the first to vote.

"I vote to deny the petition," he said.

Henry Merriam was next in order of seniority. When the Chief Justice called his name, Henry Merriam hesitated in a way that gave the impression he meant to make a statement of explanation. Then he changed his mind and said simply, "I vote to deny the petition."

Waldo Shuler was holding a paper clip against his lower lip, and his only reaction to Merriam's vote was to brush the clip softly along the length of his underlip.

"Mr. Justice McCann?" asked the Chief Justice.

"I vote to deny the petition."

Three votes against, none for. That disproportion was soon corrected. Bill Branch voted in favor of granting the petition and in rapid succession

Justices Hart, Cutler, and Shuler added their votes in favor. That made a majority of four to three against. Charles Edmunson's vote restored the tie, and left the decision to Chief Justice John Hampton.

The Chief Justice's bearing was erect and dignified, and his clipped voice was devoid of emotion.

"I vote to deny the petition for a rehearing. The petition is therefore denied."

The Chief was shuffling papers to move on to other business when he was suddenly interrupted.

"Just a minute," Andrew Cutler said.

Everyone looked toward him. Andrew Cutler was scowling.

"Everyone present at this conference table is fully aware that the opinion we have decided not to review is a sugar-coated capsule containing absolutely nothing. If this Court will not acknowledge its mistakes we are going to lose the respect of the entire country."

"The vote has been taken," Chief Justice Hampton said mildly. "Five to four against granting the petition."

Andrew Cutler's face was pale and set with repressed fury. "We are continuing to support a policy of forced racial integration. This is in direct defiance of the Fourteenth Amendment to the Constitution which so-called liberals on this Court always manage to pervert to their uses whenever it suits them. We are publicly declaring that we still stand behind a policy which is entirely unable to deal with the real racial and ethnic problems now plaguing the country. I don't believe in integration just for integration's sake. I can't see how any five judges, a bare majority of this Court, can take it on themselves to change a nation's whole way of life or force children to move to schools somewhere else—when the children's own parents have picked where they want to live and send them to school. If that isn't against the Constitution of the United States, then I'd like to know what is."

"We are glad to have your statement, Andrew," the Chief Justice said briskly to cut off the debate.

"I'm not going to let it stop here. I have been very very disappointed by the action taken today. I think we have done a shameful thing. I hoped that we were wise enough, mature enough, to review and correct past mistakes. If not, then I will now clearly dissociate myself from the majority." Andrew Cutler's thin, almost fragile body seemed to gain dimension from anger. "I am going to file a dissenting opinion from the denial of this petition."

"I fail to see what that will accomplish," the Chief Justice said coolly.

"It will set forth the reasons why I think the petition should have been granted."

The Chief twisted his head aside and pinched the bridge of his nose. It was his way of showing annoyance.

Waldo Shuler's thin voice carried clearly through the room's silence.

"I feel as Mr. Justice Cutler does about the mistake the Court made in denying this petition. The original opinion in MacDonough versus the

174

Board of Education is simply not adequate to its purpose. Therefore a rehearing should have been granted. At the very least a rehearing would have amplified and made understandable the reasons for the Court's previous decision." Waldo Shuler's brown eyes glinted out of his dark face. "However, we have decided not to grant the petition. I don't know what reasons influenced the majority. I suspect," Waldo Shuler's glance strayed momentarily to Paul Lowe, "that factors were at work that have little or nothing to do with the merits of the petition. Nevertheless, now that a decision has been taken, I believe we should abide by it. On a controversial issue such as integration in our schools, this Court should not advertise its disagreements unnecessarily. That would only create further dissension in the country at large."

"There is a question of individual conscience," Andrew Cutler said.

"Andrew, I don't imagine for a moment that your convictions spring from anything else but the promptings of your conscience. But there are practical matters to be considered also. For a rehearing petition to be denied, and for a justice to proclaim publicly his disagreement with such a routine denial, is virtually unheard of. It would cause a great deal of unwelcome publicity. You might find yourself in the embarrassing position, Andrew, of being labeled a defender of racism."

"That is not my position at all," Andrew Cutler said with a firmness calculated to offset any impression that he was weakening.

"I know that perfectly well. Anyone who knows you knows that. I'm merely saying that would be the impression the public would get. I know you don't shrink from that, Andrew. But I think it would be unfair to the rest of us to allow such an impression to remain in the public mind about one of our most esteemed colleagues."

Andrew Cutler said finally, "I strongly feel some action should be taken to demonstrate how much I disagree. But I admit that the action I propose *is* unorthodox. For that reason it might possibly give the wrong impression. I'll need more time to think it over."

Paul Lowe opened his docket book. Waldo Shuler's display of forcefulness and tact, plus his appeal to orthodoxy, had apparently won Andrew Cutler over. Paul Lowe smiled slightly as he recorded in his docket book the denial of a petition for rehearing in *MacDonough vs. the Board of Education.*

He returned to his office from the conference room at nearly five-thirty that Friday afternoon. Bill Tobin and Jack Broderick were waiting near Martha Scully's desk. All three looked at him with open curiosity.

"Petition denied," Paul Lowe said briefly. "Five to four."

Bill Tobin let out a yell and grabbed Martha by the waist. They did an impromptu dance step.

Jack Broderick said, "Congratulations, Mr. Justice."

"I don't know how much I had to do with it, Jack."

"I suppose we'll never know," Jack Broderick agreed. "But there is no question that the revised opinion you circulated was far more persuasive and logical than the original."

"Thank you, Jack."

That serious young man nodded and left the room.

Martha Scully, smiling delightedly, clasped her hands together on her waist.

"I knew you'd win," she said. "I just knew it!"

For Paul Lowe the brief sharp encounter over the conference table —resolved in a few minutes—was already fading to become one incident among many.

"If there's any credit for a victory, Bill Tobin deserves most of it. He did the work."

Bill Tobin did not hear. He was using the telephone on Martha Scully's desk and making plans in a gay excited tone.

"Mr. Justice!"

Bill Tobin was holding the phone with one hand cupping the receiver:

"Is there any chance you're free tonight?"

"I have to finish making notes on Merriam's opinion in the patent case."

A shade of disappointment crossed Bill Tobin's face. "I was hoping you could have dinner with Janet and me. It's a kind of special occasion. It's her birthday—and I'd like to celebrate today's victory."

In the narrowing frame of Paul Lowe's own recollection of the day's events, Bill's youthful zest was welcome. It was difficult to believe now that there had been a meaningful connection between the urgent hurried work of revising Edmunson's opinion and the final result of the voting at the conference. There might indeed have been no connection.

But there were no such doubts in his young law clerk's mind: it had been a victory pure and simple. In the desire to hold on to that concept, to live a while longer in the sure sense of accomplishment, Paul Lowe nodded.

"I'll call my wife," he said. "How about the Bit and Bridle Club—with champagne? I'll make one condition. I pick up the check."

"Oh, no, sir, I can't allow . . ."

"That's the condition. Sorry."

"Dutch?" Bill asked hopefully.

"I happen to know what they pay you here," Paul Lowe replied with a smile. "I can afford it better than you can."

Bill Tobin yielded. "All right, sir, if you insist. What time?"

"Say eight o'clock. I want to be home by eleven to get in a little work."

As Paul Lowe left the room Bill Tobin was speaking on the telephone in a tone that was fairly bursting with suppressed excitement.

The waiter worked the cork out of the champagne bottle with a popping sound muffled in the heavy white napkin. Then he pulled the bottle out of the ice bucket. Paul Lowe indicated Bill Tobin and the waiter poured a quarter glass for Tobin to sample, which he did in approved fashion, not ostentatiously tasting, not too casual, before he nodded to the waiter to go ahead and pour.

When the glasses were full, Paul Lowe raised his.

"To Janet Yarlton, on her twentieth birthday."

Eleanor and Bill Tobin promptly raised their glasses to join in the toast.

Janet was a pretty, brown-haired girl, rather quiet, with a gentle lovely manner and a trim figure. She was a settling influence on Bill Tobin's exuberance. From the way Bill fussed over her it was quite clear how fond he was of her. Only once did she betray her feelings and, as such revelations do, it came in an unexpected inadvertent way. Bill Tobin was excitedly telling about the victory in the New Jersey School Board case, quite swept away by his subject and making what would otherwise have been intolerably dull material somehow vibrant and full of life. Janet, out of his range, was quite obviously not hearing a single word he spoke but was so rapt with the meaning of him that what he was saying was clear to her. Paul Lowe had never seen a woman so dedicate herself in a glance— her whole spirit yielding through her eyes.

He could not help comparing this girl with Nancy, almost exactly the same age, yet so different it did not seem possible that they had lived approximately the same number of years on the same planet. His first impulse was to decide that Nancy was more intelligent, more mature. But why was cynicism with its rejection of values, its bias against emotion or involvement, more mature? Perhaps because the cynic's act of rejection implied experience enough to have discovered a root failing, a hidden canker. Why could not experience also discover a vitality that feeds, a blossom hidden in dry winter branches?

Bill Tobin had embarked on a favorite topic: the depthless state of public ignorance.

"I saw a survey the other day. A reporter went out and showed people the Bill of Rights. He didn't identify the Bill of Rights—he just told them it was a new set of laws and asked if they'd vote for it. More than half said it was Communist propaganda, and nearly two-thirds said they couldn't vote for anyone who ran on that platform."

Everyone laughed. Janet said, "That's the fault of teaching, isn't it?" She planned to be a teacher when she graduated in another year and she related most problems to her chosen calling. "They ought to have a course in every school," she said firmly, "teaching students the meaning of the Bill of Rights."

Tobin turned to Paul Lowe.

"What do you say, sir?"

"I'm rather inclined to say it's a matter of caring. People care about what directly affects their lives. The job, the house, the children—the entertainment they can find for their off hours—TV, movies, occasionally magazines and seldom books. The failure may be teaching as Janet says. But then we have to teach them not only what the Bill of Rights is, but show them how and where it affects them in their daily lives. *If* it does."

"You know it does, sir."

"We've been trained to think so, Bill, as lawyers. But I have a feeling that the majority of people at the time were hardly aware of it when the Framers drafted the original Bill of Rights. The majority was occupied then as it is now, with the small events of their day—the dinner to be made, the crankiness of the boss or the customer who didn't pay, the chimney that got stuffed up, the horse that threw a shoe. When these cares were disposed of they wanted to have some fun. If they had had TV then, they certainly wouldn't have tuned in a public affairs show about the Bill of Rights. They'd have tuned in their own Bob Hope or Red Skelton—or a good adventure show like Colonel Washington in the French and Indian War."

Bill Tobin was delighted. He gave Janet a look that said clearly, "See what kind of man I'm working for!" Paul Lowe smiled at Eleanor, including her. She had said nothing but she radiated content. This was her kind of evening. Her man pre-eminent—and herself sharing plaudits as his wife. In a confiding moment she had once told him what her mother said; "Marry a man who when you meet your friends ten years from now you can say, 'Look what I've got!'"

Bill Tobin said, "You're right. I wonder what would have happened if we had had television a hundred years or so ago. How many people would have tuned in Lincoln making the Gettysburg Address?"

Paul Lowe said, "The question is, how many would have tuned him out?"

Later, the discussion drifted to modern marriage. It was a topic that fascinated Bill Tobin and Janet; they exchanged looks when anything was said that might bear a relation to them and their intimacy. Their fingers touched on the tablecloth. Eleanor said that marriage was the only real happiness for two people and the sentimentality of that remark which might have occasioned at least a snicker or a flicker of protest only brought a fresh and tender exchange of looks.

Suddenly Paul Lowe had enough. He signaled to the waiter.

"Anyone care for a brandy?"

All said no.

"I'll have a check then," Paul Lowe told the waiter.

His gaze went beyond the waiter to the entrance. Katherine Prescott was entering with a tall man—Tom Jeffreys—as her escort. She wore the same coat she had worn the night they dined at the country inn in Maryland. As the waiter moved away, Paul Lowe saw her go down a side aisle along the banquette tables. He felt a congestion in his chest. His lips were dry. Tom Jeffreys helped her take off her coat at the table, polite and attentive. Give him his due, distinguished-looking fellow. One of the bright trivial men of TV whose whole art was in communication but who had nothing to say. That's why they attach themselves to causes, Paul Lowe thought, inflating themselves like frogs.

178

She sat down, facing him, at an angle where she did not see him. She laughed at a remark Tom Jeffreys made. Absolutely her best feature—flashing white teeth, perfect tapering curve of lips, a happy transformation! What had Jeffreys said to her?

"Paul."

He turned back to the table. Eleanor had spoken, the waiter was hovering. The check was on his left.

"Oh, yes. Thank you." To cover the awkward moment he studied the check, then took out two twenty-dollar bills and paid the waiter. The bill was thirty-four dollars and he told the waiter to keep the change.

On the way out, he used an aisle that emerged two tables away from where Katherine Prescott was seated. She saw him, brightened, and signaled.

Paul Lowe went over with Eleanor.

"Mr. Justice, how are you?" she said. Then, as Tom Jeffreys rose from his chair: "You remember Tom, don't you?"

"Of course." Paul Lowe shook hands. A swift reappraisal—tall, lean, handsomely boned face with slightly freckled skin, reddish brown hair. "Of course."

"Did you get the proofs I sent you?" Katherine asked.

"I meant to send them back but I've been busy."

"No need. I've got lots more. I really wanted to know if you approve."

"They were flattering."

"I've had two book offers already if I care to expand them. Like they say—hitch your wagon to a star."

"If it isn't a falling star," Paul Lowe said. "Hard to tell sometimes."

"I wouldn't worry." Tom Jeffreys' rapid speech was clipped pseudo-British. "I've had my antenna out and I've been getting signals, Mr. Justice. Everyone in this town knows that you've won your spurs on the Court—in jig time."

"Have I?"

Jeffreys nodded. "Would you like to hear a more exact description—right off the grapovine?"

"I reserve the right to dissent."

"Let's see. It goes something like this. Not quite as thorough as Shulor, not quite as wise as Edmunson, but you combine their best qualities. Hard worker. Opinions are clear, not too technical, and show a good grasp of the law."

"I might demur on a point or two." Paul Lowe smiled pleasantly. "Well, enjoy your dinner."

Katherine said to Eleanor, "It's been very nice to meet you again, Mrs. Lowe."

Eleanor smiled and murmured, "So nice."

Tom Jeffreys took Eleanor's hand between both of his—how did some people guess that his wife could safely be patronized?

"Mrs. Lowe, you must be proud of your husband. He is on his way to becoming a great man."

"Well, I think so."

Tom Jeffreys released her hand.

"From the look of things," he said to Paul Lowe, "there are some really difficult cases coming up. None of them will be easy to decide."

Paul Lowe shrugged. "The only reason we've got a Supreme Court at all is because there has to be a place where hard cases are decided. The easy ones don't get to us." He nodded slightly to Katherine. "Good evening, Miss Prescott."

Bill Tobin and Janet were waiting in the entrance doorway.

Eleanor said, "She was at the party at the Hardmans'. I remember her. What did you say her name was?"

"Katherine Prescott."

"A newspaperwoman?"

"She wrote a series of articles about me. I thought I told you."

Eleanor twisted her head to look back. "That man she's with—he seems to like her. Who is he?"

"Tom Jeffreys. A TV commentator."

"Are they serious about each other?"

They went out the door of the restaurant into a mild damp evening. Along the street was a row of uniformed and disciplined linden trees.

"As a matter of fact," Paul Lowe said, "I believe they're engaged to be married."

Eleanor held his arm tightly.

"Isn't that nice?" she said.

13

He had been flying almost two hours, with no destination, wheeling and turning in darkening air. The instrument panel lights glowed dully. As the plane banked the rich red glow of a dying sun invaded the cockpit.

The sensation of being suspended in space had not brought its accustomed release. He felt like a sightseer at the Foucault Pendulum, with the proof of the movement of the earth before him, but without a corresponding sensation in his own body.

I have not been able to stop thinking about her.

In twilight the buildings marched to Arlington and Fairfax on one side of the Potomac and to Montgomery and Prince George on the other side. His view encompassed the Washington Monument, stately pillar, the floodlit National Archives Building, and the marble palace of the Supreme Court. Then the white-domed Capitol—pure and white and shapely as a woman's breast.

When I saw you again, something I thought had been sleeping awoke; it began the struggle to escape.

In purpling light the wide panorama below him was a land emerging from colored mist. Yellow lights ran in straight avenue lines then were broken and scattered and became wandering pinpoints in the dark. In moveless woe, Abraham Lincoln sat enshrined amid the words of the Second Inaugural while below skaters glided past on the frozen Reflecting Pool and admirers mounted the steps to his shrine.

Tossing all the night hours in blind fear, I watched the shape of what I most dreaded, most desired.

In Washington April is the cruelest month. The shad run in the Georgetown Canal and the herring in the Potomac, and the willows along the river turn tufty green.

Turn and turn says the golden pointer, yet remain stable, permanently established on the brink of something. What? In equilibrium there should be rest.

Sunlight shone in her face when she smiled. In the shadows of a dress bare skin waited with heavy heat.

Paul Lowe in his leather flying jacket narrowed his eyes and cleared his throat, aware of the danger, the pervasiveness of desire. Think of something else.

What else? What else? Drown thought in amniotic fluid. Women are the devil's enticements. When the stick is in the bag a woman gives it life or lets it die.

With a shuddering groan the last saving thought slipped away. He could not maintain the isolation of his other-thinking. His mind had become a battleground of turbulent and consuming emotion—no, his mind was still, vanquished, while emotions cast brilliant destroying images upon it.

He called Approach Control and told them he would be landing. Dulles Airport appeared, a giant yellow hammock of light slung against blue dark night. The control tower hovered—a black temple on a stout pillar of orange flame. Its radar eyes swept the runways and the skies sixty times a minute.

He passed the tower on the approach and saw the concealed lights below—the mere mechanism creating a poet's vision. Then the plane came down on the runway and the small shock of running wheels was beneath him. No pause, only the racing and racing. The plane slowed and stopped, but his own inward momentum continued. The drive to go was greater than his fear.

In the airport he found an empty phone booth. The dial slipped noiselessly back and forth beneath his finger.

"Hello."

"Katherine? This is Paul Lowe."

Her reply did not come immediately. Then: "What a lovely surprise. Where are you?"

Not why did he call, but *where are you?* In deviant questions answers are concealed.

"At Dulles Airport. I just landed a few minutes ago and was thinking about something you told me at the restaurant last night. I'd like to talk to you."

"Now?"

"I'm free now."

"All right. Come on up."

"I'll be there in twenty minutes."

After he hung up he held the receiver for support, for maintained contact. At the moment he dialed her number he had not known what he would say. Repeating the conversation in his mind he was aware how transparent the excuse seemed. The palm of his hand came away from the receiver with deliberation, leaving a small moisture patch on gray metal. He wondered whether to call Eleanor. Better not. Then she would know he had landed and expect him home.

Outside Katherine Prescott's apartment he pushed the doorbell and heard a musical clang in the apartment. He faced the door, measuring the waiting period by the strokes of his heart. He rubbed his fingers against his palms.

182

She seemed an unbearably long time answering. Then the door opened partly. She was in dusky light.

The door swung wider. "Won't you come in? Don't mind what the apartment looks like. I did everything I could to make it presentable in twenty minutes."

She had not succeeded. Beyond the tiny foyer a vacuum cleaner leaned against a wall and a newspaper was open with the sections nearly covering the top of a table; lamplight near the sofa betrayed crumpled pillows and an ashtray littered with ashes and cigarette butts.

As he entered the living room, with a quick motion she snatched something from a chair. He had a blurred impression that it was a limp beige stocking.

Katherine wore a full-length green housecoat that was decorously provocative, almost reaching to the floor and buttoning high up to her neck, but clinging to every movement of her body. When she walked the hem lifted to show feet bare in sandals.

She made a short nervous gesture at the room. "I warned you about my housekeeping. When I'm not expecting visitors, I let everything go to pot. I really think if no one came for a month they'd finally have to dig me out of the debris."

"I don't mind at all," he said. At home he set rather exacting standards, but her sloppiness seemed part of her, and therefore exciting. Did he connote it with sexual behavior? An interesting vulgar concept.

She lit a fresh cigarette and shook flame out of a match. Searching for a place to put it down, she saw the ashtray on the sofa and groaned as she dropped the match into it.

"Well, now you know the worst. When I'm alone I'm a stationary object. I move everything I need around me so I don't have to move. I just took a bowl of fruit out of the kitchen. Would you like some?"

"No, thanks."

"How about coffee? I can make it fresh or warm up what I have from dinner. Have you had dinner?"

"No—but I'm not hungry."

"I'll confess all. Cold roast beef—ordered up from the delicatessen. If that interests you, it's yours."

"I really have no appetite."

"I'll put it out. Then it'll be there if you want it."

"Part of your not moving theory?"

She smiled. She was not offended. "I can't help it. I try to make up for it by being competent in other things. Or so I tell myself."

He waited for her in the living room on the sofa. The crumpled pillow must have been where her head lay under the lamplight. He found a book half under the sofa: *Is He Popenjoy?* by Anthony Trollope.

She came in with a small metal tray bearing two cups of coffee and a plate of rare roast beef slices with some English water biscuits and a quartered apple.

Paul Lowe showed her the book. "Why are you reading Trollope?"

"Haven't you?"

"Never."

"You should. Dickens without incident. But without caricature too. I've read it before. And I can't put it down now that I've started again."

"I didn't know you were such a literary girl."

"I'm catching up on my education. I had only two years of college before I quit to become a journalist. Or that's what I intended to become. What did the city editor say?—'You'll never become a writer so stop trying'—to Hemingway and Ring Lardner. I think it was Hemingway and Lardner."

"What did he say to you?" He was hanging on as her conversation went careening around sharp turns.

"He said, I need a secretary who can type eighty words a minute, take steno and work twelve hours a day. I said, I'll take it. I could type forty words a minute and I didn't know steno from hieroglyphic. But I could write a better letter than he could. When I brought correspondence typed back to him he was glad he had said what he meant so clearly. Never questioned it. Man's ego is a dark and wondrous thing. Easily flattered, though, and easily domesticated if you use the proper bait."

"What is proper bait?"

"Isn't there some sort of statute against self-incrimination, Mr. Justice?"

"My name is Paul, remember?"

"Well, isn't there?"

"Yes. Loosely called the Fifth Amendment."

"You're making fun of me." She gestured toward the tray. "Have something to eat, will you? I get nervous when men aren't eating. It's a woman's first line of defense."

She wore no makeup but her dark beauty needed no artificial aid. A vivacity seemed to whir in her. He was intrigued by her frank acceptance of a potential danger in being alone with him. "A woman's first line of defense." Did she know why he had come?

He began nibbling at the roast beef, dividing a slice with knife and fork and munching at it.

"It's good," he announced.

"Thank heaven for delicatessens. Or I'd starve to death between dinner dates."

"Don't you cook?"

"Marvelously. But for the most part I eat in restaurants or order from delicatessens and pizza parlors. It really doesn't pay for a girl who lives alone to cook."

"Then a girl shouldn't live alone."

"I don't usually. And I do cook for Timmy when I'm home."

"Oh, yes, your son." He had forgotten the boy. Despite her general incapacity as housekeeper, it did not seem incongruous that she should be a good mother. There was warmth and gentleness in her, combined with intelligence and a high level of intuitive understanding that would enable her to communicate with a child. Most important, there were no rough neurotic edges to her personality that would have to be rubbed smooth by friction with someone dependent on her. "Where is Timmy?"

"At school back home. I expect he'll be here for the Easter holiday. I can't wait to see him. I never seem to see enough of him."

"Why don't you?"

She made a rueful face. "Work, for one thing. Race Hardman liked that series so much he gave me another assignment. The Making of a Decision. He wants me to write up the factors and personalities behind the Court's decision on the North Platte River. I suppose he thinks talking to you has made me some sort of expert on the Supreme Court."

Paul Lowe laughed. "I expect to become an expert myself—in ten or twenty years."

"Do you think it really takes that long?"

"At least."

"But why should it? Oh, I know it requires a knowledge of the law, but outside of that what's needed but a fairly good idea of right and wrong?"

"That's all that is needed. But finding what is right or wrong is probably the most difficult job in science or philosophy—or law."

"It can't be all that difficult. I know what's right and what's wrong— at least in most cases."

"What's your method of finding it out?"

"I just know, that's all."

"What you have just made is a personal ethical statement which is emotive and hortatory rather than cognitive."

"I have?"

"And of course what is required for judgment is a method which will be valid and accepted by nearly everyone for testing whether a theory— or a law—specifying determinate good values can be shown to be right or wrong, true or false. We need to provide legal means to resolve the inescapably ideological problems of our time. It is with these matters that the Supreme Court is supposed to be concerned."

"Oh, dear," she said, "it may take you ten or twenty years just to learn how to put the problem in plain English."

"Now you see what I'm up against," Paul Lowe said complacently.

"You poor man. Try to eat a little something. You'll need your strength to do all that fuzzy thinking."

He finished the last of the roast beef and holding a quarter slice of vampire-pale apple took smiling bites of it. She came to the sofa to sit near him.

"Something you wanted to talk to me about," she said. "What is it?"

The hypocrisy he was capable of had to be on his own initiative and without challenge. He could rarely lie in response to a direct question.

"It doesn't seem important now."

"Oh." She waited, with her hands in her lap.

"You must know why I really came," he said.

She said quietly, "Last time was a mistake. We both knew it."

"I haven't been able to get you out of my mind. When I saw you last night with Tom Jeffreys . . ."

"Please," she said. "Please." She looked away quickly.

"It's true. There's no use denying it if it's true. I'd cheerfully have killed him."

The extravagance of that made her smile. "Poor Tom. Do you know why we were having dinner last night?"

"No."

"We were calling off our engagement."

There was no controlling his delight. "Really?"

"It's been off again on again and finally I made up my mind it wasn't fair to keep him on a string like that. I'm not in love with him and, though I've tried, I never will be. I don't seem to have any talent for falling in love with the kind of man who's right for me."

"What kind is that?"

She looked at him and remained fixed, except that her hands moved, unsure and groping. He took her hand; their fingers met like twining bodies.

"Oh, God," she said, "I wish I had sense."

He moved beside her and from the first kiss it was as though a switch had been turned on and deep controlling currents poured simultaneously through them, moving them in ways over which they had little or no control. She made no attempt to resist or to hold back. Her warmth excited him. His hands touched parts of her body like separate places on a high tension wire, receiving powerful jolts that inflamed and over-whelmed. He was shaken, a spasm wrapped convulsively around his bowels. Soon her excitement more than matched his.

She turned and in half secrecy unhooked the catch of her housecoat, revealing the long vertical meshed line of zipper. He pulled the metal tab down and green material folded away to reveal her bare back and the knuckly path of spinal cord. Her skin was white and smoothly molded. He slid his hands wonderingly up her back. Her arms close to her sides shielded her until the coat lay about her hips like the folded raiment of a Grecian goddess. He turned her slowly toward him—she was tremulous, shyly bold—and her breasts, slightly pink, full and pendulous, stirred against his chest. He moved her back until she was lying on the sofa with only her thighs turned so her feet touched the floor. He kissed her lips, her cheeks, down over her bare shoulders until he lay his fevered cheek against the swelling bosom. Richness overpowered him. His face lay upon a cleft of bosom surrounded by soft flesh like white talcum or deep deep yielding snow against his temples. He was gently sinking in a mysterious and supple bed, lying at full length while weightless sinking enveloped his body. His hands traced out the inward curving of narrow waist, hips, the full spongy outcurve of buttocks. She was wearing nothing beneath the housecoat.

Her voice was small and dry. "Wait."

He sat up flushed and unsure. She went to pull down the window

186

blinds, turn out the lamp. In the darkness her robe fell. She put her hand in his as he guided her to the sofa. He touched breasts tipped with desire. She lost her self-possession and the swift indecent modesty of her response was a surprise and a revelation. They were caught in a rhythm of turbulence that mounted with every gesture, sigh, touch. Her body was slippery with a slight warm moisture. The hollow of her back arched, thighs whispered, wriggling, and the crest of his erection grazed her belly. Her arms suddenly clenched him. "Do it," she breathed. He felt their full coming together as he plunged into her. He closed his eyes and was bathed in formless motionless translucent liquid, held like a floating specimen in a jar, and with a painful confused climbing effort he rode her until his breath came sharp and tight and parched in his throat and his whole strength could not contain himself and still he rode her until her sobbing breath caught and became a choked wail then he let himself go with a wild raving sundering release that drove her panting and cursing with exaltation before the crisis passed and all was descending, shuddering down into the final wheeze and sough of exhausted love.

She lay on the couch, the green housecoat draped over her middle and her head resting on a pillow, smoking a cigarette with focal intensity. Her eyes were narrow. She lay without moving while he dressed quietly. He was adjusting his tie before the mirror when she said:

"Do you have to go now?"

"I'm afraid so."

She sat up, holding the housecoat to her body while with one naked arm she reached out to stub out her cigarette. "No complaints. I knew exactly what I was getting into."

She ground the cigarette out with more than needed vigor.

"Katherine, I'm sorry."

"Of course you're not sorry. Neither am I. It's just that one part of myself hates another part. It doesn't change anything. But it gives satisfaction to my diminishing better self."

He went over to sit beside her. He lifted her hand and brought it to his lips. "Both your schizoid selves suit me fine."

She smiled. "You don't have to continue making love to me. That's all over—for the time being. Now we both need time to figure out how much damage this will do to our lives if we let it continue."

"I don't think we can stop it. Or at least I can't."

"I appreciate your saying that, darling, but we are going to have to be practical. This may be the very last chance we have to attempt anything even remotely practical. We ought to take it before everything whirls away."

She slipped one arm and then the other into her housecoat and drew it on. He bent over and tried to kiss her but she moved away slightly.

"I should begin by saying, right off, that there is every danger I am going to fall in love with you—if I haven't already," she said. "Women are like that—unable to make any worthwhile distinction between passion and love."

"Isn't it a bit too early to start drawing up a balance sheet?" He leaned over to kiss her bare back before she found the zipper and worked it up.

"It's more than likely too late," she said. "I probably should have warned you. In addition to all my other failings I am also incurably sentimental—particularly about men who mean anything to me."

"How many have there been?" He kept a jesting tone but he was in earnest.

"I'm not going to tell you. Not yet. There haven't been as many as you probably think. I don't make a great unnatural fuss about sex but I do make a condition that keeps me relatively chaste. I have to like the man—enormously—before anything happens. I can't imagine anything more horrible than going to bed with someone who doesn't really interest me. For me, lovemaking is too intimate a function to share with comparative strangers."

"You're all through adventuring. From now on it's me."

She took his head in her hands and kissed him.

"You mustn't become possessive," she said. "I very quickly become very dependent. That's my need—someone to look after me. You don't want me to get a fix on you too soon, do you?"

"Yes," he said.

As he turned the key in the lock, high heels clicked rapidly across the flooring. He opened the door and Eleanor met him.

"Paul, I've been trying to get in touch with you. Where have you been?"

"What's the matter? I'm not that late, am I?"

"It's after ten. I didn't know what to do. I even called the airport. They said you brought the plane back before seven."

"I met a couple of fellows and we had dinner and a drink together. I told you not to expect me any definite time. What is this all about anyhow?" Guilt made him touchy.

"It's Nancy. Arthur called a while ago. He sounded half out of his mind." Her voice broke. "She's in the hospital."

"Nancy? What's wrong?"

"A near miscarriage. Nancy's all right. They're trying to save the baby. Arthur wanted to talk to you."

"Shall I call him?" Paul Lowe had his coat off and was in the living room. He noticed a suitcase standing near the door. "What's this?"

"I told Arthur I'm leaving right away for Boston. Nancy needs me, and I have to go. But I couldn't leave without seeing you."

He was having difficulty taking it all in quickly, sorting out impressions. Nancy and Arthur. A miscarriage. There was almost no danger in a hospital with proper medical care. How would this affect things between Nancy and Arthur? If the baby were lost, that is. Then one thought forced itself upon him with more energy: if Eleanor is out of town I will have time to spend with Katherine. The idea of being with her again was luxurious.

188

The more he examined the content of his own mind at particular moments, the more it appalled him. He wondered if other men were better than he, or merely disguised their true motives, clothing their actions in necessity or virtue.

"Are you leaving right now?" he asked.

"I thought I would. If you could drive me to the airport."

Only then did he experience a feeling of responsibility shirked.

"Wouldn't you like me to come with you?"

She was so pleased, she had obviously been hoping he would make the offer. "Paul, would you? It's you Arthur wants to talk to—and Nancy needs you."

"Of course I'll come."

"How about your work? That's so important. Nothing must interfere with it."

"Tomorrow's Sunday. I'll take my work along with me, and I can be back in Court Monday morning."

They moved down the hospital corridor past a starched nurse, crossed a connecting passageway to another corridor. Arthur came toward them. He wore a wrinkled brown suit, and his shirt collar was open. In the bright unsparing light it was clear he needed a shave.

He came to them, blinking nervously.

"Thank goodness you're here." He shook hands with Paul Lowe and hugged Eleanor briefly.

"How is she?"

"For the moment all right. The next twenty-four hours, they say, will tell whether she keeps the baby." Arthur's eyes were rimmed with red.

"It's going to be all right. You'll see," Eleanor said, touching his arm.

He smiled at her gratefully.

"You ought to get some rest," Paul Lowe said. "Is she having visitors?"

"They don't want her to. But she refused to sleep unless Tessie stayed in the room with her."

"Tessie?" Paul Lowe said.

"That friend of Nancy's I told you about. Tessie Samuels."

"Can we see Nancy now?"

"Not now. She's asleep."

"What's the last time you slept?"

"I don't know." Arthur's thick curling brown hair stuck out untidily. "They say this started at three o'clock yesterday afternoon. I didn't hear about it until last night. I got here as quickly as I could."

"And you've been here since?"

Arthur nodded. "I talked to the doctor this morning. He said it's a good thing they got her to a hospital quickly. If there'd been any delay she wouldn't have had a chance. She was nearly unconscious when she arrived. She's already had a transfusion."

"Can I talk to the doctor?"

"He isn't here now. He'll be back in the morning."

"Is there any danger?"

"Not to her. Not any more. But the baby . . . touch and go." Arthur smothered his feeling with indignation: "That Tessie Samuels shouldn't be with her. Nancy needs rest."

"How did Tessie Samuels get involved?"

"She came with Nancy to the hospital. Nancy's been staying in her apartment. They're thick as thieves."

"It's probably just as well there was someone around when the hemorrhaging started."

"Don't ask me to be grateful to Tessie. She doesn't like me and the feeling is mutual. She's behind a lot of the trouble Nancy and I have been having."

Eleanor touched Arthur's arm. "I know what you've been going through, Arthur. You've been wonderful. When Nancy is well again she'll appreciate everything you've done."

Arthur shook his head. "She blames it all on me. She wouldn't be going through this if it weren't for the baby. If I'd let her do what she wanted . . . But I wanted my child, that's all." Arthur was close to tears. "Now it looks as if I may lose that too."

"Have you eaten anything?" Eleanor asked solicitously.

"Coffee."

"Is that all?"

"I guess so."

Eleanor gave Paul Lowe a signal.

"Let's have something to eat," he said. "There must be a coffee shop near a hospital. What room is Nancy in?"

"Five seventeen."

"I'll sneak past and take a look at her first," Paul Lowe said.

Arthur led the way down the corridor, past the nurses' alcove to a door partly open on the right. A wall plaque testified that the room had been donated to the hospital by one of the Kennedy family.

Paul Lowe slowly pushed the door wider. There was no sound. The room was almost completely dark, with blinds drawn and curtains over the windows. Someone was seated in a chair in the corner—a woman, her legs reflected the illumination from the hall. The hem of her skirt barely covered her knees and her rather thick legs ended in zippered boots.

As Paul Lowe's eyes adjusted to the darkness, he saw a misty white shape near the high bed on the right. A moment later the nurse came toward him with her finger at her lips. She motioned him outside and closed the door behind them.

"She's asleep," the nurse said.

"I'm her father. How is she?"

"The hemorrhaging has stopped. They've given her drugs and she's under sedation. She's been fighting sleep but I think she's good for the night now."

"When can I see her?"

"Not until the doctor comes in the morning. I'd say about half past eight."

"Isn't there someone in the room now?"

"Miss Samuels. Your daughter insisted that she be allowed to stay. The doctor consented to it only because he didn't want to upset her. She's still quite weak."

"Is Miss Samuels staying all night?"

"I think so. Yes." The nurse shrugged as though to say there was nothing she could do about that.

"May I look in?" Eleanor asked.

"If you want to, just for a moment. You mustn't risk waking her."

Eleanor went to the door, glanced in quickly and backed out, leaving the door half open. Paul Lowe reached for the knob to pull the door closer shut. In the room the woman was resting her head against her hand with her elbow on the chair arm. Now she slightly changed position and for an instant looked directly at him. Her eyes were unnaturally pale and seemed to generate their own light in the darkness. He had a distinct impression of real malevolence in that unblinking stare out of gloom.

The door closed her from view.

"I'll be here in the morning," he told the nurse.

They were seated in a chromium-edged booth in a small coffee shop. At the nearby counter were truck drivers, men in lumberjackets and work pants, a policeman with the collar of his uniform open, a drawn and tired-looking woman who slumped spiritlessly on her stool and drank coffee from a cup she held in both hands.

The waitress brought coffee before taking their order. Arthur sipped the coffee and munched dutifully on a hard roll. He had no will to recover lost strength. His weariness went too deep—an ague of the skeleton, a wearing out of the soul's marrow.

"It's funny," he was saying in a low tone, "but I remember saying that if I had to choose between Nancy and the baby I wouldn't hesitate. I had that choice last night—or thought I did. And it's true. I'd have chosen Nancy. I didn't even think about the baby until Nancy was out of danger."

"I know you love her," Eleanor said. "I'm sure she loves you, Arthur. Nancy's a high-strung girl. This is just a phase she's going through."

"I didn't want my child to die. I didn't want Nancy to kill our baby. Is that so terrible? Why doesn't she want our child? That isn't natural for a woman, is it—not to want to have a child?"

"When the baby is born, things will be different," Eleanor said. "Lots of women think they don't want a child and then, when they're holding a baby in their arms . . . well, it's all different."

"Tessie Samuels," Arthur said bitterly. "She's the one who poisons Nancy's mind against me. But Nancy won't listen to a word against her. She doesn't care any more how I feel. My feelings don't count. It's only her and Tessie." Arthur's voice rose. "I love her! Doesn't that count for *anything?*"

At half past eight in the morning Paul Lowe and Eleanor were waiting in the corridor of the hospital. The doctor, a moonfaced man carrying the black satchel of his trade, emerged from Room 517.

Paul Lowe walked over and intercepted him before he reached the elevator.

"I'm Nancy Montgomery's father. How is she, Doctor?"

"Coming along fine," the doctor said. "Completely out of danger."

"And the baby?"

"The baby's going to stick around and be born on schedule." The doctor smiled. "By the way, sir, aren't you our new Supreme Court justice?"

"Yes."

"A pleasure to meet you." The doctor shook hands. "But I have to tell you I don't approve of what some of you fellows are doing down there. This country's gotten along all right so far. It doesn't need too much tinkering with."

"I'll try to bear that in mind," Paul Lowe said, smiling.

When he and Eleanor entered the hospital room, Nancy was sitting up in bed. She was very pale. Her long blonde hair hung down loosely to bare shoulders in a white nightgown. Eleanor crossed to her bed and hugged her while Nancy kept an arm about her mother's shoulder. She smiled at her father and indicated the woman sitting in a chair nearby.

"Dad, I'd like you to meet a friend of mine."

Eleanor broke off her embrace and stood up.

"Mother, this is Tessie Samuels."

"How do you do," Eleanor said, blinking her eyes.

Tessie Samuels was a short, plump darkhaired woman with definite straight black eyebrows and a ruddy complexion. She used no makeup. Her dark hair was cut short and drawn away from her ears. She wore a gray tweed suit with a tailored white blouse and the suede zippered boots Paul Lowe had noticed the night before.

She turned forthrightly to Paul Lowe after greeting Eleanor.

"I'm one of your admirers, Mr. Justice," she said. Her voice was husky and soft but her hand had a firm cool grip.

"I'm surprised we haven't met before. I understand you're a good friend of Nancy's."

Nancy said, "I hope you haven't gotten your information from Arthur, Dad. He's paranoiac on the subject of Tessie. A case of instant and mutual dislike."

"I'm sorry to hear that," Paul Lowe said.

"By the way, where is my darling husband?" Nancy inquired.

"Downstairs. He wasn't sure you wanted to see him."

Nancy said dryly, "Such sensitivity. I'm surprised. I thought he'd try to visit here with you, hoping I wouldn't make a scene in front of my own dear parents." She glanced at Tessie, smiling, and Tessie returned a brief twisted smile.

Paul Lowe said, "He's been deeply concerned about you, Nancy."

"Oh, Dad, I'm not up to a moral lecture this morning."

"I don't see how you can be so cruel to your own husband," Eleanor said.

"You might consider, Mother, that I wouldn't almost have died—if not for him. It's his baby that's striking back—probably trying to kill me because I wanted to do the same thing to it."

Eleanor said reproachfully, "Arthur hasn't slept at all since they brought you here. You ought to see how he looks. No matter how bitter you might think you are, you couldn't help feeling sorry for him."

"I can imagine how he's carrying on. Arthur is the strong silent type who never found out how much healthier it is to fight than suffer." The idea amused her cruelly. Briefly, a flash of dark exasperation succeeded it. "God, I don't know how I lived with that man as long as I did! I just wouldn't admit to myself how bad things were."

Paul Lowe said, "You might at least let him see you. I think he's entitled to that."

"Arthur? He isn't entitled to anything, except a divorce. I'm going to give him that as quickly as I can."

He felt himself grow stiff with resentment but tried to avoid showing it. "It might be better to discuss this privately, Nancy."

"I can't see why it would be."

"We don't have to parade all our problems in front of other people."

"Tessie?" Nancy asked incredulously. "She knows a lot more about me than either of you do. More about Arthur too."

"I'm sure Miss Samuels is a good friend," Paul Lowe said.

Nancy's throat worked in the convulsive swallowing movement that betrayed her stress. "I didn't ask you or Mother to come here."

Eleanor made an unconscious straightening-out motion with the bed-covers. "You mustn't excite yourself, dear. That's bad for you."

"Why don't you both go away and leave me alone? In fact, why don't both of you mind your own goddamn business?"

Tessie Samuels said sharply, "Nancy!"

Nancy might have been struck in the face. As she looked at Tessie her slight flush faded to marble whiteness.

"Your mother's right, dear," Tessie said calmly. "Too much excitement *is* bad for you."

Nancy drew the bedcovers up to her shoulders. She lay back and closed her eyes. "I want them to go away."

Tessie Samuels turned to Paul Lowe and Eleanor. "Perhaps you should go. She does need rest. The doctor did say she must have absolute quiet."

Eleanor said indignantly, "We don't need to be told what to do. Nancy is our daughter."

Nancy screamed, "Mother, will you get the hell out? Will you? *Will* you?"

Nancy was sitting bolt-upright in bed, her mouth open and distorted with rage and her blonde hair atumble across one cheek.

Eleanor physically winced from the violent outburst. She grew rigid.

"All right," Paul Lowe said quietly. "If that's what you want, Nancy, we'll go."

Tessie Samuels rose and walked to the door of the room with them. She said, "I'm sure it'll be better in a few days. Nancy isn't herself. She's under sedation, you know. It's been very difficult for her."

Paul Lowe said, "I appreciate what you're doing for her, Miss Samuels. She needs someone with her. Let us know if there's anything Nancy needs, won't you?"

"Of course," Tessie Samuels answered.

Outside, as the door closed behind them, Eleanor gave him a questioning, betrayed look.

"How could you talk to that woman the way you did?"

"There was nothing to be gained by talking any other way. Besides, she's right. We had to leave. Nancy was working herself into a real hysteria."

Eleanor began to whimper. "She doesn't care about us any more. She cares more about that woman than us."

He thought: Can we prevail by citing the dubious privilege of parenthood? That would invite repayment in the hard coin of humiliation. Far better to accept defeat graciously. There would be compensations. Eleanor could dwell on the many sacrifices over the years, remember selfless love, mourn the undeserved rejection of one who gave all, asked nothing. She would learn the piercing sweet joys of martyrdom—which, after the first payment is made, are more stable and cost less than any other comparable pleasures.

As they went down the hospital corridor he gave Eleanor a handkerchief to wipe her eyes.

Arthur seemed to shrink a little when he heard the news.

"I don't understand why she's so angry with me," he said and shook his head slightly. "I don't understand it. But I'll do what she wants. I won't try to see her."

"We're leaving for the airport now," Paul Lowe said. "Do you want to come with us?"

"I'm going to stay right here at the hospital until it's definite about the baby being all right. I'll have a talk with the doctor this evening. If he says it's safe to go, then I'll leave."

"Call us if there's any news," Paul Lowe said. "As a matter of fact, call anyhow. I'd like to talk to you."

"Meanwhile get a little sleep," Eleanor said. "You can't keep going like this."

In the taxi on the way to the airport Eleanor had a prolonged bout of the sniffles. Her nose became red and she used up his handkerchief and resorted to stray crumpled wads of Kleenex which wore red smudges of lipstick.

He kept his arm about her, and her cheek rubbed makeup onto his coat lapel.

194

Perhaps he should weep, too, as Eleanor undoubtedly wanted him to do. The weather was right for it. A brown grimy day. Boston weather.

In the airport, when he returned with the purchased tickets, he told Eleanor, "We've got about thirty minutes before takeoff."

Definite information revivified her.

"I'd like to go to the ladies' room and make myself presentable."

"I'll meet you at gate two," he said.

He watched her go off to repair the damage to her appearance. When she was out of sight he stood in the blaring glare of the terminal while crowds jostled him on their way to everywhere. He was uncertain but impelled.

Finally he went to the bank of telephone booths. After dialing the number he waited with impatience. The phone rang twice, three times.

He was reluctantly about to replace the phone when he heard the receiver at the other end being lifted. Anticipatory delight ran through his veins.

"Hello."

"This is Paul. I didn't think you were in."

How wonderful the way her voice lifted. "Paul! It's so nice to hear from you."

"I'm in Boston, at the airport. I'll be flying back shortly. I should be in just after noon."

"I've missed you terribly."

He had to shun the power of memory—dragging so many unwanted things with it, summoning all of her to his mind. He had possession only of her voice.

"I think I may be able to see you this afternoon. Have you anything to do?"

"I was trying to clean my apartment. I had a terrible guilt after you left me. That's what I was doing when you called—washing dishes, so I didn't hear the phone. That's what I was going to do, try to clean up some of the mess."

"Can you leave it for tomorrow?"

"If *you* don't mind."

"I won't see anything but you. I shouldn't say this but I'm afraid you've got me in terrible shape."

"I'm glad," she said in a thrilling low tone. "Yes—*yes*—do come!"

"I'll see you about one o'clock," he said.

14

Paul Lowe glanced at the box reserved for friends and relatives of the justices. Eleanor was seated primly erect amid the early arrivals. Mrs. Gabriel Hart was there, and Mrs. Henry Merriam. As he watched, Mrs. John Hampton arrived and spoke a few polite words to each of the others. These three wives were the regular visitors; Eleanor came only occasionally. In the past few weeks, though, she had been showing up more often— probably a direct consequence of the fact that she was seeing less of him in the evenings, a reflex of possessiveness in which she established her right to a certain number of hours in his day. . . . Eleanor was lonely and missed him. There was no reason to question her love for him. She loved him in the thoughtless way in which one embraces the inevitable.

Today she was wearing the new flowered hat she had bought for Easter. Last Sunday had been a happy day for her. She had worn a new outfit in a pale gray-blue shade and they had gone to church together in the morning. New outfit, old religion. Something new, something old, her suit was blue—and what was borrowed was himself. He had been hers for the day, and even then only in physical presence. His attention was centered elsewhere—with Katherine. He no longer felt guilty or ashamed of it. What had happened to him was a simple and overpowering discovery, that for people in love there is no way of telling right from wrong. Objective judgments are made by others; for lovers there is no standard except the depth of their feelings. There is no need for them to ask; all answers exist in them.

That did not exclude a kind of affection for Eleanor. He was fond of her and wanted her to be happy—or at least to remain unscathed. He did not know how she could escape involvement or eventual injury but if there was a way to arrange that he would do it. Yet he knew the days ahead carried many ambushes and at one place or another along the way she would become an innocent victim. The only alternative was a future without Katherine, and that was unthinkable.

He slumped lower in his chair to await the completion of the admissions to the bar.

The ordeal was by now, the first week of May, numbingly familiar. Each attorney stepped forward, his sponsor spoke for him, the Chief

196

Justice greeted the applicant by name and welcomed him to practice before the Supreme Court.

In the courtroom, silence fell. The admissions ceremony was completed. Chief Justice Hampton nodded to Mr. Justice Branch, who then began to read his opinion in the Chapter Ten Bankruptcy case. After the first few sentences Paul Lowe was hardly listening. He knew what the opinion contained and the Court had been unanimous in support of it.

Beside him, Edward McCann was making notes, scribbling away in the concentrated glare of the tiny reading lamp before him. Paul Lowe glanced over the visitors' section and caught Eleanor's eye. She smiled. At this distance she seemed young and pretty and he could see the resemblance to Nancy. *Nancy.* A vaporized discontent suffused the air about him. His daughter Nancy had left the hospital two weeks ago with the child secure in her womb and no longer any pretense of a marriage. Arthur telephoned the day she left. She had not told him where she was going, but Arthur was certain she had moved in with Tessie Samuels. Arthur sounded very solemn and very defeated. Paul Lowe advised him against trying to see Nancy right away. He said, let her have a while to think things out and she may come back. He did not believe it and probably Arthur didn't either.

Chief Justice Hampton was now looking down the bench toward him. Hampton nodded. Paul Lowe gathered printed sheets on the counter before him.

"I have for announcement," he said clearly, "the opinion and judgment of the Court, in number 192, J and B Corporation versus the United States."

He began reading the facts of the case. J and B Corporation held a patent on a machine that prepared fruit for juice in one continuous operation untouched by human hands. It was an ingenious device that worked equally well for all kinds of fruit—stemming, splitting, peeling, and coring as needed. J and B Corporation wanted to acquire new patents on each one of the separate processes. It wanted these patents in order to prevent rival concerns from making cheaper variations of their machine. With certain kinds of fruit all the functions were not necessary—it is necessary to peel but not to core a banana—and obviously a cheaper machine could be made that did not perform all the functions of the J and B patented device. To allow such a cheaper machine to be made by rivals of the J and B Corporation, argued their counsel, would be an obvious infringement of the original patent.

The United States Patent Office had rejected this argument and refused the J and B Corporation's application for further patents because the corporation did not intend to make the cheaper machines itself but only intended to prevent their manufacture by others. The Patent Office's decision had been upheld by the Court of Customs and Patent Appeals.

The J and B Corporation had then appealed to the Supreme Court from this decision.

Paul Lowe read his opinion carefully; it was short and he did not need to skip words. There was no particular pattern to follow in announcing decisions. Oral pronouncements varied from one justice to the next. Waldo Shuler preferred to speak without consulting either his written opinion or his notes and he would verbally insert lengthy remarks and citations which had been omitted from his writing. Edmunson usually outlined the facts briefly, announced his judgment, and remarked that the written opinion was on file with the Clerk where anyone could read it.

Paul Lowe took a middle position: he read his opinion but when necessary skipped the more intricate sections. After discussing the facts of the present case he moved on to read the decisive section of his opinion:

"Article One, Section Eight, Clause Eight, of the Constitution has been used in support of the plaintiff's position. It is certainly true that this clause guarantees to inventors the exclusive right to their properties. However, before this guarantee is mentioned, a condition is stated. That condition therefore must be our guide. Clause Eight clearly says that the exclusive right of inventors to their properties is granted in order to promote the progress of science and the useful arts. The holder of a patent is therefore not in possession of merely another form of private property. His right of possession exists only to serve a public purpose."

By then the drift of his opinion was unmistakable. Peter Daris, the Solicitor General, seated at the table facing the justices' bench, had finished reading the slip opinion. He sat back and smiled approvingly at Justice Lowe on the bench.

Paul Lowe adjusted his reading glasses to continue: "The fact that the J and B Corporation has no intention of manufacturing the cheaper machines but only wants to prevent their manufacture by others is inconsistent with the requirement that a patent grant must 'promote the progress of science and the useful arts.' The holder of a patent is bound either to use the patent or to allow others to do so on reasonable terms.

"For this Court to allow another course of action might mean that future patents could be used merely to protect existing corporations rather than to encourage new discoveries that will be used for the common good. In this way an entire technology might be blocked off. A patent is not granted for a discovery to be suppressed or withheld, but to be made and used. A patent is a private possession that is held in trust for use in the public welfare.

"Let us suppose that the argument advanced by the J and B Corporation was carried out to its logical conclusion and that a patent should be considered only as a private property which is exclusive and fully protected by constitutional guarantees. If in the future someone discovers a patentable cure for cancer—will he have the right to withhold it? There is no difference in principle if in the case before us we allow patents to be suppressed because of some immediate gain to the patentee. Therefore: the decision of the U. S. Court of Customs and Patent Appeals is affirmed."

Paul Lowe finished reading, removed his glasses, and put them down beside the opinion on the desk counter before him. As he glanced up he found Eleanor's gaze fixed on him. Her evident pride in him made him uncomfortable. He did not deserve it. Her approval became a form of accusation because it judged him to be something more than he was.

He began to count after the first few attempts. Push, hold, relax. Poised above the floor on his arms he would hang suspended, then bend his elbows and lower his body and with his arms close to his body raise himself again. He kept his head down. He wore a white T shirt, gray shorts and sneakers, and a bulky towel wrapped around his neck to encourage perspiration. Push, hold, relax. He counted ten push-ups.

Nearby in the exercise room Gabriel Hart pumped vigorously on the exercycle. He waved to Paul Lowe, while his short hairy muscular legs churned swiftly.

Paul Lowe's chest began to feel warm. On the twelfth push-up his breath grated in his throat. Push, hold, relax. On the fifteenth count he felt the soft jounce of his abdomen. Push, hold, relax. On the nineteenth count he was barely able to lift himself and he came to a stop at twenty.

As he stood up, Gabriel Hart ceased pumping on the exercycle. Apparently he had been in an unadmitted contest, refusing to stop until Paul Lowe stopped.

Gabriel Hart eased himself off the exercycle with a sigh of relief.

"Trying to get back into condition. Just about this time each year I start going to pieces. I'm planning to do some surfcasting over the weekend."

"When are you leaving?" Paul Lowe asked.

"I thought I'd sneak away right after Friday's conference. I'm pretty well caught up on my work."

Paul Lowe wiped his forehead with the end of his towel. "Better not let the *Harvard Law Review* find out. They're always telling us how overworked we are."

Gabriel grinned. "It's a grind, but there are worse jobs. Being a United States Senator is one of them."

Gabriel Hart had been Senator from New Hampshire before his elevation to the Supreme Court, and at one time had also been a president of the American Bar Association. In most conversations he found an opportunity to mention the fact.

"Didn't you like being a Senator, Gabriel?"

"The pressures were too much. So much going on that there was hardly time to think. And you always have to worry about pleasing your constituents. Always some local fireman or other coming to visit and expecting red-carpet treatment. And every few months you have to go home and cultivate the voters. Explain to them why you voted for such and such a bill. Of course they never understand why anyhow. Their mental horizons are one hundred and twenty-five feet by eighty—the size of their home lots. Try to get them to understand why you have to vote for increased taxes to pay for a war in Southeast Asia. It just never seems important to them."

"I imagine a lot of the decisions we make on the Court don't seem very important either."

Gabriel Hart's countenance wrinkled like a prune. "But we don't have to worry about the voters. That's the difference. Our jobs are for life. They can't turn us out after six years because they don't like the way we comb our hair."

A scanty fringe of brown covered Gabriel Hart's round bald dome. He was not a prepossessing man and still resented his defeat for re-election by the good-looking young mayor of Portsmouth. Gabriel Hart had been defeated for re-election by the heaviest plurality in the history of the state. "They didn't even have to count the votes," Edward McCann once told Lowe acidulously. "They just weighed 'em."

Paul Lowe said, "Well, the Senate's loss was our gain. You were a fine Senator, Gabriel, but now you're a distinguished justice."

Gabriel Hart flushed with pleasure. "That's a real compliment coming from you, Paul. I admire your ability even though I can't agree with many of your opinions."

"You voted with me on the J and B patent case. Do you know that's the first time I ever carried a unanimous court? It gives me hope that you poor benighted heathens may yet be saved."

"It wasn't an important issue. I went along in the hope it would convince some hidebound members on your side to see our point of view once in a while."

Paul Lowe laughed. "I guess we should be grateful that we get as many unanimous decisions as we do."

Gabriel Hart shook his head testily. "In an important issue these five-to-four decisions are pretty annoying. For example, I frankly don't understand the reasoning of the majority in something like the Cardinale case."

"Edmunson is writing the opinion for the Court. Maybe he can make it clearer to you."

"Waldo Shuler is writing the dissent. I'd like *you* to keep an open mind until you read what he has to say. I have a hunch you'll be impressed. You might even change your mind about the whole problem of what we should do with draft dodgers like George Luis Cardinale."

Paul Lowe said, "I need a shower. I've worked up a sweat."

"Just wait and see, that's all I'm saying. Be flexible. That's the way to realize your full potential as a justice of this Court, Paul. Take my word for it."

"I'm afraid we'll just have to agree to disagree, Gabriel."

Gabriel Hart fell soberly into step with him as they left the exercise room for the adjoining tiled shower room.

On Monday evening Paul Lowe worked late in his office. It was quiet; Martha Scully, Bill Tobin and Jack Broderick had gone home.

Jonathan Carter came to the door. "What time shall I bring the car for you, Mr. Justice?"

200

"Don't bother, Jonathan. I'll be working late again tonight. No sense your waiting for me."

"Good night, Mr. Justice."

"Good night, Jonathan."

When Jonathan Carter had gone, he picked up the telephone and dialed Katherine Prescott's number.

"I can get away for a couple of hours. Shall I come over?"

"Yes. Yes, please."

"I'll be there as soon as I can."

She never seemed to have anything to do that would interfere with his seeing her. Once when he asked her about it she told him, laughing, that she lived the life of a recluse. Of course that wasn't so. Inadvertently he learned the lengths to which she would go in order to see him. She still occasionally dated Tom Jeffreys and he had invited her, a week in advance, to dinner at the Bit and Bridle and later to a concert at which her favorite violinist, Isaac Stern, was to play. When she told Paul Lowe about the invitation, he urged her to accept because there was no possibility of his seeing her that particular evening. Then he forgot about it. On that evening he had a small chore to perform for Eleanor on his way home—to pick up a pair of earrings she had purchased at a jewelry store. Katherine's apartment was only a short distance from the store. He called her to suggest that they might be together for an hour or so. She accepted eagerly. On his way home he suddenly remembered this was the evening of her date with Tom Jeffreys and he had delayed her far past the dinner hour. The next time he saw her he reproached her for not mentioning it and discovered that after his unexpected telephone call she had called Tom Jeffreys and told him she was ill and could not keep their appointment. For a brief meeting with him she had sacrificed her entire evening and treated Tom Jeffreys with unpardonable rudeness. Paul Lowe was flattered and a little disturbed because he realized that in similar circumstances, for a stolen hour of intimacy with Katherine, he would have done exactly the same thing.

In these few weeks he had committed himself beyond the limits of his nature; he had uncovered the heart of his former remoteness. He had found something new that was not lust or a need to conquer, a gentler emotion that beat strongly in his veins. When he held Katherine in his arms he was actually afraid of the power of this new and unaccustomed feeling. When he left her at night he would drive slowly around the block of her apartment building, unwilling to part, frustrated because he was leaving her. He would look up at her lighted window in the hope of catching some glimpse of her. Finally he would drive home with nothing in his mind but a private vision. He and Katherine, married, in the same house together. Her son Timmy was sometimes there, a vague obedient child who came and went as Paul Lowe's vision summoned him. Even in his imaginings he was unwilling to share Katherine's affection. Their marriage was a curiously solitary one—he never pictured them together with friends or at parties. He always saw the two of them alone except for the occasional materializations of that obedient son.

He picked up the telephone and dialed his home number.

Eleanor answered. "Hello."

"Hello, dear. I'm afraid I have to work late again tonight."

"Darling, you mustn't drive yourself this way. You're going to be all worn out."

"It's near the end of the term. There's only a few more weeks and we have to wind up a lot of work."

"When do you think you'll be home?"

"Don't wait for me. It may be close to midnight."

"Be sure to wake me when you do come in."

"I will, dear."

He turned out the light in his office and stood for a moment in the doorway, looking at the now familiar room with its wide desk, fireplace, and the wall lined with books. Then he passed through the silent outer room where Martha Scully and Jonathan Carter were usually stationed. In the building corridor, deserted and shadowed, a square patch of light fell from a door a short distance away.

He walked down the corridor and looked in to Charles Edmunson's office. The central room was empty but the overhead light was shining. He heard a faint stir of movement from Edmunson's office.

From the doorway he saw Edmunson at his desk, the large gray head bowed over the desk. He was writing with a black fountain pen on yellow foolscap paper. He started a new line, stopped, went back to cross it out.

When Edmunson raised his head his gaze was focused inward and a moment passed before he noticed Paul Lowe standing in the doorway.

"Paul." He put down the fountain pen. "I didn't know you were working late tonight."

"I was just leaving. Do you have a minute to talk?"

"Of course."

Paul Lowe crossed into the room and sat down.

"It's the Cardinale case." He told Edmunson of his meeting with Gabriel Hart in the exercise room. "Hart is apparently hoping Waldo Shuler will come up with a strong dissent to win at least one vote away from the majority. It isn't beyond the realm of possibility. We only had a five-to-four majority in the conference. And Waldo will be operating from a position of strength."

Edmunson considered this thoughtfully. "I think I'm fully aware of the necessity of answering Waldo."

"Then I'm not worried. When you're at your best—not even Waldo Shuler can touch you."

Edmunson shook his head a trifle wearily. "I almost wish the Chief hadn't assigned me to write the opinion for the Court."

Paul Lowe gave the old man a puzzled stare. "You're the natural choice. He couldn't have chosen a stronger spokesman for our side."

Without raising his head Edmunson stared at the yellow sheets covered with scrawled lines of ink.

"I might as well tell you, Paul. I've been working on the Cardinale case all week. I'm not at all satisfied with it." His fingers closed crablike on the top sheet and crumpled it. "I may have to tear up everything I've written."

He watched Edmunson drop the sheet into his wastebasket.

"What seems to be wrong?"

"All I've written is a crotchet of legalisms. I can't find a clear line to follow."

"I'm sure it'll come to you."

"The answers don't come to me the way they once did. I've never tried so hard before with so little result." Edmunson clasped his hands before him on the desk blotter. He stared at his twined fingers as though he were studying the convolutions of an argument. "I used to see the line I wanted to follow at a glance. Now I have to unravel it thread by thread. It's all part of getting old, Paul. A part of my mind simply doesn't function as well. And what seems to be going first with me is the integrative power."

"Before you decide you're starting to disintegrate like the one-hoss shay, you might weigh the possibility that you've simply been working too hard."

Edmunson smiled faintly without replying.

Paul Lowe said, "Why not call it a day and tackle the problem of the Cardinale case again in the morning?"

"I can't. I have to prepare a lecture I'm giving at the Columbia Law School tomorrow night."

"You can cancel it."

"I wouldn't like to disappoint them. I'm going up there to disabuse some young minds of the idea that there is any connection between justice and the kind of law they learn in a classroom. I want to tell them that while compassion may be a means, objectivity must be the end. Those young idealists need a healthy dose of skepticism to clean out their insides."

"We need your best thinking on the Cardinale case. You can't give it your best if you spend yourself in too many directions."

Edmunson smiled sadly. "The Cardinale opinion is the last one I'll write this term. I would like it to be a good one, too. I tend to think of any important piece of work I'm doing these days as my valedictory."

"Your valedictory is a long way off."

Edmunson's lips seemed to be speaking from a graven mask. "I'd like to die in harness the way Harlan Stone did—sitting on the bench in the act of reading one of his opinions. A man should not have time to prepare—death should overtake him in the midst of his labors."

"We'd all like that, Charles. But it's more important that the labor we're doing at any given time is the very best we can do. In my judgment, the Cardinale case is one more chance to lay a milestone along the path to a truly democratic society. A society that isn't afraid to allow dissident voices —and has room even for malcontents and misfits. I'd like to see that message put as strongly as I know you can put it."

"I'll do my best, Paul. But I have to keep the engagement at Columbia Law School. Those young men are the best hope we have of keeping the law from ossifying. But they need the courage of their youthful vision. I want to tell them not to believe that the doctrine laid down by the Framers is holy scripture. They can be reverent, but they also have to keep alert to find new meanings in the old sacred words." Edmunson's fingers strayed to the bushy white hair at his temples. "But you're right. I need to let up a little. After that Columbia lecture, I'll give all my attention to writing this opinion."

"Good. It will have to survive careful scrutiny, even on the smallest legal points. Whatever Gabriel Hart's or Andrew Cutler's capacity as justices of the Supreme Court, they are very capable lawyers. And they're going to go over what you write with a very fine-tooth comb."

After a long moment Edmunson nodded. "Right now, I need to get some rest. I haven't been sleeping well. I feel like an old parchment stretched to the bursting point to wrap up a miscellaneous assortment of aches and pains." Edmunson turned off his reading lamp. "Everything seems to be getting harder. But do you know what's hardest of all?"

Edmunson stood up and Paul Lowe helped him into his jacket. The old man moved with arthritic slowness.

"What is?" Paul Lowe asked, not knowing what to expect.

"Trying to accept the loss of friends. I sit and run over the list of names of the ones who have gone, see their faces, remember things they said, fights we had, triumphs or defeats we shared. I can't believe that I won't step out of this office and meet them in the hall. Or pick up a telephone and hear them speak."

Paul Lowe was a little embarrassed by the old man's futile attempt to confer life upon his dear departed. He felt sorry for Edmunson and this emotion was not one he had ever felt for the great man.

He said, "I imagine that is difficult to bear. But it's part of life."

Edmunson said, "It's one reason I won't mind dying. At the end I'll be so surrounded by ghosts that their world will seem at least as real to me as this one."

Edmunson paused in the doorway of his office and looked back uncertainly as though someone were in the room to whom he wished to say goodbye.

"At least as real," he repeated.

Paul Lowe, about to switch off the light in the office, hesitated as Edmunson looked straight at him for the space of several seconds. The dark sag of flesh beneath the old man's eyes was noticeable and the folded skin on his cheeks was purplish red.

Edmunson's hand closed on Paul Lowe's arm with almost painful force. "We have to be sure that what's been accomplished isn't undone. There are important decisions coming before this Court. I want to play my part in deciding them. But I don't know how much longer I can hold on. Help me see it through, Paul."

Paul Lowe snapped off the room light.

"I can't help worrying," he told Katherine later that evening. "He's always been remote—it's a part of his being Olympian. But now the remoteness is a little less overpowering, less omniscient—and more strange."

He sat in a corner of the sofa in her living room. She was seated on the floor at his feet. Her head leaned slightly against the inside of his knee. The warm pressure of her against his leg was pleasant, an echo of the senses.

"Perhaps he's just been working too hard," she said.

"Perhaps. At his age he can't possibly do the same work he did when he was younger."

"If Edmunson is forced to retire, how would it affect you?"

He winced. "I'd be writing more dissents than I am now, for one thing. And probably Waldo Shuler would become the new leader of the Court."

"That isn't necessarily a bad thing, is it?"

"Waldo Shuler simply doesn't think that the Supreme Court has the power to decide a lot of the questions we've been deciding. He doesn't think that the Framers intended the Court to have such power."

"He's wrong," she said. Then her definiteness seemed to startle her. "Isn't he?"

Paul Lowe said with a grin, "It's one of the most hotly debated points in constitutional politics."

"Why should it be?"

"Oh, lots of reasons. Having to do with the problems of power in a democratic society. It involves the relations between the rights of the majority and the minorities, the balance between the values of an aristocratic elite and the masses, between law and politics, between the states and the federal government, among the executive, legislative and judicial branches of government within a federal system. Things like that."

"I am about to make the unmistakable sound of someone falling off the deep end."

"Well, you asked for it."

She shrugged. "I wanted to be sure that what I believe in the first place is right."

Because she was intuitive her politics were intuitive, proceeding from sympathy rather than logic. She could be inconsistent in particulars yet maintain a steady underlying consistency in her beliefs. He had long since discovered that she could be influenced only in the way a compass needle is affected by the presence of a local magnetic field—after wavering she returned to true north. True north was for her a hatred of repression, a distrust of concentrated power, an attachment to minorities in race and religion, a fear of extremism and a love of freedom combined with an impatience about the means to attain it.

"Are you convinced now that you were right in the first place?"

"Thoroughly."

"Are you sure I couldn't unconvince you again?"

"You don't have much faith in my powers of resistance."

He touched her hair. "Should I have?"

She smiled. "I wasn't talking about that. You're a vulgar man."

He put his hand beneath her chin and lifted her face to kiss her. Then he kissed her again with sharpened meaning.

With his arm about her waist he lifted her to the couch beside him. She pressed her cheek against his face. Desire came upon him wave by wave. She responded with increasing excitement. The urgency of passion washed through his blood and picked his senses bare. Before long she was lying back on the couch ready to receive him. He took her. It was the most consummate act of lovemaking he had ever known.

For a long shuddering interval absolutely nothing else in the world mattered. When they parted they were shaken as by a glimpse of an enormous tragedy—they were like two survivors of a terrible wreck. He lay turned to her, almost touching, not quite.

"I love the feeling of your bare skin," she said. She clasped her arms behind his head. "I've decided that I'm really a very passionate woman. I never used to think so, but now I've decided I am. I've probably been ever since I was a child. You know what I would do sometimes?"

"What?" He was depleted, surrendered out of himself.

"I would pick up a pillow and bite it. Really. Hold it by the edge and clench my teeth in it. It was a kind of fit that wouldn't pass for a minute or two. Do you think a psychiatrist would say that was adolescent sexuality?"

"I'm glad you've outgrown pillows."

"Did I really bite you?"

"Look." He showed her the neat indented arc on his shoulder.

"Oh, my! Did I hurt you?"

"Terribly."

"I'll kiss it."

"That's much better."

They slept. Her black hair was soft against the side of his neck, and his arm was about her shoulder. When he awoke the room was still in complete darkness. He made out the illuminated hands of a small clock on a bookshelf.

He sat up suddenly.

"What's the trouble, dear?"

"It's late."

She came fully awake. "What time is it?"

"Past two in the morning." He was already starting to dress.

"Oh. What are you supposed to be doing?"

"I'm supposed to be working late in the office."

"At this hour?"

"It's all right. She's probably asleep. If I don't wake her she won't know what time it was when I came home."

She turned on the table lamp near the sofa. The shaded light on her face made her look pensive. She watched him dress.

He did not want to appear too much in haste. He stopped to look at himself in the mirror over the dining table, and crossed his tie end with deliberate slowness to form a knot.

"What are you doing this weekend?" he asked.

"I don't have any plans. I thought of going home to see Timmy."

"There's nothing wrong at home, is there?"

"No, but I've been neglecting him shamefully. I talk to him every day but it isn't the same as being there."

"I had a different idea. How would you like to spend a few days away together? Just the two of us."

"I'd love to. But you can't."

"I've been thinking a lot about it, and I've figured out a way." How ingenious his mind was to satisfy his desires! "Race Hardman has a home in St. Thomas. He uses it only for a month or two in the winter. He's told me I can have it any weekend I can get away."

"Oh." She sounded dubious.

"What's the matter?"

"His invitation certainly doesn't include me."

"No one will know. Race told me his place is on a deserted end of the island. It's a completely private estate."

"There must be someone around."

"The caretaker lives in town. Race told me he's an old man in his eighties and never talks to anyone. And there aren't any other servants. . . . Darling, it's a risk anywhere but less of a risk in a place like this. We won't even go out for dinner—and there's a private beach where no one ever shows up. This is a retreat for Race when he wants to cut himself off from everything. There isn't even a telephone."

"It sounds wonderful."

"I've never had any real time with you. After our weekend you can go to Timmy. He'll wait a few days longer to see you, won't he? I want this very much."

Her finger traced a line in his cheek. "Then it's settled. Of course I'll go with you."

He kissed her. Suddenly he was lighter, freer.

"I'll charter a plane," he said. "We can fly down to St. Thomas on Friday."

"Not in a private plane."

"I'm a good pilot. It isn't dangerous, you know."

"Yes it is—but not in the way you mean. If we go it will have to be in separate planes and we'll meet later in the airport."

"Do you think we need to take all those precautions?"

"We can't be too careful. Not with someone in your position."

"I just hate all the deception."

"I know. So do I. But it's necessary if we're going to do this crazy thing at all. And I do want to, darling. Suddenly there isn't anything I want to do more." The decision taken, her mood rose joyfully. "I can't believe it. A whole weekend with you!"

"Someday I'll take you flying in a small plane. I think you'll like it."

"I know I will. I've heard so much about the freedom you're supposed to feel when you're flying—but in those big commercial planes it's mechanized freedom. You don't ever breathe real air. And I hate instant coffee."

She was so different from Eleanor.

15

When Paul Lowe left Washington the morning air was slightly chilly and a fine mist was drizzling. In San Juan, Puerto Rico, the soft air was warm and laden with perfume.

At San Juan he was transferred to a two-engine plane for the short trip to St. Thomas. Soon the plane was skimming a thousand feet above the transparent blue Caribbean. Wavelets folded into each other below, leaving a small lacework of white on the sea. Occasional coral heads loomed visibly beneath the water. Then small irregularly shaped islands appeared, covered with glowing emerald color like separate stones in a necklace. The islands were peaks of an underwater mountain range that extended in a gigantic underwater shelf outward from Puerto Rico. Beyond the shelf was a sheer dizzying drop culminating in the Brownson Deep—the deepest spot charted in the Atlantic Ocean—a precipitous plunge to thirty thousand feet below the surface.

The plane flew on over shallow winding channels of blue water that skirted the awesome depths. White triangular sailing craft veered below.

The St. Thomas airfield came into view, enclosed in a valley between rounded peaks. A concrete catchbasin was set into the sloping side of a hill to catch rainwater. The plane came in over the golf course, past the catchbasin, and settled down on the runway.

Katherine's plane arrived ninety minutes later and they met in the echoing high-ceilinged indoor parking area adjoining the terminal. He stowed their luggage in the rear trunk of a rented Volkswagen. The girl at the car-rental counter had given him a map of the island with instructions on how to reach Buccaneer Bay.

He had never driven a four-shift car before but he obeyed the diagrammed instructions pasted on the instrument panel. They stopped briefly in the town of Charlotte Amalie. Race Hardman had given him an address in the town which turned out to be a rather tumbledown wooden shack. While Katherine remained in the car half a block away, he spoke with the shy young Negress who answered his knock at the door. She told him that Race Hardman's caretaker was out walking his dog but he had left the key for the estate house—together with word that all was in readiness for Paul Lowe's stay.

Soon the Volkswagen was beetling along the road again. The afternoon sun beat down strongly through the open sliding panel in the roof. The sky was clear blue and the cottages along the way were pink and white; the breeze smelled of exotic flowers.

He glanced over at Katherine. She had tied her dark hair back with a bright pink kerchief.

He shifted to low gear and the sturdy Volkswagen grumbled steadily upward over a road that curved around the height of the mountain. Below them suddenly appeared the sparkling lemon-colored town of Charlotte Amalie. Ahead was the splendid glittering panorama of the sea.

"Can we stop a minute?" Katherine asked.

He pulled the car to the side of the road. She put her head against the back of the seat.

"I won't object if you'd care to make this one particular minute last forever," she said.

"Done!"

She laughed. "That's what I've always wanted. A man with power."

He kissed her. A honk startled and interrupted them. Behind them a pickup truck had stopped. He waved to the native driver cheerfully, and the driver's surly expression changed. He grinned and waved back. As Paul Lowe started the car up again, he pulled to one side to allow the pickup truck to pass by.

They circled the road higher and higher to the top of the mountain. Far below the ocean seemed to lie as still as the Caribbean. The view stretched past Magens Bay with its curving ribbon of perfect beach to the outer channel where Sir Francis Drake once sailed with his bold men. They followed the road downward steeply over broken patches of asphalt and short intervals of plain dirt surface. Foliage grew thicker. They passed a mule tethered to a sapling and munching guinea grass. Nearby a great torch cactus rose twenty feet high. The road narrowed abruptly, became two parallel tracks of concrete, and finally turned into a path almost overgrown with jungle foliage that climbed the shoulder of a hill and ended. The jungle had not reclaimed its own; the patience of the men who had built the path must simply have given out.

A small wooden sign shaped as an arrow was planted in the ground nearby. The sign had a name painted crudely in white: HARDMAN.

"Apparently we walk from here," Paul Lowe said.

"What about the car?"

"We'll leave it here. If anyone wants to steal it, let him. If he can get it out of here again, he deserves to keep it."

They had to make their way through fifty yards of dense tropical foliage to the top of the hill where they looked down on a small valley fronting the Atlantic Ocean. Along a wide beach white rolling combers broke with crunching power, sliding over retreating cascades of water and swirling broadly up onto the sand.

Amid a grove of palm trees they saw a flat-roofed wide beach house surrounded by terraces.

"Home?" Katherine asked.

"It better be," he said. "I was about to plant a flag and claim the territory in the name of the United States of America."

They went down a narrow trail toward the house. Except for the palm trees planted at measured intervals, there was no foliage. The sandy site was absolutely level. A setting sun lengthened the shadows of the tall palm trees. The tall commingling fronds gave the appearance of an immensely high arbor.

"It's a beautiful setting," she said.

"I'll appreciate it more once I unload some of this luggage I'm carrying."

The house was made of concrete blocks, large and durable-looking, and the terrace had a chaise longue, several chairs, and a small iron table with a parasol of a metallic material. The terrace completely surrounded the house like a moat about a fortress.

"Brrr," he said.

"Built to last," Katherine said. "With a minimum of maintenance."

"So are prisons."

"I'm going to like it," she announced.

The long deep rumbling roar of combers swept in from the Atlantic.

That night, with logs flaming red in a high fireplace, they dined at a ceramic table covered with figured placemats. Katherine had discovered the kitchen freezer well stocked, and after consideration they decided on chicken breasts and livers. She sautéed them in wine, with small slices of ham inserted between the chicken breasts. Paul Lowe took a 1961 vintage Chablis from the wine rack.

Midway through dinner Paul Lowe paused appreciatively. "Where did you learn to cook like this?" he asked.

"I chose cooking in high school instead of gym. I've continued with it, off and on, in place of exercise. I don't really go in much for competitive sports." She shook her arm. "See? All flab. There's too much of me."

"I categorically deny that."

"I wish I could diet. I have an absolute lack of will power. When I get frantic I don't eat at all. I live on diet pills and grapefruit juice and sometimes even join classes where all the women stand up and swear an oath, " 'I, a plumpie . . .' "

"A plumpie?"

"Reducing salons don't like the word 'fat.' Fat is carbohydrate. The diet I liked best was by a naturopath who believed some foods were cannibalistic and ate other foods. When I finished a big dinner I had to force myself to eat certain kinds of fruit that were supposed to go right down and devour all the other foods. I could have stayed on that diet forever if it only worked. But I gained four cannibalistic pounds. Now I diet when alarmed."

Two tall tapering candles were on the table, and the only one light in the room came from a square lamp in a corner. The flaming logs wove constantly shifting patterns of light and shadow. She was wearing a long wraparound robe of gay colors, chiefly yellow and pale blue and white. Her face was flushed, and her hair, flowing down to her shoulders, was black as a Rembrandt black—other colors were in it all contributing to its blackness.

He finished the last of the chicken and touched his mouth with a napkin. "If you really want to diet, you'll have to train yourself never to sample your own cooking. That was delicious."

"Wait until you try my gnocchi. I was married to an Italian, you know, and even he admitted it was good."

"Isn't it a pasta dish?"

"But with a special something. My husband's mother gave me the recipe. He always said I couldn't make it as well as his mother did. Everyone else thought it was wonderful. I don't know what his mother could have done to it, but I suppose she kept back some special secret. Like stamping around on it in her bare feet."

He tried to make the question seem casual: "How long were you married?"

"Oh, eighteen months. Counting the times we broke up. I only lasted that long because I discovered I have an inhuman capacity to take punishment."

"Did he really hit you?"

"Who told you? Oh, Tom. Well, it's true. He hit me and I slung pots and pans back at him. It was a merry brawl. I probably would have left him in a few months but then I was pregnant so I tried to last it out. The day we brought Timmy home from the hospital my husband went out and stayed out until four o'clock in the morning. Came home roaring drunk and tried to make love to me, although he knew the doctor had said not to. That's how he was. He prided himself on being a good animal—those are the words he used. A good animal. One of the few times he showed a gift for words. He must have really been something in the war."

"World War II?"

She shook her head. "Korea. He was only a few years older than I am. Had a Distinguished Service Cross and he never let anyone forget it. Particularly men who hadn't served in the Army. He'd strike up a conversation in bars with total strangers by asking them if they'd ever been in combat. If they hadn't, he accused them of being cowards. Fortunately for him he was built along the lines of a Sherman tank and had a very heavy fist. But it became pretty tiresome and finally I refused to go to bars with him any more. That was almost the last I saw of him because bars were where he lived."

"Have you seen him since?"

"He had custody rights and was supposed to pay a staggering sum like fifteen dollars a week toward Timmy's support. He didn't pay, and he didn't use his custody rights either. Finally my lawyer made a deal with him. I'd forget what he owed me, and any future payments, if I could have complete custody. He took the deal and that's the last I heard of him." She picked up the dishes, placing one carefully on top of the other. "No—that isn't entirely true. I did hear that he married again, some Italian girl. They have two kids and for all I know are living happily ever after somewhere in Greenwich Village."

"Are you curious about him?"

"I can't really remember what he looked like. Well, a little. Tall and dark and broad and hell on women. Some women. I had a terrific physical yen for him."

She went off to the kitchen. Paul Lowe sat alone in the stone room while the fire yellowed and the windows turned black against a sky with white clouds. He thought about Katherine with her former husband and his breathing became tight. From the kitchen he heard the clatter as she loaded dishes into the dishwasher.

He had brought Edmunson's opinion on the Cardinale case with him. Slumped on the cushions of an iron chair with his legs stretched out, he worked. There were about twenty-two printed pages and long before he reached the end he was impatient. Creases of doubt formed on his forehead. He slipped his reading glasses down and read the lines at a lower angle.

George Luis Cardinale, a naturalized American citizen, had gone to Brazil to evade military service. On his return to this country after an absence of a few years, he pleaded guilty to a charge of draft evasion, was convicted and served a prison sentence. Later, when he applied for a passport to leave the country on a trip, the application was denied by the Passport Board of Review on the ground that he had forfeited his citizenship when he left the United States to evade military service. Cardinale, through his attorneys, went to work to obtain a declaration of his citizenship and to force the Passport Board of Review to issue a passport to him.

The lower court refused to do so. That decision was then appealed to the Supreme Court.

Cardinale's lawyers did not do a good job on the case. They were mainly New York City personal-injury lawyers with no experience in appellate advocacy. Furthermore, the main ground dealt with and argued before the lower court was a procedural point not related to the main issue. So the case came to the Supreme Court without the usual thorough research and legal briefing or benefit of well-reasoned lower-court opinions.

In arguing before the Supreme Court, Solicitor General Peter Daris had followed his usual adroit practice of not meeting any arguments which had not been effectively stated by the petitioner. Peter Daris' brief was very carefully contained and simply ignored the constitutional implications of the petitioner's poorly phrased arguments.

Therefore, when he came to write the opinion, Charles Edmunson had simply started from scratch. His description of his own opinion as "a crotchet of legalisms" was accurate. He had covered a good deal of ground and advanced strong arguments but his opinion lacked the strong simple clarity of Waldo Shuler's dissent. Shuler's dissent consisted of thirteen persuasive pages, virtually seamless in argument. Paul Lowe had read it before leaving for the weekend.

Gabriel Hart had cackled over it like a proud bald hen.—Can you answer this, Paul? If you've got an open mind you'd better take a second look at your position on this case.

Paul Lowe removed his reading glasses and dangled them between thumb and forefinger. Katherine was seated cross-legged on a sofa cushion before the dying fire.

She looked up at once. "Anything the matter?"

"I'm trying to analyze something."

"What is it?"

"An opinion by Edmunson in a rather important case. Something's wrong with it that I can't put my finger on."

"Can I help?"

"I don't think so."

"You're right. My head isn't put on straight for figuring out legal problems."

"I wouldn't say that. I had pretty good luck with your abracadabra witch doctoring before—on that bus broadcasting case."

"Mmmmm. When you keep talking I do make sense of what it's all about. Then if something's wrong, I feel it right in the pit of my stomach. If you have any call for stomach-thinkers let me know."

"You may hear from me a bit later."

She smiled at him. "Keep in touch," she said.

She went back to work on the cryptogram she was doing. She was particularly expert at ciphers and puzzles. Once he had tried to match her at this, and quickly discovered that his better vocabulary and training in sequential thought were of no avail against her swift divination. She flashed to solutions that he would have labored at for hours. Answers leaped to her from an occult store of wisdom.

He continued to stare at the fire, recalling the effect that Shuler's argument had made on him. Shuler had begun by pointing out that a country must have some way of dealing with draft evaders and the Constitution provided such a way; it is part of the power to make war which is inherent in the very fact that the United States exists as a nation. No one may quarrel with the power of Congress to make war, and therefore no one may quarrel with the effective exercise of that power. One way Congress chose to exercise its power was to take away the citizenship of anyone who refused to serve in the armed forces. This was not an unusual remedy for the situation. There were a number of reasons, outside of draft evasion, for which citizenship could be taken away. A man could lose his citizenship by taking an oath of allegiance to another country, or taking a job in another country for which only citizens of that country were eligible. If convicted of treason, or if as a member of the armed forces he was convicted of desertion in time of war, he would also lose his citizenship. If these were all approved reasons for depriving a man of his citizenship, was it not equally justifiable to take away citizenship from someone unwilling to perform his duty to his country in wartime?

Further on in the thirteen-page written dissent, Waldo Shuler reverted to his thesis that if Congress has the power to make war it must have the power to make war effectively. One way of doing that—a vitally necessary way, Shuler observed—was to maintain the morale of the armed forces. What would happen, he asked, to those serving in the armed forces if they knew that draft evaders who shirked their duty were getting away with it? Would not the men in uniform feel they were being discriminated against and wouldn't that reduce their military efficiency? When Congress passed a law that took away the citizenship of draft evaders it was merely taking steps to preserve the security of the nation. Since one of the basic purposes of the Constitution was to provide for the common defense, any Congress that failed to do so would fail in its duty. No judge of any court had the right to tell Congress that this duty should be abandoned.

Katherine turned, putting aside her cryptogram. It had held her no more than ten minutes.

"You have an unhappy look on your face," she said.

"I was just disagreeing with Waldo Shuler and I can't figure out why." He smiled ruefully. "Someone said that making a judgment is merely the act of finding bad reasons for something we believe on instinct. I guess I'm as guilty of that as anyone else. But so far I can't even come up with enough reasons, good or bad."

She picked up her sofa cushion and came over to plunk down near him. "Tell me about it."

"You really want to know?"

"I'm fascinated."

"Is your stomach all primed to tell if something is wrong with Shuler's opinion?"

She nodded. "If I get up for a Bromo-Seltzer, he's doomed."

He told her the facts as clearly and succinctly as he could. When he had summarized Waldo Shuler's arguments, he saw a frown gathering between her eyes.

She was silent for a moment.

"No symptoms yet?" he asked.

"Not a quiver. I don't feel sorry for this George Luis Cardinale. A man who wouldn't serve his country and who then turns around and cries that he was deprived when they wouldn't let him be a citizen any more. I'd say let him have his passport and then don't let him back in the country."

He laughed. Her intuition led into some strange blind alleys.

"That answer would satisfy no one. Cardinale would have to be declared a citizen in order to get a passport. Once he was declared a citizen, how could we keep him out of the country?"

She bit her lip. "What does Edmunson say?"

"He believes George Luis Cardinale should get his citizenship back and his passport with it."

"And you agree?"

"Yes."

"Why? Did Cardinale have a good reason for evading the draft?"

"He was a pacifist. But that doesn't matter. The principle is the same even if he were a coward."

"Then I must be wrong. What are some of your reasons?"

"They're Edmunson's reasons. I only happen to agree with him."

"Tell me what he says."

"I don't know if I can do him justice. He wrote a twenty-two page opinion."

"I wouldn't understand that if I read it. I think I can understand you."

"Well, I'll try, if you're really interested. Charles Edmunson points out that there are laws in existence which provide ways for dealing with draft evaders—and none of these laws mentions loss of citizenship. George Luis Cardinale was tried and sentenced under those laws. The Passport Board's decision that he had lost his citizenship was really a kind of afterthought, something imposed on him later in addition to his prison sentence."

"That isn't very fair, I guess."

"Edmunson also says that for the Congress to invoke such broad powers it has to prove some connection between the kind of powers invoked and the nature of the offense."

"Hmm. Lawyer talk. I don't even know what it means."

"It means there's got to be clear proof that the security of the nation is involved before a law can be justified that takes away a man's citizenship. Otherwise anyone might claim that the security of the nation is involved in almost anything."

"For example?"

"It might be involved in our inability to bring back people legally who have fled the country for other reasons."

Katherine stirred restlessly. "I suppose it's very logical. It just doesn't get through to me."

"Don't you think that the right of Congress to take away a man's citizenship is pretty remote from the duty of Congress to defend the country?"

"I guess so," she said dubiously.

"And even if Congress claims it has that right—even if the power to do so *is* inherent in the very fact that the United States *is* a government—it still is no basis for saying that the same power has been granted to the Passport Board of Review."

"I see that," Katherine said hopefully. "Yes, that makes sense. But it still doesn't answer a basic question for me."

"What's that?"

"What are we going to do with draft evaders? We can't pat them on the head and let them go, can we?"

"Edmunson says George Luis Cardinale should be tried in the courts. That's where he *was* tried and convicted in the first place. Now if the government also wants to take away his citizenship that issue should be tried in the courts too—under the due process of law that's guaranteed by the Constitution. That's where both sides will get a fair hearing. That's where George Luis Cardinale will be given certain rights—where he can call witnesses in his behalf, have the government's witnesses cross-examined, and let the whole case against him be weighed on its merits by a judge and jury."

Katherine sat up, hugging her knees. "I always did like that old man. I don't know why, but I do think he's right."

"Because you want to think so?"

She nodded. "With me, it doesn't make much difference."

"With me," Paul Lowe said heavily, "it makes a good deal of difference."

"I have to admit that Waldo Shuler's arguments make a lot of sense too."

He nodded. "If you had legal training and read his opinion you'd be impressed by how closely it's reasoned—by the logic that informs and illuminates every page. It's simply a better and more persuasive job than Edmunson's. And there's the difficulty. If I think so, what will Henry Merriam think? Or Chief Justice John Hampton? Under the impact of Shuler's kind of legalistic crossfire, it's possible they'll break and run. And on this case we can't afford to lose a single vote."

"I wish I could help. But I don't know why I think Edmunson is right. I just feel it."

He got up impatiently, went to the fireplace, and used a poker to stir up the embering logs. "Edmunson himself put his finger on what's wrong with his opinion. He hasn't found a clear simple logical line. That's what he needs. A peg to hang the rest of his arguments on."

"It's like a good lead to a newspaper story. Sometimes it can be hard to find."

"And sometimes the answer is so simple. When you see it you wonder how you overlooked it." Paul Lowe put the poker back in the rack and stared at the cherry-red heart of the fire. "For want of a nail the shoe was lost and for want of a shoe the horse was lost and for want of a horse the battle was lost . . . *where* is the missing nail? That tiny missing piece."

"I'm sorry I'm so helpless," Katherine said. "This whole thing is a couple of thousand leagues beyond my depth."

He smiled grimly and went back to the chair. He put his hand on her head and turned his fingers in her thick black tresses.

"Waldo Shuler thinks the government has a right to take away a man's citizenship on the proven record of what he did. What's wrong with that? George Luis Cardinale did refuse to serve his country. He *was* a draft dodger. He went to prison for it. Why can't I agree with Waldo Shuler that this country therefore has a right to say Cardinale isn't a citizen?"

"It does seem to be just another way of punishing him," Katherine said.

"I know, but . . ." He broke off suddenly to stare at her. "What did you say?"

"It's another way of punishing him," she repeated.

"*Punishment!*"

"What?"

"You've done it. Given me the clue. The right answer to Waldo Shuler."

"I did? How?"

"If this offense—draft evasion—is singled out, how can anyone claim it *isn't* punishment? Why should this one failure as a citizen be singled out more than a failure, say, to pay taxes or even to testify under oath? We send a man to prison for those offenses but we don't take his citizenship away. Why should *this* offense be singled out? And if it is, how can anyone say that it isn't punishment?"

"I don't know what you mean."

"Punishment has to be meted out by courts. It *has* to be controlled by due process. That's in the Constitution." His voice twanged like the string on a guitar. "Shuler cited Savorgnan versus the United States, Perez versus Brownell, and Mackenzie versus Hare—all to prove that Congress has the power to denaturalize a citizen without a trial. But the Cardinale case isn't like those." He stood up suddenly. "In this case citizenship was taken away as a *penal* action. The only significance of doing it is as punishment. If it isn't punishment, what possible effect would it have? It exists for the same reason as the gas chamber and the electric chair—and some of the same arguments could be made for them. *They* could be said to assist the morale of law-abiding citizens!"

He clasped the palms of his hands together. Katherine was leaning back, smiling at his excitement.

"Waldo Shuler said we'd have to examine the motives of Congress in making the law. But he's wrong! Congress could have any motive. Any motive at all. To defend the country or protect the security of the armed forces or heaven knows what. The motive doesn't matter. The law is *punitive*. So it has to be tried in the courts. Don't you see that?"

"No. But I'm willing to."

"It's simple. If we let Congress have the power not only to make laws, but to *punish*, anything might happen. A Congress might come along someday and decide that if you don't vote you will lose your citizenship. How could we stop that? There's only one way to do it. Prevent Congress from dealing out punishment without due process of law. Congress cannot be a judge. Congress can only make laws but the courts have to decide who will be punished under them."

"I'm beginning to understand, dimly."

"Punishment is the key. Taking away a man's citizenship is the worst kind of punishment. He becomes a man without a country—without employment—without a home. He's under a life sentence he can't even appeal."

Her gaze followed his restless pacing. In the fireplace a log hissed, crackled and collapsed in fiery ruin.

"It sounds terrible," she said. "But why shouldn't draft evaders be treated terribly?"

Other arguments fell into place. "Who will this kind of punishment hurt the most? Draft evaders who run away and stay out of the country and never repent? No! They don't care if they lose their citizenship. This hurts the men who change their minds and come home, who repent what they did and pay for it with a prison term. It singles out for the harshest punishment the very men who want forgiveness and a chance to expiate their crime. It doesn't even touch the ones who stay unregenerate, the ones who don't care if they stay expatriated forever."

Katherine said, "Do you know what it's like to watch you march around like this?"

He halted his restless pacing. "I'm sorry."

"It's marvelous," she said. "I'd follow you anywhere. To the barricades."

He looked down at her. He held his hand out and lifted her beside him. "I have a much better idea," he said.

In the warm afternoon sun a brown animal with fluffy hair moved swiftly out of the shade of an umbrella tree.

Katherine, lying prone on the sandy beach, sat up quickly. "What was that?"

He caught a glimpse of it out of the corner of his eye. "A mongoose."

"It looked like a rat."

"More like a squirrel."

"All squirrels look like rats," she said. "I hate *slinky* things. What is it?"

He rolled over on his back. "Actually, it's a member of the cat family. And a very useful little animal. It kills snakes and eats garbage. Everything, I'm told, except sauerkraut."

She shuddered. "Sometimes I wish nature weren't so damned abundant."

She wore a two-piece bathing suit in a speckled black and white pattern. Her slender waist was bare to the midriff. There was a small patch of blue varicosity at the back of her left knee—a vein in white marble.

"I like that suit," he said.

"I hope so. I paid twenty-eight dollars for it, just to impress you."

Remembering last night, he felt a yearning that was quickly translated into tenderness. He sat down beside her and rested his hand on her knee.

"After giving the matter proper judicial consideration," he said, "I wish to announce that I'm very much in love with you."

She smiled. "You belong on the Supreme Court, sir. You make such final decisions."

"Andrew Jackson once said of a John Marshall decision, 'Mr. Marshall has made his decision—now let him enforce it.' I'm prepared to do that."

She rolled over onto her stomach and rested her chin on crossed hands. "How?"

"I wouldn't be the first justice of the Supreme Court to get a divorce."

She glanced up, startled, and smiled uncertainly. "You're trying to be sweet, but you don't have to say that."

"Would you marry me if I were free?"

"That's rather a hypothetical question. Besides, I refuse to answer on the ground that it would very probably incriminate me."

"I'm serious, Katherine."

She looked down. "I don't know your wife so when I try, I manage to avoid thinking about her as a person. But what do you think she would say if you told her you wanted a divorce?"

"I don't know."

"How would you tell her?"

"I haven't thought about it."

. . . I want you to know, Eleanor, that I am not anxious to hurt you in any way or to be unkind. But the fact that a few words of the tribe were once spoken over us does not make us truly husband and wife. We need so much more than we have any hope of giving each other. If we continue with our marriage under these terms, we will have nothing to expect but wounds and nothing to show but scars. Is that kindness—merely to postpone cruelty?

He ceased communicating with Eleanor in his mind. He said, "All I know is we can't go on this way forever."

"I don't say it will be forever. Sometimes I think I won't be able to stand it another minute. In the middle of the night I've had to fight to keep from crying out with the knowledge that you're in that house with her, sleeping in the same bed."

"Dearest . . ."

"Don't say it, Paul. I know you've been with her that way. It's part of the price I pay for having you at all. I don't have any right to you and sooner or later I will have to find a way to live without you. . . . But I'd rather not think about that, just now." Her eyes brimmed. She drew a quick shallow breath. "Oh, Paul!"

She turned on her back and her bare arms went about him. After a moment she let him go and pressed her face into his shoulder.

"I've become a monster," she said. "The sort of woman I've always despised. But it doesn't help to know when you're being selfish, does it? I didn't mean to fall in love this way—it's more than I bargained for." She drew back, her mouth open with the unhealable suffering of the self-accused. "But I can't help myself. I really can't!"

With his hand on the back of her head he pressed her to him, held her close. This was what he needed—her painful emotion with himself at its center, absorbing like a sponge, swelling with ingested meaning. Alone he was small and dry—open pores waiting to be filled. The intellect is a passion too—but how empty, how empty, compared with this!

He moved his hand across her shoulder, and the strap of her halter slid over. The strap left a wide ribbon of pink against white skin. As he kissed her shoulder he suddenly was aware that she had turned her head. She was listening, and then he heard it, at first a sound indistinguishable from the roaring of the nearby breakers but then the shorter gutturals became clear and he recognized a dog's deep-throated excited barking.

There was a snarling undertone he didn't like.

He looked up. "You'd better get inside the house."

A dog burst out of the brush. He was a lean powerful police dog and his jaws were open to reveal the flashing line of sharp teeth.

Paul Lowe put Katherine behind him.

"Hey, Iversen," a man's quavering voice called.

Through the outer fringe of palm trees came an old man in a white sportshirt and cotton duck trousers.

"*Iversen!*"

The police dog halted, trembling. The fierce-looking mouth drew back over razor incisors.

The old man was carrying a rope with a collar. He fixed the collar into place on the dog's neck and patted the sleek brown coat.

"My name's Donlin," the old man said. "I'm the caretaker here. You must be the fella Mr. Hardman says he was expectin'."

"That's right. Paul Lowe is my name."

Donlin straightened and stared at Katherine with opaque eyes. "I came over today to see if everything was all right. Mr. Hardman didn't mention you was bringin' your missus."

"Didn't he?" Paul Lowe asked.

"Well, I'm pleased to meet you, ma'am."

"I'm pleased to meet you, Mr. Donlin."

Donlin held the rope short, reining the dog close. "Iversen broke away chasing one of the iguanas," he said apologetically. "Every time he sees one he gets excited. He wouldn't have done you no harm."

"I hope not," Katherine said.

"Iversen just likes to scare strangers. I'll keep him tied up good and proper until you've gone. You find everything all right?"

He answered, "Everything was fine, Mr. Donlin."

"That's good. I had a cleanin' woman in the other day to get it straightened up. And there was everything you need in the freezer."

"We found everything, thank you," Katherine said.

"Didn't know there was goin' to be the two of you," Donlin said. The back of his hand holding the rope was high ridged with veins.

"Iversen," Paul Lowe said. "That's a queer name for a dog."

"Mr. Hardman give it to him." Donlin's hand holding the rope shook as the dog's lean body shook. "Iversen was the name of the first governor of the islands. Got hisself killed sailing back here from Denmark. Convicts on board the ship mutinied. Raped his wife, tossed him and his baby overboard." Donlin's mouth parted in a mirthless grin over irregular teeth. "Rough folks on the islands in those days."

"From what we've seen, things seem to have gotten better," he said.

Donlin cackled. "Can't say that for sure. Well, hope you and your missus have a good time. Leave the key under the mat when you go."

He left, holding Iversen on the short rope leash. The dog padded with deliberate gait, the muscles in his shoulders and haunches bunching, knotting, unwinding as he kept slow pace with his master.

Katherine was close to tears.

"It's all right, dear," he said. "I'm sorry the dog frightened you."

"It isn't that."

"What is it, then?"

"I wish the caretaker hadn't seen us."

"It doesn't mean anything. He has no reason to mention you were here. Besides, he doesn't see Race Hardman for months on end."

She shook her head. "I guess I just feel guilty, no matter how much I try to tell myself I shouldn't. I try to pretend there isn't any ethical problem involved—that I just happened to fall in love. But underneath everything, I know we're in the wrong. And that isn't the worst. The worst is that most of the time it doesn't seem to matter."

He put his arm gently about her waist. She was trembling. Her head rested lightly on his shoulder as they went into the house.

He drove to the airport. She kept one hand tightly on his arm. Even on the mountain driving she did not let go while he kept both hands on the wheel. From a high vantage point the harbor boats shone in the sunlight, fishing boats and colorfully painted houseboats clung to safety near the shore, and farther out giant passenger liners waited massively.

On the narrow roads the chugging Volkswagen sounded unnaturally loud. Leaving a place, small noises are magnified like tiny voices calling you back. A cloud shadow slid down the slope toward a rust-colored freighter tied up in the harbor quay.

The car wound down the mountain road. Bluebeard's Castle rose on a promontory across the way, standing like the pirate himself on a quarterdeck looking down upon a motley crew of decaying houses and steep narrow streets.

In a few minutes they arrived at the airport. He drove into the huge covered shed and parked.

"This is where we have to say goodbye," she told him.

"No," he said. "I'm going to wait with you for your plane."

"That's nearly half an hour. And we shouldn't be seen together."

"It's all right," he said. He wanted to offer this small daring as proof of how much he cared about her.

They went to the counter to settle accounts with the car-rental agency. The girl on duty was trim and blonde and efficient. She wore a tailored blue jacket and visored cap. He was signing the charge sheet when he heard:

"Mr. Justice! What a pleasant surprise!"

He finished signing his name but the letters became elongated at the end as his pen slipped on sudden moisture in his fingertips. He placed the pen down carefully. He had not recognized the voice. When he turned he saw a darkhaired woman, rather short and shapeless in a black suit with cloth buttons and a perky Tyrolean hat with colored feather. She was standing beside a light blue traveling case.

He saw her legs encased in zippered suede boots. He remembered the boots.

"I'm Tessie Samuels—your daughter's friend," said the husky soft voice.

"Yes, of course. Miss Samuels."

Her handclasp was firm and cool and sure.

"I work for a public relations firm," she said, her eyes including Katherine. "One of our clients is opening a branch store in the Virgin Isles Hilton. I had to come down to attend the gala opening." As she finished speaking her gaze moved frankly toward Katherine.

Paul Lowe said, "Miss Samuels—I'd like you to meet Katherine Prescott."

"How do you do." She shook Katherine's hand with an abrupt gesture.

Katherine said, "How do you do."

He was pleased to note how well Katherine withstood the shock. She even managed to smile, but color heightened along her cheekbones and a pulse throbbed noticeably beneath a spray of dark hair at her temple.

"Have you been here long?" Tessie Samuels asked.

"Just a few days."

"Oh, I see." *She saw.* "I left Nancy yesterday. You'll be glad to know that she's coming along beautifully. She's put on weight."

"I understand she's staying with you now."

Tessie Samuels' face wore the enameled look of someone who has resolved a final incredulity.

"Until the baby is born." The quick clichés became tedious; she struck. "How is Mrs. Lowe?"

"She's fine."

"She didn't come down with you?"

"No. I had some work to do on an important case and I flew down here to be alone." There was no putting it off any longer. "By chance, I met Miss Prescott. She's a newspaperwoman who did a series of articles about me."

"I seem to recall. Nancy showed them to me." Her focus shifted its weight to Katherine. "Very well written, I thought."

"Thank you."

"Do you have time for a drink?" Tessie Samuels asked.

Her question included Katherine but Paul Lowe avoided the trap of answering for both.

"I'm sorry, but I'm afraid I haven't time. I have a lot of things to attend to."

"Oh, too bad." Her glance strayed to Katherine again. "I intend to call Nancy tonight. I was hoping if we had a drink I could report all about you."

"Give Nancy my love, won't you?" he said.

"She'll be so surprised to hear that I ran into you," the slightest pause, "and Miss Prescott."

"Where are you staying?" Paul Lowe asked.

"Where else? The Hilton. Where did you stay, Mr. Justice?"

"At a friend's house. Well, Miss Samuels . . ."

"You're not running off?"

Katherine said, "I'm afraid they're announcing my plane."

The gravelly raucous announcement came over the loudspeakers.

"Are you going on the same plane, Mr. Justice?" Tessie Samuels inquired.

"No. I'm taking a later one."

"Justice Lowe was kind enough to drive me to the airport," Katherine added.

"How lovely," Tessie Samuels said. Then because it was too good not to bear repetition: "How very lovely."

"They're boarding now," Paul Lowe said to Katherine. "You have to go."

"Don't let me keep you, then," Tessie Samuels said. She twiddled her fingers. "Have a pleasant flight, Miss Prescott. Do you know where I can get a cab?" she asked Paul Lowe.

16

In his office Monday morning Paul Lowe tried to keep his attention from private anxieties. He had before him the opinion of Henry Merriam in *Victor Reit vs. New Jersey*, a state bank robbery case. It had taken Merriam five pages to explain the complex details of what had begun at a few minutes past midnight the previous November when the state police broke into an apartment and arrested Victor Reit, suspected of possessing stolen bank notes. A search of Reit's apartment uncovered several bundles of the missing bank notes. The question for the Supreme Court to decide was this: if the police acted illegally in making the arrest, and later in conducting a search without a search warrant, could Victor Reit's confession, which was obtained shortly after he was taken into custody, be introduced into evidence against him at his trial?

Justice Merriam's opinion held that the evidence acquired illegally could not be used:

The Constitution forbids the police to make an arrest unless they have "probable cause" to believe a felony has been committed by the man they are arresting. There was no such "probable cause" in the case before us, and therefore Victor Reit's arrest, and the subsequent search of his home, was illegal. No court can permit law enforcement agents to secure convictions as a reward for violating the law. This rule was originally laid down when the Court prohibited the use of evidence acquired in violation of the Fourth Amendment's ban on unreasonable searches. Subsequently, this rule has been expanded to many other forms of police activity.

Merriam cited statistics to show that every year as many as a hundred thousand arrests were made based on mere suspicion:

The time has come to enforce Constitutional safeguards and enjoin not only federal agents but local police officers from continuing to make such arrests. The effective way to do this is to forbid the use of evidence of any kind whatsoever, including confessions, acquired as the result of any such illegal arrest and seizure. We cannot encourage lawlessness in those who are sworn to uphold the law.

Paul Lowe finished reading Henry Merriam's opinion. He wrote a note to Merriam asking him to mention that, in reaching this decision, the Court was protecting the liberties of all citizens, and added:

"Unfortunately, in this instance, it has to be done even though it involves an admitted criminal. But the question the Court must decide is whether the constitutional guarantees of due process of law have been properly observed, not whether a specific man is guilty in a specific case."

As he finished writing the note, his private anxieties surged forward. He had dammed them back but at the first break the torrent rushed through to inundate him. Would Tessie Samuels tell Nancy?

He put his pen down and forced himself to pick up the dissent on the Victor Reit case written by Andrew Cutler. He held the printed pages in reading position but could not focus on them.

Of course Tessie Samuels would tell Nancy and Nancy would tell her mother—she inevitably would. Eleanor would be shocked into vindictiveness. There was no measuring the pride of a woman who secretly believes herself unworthy; she lives in her pride like a dwarf in a castle.

Victor Reit vs. the United States. He made a wrenching effort to concentrate on Andrew Cutler's dissent. Andrew Cutler argued against the Court putting any further restraints on police investigations:

The test of "probable cause" in an arrest has to be interpreted with the utmost liberality. ["Liberality" was one of Cutler's favorite words; he used it as though to counter an unspoken accusation against him.]

In the present case the distinction between "probable cause" and mere arrest on suspicion is so narrow that the officers might unintentionally have crossed over it to make an illegal arrest. On such tenuous ground to prohibit the use not only of evidence of a felony having been committed, but even of the confession later made by the defendant, will unreasonably hamper law enforcement and put the Supreme Court plainly on the side of criminals in their brutal war against society.

Paul Lowe sat back in his swivel chair. Having read the two opinions, he was certain the liberal majority would hold. Chief Justice Hampton, Justices Edmunson, Merriam, McCann and himself had voted together in the conference. Justice Bill Branch had been absent, but Paul Lowe now considered it likely Branch would end up on the majority side.

Suddenly he put his hand to his face. He saw Katherine. The air was touched with the murmur of her voice.

Martha Scully said, "Mr. Justice?"

Slowly he removed his fingers from the bridge of his nose. "Yes, Martha?"

"I have a note from Mr. Justice Edmunson." She came from the doorway to deposit the open envelope on his desk.

226

When Martha left, he opened the loose flap and removed a sheet of paper with a handwritten message.

Dear Paul:
Thank you for your suggestion in re the Cardinale opinion. The concept of punishment may be just what we need to tie it all together.
CE

Paul Lowe smiled without amusement. It occurred to him that punishment might be a ruling concept that can tie everything together. We are all obsessed by it. Even in our games we set penalties. Go back two spaces and pay the jailer. In our work we flog ourselves beyond endurance. "He doesn't know when to stop." We purchase success with coronaries and our children with sacrifice. Parents we reward with duty—shed like blood in their service. In love we demand payment in proofs, ever more painful proofs.

Our God is a jealous God who made us in His image yet He always punishes us for being what we are. Or did we make God—create Him *only* to punish us?

He stood up. He had to beware of self-pity, that destroyer.

Late afternoon, in the supermarket, he stood idly leafing through magazines at the rack while Eleanor hustled about the aisles with her wire cart. He watched her gravely make a choice between competing brands of maple syrup. Tomorrow would be thin little pancakes for breakfast. Certain rituals she performed in the same way that primitive women made burnt offerings to placate the angry gods.

She moved on with the cart, her hands darting here and there among the high-piled counters to emerge with her catch. The cart began to heap up with the week's provender. She trusted no one else to do her shopping. No one could have done it as well or as economically, she was convinced. For a moment in a space between precariously stacked groceries she appeared and seemed to be one with the cans and the packages and the boxes and the jars, a symbol, relentlessly purposeful in search of an ever more mechanized efficiency.

Eleanor would not forgive infidelity. He was sure of that. It would be unendurable to her. Her pride was too easily wounded, and this blow would be directed not at her real self but at herself magnified—at Mrs. Paul Lincoln Lowe. She was far too proud and therefore far too vulnerable. Or far too vulnerable and therefore far too proud. The consequences were the same. She would exorcise her anger in her power to change his life.

If there was a divorce, it would not be a quiet one and there would be no reasonable settlement. She would exact the full price of her humiliation. He couldn't blame her for that. The fault was not hers and she had a right to set hard conditions.

Nevertheless he resented her power over him.

After dinner, the telephone rang.

"Hello."

"Hello, Dad." Nancy sounded toneless and distant.

"Where are you?" he asked.

"Dulles Airport. I just arrived with my friend Tessie Samuels. I thought I'd run up to see you."

Paul Lowe released a breath. She had not wasted a moment's time.

"Who is it?" Eleanor asked.

"It's Nancy," he told her.

"Nancy!"

She got up quickly to go to the telephone.

"Nancy darling, what a lovely surprise . . . Where are you? . . . *Here!* Marvelous! . . . She is? . . . Of course come up. We've already had dinner but we can give you something. . . . Well, we'll see. Come as quickly as you can."

Eleanor, beaming, replaced the phone in its cradle. "Isn't that nice? Nancy sounded wonderful. She's here with her friend Tessie Samuels."

"I thought you didn't like her."

"I might have been wrong. Tessie Samuels has been very nice to Nancy at a time when she needed it most. Oh, I know that Arthur said she poisoned Nancy's mind against him. But I don't believe that. It's only natural for Arthur to try to blame someone. I don't think Tessie Samuels had anything to do with the breakup of their marriage. The reasons are never that simple, are they?"

"Usually not."

He was tempted to add: no matter how complex the reasons, marriages do fail, however, and sometimes marriages fail without the fact ever being ratified by the solemnity of a divorce. His father, Thomas Garfield Lowe, over-serious, dedicated doctor, kept his marriage alive until he fell dead. His wife, Paul's mother, had revered his memory. The father's portrait in oil hung above the mantel on the fireplace; he was rather handsome with his slightly drooping mustache and inexplicably sad eyes. He had died when Paul was seven years old. Only years later did Paul discover the truth behind the pigmented sorrow in his father's eyes. Thomas Garfield Lowe drank too heavily, loved his sons, resented his hypochondriac wife, occupied himself furiously to keep from thinking. In leisure moments he played the violin, and at thirty-four years of age died in a meningitis epidemic, thereby mercifully avoiding the Great Panic, the Great Depression, the Great War, and the long dregs of unhappiness.

"In some ways," Eleanor said, "I can see where Nancy's friendship with Tessie Samuels might be very good for her. She needs someone like Tessie, don't you think so?"

In a curious way he began to feel free to say what he liked.

"I don't particularly like Tessie Samuels."

"You don't usually make up your mind about people quickly," Eleanor said in a slightly reproving tone. "I had the same first impression, but first impressions can be wrong. Nancy has told me a little about her. Her father is Judge Samuels—a very fine man. She comes from a very fine family."

"I'm sure she doesn't like me either."

Eleanor's gaze faltered. "You're imagining that, Paul. What reason would she have?" Eleanor picked up her handiwork. She plied the needle through the woven cloth vigorously. "Well, no matter what, I know you'll be especially nice to Miss Samuels—for Nancy's sake."

Seated in a chair opposite, he was thinking that he should have told her before this about the meeting with Tessie Samuels and made some attempt to explain Katherine's presence with him. Eleanor had already marked Katherine as the kind of woman he might be interested in, so there was no chance to avoid suspicion but if he had told Eleanor the confession itself would have helped to allay suspicion. Why had he delayed? He was reminded of those poor bastards who held to a mooring line as a balloon suddenly ascended, breaking from its mooring. When they were carried skyward they had a brief choice—drop off and suffer minor injuries or hang on and hope something would happen to save them. The balloon might miraculously descend again or the rope be drawn up or anything, anything! . . . One by one they fell to their deaths. We never let go in time.

When the doorbell rang, Eleanor started up to answer. He gestured for her to stay, then opened the door himself to confront Nancy.

She was chic and tall beside the short stocky figure of Tessie Samuels. Nancy wore a turquoise jacket and a loose-fitting skirt, and she did not look pregnant except below the waist where a small round protuberance showed.

"Hi, Dad." She offered a cool cheek to kiss as she entered. "You know Tessie, don't you?"

Tessie Samuels wore a bulky-looking short coat over her green wool dress. She was wearing those same zippered suede boots.

He smiled. "Of course. We met yesterday in St. Thomas."

"You did? You didn't tell me, Paul," Eleanor said. She appeared to be puzzled by the strange omission.

"I forgot."

Tessie's glance flickered to Nancy, then back. "It's nice to see you again, Mr. Justice."

"You've never been to St. Thomas, have you, Nancy?" he asked. "You ought to go sometime. It's your kind of place."

Nancy's eyes were lambent with mockery. "Is it?"

He helped Nancy remove her jacket. "Lots to do. Some of the loveliest beaches in the world. Water so clear you can see a dime fifty feet down. Even read the date on it. Great snorkeling."

Eleanor and Nancy embraced.

He assisted Tessie Samuels out of her bulky coat.

"How did that public relations chore you were doing down there work out?" he asked.

"I only had to attend the opening," Tessie Samuels said. "Everything came off on schedule."

Eleanor turned to Tessie. "It must have been quite a surprise meeting my husband, Miss Samuels. Where was it?"

He said, "At the airport."

He was perversely enjoying these final moments. Before the firing squad, refusing the blindfold with cool insolence, calling out "Ready-aim-fire" to his executioners.

Eleanor was smiling at Tessie. "Well, that was quite a coincidence." She couldn't seem to get over it.

"Yes, it was," Tessie said.

Eleanor turned to Nancy. "Have you eaten anything? Wouldn't you like me to get you something?"

"We had dinner in Boston—before we left. We don't want a thing, Mother." Nancy glanced into the wall mirror and touched her hair. "Tessie hasn't seen your new home. Why don't you take her on the grand tour?"

"Well, I'd be glad to," Eleanor said. "But perhaps Miss Samuels isn't interested."

"You seem to have a lovely place," Tessie Samuels said. "I'd like very much to see it, Mrs. Lowe."

Eleanor asked, "Are you coming, Nancy?"

"I'm walking for two these days. It tires me out. I'll just stay and visit with Dad."

As soon as Eleanor and Tessie Samuels left the room, Nancy seated herself carefully on the sofa and crossed her legs.

"Do you have a cigarette?"

"There's one in the box next to you."

Nancy chose one. She waited with lidded amusement while he held a lighter to the cigarette and she touched his hand lightly as though to steady it.

She glanced up at him. "You don't have any nerves, do you? Your hand is steady as a rock."

"Do I have any reason to be nervous?"

She blew out smoke. "I notice how eager you are for a showdown. That remark to Tessie about meeting in St. Thomas. You were practically asking for it." She sat back and spread her arms along the sofa. "What sort of woman is she?"

"Who?"

"Katherine Prescott. I remembered her when Tessie mentioned her name. She's the newspaperwoman who wrote that series of articles about you. But I forget what she looks like. Good-looking? Younger than Mother?"

He stared directly at her. "If you think you can play cat and mouse with me, you're mistaken. If you have anything to say, say it."

"Do you actually expect to brazen it out?"

"Miss Prescott and I met by chance in a lunchroom near the airport."

Her voice sank down to ironic sibilance. "I admire your gall. It's one of your most endearing qualities."

"I find this particular attitude of yours, Nancy, among your most irritating qualities."

"I suppose this is all part of the picture of Paul Lincoln Lowe. Nothing chips away that monument of insincerity. You've been acting a great man for so long it's become second nature." She reached to an ashtray to twist out her cigarette. "Now you manage to screen out all the things Paul Lincoln Lowe isn't supposed to feel. There must be some little remnant of you hidden away that is really you. Under that rusty cowpoke exterior there has to be. If so, I want to talk to it for a minute. I know you haven't loved Mother for a long time. That's all right. I've never understood why you two got married in the first place. And—don't misunderstand—I certainly don't object if you have a little fling now and then."

Her directness was disconcerting.

"But your affair with Katherine Prescott is obviously more than that. Or you'd never have taken the risk of running away with her the way you did." Her green eyes glittered. "If you should happen to have arrived at the conclusion that the time has come to end your marriage, you might just as well forget it."

He should have laughed—the congestion of laughter began in his diaphragm but something blocked it.

"It seems to me, Nancy, that you're the one who's arrived at all the conclusions."

"I'm just setting conditions, Dad—the way you did when I told you I didn't want to have Arthur's child and you forced me to go through with having it."

She had not been softened by pregnancy; the other life within her had not blunted the sharp cutting edge of her own personality. In her womb the embryo was walled off, sealed off, separate, breathing nutrient in its hostile environment like a skindiver through a little tube.

"And what are your conditions, Nancy?"

"You aren't to see Katherine Prescott again. In fact, she has to go away so there's no chance of your even starting up with each other again."

"Aren't you being just a little silly? I have no control over anything that Miss Prescott does."

"Then you'd better sit down and reason with her, Dad. You're very good at that. I'm sure you can persuade her to do almost anything for you."

He was struck by how malice added something to Nancy's beauty.

"And suppose I don't accept your conditions?"

She stared at him. "I can always bring Mother up to date on your little escapade. That will get very very messy."

"It might. On the other hand she might not believe you. She might believe me."

When she clenched her teeth her cheeks knotted. "I'm willing to gamble that. Are you?"

The door closed in an upstairs room and footsteps murkily crossed the carpeting.

"Yes, I think I am, Nancy," he said.

Do not run, walk, to the nearest exit. Amid the blazing revels, as the tinsel explodes in flames and the gay party decorations are sucked up in destroying fire and champagne bursts in the bottle, do not run, walk.

She watched him carefully to catch any nuance of meaning.

"Mother will take it into the courts," she said. "It will be a real Roman holiday before she gets her divorce. Do you have any idea of how the story will be handled in the newspapers?"

He sat stony faced.

"When they're through with you, there won't be enough left of your dignity for you to stand on. If you don't resign you'll become a tourist attraction for Washington sightseers. 'That's Justice Paul Lowe—*he's* the one.' Something unintentionally humorous will turn up in nearly everything you say—'Isn't he someone to talk about morality of contract—with *his* morals?'"

The sharp *klock* of high heels moved onto the wooden flooring above them.

"The tabloids will have a delicious time of it," she said. "Katherine Prescott will get her share of the notoriety too. She'll be the Other Woman—and that label will stick to her for a long time."

He said, "This is beginning to sound like some sort of obsession with you, Nancy."

Nancy laughed. "Should I talk to my analyst? I've discussed you a lot with him in recent weeks, Dad. He says I feel betrayed because I had a false image of you—kind and good and noble—and then I blamed you for not having been that way when I needed you to be. But you taught me that image. You brought me up on it. And that's a form of betrayal, isn't it?"

"I never pretended to be anything but your father, Nancy. You might understand me better if you expected less."

"Ah, the gentle wise parental voice. It doesn't help. Neither will the stern parental voice. I know all the variations, Dad, and none of them frighten me any more. I've grown up. I'm not your daughter—I'm your enemy. If that makes me unnatural, you've only yourself to blame for it. You betrayed me first."

"If you think that, I feel sorry for you, Nancy."

"Don't be. You're the one likely to find himself standing in the forum with his pants down. Well, what is it going to be, Dad? Are you going to be sensible and send her away?" She made a curiously stiff movement with her arm, an unwonted awkwardness. "Or are you going to keep on with your juvenile daydreams about starting life all over again with a woman you love, love, love."

He heard footsteps moving slowly down the staircase.

Nancy's voice turned like a knife to its sharpest edge: "Remember—it's your whole future."

Eleanor appeared in the doorway with Tessie Samuels.

"What are you two talking about?" she asked.

"Everyone's future," Nancy said brightly. "What else is there to talk about? I was telling Dad that Judge Samuels—Tessie's father—predicts he'll be one of the strong men of the Supreme Court. The natural heir to Charles Edmunson. Isn't that so, Tessie?"

Tessie Samuels said to Paul Lowe, "My father is one of your admirers, Mr. Justice. He's read all your opinions."

"That's very patient of him."

"He says you'll take Edmunson's place because the liberals on the Court will need a new leader when Edmunson retires. He says the Chief Justice isn't temperamentally suited to be the leader of any one faction, and Justices Merriam and McCann aren't strong enough."

Paul Lowe said: "I wouldn't like to disappoint Judge Samuels. But I'm having enough trouble holding my own."

Tessie Samuels answered with a thin, superior smile, "My father usually knows what he's talking about. It's possible you're too close to the situation to appraise it impartially."

"I suppose we'll just have to wait to see who's right."

Tessie Samuels lapsed into an unpersuaded silence. Obviously she had a close and admiring relationship with her father and accepted his judgments submissively. In their brief exchange Paul Lowe caught a glimpse of a child, patterning herself after the strong parent, copying him, willing herself to be more like him. It would account for some of Tessie Samuels' self-conscious masculinity.

Nancy said, "Mother, you know something? I *am* hungry, after all. Are you hungry, Tessie?"

"I'll eat if you want to," Tessie said.

Eleanor and Tessie Samuels led the way toward the dining room. Nancy lingered behind with him.

Nancy said, "I won't tell Mother anything yet. I'll give you a chance to think it over."

Only the dullest do not contemplate the chance of escape—but, still, the main thing to avoid is panic. Do not run, walk.

"That's very considerate of you."

A slow smile wrinkled her lips. "I know you, Dad. Judge Samuels is right when he says you have a chance to be a great man, and that's too important for you to risk. . . . I wonder, did Abraham Lincoln have a daughter? If she could be alive today, how would she feel seeing him all permanent in granite? Would she join with the idolaters—or try to knock a few stone flakes off his statue?"

He said, "Whatever she did would reveal a lot more about her than about him."

She put her arm through his, and laughed gaily. "The man with the answers," she said as they entered the dining room.

Katherine sat quietly for a time until the difficulty of speech began to thicken between them. It was raining outside her apartment windows. Now and again a spray of water lashed like a cat-o'-nine-tails at the windowpane.

She stared unseeing at the darkness and hugged her elbows.

He sat upright, outwardly composed. Within himself he was shivering as though he were somewhere outside in the rain. The illusion became so real that he almost felt wetness on his face and hair, and raindrops sliding down his cheeks to the mouth corners.

Finally he broke the silence, "I don't believe Nancy will make trouble when it comes right down to it."

The words sounded forced.

"My poor darling," she said. "It's exactly what Nancy will do."

"Why do you say that?"

"Partly because she wants some sort of revenge against you. And partly for a reason she would never acknowledge." Katherine turned to him sadly. "She's in love with you in the same way I am."

"Ridiculous!"

"She puts up with Eleanor as a rival because she knows you don't love her. But she won't accept anyone else—not as someone to share you with."

Was it so? That was the subtly poisonous attraction of an explanation drawn from the unconscious—particularly someone else's unconscious. How could it be refuted? Its logic was unanswerable because it ran deeper than the logic of the conscious mind.

Sometimes he longed for a bright clear pre-Freudian world.

"Whatever she does about us, I'm prepared for it," he said. "I won't let anything stand in the way of being with you."

She shook her head. "I can't let you destroy yourself. Your work is too important."

"Not as important as you are."

"When you talk about it, when I see your excitement about it, I could be jealous if I didn't admire you so much for being the way you are."

"You don't have to be jealous. Not of anything."

But her intuition was right. His duties on the Supreme Court had become not merely his appointed task but something that existed in and permeated everything. He never saw the palatial marble building without a queer pride that his desk was somewhere inside, that he was, even in the smallest way, one reason for its being there. He never read the names of any of his predecessors, or paused before their likenesses preserved in stone, without a sensation of being among friends, co-workers, equally concerned with him in a common enterprise: the law, the growth and stability of law within a nation founded on laws. Only a hundred men had served on the Supreme Court since its inception, and the strongest bond linked him to them all. It seemed to him they were, at the same moment, in a great hall, visiting and talking with each other (their thoughts and opinions, the visible impact of their personalities, were in the record) and the accident of their separation from him in time was no more meaningful than the accidental seating location in the great hall—some nearer, some farther away. At any moment he might cross over to them, or they to him.

Katherine said, "Nancy is angry enough—disturbed enough—to do anything if you try to cross her. She has to believe that her ultimatum has worked."

"What are you suggesting?"

"I should go away for a while."

"No!"

"Paul, I have to go home to be with Timmy, anyhow. I can stay there longer than I planned. I'll ask Race Hardman for a temporary reassignment."

"How long would you be gone?"

"As long as necessary. Until Nancy isn't suspicious any more."

"And what will happen to us while we're separated?"

I can tell you, he thought. We won't intend anything to change, but it will change whether we intend it or not. You won't share any of my problems and I won't share yours; we won't communicate the little things to each other that are the most important in a real intimacy—that don't even need to be said, but are told with a look, or a gesture. Or even a silence. Time will pass, and doubts will grow until our separation takes on a character of its own, becomes an established fact. And we'll never understand how everything got to such a state because we never wanted it to.

She said, "I can accept it because it won't be forever. I know I love you, and that's enough for me. People can do anything if they're in love."

In any event, he thought, he could propose no better answer. The problem was difficult, and Katherine was offering a kind of solution. She was saying: wait, see how things work out, allow dusty enmity to settle.

"I'm not sure I can be away from you very long, Katherine. I'm not sure I have the strength. But I suppose I could try it."

She looked up, her expression barely closing over pain. "I'll miss you terribly. But it's the best way. We have to do what's best, don't we?"

"On one condition." He stopped near her and took her hands. She stiffened, waiting for what he would say next. "If I can't stand it, will you come to me? Whenever I send for you?"

"Whenever you send for me," she said quietly.

Unexpectedly, entirely without warning, he was truly shaken by the fact of this impending separation. Their remaining time, this brief hour together, became unbearably poignant to him. He wanted to extend it by intensely experiencing it.

Still holding her hands, he raised her to him. He kissed her. How yielding she was! Everything was now tremendously confused. He thought, through a maelstrom there is no sure guide but instinct. The slow thunder of her heart was beneath his hand. For a moment she was cold—her coldness penetrated him—then her beating heart quickened its rhythm and the strength of his desire made the room warm.

17

He would not have believed how much he would miss her.

Nothing availed against the power of memory. In odd and unexpected ways he called her back—that wonderful way in which laughter lit up her face, a mocking curtsy she once made, the small globules of water on her skin after swimming, her serious intent look while plucking an eyebrow before a mirror, how she held a menu too far away, and how candlelight illumined the almost poreless perfection of her cheek. These images intruded into his mind to call him away from the present task, to make other people's voices sound distant and their faces go out of focus.

In the first few weeks he turned to work as an escape from bedeviling thoughts. When he was assigned an opinion he labored day and night until the draft was ready for the printer. He was indefatigable, read every source, tracked down every citation. Lawbooks were scattered on the floor of his office with tiny white papers sticking out like flags from the pages he wanted to consult.

When he was not researching or writing an opinion, he invented tasks to occupy the hours. He would play with simple statistics like a bank teller counting over the cash in the till.

One morning he said to his law clerk, Jack Broderick: "I'd like to know exactly how many lawyers the Court has admitted this term."

"Yes, Mr. Justice," Broderick said, mystified.

He did not explain why he wanted the figures. He relied on the mysterious power of status to keep his request from seeming nonsensical. Oddly enough, the facts—1647 lawyers—later proved useful during a debate in conference on ways the Court could cut down its work load.

After that debate while he was discussing the disposition of the various cases with his law clerks, he suddenly said to Jack Broderick:

"I'd like you to do a breakdown of cases we've handled this year by categories."

"Which categories, Mr. Justice?"

"Well, roughly—it'll have to be rough because of overlapping—break them down first into cases that deal with business. You know what I mean, interpreting Acts of Congress that relate to business—those cases dealing with labor laws, antitrust suits, and tax laws. Then give me an estimate, as accurate as you can make it, of how many of our cases deal with the conflict between the federal government and the states. I suppose the final category would deal with cases that involve some claimed interference with the constitutional liberties of citizens."

"You want this breakdown on all the cases handled this year, Mr. Justice?"

"I tell you what you can also do. Let's have a similar breakdown of the cases handled five, ten, and fifteen years ago. That'll give a basis for comparison on how the nature of our caseload is changing."

"Do you want Bill Tobin to give me a hand on this?"

"I don't think it'll be necessary. I'll be keeping Bill busy on some other things."

Jack Broderick answered a shade wearily, "Yes, Mr. Justice."

His loneliness was hardest to bear when he was not working at all. At home, he tried to be especially kind to Eleanor but that sort of kindness, expressed in politeness, in consideration, confirmed the fact that they were living together as intimate strangers. If, as he often thought, there are two codes of right and wrong conduct—one written and the other unwritten—it was against the codified written charge that he could offer a defense; he was an adulterer yet felt himself to be innocent. It was in the unwritten guide that he condemned himself, in that markless ledger wherein he kept his emotional debts. His behavior toward Eleanor was too correct and therefore cold and to be cold toward those whom we are supposed to love is cruelty.

At night he would lie quietly in bed, staring at the ceiling, trying not to disturb Eleanor lying beside him, trying not to think about Katherine. In the morning he rose early, having slept no more than three or four hours, and had two cups of hot black coffee for breakfast. Long before the commuter swarm had begun to crowd the streets, he left for the Supreme Court.

One morning he arrived at six-thirty, and had been hard at work for nearly two hours when his law clerks arrived. When he came out to Martha Scully's desk, he heard their voices through the partly open door of the office.

Bill Tobin said, ". . . not as much of a scholar as say Edmunson or Waldo Shuler—but he's more soundly based in constitutional law and precedent than Edmunson is, and his whole philosophy is a hell of a lot more daring and, well, pungent than old mossback Shuler."

"That's your personal opinion," Jack Broderick answered sharply.

Paul Lowe started for the open door to let the young men know that he was in the office. Before he could reach it, Jack Broderick's high clear impatient voice continued:

"Some of the assignments he's been giving me lately, I wonder if he knows what he wants. He's storing up all kinds of miscellaneous facts that can't do him or anybody one damn bit of good."

Paul Lowe paused. At this point he could neither advance nor retreat.

238

Bill Tobin answered sharply, "It's possible, Jack, that you're in no position to tell."

"Who's in a better one? I work with him every day."

"Maybe you're too close. You need perspective. All I know is that the people who do have perspective are practically in raptures. They say he's the best new justice in the whole recent history of the Court."

"Who says that?" Jack Broderick inquired disdainfully.

"The law review journals for one. There must've been a dozen articles about him."

"Frankly, I don't know what they base that kind of statement on. I haven't read anything of his that's going to go ringing down the ages."

"He hasn't had that sort of case yet. But when the right one comes along, you can bet he'll do right by it. Just one big issue and he'll put his name in the history books along with the best of them."

A rustling movement inside the clerks' office indicated that the two young men had taken their places at their desks. Martha Scully might arrive at any moment.

Paul Lowe tiptoed quietly to the corridor outside the office. Then he turned and entered briskly with as much clatter as he could reasonably make.

He went to the door of the clerks' office to look in.

"Good morning, gentlemen."

"Good morning, Mr. Justice," Bill Tobin said.

"Good morning, Mr. Justice," Jack Broderick said.

Both young men smiled cheerily.

He sat staring at typewritten words on the paper in the machine before him:

It has been argued that we must permit Congress to take any steps necessary to preserve the security of our nation. But the question we must also ask ourselves is: What kind of nation do we wish to preserve, and how? The only way to preserve a democratic government is to keep it fully responsive to the needs of its people. That means leaving them wholly free to declare what they need as well as what they fear, what they wish to change as well as what they wish to maintain. For every value to be obtained some sacrifice must be accepted. We dare not exchange liberty for government.

He was writing an opinion assigned to him in *Dyke vs. Representative Charles Albert*, the Chairman of the House Un-American Activities Committee.

He had stopped because he had the early symptoms of what he feared was going to be a severe headache.

The intercom buzzer sounded.

Martha Scully said, "Mr. Justice Branch is here to see you. He said not to interrupt if you're busy, Mr. Justice."

"I'm not too busy to see him."

A moment later Bill Branch entered the office. Paul Lowe swung about in his black leather swivel chair.

"Good morning, Bill. How are you?"

"I'm fine, Paul. I heard your typewriter clicking away when I came in a few minutes ago, so I waited for a pause before I asked Martha to ring in."

"That's nice of you, but I really don't mind occasional interruptions."

Bill Branch sat against the edge of the desk. "Been going at it pretty hard of late, haven't you?"

"There's a lot to do."

"Of course I shouldn't complain. Having a workhorse like you around is always a blessing. You take up the slack left by us worn-out, spavined and broken-down equines."

"Everyone seems to be pulling about the same load, Bill."

Bill Branch was the kind of man who was rarely called William even by strangers. He was heavy-set, graying, jowly and friendly. His nose seemed to have been carelessly molded out of putty and attached to his face, and there were innumerable tiny red veins in his cheeks. He was careful of his health and physical appearance. He visited a Turkish bath twice a week, played golf on Sundays, and dressed in expensive suits cut to his measure by a private tailor. The jackets fit sleekly over his full torso, but no trousers could do much for the thin, set-wide-apart legs which protruded from his thick body like penciled lines in a man's figure drawn by children.

"You've been averaging an opinion a week. That's a good deal more than your share." Bill Branch rubbed his shapeless nose amiably. "I've just read your opinion in Voorhis versus the *Daily Record Mirror*. As you know, I wasn't at the conference when the voting was held. I think I might go along with you, if you can clear up a couple of points for me."

"I'll try."

When Paul Lowe had finished with his explanation, Bill Branch sighed and announced in his gravelly voice, "I'll join in your opinion this time. Then if your clear rule doesn't prove out in practice I'll take the next chance I get to make my own position clear."

"I'm glad I heard your objections, Bill. I'll include a passage on the safeguards that are built into the law to assure a fair trial, regardless of what kind of publicity a defendant gets."

"You'll carry the Court with you on this one." Branch smiled. "That makes quite a winning streak for you, doesn't it, Paul?"

"I've just been lucky enough to pick the winning side."

"More than that," Bill Branch said. "More than that. By the way, are you planning to go to Dolores Hardman's party next Saturday night? It'll be a splashy blowout."

"My wife is looking forward to it. So I guess I'll be there."

"You'll have a good time," Bill Branch said. "According to the society columns, Dolores' parties are always the big event of the social season. But I go there for the same reason I watch tropical fish in a tank. Such weird specimens turn up. . . ."

Shortly after Bill Branch left, Martha Scully brought in the mail. There was a light blue envelope, in the familiar handwriting, marked *Personal*. He waited until Martha left the office before he ripped open the envelope.

Dearest,
    I've been invited to Washington to the party at Dolores Hardman's. I'm sure Race arranged for his mother to ask me, so it's really something of a command invitation. I'm leaving Lincoln Friday morning. Is there any chance at all we can see each other?
    I've missed you desperately.

KATHERINE

The buzzer sounded to warn him that five minutes remained to the opening of Court. He did not hear it. He remained seated at his desk until Martha appeared anxiously in the doorway.
    She said, "You'd better hurry, Mr. Justice."
    Paul Lowe grinned foolishly at her. "Martha, don't worry about me. I'm fine."

At a few minutes past nine o'clock Saturday evening, he sat with Eleanor in the rear of the Chrysler sedan halted at the south gate to Dolores Hardman's estate. They were waiting for their credentials to be checked. Ahead in a Jaguar convertible was a swarthy man in a bright-colored turban with a coronet of jewels set into the top. The woman with him, somewhat lighter of complexion, had her long thick intensely black hair drawn back tightly and held together with a diamond-studded comb. She wore a sari that left one brown shoulder bare.
    "Who are they?" Eleanor asked, beside him in the car.
    "Probably some major diplomat from a minor country. The kind who recently renounced his titles, kept his privileges and, having freed the slaves on his estates, accepted a lush job at the UN so he can tell Americans why we're not a true democracy."
    "Do you think that's his wife? She's handsome."
    The Jaguar passed through the gate. Jonathan Carter pulled their car up to the gate. Before Jonathan showed their gate pass the guard, smiling, peered into the back seat.
    "Mr. and Mrs. Justice Lowe. Go right ahead."
    Eleanor tugged the edges of her mink wrap with satisfaction, and smiled. Nothing reassured her so much as to be recognized. He did not spoil her pleasure by telling her that the gateman had a list of the guests' cars with the license numbers to help him in making the identification.
    They got out of their car at the porticoed south entrance and entered

the Hardman mansion between two huge white pillars. In the reception room forty or fifty guests were gathered, in two main clusters near the large fireplaces at either end. Servants were passing among the guests with drinks.

In the group Paul Lowe recognized Henry Merriam and Waldo Shuler and Gabriel Hart; Senators Vance Murdoch, Otto Binder, Tom Sherman and George Walsh, and Attorney General Keenan. Their wives wore their most expensive floor-length gowns and whatever jewelry they had been able to dig out of vaults, beg, borrow or rent. Glitter was the word for guests at a party by Dolores Hardman. Dolores was in her seventies, a tiny, regally gray-haired lady of insufferable wealth and domineering manner, who owned a collection of fabulous gems, including the world's most notorious diamond necklace. She had earned the reputation of giving the best parties in the city that often seemed devoted to nothing else but parties. Her home was in Alexandria, a few miles south of Mount Vernon with a commanding vista of the Potomac. Here gathered leaders of government, of the military, grande dames of society and presidents of mighty corporations. Paul Lowe had met Dolores Hardman only twice. Beneath the assumption of superiority which wealth and manner and family inheritance conferred upon her, he found her a rather silly woman whose chief interest in life was her jewelry collection and her conspicuously different hairstyles. Tonight she wore a high sweeping pompadoured wig, festooned with sparkling jewels, so intricately wound and coiffured that she walked beneath it like a native woman carrying a particularly fragile basketful of produce.

In the first twenty minutes Paul Lowe exchanged greetings with the Speaker of the House, the Attorney General, the Assistant Secretary of Commerce, a four-star general, a well-known author, a prominent minister in the Italian government, and two influential members of the press, including Teddy Strong, the chief editorial writer for the *Times*. By this time the crowd had multiplied seven fold and other guests were still arriving (he waved hello to Martin Gannett, the president's appointment secretary).

Eleanor was in a corner, in conversation with Chief Justice John Hampton and Susan Branch, who was Bill Branch's wife. Paul Lowe started to go over to them, but was detoured by three women who wanted to meet him. They turned out to be, respectively, the wife of a Congressman, the daughter of the chairman of the National Advisory Committee, and the president of the Women's Trade Union League.

When he did break away during a conversational lull (the conversation had been mostly lull) he arrived to overhear John Hampton discoursing on the need to cut down the Court's work load to insure maximum efficiency.

"Something will have to be done soon," John Hampton said, touching his black-gray hair in an abstracted way. "I've talked to my colleagues about cutting down on the length of written opinions and giving up the writing of so many separate opinions and dissents. But that isn't enough."

"I really don't see how you all do as much as you do," Eleanor said.

Susan Branch added, "Sometimes I tell my husband, 'Bill, it can't keep on this way, can it?'"

John Hampton smiled a bit wanly. "There are other solutions, of course. I personally believe we should ask Congress to take away federal jurisdiction over cases which come into the district courts simply because they involve citizens of two different states. That category was once important but it's steadily diminishing. I can't see any real harm if we drop such cases altogether. Don't you think so, Paul?"

"It would certainly be a timesaver," Paul Lowe said.

"In the end, however," John Hampton said, warming to encouragement, "we're going to have to lead the lower courts, help them to make rules of procedure that will cover cases which otherwise might involve the Supreme Court. I've been giving it some thought recently. The next time I meet with the lower-court judges I'm going to concentrate on working out ways to improve the operations of the entire federal court system."

Eleanor's smile had taken on a fixed quality and the intense focusing of her eyes told Paul that her physical responses were locked in place while her thoughts wandered. She looked lovely in a maroon-colored dress with long flowing lines accentuated by the fall of a drape from one shoulder down across her waist in a cascade of pleats to the hemline. Three hundred and forty dollars. If the cost of outfitting all the women at Dolores Hardman's party was added up, he thought, there would be enough to take all the children of Appalachia out of rags.

Someone plucked at his arm.

"How're you doing, Mr. Justice?"

Bill Tobin, with his girl Janet Yarlton, was standing near. Bill looked more pale than usual. Beads of perspiration dotted his upper lip and gathered on the level plain of his forehead where the hair had receded.

"Bill. How nice to see you here!" Paul Lowe said.

"I thought I'd surprise you. My girl—Janet Yarlton, remember?"

"Of course. How are you, Janet?"

"She's the one who got the invitation. I'm just her escort."

"Do you know the Hardmans?" Paul Lowe asked Janet.

"Yes," Janet said. "My folks are cave dwellers—real old-line Washingtonians. Part of the group that used to drop their cards at the White House to let the President know they weren't mad at him."

"I understand Justice Frank Joyce will show up later tonight," Bill Tobin said. A sudden swell in the crowd forced him close to Eleanor. "Oh, how do you do, Mrs. Lowe." He managed to hold his drink safely away from Eleanor.

"First time I've been to one of these extravaganzas," he said. "It's real camp, right down to the handwritten invitations in fine Spencerian script. I thought that kind of writing went out with George Washington and James Madison."

"I think it's a very impressive party," Eleanor said.

"You ain't seen nothing yet, Mrs. Lowe," Janet said. "Wait until someone starts to climb the chandelier and throw down light bulbs. This is one of the last great social events of our age. After us, the deluge."

"How will we know when the end is coming?" Bill Tobin asked.

"It'll rain champagne for forty days and nights," Paul Lowe said.

Servants carrying trays of drinks moved through the narrowing aisles of people. Paul Lowe pursued one fellow and captured a bourbon and soda from the tray.

By then he had lost Eleanor and the others. He was alone with Susan Branch.

Susan said, "Your wife is a very pretty woman, Mr. Justice. You must be very proud of her."

Susan Branch was a round-faced plain woman with soft brown hair streaked with gray. Everyone said she was very sweet. "Isn't she sweet?" is what everyone said about Susan Branch.

"Oh, yes," Paul Lowe said. "I am. I'm very proud of her."

He was a little drunk and more than a little anxious by the end of the first hour. Each time he glanced at his watch he discovered that only a minute or two had passed. His nervousness increased. Although Katherine was not usually punctual, he had counted on her being punctual tonight.

Then an undertone of depression set in. She was not coming. Something had gone wrong. He made frequent trips to the bar in a corner of the huge room. He had consumed half a dozen bourbons without experiencing the slightest relaxation of tension.

Where was she?

She was flying in from Lincoln. Perhaps the plane was down somewhere. Even now, as he stood here, worrying, she might be dead in the wreckage somewhere. He would not allow such thoughts! . . . *But where was she?*

Would he have heard if a disaster had happened? Not necessarily. They might not inform anyone at the party. It might take hours. . . . On the next trip to the bar he saw Brenda Hardman hopelessly mired in desultory talk with a man from the Department of Interior who was outlining to her the need for conservation of natural resources.

Brenda Hardman gave him a pleading glance.

Drink in hand, he moved in. "Brenda, dear, you're looking spectacular tonight."

She wore a simple long black gown with a bow at the bosom. Her skin appeared startling white against the black. Jeweled earrings glittered, a tiara shimmered in her hair.

"Thank you, Paul. Do you know Peter Wyatt? He's from the Department of Interior. Mr. Wyatt, this is Mr. Justice Paul Lowe."

"I'm very honored to meet you, Mr. Justice. I've been following your work on the Court with great interest. Very great interest."

After a few moments of stilted conversation Peter Wyatt left.

"I don't know how to thank you," Brenda said. "I was starting to go numb. The numbness was already up to my chin." Her cupid's-bow mouth wrinkled pettishly.

244

He could not keep his attention on what she was saying. His glance roamed the huge room, searching, searching through familiar and unfamiliar faces for the one he wanted to see.

"You're a good friend," Brenda sighed—a fluttering breath. "You know, this is only the third party I've been to since the one we gave for you when you arrived in Washington. How long ago was that?"

How long it seemed!

"Seven months," he said.

"You see? Race wouldn't have come to this party if it weren't being given by his own mother. I don't know what interests him any more. Except business. Did you know he's negotiating to buy the Starnes chain?"

"I'm not surprised. I expect Race to be the most powerful publisher in America someday."

Brenda shook her head. "I'm worried about him. His gastritis is so bad he hardly eats. And he's away from home so much I don't think the children know who their father is any more." Her lower lip trembled.

Paul Lowe felt little sympathy for her. She had a problem, but everyone in the wide green world had problems. There was no sense in peddling one's troubles like wares to the casual passer-by. Besides, what did she understand of the meaning of real trouble? How old was she? Race was thirty-eight, and Brenda might be ten years younger. A young beautiful woman with everything. Half the population of the world was going to bed hungry every night. Children were crying for a handful of rice, a saucerful of milk. Disease and war were maiming and rending old and young with untellable agonies.

Suddenly he could not listen to Brenda any longer. He looked for succor. Bill Tobin's tall head appeared amid surrounding heads.

Paul Lowe nodded to him and Bill Tobin came over.

"Bill, have you met Brenda Hardman? At the moment Bill works for me," he told Brenda. "But he'll be free of bondage in a few more weeks. In the fall he starts on what will be a memorable career in the law." He held up his empty glass. "Excuse me—I think I need a refill."

He left to continue his search. Katherine might already have arrived and in the midst of the continual uproar, the ceaseless shifting of (God!) how many people, she might be looking for him. He clung to this hope while fear rose through the hazy light of chandeliers, through the moist warmth of too many humans gathered in a single place, exchanging their body heat and tepid conversation.

On the way to the bar he was watching everyone, looking past everyone. John Hampton and Bill Branch were talking with Attorney General Keenan. John Hampton stood very erect, very dignified—the physical reflection of a natural hauteur but also, Paul Lowe knew, an attempt to offset an increasing portliness of stomach. He saw John Hampton look up at him suddenly, and notice the empty glass in his hand. There was no fathoming John Hampton's expression.

At the bar Paul Lowe waited behind the Secretary of the Navy and a young Congressman from Oregon. As he was turning away, with a newly filled glass, Bill Branch came over.

"How do you like the party so far?" Bill Branch asked.

"It's fine."

"I'm not enjoying it much. The Chief has had my ear and all he talks is Court business."

"I had a session with him before."

"Still, it's better than trying to pump up a conversation with his wife. All Jane Hampton cares about is horses. After a while I felt like I was growing a tail. What're you drinking, Paul?"

"Bourbon and soda."

Bill Branch nodded. "Haven't you been on the sauce pretty heavily tonight? I think the Chief's noticed it." Branch's light gray eyes were serious. "Forgive me, Paul. All my friends know I'm the last one to give advice. How can I? I've been Peck's Bad Boy as long as I can remember. But I'd hate to lose my title to you."

"I'd say I still have quite a long way to go to catch up," Paul Lowe said quietly.

Bill Branch chuckled. "I'm only trying to be helpful. I wish somebody had talked to me ten years ago the way I'm talking to you now. Time and the quart spare no man."

Paul Lowe glanced around the room at the people gathered in groups, talking with forced animation, and abruptly he saw them all as gossiping housewives chattering to each other over a back fence. And their gossiping was all about him. How could he strike back? There was no way. They were invincible in their sobriety.

He saw Eleanor and waved.

"There's my wife. Excuse me, Bill."

Eleanor came forward to greet him. "I've been trying to find you, darling. Frank Joyce came in a little while ago." She glanced significantly at the glass in his hand. "Don't you think you've had enough?"

"No," he said mocking her tone, "I don't think I've had enough." His anger flowed down his shoulders and into his arms. "Damn it! Why can't people leave me alone?"

He turned and left her standing there. He set off across the crowded floor, walking slowly, apologizing through the crowd as he kept bumping into people. Someone turned into him and sloshed his drink.

"Oh, I *am* sorry."

"It's all right," he said.

He blinked to clear his vision of a slight fuzziness. The young man who had spilled his drink was good-looking silver-haired Peter Daris, the Solicitor General, who was with his usual companion, Laura Connell.

"That was clumsy of me," Peter Daris said. He took his handkerchief out and brushed Paul Lowe's jacket. "I'm afraid I wasn't looking."

Paul Lowe managed a grin. "Let's not make a federal case out of it, shall we?"

Peter Daris laughed, and so did Laura, and as Paul Lowe pushed on he was aware with peripheral vision that they were talking about him, and smiling in friendly fashion. He was all right, perfectly all right, perfectly in control.

Katherine was coming toward him.

For the space of a second he could not be sure. He plucked at the lapel of his dinner jacket and rubbed his thumb and forefinger afterward as though to assure himself of his own physical presence in the same room.

"Katherine," he said under his breath.

The tall lean figure of Tom Jeffreys was at Katherine's side, his handsome masklike face somehow seeming naked above the faultless dinner jacket. Paul Lowe felt rumpled. He pushed his hair back with his free hand and some of the drink he was holding spilled.

She came directly to him and stood, smiling a little. She was real.

"Mr. Justice," she said, "how nice to see you again. You know Tom Jeffreys, don't you?"

"Of course. Hello." Switching his drink to his left hand he shook hands with Tom Jeffreys. "It's been a long time," he said to Katherine.

"Well, yes. I've been out of town. I only came back for the party. It's not the sort of affair you can ignore, is it, especially when the hostess is your employer's mother? Though as it turns out I very nearly did miss it, after all."

"My fault," Tom Jeffreys volunteered. "A last-minute emergency at the studio. A big shakeup in the news department—and I couldn't get away."

"I almost left without you," Katherine said in smiling reproof.

Paul Lowe knew the message was meant for him as explanation and apology. He stood stockstill, his senses overwhelmed by the simple fact of her being there and speech blocked by the many things he wanted to say. People shimmering in the hazy light drifted past, shoulders touched him, he was jostled—the presence of all other people annoyed him.

"I'm glad you could make it," he said.

Katherine looked around the huge overcrowded room. "I'm not sure anyone will ever know whether I was here."

"I will," he said.

She said lightly, "How gallant," but her glance warned him against saying more.

Tom Jeffreys gave Paul Lowe a quizzical stare. Then someone passing by grabbed him. Tom Jeffreys turned aside to talk.

Paul Lowe said in a tense whisper, "I must see you alone."

"Yes, I want to. But where?"

"I don't care. I can't talk to you in this crowd."

A voice called to him: "Paul! Paul Lowe!"

He turned. Frank Joyce was standing at the left of the fireplace at the far end of the room. Mr. and Mrs. Walter Schonberg were with him. Walter Schonberg was emphasizing a point with a pudgy finger that jabbed toward but never quite reached Frank Joyce's pleated shirt front.

Frank Joyce laughed softly at what Schonberg was telling him and then smiled and waved to Paul Lowe.

He waved back, and smiled, but when he looked for Katherine again she was gone. Then he saw her, a few feet away, with Tom Jeffreys leading her by the hand as they sidled through a narrow space in the crowd.

He would have called out but the distance widened and people closed in behind her like water surging together after a boat's passage. He saw the top of her head, and for a moment was tempted to plunge into the boiling sea of people after her. But a microscopic pinch of caution remained. He thought: I'll find her later. We'll be together—later.

Frank Joyce had a saintly appearance, made more striking by a crowning aureole of white hair that had become almost ethereal since Paul Lowe last saw him. He was shrunken inside his tuxedo jacket and his neck appeared too stringy to fill out his collar.

Paul Lowe came up beside him. "Mr. Justice Joyce, I believe."

"Paul!" With the familiar, quick, almost childlike affection Frank Joyce threw his arms about Paul Lowe's shoulders. At close quarters Joyce's body felt as though it were made of some hollow weightless material that was not flesh and bone.

"It's good to see you," Paul Lowe said. "Especially looking so well."

"I feel better—much better, Paul."

"I wanted to come to see you, but I was told your doctor didn't encourage visitors."

"This is the first evening I've been allowed out in a long time. My doctor's been treating me like a piece of fragile crockery."

"Just as well. He pulled you through."

"I talked to Bill Tobin earlier this evening. You can definitely count him among your admirers, Paul." Joyce smiled his shy smile. "In fact, if you'd care to, you may count me among your admirers too."

He flushed. "I don't expect to fill the shoes that were handed to me."

He was touched by Frank Joyce's compliment. Joyce had been one of the giants, an almost mythical figure, when Paul Lowe first came to the Supreme Court as law clerk to Edmunson. He could never have foreseen a time when they might speak, even remotely, as equals.

Joyce shook his head regretfully. "I always complained about the Court when I worked there. Called it the marble prison. But I was unhappy to leave, and I still miss it."

"Even in the little time I've been there," Paul Lowe said, "I can understand how that would happen."

"I think, Paul, it's because being a justice of the Supreme Court is rich in the satisfactions that a lawyer in private practice—or a politician—can never experience. The Court is one of the very few professions which enable a man to keep his integrity—and devote himself to fulfilling the inner life."

Amid the plush magnificence of Dolores Hardman's home, it was typical of Frank Joyce to discuss the satisfactions of the inner life. He was unworldly in the best sense—the material grasp never even caught at his coattails. He existed in a domain of pure spirit. How could he ever be Frank Joyce's equal? The old man's gentle serenity made Paul Lowe feel like a primitive—a raw, hungry, burly figure.

Several people descended on Joyce at once and he murmured an apology before he was taken away. Paul Lowe looked after him, thoughtfully.

"Remarkable man, isn't he?" Walter Schonberg asked.

"Yes," he said.

Walter Schonberg removed his cigar from between his teeth. "Well, God made us all different people. And that's a good thing."

It was so easy, Paul Lowe thought, for men like Schonberg who fully accepted themselves. There seemed to be a simplicity, a unity, to their characters that he envied. It was hard to believe that the seething turmoil he found within himself could ever be brought together into the coherence of a single identity.

There should be some calculus of desires—a measure by which he could know that one desire was this much greater than another. Katherine—his need for her was measurable in its intensity. But how much less was his need for other things? To do useful work, to achieve some fungible end, to let his life stand for something more than an allotted number of years in which to indulge his pleasures, to be a guardian, not destroyer, of that most sacred Ark in which men have carried for generations the enduring relics they call their morality. *If I am not for myself, who will be for me? If I am for myself only, what am I?* The Talmud had been a milestone along the path from the dark caves. But the answer to his dichotomy was not to be found in books. Ape and saint struggled within him, coupled by the tail.

Walter Schonberg was exchanging pleasantries with several friends. Now he turned back to Paul Lowe.

"There are refreshments in the other room. Shall we?"

The crowd began a slow eddying flow toward the dining room. Katherine, with Tom Jeffreys, was already nearing the high-arched entrance.

"By all means," Paul Lowe said.

In the huge semicircular dining room marble columns along two walls flanked individual busts of deceased Hardmans. There was Brewster Hardman, land-grabber and railroad tycoon; Earle Hardman, who served as an aide to McClellan in the Civil War; and Juniper Hardman, so-called frontier wit and humorist who after a few years in the West retired to a comfortable mansion on Long Island to write of the roistering days; and George Hardman, Race's father, who had founded the chain of newspapers that Race was still expanding.

At a massive horseshoe-shaped table beneath an American flag made of red, white and blue flowers, an incredibly lavish buffet was set forth. There was caviar flown in from Poland, and salmon from Alaska and fruit from Hawaii. At regular intervals along the horseshoe table were decorative wreaths that spelled out the names of various states in the same red, white and blue flowers. These floral displays divided the salmon from the boiled Maine lobster, and the lobster from the Virginia ham, and the turkey from the fresh strawberries and macadamia nuts.

At the opposite side of the room, and along both walls, small tables had been set up. At each place setting the doilies were shaped like bright blue stars. Imprinted on each gold-rimmed service platter was a fifty-star flag.

Dolores Hardman preceded Paul Lowe to the feast. "Do you like the patriotic motif?" she asked.

"Very much. Where did you get the idea?"

"It's a mark of respect to our guests of honor. The Senators from Hawaii and Alaska. I thought it would be a nice touch since they're from our newest states, you know. But I *was* worried about the caviar."

"Were you?"

"Everything else is native, you know. I wondered if it would be disloyal to have Polish caviar. But then our relations with the Poles are improving, and there's simply no question that they have the best caviar. Don't you think so, Mr. Justice?"

"I certainly do."

"I hope everyone is having as good a time as I am."

"I'm sure they are. It's the very best spring party you've ever given, Mrs. Hardman. I'm sure they'll be talking about it for a long time."

Dolores Hardman gave a coquettish inclination of her head that endangered her towering coiffure. "Do you really think so? How sweet of you to say so, Mr. Justice. Be sure to try some of the Alaska salmon. It was flown in just this afternoon."

Under Dolores' watchful eye, Paul Lowe heaped his plate with delicacies. But when he moved out of her range of vision he put the plate down at an empty table setting and headed toward the bar in the other room. He ordered a bourbon and branch water and sipped it, waiting to see if Katherine would come out to meet him.

"Mr. Justice!"

Janet Yarlton came toward him. He noticed for the first time how demurely attractive she was in the high-necked dark brown evening dress with copper earrings and on her slender arm, a copper bracelet. "I've been looking everywhere for Bill. Have you seen him?"

"He's probably looking for you. Why don't you stay in one place for a while and let him catch up?"

Janet brushed her hair back in place behind her ear. Her delightful smile vanished into quick irritability. "I hate parties like this. You can never *find* anyone."

"If I see him, I'll fire off a rocket," he said.

He finished his drink but Katherine did not come. He ordered another and took it with him to one of the small uncomfortable gold chairs that lined an entire wall. He sat down, holding his drink, and stared ahead until suddenly he was aware of someone sitting down beside him.

"Hello," she said.

He took a deep swallow of his drink. "I was wondering when you'd show up."

"I saw you come out here, Paul, but I couldn't think of an excuse to leave my table right away."

He couldn't help being surly; he *felt* surly. "I didn't know Tom Jeffreys was bringing you tonight."

"He was invited also, Paul. I could hardly tell him I'd prefer to go alone."

"You'd have gotten here earlier if you had."

"Darling, you're not jealous."

"Of him?"

"You *are* jealous."

"This is the first time we've seen each other for three weeks," he said. "I didn't believe you'd be so late."

"Dear, what's the matter with you?"

He finished his drink. A teleprompter in his brain had ceased sending messages and there was suddenly nothing for him to think about. It was a curious sensation of utter blankness which fortunately lasted only until she spoke again.

Katherine said softly, "It may be time you called a halt."

"To what?"

She nodded her head toward his empty glass.

"Oh, for God's sake, you too? I know how to hold my liquor."

Farther down the row of gold chairs people were turning to look. Katherine said, "Please don't have any more to drink, for my sake."

"I'm all right. Don't worry 'bout me."

His voice was slurring. That's what happened when he was accused of something—he began to act that way unconsciously. Un-con-scious-ly. Each separate syllable stated itself distinctly inside his head.

Suddenly Katherine said, "Tom, you'd better take me home."

Sure enough, Tom Jeffreys was there. Paul Lowe looked up at the lean face with prominent bones like a death's head.

"Y're not going home," Paul Lowe said.

"I can't really talk to you in this condition," Katherine said. She sounded near tears.

"You jus' wait a minute." He reached for her but his arm swung in empty air. She was standing, with Tom Jeffreys beside her.

Katherine hesitated. "Please try to get control of yourself."

"Don't argue with him, Katherine. It won't do any good. Can't you tell he's more than half out to sea?" Tom Jeffreys had very quickly abandoned his respectful tone. "Let's go, Katherine."

"Keep out of this, Jeffreys," Paul Lowe said. "If she wants to go, let her say so."

He was having trouble with the letter s. He heard it come out "shay." Well, not as bad as that.

"She *is* saying so," Jeffreys said coldly.

"Someone appoint you her guardian? Who the hell are you?"

That came out with no slurring and quite deliberately rude. His control was limited; he couldn't afford to waste it on politeness.

Tom Jeffreys' long nose seemed to quiver. "For heaven's sake, stop making a spectacle of yourself!"

"F'r two cents, Jeffreys, I'd punch you right in the mouth."

He knew he would do nothing of the kind but he enjoyed threatening to do it. The element of danger fascinated him. Nothing would remain but the early dawn with pistols.

Tom Jeffreys' slightly yellow teeth bared. "If you care anything at all about the dignity of your position you'll leave now—while you can still move under your own power."

Paul Lowe pushed himself erect—too quickly—and waited for dizziness to pass.

"You'd better apologize, Jeffreys."

"Well, I'm not going to," Tom Jeffreys said.

The air pulsed with deeply rhythmic sound. After a moment he recognized the bass undertone of an orchestra. He heard better in the low register than the high and only occasional thumps came through to him.

"Tom, please take me home," Katherine said. "Now."

"He's not going anywhere 'til he apologizes," Paul Lowe said. "He's been too goddamn insulting."

"Are you serious?" Tom Jeffreys asked. "You're a disgrace, Mr. Justice." How cynical he made the title sound! "And somebody has to tell you so."

Yes, Paul Lowe thought suddenly, it should be the verbal slap every time. Not a slap really—for it went beneath the skin. The poisoned needle —quickly in—then watch the slow writhe on the syllabic point, the ridiculous dying.

If with no warning he clubbed Jeffreys, would he knock him down? Probably. He was a little drunk, and not in the best of shape. Tom Jeffreys was a dozen years younger and several inches taller, but he was that lean nervous type who smoked too much and flinched from physical contact. His sport would be tennis. Quick stop and start, graceful run, musical *ping* of taut racquet strings on a high-bouncing ball, delicate vibrating impact on wrist nerves.

"I'll give you one more chance," Paul Lowe said. "Y'd better apologize."

It could have ended there if Tom Jeffreys had shut up, or if he had started to leave. Everything would have been fine if Jeffreys had not chosen this particular moment for one last sarcastic comment.

He said, "I'll look forward to reading about a nasty little episode in the gossip columns tomorrow. 'Distinguished justice of the Supreme Court gets falling-down drunk!'"

Tom Jeffreys was a bit too close as he said it, his wide mouth ugly in close-up, the fair freckled skin as mottled as a tiger's. Paul Lowe struck almost in self-defense, half clubbing. Jeffreys' eyes snapped wide open with astonishment and Paul Lowe saw his own fist frozen forever against the bony angle of Jeffreys' jaw. Then Jeffreys' face vanished out of his range of vision and he heard Katherine utter a small stifled scream.

A woman's voice: "I saw what happened. He hit him!"

A man's voice: "Nothing of the kind. They're both drunk!"

"Who is it? What's going on?"

He was hemmed in. Then he saw Bill Branch help Tom Jeffreys to his feet and brush off his tuxedo jacket.

Someone asked, "Was it a fight?"

Bill Branch answered, "Of course not. Mr. Jeffreys slipped. I saw it happen."

A woman said, "I didn't see anything like that."

A man said, "First thing I knew he was lying on his back."

"Are you all right?" Bill Branch asked Tom Jeffreys.

Tom Jeffreys, looking furious, kept his voice to a low grated whisper, "He's crazy, I tell you. Blind drunk and crazy!"

Bill Branch turned to the crowd and spread his arms to hold them back. His gravelly voice rose: "There's nothing wrong. Really. Let's not make something out of nothing."

Someone must have alerted the orchestra for the music abruptly became loud and clear with its treble register intact. Bill Branch took Paul Lowe by the arm and started through the crowd. He could not see Katherine anywhere but he caught a glimpse of Eleanor, pale and distraught, and smiled reassuringly at her.

Oh, boy, he thought suddenly. It was all he could think. Oh, boy.

18

In trying to piece the whole thing together, he could not remember leaving Dolores Hardman's estate. He could see himself arriving home, very tired, and Eleanor sniffling while they were undressing to go to bed. Then sleep had mercifully driven out the shadowy imprint of the immediate preceding hours.

His next clear recollection was Sunday morning, and a breakfast of tomato juice and black coffee, and the telephone ringing.

It was Nancy. She sounded amused. "I've been reading about you in the paper this morning."

"What paper?" he asked. He was annoyed at Nancy's attitude. There was a faint throbbing ache just above the bridge of his nose.

"Oh, you weren't in time for the regular respectable sheets. Their Sunday editions were all made up. But one of the scandal sheets that comes out on Sundays managed to include an item." Nancy giggled. "Tell me, Dad, did he fall or was he pushed? It isn't too clear from the way the story was written in the *Capitol Tattler*."

"Nothing happened at all, Nancy."

"It says in the paper . . ."

"I don't care what it says in the paper, Nancy."

"I'll read it to you. 'The big hubbub in the nation's capital this ayem concerns the altercation between our newest Supreme Court justice and a TV news commentator, who ended up on the floor wondering "wha' hoppen?" Such goings on.'"

Fortunately, there was no mention of Katherine Prescott, and Nancy had no reason to suspect anything. He blinked his eyes, which felt as though they had been rubbed with grit.

"They're trying to make a story out of nothing. There won't even be a mention in a reputable paper like the *Times*."

"The *Times* doesn't believe in gossiping about people—only countries. Well, since you're apparently not going to tell me the real story, I think I'll put my faith in the yellow-press version. It's a lot more interesting."

"I'm glad you're enjoying it, Nancy."

"It's always such fun when your father gets his name in the papers. By the way, this is the last you'll hear from me for a while unless I get the urge to write. I'm leaving for a vacation in Paris next week with my friend Tessie Samuels."

"What about the baby?"

Her voice was brittle with challenge. "What about it?"

"Do you think it's wise to travel in your condition?"

"The baby's not due for seven or eight weeks. I'm not about to become a recluse for the sake of that little brat."

There was nothing to be gained by arguing with Nancy—there never had been.

"Would you like to talk to your mother?"

"No, but give Mother my love, won't you? And tell her to keep her guard up. I understand from reading the newspapers that you're developing a splendid left hook."

Across the table from him, Eleanor had been holding a glass of orange juice to her lips and watching him through the top half of the glass to which tiny bits of orange pulp still clung. He put the telephone down and she put the glass down.

"Didn't Nancy want to talk to me?" Eleanor asked.

"She sent her love. She said she's leaving for Europe with Tessie Samuels."

"Oh, Then we'll be able to see her before she goes."

"She didn't seem to want to see us."

Eleanor's slightly protruding tooth pressed into her lower lip. "I'm sure she wanted to see us, Paul. Why did she bother to call?"

"She wasn't calling us out of concern—just curiosity."

Eleanor's attention was diverted to a fresh anxiety. "She knows about it, doesn't she?"

"Yes."

"Oh, dear."

"I wish you'd stop acting as though the end of the world had arrived. It hasn't. It's just some gossip columnist in a weekly tabloid who didn't even mention me by name."

"It's just such a terrible thing to happen to a man in your position. I was up most of the night thinking how unfair it is. You're so vulnerable when you have a name that makes news."

He was sure she did not know the truth about what had occurred at Dolores Hardman's party. Probably the reason seemed clear to her—she was aware that he had been drinking enough to have lost control and if he lost control then he lost responsibility. What was important to her now was to protect his reputation, their home, her social status. In her frustration at realizing how helpless she was to do anything she found genuine emotion, and the emotion in turn gave her a higher degree of articulateness. "You're so vulnerable when you have a name that makes news." Not a profound or even particularly keen insight but true and clearly expressed. All the middle-class powers of her mind were harnessed by the force of sincerity.

The next telephone call was from a reporter on a news service. He was checking the item the gossip columnist had printed. Paul Lowe told him he had no comment to make because there was simply nothing worth making a comment about. The telephone rang again a moment later. This time the call was from a reporter for the Washington *Post*. Paul Lowe told him what he had told the news-service reporter. The next call was from a syndicated columnist who specialized in politics on an informal gossipy level.

"It must have been a wonderful party," the columnist said with a noticeable acidity. "Dolores' parties are usually such bores. I'm really sorry I missed this one."

When Paul Lowe hung up he told Eleanor, who was then sipping her coffee, "I'm going down for a walk. If anyone else calls, tell them I've gone out for the day."

"All right, dear."

At a large corner drugstore that was open on Sunday, he entered and went to a telephone booth. He dialed the number of Katherine's apartment. The phone rang and rang with no answer.

At five o'clock that afternoon, while Eleanor was listening to the hourly news report on the radio, he risked another call from his library. Again, no answer. He went out to find Eleanor in a somewhat more cheerful mood. The news report on the radio had made no mention of the incident.

"I'm going to try to do some work," he said.

"We'll have a quiet dinner at home," Eleanor said. "At about eight?"

"That will be fine."

By the time dinner was over he was obsessed with the need to talk to Katherine.

"I think I'll go out for a while," he told Eleanor.

"Do you want me to go with you, dear?"

"I'd rather be alone if you don't mind. I want to think out a problem that's puzzling me."

After walking a few blocks he hailed a taxi and gave the driver Katherine's address. Outside the building he looked up at the window of her apartment. There was no light in the window. It was nearly ten o'clock. He rode the slow creaking elevator upstairs. At the door he pushed the bell again and again, heard the empty clanging inside. Finally he went downstairs and rang the bell of the superintendent's apartment on the ground floor.

A short, squarely built man with a pencil mustache answered the door. He wore a white shirt, suspenders, and a pair of dusty trousers.

"I've been trying Miss Prescott's apartment. There doesn't seem to be anyone home."

"She left early this morning."

"She left? Where was she going?"

"I'm sure I don't know, mister."

"Did she say how long she'd be gone?"

256

"All I know is, she was carrying a suitcase. I helped her put it in the taxi."

"I see. Thank you very much."

When he emerged again onto the street, he was dazed. Why would she run away, without a word? No matter how great her haste there would have been time to telephone. Then he realized it was impossible for her to talk to him at his home. They never could do anything in the way lovers could. They were trapped in a maze of marriage, career, conflicting interests. They could not even plan a day together over this weekend without having their plans knocked flat by something unexpected. They had spanned two thousand miles of separation, only to be separated again. Why? It must have some connection with the drunken brawl at Dolores Hardman's, but while he was ready to admit that was his fault (entirely his!) she might have stayed to hear him explain. She needn't have gone home. Perhaps she hadn't. Most of his hope was dying, but was not quite dead.

He spent the rest of the night in anxious indecision, sleeping little, and very early Monday morning went to his office in the Supreme Court building. He tried to work but could not concentrate on the common-law rule condemning contracts in restraint of trade. He heard Martha Scully arrive, and soon afterward the mail. When she brought the mail to him, there was a light blue envelope marked *Personal*. It was postmarked Sunday and had been mailed from the airport.

Dear Paul,

I know that what happened was only because I was there. I should never have come. If there were some way I could make it up to you—but this is all I can think of. I'm leaving Washington today, going home. You have enough burdens, and all I seem to do is add to them.

KATHERINE

For the remaining hour and a half before Court convened he kept trying to telephone her at home in Lincoln. There was no answer. He made the last call to her a few minutes before the buzzer warned him it was time to go to the robing room.

As he entered the robing room a few minutes before ten o'clock, there was a distinct pause in the muted flow of conversation. He began shaking hands all around—the Chief Justice grave and nodding slightly without speaking, Henry Merriam winking at him. Waldo Shuler's clasp was abrupt and almost absent-minded. Bill Branch wrung his hand with more than ordinary enthusiasm. Edward McCann grinned and gripped Paul Lowe's arm slightly for a moment with his free hand. Andrew Cutler's look was forbidding and distant. Gabriel Hart was nervous and his small hand was damp.

Charles Edmunson was at his locker being helped into his robe. He offered Paul Lowe a large hand and a solid grip.

"Anything I can do, Paul?" he asked gently.

"I don't think so."

"It will pass. That's what to keep in mind. It will pass. There's not one of us who hasn't had his share of similar publicity. I remember when they broke the story that I was a member of the Universe Club which had what they claimed was an anti-Catholic and anti-Semitic admissions policy. I was in danger of being named Bigot of the Year."

"I believe it's time, gentlemen," Chief Justice Hampton said.

On the signal they left the robing room. In the corridor Edward McCann fell in beside him.

He said, "I understand that this fellow Jeffreys is threatening some sort of legal action. For assault. Have you heard anything about it?"

Paul Lowe was too shocked to reply at once. He thought: that would put the entire affair onto the front pages, promote it right out of the gossip columns.

"Where did you hear that?"

"A reporter from the New York *World Journal* who called me this morning. He said it was just a rumor, so far. He'd been unable to confirm anything except that Jeffreys had been to see his lawyer. But I thought I'd pass the word along."

He winced. "If Jeffreys goes through with it, it will be the first time a Supreme Court justice ever was hauled into court as a defendant in a criminal trial."

"Let's hope it doesn't happen. With the kind of publicity the Court is getting these days, it'd be hard to get you a friendly jury."

McCann opened the door and entered the anteroom behind the Court bench.

Andrew Cutler held Paul Lowe back a moment.

"A man I know in the CBS news department called me this morning," he said.

"Did he?" His tone was a bit aggressive. He was starting to feel badgered.

"Early this morning. Before I left for work. He wanted to know my reaction to the incident that's supposed to have happened at Dolores Hardman's affair Saturday night."

"What did you tell him?" he asked with patient menace.

"That I wasn't present. Off the record, I added that I hoped the report wasn't true because it would be a bad blow to the prestige of the Court."

He managed to repress anger. "I see."

"Of course I don't know the facts, Paul. But if it is true, I consider the entire episode . . . disgraceful." Cutler was icily patronizing: "We do have an obligation to maintain the good name of the Court."

"As you say, you don't know the facts, Andrew. I would think you'd learn by now that it pays to get the facts before you form an opinion."

Andrew Cutler's face froze in a haughty unspoken reply. They went into the waiting room. The Marshal's voice came from the other side of the maroon curtain:

"The Honorable, the Chief Justice, and . . ."

He consciously straightened his shoulders. When the curtains parted, he entered with Edward McCann and Gabriel Hart through the far left opening in the curtain and went directly to his chair.

The spectators' section was filled but there was no unusual noise or motion in the packed courtroom. What had he expected—a Roman carnival, a mob shouting for his head? He should not have been rude to Andrew Cutler, a man with antennae far too sensitive to the proprieties. He should have realized that Cutler was not speaking from an offended moral sense so much as from a desire to protect the Court.

"May God bless this honorable Court. Please be seated."

The page pulled out Paul Lowe's chair for him to sit down. For a moment after he was seated he did not dare to raise his eyes. When he did, he was certain that a majority of the spectators in the courtroom was looking at him. He was a stationary target for all eyes, up here on the bench in his unprotective robes of dignity. In the front row a woman in a polka-dotted dress leaned over to whisper to the woman seated beside her, and the other woman smiled and nodded in return.

Unwillingly, Paul Lowe had a dreadful image—a slow wounded lame moose, head and antlers bowed, waiting to be ripped and torn by a wolf pack. . . .

This Monday morning was the longest he ever remembered in a courtroom. Each lawyer at the lectern presenting his case seemed to be talking in slow motion. He wondered if the Chief Justice was not allowing the lawyers more time to present their arguments than had been scheduled. When an argument was concluded, and the red light glowed on the lectern to signal that time was up, he could hardly restrain himself from saying, "Thank God." He watched impatiently as the lawyer and his associates at the table gathered up their papers and departed. The next lawyer approaching the lectern came as a thief bent on stealing that most precious of all commodities, that fluid in which all else flowed, Time.

Finally the noon hour arrived. He rose with the others, but did not go to the justices' dining room. He had arranged to have lunch alone in his office.

When he entered, Martha Scully was at her desk, typing rapidly. She looked up, smiled without a word, and went back to her work. He escaped into his private office and closed the door.

He read again Katherine's short note to him. She could put any face on it that she cared to. The truth was she had abandoned him. Just when he needed her most! He crumpled the letter to throw it in the wastebasket, hesitated, then flung it angrily. He removed it again, intending to tear it to pieces to remove the incriminating evidence. Instead he smoothed out the wrinkled note on the desk blotter and read it again. Seeing her again after three weeks—three impossibly long weeks—had awakened barely dormant feeling. He had endured the torpor of her absence while in his deepest self he had continued to possess her.

And for her to leave him now! He felt a choking in his throat. It was unjust.

The buzzer sounded. He was due back in the courtroom. The half-hour lunch recess was over. He pushed back the chair and stood up; he had not touched his tray of food.

Within an hour of his return to the courtroom his mood had turned sharply irritable. Again and again he broke in on a lawyer's argument. This conduct was expected of Waldo Shuler, whose reputation for harassing lawyers was legendary, but Paul Lowe had never allowed himself to indulge in it. Today he could not avoid it. The lawyer before the Court was tediously, unbearably long-winded, and Paul Lowe's temper was short.

Once he interrupted the lawyer to tell him he was frankly sick and tired of watching him perform a Maypole dance around the issue:

"I would like to see you establish *some* connection between justice and the kind of rule you are proposing."

The lawyer was a pleasant-looking man, about forty, with horn-rimmed glasses. He replied, "I'm not trying to put forward an ideal, Mr. Justice Lowe. I simply want a rule that accords with the Constitution of the United States."

Paul Lowe said with an ironic edge to his voice, "There's no doubt where you'll come out on this issue—exactly where everyone has come out for a hundred years. But we must remember that the doctrine as laid down by the Framers is not Holy Scripture."

The lawyer flushed. "I won't debate legal philosophy with the distinguished Justice. I'd rather debate the facts involved in the present case."

"Very well. I will describe for you the basic position you've been defending here for the past half hour."

In a few staccato sentences Paul Lowe outlined the lawyer's position and pointed out where he had wandered from the central issue to be decided.

"Isn't that it?"

The lawyer's face was crimson. "Yes, Mr. Justice, that's about it."

"That took me two minutes. Why did it take you half an hour?"

Charles Edmunson broke in, "That was an impressive performance on your part, Justice Lowe. But we must allow counsel to get where he is going at his own pace."

"I simply want him to bear in mind that the shortest distance even between two legal points is still a straight line."

The spectators tittered. Chief Justice Hampton irritably fingered the bridge of his nose.

Charles Edmunson said, "I'm sure counsel will arrive at a full discussion of the relevant points before concluding his argument. I am inclined to hear him out without any further interruption."

Paul Lowe stared down the bench toward Edmunson. He resented Edmunson's rebuke. Perhaps the snail's pace of this kind of legal argu-

260

ment was more suited to the antiquated rhythms of an old man's mind; but there was a need for rapidity and vigor—youth—if the pressing work of the Court was to be done.

"Justice Edmunson, I too am interested in hearing him out, even if I have to *show* him the way out."

Why was he speaking this way? He sensed an angry spirit striding forth out of him.

Charles Edmunson answered with a growl, "This hour is devoted to hearing arguments of counsel. The arguments of the justices of this Court should be heard at the appropriate time and place—in the conference room."

Along the length of the bench the other justices drew back instinctively out of the line of fire.

Paul Lowe said in a flat barking tone, the words like separate pistol shots: "We cannot allow the proceedings in this courtroom to proceed at a . . . sleepwalker's pace."

Edward McCann drew in a hissing breath. There was a distinct murmuring in the spectators' benches. All those who regularly covered sessions of the Court were aware that Charles Edmunson occasionally dozed off during dull bouts of oral argument.

Chief Justice Hampton said, "Counsel will proceed."

Paul Lowe sat back in his chair and pushed a pencil behind his ear. Blood pulsed in his ear lobe against slick smooth wood. He wished for some destruct button to obliterate words already launched. He wanted to make amends, to apologize, but he could not think of anything to do or say. In such moments, he thought with remorse, a man's true character reveals itself. His slow-building anger, directed at himself, had abruptly and dramatically turned into senseless attack on Charles Edmunson. Edmunson—of all men!

What could he do?

He began to compose a letter in his head to Edmunson:

My dear, dear Charles . . . You must know how much I admire you. . . .

He would not write a letter. He would find another way.

The danger was in multiplying blunders—and he had lost his guide through the maze of what was right and what was wrong. He had to get his emotional bearings.

Where was Katherine?

Race Hardman poured from a long-necked brown bottle with a steady careful hand. Wine brimmed up, amber and swirling, in the delicately rounded glass.

Race handed the glass to Paul Lowe.

"One of my favorites," he said. "If you like it, I'll send a case to your house."

He waited anxiously while Paul Lowe tasted it. The wine was tart, light, with a mellow center.

"It's very good," Paul Lowe said.

Behind his thick spectacles Race Hardman's gray eyes sparkled with vicarious pleasure.

Both men were seated in the library of Race Hardman's home in Georgetown. It was a warm day and the paneled doors leading to the garden were open.

"I wish I could join you," Race said. "But the doctor is firm. No more than one glass a day. I try to save it for dinner. But I enjoy watching other people enjoy wine." He stopped talking to watch Paul Lowe take another sip. "Have you heard anything more from Tom Jeffreys?"

"No. Should I have?"

"He intends to bring you into court on an assault charge."

"I've heard that rumor."

"It isn't a rumor, Paul. There's been backstage maneuvering going on to prevent it. Even the Attorney General—Phil Keenan—has interceded with Jeffreys on your behalf. He gave Jeffreys to understand that he was speaking for the President."

"It was nice of him to bother. Do you really think it's necessary?"

"Yes, I do." Race Hardman watched Paul Lowe carefully as he took another sip of wine. "As far as I can tell, this Jeffreys fellow is something of a bastard."

"How do you know? Have you talked to him?"

Race Hardman nodded. "I called him when I heard he was considering filing a criminal charge. I asked him to consider the kind of publicity that would result from a justice of the Supreme Court being brought up for trial."

"What did he say?"

"He said you deserved exactly that kind of treatment. I think there's something else bothering him, Paul, and my guess is that it has to do with Katherine Prescott."

Between Paul Lowe's fingers the stem of the wineglass was fragile. He could easily have snapped it.

"Katherine Prescott?"

"Now don't be silly enough to deny it, Paul. I've known about you and Katherine ever since you spent the weekend at my place in St. Thomas."

"Were you checking up?"

"Not at all. My man down there—you met Donlin?—has to make sure my guests' needs are taken care of, and to do that he has to know how many guests there will be. I told him there would be only one. You. When he told me there was a woman also, and described her, it was perfectly clear she was not your wife. She did fit Katherine Prescott's description, though, and when I discovered Katherine was out of town that weekend everything added up pretty clearly."

"How did you discover that? A little further spying?"

"There's nothing intrinsically wrong with *knowing* anything, is there? You'd be surprised at some of our methods for gathering hard news, and you'd be more surprised at how much we choose not to print. The only possible harm can come from what use you make of what you know. Facts are like bullets, Paul—totally inoffensive in themselves. I give you my assurance that I have not the least intention of shooting at you. Quite the opposite, in fact."

"But you have the ammunition if it becomes necessary."

"Finish your drink and don't be an ass. Katherine is a darn attractive woman and I am not a puritan."

"Frankly, Race, I don't understand why you've gotten yourself involved in my personal affairs."

"That answer should be obvious. I'm fond of you. But of course it's more than that. I have a sense about people, Paul—a sense of touch. I literally have it, perhaps because my eyes are so bad. I can touch what a person is. You may be a great man, Paul, and I've known it from the first moment we met. I touched your mind and it's an uncommon mind. As your friend I can't stand by and watch you go down the chute to certain disaster."

"I'm sure you mean well. But I'd appreciate your letting me handle my own problems from now on."

Race Hardman shrugged. "You'll have to do something about Tom Jeffreys. But that will be easier to do now that Katherine is out of the picture."

"How do you know that?"

"In a way, I may have been responsible for it."

The clocks struck the hour of seven—in the library and in the corridors beyond. A white frothing heated mixture was seething within him.

He asked tightly, "When did this happen?"

"Right after that unfortunate brawl at my mother's party. There was a good deal of confusion. When you left I managed to have Tom Jeffreys escorted home and I undertook to see Katherine home myself. We had a very enlightening talk about your relationship."

He stared at Race Hardman as though he were some strange wild animal.

"Race, what gave you the right to talk to her about me?"

Race Hardman continued as if he had not heard the question: "I can't vouch for her exact words but in effect she told me that she was very shaken by what had happened at the party, that she suspected it might be partly her fault, and that she did not want to hurt you in any way. I told her it was naïve to think she would be able to conceal her relationship with you for very long. Not in a city like Washington. When they first laid out the streets of this city they put in the routes for gossip to travel. And as the newest justice of the Supreme Court you're a prime target. She asked what I thought she should do and I suggested that she leave Washington as soon as possible."

The enormity of what he had done!

"Where did she go? I've written her letters but she hasn't answered. And the telephone at her home is disconnected."

"Paul, I'm not going to tell you. It's better if you don't talk to her.

Nothing can change the fact that you're married and she's the other woman, or that you're an important man and the end result of any long-term affair would probably be to wreck your career."

He hated Race Hardman at that moment, hated everything about him, his home, his books, his wealth, even his ailments—most of all his languid air of worldly wisdom.

"I've had just about all the advice from you that I'm going to have, Race. Who the hell do you think you are?"

Race Hardman turned a heavy ring on his finger—the ring his father had worn. A totem, Paul Lowe thought. In some primitive tribes the natives believe that you acquire the wisdom of your father if you eat his brain. In more advanced societies a man wears his late father's ring.

Race Hardman said, "When you've had time to simmer down you'll realize I've been acting as your friend. I'm sure Katherine thinks so. Women are wiser in these matters—their natures are more romantic but their actions are more practical. A prolonged separation is the best thing that could possibly happen to you right now. Believe me, Paul, I know how difficult such a separation can be."

"Do you?"

"Yes. And I'm prepared to help with the problem."

A wonder the question didn't stick in his throat: "How do you intend to be helpful, Race?"

Race Hardman answered imperturbably, "You'll need something to keep your mind occupied, especially for the summer while the Court is shut down. Actually I got the idea from something Katherine wrote in one of her articles about you. She gave an interesting account of your wartime experience in the China-Burma theater."

"Race, you're fantastic. I wouldn't believe you existed if I weren't talking to you."

"I thought you might enjoy spending your summer recess on the other side of the world," Race Hardman said. "A lot of changes have been taking place in Burma. Mostly Red, I'm afraid. There's a shocking ignorance in this country about the situation there. My guess is that things will explode very shortly."

"Is it possible, Race, that you think I would take your suggestion seriously?"

Race Hardman smiled. "My idea is not for you to do another series of political or economic background articles. That pseudo-expertise is what all the foreign correspondents turn out. I'd like a sort of Return of the Native piece. What Burma looks like to you twenty-odd years after the war."

"I'm not interested!"

"Paul, hear me out. All you have to do is revisit some of the old scenes, talk to some of the people if they're still alive—show us in the course of a personal memoir the human side of the changes going on over there. You can get a natural human-interest angle—make an expedition to the site of your plane crash. That could be very interesting."

"It's out of the question."

"Don't make up your mind too quickly, Paul. I've spoken to the people at *Life* magazine and they're very interested. I can guarantee a big newspaper syndication. It can be a very attractive deal—and will help to get you through a difficult period. It's always difficult when you're getting over a love affair, Paul. Don't think I don't understand and sympathize."

His anger which until now had been a kind of physical stimulation was nearing the hallucinatory stage. He could scarcely credit what he was hearing. This mannered oaf—this elementary snob with a fancied superiority founded not on intelligence but on caste, inbreeding and ancestor worship! This poseur with his uncultivated yearning for power and his cultivated palate for fine wines! This monomaniacal man of business with his pedant's greed for information which he stuffed into a brain that never echoed to anything but the assuring rattle of facts—*this* creature was measuring *his* needs and assessing what to do about *his* problems!

"There's only one thing I want from you, Race."

"What's that?"

"Katherine's telephone number. I know you have it."

"Of course I do. But I'm not going to help you make a confounded fool of yourself."

He heard his voice tremble, "Race, you're a damned meddling fool. You're going to stay out—entirely out—of my personal affairs."

Race Hardman seemed to be aware for the first time that Paul Lowe was angry.

"As you will," he said.

"Her phone number, Race."

"She doesn't want to hear from you."

"Race, I'm trying to be patient, but . . ."

Paul Lowe stood up. Race Hardman blinked and held up a hand in graceful surrender.

"All right," he said. "If you're going to be melodramatic about it. I have it here."

Race Hardman rose, went to a rosewood desk in the library, opened a drawer and took out a maroon covered memorandum book.

"It's her father's house. She and her son Timmy are staying there. I understand the boy isn't well."

He gave the number to Paul Lowe, who repeated the digits, moving his lips to compel them to remember. Then he nodded and started for the door.

Race Hardman said, "You can call from here if you like."

He hesitated.

"You needn't worry about anyone overhearing," Race said. "It's a private phone in this room. No extensions."

He nodded.

Race Hardman returned the memorandum book to the desk. "I'm sorry if you've misunderstood what I tried to do, Paul. My hope is that in time you will come to appreciate how earnestly I have tried to be your friend."

He said nothing.

Race Hardman started for the door. As he reached Paul Lowe he stopped and held out his hand.

"Forgive me?"

After a moment, Paul Lowe shook hands abruptly.

"That's better," Race said, smiling. "Do keep this Burma thing in mind, will you? I'm serious. It would be a wonderful opportunity for everyone concerned."

"You never give up, do you?"

Race Hardman's smile widened. "That's one secret of my success." He left the library, closing the double doors behind him.

He picked up the telephone and dialed. The receiver gave back small whirring twisting sounds as the relays were connected. Then there was the altered sound of another phone ringing. Finally, the ringing stopped:

"Hello." A man's voice.

"May I speak to Katherine?"

"Who's calling?"

"A friend."

The phone was put down—he heard the clacking noise. After a minute it was picked up again.

"Hello," Katherine said.

"It's Paul."

Total silence.

"I had to talk to you, Katherine." He spoke quietly, afraid that she would hang up. "I wrote but you didn't answer. I haven't heard from you since you left Washington."

"I sent you a note when I left. I tried to explain."

"Your note didn't explain anything. I found out from Race Hardman what really happened. I'm calling from his home. He told me that he spoke to you after the party."

"It wasn't anything he said to me, Paul, so much as that he *knew*. It made me realize how foolish we were to hope to keep people from knowing." Her voice began, lost control, stopped, began again on a new and desperate note: "Oh, Paul. Don't you see? It's Race Hardman today and someone else tomorrow, and once gossip starts it never ends. It wouldn't be long until Eleanor knew . . . and then it would get into the newspapers and they'd crucify you. Paul—I meant it when I said I didn't want to add to your burdens, and yet that's all I seem able to do."

"I must see you, Katherine."

"No." The single word seemed all she could manage.

"Why not?"

"That would start it all over again." She hesitated. "I can't talk to you now. My father is right in the next room."

"I don't care. I have to see you."

"We can't." Her voice was threaded with the color of tears. "Don't you see that we can't? You have important work to do—a great future. It would wreck everything."

"Without you, I don't have anything, Katherine."

The quick turn to sentiment, syntactical gambit, an appeal to the utterly subjective through grammatical inversion.

"Paul, I'm trying hard to be sensible when I don't want to be. You must help me. Don't you know that I want to go out right now, this minute, and get on a plane and go to you?"

"Then do."

"It isn't possible." Her voice was hushed and vibrant.

"Then I'll come to you."

"Paul!" Her breath fought in her throat. "Paul, I haven't told you but when I came home I found Timmy sick. He has bronchial pneumonia. My father was looking after him with a housekeeper. I can't leave him now and I wouldn't. And when he's better I have to take him away for a while. I promised. And he'll need a long rest to get back his strength."

"That isn't your real reason."

"No, but it's true all the same. Darling, we agreed that we had to wait for a while. That's even more true now. I love you far too much to let you sacrifice your career for me."

He felt sullen with betrayal. "I need you, Katherine."

"Don't, Paul. Please. *Please.*"

"Katherine, anything may happen if we wait longer. We may lose each other forever."

"Not if we love each other."

He would have been content to feel the pounding tension and the pouring release he had known with her. For those few exquisite minutes he would exchange everything—whatever subtracted from the total of masculine vigor.

In moments when he felt most committed he could stand apart from himself, a stranger. In the garden outside the library a red-throated robin hopped from a brick wall to a flowering dogwood tree. Through the open door a mild breeze sent warm quivering waves around him.

"I hope you're right, Katherine."

"We can't lose what we have, Paul." Her whisper came close to the phone. "I'm going to hang up. I do love you, Paul. I do!"

The telephone clicked at her end. He held the receiver to his ear to keep the link between them unsnapped. Frustrated desire shook him— set his emotions flying to settle into new patterns. He turned the black metal receiver against his face and waited through an intermittent buzz to a low-pitched unending whine. Finally he replaced the instrument in its cradle.

He went into the garden. A hornet, a moaning knife, cut close to his ear. There was no other sound.

He was removed, not a part, outside of, not included in life. Nothing was important; nothing concerned him. He enjoyed the sensation. At least he could be free of tyrannical self-questioning, the imperious sovereignty of doubt. If I doubt not, can I exist? (The warm spring day existing entirely without him, with no visible sign of him to be found, held no terror.) He wished to cling to the present feeling, put it somewhere that he could take it out again. In this moment, selfhood gone, ecstatically at peace, a sharp thought pierced him.

Was she really gone? *That* was hard to believe.

19

The final decision of the term was delivered by a unanimous Court. Gabriel Hart wrote the opinion for the Court in which a state law providing for different treatment to be accorded voters in different senatorial districts was held unconstitutional under the equal protection clause of the Fourteenth Amendment.

As soon as Gabriel Hart finished reading his brief announcement, Chief Justice Hampton spoke:

"The other opinions and orders of the Court have been filed with the Clerk and will not be orally announced. All cases submitted to this Court for this term having been disposed of, and all business before us concluded, it is ordered by the Court that all cases on the docket be, and they are hereby, continued to the next term."

John Hampton nodded to Marshal Robert Perry. The Marshal rose and his voice rang out in the half-filled courtroom:

"This Honorable Court is adjourned to the time and place appointed by Law."

The justices quickly left, filing out through the maroon curtain.

In the anteroom Edward McCann did a small jig. "Well, nothing ahead but four glorious months of baseball and romping with the kids. I can hardly believe the day has finally arrived."

They crossed the corridor to the robing room. Paul Lowe's colleagues were in an unusually festive mood.

"I've got the boat all chartered," Gabriel Hart said to Edward McCann. "We're going to cruise the Bahamas for six weeks. Fishing and loafing on deck in the sun."

Paul Lowe asked the Chief Justice, "What are your plans, John?"

"Oh, I'll be staying home mostly. I'm writing a book, you know. My wife and I will spend a few weeks on her family's horse farm in Kentucky. We'll get in some horseback riding. It's beautiful country."

Bill Branch grunted. "If you really want beautiful scenery, come out West. It's still the only unspoiled section in the whole United States— the only place where you can drive fifty miles without seeing a motel or a hamburger stand. I own a shack where the nearest telephone is eighteen miles away. And it's a party line at that."

Standing at his locker, Henry Merriam chuckled. "After eight months cooped up in this legal monastery, I am positively craving some pleasant society. My wife and I intend to go to at least twelve parties a week. And we'll throw fifty of the fanciest dress balls you ever saw. You're all invited to everything. That includes you, Andrew."

Andrew Cutler removed his black robe and smiled frostily. "No, thank you, Henry. I've accepted a number of speaking engagements for this summer. I intend to be quite busy."

Paul Lowe crossed over to where Sam Davids, the locker-room attendant, was helping Edmunson out of his robe.

Charles Edmunson said, "It makes me weary just listening to these youngsters carrying on with their busy schedules."

"What are your plans, Charles?" Paul Lowe asked.

"I intend to sit still with a book in my lap in my most comfortable chair for a month or two. Then I'll try to get up strength to open the book."

Sam Davids moved on to assist Bill Branch with his robe.

Paul Lowe said, "Charles, I can't tell you how bitterly I regret a remark I made from the bench a short while ago. I've been trying ever since to think of some suitable form of apology."

Edmunson's bushy eyebrows lifted quizzically. "I'm sorry to say I don't recall what you mean, Paul. My memory is really terrible in some matters." A warm twinkle in the large pupils of his eyes belied the words.

Paul Lowe said, "These past months, working with you, have been the most rewarding of my life. You've taught me a great deal. More than I can tell you, Charles."

"I think it would be fairer to say we've learned from each other. I trust we'll see each other sometime before October." Edmunson's large hand grasped Paul Lowe's hand tightly. "And I hope that whatever personal problems have been disturbing you will have been resolved before then."

"Thank you. I'm sure they will," he said.

Behind him, where Bill Branch was standing with Waldo Shuler, he heard Waldo's high cackle of delight.

"No use trying to win me over, Bill," Waldo Shuler said. "My wife and I are heading east, not west. Greece and Israel this time. She wants to see where Moses started all this law business on Mount Sinai. And I want to see the holy places where Plato trod." As Paul Lowe turned, Waldo Shuler included him in the conversation: "My wife says I'm a bad Jew because I admire Plato more than Moses."

"Doesn't she know Moses was an Egyptian?" Paul Lowe asked.

"I told her that—but she didn't believe it until she got the word from Cecil B. De Mille. I wish Cecil B. had made a movie showing that if Plato had only been born a little further south he'd have been Jewish. That would have made everything simpler for me. But if I tried to tell my wife something like that she'd break a Torah over my head."

Leaving Bill Branch to follow with Edmunson, Waldo Shuler walked with Paul Lowe from the robing room.

"How about a game of chess in my office?" Waldo asked.

"I don't know if I can make it this afternoon."

"Afraid of getting your head beaten in?"

"Something like that. All your latent sadism comes out when you get a chessboard in front of you."

"I've got someone coming at four o'clock," Waldo Shuler said seriously. "I'd really appreciate it if you could find time for a game before that."

Paul Lowe was aware now that something more was intended than a chess game. "All right, if one more victory is that important to you."

Waldo Shuler's quick smile came and went. "You can't tell. One of these days you may even come close."

At a few minutes past three o'clock Waldo Shuler announced with satisfaction, "You've got yourself into a trap."

Paul Lowe studied the chessboard for a moment. "I don't see where."

"You will."

Paul Lowe moved a knight to counter the only threat he could see on the board.

Waldo Shuler reached toward his black bishop. "Everyone announced what he was doing this summer. I notice you didn't."

"Because I'm not sure."

Waldo Shuler moved the black bishop to capture a knight. "No plans?"

"Nothing definite." A glance at the new situation on the chessboard reassured him. "That move will cost you your bishop," he said. He swept across with his bishop to take Shuler's black bishop and sat back, content. "I'll probably visit relatives back home in Nebraska. Beyond that I'm open for anything. I may just spend the summer boning up to give you a real trouncing in chess."

"That's the spirit." Waldo Shuler advanced a white pawn into the knight's fourth square. "You'll never do it. But I admire a man who resists the inevitable."

"You're so modest." He began to suspect Waldo Shuler might have deliberately accepted the sacrifice of his black bishop.

Waldo Shuler said, "Modesty is a virtue only when you have no other." He nodded approval of Paul Lowe's parrying move—the bishop to the king's second square to defend the king. "If I'm a superior man, it would be wrong for me to pretend I'm not." His white knight swooped to the queen's fourth square. "For ordinary people it's different. It's wrong for them to be boastful, because they have nothing to boast about. Modesty becomes them."

Paul Lowe suddenly realized two of his black pieces were being threatened. He sighed. "I'm going to have to find some other game where I can take you down a peg. I don't think I'll ever do it in chess."

"Keep trying." Waldo Shuler fingered the scar over his left eye. "I understand that Tom Jeffreys is going to the district attorney tomorrow to file a complaint against you."

Paul Lowe continued to study the problem on the board but the major part of his attention focused on what Waldo Shuler was saying.

"Is that so?"

Waldo said, "At least that's what he told the Chief Justice when the Chief called to try to persuade him not to."

He felt perspiration on his neck. John Hampton—that severe, impartial man—what a wrench it must have cost him!

"A lot of backstage maneuvering has been going on, Waldo. Why wasn't I told about it?"

"There wasn't much you could have done."

"I could have saved everyone else the trouble by talking to Jeffreys myself."

"Tom Jeffreys has been too angry even to talk to you, Paul. He knows he can do you a good deal of harm and for some reason he's not only willing but anxious to do it."

"Then why hasn't he done it already?"

Waldo Shuler watched Paul Lowe take a king's pawn with his knight. "I think all the influence being brought to bear has made a little headway with him. Another friend of yours—Race Hardman—stopped to talk to him at his club yesterday afternoon. Race Hardman reported to the Chief that Jeffreys is willing to admit that you might have suffered a fit of lunacy."

"Thank you," Paul Lowe said dryly.

"Race Hardman thinks that if you go to Jeffreys in person, hat in hand, and eat a huge portion of very humble pie you can probably persuade him to change his mind about pressing the criminal charge."

"Why didn't Race tell me this? I know him better than the Chief does."

"Race doesn't think you hold him in very high regard at the moment. Anyhow, the Chief wanted to talk to you, but I thought it might be less embarrassing if I did."

"And what do you advise?"

"Crawl. It will be painful, but a lot less painful than the consequences of having your private life on display in a courtroom."

"What do you think would happen if it actually went to court?"

Waldo Shuler said softly, "Paul, you got drunk and hauled off and belted him. Fortunately it happened so quickly that not too many people saw it. God knows what will happen, though, if they subpoena witnesses. They can undoubtedly prove that some kind of assault took place. What are you going to claim? Self-defense?"

"I might claim provocation."

"And even if you win you'll lose. Public men have to cultivate their vices in secret, Paul. Once you're accused of something the public thinks it's proof of guilt."

"I don't know if I can apologize, Waldo."

Waldo Shuler put a hand to the back of his neck and stretched his neck against it. His chronic ailment, a stiff neck, was bothering him.

"Think about it, Paul. Tom Jeffreys is having dinner alone at his club this evening. He's been told you might show up, thoroughly ashamed and willing to make amends. Whether you do or not is up to you, of course." Waldo examined the chessboard again with interest. He nodded gravely. "That was a good delaying move you made. But it won't help in the long run."

Waldo Shuler moved a pawn to king's bishop's fourth square. It was the opening of an inexorable winning combination. Within a few minutes a paralyzing double attack was under way and Paul Lowe was helpless. He looked over the board in the hope of spotting further moves but the wicked anticipatory leer on Waldo's face told him he would find nothing.

Finally he said, "All right, Waldo. You win."

Waldo Shuler rubbed his hands. "Your mistake was letting yourself be forced into an unprotected position. That's a weakness to watch out for in the queen's Indian defense. Matter of fact, it's a weakness anywhere. The thing to do is return, if you can, to where you made the wrong move and patch it up as best as you can."

Paul Lowe moved his chair back from the table. "In other words, go to see Jeffreys."

"Did I say that?"

"I suppose I'm just being stubborn. It's the only thing to do."

Dimples appeared at Waldo Shuler's mouth corners. He was delighted as a child. "I've always known you were a practical man who sees what has to be done and does it." He stood up. "That's why you don't belong with those fuzzy so-called liberals on the Court. You belong with me."

"Tell me why you got yourself involved in this, Waldo. To win me over to your side?"

Waldo Shuler patted Paul Lowe's cheek. "It's because I like you, Paul. I can't help liking you. You play a good game of chess and you're a good bitter loser." He became serious. "Can I give you a last bit of advice?"

"Of course."

"Tell Jeffreys you'd been working too hard, that you were upset about personal troubles. . . ."

"What personal troubles?"

"What's the difference? Everyone has them. Tell him you had too much to drink, even. Let him be superior to you for a few minutes. It can't hurt you and it will do wonders for his ego. You flatter a man's ego, Paul, and it's hard to keep him for an enemy." He had lost all trace of his customary whining tone. "Give me a ring later, won't you? I'd like to know what happens."

"I will. And—thanks, Waldo."

"Don't mention it. You may do me a favor sometime. After all, I'm only helping you so it will put you under obligation, right? You have to watch me, Paul. All my enemies will tell you I'm the Jewish Machiavelli."

Tom Jeffreys was not in the dining room of the Bath and Tennis Club when Paul Lowe arrived. He found him seated in a wicker chair on the terrace that commanded a view of the Potomac. Jeffreys had put a cigarette to his mouth and was holding a lighter flame to it. Only his eyes moved when Paul Lowe came over to him. Then he deliberately snapped shut the cover of the lighter and put it into his pocket.

"I was told I might find you here," Paul Lowe said.

"Have a seat, Mr. Justice." Tom Jeffreys' face was impassive but his voice was clearly hostile.

He sat down in another wicker chair facing Jeffreys. "I believe I owe you an apology for what happened at Dolores Hardman's party. I admit that I was drinking too much. It certainly wouldn't have happened if I were sober."

"That's a pretty disgraceful confession for someone in your position to have to make, Mr. Justice."

"Yes, it is."

"And I certainly hope you don't think a statement like that is going to make up for what you did."

"I came here to find out what would, Mr. Jeffreys."

"You could have really hurt me. As it was I had to go to the dentist the next day. He found I had two loosened teeth."

Paul Lowe maintained a sober and concerned look. "I'm very sorry to hear that. I really am."

"I've talked to my lawyer. He said if I felt strongly about it I should see the district attorney."

It was quickly becoming apparent that Tom Jeffreys wanted to soothe his wounded pride in the balm of this triumph—and it would not be wise to deny him the full measure.

"I certainly don't blame you for being angry," he said.

"If I did go to the district attorney, the publicity wouldn't do the Court any good. Especially at a time when so many people are saying some members ought to be impeached."

"That's perfectly true." Obscurely, irrationally, he was becoming annoyed with Tom Jeffreys. Somehow, they were both co-conspirators in this trouble which had involved so much better, more worthwhile human beings; they were victim and aggressor joined in an enclosed act, unaware of how their struggle was affecting others.

"I got a lot of phone calls from a lot of important people," Tom Jeffreys said, "advising me to be a good fellow and forget the whole thing. But I was just about to go ahead with it when Justice Shuler told me how anxious you were to meet me. I thought the least I could do was to hear you out."

"I don't know what else I can say. It was a terrible blunder. Of course I was drunk or I never would have swung at you. I have no reason to want to do you any injury."

"I can't imagine what reason you would have."

"I have none."

"Then it was a damn silly thing to do. Drunk or not. I hate to think that men in your position don't have any better control over what they do."

"I haven't had a drink since it happened—and I won't be having any. I had a lot of personal troubles at the time."

Jeffreys had been angrily enjoying the whole episode, reveling in the intimate ritual of yielding forgiveness—the layman granting absolution to a prince of the church. Now his mood changed. Thoughtfully he exhaled smoke through both nostrils.

"Katherine Prescott called me a few days ago," he said.

"Oh."

"You two have become rather good friends of late, haven't you?"

"I've always thought she was a lovely woman."

Tom Jeffreys dropped ash carefully into a standing tray beside his chair.

"Katherine was very concerned about you. Very concerned."

"I'm sorry to have upset her."

"She asked me not to do anything that would hurt your career. She's a great admirer of yours, Mr. Justice."

"I'm pleased to hear that."

"Actually she said that no matter how angry I was, I didn't have the right to do anything that would in any way affect the work you're doing."

"I was wrong, and you had a perfect right to be angry."

"Nevertheless, what Katherine said did have some influence with me. I'm very fond of her. We were engaged to be married, you know." Tom Jeffreys stared off thoughtfully at the dark blue waters of the Potomac, riven with lances of moonlight. "As I say, I'm very fond of Katherine. I wouldn't want to see her mistreated in any way."

"I should think you wouldn't."

"She's always attracted men and I imagine some of them make the mistake of thinking that she's easygoing or accommodating. She isn't like that at all."

"I'm quite sure she isn't." Heat began to speckle the pores of his cheek.

"Since her marriage ended three years ago I don't believe she's even dated anyone except myself—and one other man. And I don't think she's been serious about anyone but me. This other fellow was an Ambassador from one of those middle eastern countries and Katherine met him at a diplomatic party. You never saw such an unlikely-looking couple."

Paul Lowe recognized that this other man was being used as a deputy for himself, and that Tom Jeffreys was exorcizing the possibility of his having been Katherine's lover.

"It's hard to explain these things."

"I'm not worried about Katherine, not really. She knows how to handle herself. But," he looked directly at Paul Lowe, "I certainly would not like her to become involved with the wrong man."

The moon had imperceptibly climbed higher. A pale slice of light fell on the dark floor of the terrace.

Paul Lowe said, "That isn't really what we met to talk about, is it?"

"Have you been seeing Katherine?" Tom Jeffreys asked abruptly.

He waited through a pang of resentment, and then the sour wash of having to repress it. "I'm not sure this is any of your business, Mr. Jeffreys. But as you know Katherine did a series of articles about me—and then there was some sort of follow-up piece on how the Court arrives at

275

a decision. Naturally we had to meet several times while she was writing the articles. I have only the highest regard for her."

"That isn't what I meant," Tom Jeffreys said. "But . . ." he ground out his cigarette with deliberation, "I suppose it *is* none of my business."

"You have my apology for what happened at Dolores Hardman's party. What's the next step?"

A portly man in a tuxedo came out on the terrace and the boards creaked softly beneath his weight until he found a seat.

"All things considered," Tom Jeffreys said slowly, "I'm going to consider the incident closed. You have my word that I won't press charges or take any legal action."

"That's very decent of you."

"I'm not the type who holds a grudge, Mr. Justice."

After a moment's hesitance Paul Lowe held out his hand. Tom Jeffreys took it. His handclasp had an oddly tentative quality—probably because he regretted that the episode was at an end. The nature of a triumph is to end even as it is achieved. If there had been a way to prolong it Tom Jeffreys would doubtless have done so, savoring and resavoring the honey flavor of *noblesse oblige*.

On their way back from a vacation in Bermuda, Ken and Sheila Norris stopped off in Washington to have dinner at the Lowe home on Volta Place. It was two days after Court adjourned.

As soon as the dinner dishes were cleared away Sheila Norris turned to Paul Lowe and said, "Ken is about to launch on another of his crusades. You're his best friend, Paul, and I want you to talk him out of it."

Sheila was a blonde woman, once pretty, who still wore the sort of dresses, hairstyles and cosmetics that had once served to enhance her good looks but now merely emphasized their absence. Her thin blonde hair was piled high atop her head and was secured with a tortoise-shell comb, and her clinging dress revealed a widening waist and hips. The deep red color of lipstick accented the too thin straight line of her lips, and the highlights of rouge on her cheeks pointed up a sallow skin.

"Ken usually seems to know what he's doing," Paul Lowe said.

Sheila said, "It was a lot better when you two were law partners. You were the sensible one, Paul. You wouldn't work for weeks and weeks without getting paid for it and end up being called a Red or something."

"This case has nothing to do with politics," Ken Norris said softly.

"What does it have to do with?" Paul Lowe asked.

"It's a simple matter of whether a man has a right to a fair trial."

"Maybe you'd better tell me a little more about it."

"I'm dying to. I just don't know what the usual fee is for consulting justices of the Supreme Court."

"Oh, I'll settle for half what you get out of it."

"Fair enough."

Ken Norris lounged on the curved sofa, with one leg stretched out. His body seemed to have a curious sort of formlessness which enabled him to adapt to the shape of furniture.

He said, "This case is probably unique in American criminal law, but from all the attention it's gotten in the newspapers you'd think William Weaver had been sentenced to a ten-dollar fine for being caught with his hand in a cookie jar."

"I gather William Weaver is your client."

Ken nodded. "I got involved through Everyman's Legal Guild. Naturally as a director of the organization . . ."

Sheila sniffed disdainfully. "That's how they pay him. With a title. My husband is a pushover for a title."

"Sheila, please," Ken said. He turned to Paul Lowe. "Let me tell you a little about William Weaver first. He's a slightly subnormal young Negro of twenty-six who is something of an habitual criminal and has spent seven of his adult years in prison."

"You see the kind of clients he takes?" Sheila asked indignantly.

Ken Norris smiled slightly at Paul Lowe. Their long years of friendship had made communication between them effortless. Ken's look said: don't worry about Sheila—she isn't bothering me. Paul Lowe knew this was true. Ken had taught his wife early in their marriage to keep her distance, even when criticizing, and in return she could expect him to do the same. Too close a relationship would have jeopardized all. Sex, their great bond, was kept in the area reserved for such matters—a zombie that could lie dead yet be revived by sorcery when needed to perform its task.

"My wife has a crusade of her own going," Ken said. "She's against my taking on any more clients who haven't got any money to pay me with."

"Tell me more about William Weaver."

"Well, promptly on his release from prison he stole a car, picked up a young white woman at a bus stop, drove her to a road near a lonely cemetery and raped her."

"He certainly needs the help of a good public-spirited lawyer. A *darn* good lawyer."

"When Weaver was booked on the rape charge he had a lawyer named Patrick O'Hara. But William Weaver didn't make O'Hara's job any easier by committing several incriminating verbal blunders."

"Such as?"

"He volunteered that he couldn't have been guilty of raping that white girl because he never entered her body at all but made her copulate with her mouth on his penis."

Eleanor gave a startled gasp. Sheila Norris rewarded her with a triumphant glance.

"What happened?" Paul Lowe asked.

"After several adjournments a trial was held, and a verdict of guilty was returned. The state law provides that rape when there is bodily harm to the victim is a capital crime. So William Weaver was sentenced to die in the electric chair. In the ordinary course of events he would probably have gone to the chair and that would have been the end of it."

"He had a right to an appeal."

"That's where the case starts to get interesting. It went up on appeal to the state supreme court. The appeal was denied on the basis of the transcript of the testimony."

"So far a pretty cut-and-dried case."

"Except that this happened in a southern white town. The official court reporter was a white woman of pretty strict religious training. Naturally she was horrified by the explicit detail in the official testimony of how the rape occurred. Not quite so naturally, when the time came to transcribe the filthy details she just couldn't bring herself to do it. And because she was afraid of losing her job she didn't ask for someone else to do it. She simply skipped the obscenity."

"She did *what?*"

"I told you it started to get interesting. Weaver's attorney—Patrick O'Hara—noticed the omission after the appeal was denied and brought the matter to the attention of the trial judge. That honorable gentleman merely ordered the omitted testimony transcribed and added to the transcript by another court reporter."

Paul Lowe ran his fingers back through his sandy hair. "Was anyone present who represented William Weaver when the additional testimony was transcribed?"

"You get the point, Paul." Ken Norris grinned. "The answer is . . . no."

"Go on."

"Attorney O'Hara claimed the whole process was illegal because testimony was added to the record without a hearing in which the defendant's rights were represented. O'Hara also pointed out that in view of the clear evidence of the lady court reporter's feelings in the matter, no one could even be sure she had taken down the original testimony correctly. So the appeal to the state supreme court had been denied on the basis of not only an incomplete, but quite possibly an inaccurate, transcript of what actually took place at the original trial."

"That should be enough to get William Weaver a new trial."

Ken Norris grunted. "The trial judge wouldn't even hold a hearing on the problem of the transcript. He said the transcript had been complete enough for the state supreme court to rule on the appeal and, besides, the additional material would only have hurt the defendant's chances. Attorney O'Hara then asked the state supreme court to order such a hearing. They refused."

"On what grounds?"

"They upheld the trial judge's contention that the transcript had been complete enough for them to make a fair disposition of the case on its merits. However, they affirmed by a tie vote. Two judges dissented—and said a new trial should have been ordered, and one judge wasn't sitting."

"Where do you enter in?"

"Right there. Patrick O'Hara couldn't afford to devote any more of his time to the Weaver case. He was working without pay and the legal complications were starting to drag out. So he asked Everyman's Legal Guild to take over."

Sheila Norris said, "If you'd pay half as much attention to the needs of your own family as you do to cases like this, we'd be rich by now." She turned to Paul Lowe. "Don't you agree with me, Paul? I'm not against Ken's taking up causes but there has to be a limit."

Sheila did not begin to understand that this quality of involvement was one of her husband's most attractive traits. He was constantly getting mixed up with organizations whose very names often spelled out their futility and whose membership varied from unworldly to sinister. But without this naïve eagerness for anything smacking of social reform, Ken's critical intelligence would have led him directly into a swamp of cynicism.

"As a judge," Paul Lowe said to Shelia, "I can't help being grateful that there are still public-spirited lawyers like Ken around. I don't know what we'd do without them."

Sheila rolled her eyes impatiently. "I should have known better. You men are always trying to remake the world no matter what it costs your family."

Eleanor gave Sheila a glance of sympathy and unspoken understanding.

Ken Norris stretched comfortably. "No use fighting them," he said to Paul Lowe. "Women have this trade union. All you need for membership is mammary glands. Well, Paul, what do you think? Does William Weaver stand any chance?"

"Probably not much. But in view of what you've told me, he certainly rates a new trial. The error made at his trial couldn't happen again in a million tries, but it was made and there's simply no way of knowing how the appeals court would have acted if they had the full original transcript in front of them."

"That's my position. I'm going to use every legal means I can beg, borrow or invent to see that he gets a new trial."

"It may be a busy time ahead," Paul Lowe said.

"And a poor one," Sheila said pointedly.

"We can afford to lose a few months," Ken Norris said. "William Weaver is in danger of losing a lot more than that."

He was able to sleep late on Monday morning for the first time in months. He woke at ten o'clock, breakfasted, and lounged in the living room in striped silk-shantung pajamas, reading a book in an easy chair, his stockinged feet resting at attention on a hassock before him.

The telephone rang.

Eleanor said, "It's for you, dear. From the White House."

He took the telephone from her.

"Hello."

"Mr. Justice Lowe?"

"Yes." He recognized the voice.

"This is Martin Gannett, calling for the President. Would it be convenient for you to meet him at eight o'clock this evening?"

"Of course. Any special reason?"

"The President told me only that he'd like to have a private discussion with you. Would you come to the northwest entrance? The President will be in the library."

"I'll be there at eight o'clock," he said.

The clock was chiming the hour when Paul Lincoln Lowe entered the library to find President Lamont Howard standing beside a bookshelf in a far left corner of the knotty pine library. The President was wearing black-rimmed reading glasses and held a book in his hand. He put the book back on the shelf and came forward to greet Paul Lowe.

"Paul. It was nice of you to come on such short notice."

"Oh, I always manage to find time to see the President of the United States."

Lamont Howard chuckled. He removed his reading glasses and slipped them into the breast pocket of his rumpled gray suit.

"I thought I'd get hold of you before you went scooting off for the summer. Once people scatter out of Washington it's a mighty tough job locating them again. The summer in Washington always reminds me of the years when Eisenhower was President. Where did everybody go during those years? There never seemed to be anyone around." The lines in the President's face coalesced in a smile. "No one but Republicans—and they don't count."

"You'd have had no trouble locating me. I'm sticking close to home."

Lamont Howard gave him a surprised sideways look as he led the way to two armchairs flanking a coffee table strewn with books and magazines.

"Not planning to go anywhere?"

"I was talking to my wife about that this weekend. We decided to spend the months of June and July back home in Lincoln, Nebraska."

"Doesn't seem like a very exciting vacation."

"My wife wants to visit with her mother and sister. And I'd like to see a number of my old friends."

What would the President say if he said he was also planning to spend the summer in Lincoln because a woman named Katherine Prescott would be close by?

Lamont Howard said, "Race Hardman was here for lunch today. We had an interesting talk. Among other things he mentioned that he was trying to persuade you to go to Burma on a project of his. Something to do with revisiting the places you were at during World War II."

"Race is always brimful of ideas. I didn't take that particular suggestion seriously."

The President's small eyes twinkled. "I wish you would, Paul."

He sat down and indicated the chair for Paul Lowe to take.

Paul Lowe said, "Don't tell me the President of the United States is helping Race Hardman conduct his business affairs."

"The only business I'm interested in is in running this country. But a good deal of the security of our country depends on what's happening—or is about to happen—overseas. Burma is a real trouble spot. My reports indicate a full-scale revolution may break out there any time. That revolution will be Communist inspired. And it will have a very good chance of succeeding unless the Burmese government moves quickly. We want to back up their army with enough guns and money to crush the rebellion before it gets a hold—and before Red China starts helping out the revolutionaries."

"It sounds like a serious problem, Mr. President, but I don't see how I can be of any help."

"You can, though. Here's the situation in a nutshell. The current President of Burma, U Ba Saw, is a fine fellow—a pacifist, an admirer of Gandhi, a philosophical Buddhist. He would make a great professor on Southeastern political affairs at some university. But as President of a whole country . . . well, that's a different story. He won't stand up to the Commies the way he ought to. So far he's refused to accept any help from us at all. We've offered to outfit five whole divisions, send advisers, the works. He won't hear of it. Says he doesn't want his country to become another Viet Nam."

"We have an Ambassador on the scene, don't we?"

Lamont Howard grimaced. "A good friend of mine, Mark Branford. His chief qualification is that he contributed a hundred thousand dollars to my last campaign. That's why he's in Burma. In fact, the only reason we sent him to Burma is that everything looked peaceful there at the time. We didn't count on the situation changing so rapidly."

Paul Lowe smiled. "Maybe what you need is a new Ambassador."

"I can't yank him out yet. He's happy and he thinks he's doing a wonderful job. I sent Roger Mayburn—my Assistant Secretary of State—over there to see what he could do. He got nowhere because the reason for his trip was too well publicized. Everyone knew he was there to push the Burmese into accepting more American help. Before he arrived they had big protest meetings under way, and by the time he got there the pressure was building up to send him packing. He had to work in a goldfish bowl. President U Ba Saw would never even meet him without at least three of his ministers around—and at least one of them was always a known Communist sympathizer. Mayburn might as well have been handcuffed and gagged for all the good he could do."

"You think I might do better—in an unofficial capacity?"

Lamont Howard grinned. "I'll fit you out with all the documents. A letter from me to U Ba Saw—plus all the evidence we've uncovered of the Communist revolution brewing in his country—and some plain talk from our military men on how much he'll need, what we're prepared to give him and when it'll be delivered. All he has to do is say the word."

"This is not my sort of job, Mr. President. I don't know if I can handle it."

"Paul, my bet is that you'll do it as well as any man in this government. And the best part is that no one will know the real reason you're there. The assignment from Race Hardman is a perfect camouflage."

Other possibilities of camouflage instantly occurred to Paul Lowe. There would be an enforced separation from Eleanor, and after such an interval it would be much easier to convince her that he wanted a divorce for reasons that did not involve another woman.

"Mr. President, if you want me to do this, I can't refuse. All I can promise is to do my best."

"It's simple enough, really. Our part of the job won't take long. Just make sure U Ba Saw reads the stuff I'm sending with you and get his personal reaction to it. If he's vacillating, try to make him see it our way. The whole discussion must be informal, but it may help to open his eyes to what's going on in his own country—how much danger they're in."

"One question. When do I leave, Mr. President?"

"As soon as possible. You're a good man, Paul. I wish I had a dozen more like you. Don't worry about your ability to handle this assignment. The way you've been operating on the Supreme Court proves you're a born diplomat."

"I'd prefer to have you say I was a born judge."

Lamont Howard laughed. "You're both. I understand that everybody is supposed to be mad at everybody else over there on the Court but nobody's mad at you."

"I wouldn't go so far as to say that, Mr. President."

Lamont Howard shrugged. "All I know is what I read in the confidential memos. . . . How would you like one of my world-famed martinis?"

"I usually drink bourbon."

Lamont Howard stood up. "I heard about that too."

"In the same confidential memos?"

"I have spies all over." He crossed to the concealed bar. "It won't be too hard for you to lay off that stuff while you're overseas, will it?"

"I don't have a drinking problem, Mr. President."

"I don't mind anyone having a little belt now and then. But you have to be careful when you aren't among friends."

"What happened that night at Dolores Hardman's was an exception. I haven't been drinking since."

The President took from the bar a cocktail shaker, two glasses, a bottle of gin and a bottle of dry vermouth. "Good. I'm glad to hear it." He began to pour the gin and vermouth into the shaker. "My martinis are what I will be remembered for by posterity. Wait'll you taste one. I only serve one to a customer. If I served any more I could end up ruling the world."

Eleanor went from the bedroom to the bathroom carrying her bra and panties. Watching her, Paul Lowe was reminded of that time many years ago when he had entered a room to find her, similarly unattired, with a nurse helping her to the cot in the doctor's office. She had just had her abortion.

He lay back on the bed, his hands clasped behind his head on a pillow, with only a sheet covering his nakedness. The physical part of lovemaking had ended but the overtones went on like the sound of music in a concert hall when the musicians have ceased to play.

He heard the toilet flush, a loud gurgling noise, then a swirling rattle.

Eleanor came out of the bathroom. She had not put on her nightgown. Her nude body was lean, a slight protuberance at the abdomen, a relaxing of the shoulders, a pendulosity of the breasts—but still a good figure for her age. She went to the dressing table and Paul Lowe got out of bed and went into the bathroom.

He stared at himself in the bathroom mirror. Even in the indirect soft light he looked haggard. He turned the faucet and ran hot water into his hands and buried his face in the cupped heat. Indescribably delicious. Under his skin the tiny capillaries greeted the life-giving warmth.

He reached for the towel.

—Are my breasts too small? the girl asked.

—They're perfect.

He wiped his hands on the towel. The narrow inside panel of the bathroom door had a full-length mirror. He saw himself in it, Harriet standing beside him. She flaunted her small exquisitely formed body in the full-length mirror.

She put her hands beneath her breasts.

—I think they're too small. I wish I had a size thirty-eight. How big is Eleanor?

—I really wouldn't know.

Her dark eyes were smoky and her tousled blonde hair was partly damp.

—You never talk about your wife, you know that?

—Do you think there's a reason?

—Of course there's a reason. Papa Freud sees all and knows all. You know what I think the reason is?

—What?

She blew the hair out of her eye, squirting breath up from a corner of her mouth.

—You hate her.

—I don't. You're wrong.

—All right, pussycat, so you don't hate her. Then why did you come panting after me? Just because my gender is feminine and yours is masculine?

—Maybe.

She laughed—a laughter infectious but a little frightening.

—More than that, darling. You're not a goat, you know. In fact . . .

Her teeth were white and her mouth a perfectly formed orifice, as she regarded him too deliberately.

—You're not nearly as good a lover as Stephen.

Nothing was forbidden to Harriet. Her tongue was forked.

—I'll get better. As soon as I stop thinking you're the most beautiful piece of crockery I've ever seen.

—Why do you crock me? I'm married to one of your very best friends.

She dared him, eyes dancing.

—I don't consider Stephen Korwitz one of my very best friends or anything like it. We just happen to be in the same class at law school.

—Boola, boola, boola, boola.

Naked sprite doing the cha-cha to the rhythm of the Yale song. Harriet was a creature of odd if not impossible contradictions. Her moods varied so wildly from meeting to meeting that he never knew what his welcome would be. She could be full of lustful greeting or watch him with distant calculating amused eyes that laughed far back in the corridors of her mind.

But there were moments with her—no less rare for being brief—when he had a sense of joy, disporting with laughter in his skin.

He dried his hands on the towel.

The affair so many years ago with Harriet had been a prevision.

With Katherine promise had become fulfillment. In his parched nature he found unexpected springs among famine roots. He shook off part of the heritage of the long-dead overdedicated father, and a mother drowned in pneumonia but long dying of trivia. He gained eyes to see without the shadows of other things forever waiting attendance, without the terrible double vision that was created by the mind behind the eye. He saw his love plain without the lies created by the brain as it groped for meaning in its own depths. *Omnia vincit amor.* He had always thought that a lie, and no better for being a lie in Latin—every language must provide for mendacity. But he was wrong. *Res ipsa loquitur.* The thing speaks for itself. Does the harvest ask why it is growing?

If there is no love, *Hamlet* is a ghost story. . . .

Eleanor was sitting before the dressing table mirror, naked, with one leg crossed over the other. With her fingers she applied cream to her cheeks with small circular strokes.

She saw him watching her in the mirror and smiled with a question in it.

"Is anything the matter, dear?"

"I was only watching you."

"Oh." The fingers moved more swiftly in rounding cream into a cheek. Her smile became satisfied.

She was good in bed. She had overcome the initial frigidity carefully instilled in young virgins—the art of the controlled response, the not-quite surrender, the step-by-step consent leading to a final overwhelming no. Now Eleanor could have sex and be happy. She could abandon control, hold back nothing, lift him into potency, deliver on schedule the final yes—yes—YES. She knew how to enjoy the wallowing in an afterglow of emotion. For her a sexual encounter had become a form of moral obligation—she was obliged to make it amount to something.

But he could predict each of her reactions, as she could predict each of his preliminary moves. They had long since ceased to hear the beating of their hearts.

"Eleanor," he said.

The gently circling fingers halted at a cheekbone. "Yes?"

"You haven't asked me what happened when I met the President at the White House this evening."

284

She put her hand down. "I was beginning to think you weren't going to tell me. That it was one of those government secrets you can't even discuss with your wife."

She lived in a small circle within a multiplicity of larger circles, surrounded by many areas she felt forbidden to enter.

"No, I can discuss it with you. But I don't think you should mention it to anyone else."

He had previously mentioned Race Hardman's offer. Now he told her why the President wanted him to accept.

"What did you tell him?" she asked.

"I could hardly refuse. After all he is the President." He knew her reverence for authority.

Absently she began to stroke the skin beneath her eyes. "Then you're really going? Must you leave right away?"

"We can have a little time together."

"How much?"

"Perhaps a week. I have to make arrangements."

"That won't be time enough to visit Lincoln. Mother and Natalie will be so disappointed."

"It can't be helped. There'll be time after I come back. I don't expect to be gone more than six or eight weeks."

"I don't know what I'll do without you."

He stopped to gaze at her hand making its way along the natural curve of the ointmented skin surfaces. Was he that important to her? Is habit speaking—or the heart? *Love for love I canna gie.* By occupying her time, her body, I am keeping out worthier contenders for her affection.

"It won't be as long as you think," he said. "And you'll be with your mother and Natalie."

Eleanor sighed; bare breasts rose and fell. She turned back to the mirror; her mouth trembled. "I was counting so much on having these next few months alone with you. I've hardly seen you at all."

Dutifully he went to her. He sat beside her on the dressing table bench that was not really large enough for two. He held her hands.

"I'll write you as often as I can. It isn't going to be forever, you know," he said, and as he said the words he realized fully for the first time that it was going to be forever. People grow apart and when the growing apart has gone on long enough there is a chasm which divorce only confirms. The true sin is attempting to live without love.

He welcomed the impending separation as the beginning of his escape from old patterns, back to a time and a place where his personal dilemmas had been simpler, more sharply defined, far less threatening—back to his youth. Now that his Burma journey was about to become a reality, no longer a fanciful idea somewhere on the stellar reaches of improbability, he was excited about the prospect it offered for ending the old and beginning the new.

Only a few more days. Then he would be in a plane, putting distance between himself and the moral noose which had been tightening about his throat.

20

On June twenty-fourth Paul Lincoln Lowe arrived in Rangoon. He was met at Mingalodon Airport by an official delegation from the United States Embassy. The head of the delegation was a lean man with a long worried face. His protruding kneecaps made him look slightly ludicrous in shorts.

"Mr. Justice, this is a very great honor," he said. "My name is David Moss. The Ambassador asked me to convey his regrets that he could not be here in person to meet you. I'm sorry to say that the Ambassador is indisposed at home."

"I hope it's not serious," Paul Lowe said.

"Well, actually, it's a comparatively mild case of amoebic dysentery. He'll be up and around in a few days. Meanwhile he has given me instructions to do everything possible to make your visit a pleasant one."

"Thank you, Mr. Moss."

They crossed the airfield. The heat was shocking—as though he had suddenly turned a corner into a molten wind that took his breath away.

On the crest of the hill above the airport the golden surface of the Shwe Dagon Pagoda shone like a burnished lamp. Twilight had passed swiftly. A sky crimson-laced with delicate black clouds had suddenly plunged into a mauve-colored darkness.

As they entered the main building in the airport, David Moss said, "I've arranged for your luggage to be checked through without the usual formalities. You've no idea how endless they can be in this country."

"I appreciate that. Where will I stay?"

"Of course you'll stay at the Embassy, Mr. Justice. There'll be a reception tomorrow night. We've invited some of the most prominent Burmese officials. The President of the Union of Burma, U Ba Saw, has promised to be there."

"I've heard a good deal about U Ba Saw. He must be an interesting man."

"Oh, yes. Is it true, Mr. Justice, that you intend to write a series of articles on the political situation in this country?"

Paul Lowe said, "I'm afraid in the short time I'll be here I couldn't become very well acquainted with the political situation. All I hope to do is jot down some personal impressions. With photographs." He chuckled. "*Some* photographs. Luckily the new cameras take good pictures practically by themselves. So I leave the art to the cropping."

They sat down on a hard wooden bench and waited for the luggage to be delivered from the plane.

"How long have you been in Burma, Mr. Moss?"

"Six years."

"You see? No matter how I tried, I couldn't cram into a few weeks all the experience someone like yourself has gained in six years."

David Moss's adam's apple bobbed in a corded neck. "Well, it's true that Burma does present a different problem from any other country in Southeast Asia." He turned to Paul Lowe with a popeyed intensity. "The Burmese have very little in common with their neighbors in bordering countries. For every citizen of Burma who visits Thailand, for example, there are more than two hundred who visit the United States, England, or France. There's so little *communication*. Did you know that a telegram from Rangoon to Bangkok—a distance of five hundred miles—has to be relayed by way of London?"

"Not a very efficient method of sending a telegram, is it?"

"It certainly isn't. That's one quality the Burmese particularly admire about Americans—our efficiency. They realize that American know-how has made us prosperous. As the Ambassador was saying to a group of prominent Burmese businessmen just the other day, the people of the United States comprise only ten percent of the world's population but we account for one-half of the world's production. The answer to that is our know-how, our efficiency."

"I can see where Burmese businessmen would appreciate that message," Paul Lowe said wryly. "How about the working people—the peasants? How do they feel about the United States of America?"

"Oh, we're a never-never land to them. They simply can't imagine that we worry about things like food surpluses and having too much of everything. It's inconceivable to them that the ordinary working man in America has a car, a television set, and owns a fine modern home. That's positively staggering to people who have such limited opportunities."

"Isn't there a danger in that?"

"A danger, Mr. Justice?"

"If the ordinary people in Burma know that our banquet table is laid out for a feast, won't they resent us when we offer them only the crumbs?"

David Moss blinked. "That's an interesting question, Mr. Justice. I'm sure the Ambassador will be very anxious to talk to you and give you his own viewpoint. . . . Ah, there's your luggage now. I'll have it moved out to the car right away."

David Moss jumped up and crossed to the railing where he held an animated discussion with a porter and a customs inspector. Paul Lowe smiled sadly as he watched him. David Moss could be quite officious within small limits but would never never exceed his authority—he was the type of man whose name after a short time escaped you, one of those who never reach a position of importance or belong to the inner circle, who are always too anxious to please and slightly in the way of their superiors. Married? Probably to a woman like himself, plain, stringy, anxious and hovering—an indistinct couple to be invited only if need arose for a pair to fill out the invitation list and someone remembered "the fellow with the bony knees and that white-faced sad-looking woman."

Because he had been unkind in his thoughts, Paul Lowe became especially attentive as David Moss led the way to the chauffeured limousine waiting outside the main building. David Moss told him about the Golden Pagoda which had been built to enclose the eight sacred hairs of Buddha.

"Sounds very much like our own early Christian churches," Paul Lowe remarked. "They were usually built around some sacred relic of the Martyrs."

"Why yes, that's so, isn't it, Mr. Justice?"

During the drive away from Mingalodon Airport, David Moss continued to point out the sights in a matter-of-fact, uninteresting account. Paul Lowe's interest shifted quickly from the streets with doughty British names, Phayre and Fraser and Strand, and from the tall obelisk of the Independence Monument, to his own impressions: a sweltering and dusty town, half drowning in squalor. In the side lanes he saw refuse piled, and dogs and crows prowling and picking through it.

The limousine passed skeletal half-dressed men barely propped up against the walls of buildings. Along railroad tracks and the shores of Royal Lake were row upon row of decaying squalid shacks.

The constant commentary of his host appeared chiefly to be aimed at diverting his attention:

"The people in Rangoon are very friendly, very clean. They even wash in the public fountains and you'll see them going about soaked with water, their *longyis* molded to their bodies. The *longyis* are those pieces of checked or striped material they wear about their bodies and legs. They look like shirts. The women wear the knot at the side and the men wear it in the middle. Those men you see walking so slowly carrying bowls are the *bonzes*, Buddhist priests. They always wear orange or saffron or ochre-colored clothes. Their bowls are so-called beggar bowls. Anyone who puts food in the bowl receives credit for a good deed. The priests don't beg, really—they just give people a chance to earn credits."

His slightly condescending air annoyed Paul Lowe.

"It isn't too different from paying for a Mass to be said for the repose of the soul after death, is it? Or even putting money into a collection plate at church?"

David Moss answered a bit stiffly, "I wouldn't push the comparison too far, Mr. Justice. After all, these are a very superstitious people."

"Americans are a nation of penny mystics, Mr. Moss. If we added up every American who goes to tea-leaf readers, handwriting analysts, fortune-tellers, numerologists, spiritualists, yogis, faith healers, astrologers and clairvoyants, it's possible that we'd discover our so-called lunatic fringe is the lunatic majority."

David Moss lapsed into a silence. The limousine picked up speed as it passed lurid-looking cinemas with garish posters advertising American, Burmese and Indian films. Loudspeakers from the theater lobbies made a constant raucous clamor. Vans parked in the road blared out the attractions of the various motion pictures. The streets were crowded to the brim with white-shirted, black-headed throngs that appeared to be motionless until, as if a wave passed over, the human sea moved back or forward. Through the high-pitched babble of voices motor traffic *thrummed* and bicycle bells jangled.

Paul Lowe sat with his head back against the rear seat of the car. He closed his eyes. His exchange with David Moss had put a period to the wearing travelogue and he was grateful for that. Too many impressions were flowing in too quickly and he needed to make the adjustment between the picture of Rangoon he had imagined before his arrival and the exotic reality.

The afternoon he had left Washington (a final glimpse of Eleanor as he went down the ramp—waving, all tears) Rangoon had seemed as unreal as a heat mirage. The giant commercial jet delivered him to Amsterdam, one of the most modern, most efficiently appointed airports of the Western world. There he had chartered a private plane and flown to Beirut, where he first began to feel the impact of change. The airport was a huge shed with a corrugated iron roof where dark-skinned indolent men lounged against the wall in cedar-scented sunshine. Then he flew on to Karachi, with palm trees and eucalyptus, lizards on the walls and vultures perching on rooftops. By then he accepted that he was an alien, in Western dress among people in loose white garments and bare feet. A thousand years of conquest stood between. In the autumn of 1095, at Clermont, a Pope had called the faithful: "Enter you the road to the Holy Sepulcher, convert it from the wicked race, and subject it."

The banner of Christ crucified led the way to battle and slaughter: "God wills it!"

And the high fierce answering cry: "There is no other God but God!" from the high hills of Hattin.

He had flown across the great red plain of India to Rangoon.

Now as the limousine went slowly through the hot rancid streets of Rangoon on its way to the American Embassy, he wondered whether it was hot as this at home where Nancy waited swollen with her unwanted child. He felt sorry for the poor unwelcome infant. Once out of the womb there was no place to hide in a hostile world.

Children splashed in a fountain. Their rayon garments clung to their small behinds. That first night in St. Thomas, half the world away and wide, Katherine had been changing her dress. He remembered how her black silk underthings had clung to her.

David Moss saw him watching the children playing in the fountain.

"We try to discourage them from doing that," he said. "But these people love water and in the hot weather there's simply nothing to be done with them. They even wash their dogs in the fountain. They don't understand the first principles of sanitation."

"Back home in Lincoln, Nebraska, kids splash around with their dogs in water from an open fire hydrant."

David Moss appeared to be vaguely resigned: "Yes, I suppose children *are* the same all over the world."

"'God made of one blood the whole race of men.'"

"Is that a quotation, Mr. Justice?"

"The late Pope John said it. A good man, God rest him."

"Yes, he was."

"I don't believe he would have sanctioned a crusade against a so-called wicked race, do you?"

"No, I don't think he would have."

Paul Lowe said, "Well, then, nine hundred years have brought an improvement in Popes if not in the rest of us."

David Moss arrested his consenting nod midway, as though it had suddenly occurred to him that he might be joining in a sacrilegious statement.

The limousine turned in past a barbed wire entrance that led to the American Embassy.

At the Embassy reception the next evening, Paul Lowe met the President of the Union of Burma. U Ba Saw was a small gentle wrinkled man who shook hands gravely.

"It is a very great honor to meet a distinguished visitor from your great country."

"I'm looking forward to my visit here, Your Excellency."

"I hope you will stay long enough to meet many of my people. If there is any way in which I can be of assistance, please let me know."

"Thank you."

"I have met your Mr. Justice Charles Edmunson. In your city of Washington. I was most impressed. Please give him my respects when you return there. He is a great man, do you not agree?"

"I agree."

"Even so," U Ba Saw sighed. "In my country we wish for such men to lead us. But it takes time to produce such greatness, is it not so?"

"Yes."

"Later we will talk more of this," U Ba Saw said. "Now I must not keep you from the many guests who wish to speak with you."

Native servants in *longyis* passed among the guests, carrying trays of drinks—scotch and soda, bourbon, rye. Few Burmese drank in their homes so there was no peculiarly native alcoholic drink. Paul Lowe kept a glass of bourbon in one hand and a fixed smile on his face, while he nodded and shook hands with the various people who came up to be introduced to him.

Of many he remembered two.

One was a Buddhist priest, wearing a rather short saffron *longyi* with muscular slightly bowed legs and strong-looking feet in sandals. His head was shaven, and he was tall for a Burmese, an inch or so taller than Paul Lowe.

The priest said, "At such parties the people one meets do not give a true picture of conditions in Burma."

"What are the conditions in Burma?" Paul Lowe asked.

"The houses of the poor have walls of mud, bricks or rice paper. The streets swarm with naked potbellied hungry children. Death and disease are close to our people and their lives are short. In a typical village the average worker earns less than—in your American money—one hundred dollars each year."

"What do you think should be done?"

The Buddhist priest's solemn brown face remained impassive. "There are no simple answers. However, one must emulate the wisdom of Prince Siddhartha. Prince Siddhartha was born the son of a wealthy king who surrounded the young prince with all the kingdom could offer and kept him from seeing any death or ugliness. One day Prince Siddhartha went out to a park in the city and saw three things—a decrepit old man, a sick old man, and a corpse—and these sights revealed human misery to him for the first time. On the night *his* first son was born Prince Siddhartha renounced the world and retreated into solitude to learn the causes of human misery."

"And did he learn the causes?"

"He learned that the only way to obtain peace of mind is to renounce the vanities of this world. Prince Siddhartha attained perfect peace. He became Gautama Buddha."

"A very great and very good man," Paul Lowe said. "But following his example and renouncing the world at this point won't help those poor villagers you were speaking of, will it?"

"One must always seek his own wisdom." The priest's eyes were bright brown diamonds. "This world, Mr. Justice, is a bubble scarcely worth the effort needed to comprehend its history from molten glass to blackened rock. But everything lives in the wise man's consciousness." He bowed and moved slowly away.

The other man Paul Lowe remembered was Bogyoke Shlaing, a smiling, friendly general in a uniform of brown *witsone*, with buttons of brass and epaulets. Bogyoke waved a paper fan before his face as he spoke.

"Meestah Justice," he said, "you can travel anywhere you wish in Burma. There is regular and reliable service by air to all the larger towns. Communist bandits have made many attempts to cut the railroad, but there is still regular service. There are only two serious breaks in the line from Rangoon to Mandalay but passengers are carried over these by mules."

"I'm flying my own plane," Paul Lowe said. "North as far as Mitkyina and then by foot into the mountains of the northwest."

Above them an electric fan whirred. A servant appeared with a tea basket and poured a cup of green pickled tea for Bogyoke Shlaing.

Bogyoke's smile remained friendly. "I do not think that the trip you speak of will be possible, Meestah Justice."

"Why not?"

"The military situation in the north is, ah, uncertain. There are many Communist bandits."

"I'm willing to accept the risk."

"It is necessary to assure the safety of important personages. If something should happen to you, Meestah Justice, it would be most tragic for my government. People would say, what kind of government is it that cannot assure the safety of such a distinguished visitor?"

"I've already obtained my travel permit from the Permanent Secretary of the Ministry of Information."

Bogyoke nodded. "He is not fully aware of the situation." He sipped his cup of tea. "That travel permit is, of course, subject to military approval and that means my approval."

"Surely you would not refuse to approve it?" Paul Lowe said quietly.

Bogyoke Shlaing sipped his tea. Another servant brought a plate with finely chopped garlic and an assortment of spices, and he sampled some.

Bogyoke said, "I will take the question under advisement with the Chief of Special Branch police. He will render his opinion. Then, sir, your request will be considered further."

"Look, General, I'm here on an assignment from an important American magazine and a number of American newspapers. I haven't come this far to be turned back."

Bogyoke Shlaing rested his tea cup gently in the palm of one hand. "Meestah Justice. We wish to cooperate in every way."

Paul Lowe said firmly, "I need to have my travel permit approved. I intend to leave for Mandalay within the next few days."

Bogyoke shook his head. "I regret a final decision cannot be available in such time."

"Then I'll have to ask the President himself. And if he says I can't go I'll report that fact to the people in the United States who asked me to come here. I will tell them of the inability of your government to control the situation in Burma."

Bogyoke Shlaing drew in his chin slightly. "Have I said this?"

"That's the real story, isn't it?"

"No, Meestah Justice. The army is in excellent control. But we cannot guarantee your absolute safety. That is why I have spoken so."

"I don't ask you to guarantee it. My safety is my own responsibility."

Bogyoke Shlaing dipped his head. "If you insist let it be so. I will notify military authorities in the districts you wish to visit. They will make easeful your journey in every way."

"Thank you," Paul Lowe said. "That's very kind."

"Will you care for some tea?"

Paul Lowe shook his head politely.

At shortly before midnight he was granted a private interview with President U Ba Saw. They retired to a small anteroom off the main reception hall.

He said, "Your Excellency, I have a private message for you from the President of the United States."

"A private message?"

"Yes, Your Excellency. It is for your eyes only."

With a troubled expression, U Ba Saw accepted the letter that Paul Lowe handed to him. He read the letter carefully and handed it back.

"You may tell your esteemed President that we are aware of the problem."

"Perhaps, Your Excellency, you are not aware of quite how serious the problem is. I have brought other documents with me."

U Ba Saw held up his hand. "I will consult with you in my office tomorrow, when other ministers are present."

"These other documents are also meant only for your eyes, Your Excellency. I wish you would read them now. It won't take long."

With a sigh, U Ba Saw accepted the documents. On the settee in the anteroom, holding ribboned reading glasses between thumb and forefinger, he read quietly. Finally he put down the documents. He pulled at the sleeves of his long jacket and refolded the handsome yellow silk *longyi* about his waist and hips.

"We in Asia do not understand, Mr. Justice, why Americans are always willing to help Asian people kill other Asian people."

"That is certainly not our reason for wanting to help, Mr. President."

"However, that would be the result of the military aid you offer, would it not?"

"No, it wouldn't. We offer assistance in putting down a revolt before it becomes serious, before it develops into real civil war."

"The civil war in Viet Nam would have ended much sooner without American soldiers and guns."

"It would have ended in a Communist victory. That isn't what you want, Your Excellency. Your government is firmly opposed to the Communists."

"But that is not our highest purpose. We do not believe that the Communists desire to destroy the world—and it is therefore not fitting that *we* should destroy the world merely to defeat them."

"You can't just stand by and let them take over, can you, Your Excellency?"

"We would resist if they should attempt it."

"All we want to do is help you to resist," Paul Lowe said.

"If our ideals prove worthy, the people will support us—and we shall have nothing to fear from Communism."

"I don't see how accepting aid to preserve your own government can do any harm to your ideals, Your Excellency."

"One cannot compromise with what he is, Mr. Justice. The late Mahatma Gandhi proved that a policy of nonviolence may accomplish more than a policy of violence. I do not wish to encourage strife among my people. An act of violence bears children and those children will have children. Is it not better to observe the laws of Buddha—and preserve life? That is a sacred principle of the Buddhist religion."

"Your Excellency, the Christian religion also teaches 'Thou shalt not kill.' But the law of Christ is sometimes broken to serve the needs of the state. In a practical world we have to choose practical alternatives."

"Mr. Justice, we cannot wait for others to choose the path of righteousness. We must follow it ourselves—and pray that others will follow."

There was no reason to doubt the sincerity of this small gentle man. U Ba Saw was a pacific and smiling Buddha mask over the Jekyll-Hyde countenance of the real Burma. On the one side there was the army, backed by the landlords, the wealthy and the middle classes, and on the other side the peasants, the landless, and the Communists. Neither of these opposing groups was yet in a position to seize power and for the interim they had compromised on this man for President—a folk hero whose universal popularity compelled both sides to support him.

Paul Lowe said, "Your Excellency, the United States government believes you are in a much more precarious position than you realize. I hope you will seriously consider our offer to give you the support you need."

U Ba Saw nodded politely. "We will. And we will also, of course, pray for guidance."

"May I expect an answer soon to my government?"

U Ba Saw nodded. "Now, Mr. Justice, let us not pursue our disagreements further. I would prefer to hear from you about your United States Supreme Court."

He sat back and smiled at U Ba Saw. "What would you like to know?"

"Tell me of its position in American life. What kind of cases does it dispose of? What power does your Court have to enforce its decisions?"

He scratched his temple. "This isn't going to be easy to explain, Your Excellency. But I'll try."

U Ba Saw listened carefully while he did his best. Then U Ba Saw permitted himself a small smile.

"In the city of Rangoon," he said, "there is a Chinese Buddhist temple. A visitor may kneel before the goddess and state what he desires to know. Then he takes in his hand a container of sticks and shakes them as hard as he can. When a stick falls out its markings are consulted, and the clerks in charge of the temple are the only ones who may interpret the answers. Is not this like your United States Supreme Court?"

He grinned. "There are certain resemblances, Your Excellency."

U Ba Saw's small wrinkled face crinkled. He clapped his hands with delight.

In his bedroom an electric fan whirred overhead. When he turned the fan off the room grew unbearably hot. When he left the fan on, the noise disturbed him just enough to keep him from slipping over the dividing line into real sleep. Instead he dozed fitfully.

He saw an old and powerful, wise face. Charles Edmunson. When I was younger (Paul Lowe thought) I believed that the royal road to happiness was traveled only by the wise but I have met wise men since and they are no happier than ordinary men. They suffer from the isolation that wisdom brings—the penalty of losing human contacts, of living more with ideas than with people. Wisdom itself is a form of illusion. . . .

A small and gently smiling brown face. U Ba Saw's religion forbade the taking of human life. But the Burmese soldiers fought the British. Those same Buddhist soldiers who would never have shot a mad dog or stepped on an insect fought and killed other men . . . They knew killing was unchangeably evil and that God was not with them when they went into battle. But they went. If they had been better armed, better prepared, there might have been less killing.

Idealism is also an illusion—one of the most dangerous.

He rolled in bed restlessly. He had no desire to think. He wanted to sleep.

Her face.

Her voice.

The whole delicate frame of her body suspended beneath him.

This is no way to get to sleep. He had to subtract himself from his thoughts.

He opened his eyes in a hot still bedroom.

On the morning he was to leave for Mandalay his mail caught up with him at the American Embassy. There was a letter from Eleanor, friendly, full of perfunctory reports. She was staying with her mother and sister Natalie in Lincoln. The outside of the house was being painted. She had opened a special checking account in a Lincoln bank. There had been no letter from Nancy, who was somewhere in New York with Tessie Samuels awaiting the birth of her baby.

In the mail forwarded by Martha Scully there was a short note enclosed in an envelope from the United States Senate. The note was a reply by Senator Vance Murdoch to Paul Lowe's latest inquiry on behalf of getting funds authorized for the North Platte dam. Senator Murdoch advised that the project was still under consideration although no legislative action was contemplated at this time. Senator Murdoch offered his warmest personal regards and assured Paul Lowe that he was anxious to be cooperative in every possible way. In politics an inverse ratio operated between the warmth of language and the chill of performance: a politician became friendlier as the harshness of refusal became undeniable.

The other mail was mostly from people angry at the Supreme Court and at him in particular. Purest vitriol ran through most of the letters. There were some exceptions, a few correspondents who, trying to be fair, praised him for his courage even while they damned him for his stupidity. In his first weeks on the Court Martha Scully had tried to keep this sort of mail from him but when he found out he had insisted on reading every letter. Now he sometimes regretted his insistence. The passion which motivated people to write in such insulting terms shook him. He did not blame them for thinking that he was wrong but why did none even admit the possibility that he might be right? Their absolute hatred for any opposing idea made him wonder.

The Supreme Court is trying to abolish God from the government and the schools. . . . I might fairly ask whether, if God is to be worshiped at government expense, we can keep the government from eventually deciding which ways of worshiping Him are acceptable. Is it abolishing God to cut him off from the purse strings of the state? He is not a civil servant.

The Court upholds positions which are advocated by extremists. . . . If extremists were to advocate free education and civil rights, should we oppose those things merely because they are advocated by extremists? That would grant such people a measure of control over us they could never obtain by other means. If they control our responses, they control the situation.

The Court defends the constitutional rights of enemies of democracy. . . . If a judge decides that a constitutional claim by a Communist is valid, does that make the judge a Communist? Then it should follow that if he decides a constitutional claim by a Democrat is valid, he is a Democrat. Or a Republican if he upholds a constitutional claim by a member of that party. Or a Catholic or a Baptist or a Christian Scientist or an atheist or a vegetarian or a dope peddler.

Crossing Mingalodon airfield to his waiting plane, Paul Lowe thought of a quotation which might answer such critics. He would have it printed up and mailed back to all virulent letter writers.

Quidquic solvitur solvitur secundum modum solventis.

Whatever is solved is solved according to the manner of him who solves it.

That will give them something to think about.

He climbed into the plane and waved to David Moss who stood outside the terminal building. In a moment the roar of the engine responded and the plane trembled with readiness to go. The power of mechanical things such as airplanes to carry out their function was impressive. Within a machine conflicts are reduced, friction held to a minimum, gravity counterbalanced and power measured out equal to the task to be performed.

It is different with human beings. Too much of their strength is devoted not to carrying out a task but to fighting down the opposition to it.

In the late afternoon he arrived at Mandalay airfield, the first stop scheduled on his journey to the north. A shimmering haze caused the landscapes to shift and waver as he brought the plane down past scorched hills. Along the plane's metal wing ripples of warm air moved.

As he stepped out of the plane he realized it was not the degree but the kind of heat that was different. In Rangoon the heat had been humid, uncomfortable, clinging like wet clothes, but in Mandalay, heat had a dry shape and body of its own, suffocating and dense. Beyond the airfield the sky seemed covered with a reddish tint of dust.

U Nee, a representative in Mandalay of the United States Information Service, met him at the airport in a large handsome car which flew a small American flag from the radio antenna. U Nee was an elderly man, slightly stooped, with eyes like flat brown shavings of stone. He wore linen clothes of American cut and spoke with a faint British accent.

"I have instructions from the Embassy," he said. "They are anxious for you to see what you wish. With the confirmation of the army, I have worked out a very extensive program for sightseeing. There will be a minimum of danger."

"Danger?"

U Nee sighed. "The rebels are very active. Two nights ago they burned down a small hotel only two miles from the town. It is hard to deal effectively with them. Our own police are infiltrated."

"Are the rebels Communists?"

"Not all. But there are Communists among them. The situation here is not so bad as in the north. There, the Communists control entire villages."

"Why is there so much trouble?"

U Nee shrugged. "Where there is poverty there is trouble. Is it not so? And this country for many hundreds of miles shares a common border with Red China. A powerful neighbor wields influence."

Soon they were driving along the dusty road leading from the airport to the city of Mandalay. He felt the perspiration running down his legs. He pressed a handkerchief between his palms to dry his hands but before the car reached its destination the handkerchief was soaking wet.

The car stopped before a small villa with a tidy garden, a white gate and a path of stone leading to the door. It might have been a suburban home anywhere in the Southern United States, except that it was badly in need of repairs. Plaster was flaking from the walls and a corner of the house was blackened.

U Nee was particularly embarrassed by the blackened exterior.

"The work of rebels," he said with disdain. "Two weeks ago they set fire to my house. They piled kindling at the wall and set it afire. We were able to extinguish the flames before more damage was done. Still, we are fortunate. A few nights ago my neighbor's house was entered and all his furniture wrecked and his clothes stolen." U Nee shook his head. "They grow bolder every day." He pointed to hills in the north. "That is the frontier of the rebels. It is only four or five miles from town. They come down in the night, and make life difficult for those who are against them."

"Is there no way to stop them?" Paul Lowe asked.

"We do not capture many. When we do, we try to set an example. Yesterday one was caught passing out leaflets that called upon the people to rise up and overthrow their leaders."

"What will happen to him?"

"There will be a trial and he will be shot."

As he was about to enter the doorway, "Is there a death penalty for merely passing out leaflets?" he asked.

U Nee shrugged. "If we do not deal severely with the rebels, how shall we control what they do? In these times an offense against the state must be punishable by death."

They entered the living room which had bamboo furniture and a dark polished wooden floor.

"I would like to be present at the trial of the prisoner. Can it be arranged?"

"Without difficulty," U Nee said.

"It would be interesting for Americans to read about how a trial is conducted here. If I show you how to operate my camera, will you be good enough to take photographs of what takes place in the courtroom?"

"I will be honored." U Nee rubbed his hands. "Shall we have lunch, Mr. Justice? We are having *kyatthahin*."

"What's that?"

"A delicious dish of chicken limbs jaundiced with curry. I am sure you will enjoy it. My cook has made me the envy of all my neighbors."

At five o'clock in the afternoon when the brazen heat had passed its zenith, U Nee escorted Paul Lowe to the courtroom where the trial was to be held. It was a large room with a high ceiling and two pillars at either side of a door which opened onto a courtyard.

The Judge's desk and a solid-looking high-built chair were on a raised platform. On the desk, beside a bowl in which a few incense sticks were burning, there was a small block of black wood.

"That is the court-shocking wood," U Nee said. "The Judge uses it when he wishes to command attention or is angry."

"In my country, we call it a gavel."

U Nee seemed pleased at this parallel between American and Burmese justice.

As the courtroom slowly filled up with spectators, a faint gong sounded. The Judge entered, a rather large man with a rough-hewn, ugly face, who wore a saffron *longyi* and a white jacket. His *longyi* was secured with a diamond-clasp belt and despite his considerable bulk he moved so silently that he almost seemed to glide into the room.

U Nee stepped forward to the dais and spoke with the Judge. He indicated the camera he was holding and pointed toward Paul Lowe. The Judge nodded and gave an order to a policeman in a blue cotton uniform.

U Nee returned.

"The Judge will be honored to have you sit with him. A place is being

298

prepared. I will take photographs and later I will act as your interpreter when the questioning of the prisoner begins."

When Paul Lowe reached the platform the Judge rose to shake hands.

Paul Lowe said, "It is very kind of you to allow me to be present."

The Judge replied in very good English: "We wish our friends from the United States to see how quickly and efficiently justice is done in Burma."

Two chairs, slightly smaller than the Judge's own chair, were carried onto the platform by a policeman and placed on the right side of the Judge's desk, facing the courtroom. Paul Lowe sat down with the Judge on his right.

U Nee aimed the camera and a flash of white light illuminated the courtroom. The Judge's hand quivered but he gave no other indication of surprise.

U Nee continued taking pictures while the courtroom gradually filled. Soon the crude benches were crowded with men and women sitting so closely that someone always seemed to be squeezed forward.

U Nee returned to the platform and took his seat beside Paul Lowe. The Judge lifted his block of wood and banged it on the desk. He uttered a short command.

"He says to bring the prisoner," U Nee whispered to Paul Lowe.

Two policemen escorted the prisoner in from the door that opened between the two pillars confronting the courtyard. He was a youth of no more than sixteen or seventeen, with a square face and a set jaw. He wore a short-sleeved dirty brown shirt and wrinkled canvas trousers. His brown arms were well muscled. He was brought before the dais and when the policemen released him he stood with his legs slightly apart and his hands on his hips.

The Judge asked a question. The boy's answer was short and his manner contemptuous.

U Nee continued to translate. "The Judge asked his name. The prisoner answered Zan. . . . The Judge now wishes to know if that is his real name. The prisoner answers that is the name by which he is known. Has he no family? . . . No, he has renounced his family."

U Nee's quick soft whispers enabled Paul Lowe to follow the interrogation closely as it proceeded.

The Judge asked, "What do you do for a living?"

"I am a soldier."

"How old are you?"

"Fifteen years and eleven months."

"You are not old enough to serve in the Burmese army."

"I am a soldier of the guerrillas."

"A Communist?"

"Yes."

The Judge cleared his throat loudly. He turned to Paul Lowe with a stern expression and said in English:

"You see. We already have a confession."

Paul Lowe asked, "What is the prisoner accused of?"

The Judge frowned. "I am coming to that." He turned his attention back to the prisoner. "You are accused of passing out leaflets to people on the road between the city of Mandalay and Maymyo. These pamphlets called on the people to revolt against the lawful government. Do you admit doing this?"

"No," said the prisoner.

"You are accused by two soldiers of the regular Burmese army who discovered you doing so."

"They are lying. Let them produce these leaflets they speak of."

"If you were not doing what they say, what were you doing there?"

"With several of my comrades I was searching for one who had tried to desert."

"Did you find him?"

"No."

The Judge said impatiently, "We have heard enough lies. The prisoner is found guilty and sentenced to die before a firing squad." The Judge banged his court-shocking wood. "Take the prisoner. Court is dismissed."

Two policemen moved in and took the prisoner and led him away. He went defiantly, without a backward glance.

The Judge turned to Paul Lowe and U Nee.

"This is the kind of rabble with which we must deal. It is necessary that justice should be prompt and severe with them."

"Is there a law against passing out leaflets?" Paul Lowe asked.

The Judge answered: "We have a law which forbids the committing of any action which disturbs the security of the state."

"And the penalty for breaking that law is death?"

"That is within the discretion of the Judge."

"Is there any appeal?"

The Judge's eyes lidded slightly. "There is nothing from which to appeal. He received a most fair and just trial. Would it have been different in your country?"

"Yes, it would."

"In what way?"

"There would have been witnesses called to testify against him."

The Judge shrugged one shoulder slightly. "None was needed. He admitted he was a Communist. But if he had not confessed we would have called upon the soldiers who saw him passing out leaflets."

"Would he have been allowed to question those soldiers?"

"To what purpose?"

"To discover if they were telling the truth."

"How could one know that?"

"There might be additional evidence to prove it."

"What manner of evidence?"

"The leaflets themselves, for example. If even one of them had been produced you might be better able to judge whether what was written in them *really* threatens the security of the state."

"There is no question of it. The soldiers would testify to it."

300

"The defendant denied that there were any leaflets."

"He was lying."

"How can you be sure? Isn't it possible the soldiers were lying?"

The Judge turned to U Nee with an accusing stare and spoke swiftly to him. U Nee flushed. Then the Judge turned back to Paul Lowe.

"Mr. Justice, it is clear you do not understand the conditions in Burma. The army is the guardian of the people. If we do not have faith in our army, whom would you expect us to believe?"

"I do not mean to offend anyone, Your Honor. I am merely trying to learn what differences exist between the way the law is administered here and in my own country."

The Judge appeared to be mollified.

"Is it not the purpose of a court to punish criminals?"

"Not to punish—but to decide who is guilty."

"The law says who is guilty."

Paul Lowe said, "We believe the courts must act as an intermediate body between the people and the kind of laws a legislature may pass. It is up to the court to decide what the law means and then to apply it in a particular case."

The Judge smiled expansively. "Then it is clear that there is little difference between us. We, too, apply the law. The people are entitled to the protection of judges against their enemies. A judge must interpret the law to protect them. Is this not so?"

Paul Lowe said, "It isn't quite what I meant."

The Judge's face clouded. "Then we do not understand each other," he replied.

"Perhaps that will change," Paul Lowe answered courteously. "One of our great Americans, Benjamin Franklin, said, 'The older I grow, the more apt I am to doubt my own judgment and to pay more respect to the judgment of others.'"

"That is very well said," the Judge agreed.

U Nee also nodded enthusiastic agreement, smiling with pleasure.

Paul Lowe said, "I would add that when one is looking to discover the truth he should take a flashlight and not a sword."

The Judge was highly satisfied—this remark had a Confucian ring that suited him. His voice turned soft and rather sad.

"Until the Communists came," he said, "we judges had no trouble. They have brought evil influence. They are prisoners of minds. Communism is a vehicle in which all crimes travel."

The Judge rose, shook hands with Paul Lowe and with U Nee, and left the bench.

"Shall you wish to go?" U Nee asked.

"Whenever you wish," Paul Lowe said.

The courtroom was empty of spectators.

That evening he asked U Nee for permission to visit the Communist prisoner awaiting execution.

U Nee returned with a permit from the Director General of Prisons. "The execution is scheduled for dawn," U Nee said. "The prisoner has very few hours."

"He may not want to see us," Paul Lowe said. "But there's no harm in trying."

The prison was in the middle of an enclave of barbed wire, an assemblage of buildings that resembled barracks. In the largest of the buildings was a block of solitary confinement cells in which the prisoner Zan was kept. They were admitted to the building by the head warden, a self-important little man who swung his heavy bunch of keys like the badge of high office.

The prisoner Zan was in the second cell from the entrance, a small area barely large enough to contain a wooden bed, a crude table and a bench. There was a narrow window protected with iron bars about a foot above Paul Lowe's head. The warden stood at the entrance of the cell, jingling his keys. U Nee passed on Paul Lowe's request for the warden to leave them alone. The warden, with a hurt expression, replied this was impossible. But he stopped jingling his keys.

Zan had not moved from the moment they entered his cell. He lay back on the wooden bed with hands clasped behind his head.

U Nee spoke rapidly to the boy, apparently explaining who Paul Lowe was. Zan's expression of indifference did not change. His eyes moved to rest incuriously on Lowe before he stared straight ahead again. U Nee spoke to him urgently and the boy responded with short grunting sounds.

U Nee turned to Paul Lowe.

"He says he prefers to spend his last hours in peace and quiet."

"If he really wishes that," Paul Lowe said, "we will leave. But tell him that he may do a service to the cause he believes in by helping us understand why he joined it."

U Nee delivered the message. Zan lay perfectly straight, then drew up his legs and sat up slightly, resting his head and shoulders against the wall. He spoke to U Nee.

"He asks what do you wish to know?" U Nee said.

"Well, why did he choose to fight against the government?"

The boy's answer came readily and U Nee translated it:

"Because the government is for the landlords. The people are landless and poor. The government is corrupt and does not care for the people."

U Nee wore an expression of faint distaste as he translated this message.

Paul Lowe asked, "Does he think the Communists will do more for the people?"

This time the answer was prompt, accompanied by a vigorous nodding of the head:

"The Communists will make a new Burma. Burma will be born again as a land of opportunity. There will be work for all, starvation will disappear, and people's minds will not be clouded by superstitions."

"What sort of superstitions?"

"Surely," U Nee translated, "the foreigner is aware that the town of Mandalay was built because the site was favored by astrologers. It has no other reason for existence. The climate is bad because the trees were cut down to use as fuel in making bricks to build pagodas. Fifty-two peasants were sacrificed—buried alive beneath the foundations so their angry spirits would help defend the town against its enemies. Among those buried alive was a pregnant mother—because the spirits of mother and child are supposed to unite in death to create a demon of great power and malignancy. This is what I mean by superstitions."

"But this all happened a long time ago," Paul Lowe said.

"Superstition is still in the land. It is used by our masters to keep our people in fear and ignorance. Communism will sweep away foolish beliefs and set the people free."

"Why do you not try to help the government to accomplish these ends?"

Zan turned to look at Paul Lowe after his question was translated. His small almond-shaped eyes held a look of pity.

"The government is corrupt," Zan replied. "The peasants can starve, for all it cares. The Communists are on the side of the people. The government is on the side of the landlords. They wish to keep us poor so they may become rich. They have yachts in Rangoon harbor waiting to flee if real trouble comes. Our wealth is sent away to foreigners while we have no bread to eat."

When U Nee finished relaying this, Paul Lowe said wryly, "He seems to be well supplied with answers, at least for that kind of question. Let's ask a more personal one. He said that at the time he was captured he was looking with his comrades for a deserter. What would they have done with the deserter if they had found him?"

The answer came back swiftly. "We would have brought him back to our camp."

"And then?"

"We would have called all to witness. Our captain would then walk up to him and say, 'You tried to desert.' And in sight of the others he would shoot him dead with his pistol."

"Would the man have been allowed to speak in his own defense?"

"There would be nothing for him to say."

"Would anyone speak for him?"

"Who speaks for a traitor?"

"Wouldn't he be allowed to have any trial at all?"

"That kind of pig does not deserve a trial!"

Zan was sitting upright, one leg spread out on the bed, his body turned toward Paul Lowe. His voice rang with anger. Beads of perspiration stood out on his forehead.

U Nee said quietly after a moment, "Is there anything else you wish to ask?"

Paul Lowe said, "Tell him for me that I am sorry he has been sentenced to die. Ask him if there is anything he would like me to do for him."

Zan listened to this with eyebrows slightly lifted.

"What is it possible to do?" he asked.

"If he has a family, I will be glad to write to them."

Zan stared at Paul Lowe until U Nee finished the translation. Then he drew his legs up and crossed his muscled arms just below the knees.

U Nee translated: "One understands the reason now for the white American's visit."

"What is that?"

"That he should learn the whereabouts of Zan's family so they too may be punished."

"He mustn't believe that. I would like his family to know that he is a brave man and that he went calmly to his death. I would like them to be always proud of him."

Zan listened to the translation without appearing to listen. Then he spoke.

U Nee interpreted Zan's answer. "My father is dead. He was killed by government soldiers. My mother and my two sisters will know I gave my life gladly to free my country of tyrants. They do not need to be told that. I have three brothers who also fight for our people against landlords and white imperialists. Perhaps they also are dead. No one knows. It does not matter."

Paul Lowe said, "Then tell him I wish him goodbye—and I hope his courage will not fail."

U Nee repeated this, Zan's chest began to shake. At last he fell back onto the bed and his whole body was shaking with laughter. The two men left the cell.

The head warden escorted Paul Lowe and U Nee from the building.

U Nee said, "Now you see, Mr. Justice, they are fanatics. There is nothing to do with his kind but to kill them. If you do not kill them they will kill you first."

"Zan is fifteen years old. It might be interesting to know exactly what happened to him in these fifteen years to make him believe the way he does."

"That would be interesting, but it could also be fatal. While you are trying to find out he will kill you."

"There are only two possibilities—either Zan is right or he is wrong. If he's right, something should be done about the conditions that make him willing even to die to change them. If he's wrong, something should be done to show him how wrong he is."

"That is humanitarian, Mr. Justice. But one does not talk with a loaded pistol. That is what Zan has inside his head—a loaded pistol. He is not human. When the time comes for him to die he will spit at the firing squad."

Paul Lowe said, "Perhaps. But some say that fear makes the mouth very dry."

They left, walking slowly and in silence between rows of dark barracks with iron-barred windows.

In the morning, at almost the moment the prisoner Zan went before the firing squad, Paul Lowe took off from Mandalay airfield for the mountains of northern Burma.

304

From a distance the broad sweep of mountains seemed endless. Great brown jagged peaks thrust through soft-bellied clouds with stony violence.

He pointed the plane's nose up and began to climb. At ten thousand feet the clouds were clustering about the granite mountains and the condensation of moisture from glaciers and snow peaks created further banks of mist even as he watched.

At twelve thousand feet, deep rifts appeared in the cloud formations to parallel in the sky the wild jumble of ridges and canyons below.

He glanced at the map on the seat beside him. Several peaks in his immediate vicinity soared two or three thousand feet higher than his present altitude. He kept the plane pointed steadily upward until he passed the tree line. There was no vegetation on the ridge tops, not a trail, not a sign of water, not the slightest evidence of life. He might have been flying over the beginning of the world.

Dwarfed in earthmaking silence, the tiny whine of the plane was a mosquito's buzz in a giant empty cathedral. He searched the mountains he had last flown over when he was twenty-three years old.

He had been slim, young, expecting death to come flashing and sudden in a hail of bullets in a disintegrating plane. He had not foreseen the middle-aged man disintegrating in a welter of disorderly emotions. That man, flabbily awaiting doom, would have been an enigma and a disappointment to young Paul Lincoln Lowe. That younger self, so full of hope, would not have understood how the time between could become a process of narrowing down, how the demands of the years pressed in like cholesterol in the bloodstream until there was scarcely room for life itself to pass.

On his left rose a steep wall, its sides glistening with ice. Paul Lowe's small plane winged past the ice tower's chill surveillance. In the distance loomed white peaks sparkling in the sun, further sentinels, inhabitants of some Jupiterian planet.

Directly before him spread a vista of diminishing saucer-shaped peaks. A milky ribbon of river wound its way through the range and he saw one or two irregular blue patches that were lakes.

He had a sudden queer sensation—as though he were a stranger in a city who turns a corner and finds himself walking down an oddly familiar street. Without willing it, knowing what he would see, he turned his head.

There it was. A high narrow canyon about a half mile long and several hundred yards wide that resembled a notch cut into a granite wall.

He turned the plane toward this canyon, flying directly at it. At the last moment he lifted the plane before the wings could scrape brush from the canyon shoulder. In that moment he saw, in the narrow twisting canyon bed, on a rise slightly to the left, a long smooth expanse of flat rock broken in the center by what appeared to be a blackening heap of junk metal.

Twenty-three years ago his expectations of sudden death had almost been realized here.

It was the wreckage of a P-38.

21

As his official guide for the ninety-mile trek into the mountains Paul Lincoln Lowe hired a formidable figure of a man. Kyam was six foot five inches tall. He wore a dirty maroon headpiece with wings extending out over his ears. His long mahogany-colored features were handsome despite high bulging cheekbones and horizontal eyes in which the whites were not white at all but pink. His thick dark eyebrows turned upward over the bridge of his nose and, together with a deeply wrinkled forehead, gave him a slightly quizzical appearance.

He wore rough brown canvas clothing held together with coarse string instead of buttons and scarves of red, green and blue were twined about his neck. In a scabbard at his side he carried a *dah,* a wicked-looking sword about three feet long.

Kyam hired two Palaung porters to carry the luggage, and four sturdy-looking mules to carry them all. He promised Paul Lowe that the journey to the village of Pao would take no more than six days. In the village of Pao they would find someone who knew the mountains well enough to lead them on foot to the site of the plane's wreckage.

They started out at shortly past seven o'clock on a Friday morning along a road that led to the hills. For a time the road narrowed to a trail that was almost overgrown with tangles of bamboo and creeper. Tall teak trees drooped their big leaves to the ground.

The mules did not make a mile's progress in an hour.

Kyam was not discouraged. "We shall reach the village of Pao in six days," he promised. He held up one hand and one finger to emphasize that he meant what he said.

On the trail they rode single file, with Paul Lowe behind Kyam and behind him in turn the two Palaung tribesmen on their mules. Kyam treated the Palaungs with kingly contempt. He was a Kachin and looked down upon all Mongolian tribes.

At dusk the road reached low hills covered with shapeless scrub and broken by occasional patches where an attempt at farming had been made and abandoned. Now the maize and the tea bushes were yielding back their ground to thorns and ferns.

Kyam held up his hand and the tiny caravan came to a halt. Sitting astride his mule, his long legs sticking outward, Kyam said, "We will make camp here."

"But we've only covered eight miles," Paul Lowe protested, "and there's still half an hour of daylight."

Kyam's reply had a simple dignity: "I am hungry."

Over a dinner of *tok tok chow*—pork chopped up and mixed with vegetables and fried in a pan—Kyam had an opportunity to practice the English he had learned in a missionary school. Kyam was proud of his newly acquired Christianity, and correspondingly bitter at all Buddhist priests.

"There are more *pongyis* than people," Kyam said. "They pay no taxes and do no work. They also favor bad health. In the missionary school I saw the white man's medicine. They have pills which put an end to the trembling sickness."

"Malaria?"

Kyam nodded. "One, two pills and a sick man is better. But the *pongyi* tell the people not to take the white man's medicine."

"Why would they do that?"

"They say that merciful Buddha will be offended if the insects or bugs are killed with the white man's magic."

"How do they treat malaria?"

"They put leeches on a man's forehead to drain him of his blood."

"It is hard to change old ways," Paul Lowe said. He scraped up the last of his *tok tok chow* from the tin plate.

Kyam's full red lips beneath the gracefully arching mustache pursed in a superior smile.

"If old ways let people die," he said, "old ways must go."

"I agree with that. It just may take more time than you think."

"Not if we get rid of *pongyi*," Kyam said.

On the second and third day they made good progress. On the fourth day they encountered a herd of humpbacked buffalo being driven in from the hills for the night.

"We will reach Pao the day after tomorrow," Kyam announced.

"That will be exactly six days. You will have kept your word," Paul Lowe told him.

"I am a Kachin," Kyam said.

That evening as Paul Lowe wrapped himself in his sleeping bag, Kyam moved close to him. The quarter moon was high and the dark bulk of the mountain shone faintly in the dim light. Kyam was obviously in a mood for conversation.

"Do you know how many doctors are in all of these mountains?" Kyam asked.

"No," he said. He was very tired. "How many are there?"

Kyam lit a fat cheroot. "There are no doctors. Not one. But the people need the white man's medicine."

"What happens if someone gets sick?"

"The *pongyi* pray. They pray to Buddha who they say is not a god. If he is not a god, how can he hear prayers?" Kyam touched the hilt of the *dah* in his scabbard. "I wish God would give all the *pongyi* one head so I could cut it off with this!"

"That is not the wish of a good Christian. A good Christian does not try to kill his enemies."

Kyam's pink eyes glittered malevolence. He puffed fiercely on his cheroot. "If the Communists were in power they would kill all the *pongyi*."

"They might do the same to the Christian missionaries."

"If they will limit their killing to the *pongyi*," Kyam said, "I too will be a Communist."

He tugged defiantly at the drooping end of his mustache.

The night air in the mountains was cold. Even in his sleeping bag Paul Lowe shivered. He thought about this once-peaceful land now torn with strife. It could not all be blamed on Communist propaganda. Even in this remote Kachin state, tribesmen such as Kyam knew what was going on in the rest of the world. They knew that they lacked medicines and doctors and hospitals. They knew that there were no schools for their people to learn. They wanted to be taught how to farm, how to drill wells, how to bring in water through ditches, how to plow, how to use machinery. They lived on an island of backwardness and suffering amidst a general world progress and plenty. The rudest goatherd knew what was needed and in his knowing lay such potential for violence that Paul Lowe's imagination winced at it.

He put his hands behind his head and watched the pale sliver of quarter moon through black tree branches.

On the sixth day their expedition climbed within sight of the mountain village of Pao. It was a small desolate village of bamboo huts that lay on a rocky stretch of ground between reaching cliff sides. On the far side of the village the slope ran down at a steep decline.

Nothing in Pao had changed; the village looked just as it did when Paul Lowe first saw it twenty-three years before. He wanted to rest a moment and prepare his middle-aged self for a meeting with a scene from his vanished youth.

But Kyam hurried his mule ahead, leading the way into the village. Paul Lowe followed.

Several women came out to meet them. Kyam spoke to them in Kachin dialect. The women gathered about Paul Lowe's mule, jabbering and smiling excitedly. Like most Kachin women they were elaborately dressed. They wore tight skirts of a heavy red cotton, short black blouses laced with beads, and huge neckpieces of carved silver. Their straight black hair was drawn back and tied in a small bun behind their heads. They were young women, some strikingly handsome, and wore rattan rings which hung about their waists like loose belts.

"What are they saying?" he asked.

"They are talking about you," Kyam said. "Only one of them has seen a white foreigner before. That one attended a *manau* in Mitkyina several years ago."

"A *manau?*"

"A celebration in which sacrifices are offered to the *nats*—the spirits of nature. Of course," Kyam said, drawing himself erect, "as a Christian I do not believe in the *nats*. Some say they have great powers. But the worship of them is what you say in English . . . there is a word which means backward looking."

"Primitive."

Kyam nodded. "Primitive. Nevertheless, some say the *nats* are very, very powerful."

As they came near the huts, Kyam dismounted and signaled Paul Lowe to do the same. The Palaungs also dismounted. The chattering women followed at a respectful distance. As they entered the village two wolf-like dogs leaped at them, barking furiously. Kyam beat them off contemptuously with the flat blade of his *dah* and the dogs went howling up the rocky street with their tails between their legs.

An old man came out from the entrance to the main hut. His body was spare but broadshouldered, nut brown, and stripped to the waist. He wore a soiled *longyi* of an indeterminate blue and his thin bare feet were gnarled with age. A dirty blue cotton turban was wrapped about his head. No hair showed beneath it or on the nape of his neck.

A few mangy chickens cackled and a pig as round as a beer barrel grunted nearby as Kyam and Paul Lowe went up to the old man.

"I will explain to him why we have come," Kyam said.

Kyam spoke to the old man in a language which seemed to have only the *a* vowel in combination with an unlimited number of consonants. The old man turned several times to look at Paul Lowe, pushing out his lips and chewing his gums.

At last the old man smiled and became more of a toothless friendly old man than a forbidding ancient. He began to speak very rapidly. Kyam waited politely until the old man was finished.

Kyam turned to Paul Lowe. "This old man is chief of the village. I told him that you wish to hire a guide to take you on foot into the mountain where your plane crashed a long time ago. When I said about the plane he became very excited. He wishes to know if you remember the name of the village chief who brought you and your friend down from the mountain."

"His name was Chung-jin."

When Kyam told the old man this, the old man nodded very excitedly and repeated the name, "Chung-jin, Chung-jin," and nodded again. Then he took two steps forward to seize Paul Lowe's arm and hold it tightly. He leaned close until his face was only a few inches away. The dark cavern of his mouth exhaled a foul odor and there was a stale smell from his body. "Chung-jin," he said again, gripping Paul Lowe's arm and shaking it impatiently.

The old man spoke to Kyam, and Kyam said, "He wishes to tell you that he is the nephew of Chung-jin. And he is one of the men who helped to carry you down from the mountain."

It did not seem possible. The nephew of Chung-jin had been a brawny lad hardly older than himself. This old man must therefore be less than fifty years of age.

The ague of mortality chilled Paul Lowe to his marrow.

He said to Kyam, "Tell him how very glad I am to see him again."

Kyam translated and the old man listened with his head turned slightly toward Kyam. He gave a wheezing snort of delight.

Paul Lowe said to Kyam, "Will you ask him whether Chung-jin is alive or dead?"

The answer came quickly.

"Chung-jin is very sick. He is dying. However, if you wish to see him you may."

"I wish to see him," Paul Lowe said.

The old man spoke briefly to one of the women waiting outside the main hut. She gestured to Paul Lowe and Kyam to follow her. They walked quickly, trailed by a curious crowd of naked children and women. Only one Kachin man was among the crowd, a rather wild-looking fellow with bloodshot eyes. The woman led the way, turning frequently to be sure they were following her, to a hut at the far end of the village compound that was almost screened from view by the matting of roots hanging down from a huge old banyan tree. A well nearby had a cover that was fashioned like a miniature pagoda.

The hut was in partial darkness and Paul Lowe had to wait until his eyes adjusted to the absence of light. In a far right-hand corner on a scattering of straw lay the bony remnant of a man, a brown-colored skeleton with each rib distinct and countable. The man's cheeks were caved in so the teeth made separate impressions on nearly transparent skin. The eyes were open and staring, almost protruding because of the receding skin and the deep indentation of the sockets in which they were held.

Paul Lowe moved forward in the hut to squat in the dark corner. An unbelievably thin arm stirred restlessly in the straw and two skeletal fingers picked idly at dry yellow strands.

"Chung-jin."

Eyes which had been staring upward rolled slowly over in their sockets.

"We knew each other many, many years ago. I am a white man, a foreigner. My name is Paul Lowe."

The staring eyes held no sign of recognition.

"It was during the war. My plane crashed in the mountains. You brought me down to the village and nursed me back to health. You and Miat."

Bony fingers stopped moving. The lips mumbled over each other, "Miat."

"Your daughter. She was my nurse for many weeks. My name is Paul Lowe. The American soldier."

Lids moved half down over the eyeballs, leaving only the whites.

"Miat."

310

He said urgently, "Miat is your daughter. I lived in your house when she was here with you. I was hurt and you nursed me back to health."

"Miat."

"I have never forgotten her—or you, Chung-jin. You were my teacher. Do you remember the nights we talked together? You were my teacher."

The lids blinked wide open. The whispery voice acquired a reedy undertone, "Of what use is teaching? It is enough to know the One. That is the way to Tao."

"We talked of that—and of many other things."

"Tao cannot be named. That which is named is not Tao."

Once, after the war, when asked for his religion on some application or other, Paul Lowe had been tempted to put down "Taoist." It would have amazed the official who asked him for it, but his motive had been more than the youthful desire to amaze. He had wanted to pay some small tribute to this man who now hovered so visibly near death. That withered head with unkempt gray hair had once held, clear as a fly in amber, a philosophy of a universe essentially one—reverting, polarizing, moving in eternal cycles, leveling all differences, accepting the relativity of all standards and the return of all things to the divine source. In the mountains of Kachin, living among primitive tribesmen, Chung-jin had revered the wisdom of his Chinese ancestors and had taught that science and reason were tools and not ends, that the world was spiritual and could only be known by a kind of intuitive knowledge that would never be expressed in equations.

"Chung-jin!" His voice was taut with the desire to make the dying man hear him. "I am Paul Lowe. I have returned after many years."

There was no response. The lips swallowed each other without making a sound.

"When I knew you I was young. I did not understand all you tried to teach me. There are things I would still like to know. Things you can tell me. Can you hear me, Chung-jin?"

No answer.

"This is the wisdom of Tao," Paul Lowe said. " 'Flow everywhere in the limitless, in the ocean that abolishes all boundaries . . .' " He put his hand on the old man's shoulder, on a part of bone that was sharp as a splinter. " 'Were the ocean itself made of fire, the perfect man would not feel hot. For the perfect man is a being of spirit.' "

The words sounded as strange now as they had the first time he heard them in Chung-jin's singsong recital. Such mysticism both repelled and attracted a young man with Western training and a belief in progress and the invincibility of human reason. But the years had somewhat undermined his confidence in the scientific approach to the material world. After all, what had been learned by science of the essential nature of things? The substance of matter had been pursued down through the molecule and the atom to the electron and to primal impulses which no one understood, where phenomena met on the verge of being and unbeing. The substance of mind had been pursued through the wrinkles of the brain to electrical waves that were able to record but not to interpret the miracle of consciousness. What had the scientists revealed of the beauty and sorrow of man's short life? Science had lost touch with humankind— lost the ability to do anything but inflict neurasthenic shock. Yet Paul Lowe's faith in the ability of human reason to discover truth remained basically unshaken. It seemed to him that truth would reveal itself not in a dazzling wholeness apprehended solely by intuition, but in fragments and pieces gradually and painfully acquired by rational men working to assemble tiny bits of a mosaic that would take eons, perhaps infinity, to complete.

"Can you hear me, Chung-jin?"

The head rolled listlessly on straw.

"*Leave him!*"

The command rang with scornful anger. Paul Lowe turned to see a young man standing within the dim hut. His short wiry figure was outlined against the doorway. He wore a tan shirt open at the collar and short pants that showed sturdy muscled legs.

The young man spat at the floor near Paul Lowe.

"Take your hand off him."

Paul Lowe removed his hand from Chung-jin's shoulder.

"Who are you?"

"It is my business to ask, not yours. What is your name?"

"My name is Paul Lowe."

"What are you doing here?"

"That would take time to explain."

"You will answer when you are asked a question."

"I certainly didn't come here to make trouble, if that's what's bothering you."

"I will decide that. You will explain your purpose here."

"Ask the village chief. I've already spoken to him."

"I am in command in this area. You will answer my questions."

"Not until I know who you are."

"Mengshu. Captain in the liberation forces."

"I'm pleased to meet you, Mengshu," Paul Lowe answered, rising to his feet. He had decided the best course was to be deliberately casual. There was quite enough rigidity and tension from this young man.

"Perhaps you should not be pleased," Mengshu said. "I have not decided what will be done with you. That will depend upon what you are doing here."

"I'm an American—a citizen of the United States. In my country I'm a judge." Paul Lowe spoke very clearly and slowly. "Some years ago I was a pilot and fought in the war against the Japanese. After some fighting around Mitkyina my plane and that of a fellow pilot were forced to crashland in these mountains." The words began to sound hollow and unconvincing, so he made a deprecatory gesture. "I know it is hard to believe but I have come back, after all these years, to find the spot where my plane went down."

312

Mengshu wore a cartridge belt slung low over one hip and a pistol in the holster. He put the palm of his hand against the butt of the weapon.

"You are a spy."

"I am nothing of the sort."

"Do you have proof?"

"I can show you my passport and other identification papers."

Mengshu made an abrupt movement. "Get them."

As Paul Lowe went to the door, he was relieved to hear the creak of Mengshu's shoes on the floor following him. Outside the hut Kyam was waiting and as Paul Lowe emerged Kyam came over to him.

"Say but the word," Kyam whispered, "and my *dah* separates his head from his body."

On the village street several armed young men were in evidence. One was talking to a Kachin woman at her spinning loom outside her hut. Others stared at Paul Lowe curiously. The armed men were dressed as Mengshu was, in tan blouses and short trousers, and each man wore a cartridge belt and pistol in a holster.

"I don't think that will be necessary," he said to Kyam.

He fumbled through the pack slung over the mule's sides until he found his passport, travel permit, and several letters. These he handed to Mengshu, who studied each in turn carefully. Mengshu then put them all together and gave them back.

"It is still possible that you are a spy," he said. "Your country sends guns to fight us. Why should they not send men also?" His tone sounded a shade less belligerent.

Paul Lowe said, "You see from the documents that I hold high position in my country. Is it likely they would send me to spy on guerrillas in the mountains of Kachin?"

"You would be wise not to underestimate us. We are in command here."

"I don't want to take sides politically. All I want is a guide to take me to the wreckage of my plane. I have already sighted it from the air. I know the location. But I will need a guide to show me the best route through the mountains."

"You will remain in the village tonight, under guard. Tomorrow you will be escorted back where you came from."

He answered quietly, "I don't intend to turn back."

"What *you* intend is not of importance. I am in command." Mengshu stared with a new suspicion. "What were you doing in the hut of Chung-jin?"

"He rescued me after my plane crashed many years ago. I lived with him for many weeks until I recovered from my injuries."

Mengshu's high forehead gathered a frown. "You lived with Chung-jin? How many years ago did this happen?"

"During the war. Twenty-three years, to be exact."

"You knew his daughter who lived with him then?"

"Miat. Yes."

"Ah," Mengshu said. "You knew her."

Somehow the way he said it summoned Miat's presence back—slim and brown-skinned, laughing, pouting like a child. She was a child—un-selfconscious, affectionate, and free. Miat.

"What happened to her?" Paul Lowe asked.

"She is dead," Mengshu replied shortly. He gestured to two soldiers nearby.

Mengshu gave orders. One soldier saluted with the back of his hand against his forehead.

Kyam whispered to Lowe, "Say but the word . . ."

He answered impatiently, "It's all right."

The soldiers led him to a vacant hut, smaller than the others, smelling of excrement. There was a bamboo mat for sleeping, and a rickety wooden table and a chair. The soldiers left him.

After an hour another soldier entered, a tall thin angular fellow. He put a pitcher of water on the table and left without looking at Paul Lowe, who drank a little of the water; it was tepid and tasted as though someone had been bathing in it.

He sat down on the bamboo matting. At first he tried sitting cross-legged in approved fashion but that became tiring and a cramp started in a calf muscle, so he lay down on the matting, resting on one elbow. He wished he had had the foresight to ask for one of his books.

A scratching sound attracted him. He rolled over to the wall and heard, quite clearly, a voice. Kyam must be standing right outside the wall of the bamboo hut.

"Say but the word, and I will free you," Kyam whispered.

"We will talk about that in the morning," he said wearily. "Go to sleep now, Kyam."

That night he had a disturbing dream. With part of his consciousness he was aware of tossing restlessly on the bamboo matting in the hut, but with another part of his mind he was leading a flight of P-38's in a raid on a Japanese airport. Again and again he raked the field. Dust clouds were kicked up by his six machine guns firing, and Zeros began to burst into flame on the field below. When he pulled up through columns of blaze and smoke he was alone in a sky empty of life. He cruised through a blankness without color, without sound. Suddenly out of the sun a Zero darted at him with guns blazing. He was helpless, flying at low altitude and at a cruising speed. He saw the cannon on the Zero belch. A shock hit the plane and oily black smoke rose in front of his eyes. Something danced over the fuselage like a heavy rain and he smelled cordite and gasoline. He reached up and grabbed the handle and rolled the canopy open. There was no light. His first thought was that black oil must have covered his windshield. He put the nose of the P-38 down and dived to clear it. There was no sound, not even wind racing past. He could not pull out of the dive. He waited for the shock of annihilation but it never came. There was simply nothing. After several minutes he unbuckled his belt and stepped out of the plane, fully expecting to fall through space.

But he did not fall and he did not touch the ground. There were clouds about him, gray and clinging, and everything seemed curiously deserted, silent. He did not hear his own heart beating. He walked on like a blind man, hands partly extended before him, unable to feel the ground with his feet. He began to wonder if he was alive. There was no evidence of the senses to reassure him. Abruptly he collided with something, feeling no impact, only the arrest of forward motion. With his hands he explored the strange object. Finally he traced out the fuselage of a plane and worked his way forward to the pilot's seat. He was glad to have found the plane—its mere physical presence in this featureless void was a comfort. He saw that the pilot's seat was occupied. He saw the helmet and part of the jacket of someone sitting in it. When he called to the pilot his voice made no sound. He reached out and touched the man's shoulder. The man turned quickly at the touch. Beneath the helmet there was a charred face, black as soot. The skin was flaking and the eyesockets were empty. The mouth widened in a grin. One hand closed upon Paul Lowe's wrist with an unbreakable grip.

He screamed.

He sat up in the darkness. There was no sound in the hut but the echo was inside his head. In a moment the door to the hut was flung open.

Mengshu stood in the doorway, holding a kerosene lantern.

"Who cried out?"

He considered denying it, then said, "I did. I must have been dreaming."

Two soldiers flanked Mengshu slightly behind him. As Mengshu held the lantern higher his expression changed from hostility to a pleased wonder.

"You are pale." He repeated this in dialect for the benefit of the two soldiers, who laughed.

Paul Lowe shielded his eyes. "That light is blinding me."

Mengshu lowered the lantern.

"Do not be afraid. Your life is not in danger. In the morning you will go back to Mitkyina."

"I don't intend to go back."

Mengshu's face hardened. He was about to reply when another thought apparently occurred to him. "It is dangerous in the mountains when a monsoon strikes. This is the season for monsoons. You will be much safer to return to Mitkyina."

"I'm not worried about danger," Paul Lowe said.

"Because you are ignorant of what may happen to you."

"I'm willing to go ahead without a guide if there is none available to go with me."

Mengshu's deep-set eyes reflected the light of the lantern. There was a shadow on his cheek from his highbeaked nose.

"In the morning we will see. Perhaps you will change your mind." He nodded to the two soldiers, who left. In the doorway, holding the lantern at waist level, Mengshu looked back. "Sleep well."

Paul Lowe lay back on bamboo matting in the darkened hut. The thought that had passed through Mengshu's mind had been as easy to read as though written on a teleprompter. If Paul Lowe set out on the expedition to the mountains and were forced to turn back through weakness or fear, that would be an invaluable demonstration to Mengshu's followers of the inferiority of white foreigners. It might prove to them that stories of the white man's prowess were inflated and that, without machines to aid him, he was a pitiful creature not to be feared. Such a report, faithfully circulated to the remotest regions, could be worth as much as a regiment.

The faint odor of excrement assailed his nostrils. He rolled over onto his side and settled down uncomfortably on the matting. A swinging lantern in someone's hand as he passed the hut made a quavering light on the wall and swiftly moved on.

He smiled to himself. Mengshu might unwittingly endow this whole expedition, founded on a romantic impulse, a quixotism of the Western mind which the oddly pragmatic mysticism of the Eastern mind could never understand, with a serious and even grim purpose.

The shadow of a sentry paced at the door to the hut. Paul Lowe picked up a sliver of bamboo and broke it between his fingers. If he accepted the challenge there would be no turning back. Not at any cost.

22

In the morning Mengshu arrived at the hut. A soldier opened the door and stood aside for him to enter.

Paul Lowe sat up. "Good morning."

"I have decided to grant permission for you to make a journey into the mountains."

"Thank you," he said, and stood up. "Am I also permitted to hire a guide in the village?"

"That will not be necessary. I will accompany you as guide."

"That is very kind."

"If I go with you, I am sure there will be no spying."

"Do you know the mountains well? I can show you on a map where I wish to go but you will have to find the best route to get there."

"I have lived in these mountains all my life."

Paul Lowe shrugged. "Well, I suppose that answers the question. How many of you are coming with us?"

"My men are needed in the village. We are teaching the villagers how to plant crops scientifically. They have much to learn but this year they will have a good harvest. We are also teaching them how to read and count with numbers."

"That will be very useful. Then you're coming alone?"

"I will take one man with me. The porters have unpacked the mules and are waiting. How long will it take you to be ready?"

"I won't be a minute," he said.

When he emerged from the hut the entire population of the village of Pao had turned out to witness the start of the expedition. Mengshu's soldiers were clearly in evidence among them. He thought: these soldiers are so much a part of the people that they are almost ostentatious about it. They not only look the same, except for the type of clothing they wear and the rifles, but they spoke the same language and behaved with these ignorant mountain tribesmen like older wiser brothers who had come to visit them and be of whatever assistance they could.

Not a bad approach, Paul Lowe conceded. It is not even a bad way to make friends. Solidarity—that is always the watchword. The people

317

and the Communists are supposed to grow into one rock so they cannot be parted from each other except by pulverizing the rock.

He knew why the villagers were turned out to watch his departure. Mengshu wanted the expedition to begin with as much publicity as possible so that its end would be well remembered.

I may fool you, Mengshu. He felt the steadiness of resolve settle into him. I may come back carrying my shield instead of being carried on it.

The village chief came up to shake hands with him and to speak a few words.

Kyam translated: "The chief says he wishes you a fine journey. And he says you should remember the warning which he gives to all who travel in the mountains, 'Go slowly if you wish to return.'"

"I thank him. Ask him to say goodbye to Chung-jin for me."

As the village chief received this message, he shook his head mournfully.

Mengshu, a few paces distant with a tall thin soldier companion and the two Palaung porters, gestured impatiently.

"Goodbye," Paul Lowe said.

The village chief waved a limp brown arm.

Under the solemn watchful gaze of the villagers of Pao, the expedition got under way.

Mengshu set a rapid pace. He mounted uphill trails with a heavy-hipped energetic stride, and seemed to begrudge even the brief halt for a breakfast of dried apple rings and cocoa. After they had been climbing two hours he began harrying the Palaung porters for swifter progress.

Paul Lowe kept up without complaint. He tried to regulate his breathing and betray no sign of weariness. Kyam moved beside him with an effortless long-legged stride that devoured distance.

Toward evening a fog rolled in that quickly obscured the peaks and moved down ridges and canyon walls. When the slope became steeper and the fog thickened, the Palaung porters began to act apprehensive. The swarthier Palaung spoke to Kyam.

Kyam said to Paul Lowe, "He thinks that we should make camp now. He says it is dangerous to travel in this weather."

"What do you think?"

"A Palaung is like a donkey. He knows when it is safe to go or not to go."

"I'll talk to Mengshu about it."

He moved up the trail to Mengshu.

"The porters think we should make camp," he said.

Mengshu shook his head. "We will go on. There is nothing to fear."

"Did I say I was afraid?"

Mengshu smiled slightly. "Why do we waste time standing here if you are not afraid?"

"Have it your way. Let's go on."

The drizzle was at first pleasant and refreshing but when the drops

318

continued to fall steadily, Mengshu and his soldier companion took short water-repellent transparent coats from their small traveling bags.

Paul Lowe called Kyam over.

"Tell the porters to put down the packs they are carrying."

Kyam gave the order. The Palaungs slipped the straps from their shoulders and let the heavy duffel bags slip to the ground. Paul Lowe opened them and took out compact packages in separate plastic bags that carried the various pieces of equipment. He took out water-repellent jackets for himself, Kyam, and the two Palaung porters.

He was helping one of the Palaungs to put on his jacket when Mengshu shouted impatiently.

Kyam said, "He says we are taking too much time."

"Tell him to go soak his head."

"What is that?"

"Never mind. I'll tell him." He raised his voice to carry. "We'll be ready as soon as the porters are."

They moved on in failing light, with Mengshu climbing steadily at a brisk pace. The air was dark. The ground was soggy underfoot and mud clung to their boots.

At one point the trail was blocked by a huge wall of dirt, rock and upended trees. The cliff wall beside it looked as though someone had dug into it with an immense spoon.

"This landslide did not happen very long ago," Kyam said. "The ground is soft from the rains."

"It's a good thing we weren't around when it happened."

Kyam made a rapid sign of the cross.

They picked their way carefully around the upper edge of the landslide. The last light was nearly gone. The rocks were black and slippery under their feet and tiny fresh rivulets had begun to course down the mountainside.

When they reached a thick stand of spruce trees Mengshu signaled a halt.

"Here we will make camp," he said.

They put up their lean-tos. Kyam soon had a crackling campfire going. While soft rain rustled in the tree tops, they ate dried soup, canned hamburger and dried cocoa around the fire.

The Palaungs were still eating when Mengshu started to harangue them.

"Is he angry?" Paul Lowe asked Kyam.

"I do not understand all the words when he speaks so quickly in the Palaung dialect. But I understand enough to know that he is making a speech."

"What about?"

"The United States of America."

"What is he saying?"

"He says that your country makes war on Asians because you wish to take over our land. He says if that happens the poor will become slaves and drag carts like oxen while the white men whip them."

Paul Lowe said, "Tell them for me, Kyam, that what they have just been told is a lie."

Kyam grinned. He broke into Mengshu's monologue to repeat this message. Mengshu gave Kyam an angry glance and answered him in hard syllables of contempt.

"What did he say?" Paul Lowe asked.

Kyam twirled an end of his mustache angrily. "He said I am a donkey who allows the white man to ride me and brays when I am told."

"Ignore him, Kyam. Tell the Palaungs that if my country desired to take other people's land, why are we setting free the colonies that we once owned? If they fear being swallowed up they should watch carefully their hungry neighbors, like China."

Before Kyam finished speaking, Mengshu began waving his hands and shouting. The Palaungs looked from Mengshu to Paul Lowe with interest, and the swarthier Palaung stopped eating long enough to ask a question.

Kyam said, "He would like to know who will win a war between China and America."

"I hope there will not be a war," Paul Lowe said. "Tell him it is the same with countries as with men. They can live at peace if they respect each other's rights."

When Kyam finished, Mengshu spoke quickly to the Palaungs.

Kyam interpreted: "Mengshu says there *will* be war and China will win. He says the United States has money and weapons but China is on the side of the people against the masters. He says people everywhere know that China fights for their freedom."

Paul Lowe asked, "Are the people of Tibet free now that they have been swallowed by the Chinese tiger?"

This remark struck home to the Palaungs, who had close ties to their Tibetan brothers. They looked at Mengshu with solemn distrust.

Mengshu replied: "In Tibet, only the rich monks are not happy. Their land was taken away and given to the poor. But the people are free. The lowliest peasant is now the equal of the highest and most powerful leader in the land."

"How can he be equal if he is not allowed by the leaders to say what he thinks?" Paul Lowe asked. "He cannot sit at a fire as we do and speak his mind."

"That is a lie!" Mengshu replied hotly. "Any man may speak. Only the enemies of the state are silenced."

"In other words," Paul Lowe said, "I will defend to the death your right to agree with me."

Kyam looked puzzled as he began to interpret this, and when he finished the Palaungs were plainly bewildered. Paul Lowe decided that he had better try to explain the meaning of the original statement.

"In the United States," he said, "every man is free to speak, to object and to disagree with what the government does because that is part of a democracy. This right is defended by all. No man may be persecuted by the majority for what he says or believes. Our Constitution guarantees this to all men, even to those who proclaim themselves our enemies. That is why we can give this promise: 'I wholly disagree with what you say but I will defend to the death your right to say it.'"

Mengshu answered: "Words! Words written on paper. You cannot feed people with pieces of paper. People need food, clothing, medicine."

"We try to help the people of other lands. We send them food and clothing and medicine. That is true in Burma and in many other places."

Mengshu answered harshly, "Do you think you can make the yellow man believe the white man is our friend? The white man has been our oppressor for centuries and in other lands, even as we speak, the white men's guns are killing yellow men. Why does that happen if you are our friends? If people ask for bread, the United States sends planes with bombs, jellied gasoline and poison gas. Is that how you wish to show friendship for us?"

Kyam kept up a running translation almost sentence for sentence and when he finished Paul Lowe saw that Mengshu's rhetorical outburst had impressed the Palaungs. They were nodding, and wiping their mouths with their sleeves and regarding Paul Lowe with narrow hostility. Even in these mountains ordinary men had heard of military intervention by the United States in neighboring lands. For them white men in planes had become the enemy. Every bomb that fell, every napalm fire that destroyed a village created more enemies for the white man. The word spread from village to village on whispers of fear.

"All that my people want," Paul Lowe said, "is for other countries to have the right to choose freely their own form of government. Our country was made by a revolution. We do not oppose revolution elsewhere, except where it sets up the kind of government that will forever end a man's right to choose how he wishes to be governed."

The Palaungs were clearly not interested in this reply. The swarthy one was already making preparations to sleep for the night. Kyam's handsome mahogany-colored face was burnished with the flickering orange light. He sat without speaking, poking at the fire with a partly blackened twig.

Mengshu smiled at Paul Lowe with sneering triumph across the camp-fire.

A fire of rebellion is sweeping these lands, Paul Lowe thought, and is being fanned by men like Mengshu who champion the cause of the land-less and poor. They go among the tribesmen, preaching hatred of the white men, promising land and money. They tell the poor how they will soon live in the homes of the wealthy and they even assign actual houses to them complete with furniture, for delivery in the future when the revolution succeeds. They put down their weapons to work beside the peasants and help bring in the crops, and they promise that soon there will be plows and tractors, new methods of irrigation. They offer hope to men whose lives are being worn away in hopeless poverty, and it is all very well to say that they do not intend to deliver on what they promise. How do we know? More important, how do these people know? What did men like himself, who believed in the democratic way, have to offer them instead? These people have never known democracy and its truths are far from self-evident to them. The inalienable rights with which they have been endowed by their Creator amounts to the right to live short and squalid lives, to earn a bare subsistence by backbreaking labor, and to die without having experienced a millionth part of the benefits that civilization had to offer. For these people, as they become aware of what sort of existence they are condemned to, the democratic way is slow and cumbersome. It is easier to accept from apostles like Mengshu the gospel of the flaming torch.

Paul Lowe lay down beside the fire in his sleeping bag and turned on his side. It's like the ant, he thought, which has a stomach for digesting but also has another "social stomach" for storing food to be shared by regurgitation with others of its colony. Until the ant's own stomach is full there is no use for the "social stomach"; that part of the ant's marvelously intricate organism remains idle awaiting the moment when its needs are satisfied and it can regurgitate—ethics and laws and charity. The Democratic Way.

He felt himself growing sleepy.

Nearby, Kyam tossed the blackened twig aside. He yawned and stretched his long arms. The campfire was crackling and roaring and would last the night.

In the morning, after they had resumed their climb, rain began to pelt down harder. They were ascending a small ridge and had reached an elevation above a small stream. It became black and swollen and swift even as they moved along its bank.

On the sides of the ridge, moss and lichen were wet and even the sure-footed Palaungs slipped under the weight of their packs. Paul Lowe lost his balance and slid several feet down a muddy slope. Kyam threw down a short length of rope and helped him to scramble up again.

"Are you hurt?" Kyam asked.

"No. I'm fine."

Kyam muttered irritably: "I do not like to climb in such weather. It is dangerous. We should take shelter."

"That's up to Mengshu. And I'm sure it isn't what he has in mind."

The caked mud on his trousers washed into brown trickles and was soon gone. Mengshu had not paused when Paul Lowe fell and he was already a hundred yards ahead. In the treacherous footing it took twenty minutes to overtake him.

The afternoon shadows deepened and the fog in a valley to their left began to disperse. It became an all-pervading haze of mist. Trickles of water dripped constantly from the rocks, oozed through thick sod and grass, joined and became cascades that raced downhill and shattered in tumbling white spray from the ledges. From time to time the men passing below were drenched by one of these sudden waterfalls.

As they moved up the narrow trail after one such drenching Kyam said, "The porters have fallen behind. Shall we stop and wait for them?"

"They'll just have to catch up with us," Paul Lowe answered. "Anyhow that's Mengshu's problem. Let him worry about it."

Mengshu, keeping the lead and setting a cruel pace, did not notice that the porters were missing. When he did, he reluctantly called a halt. A long time passed before the Palaungs appeared, struggling up the trail under the weight of their packs.

Mengshu upbraided the porters in a tirade which was punctuated by intimidating waves of his pistol. The Palaungs listened with eyes downcast. The swarthier one made a short grumbling answer.

Kyam said, "The Palaungs say a storm is coming. They do not wish to go any further."

Mengshu's tirade increased in volume and ferocity and he brandished his pistol almost under the nose of the swarthy Palaung. This did not appear to make any impression on the Palaungs. But when Mengshu gave the order for the expedition to get under way the porters shouldered their burdens and complied. Apparently on order, the tall angular soldier fell back to the rear of the procession to keep a watchful eye on the two porters.

The trail made a long spiral turn that came out near the crest of the ridge. From low and menacing clouds rain drove down in slanting sheets. Across the intervening valley, through the bluedark sheen of air saturated with water, Paul Lowe glimpsed a dozen huts clinging to the opposite side of the canyon wall. The huts were clustered in a hollow which had been carved out by centuries of wind and weather.

Kyam moved forward on the trail to speak to Mengshu. Mengshu merely shook his head. Kyam began to gesticulate angrily and point toward the huts. It was obvious that Kyam was urging that the expedition take shelter there from the developing storm.

Mengshu shook his head again, and finally Kyam took him by the arm to bring him to a halt. They confronted each other, the giant muscular Kachin and the short wiry Captain of the Liberation Forces. Kyam's handsome face was stern with anger and his mustache drooped soddenly. His hand rested on the hilt of the *dah* in his scabbard.

Mengshu stared at him coldly. A semicircle of raindrops fell from the visor of his cap. At last he turned his back on Kyam and moved on again without a word.

Kyam's fingers clenched on the sword and hatred masked his face as he stared after him. The porters struggled past Kyam on the trail but he stood until Paul Lowe went up and touched his arm.

"You're right. We should take shelter, Kyam, but Mengshu is not a fool. He had a reason for making us go on. He wants to prove he is a better man than you and me. He wants to shame us by forcing us to turn back."

After a moment rigidity went out of Kyam's shoulders. "Then he is indeed a fool. He is a great fool if he believes he can ever be better man than I am. He is of the Mongolian tribe. I am a Kachin."

The tall angular soldier moved up the trail toward them, a scarecrow in his transparent raincoat. Kyam fell in beside Paul Lowe and they trudged on through mud that was almost ankle deep.

He began to wonder how much farther he could manage to keep going. His bones felt weak and his knees ached and his muscles were conspiring to drag him down to rest. Each breath burned a fiery channel down his throat to his lungs. He was deafened by a roaring in his ears and the strokes of his heart shook him with a distinct and heavy pounding.

As they crossed the ridge and started up the far slope the storm broke in full violence against the cliff heights.

First, a tremendous wind sucked up from the canyon and caused a whistling explosion up the steep rocky sides. A black cloud fell over a sharp peak that appeared to puncture it and turn it into a flopping sack of water. The clouds burst open and sent huge waterspouts racing down the cliff. The wind swirled with the force of a tornado to fling water through the air.

Within seconds the expedition was inundated. One of the Palaung porters tumbled rolling down the hill within a geyser that spouted from the mountainside with eruptive power. His companion tossed off his pack and went scrambling down to rescue him. He went two strides and was swept up in a racing torrent that plunged him cartwheeling down the slope.

Paul Lowe clung to the rock wall. A swooping wind plucked at him. The rock lit with vivid glare from the lightning flashes that struck through the length of the canyon. He twined one hand tightly into underbrush and held on.

A gigantic forked and arcing display of lightning illuminated a crooked path as though invisible railroad tracks had suddenly lit up in the air. Then darkness fell, a total blackness in which the world seemed to end in the screaming fury. The noise around him multiplied beyond the limits of hearing, then redoubled until his nerves were shattered and overwhelmed.

He had no idea of what had happened to the others. Time and space contracted to this one instant and one tiny area. He felt mud shift and crawl down over his face and body like living protoplasm. When he pulled his face clear of it the hammering rain knocked his breath away.

The wind increased.

Harsh and pitiless, chilled by the mountainside heights, the wind tore and raved. He clung to his hold on the rock wall. A gullying torrent ran half across him on its way down the cliffside. A dagger of lightning bounced off canyon walls, dug in here and there and gashed a bright wound down into the darkness before it vanished. The ground quivered seismically— the ultimate betrayal when the earth deserts its mooring—and he remembered hearing of landslides set off by monsoons in which thousands of tons of mud were dislodged to bury whole villages. He imagined himself buried beneath tons of clay, never to be found. That became all too easy to imagine, so he tried not to think of it.

In the freezing wind the lashing rain turned to sleet and hail. The stings on his face and hands were like a thousand knifepoint jabs. He put one arm around his head and turned his face downward. When he looked up to catch a breath the hail sliced his flesh—tiny stones driven at great velocity by the hurricane force of the wind. He seemed to inhabit a dimension in which noise and pain had become the only reality. His hand twined in the brush seemed frozen there. If he moved his fingers he would have completely lost his hold.

When he could no longer endure, he endured.

At last the downpour appeared to slacken a bit. Then he felt someone's hand on his shoulder and he turned his head with agonizing effort.

Kyam, soaked through, his cap gone and his hair matted to his temples, stood near.

He gestured—words would have been meaningless in that uproar. What did he mean? Paul Lowe wondered. To go on? *In this?* The man must be insane. Paul Lowe's feet were numb and every joint in his body was paralyzed. He was unable to move.

Kyam gestured again, more impatiently. Paul Lowe released his hold on the underbrush and found that his fingers could move, after all. He pushed himself away from the rock wall. The act of motion shot raw pain through him, but as Kyam went along the path that hugged the cliff he followed. His boots swirled foot-deep water that seemed to be running wildly in every direction, twisting and whirling into rivulets and streams. Each time he moved his leg forward it required a separate terrible effort. He bent into the wind. Prayer bubbled at his lips. At any moment he expected to fall face down on the path and drown in the mud and water. He experienced the actual sensation of falling and smothering, and was surprised to discover himself still erect and moving forward.

The wind spiraled viciously, carrying rain briefly up with it, and he saw Kyam plodding doggedly toward a stone outcropping of the cliff. It was at least several hundred feet away. It might as well have been several hundred miles. He knew that he would never reach it. Nothing would lift his body over that demanding stretch of ground. Blood slowed in his veins. His weariness carried the seeds of death.

In that moment, as he abandoned the struggle, knowing it to be useless, an image crossed his brain of himself floating to the surface like a dead man rising from the sea's caverns. Then he saw Katherine when she heard that he was dead. Her grieving countenance accused him, gave him an impetus that carried him forward.

He would prove to her he had done his best.

He had given his all.

She could not blame him.

His feet lifted like thousand-pound weights as he forced one foot after the other. You see, Katherine? You see how I tried . . .

In the natural shelter of the cliff Kyam was sitting in a far corner, half erect, with his eyes closed. The ground was damp but solid. Paul Lowe flung himself down.

Thunder and lightning broke with renewed fury. The wind howled and raged.

In the overhang created by the rock outcropping they were protected. Paul Lowe turned over on his side and folded his hands beneath his cheek. He was alive. For the moment that was more than enough.

The monsoon blew out. Altogether the savagery of the storm lasted no more than two hours from the first steady drops of rain to the final clap of the last thunderbolt.

Paul Lowe opened his eyes and sat up. Kyam, standing beneath the lip of the stone outcropping, lifted his hand and waved toward something. The swarthier of the Palaung porters entered the rock shelter. His clothing was sodden.

He grunted a few words and flung himself shapelessly into a corner.

Kyam said, "He says that was the mother of storms."

"It certainly felt like it," Paul Lowe said.

Kyam shrugged. "I have seen worse, but only as a boy."

"I hope the others are safe."

"It is hard to kill a Palaung. They do not have enough intelligence to die. As for the Communists—they cannot afford to die. They would go straight to hell."

An hour later a mudcaked apparition appeared along the trail. It was the other Palaung. Somewhere along the way he had lost his pack, gone forever beneath mud and slime, but he was grinning happily.

Soon Mengshu and the tall soldier appeared. Mengshu was limping and his arm was about his companion. His pistol was gone. He was morose.

Kyam managed to get a fire going. While the others were drying out, Paul Lowe examined Mengshu's injured foot. There was a deep gash across the instep and the ankle was badly bruised and beginning to swell. In the duffel bag Paul Lowe found a plastic sack that contained his medical supplies: adhesive tape, bandages, iodine, penicillin salve, scissors, spirits of ammonia and aspirin. He tended to the injured foot while Mengshu watched, glowering. When Paul Lowe finished, Mengshu tried to put the freshly bandaged foot, white and antiseptic looking, back into his boot.

"You won't be able to do that until the swelling goes down," Paul Lowe said.

Mengshu made several attempts and then angrily began to unwrap the bandage.

"You can't get the boot on even without the bandages," Paul Lowe told him. "But if you take them off you have a good chance of getting an infection in that cut. It's deep. You might even be risking blood poisoning or gangrene."

Mengshu stopped unwrapping the bandage. He stood up and took a few hobbling steps.

"I can't walk like this," he said accusingly.

"I didn't think you could."

Mengshu flung out an arm. "But I must! I can't stay here."

"We can rig up something to carry you."

"I don't want to be carried!"

326

"What else would you suggest?"

Mengshu thought about this with fierce concentration. Finally he asked, "How long will it be before I can walk?"

"It's possible you've got a fracture, but I don't think so. There's probably some badly torn ligaments, and then that bad cut in your foot. My guess is that you won't be able to get around for at least a few days."

"It will be sooner," Mengshu said.

"I hope so. None of us particularly likes the idea of carrying you all the way back to Pao."

Mengshu's nostrils flared. "We will not go back to Pao."

"Is there another place you'd rather be taken to?"

"We will complete our journey."

"In view of what's happened, that isn't possible."

"I have agreed to take you there, and I will. It is settled."

In the heat of the fire the odor of drying garments mingled with perspiration odors and the air became close in the small shelter. Smoke curled up from the not quite dried wood Kyam had been forced to use to make the fire.

Mengshu hobbled to a corner with the aid of his soldier companion, and sat apart from the others. Mengshu was dejected—apparently he felt that he had lost face by allowing Paul Lowe to treat his injury. His hand occasionally strayed to the empty holster where his pistol had been. He missed the clear symbol of his authority.

As the afternoon wore on, a breeze freshened and the odors disappeared. In the fire's warmth there was a relaxation of tension. Kyam even clapped the swarthy Palaung on the back and told him he was a good fellow for having held on to his pack.

Kyam asked Paul Lowe, "What time tomorrow will we go back to Pao?"

"We aren't going back."

Kyam indicated Mengshu in the corner. "What about him?"

"It is his wish that we go on. He doesn't want to be carried back into Pao on a stretcher." Paul Lowe grinned as he squatted by the fire. "I don't blame him. It doesn't fit in at all with his plans. If anyone was supposed to go back on a stretcher, it was me."

Kyam said, "We will carry him. But it may be a rough journey. He will not enjoy it." The prospect seemed to improve Kyam's spirits. "I am very sure that he will not enjoy it."

In the morning he ached in every muscle and his eyes were bloodshot and sore. He bathed his eyes in a solution of boric acid and took two aspirin. The toll on the other members of the expedition was now apparent. Kyam complained of a severe neck pain and Paul Lowe gave him two aspirin. The tall angular soldier said that his head was hurting, and he was given two aspirin also. By then the two Palaungs were beginning to feel left out of things and came forward to register their complaints.

"My back hurts," said the swarthier one. His injury could not have been serious for within a minute of taking his two aspirin he was beaming.

The second Palaung held his arms crossed on his stomach.

"I am sick. Very sick, here," he told Kyam, and indicated that the source of the trouble was his stomach. He bent double to make the point absolutely clear.

"What sort of pain?" Paul Lowe inquired.

"A sword turning in my bowels."

The Palaung did seem to be in genuine distress, but he had no fever. Glancing over his skimpy medical supplies, Paul Lowe found nothing that seemed to promise relief from a generalized belly ache. Then he remembered that constipation is a frequent problem among the natives.

"When did you last have a bowel movement?" he asked.

The man took one hand from his stomach long enough to hold up four fingers.

"Four days?"

The man nodded. Paul Lowe gave him a dose of a strong liquid laxative.

Meanwhile Kyam and the tall soldier, working together, rigged up a carrying frame of tree branches. They wrapped Mengshu in his sleeping bag and lifted him onto it. Paul Lowe could not help admiring Mengshu's stolid impassivity. Those torn ligaments and the gash in his foot must have been giving him a good deal of pain.

As they were getting ready to leave their makeshift camp, Paul Lowe asked the Palaung how his stomach was feeling. The man's answer was a broad grin.

Kyam interpreted: "He says he is feeling fine and that you are a fine doctor."

On the trail Kyam, the tall soldier and the two Palaungs carried Mengshu on the litter. Paul Lowe had to carry the duffel bag and the weight of it on his back gave him a new respect for the durability of the Palaung porters. Fortunately, because of the litter they were carrying, progress was slow and there were frequent halts to rest. It took great skill to maneuver Mengshu's litter over the steep rocky trails which narrowly skirted dangerous chasms. They moved at a caterpillar's pace to keep him from plunging into the depths.

They made camp in late afternoon at a height of about ten thousand feet and the Palaungs went off to collect wood for the fire.

Kyam was alone with Paul Lowe, several yards distant from where Mengshu was sitting up with his companion.

"Our friend is not talking much." Kyam gave a nod of his head in Mengshu's direction.

"I can't help feeling a little sorry for him. I know he's in pain, and it's been a pretty jolting trip."

Kyam's pink eyes glittered. "You may be sure of it."

"It's hard enough for him, Kyam, without trying to make it harder."

"I do not like him."

"Why not?"

Kyam rubbed the inside of his forearm. "Because he is not a Christian. I am a Christian."

"There are many good men who are not Christians, Kyam. Among the peoples of the world Christians are a minority."

"Are you a Christian?"

"Yes, I am."

"I like you." Kyam scowled at Mengshu. "I do not like him."

The Palaungs were returning with wood for the fire. As he and Kyam went to meet them, Paul Lowe thought: perhaps the best solution is to make simple replies to complex problems. "I do not like him because he does not believe as I do." That had the virtue of simplicity and honesty and all battles fought for the mass mind have to be simplistic but also have to be honest, because the majority of men do not understand complexity but will smell out dishonesty every time. A belief must be absolute and clear for men to understand it, hold it, and still go about their business.

He was bedding down for the night when a more disturbing thought occurred to him: it may even be that to probe too deeply paralyzes the will.

Early the next morning the party reached the awesome wall of ice that Paul Lowe had flown past in his airplane. They moved with extreme caution along a narrow defile over a yawning gorge in which long shadows twisted and turned. In the distance Paul Lowe saw towering snow-capped peaks, but at this high altitude the sun was hot and direct and low humidity gave the sunlight a fierce burning power. The Palaungs wore sunglasses with wooden frames—these dark-skinned people were affected in the eyes by strong glare. Paul Lowe wore wraparound dark-tinted glasses with prescription lenses. Kyam and Mengshu and the soldier wore ordinary sunglasses. Occasionally Mengshu put his arm across his eyes when, lying face up on the litter, he was forced to stare up directly into the strong light.

Despite his handicap, Mengshu proved to be a fine guide. He led them to their destination as surely as a taxi driver through the District of Columbia.

As they climbed toward the entrance to the narrow canyon an eagle floated silently overhead on outspread wings. There was no sound, not even a wind.

Sunlight paved a bright path almost to the mouth of the canyon where the darkness abruptly took over.

Paul Lowe's heart beat with a muffled excitement and a kind of foreboding. This was the climax of his queer quest. The foretaste of its meaninglessness already assailed him, as sour a taste as medicine in the mouth. . . .

The P-38 was a rusting pile overgrown with creepers and straggly growth until it seemed like an iron vegetation. Its shape was barely distinguishable, the broken fuselage, the open space of the cockpit, a part of the tail section. He touched the rim of the cockpit, half expecting to be catapulted back through time by the mere gesture. Dark red flakes of rust came away on his hand. The cockpit was half full of dirt in which small fernlike plants were growing. He touched the control stick. He felt the swift sick sinking in the pit of his stomach and relived those few desperate moments.

The world is the least difficult enemy. The devil is the hardest to understand. The flesh is the most tenacious. . . . And when all three are conquered, no more war remains in the soul.

No more war remained in his soul, but he had conquered nothing, least of all himself. Deskbound, chairbound, ease-wrapped, all he could claim was that he had survived. But those who survive in the mountains can perish lingeringly of equations and the moral law.

What had he accomplished in the war? That was the real question. It was a poser. He had nearly lost his life in the service of something, and with the least effort he could remember those who had lost their lives. Off they went into the wild blue yonder. Jimmy Jamar, "the champ of MIG alley," who went down in a spinning smoking dive out of a sky filled with little red and silver planes. Hank Morritt, whose plane skidded off on the right wing during a crash landing and whose cockpit hood wouldn't open until the fuselage lit up like a flaming banyan tree. Bob Hastings, the laughing blond boy who had loved practical jokes and in the midst of an air battle heard the order, "All clear, pancake." When he tried to obey the code command to land, a Nakajima-97 got on his tail and shot him to pieces. Dying in the hospital, Bob cursed the radio operator who had given him the command. But there was no such message on the radio log. An English-speaking Japanese pilot had transmitted the order on the Tenth Air Force frequency and pulled Bob Hastings into a trap.

The broken skeletons of planes and men had littered the landscape from Rangoon to Mitkyina and beyond.

But Paul Lowe had outlasted the war and now that whole gigantic enterprise was a part of his education. It had taught him a lot. You learn in a war if you live and he had learned that he would have to acquire a new set of allegiances. He could no longer afford to be loyal only to his own interests, or those of his family, or his town, or his state, or his nation or his race. He had to give absolute loyalty not even to humanity considered as a whole because there was no such humanity except in the sentimental yearnings of Utopians and the pious visions of saints. He had to devote himself utterly to the principles which bound the struggling mass of mankind together, which kept the lines of communication open and kept the pitiful collective intelligence of the sublunary species working against desperate odds to keep its precarious hold on a planet that was itself a ridiculous speck of dust floating in the midst of inconceivable hostilities. And he had to be aware that his true allegiance must reach beyond the principles, no matter how wise or eternal they appeared to be, to the rational mind casting aside what it had learned and seeking to learn more, accepting nothing but change, and offering nothing more than the joy of the search to justify its ceaseless searching.

The others had halted and were waiting a short distance behind him.

330

Mengshu was standing up from his litter and was watching him with frank curiosity.

"I would like to take photographs," Paul Lowe said, "but the light is not good now."

Kyam answered, "We can make camp here if it is your wish."

Paul Lowe glanced at Mengshu who said nothing but kept regarding him with narrow interest.

"I suppose it's as good a place as any," Paul Lowe said.

That night he returned to the wreckage of the plane. In pale moonlight the rust and decay were not so plainly visible and the structure seemed almost intact. Imagination filled in the shadowed places. In that cockpit he had been forced for the first time to confront the naked probability of death, not the challenge or the romantic illusion, but the probability. Youth does not survive certain thoughts and the overwhelming nearness of death is among them. His youth had ended here.

He heard a footstep behind him. Kyam came toward him, his long shadow following in the moonlight.

"I saw that you were missing and came to look for you," Kyam said.

"I was about to return," Paul Lowe told him. "I could not sleep and came here a while. Are the others asleep?"

"I believe Mengshu is pretending sleep."

Paul Lowe pointed to the north, toward the snow-capped mountain peaks.

"Is that China?"

"That mountain is the border. Beyond it is China."

"If the Chinese decided to come across, it would be hard to resist them."

Kyam touched the hilt of the *dah* in his scabbard. "Yes, but many would die. They would swim in their blood." Kyam looked away from the snow clad mountain. "Will you return to the campfire now? It is cold here."

"I'll come back in a little while. You go to sleep, Kyam. I'll be all right."

A few minutes later, starting back from the canyon, he glanced up and saw on a small mound nearby a silent figure watching him. Mengshu was leaning on a short sturdy tree branch and his white bandaged foot was tilted at the heel.

"I have been wondering about you," Mengshu said. "It is clear to me now that you are not a spy."

"I'm glad you're convinced of that."

"You have really come all this way to see this plane. Why?"

"I can't give you an explanation that would satisfy you, Mengshu."

"I know the answer. It came into my head a short time ago, while I was standing here. Like all white men you worship the machine. The machine is a god to you."

He laughed. "You're wrong. It's nothing like that, Mengshu."

"Then what is it?"

He indicated the blackened pile of rusted metal. "I killed two men in other planes before I crashed here. I saw those men go down in flames and that sight is one I would prefer never to see again."

Mengshu's bronze face glowed in the moonlight. "War will come. The white man will never be a ruler again in Asia. Our side will win because we belong here—this is our land. If you try to oppose us, we will destroy you no matter how many machines you send against us."

"There is a better way, Mengshu."

"The land has to be taken from the rich and given to the poor. That will take fighting."

"And will that solve the problems? You will need machines to work the land, and men who will know how to work the machines. Educated men. You will need schools, and better houses to live in, and better clothes to wear, and better medical treatment."

"All that will come. It cannot be done in a single year."

"Of course it can't. You have to keep trying to bring it about. That is what a government is for, Mengshu."

"That is a lie. Your government does not care about people."

"Our people set up the government in the first place, to serve their needs better and to help them get what they want. If the government does not concern itself with what the people want, then it is a bad government and the people will demand a change."

Mengshu stared at him suspiciously. "You are trying to sound like a Communist."

"No, Mengshu. I believe that people should demand that the government serve them. To do that they need the right to be heard so they can make their needs known. I don't believe your leaders will allow anything to be heard if it is unpleasant, or if it disagrees with them or makes trouble."

Mengshu stiffened. His hand clung tighter to the stick that supported him. "Only enemies of the state will be silenced. That is proper. Those who stand in the way of progress will be eliminated."

Keep the lines open, Paul Lowe reminded himself, because if the lines go down that will be an end of all communication. But he was a little discouraged. He could guess Mengshu's opinion of him: one of those liberals whose cloying faith was in words rather than deeds, the kind that would have to be purged in order to free the revolution of certain illusions. Mengshu would replace the facile gentle optimism of those who merely meant well with the caustic revolutionary optimism of those who were true guides to the future.

This Paul Lowe understood, and yet he sought for a ground on which he and Mengshu could meet. The same process which had led them to opposite conclusions might lead them back again to find their common humanity. Perhaps, as Mengshu supposed, a cauterizing flame had to pass over men and the answers be discovered in killing agony and apocalyptic despair. But even if the new world was born out of a destructive vigor there would have to be in it the essential ingredient that was in everything done by homo sapiens in behalf of homo sapiens: the integrative power

332

of the individual reasoning mind. While that power was present there was always hope because the ability to reason for oneself is the source of all rebellion. If the whole world were temporarily persuaded to think as Mengshu did, or as Paul Lowe did, it would not be a better place. In fact, it would be much worse—a place that would lose charm and variety even for the victors.

Yet if this bitter cup may pass, let it.

"Shall we go back now?" Paul Lowe asked.

Mengshu pointed with his cane stick. "You go. I will follow."

He understood the reason for the order. Mengshu had great difficulty in walking and did not want a witness to his weakness.

After taking photographs the next day they broke camp. Mengshu was again forced to take his place on the litter. His leg was worse. During the night Paul Lowe had heard him gasping and wished that he had included morphine in his medicine kit to ease the man's suffering. It was clear now that the leg was probably broken—he suspected one or more fractures in the ankle—and last night's short walk had cost Mengshu dearly.

The return journey to Pao was arduous and painful. Mengshu's injured leg kept giving him torment and the continual jouncing of the wooden litter was unbearable to watch. Mengshu did not complain. He lay hour after hour broiling in the sun and freezing in the cool winds that blew up as the day was ending. He did not utter a sound. The shock and exposure had brought on a fever and there were times when he seemed to be dozing but must have fainted.

It took them a week to complete the return to the village of Pao. They traveled little more than a mile an hour and on the last day they completely ran out of their supplies of food.

They were half a mile from the village when Paul Lowe saw the chief and several other men coming out to meet them. Mengshu shouted angrily at his litter bearers until they put him down. Assisted only by his makeshift cane, he slowly and painfully staggered down the slope to meet the chief.

The chief gravely shook hands with Mengshu, then greeted Paul Lowe and Kyam. He spoke a few words.

Kyam interpreted: "He says he is happy that we have come back safely from our journey. And he hopes that for you the homecoming will not be saddened by the news he brings. Chung-jin is dead."

"Would you tell him that I am grieved to hear it," Paul Lowe said.

As Kyam translated this reply, Paul Lowe realized that Chung-jin's death had not really caused him sorrow. Chung-jin was unreal, a figure out of a dream, but his own body was aching and shivering with the morning cold. That was real. So was the rust-colored mountain and the strange wild-looking Kyam and the Palaung porters, and these people from the village of Pao with their poor huts straggling down the steep inhospitable slope.

A little distance away Mengshu was standing, stockstill, pressing his thin lips tight and staring in front of him.

Paul Lowe said to Kyam, "Tell them Mengshu has a very bad leg. It is probably broken and he will need a doctor. If they know where there is a doctor we will go to him and bring him here."

On Kyam's face was an expression of bewilderment, the unhappy helpless look of a man betrayed.

"There is no doctor in the mountains," he said. "It is a week's journey to bring one here. Perhaps longer, even if a doctor would come."

"We will need fresh provisions then. For the journey."

Kyam regarded him with mingled curiosity and disgust.

"If you had broken your leg," Kyam said, "Mengshu would have left you to die in the mountains. The plague take him! Why should we bother ourselves for him?"

"Because," he said, appealing to an authority Kyam would respect, "it is a Christian thing to do."

Kyam lapsed into sullen acceptance. He began to translate Paul Lowe's message to the village chief.

Paul Lowe went over to where Mengshu was standing. Under a film of pain that glazed Mengshu's eyes, he thought he glimpsed a man, perplexed, a little frightened, but resolute.

"You were a very good guide," he said, and held out his hand.

Mengshu's suffering had washed from his face the expression of authority and command. In the clear morning light Paul Lowe saw that he could not be more than twenty years old, a mere boy with a stern, sickly face.

Mengshu ignored the outstretched hand. He placed his weight firmly on his injured leg. "Why are we standing here? Let us go down into the village."

Scorning to be carried on the litter, Mengshu began to limp down the trail. Paul Lowe winced watching him, knowing what price was paid in agony to walk on that injured leg. Then he followed, and after a moment so did Kyam and the villagers. The Palaung porters brought up the rear.

It was half a mile but somehow Mengshu made it. He only limped a little when they reached the first of the straggling huts and passed the silent and curious villagers who had gathered to watch them.

Mark Branford, the United States Ambassador to Burma, was a courteous and amiable man. He was the son of a wealthy textile manufacturer and he had inherited his father's fortune along with the good sense to leave the care of it in capable hands. That left him free to pursue a career in public affairs. Unfortunately, Mark Branford was no better suited for public affairs than for textile manufacturing.

Nevertheless he was a gracious host. Paul Lowe dined with him and David Moss on the evening after his return to Rangoon. The Ambassador ate heartily, having apparently recovered completely from his siege with amoebic dysentery.

334

Through the tall window of the dining room Paul Lowe could see glowing rice-paper balloons floating through the night.

"They're celebrating another of their festivals," David Moss said. "An interesting effect, isn't it? They make a giant balloon of rice paper and paint it and hang candles beneath the opening in the bottom. Then they hold it over a bonfire until the balloon fills with hot air and they send it off glowing with candlelight inside it."

"Ingenious," Paul Lowe muttered.

"Oh, yes," David Moss agreed, "for a rather primitive people they do come up with clever ideas."

Through the open window there drifted a spicy smell that Paul Lowe would forever afterward associate with Burma. It was a smell that perfumed all its cities with a strange musky fragrance, compounded of teakwood, of opium, of people with coconut oil in their hair and sandalwood soap on their bodies, of bazaars crowded with human life and of horned buffaloes wading in the *klongs* along the road, of fruit that was overripe and earth that was humid and rich.

"In some ways I'm going to be sorry to leave here," Paul Lowe said.

"When do you plan to leave, Mr. Justice?" David Moss asked.

"As soon as I can arrange my audience with U Ba Saw."

"I've already made your request known," Mark Branford said. "We should have definite word within a day or two."

After dinner David Moss excused himself with an "It's been very pleasant to meet you again, Mr. Justice," and Paul Lowe retired with the Ambassador to his private office in the Embassy building.

"The President has told me," Mark Branford said, "that you will report to him on how the situation looks in Burma. I've tried to keep Lamont up to date but of course I don't blame him for wanting more information. It's very touch and go here. Very touch and go."

"Have you made specific recommendations on what should be done?"

"Oh, yes. We are on top of the situation all the time, you see."

"What action have you recommended, Mr. Ambassador?"

"Well, I've told Lamont that we simply have to bring U Ba Saw around to realize that we're his friends and that any military assistance we give his government isn't going to be a cloak to cover up some advantage for us. U Ba Saw is personally a very fine fellow but his big fear is colonialism, you see. Like most of his people he's suspicious of Western colonialism. He looks behind everything we do to find some secret motive which is tied up with it. It's very unfair, of course."

"Apparently he doesn't share our government's view of the serious nature of the Communist threat in this part of the world."

Mark Branford finished lighting a cigar and flicked the flame out of the match. "He'll end up on our side, I'm sure of that, but you have to remember that these people come from an older and more patient world. They can't understand our constant demands for action. They like to take their time about things."

"President Howard seems to think there are urgent reasons for taking action now."

"And so do I. So do I. But it's a curious thing, when you talk to these people you find they don't have any sharp edges. They're more philosophic, if you know what I mean. And they're not likely to be shaken by sudden revelations. Even if I could prove there was a Communist conspiracy about to take over the country, men like U Ba Saw would still think they could make their peace with it."

"And you don't think that's possible?"

"Emphatically not. Rule or ruin, that's the Communist's motto. They're impossible to talk to when they're dealing from strength. When they've got you in a vise they keep closing in. And eventually they control the whole situation."

"How can we prevent matters from getting to that state, Mr. Ambassador?"

"We're doing our best. But we have to move with a prudent sort of caution. We don't want to get ourselves overcommitted here and of course in the last analysis the Burmese people have to help themselves." Mark Branford blew out a reflective concealing cloud of smoke. "On the whole I'd say that I'm not too alarmed about the way things are going at the moment."

Ambassador Branford's understanding of the problems in Burma had been gleaned during two or three trips outside Rangoon, always by scheduled airlines to major cities where he met and talked with people from approximately the same power stratum of society. At dinner Paul Lowe had learned that Mark Branford was aware "the hinterlands are seething with unrest" but his fears were well diffused by a basic conviction that the Burmese were a passive people whose chief interest was not in revolution but in pursuing a contemplative way of life.

Mark Branford said, "We have to go along with U Ba Saw for the present and try to influence him in little ways to see our point of view. I've met with him twice and I'm going to have another serious talk with him in the near future."

"Will you discuss anything with him outside of the problem of military assistance? After all, I understand the Burmese sell one-third of their rice crop to Red China. We can't expect them to turn their backs on that kind of trade. It may be a chief reason they cling to a neutralist position between us and Red China."

Mark Branford nodded sagely. "You're probably right that we should concentrate a bit more on the economic realities. Of course we could do a lot in the way of giving economic assistance. As I've told them again and again, America is a rich country and we produce more than the rest of the world put together. But we're not a Santa Claus. And trying to be one could be dangerous in the present situation."

"Why dangerous?"

"Well, we can't ship in enormous quantities of material to these people until their political setup is more stable. If anything did happen, and there was an unfortunate change in government, our effort would be wasted. All that we'd do would simply be to help our enemies. It's ticklish diplomacy, you see that, don't you?"

"We can't stand by and wait for a revolution to come, can we?"

"Of course not. On the other hand, we can't make these people do exactly what we want. We can't twist their arms. I have come around to the view that no show of force is going to impress them. You mention the atomic bomb to them and they're not impressed. They just look at you with plain hatred. We have a lot of missionary work to do in that area. I hope you'll make some of these difficulties clear in your report to the President. Tell him that we're staying with the situation here as it develops. We're right on top of it."

It was apparent that nothing more was to be said to Mark Branford. Paul Lowe smiled a bit grimly and accepted the cigar that the Ambassador offered.

The next morning a letter arrived from Eleanor, a long hastily scrawled missive that clearly reflected her agitation. She had learned two weeks after the event that Nancy had given birth to an infant daughter at Doctors Hospital in New York. Shortly after Nancy left the hospital she had taken the baby up to Boston and left her with Arthur. The very next day she had flown off to Europe with Tessie Samuels. The only word from her since then had been a postcard from Rotterdam in which she said she intended to spend the rest of the summer in Paris, and in which she made no mention of her daughter at all.

Such indifference grieved Eleanor who had never succeeded in dulling her responses to Nancy's errant behavior. But at this point the tone of the letter began to improve. Eleanor had flown up to Boston to see the baby and reported "she is really the most beautiful baby I've ever seen." It was not reliable testimony. Eleanor was preparing herself for her new role as grandmother.

On the afternoon of his third day in Rangoon while Paul Lowe was resting in his spacious bedroom on the second floor of the Embassy building, a servant came to announce that a message for him had been delivered by hand.

It was the answer he had been waiting for from U Ba Saw, President of the Union of Burma.

My dear Justice,

I regret that the urgency of business prevents me from making an appointment to see you again.

However, I wish you would inform President Lamont Howard that we are fully aware of the strength of Communism in our country and prefer to deal with it in our own way. The anxiety of your country about Communism is something which we in Burma simply do not understand. When a nation becomes obsessed with fear it suffers from what is similar to a paranoid system in an individual. The paranoid man can be very intelligent, can reason logically about many things, but never about that isolated part where his paranoid delusion is involved.

We in Burma reject the belief that the world must be divided into two hostile camps. There is room for others to exist and have an importance of their own.

As a further message to your President, I wish you would remind him that America has truly nothing to fear but fear itself.

On a personal basis, I enjoyed our meeting. I hope you enjoyed your stay in Burma and will soon return.

Sincerely

U BA SAW

On the wide bed, beneath an electric fan, Paul Lowe read U Ba Saw's letter. It might have been headed, he thought wryly, *Failure of a Mission.* He had not been able to penetrate far into U Ba Saw's serenity. Perhaps this was because of a dichotomy in his own views—between the public man and the private man; the role that he had assumed and the man he was.

In his slippers he padded across the polished wooden floor and opened wide a deep window that was covered with wire mesh. He was starting to compose an official report to President Lamont Howard. Mr. President, it is my conviction that . . . no, "conviction" was too strong. In a world of shifting values one is entitled to nothing more than a tendency to believe. But how could one say he had "a tendency to believe" in a situation where if the answers were unsure the disasters were certain? Mr. President, we may not be able to convert the Burmese people to our brand of democracy or our brand of private capitalism. These people want a government that will accomplish something for them, even if that government does not guarantee the full enjoyment of all their liberties. Our laws would not work here because the social conditions are entirely different. Unlike poetry, a law cannot be written about things which do not exist. The law is not a revelation but an ordering of events. It will not help us to rebuke or reproach these people because their priorities are different from ours. We would not change our ideals to suit them, neither should we expect them to change their ideals to suit us. . . .

He could see President Lamont Howard's face when he received that message. The President, rightly, wanted to keep Burma among the friends of the United States, and all Paul Lowe was able to tell him was that we might have to settle for not having Burma as an enemy. . . . The fan in the room churned heated air and perspiration ran down his neck into his collar.

23

One of the most stirring sights for any returning traveler is the White House glimmering in morning light like a sculptured white coral in a sea of green trees. The vision filled Paul Lowe's eyes with wonder and tears.

A policeman came out of the little white booth at the entrance to the White House driveway. He opened the tall iron gate and came over to the cab to check Paul Lowe's credentials.

"Go right in, Mr. Justice."

The cab backed out of the driveway. Paul Lowe went up the broad marble steps beneath the brass-trimmed lantern that hung from the high ceiling of the portico.

A few minutes later Martin Gannett ushered him into the President's oval study on the second floor. Lamont Howard was looking somewhat thinner.

He shook hands cordially. "It's good to have you back, Paul. I hope you didn't have a bad trip."

"It was disappointing, Mr. President."

The President sat in his swivel chair and Paul Lowe took a seat on the sofa opposite.

"I gathered as much from your official report, Paul. It arrived a couple of days ago in the diplomatic pouch and I've had time to study it and go over it with some of my top advisers." He hitched himself erect in his chair. "But there's still no substitute for talking a problem out, between friends. I'd like to know how bad you think it is for us over there."

In the next half hour Paul Lowe gave the President a full report on his meeting with U Ba Saw and his estimate of the political situation in Burma.

"Of course it's impossible to form any reliable judgments in so short a time, Mr. President. But my impression is that Ambassador Branford is somewhat out of touch with the realities. He doesn't realize how explosive things are—or why." Paul Lowe smiled ruefully. "I must admit that I don't seem to have done much better in the way of getting our message through to the Burmese leaders."

"That may not be your fault, Paul. You were carrying the sort of message they don't want to hear." He added with sudden vexation, "If only I could make them understand that we only want to help. I've tried every approach I can think of. It's like talking to a bunch of sleepwalkers who don't want to be waked up to the danger they're in. I wish I knew what else to do. What would you do if you were in my place, Paul?"

"I think I'd try to change our tactics, Mr. President."

"How?"

"Well, to begin with, it isn't doing any good to keep telling these people that we're the most powerful country in the world with the highest standard of living. That's Ambassador Branford's approach and it's like boasting to poor relatives. They undoubtedly resent the fact that we *can* produce as much as the rest of the world put together."

Lamont Howard nodded sadly. "Mark Branford is a good friend of mine and a nice fellow. But every time he opens his mouth his foot falls out. Still, I can't believe that winning over the Burmese to our side is going to be a simple matter of public relations—or saying the right thing at the right time. What can we do in a practical way to show them we're their friends?"

"They need our help badly, Mr. President. We've got to make them realize that we're willing to give them the kind of practical assistance they need, working through their institutions and their leaders, without setting any kind of political conditions. Even if that means allowing them to set up state socialism and adopt a neutralist position in world affairs."

The President hunched forward. "That's a stiff price to pay, Paul. We could wind up just standing by while the Communists take over everything without having to fire a shot."

"I don't think we can afford to stop with just offering cooperation to government leaders, Mr. President. Above all, we have to work at the grass roots level where the support of the people is won. That's what the Communists are doing. The Burmese people don't ask us to send arms to train their soldiers or pay their military bills. They need us to work with the peasants, teach them to read, help them to bring in the crops. They need regiments of doctors, teachers, engineers, as well as skilled laborers to instruct them in new trades."

He had struck the right tone for the President. In Lamont Howard's mind a moral problem did not become real until he could translate it into terms of its practical handling. Only when the raw material of morality was processed in a political machine did the President truly recognize its existence, but what was fed into the machine he understood fully because he was a pure function of the machine.

"I guess we could work up an aid program along that line," Lamont Howard said. "I could probably wangle it through Congress pretty quick too. Do you think that would make any real impression on them?"

"No one can be sure. But I believe it's our best hope of stopping Communism in its tracks. In fact, I can't see any practical alternative."

"There's always one alternative, Paul. We can maintain an anti-Communist government in power by direct force of arms if it comes right down to it."

340

"Yes, we can do that whether or not such a government supplies the wants of the people. But there are two things we will never do, Mr. President. We will never make such a government work for very long and we will never make it popular."

The President swung about in his chair. "Paul, it's a difficult problem. I've got a lot of factors to consider. But it sure couldn't do any harm to try to make a move in the direction you're proposing." Lamont Howard stared at him. "Would you consider taking on a job?"

"What sort of a job, Mr. President?"

"I've had an idea for a long time that I might appoint someone to be a sort of super-ambassador—reporting directly to me on how the situation looks in different countries."

"That isn't in my field of competence, Mr. President."

"Your first assignment would be Burma. You could try to work out a new approach to the problem over there, and get some of the fossils in the State Department to give a good hard shake to their ossified ideas."

"I'm not really qualified to do that. And there's an additional problem."

"What's that?"

"I'd make suggestions. But they wouldn't amount to very much unless they happened to be what you wanted to do in the first place."

The President chuckled but his expression remained serious. "I'm a reasonable man, Paul. We don't have to agree on everything. It would be useful for me to get a different viewpoint once in a while."

Paul Lowe said gently, "Mr. President, I'm afraid we would approach too many matters from a wholly different angle."

"I'd try to see it your way when that happened. The Lord knows our present policy isn't working out so well that I couldn't afford to try something else."

"I'm flattered, Mr. President, and I appreciate your confidence in me. But I'm very happy on the Supreme Court. I was never much of a politician. I'm more at home as a judge—a completely different kind of animal."

The President's glance sharpened. "Your personal happiness isn't the most important thing in the world. In times like these none of us has the right to turn down a chance to help save the peace."

"There are other men who can do more for that cause than I can, Mr. President. I believe I can be more useful on the Supreme Court than anywhere else."

"Our people are good and sick of having our boys killed in Southeast Asia without any end to it. I'd like to keep our country from getting any deeper involved over there than we are right now. I don't know if we can do that, Paul, but I'd sure like to." The President rubbed his hand wearily over his face. "I need someone to help me try, Paul. Promise me to think about this assignment, won't you?"

"Of course, Mr. President."

"But give me an answer as soon as you can. In a few weeks at most."

The President was silent for a while. "As you know, the hour is getting late."

The President's lined face looked very tired.

In August the city of Washington literally broils in heat. During the drive to his house on Volta Place the noonday sun was making the asphalt in the streets gummy. He was looking forward to a shower and a nap on the sofa in the dark quiet of his home.

He entered the front door with his key, expecting the pervading smell of mustiness that always accompanies a long-closed home. But there was no such odor. As he crossed the carpeting toward the living room he saw dust motes in the sunlight from the window. The windows were open and the blinds drawn up.

He turned as Eleanor entered the living room. She came to him with fire in her cheeks and sparkle in her eyes.

"Paul!"

He was so startled at her presence he was unable to react.

She kissed him on the cheek.

"Aren't you glad to see me?"

"How did you know I'd be here? I only sent you a telegram when I landed in New York. That was two o'clock this morning. You didn't possibly have time to get here from Lincoln."

She laughed at his surprise.

"I've been here since yesterday, darling. I telephoned the Embassy in Rangoon. I hadn't heard from you and I was worried. I found out that you'd left the day before and were flying to London to book passage on a jet home. So I came right home to get everything ready for you." She flung her arms about his neck and really kissed him. "Isn't it wonderful to be together? You're really *home*, Paul." Her arms tightened. "I can't begin to tell you how I've missed you."

His perfunctory hug signaled an end to the embrace. Her arms uncoiled.

"What's the matter, darling? Are you upset about something?"

"No. I'm trying to adjust to the fact that you're really here."

"While you're doing it, you may as well get all the gossip. I talked to Nancy a few days ago too. She's in Paris. She's apparently had some sort of quarrel with her friend Tessie Samuels that she didn't want to talk about. But she's met a marvelous new man."

"How about the baby? I had a telegram that she was born in August."

"August seventh. Nancy left the baby with Arthur in Boston. He has a nursemaid to look after her. I hope we'll have time to go up to see her."

He was thinking: poor Eleanor. Again: poor Eleanor. He did not know what had started this wave of sympathy toward her. Perhaps the fact that because she was here he would have to tell her; or perhaps the fact that she appeared to him to have lost another shade of youth, to be a trifle wearier, bending a bit more compliantly to the years; or perhaps because she was so willing to be friendly, so ready to accept kindness rather than love. Or perhaps only because her desires were small and transient and easily satis-fied.

"Where's your luggage?" Eleanor asked suddenly.

"I checked it at Dulles Airport. I had an appointment with the White House this morning and didn't know where I'd be staying tonight."

"We can pick it up later, then."

Paul Lowe nodded.

He would have to tell her without delay.

She sat on the living room sofa, with her legs curled under her and her hand clasping her ankles. She chattered on about Nancy. Her sallow skin seemed to have more color, or was it the flush of excitement? She was happy about Nancy's new man. She thought it would mark the beginning of a new life for Nancy if she married this man she had met in Paris. Eleanor put such store by this child who despised her. Paul Lowe wondered if the other child—the one they had chosen not to have, who perished microscopically in the womb—would have received such uncritical affec-tion. Probably. Eleanor could not divide her affections any more than she could divide her body. She truly did not exist in her own right. Her loyalties were herself.

In the room the echoes of her voice softly came and went. His heart began to beat powerfully. He wondered how to begin to tell her and he kept waiting for an opportunity.

She chattered on. Now it was about the house, and the condition it was in when she arrived and what she had done to prepare for his home-coming. That speck of white tooth showing in a corner when her lips were closed . . . once that had driven him to distraction with a desire to kiss her mouth. And those greenish-brown eyes had held such depths of mystery until he struck bottom in their shallows.

He began to wonder if he would be able to tell her. He could place the blame on no one but himself. Was he worse than other men—or were they better able to ignore or conceal the scarlet line of sexual adventure that ran through the fabric of their natures? If the truth were known, he probably belonged with the majority. He was not a libertine—in over twenty years there had been only four women, and one of them had been his wife. Miat had been an episode that happened far away and long ago—a lovely interlude of no significance. Harriet had meant more but their affair was short and intense and physical. And now there was Kather-ine.

There was no way to put it off any longer. He went to the bar and poured himself a drink, dropping in ice cubes with plunking noises and gurgling bourbon over them until the glass was full.

"Would you like a drink?" he asked. His back was still to her.

"No, thank you, dear."

He turned. "Eleanor, there's something I have to talk to you about."

"You sound so serious."

"It's very serious. It has to do with us."

343

"Is something wrong?"

"I'm afraid so."

She waited in a solemn silence. Still waters run deep, her mother always said about Eleanor, mistaking her silence for dimension. Well, he had rescued her from that monstrous woman's clutches when he married her. No matter what was ahead for Eleanor now it would be better than sister Natalie's fate. Natalie had failed to escape. There had been no rescuer. Mother had seen to that. Until Natalie was thirty, Mother had read her mail and torn up letters from boys she did not approve of. He shook off this transparent sort of self-justification, recognizing it as his own fear of inflicting pain.

"I haven't been happy for some time, Eleanor."

"I don't understand." She really didn't. "Why haven't you been happy?"

"That's one reason I went away—to find the reason."

"Was it anything I've done?" She reached for a cigarette.

"No. No, of course not."

That was true. He might have gone along for years, attracted to other women but doing nothing more than play the small flirting game whose chief object is reassurance that we are still pleasant to look at, not old.

"Then I'm afraid I don't understand," she said. She lit her cigarette shakily. His tone had begun to alarm her.

Was it Katherine Prescott? he wondered. Certainly not her alone. There had been other women, at parties, on street corners, at supermarkets, seated nearby in theaters, anywhere, women who for a combination of unexplainable reasons had struck him with a force that took away his breath. Women with a look of meaning in their eyes. They had all disappeared into the innumerable avenues that lead away forever. He had been vulnerable. He had been waiting. Any one of those women might have been the one he was searching for. Yet he believed what he felt for Katherine was unique, could not have happened with anyone else; he was caught with her in a web so intricate that no strand could be pulled without causing a hopeless snarl in everything he felt and everything he was.

"I've come to the conclusion that I don't have anything to give you any more," he said.

There it was, spoken and palpable—the cruelty, the necessary cruelty.

She puffed nervously on her cigarette. "What?" she asked. He wished that she would not smoke. Nicotine was staining some of her teeth.

With his drink in hand, cold comfort, he faced her. "This isn't a sudden decision, Eleanor. It's been coming on for a long time."

"I don't know what you're talking about."

She was composed, aloof, but fueled from within by churning undefined excitement.

"We can't go on together any longer."

"Are you playing some kind of game with me, Paul? If so, I wish you'd stop."

"What I'm asking for is a divorce."

"This is a crazy mood you're in. I know what you're like when you're in one of your moods. Are you feeling well?" Her speech stuttered. Her movements became staccato: quick puff at her cigarette, swift exhalation, the knocking off of an ash that hadn't yet formed on the cigarette tip.

"This had to come as a shock but it can't be entirely unexpected." His throat was hoarse and his Midwestern twang seemed to him more noticeable. "I'm putting into words something we both must have been thinking for a . . ."

"It isn't true," she said faintly. She looked ill. "I had no reason to think anything. No reason at all."

"I don't believe that's being honest with yourself."

"Don't you know how I love you? Don't you care?"

"Eleanor, please . . ."

"You don't care or you couldn't say these terrible things." Out of her anguish she exclaimed, "I don't have anyone but you!"

"I haven't stopped caring about you," he said. He wanted so much to be kind to her. He felt so guilty. "I'll always be around if you need me. I just can't be married to you any longer."

"I know what it is!" The sofa cushion creaked. "There's some other woman." She stood up suddenly. "You've gotten involved in a cheap affair with some . . ." hurt and anger sought the word, ". . . some harlot!"

"Eleanor, it will be a lot easier if we try to talk about this like two sensible people."

She was trembling taut, a bow ready to let fly. "Sensible!" All she could do was repeat the word. "*Sensible!*"

It must be frustrating to be inarticulate with rage. In order to blunt the keen edge of his present awareness, a part of his mind was working in this oddly detached way. Of all emotions, he thought, rage calls for symphonic language. Poor King Lear struggling with the tempest had been able to match it blow for blow; the crazed old man must have found satisfaction in that.

"I don't believe any of this is happening," she said. "I won't believe it!" She was close to tears but trying to maintain analytical calmness.

"It isn't anyone's fault, Eleanor. It's just something that happened to us."

Her face began to shatter. He averted his eyes.

"You can't treat me like this, Paul. I won't let you!" Her voice snapped, "Don't I mean *anything* to you? Don't you *care* what you're doing to me?"

Deeply stirred by her appeal, he was at the same time somewhat restrained by her pity for herself. Self-pity creates a wall around the sufferer, shutting out sympathy like a powerful electrical repulsion.

He touched her shoulder. "Right now you need to rest. We can talk more about this later."

"Don't touch me! Take your hand off me!" She lifted her face and curiosity peered like Caliban out of a dark cave. "*Who is she?*"

This was the moment for him to deny all. This was the moment that would not come again.

"Who she is doesn't really matter," he said.

345

Her mouth fell open with shock. Her hand fluttered near her chest. She reached out, found a chair and sat down. Her hand dislodged the floral covering from the chair arm; it lay on the floor like a fallen battle standard.

"There is someone else. I should have known it." She shook with a spasm of revulsion. "How could you?"

"It isn't anything I planned, Eleanor."

"How did you meet her? How long has it been going on?"

A new element was introduced. Simple duration. She wanted to measure infidelity by the week, month, year, to the full stretch of villainy.

"I won't discuss that. I'm not going to hurt you any more than I can help."

"I demand to know! I have a right. What's her name?"

"No," he said. "I won't tell you."

"*No!*" She reacted with violence to the word's indignity.

She leaped up and reached the bar in length strides. Her arm swept like a croupier's stick. Bottles and glasses plunged from the narrow top. The bottles hit the carpet with thumping solidity but there was a splintery sound of breaking glass. Then the ice bucket struck and rolled spilling its square ice diamonds. The flower design in the rug turned black as water penetrated its tendrils.

The shock was transferred into a new thought: rage does not need language. The physical response will suffice.

"A divorce!" she cried, summing up all her concentrated fury. "You'll *never* get a divorce! Never!" She shrieked rejection, triumphant in outraged virtue. "Oh—*no!* I'm not going to be turned out so you can bring some other woman to sleep in my bed!"

"Eleanor, please . . ."

"Just a pleasant divorce and I'll never be heard from again! You can't send *me* packing with money, Paul! It won't be as easy as that." A livid color suffused her face. "You won't get away with anything. You'll pay! You'll pay with all you've got!"

He had never seen her like this. He would never have believed her capable of such an outburst.

A convulsive shudder ran the length of her body. "I hate you!" she shouted, and with an unintelligible cry she fled the room.

She ran up the stairs.

At the foot of the staircase, looking up, he did not know what to do. He did not know why he continued to stand there or what he was waiting for. Perhaps he expected her to return, or perhaps he thought that if he did not move she would at least sense his presence there demanding her return.

An hour later she allowed him into the bedroom. She opened the door and stood aside for him to enter. Her face was empty, puffed with crying.

"Are you all right?" he asked.

She smoothed her dress. "I've been thinking. I've come to a decision."

346

"What is it?"

In an effort to gain more control she opened the cigarette box. When she put a cigarette to her lips he tried to offer a match but she avoided him. She sat on the bed and struck her own match. The flame trembled and died in the transfer of its glow.

"I want to be fair," she said firmly.

"I know that."

"I'm sorry I made such a scene. I never expected anything like this from you, Paul." She blew out jagged smoke. "But I know you well enough to know this isn't your fault. You may be weak but you're not evil or cruel."

That speech—how admirably designed to serve multiple ends. *I'm sorry I made such a scene.* As you know, Paul, I am reasonable and sweet-tempered, slow to take offense and quick to apologize. At least pity is owed to me. *But I know you well enough to know it isn't your fault.* The years we've shared, the trials we've undergone, have proved to me that you're a better man than you now seem. *You may be weak.* I am not blind to your forgivable flaws. I will hold up the shield of love until this momentary aberration passes. *But you're not evil or cruel.* If you deny this, you accept an accusation that will strip away your prized humanity.

And all this without a conscious thought on her part, without fore-planning. How miraculous women are in matters of the heart!

He waited for her to continue.

"Whatever happens from now on, the picture of you—and this woman —will come between us. But I've decided not to allow this mistake—no matter how senseless, how awful—to ruin what we have. I'm going to make every effort to forget it happened . . ."

"Eleanor . . ."

". . . but only on one condition. You must never see this woman again. I don't say it won't be hard for me. But I want to save our marriage. And I'm not willing to let it be destroyed because of some cheap affair."

He answered steadily, "I can't accept your condition, Eleanor. A divorce seems the only honest way out."

She paused, staring. "I've just told you that I'm willing to forgive and forget. And you can stand there and say that you won't meet me halfway. What kind of a man are you?"

"There won't be any trouble about a settlement. Anything that's fair will be all right with me."

"I couldn't be that wrong about you. You're not the sort to throw away all the years we've had together, just to run to some strange whore and climb into her bed."

"We'd better stop this, Eleanor."

She bit her lower lip; the slightly protruding tooth rested on red flesh like a tiny pearl in a red velvet case. "I never believed you were like other men. But I see now that I misjudged you. You're like the rest in at least one way. Sex is all you think of. Sex, sex, sex!" She closed her eyes and lay back on the bed and was suddenly completely still. Then her knees opened slightly in a wanton pose. "Well, if that's all you want, we've had good times. You can't say we haven't."

A thick pressure filled Paul Lowe's head and his forehead became hot. He was so embarrassed for her that he could not look in her direction.

"Eleanor," he protested. "Please!"

She opened her eyes. "Is she better than I am in bed? Is that why?"

"I won't stay and listen to this."

Her eyes flashed emerald fire. "Is she younger and prettier? Well, it doesn't last! It's all the same. We're made the same way. One night you'll look at her and you won't want her either."

The pounding in his skull increased.

"For God's sake, stop it!"

"Oh, I'm hitting home! This hurts you, does it? I'm glad to see something does. I was beginning to wonder if you had any feelings."

It was worse than he had imagined. But what was revealing was that he could not be angry with her. If he had been capable of anger it would have meant there was unspent feeling between them. All he knew was pity, real compassion for her. And he was made ill by the cheapness and the violence of the quarrel . . . There was nothing else.

In silence he heard the room rustle. Eleanor had changed position— she was sitting up on the bed. In the slow deliberateness with which she put out her cigarette he divined a change in her mood. She appeared to be satisfied that she had taken her mite's bite of blood, and was ready to move on to a new phase.

"I realize that when something like this happens," she said, "the fault isn't entirely on one side. I must have failed somehow."

"That isn't so."

"It must be so or we wouldn't have come to this."

"None of this is your fault, Eleanor. I won't allow you to take the blame."

"I don't mind, because it's true," she said. "I'm willing to work at what I've been doing wrong. I'll need your help. You'll have to tell me what to do to make you happy." She smiled the sad smile of virtue. "Apparently it isn't enough to say that I love you. Because I do, you must know that."

"Eleanor, maybe you did love me once. But if you ask yourself honestly, you'll realize it's been over for us for some time. We've been going through the motions, that's all."

"Speak for yourself, Paul. You can't speak for me."

He was exhausted, unwilling to play this desperate game any longer. He had no answers—and her arsenal of questions was still full.

"We owe each other one more try," she said. "That isn't much to ask. We have twenty-three years invested in each other, Paul. I want to save them. Don't you want to?"

Perhaps they were using the same words to mean different things. The trouble with marriage, Arnold Bennett said, is its *dailiness*. But in Eleanor's

348

lexicon this quality was what saved a marriage. All the days and nights were weighed in the scales, to equal the sum of love. But for him love had to be a counterweight on the other side and without it the balance dipped down and down, grain by grain, hour by hour.

"I can't, Eleanor. I simply can't live with you. If I pretended I could, and went on from here, you'd end up hating me for it. There's nothing either of us can look forward to."

"How can you be so coldblooded? How can you talk to me as though I were a stranger?"

There were thousands and thousands of such queries still to come. He saw them stretching out into infinity, the numberless pages of some psychological questionnaire. No matter how he answered, with truth or with kindness, there was a small grade entered against each reply and the score added up tiny merit by tiny demerit until in the end he inevitably would lose and be classified. A brute.

"I'll help you in any way I can. You deserve that. I'll always do the best I can for you."

She began to cry a little. He wanted to shield her from further harm, even at his hands. The kindest thing was to go.

"Dear, I'm going to leave now. But I'll call you later and if there's anything you need . . ." The words sounded foolish. He broke off. It was so much easier to be kind than to be kind to a particular person.

She held herself stiffly, watching him with a kind of hatred while tears made glistening streaks down her cheeks.

"I warn you, Paul, if you go out that door I'll never take you back."

For just a moment she was Eleanor Olson, the prettiest girl in school, and no boy could push her around. He felt protective and tender toward the recaptured image, and terribly sorry for her because she could not maintain it.

"Goodbye, dear."

He went to the door.

"You'll never be happy with her. I promise you that!"

He opened the door and stepped into the hall.

"Get out!" she screamed after him. "I don't need you!"

He had gone a few steps down the hall when a heavy object hit the inside of the door and fell with a loud noise to the floor.

Downstairs, while he was taking his clothes from the closet, he stopped to listen. Footsteps creaked on the floor in her room. After a few moments the footsteps ceased and there was a deep sigh of bedsprings. After any sort of emotional upheaval Eleanor was fatigued—it was too much exertion for her either to repress or express emotion. She would be lying in bed and staring at the ceiling.

He went on with his packing. He could not risk going back although he would have liked to tell her something reassuring. But what? He was destroying the only achievement of her life by ending their marriage. It was a testimony to the grasp of false consciousness that she was still unaware of how little they had in common. She had kept on turning the pages of a calendar and somehow succeeded in concealing from herself the knowledge that all the dates were blank.

They had been dying the slow death. This moment, dreaded but necessary, was a quick scalpel that killed or cured. Now would come the surgical sense of release and at the same time the keen emptiness of something taken away, the longing of the patient for the tumor that was killing him.

There had been nothing else to do. It was not Eleanor's fault, nor Katherine's, possibly not even his. When the last excuse is spoken, the final explanation revealed, we find that we reach out toward life because our need is to survive.

24

Paul Lowe moved into a hotel on K Street only a few blocks north of the Supreme Court building. He worked on the articles he was doing about Burma for *Life* magazine and newspaper syndication. Work was therapy. No matter what the upheavals or travail of the divorce negotiations he could find a respite at his desk where work was waiting for him.

On September ninth, two days before the deadline, he delivered the articles by messenger to Race Hardman's home.

That night was the first in weeks in which he slept more than a few hours. He awoke refreshed and in his bathroom mirror he noticed a little color in his cheeks and his eyes looked brighter.

Race Hardman telephoned the hotel that afternoon.

"Paul, I've just finished reading your articles," he said. "I'd like to talk to you about them. Where and when?"

"Any place you say."

"How about my club? It's quiet there and we can talk."

When he arrived at the Universe Club, a quiet building on Embassy Row with no sign to identify it, he checked his hat and asked at the desk for Race Hardman.

"Mr. Hardman is in the steam room. But he's expecting you, Mr. Justice, and asked if you'd mind waiting in the lounge."

The lounge was a spacious room with a very high ceiling, and lifesized oil paintings of deceased Universe Club members in stiff and distinguished array along the walls. There was a double tier of bookcases, many small dark tables with newspapers and magazines, and a phalanx of huge black leather chairs.

He sat down and when a waiter appeared, he ordered a drink.

There were only two people in the room, both white-haired men in their seventies. One was reading *The Wall Street Journal,* and the other was ensconced in a chair at a window, looking out with monumental patience.

There are all sorts of endings, Paul Lowe thought, and the ending amid well-upholstered luxury can be as quietly desperate as any. Possibly these men would not have agreed that they were desperate—because for them monotony might be a refuge, a routine to be established and maintained in the same way that younger people maintain themselves with work and mechanized pleasures, the motion picture theater, TV screen, Sunday drive in the car, dinner at a restaurant, playtime with the children. The trick is to use up strength little by little so that we can go to bed tired. But underneath, and all men know it, there is another existence, running like a dark powerful stream full of danger and delight, fetid, torrential, self-engulfing, into which we enter at our peril because there is no turning back. Once the plunge is taken the risks must be accepted.

He felt a tingling sensation begin in his arms and shoulders and move into his chest. Katherine, he thought.

He was sipping his bourbon when Race Hardman appeared. Race wore a dark blue blazer and slacks, and a white shirt open at the collar to show a yellow ascot. He sank gracefully into the adjoining chair.

"I'm sorry to be late," he said. "But when that masseur gets to work he really gives me a workout." He flexed his shoulders. "I can still feel it aching inside."

"You're looking very sporty today, Race."

Race peered at him through his thick glasses. "Oh, I'm feeling fine. You look a bit granitic, though. That adventure in Burma must have taken something out of you. It's left you a bit more stern and Oriental. A cross between an unsmiling Buddha and a Western sheriff."

"That's the way I've always looked. You just haven't seen me for a while."

Race Hardman smiled and said, "Incidentally I've had copies of your articles made and sent them over to *Life*. They already have the photographs you took, don't they?"

"They didn't seem too pleased with those. But I tried to warn them I wasn't a photographer." He finished the last of the bourbon and put the glass on the table. "How about the articles? Are they the sort of thing you wanted?"

"Oh, they're fine," Race Hardman answered readily. "I like your impressions of the people and that stuff about the monsoon was good." He signaled the waiter and ordered a plain club soda. Then he turned back to Paul Lowe. "It's the damnedest thing, Paul, but I got the feeling that you had a real grasp of the political situation over there. I know the President feels the same way."

"Have you been talking to the President?"

"Yes, and you registered very favorably with him, Paul. He says you have an independent mind."

"That's ominous. It's my impression that Lamont Howard approves of only a limited amount of independence."

"Well, there are times he appreciates it more than other times," Race Hardman answered dryly. "Right now he's in an appreciative mood. He's aware that the man he's got over in Burma is a docile incompetent. And the military men he sends over there from time to time have bombs where their brains ought to be. He needs someone who's capable of a more flexible approach." The waiter brought the bottle of club soda with a glass on a tray. Race Hardman was silent until he left. "He needs *you,* Paul. Have you given any further consideration to the job he offered?"

"Yes, I have. But I'm inclined to think that I'm needed on the Court. Last session there were a disquieting number of five-four decisions. I don't expect things to get much better this year, since Bill Branch seems to have definitely joined Waldo Shuler's camp. That means Edmunson's liberal coalition can't spare a single member."

"Do you think the President would appoint a conservative justice in your place if you resigned?"

"You know he would, Race."

"But it's bound to happen sooner or later anyway. Edmunson can't keep going much longer. Another year at the most, and the President will have to appoint someone to Edmunson's chair."

"I hope it won't happen that soon."

"You can't prevent it. And if you accept the President's offer you can do yourself a lot of good politically. Foreign policy is the most important single issue in this country, Paul. That's where the reputations are being made. It's the way up the ladder for any ambitious man."

"I'm not that ambitious, Race. And I'm not at all sure I could acquit myself creditably in that field."

"Why not?"

"I'm not adept at that kind of maneuvering. For example, I couldn't have done what we did in Burma some years ago when we connived with Li Mi and his Nationalist Chinese against them shortly after they won their independence."

Race Hardman blinked. "That's not official, is it? No one has ever come right out and said we did that, have they?"

"But it's one reason the Burmese people won't take a stand with us against Red China. Unfortunately, I understand their point of view. I suppose that's what is meant by judicial temperament. One tends to see both sides of the coin."

"There aren't two sides when it comes to war or peace, Paul. And peace is what we're talking about. Take the President's offer and you'll be number two man in the State Department—wielding as much influence as the Secretary himself. And when the national political convention comes around in a couple of years you'll have a name they have to reckon with."

"I promised the President to consider it. I'm still doing that, Race. That's the only answer I can give you right now."

Race sipped his glass of soda. Then he asked cautiously, "By the way, where shall I address the proofs of your articles when I've finished editing them? I notice you have a new telephone number."

"I'm staying at a hotel." Paul Lowe mentioned the name of his hotel.

"Is Eleanor there with you?"

"No, she isn't." His voice seemed loud in the nearly empty lounge. The painted replicas of Universe Club members looked down with grave disapproval. "We've separated. Eleanor is going to get a divorce."

A flush stained Race Hardman's cheeks, standing out like bitten patches on the clear skin. "I'm sorry to hear that, Paul. You and Eleanor are two of my favorite people." He blinked. "Have you talked to Katherine?"

"Not recently. Not since I came back, as a matter of fact."

"I'm assuming that Katherine is the reason for this."

"There are a lot of reasons, Race. Our marriage simply wasn't working out. But I hope Eleanor and I will remain friends."

"Paul, I've watched too many marriages break up and no one ever remains friendly. It's too much to hope for. That's why I hope Eleanor won't find out about Katherine—at least until after the divorce is final."

"I'd like to keep Katherine out of it. I haven't even called to tell her about the divorce."

"That's wise, Paul. There wouldn't be any point anyhow. She's not at home."

"Where is she?"

"She took her son—he's been sick, you know—to a ranch in Arizona for a few weeks."

"Will you be in touch with her?"

"Probably."

"Don't tell her anything about my divorce. I'd rather she heard it from me."

"I won't breathe a word. In return, I'd like to get a promise from you, Paul."

"What?"

"Don't do anything foolish like trying to find out where she is and going to her."

"I have no intention of doing that."

"I don't know why I have this feeling that I have to protect you from yourself but for one of the smartest men I know you do some pretty dumb things. Until the divorce is final you'd better live like a monk. You understand the reason for that."

"Yes," Paul Lowe said. He also understood that Race Hardman's warning did not proceed out of a personal morality, a sense of moral equilibrium, but out of a belief that reputation must be preserved at any cost, that the credentials of a good character had to be in order and ready to be presented at short notice. Race conducted his own public life in a manner that was above criticism—and no one except a very few intimate and trusted friends knew of the clandestine visits to certain houses on the fringes of the slum district. Paul Lowe knew this because Race Hardman in a drunken careless mood had once tried to persuade him to go along. At the doorway of the house while Paul Lowe was still arguing with Race to go home and sleep it off, a blowsy redheaded Negress in a floral nightgown, smiling with pink lips, pink mouth, her fingernails enameled pearl, had come to draw Race in after her. Her bare feet were in heavy tufted sandals and she led him in as he giggled helplessly. "Meestah Peacock" she called him and the name's erotic significance reduced Race Hardman to an infantile delirium of delight.

That had been five years ago, and neither of them had since referred to the incident. He wondered now what Race Hardman would say if he did mention it. Race would doubtless freeze into an offended crystalline anger and that would be the finish of their friendship. No one could attack Race Hardman's dignity—that was a strike into the vitals.

The initial separation from Eleanor did not mark the end of his marriage. It was the beginning of similar emotional scenes on a diminishing scale with occasional flareups that almost brought the conflict back to maximum intensity. During the weeks after he left the house on Volta Place there were a series of acrimonious lunches, some embarrassing phone calls and letters from Eleanor, some humiliating entreaties in person which ended in one near-disaster when he drove her home afterward and she would not get out of the car until he agreed to enter the house with her.

He went with her, to avoid a scene and out of curiosity as to what she would try. What she tried was to seduce him. It was a terrible moment for them both. He finally struggled free of her embrace and told her gently but firmly that there was nothing to be gained, nothing whatever, from this sort of behavior. He appealed to her pride but touched her sense of shame. When he left her she told him that he could not return to the house, ever, unless he telephoned for permission. If he needed anything, such as clothes, or if there were any messages, he could leave word with the answering service and she would be sure his request was taken care of. Her coldness was face-saving after so much heat.

Shortly afterward they went to a lawyer. The meeting, which was supposed to discuss a property settlement and the amount of alimony, became something else when the lawyer made a dutiful attempt to effect a reconciliation. Eleanor had accumulated such reserves of resentment that she spilled venom. The meeting ended on a bitter and quarrelsome note, and the lawyer was convinced that there was no reasonable hope of bringing them together again. He suggested that they engage separate attorneys in Lincoln to handle their respective interests. He also suggested that Eleanor file the suit for divorce and that the grounds might be extreme cruelty—the minimum acceptable in the State of Nebraska.

With the articles on Burma finished, there was no work for him to do until the first Monday in October, when the new session of the Supreme Court would begin. The days became unbearably long. He was anxious to get back to the sort of demanding labor that would leave him less time to reflect on personal dilemmas.

A few days after his conversation with Race Hardman he saw Eleanor off on a plane to Lincoln, Nebraska. In the airport she scarcely looked at him until the time came to part at the gate.

Then she said tightly, "Don't you dare kiss me goodbye," and strode off down the gangway to the plane. He watched her go, touched by this odd streak of gallantry in her.

He returned to his hotel room and tried to read without success. He turned on the television set and mindlessly watched mindless pictures.

At three-thirty in the morning, Frances Langford was singing to him from a thirty-two year old musical comedy. Finally he turned off the screen.

In bed, he thought of Katherine and he could have sworn her fragrance was in the room. I'm starting to have hallucinations, he thought; he turned to the wall where hazel eyes welcomed him and a soft white throat rose above lovely breasts. How could unreal visions have such power to quicken his pulse? He would not allow himself to think of it. He was like a schoolboy waiting impatiently for the drudgery of the classroom to end. So little remained now to keep them apart. The prolonged time of separation would soon be over and he would see Katherine again.

A chilling thought occurred to him: what if something had happened to change the way she felt? Perhaps she did not want him any more. But she *must*. Perhaps she had met someone else. Impossible! There was no one else for him so there could be no one else for her. How did he know? The same causes that had kept him faithful must have been working in her. Same causes—same effects. Nothing could alter a true emotion. Nothing! He did not believe that. He had often witnessed the death of love. Time was the destroyer. If Katherine and he met after years, would they be the same with each other? Of course not. Even a little time changed something. So many things began from nothing and returned to nothing. A year ago he and Katherine had not even known each other. In some distant future . . . who could predict? Human relationships are unpredictable. Love between people does not grow as inevitably as an oak from an acorn; there are simply too many possibilities. Numberless possibilities. The human acorn could as well grow into a hedge row or a cactus plant.

They had been together, and were now apart. Why? Everything was so trivial—that unfortunate accidental meeting at the airport in St. Thomas, the drunken encounter with Tom Jeffreys at Dolores Hardman's party, her son Timmy's illness. Real events but as light as air, lacking in substance, and yet enough to build a wall between them. He might have died in a foreign land without ever seeing her again. There would have been some corner of a foreign land forever Katherine's.

He listened distractedly to his own mind recording this inconsequential chatter, linking on and on. . . .

In the morning he stopped by the house on Volta Place to pick up his mail. A huge package had arrived from his office containing a large part of the summer's accumulation of cert petitions with the memos prepared by his law clerks.

A note accompanying the petitions was from Jack Broderick, his law clerk, who said that the session ahead looked like the busiest in the Court's history. More than fourteen hundred petitions for certiorari were on hand. There would be batches arriving every week from now on until the official opening of Court.

The other mail was uninteresting—the usual collection of notes from friends and from acquaintances, and the usual volume of crank mail from people he had never known or met.

There was a short friendly letter from Ken Norris;

Dear Paul,

Obviously my last two letters fell into a well because you haven't answered them. If you are dead, send a postcard. If you're alive, I advise you to put aside all irrelevant business at once and get down to the hard labor of keeping up with your correspondence. How many old friends do you have that you can ignore *me* like this?

Write!

That's an order from

KEN

Judging from the tone of the letter Ken did not know anything about the impending divorce. Eleanor was in Lincoln but she might not be in a mood to communicate with friends. It would not be easy to tell Ken about the breakup in a letter but it would be far more difficult to tell him over the telephone. Although Ken Norris was his closest friend he had not told him anything about Katherine. Over the telephone Ken might ask questions that would have to be fended off with dishonest answers. But a letter could say as much or as little as one wished.

Paul Lowe returned to his hotel and sat down at the desk in his room to reply to Ken. He was writing the letter when his telephone rang.

"How are you, Paul?" It was Waldo Shuler. "I didn't know you were in town until I read about you in the *Capitol Tattler* last night."

"I didn't know there was anything about me. Why am I being honored with a mention?"

"Would you like me to read it to you? I've got it around here someplace."

Paul Lowe could almost see Waldo Shuler fitting his glasses in place before he heard the rustling of paper at the other end of the telephone.

"Here it is," Waldo said. " 'Mr. Justice Paul Lowe is staying at a fashionable hotel on K Street. His Georgetown home is vacant, and Mrs. Lowe is in Lincoln, Nebraska, Thinking Things Over. Could be that the marriage of our junior justice on the Supreme Court has finally reached Splitsville— on the Rocks?' "

"If I can make an item in the town's most widely read gossip column," Paul Lowe said, "I must be famous. 'Splitsville—on the Rocks.' A colorful vocabulary."

"If you ask me, these columnists can't read or write real English. That's why they invent a language of their own. If you took away their three dots they'd be practically speechless." He paused. "Is it true, Paul?"

"My wife is in Nebraska. And I'm here at the hotel."

"All right, it's none of my business. But I'm glad you're in town. So far as I know, none of the others has arrived. They won't be here for another week or two. So why don't we have dinner? Come to my house. My wife learned how to cook in the hardest school of all—mine. I promise you a fine meal and we'll sneak in a game of chess later."

"Thanks, Waldo. I'd enjoy that."

"Pick your night."

"How about Thursday?"

"Thursday is fine. About seven."

Anna Shuler came in from the kitchen wheeling the serving cart. Anna was a formidable woman, almost two hundred pounds, who wore a black tent of a dress and a copper necklace and earrings. She had dark hair, dark eyes, and a flawless complexion that indicated she might once have been pretty.

"Ah," Waldo Shuler said, rubbing his hands with anticipation. "My wife calls this her bread-and-butter soup. Wait until you taste it."

His daughter Sara said nothing. She kept her head slightly down and her eyes fixed on the table. She was fifteen, very thin but attractive in an old fashioned way. She wore her hair in a bun on the back of her neck.

The bread-and-butter soup was delicious, a rich and meaty mixture.

Waldo Shuler wiped his mouth with a napkin. "How did you like it?"

"Fantastic," Paul Lowe said.

"Wait until you try the stuffed veal with the noodle pudding. I don't believe it myself even though I taught her everything she knows. In French and German and Italian cooking I've got her beaten, but she has a feeling for Jewish cooking that no one can equal—not even me. You can't argue with five thousand years of tradition. A really good Jewish cook gets something through the genes. She doesn't cook food—she has a love affair with it and then puts it on the table."

The stuffed veal with noodle pudding was, as Waldo Shuler had predicted, a gastronomic experience. Daughter Sara bent studiously to her plate, using her fork and knife with quick movements that made the act of eating seem furtive. In between mouthfuls she had a habit of chewing her lower lip that Paul Lowe found distracting. He made one or two attempts at conversation with Sara and got nothing back but a mechanical and toneless response that finally discouraged him from trying.

"Did you get your bundle of certs in the mail?" Waldo Shuler asked.

"I picked them up the other day. Looks like a busy session."

"Oh, we'll winnow 'em down. We've got a whole week of conferences before Court starts hearing cases ten days from now." Waldo Shuler fingered the scar over his eye in a worried gesture. "But there are a lot of touchy and difficult problems on the agenda."

"Nothing particularly new in that, is there, Waldo?"

"One thing is new. The atmosphere in which we're going to attack the problems." He guided a forkful of pudding to his mouth and chewed thoughtfully. "We've inherited a lot of bad will, Paul. The way I look at it, it's something like pushing that snowball up a hill. We've been pushing and resistance has been getting bigger all the time. It wouldn't take much to make that snowball turn right around and roll over us."

358

"We can't worry about that, Waldo. We have to do our jobs."

"It wouldn't be the first time we kept a thermometer in the public's mouth to see how hot under the collar it's getting. Remember the New Deal Court—and the 'switch in time that saved nine'?"

"The situation was different then. The Court was vetoing all attempts to deal with the Depression. And Congress was about to pass a bill to reorganize the Supreme Court."

"There's a pretty big minority in Congress right now that's pushing for a constitutional amendment to limit the powers of the Court. After the elections in November there are going to be some new voices added to the clamor. The uproar is coming in from all sides, Paul. Civic groups, newspapers, magazines—even lawyers. The leader of some Bar Association out West said the other day that the Supreme Court is a stalking horse for the Communist conspiracy in this country."

"We can't worry about the crackpot fringe, Waldo."

"It isn't only the crackpot fringe. Have you been reading the newspapers? In almost every state of the Union a politician will be running for office on a platform of denouncing the Supreme Court. It isn't only in the South, where they hate us for civil rights, but in the North, West and East where they're saying we're soft on Communism. If the international situation gets any worse, that kind of pressure will build up."

"What do you think we should do, Waldo? Refuse to declare what we believe the Constitution says? We can't simply abandon our duties."

"When the Court opens I think we ought to work on repairing our image."

"What sort of image do you think we should have, Waldo?"

"The Supreme Court is supposed to be made up of justices who are fair-minded, impartial, hardworking, serious-minded legal scholars. A justice of the Supreme Court can't be a partisan."

Anna Shuler and daughter Sara cleared away the plates. There was apple strudel for dessert, hot and flaky, accompanied by cups of furnace-hot tea.

"Good, huh?" Waldo Shuler asked with a mouthful of strudel.

"Great."

"It's a wonder Jewish men don't die of indigestion by the time they're thirty. All Jewish cooking tastes wonderful and practically nothing is digestible."

Paul Lowe tested the sides of his teacup with his thumb and middle finger. It was scorching hot.

"Have you been trying to fatten me up for the slaughter, Waldo?"

"What's that mean?"

"All this talk about the fierce climate of public opinion. The suggestion that we should crawl into some sort of dugout shelter for the duration. Could that be just another attempt to win me over to your side?"

Waldo Shuler answered somberly, "I'm like any good salesman. I like to peddle my product. But this time I'm really worried."

"All right." Paul Lowe smiled. "I was just starting to wonder if you were practicing the same black magic on me that won Bill Branch over."

Waldo Shuler opened his palms outward. "See? Nothing up my sleeves."

"That's what a magician always says—just before he picks the jack of spades from behind your ear."

Anna Shuler and daughter Sara enjoyed this. Anna Shuler's enormous body swelled with repressed laughter. Daughter Sara sniffled into her hand.

Waldo Shuler sighed. "I wish I could think it wasn't serious. But this kind of real crisis shows up regularly every thirty years or so. The trouble lies quiet in the interval, building up a head of steam. And now it's time again for a real blowoff against the Court."

"If it comes we'll survive it, Waldo. Since the first days of the Republic there have been attacks on the Supreme Court. Remember the toast: 'To the Judiciary of the United States—independent of party, independent of power, and independent of popularity.' That was said a hundred and sixty years ago and it's still true. For a Court that can't use physical force to carry out any of its decisions, has no taxing power, and has to rely on Congress to supply its funds to stay in business and the President to see to it that anyone listens to what it says, we haven't done too badly."

Waldo Shuler shook his head dolefully. "I'm still worried. I'm not kidding, Paul. We all have to pull together to get the Court through the storms ahead."

Paul Lowe's mail that morning had brought a dozen copies of a cartoon that had recently appeared in a right-wing tabloid. It showed the Supreme Court as a puppet with Charles Edmunson as puppet master and in the foreground an evil blackbearded audience of one, labeled The Kremlin, giving the performance his enthusiastic approval. Over a million copies of the cartoon had been reprinted and many of them were being mailed directly to the justices of the Supreme Court. Most of the cartoons were addressed to those justices who voted with Edmunson in the so-called liberal coalition on the Court.

Waldo Shuler might be justified in worrying, Paul Lowe thought. Most of the letters were from people who were doing more than exercise their American right to entertain a low opinion of him. The letter writers were rabid with anger *and* frustration, and there was no worse combination than that.

On the whole the Supreme Court was becoming a battlefield where a part of the war for men's minds was being fought. The Founders had faith that the benefits to be gained from a free interchange of ideas far outweighed the dangers. "I have sworn an oath upon the altar of Almighty God to combat every form of tyranny over the mind of man." Paul Lowe shared Jefferson's faith—and he wanted, more than anything, to have the right to continue to fight for it.

It was then he decided he would have to tell the President he would not resign and accept the offer of another post. He was going to stay on the Court and wage the battle for what he believed with whatever powers he possessed.

"I can see I'm starting to worry you, too," Waldo Shuler said.

360

"A little."

"It's something to worry about, believe me, Paul."

"Would it make you feel better to beat me in a game of chess?" Waldo Shuler brightened. "How about it?"

Paul Lowe nodded. "What have I got to lose but self-respect?"

25

At precisely ten o'clock on Monday morning, the second week in October, the red velvet draperies behind the justices' bench parted with a flourish and the Marshal banged his gavel.

"The Honorable, the Chief Justice, and the Associate Justices of the Supreme Court of the United States."

Eight justices stepped quickly through three separate openings in the draperies.

The Marshal intoned:

"Oyez! Oyez! Oyez! All persons having business before the Honorable, the Supreme Court of the United States of America are invited to draw near and give their attention, for the Court is now sitting."

The page boys pulled back the chairs. The eight justices waited in their places. One place of the nine was empty. For the first time in his long career on the Supreme Court bench, Charles Edmunson had been unable to attend the opening. He was confined at home suffering from the aftereffects of a badly infected tooth that had been extracted only that morning. His tall black chair beside the Chief Justice's looked oddly abandoned with no one standing behind it.

The Marshal said, "God save the United States and this Honorable Court."

Edward McCann bowed his head as the Marshal called upon God's help. Covertly glancing down the line Paul Lowe saw that the Chief Justice and Henry Merriam at the far right of the bench had also bowed their heads. The liberal bloc was well represented in this mark of reverence to the Deity. There was a divided vote among the conservatives. Gabriel Hart and Andrew Cutler stood with heads bowed but Waldo Shuler and Bill Branch stared straight ahead until the Marshal finished speaking. Then all the justices took their seats behind the bench.

While the Chief Justice was occupied with the ceremonies of admitting new lawyers to practice before the Court, Paul Lowe glanced out over the courtroom. After the ceremonial opening the preceding week the preliminary work had been finished in the conferences. Now they were beginning a regular schedule. For the next few months, each two weeks of arguments would alternate with two weeks of recess during which opinions would be written, read, debated, rewritten and circulated again.

In the second row of the public section a woman caught his attention. She looked a little like Katherine. She was seated slightly to the left, two seats from the aisle. Paul Lowe could hardly keep his eyes off her and was finally forced to stare down at his desk to avoid attracting her attention.

Blood was pounding at his ears and mounting to his face.

God, how he missed Katherine!

When all the lawyers had been admitted, Chief Justice John Hampton announced the first case to be heard:

"Number 28. Grange Trust Company versus the Federal Reserve Board."

Paul Lowe had before him his typewritten notes on the briefs that had been filed with the Court Clerk by the competing attorneys. The Forstmann National Bank wanted to establish a branch by means of a holding company, enabling it to avoid the geographical restrictions of the National Banking Act. The Federal Reserve Board had approved the plan, but a competing bank, the Grange Trust Company, promptly moved to prevent the branch from opening for business. In the resulting legal tangle all parties finally had to seek a definitive answer from the Supreme Court.

The attorney for the Grange Trust Company took his place at the lectern that stood directly in front of the Chief Justice's seat at the center of the bench.

Above his desk a fly buzzed almost directly over the complicated black veining of typewritten sentences on the page. Paul Lowe looked to where the Court's official reporter and several newsmen were seated at small desks below and in front of the bench. If all the cases in a year were like this one, he thought, I would go out of my mind. The issue was technical and hardly anyone except the parties themselves cared how the decision would come out. Most of the newsmen were down in the press room on the ground floor, going through the list orders that had been filed with the Court Clerk and looking for an item of interest to the general public. This morning the result of the labor of the previous week had been made known. The Court had disposed of more than four hundred cases, rejecting all but thirty-seven outright. Of the thirty-seven, there had been eight in which the judgments of lower courts were summarily affirmed and five in which the judgments were summarily reversed. That left a total of twenty-four cases in which the Court agreed to give plenary consideration to the issues involved and arguments were scheduled for later in the year.

Still, the fly buzzed. Keeping his eyes downcast, Paul Lowe reached out with a free hand. He hoped this maneuver would outwit the pasty intruder. Think I can't see you, don't you?

The attorney at the lectern was saying, "The respondent's attempt to find support for the Federal District Court's asserted jurisdiction under the Administrative Procedure Act . . ."

Now.

A quick flip of the wrist and the palm of his hand trapped the fly against the desk top. Smiling, the fly fell dead. Not wounded, sire, but dead.

He swept the carcass into the wastebasket.

When they recessed for lunch, Edward McCann walked beside him through the corridor on the way to the private dining room.

"Well, how does it feel to get back in harness?" McCann asked.

"I'm enjoying it. It's just bad luck that we had to hear a banking case on our first morning."

They entered the dining room where lunch was waiting. As Paul Lowe was methodically cutting up his Salisbury steak, Edward McCann leaned over to put a fleshy arm on the back of his chair.

His voice was low and confidential. "By the way, has anyone spoken to you about Edmunson?"

"What about him?"

"The Chief told me yesterday that the Old Man has had a rough summer. Had a couple of minor sinking spells. The Chief doesn't think he's snapped back from them. Have you noticed anything?"

At the conference last week, Edmunson had not seemed to be quite his old self. But this was not a thought he wanted to share with anyone.

"He looks about the same to me," Paul Lowe said.

McCann nodded, relieved. "He's no spring chicken. But my father at eighty-one is as spry as ever and I've got an uncle who still goes to work every day and plays cards with his friends at night. Not to mention my maternal grandfather and grandmother, bless 'em, who are in their nineties."

For generations the McCanns had been reproducing like rabbits. Both of McCann's parents were still living and so were two of his grandparents and as nearly as Paul Lowe could make out McCann had at least four brothers and three sisters and an almost infinite amount of nieces and nephews.

"I'm sure the Old Man is good for a couple of years yet," Paul Lowe said.

Edward McCann sat back in his own chair and the wool of his trousers stretched over his flattened thigh.

"That's what I told the Chief," he said.

Paul Lowe smiled. "Did you cite the precedent of your own family? You can use them to convince anyone of almost anything—especially longevity. Just between us, Edward, do you have any relatives who would prove man's life on earth is short and full of trouble?"

McCann said, "That would be Uncle Timothy. Dead at fifty-three, and hardly enough insurance money to bury him. Of course he didn't go of what you might call natural causes. He fell off a trolley car on a hill in San Francisco and broke his neck. So Uncle Timothy was something of an exception. The rest of us all suffer from the Curse of the McCanns. We're Catholic, we live practically forever, enjoy sex, and confine our activities to our wives. The end result of such a Curse as you can plainly see, is children."

"Your tribe'll end up inheriting the earth."

McCann nodded soberly. "My great-uncle Duncan used to say that in a thousand years there'd be only two races left on earth. The McCanns and the minority."

By the time Court adjourned at two-thirty they had also heard cases dealing with a federal law regulating trade with the Indians, and a state law which permitted a child to be adopted by foster parents without prior notice to the mother, who was under treatment in a sanitarium.

Paul Lowe returned to his office to face the accumulated petitions and briefs to be read, notes from other justices to weigh and consider, letters to be answered. Martha Scully was hard at work at her desk in the main office and she scarcely looked up as he entered. It was amazing. This first official day on the Court was proceeding as though this had been the routine for weeks. In the clerks' office he heard the clatter of a typewriter. That was the only change—Bill Tobin was gone. Tobin's replacement was a tall, good-looking, self-assured young man who had been recommended by Ken Norris. The young man's name was Harry Temple.

Paul Lowe had been working almost two hours when he heard a cheerful mingling of voices in the outer office, one masculine and exuberant, the other Martha Scully's, controlled but amused.

The next moment the door to Paul Lowe's private office swung wide open. Ken Norris crossed the room quickly to wring Paul Lowe's hand.

"Paul!"

"Ken, I didn't have any idea you were in town. Why didn't you let me know?"

"It was a last-minute decision. I'm running around on behalf of William Weaver." Ken sat down in a chair and extended his short legs before him. "The money isn't coming in and I've used up too much of Everyman's Legal Guild treasury so I came to Washington looking for a few fat cats with consciences."

"There ought to be enough of that breed around."

Ken shook his head discouragedly. "A lot of people resent my trying to do anything at all for Weaver. They seem to think he should die just because he's socially undesirable."

"How is the legal end of it going?"

"Oh, I've lost all the skirmishes. But I may still win the war. I won't bore you with the legal stratagems by which I've tried to keep the poor bastard out of the hot seat," Ken Norris said. "It's been so close a couple of times that even *my* legal bottom got a little burned. But he's still alive and I still haven't played all my cards."

"Suppose everything fails, Ken. Are you prepared for it? You've put a lot of time and effort into this, but there's a very good chance you won't win."

Ken managed a grin but his eyes didn't join in it. "Oh, I'll stand by bravely while William Weaver goes to his death for a crime that isn't half as serious—and a lot less permanent in its effect—than murdering a small boy after having kidnaped him for ransom."

"Why pick that analogy?"

"I was thinking of Loeb and Leopold. They had fifteen million dollars and Clarence Darrow, so they weren't executed but packed off to prison.

Poor William Weaver has not one red cent and has yours truly instead of Clarence Darrow. A staggering disproportion. And that's the real reason that William Weaver probably will enjoy the privilege of being legally murdered. The privilege is reserved for poor bastards like him."

"That's a pretty cynical statement, Ken. I don't mind your getting involved with William Weaver, but I am going to mind if it makes you bitter."

"I don't know whether it will make me permanently bitter but I'm certainly entitled to unload a wagonload of moral indignation. That's the only satisfaction I'm ever going to get out of this case. I haven't earned a dollar since I took it and I'm not likely to for some time to come. But I can't quit, because at this moment no one stands between William Weaver and the electric chair except me. And if he dies, it will be punishment not according to the degree of the crime but according to the degree of poverty. That's enough to shake any man's faith in equality before the law."

Paul Lowe steepled his hands and looked over them at the bookshelves in his office with the fat closely aligned beige-colored volumes with embossed black and red titles.

"Well," he said, "I don't think you're going to get anywhere arguing equal protection of the laws. But there might be an Eighth Amendment question here."

"How?"

"Cruel and unusual punishment is forbidden by the Eighth Amendment."

Ken Norris stared at Paul Lowe for a moment. "The question would be whether the Constitution forbids the deliberate taking of a man's life by the government."

"Or whether it forbids the death penalty for any crime less than murder. That's a narrower question."

Ken rubbed his slightly pockmarked chin. "Either way it's a large-sized question. I'd have to challenge the whole concept of capital punishment."

"But the Supreme Court has held that the Constitution forbids the levying of any penalty which is unduly harsh in relation to the crime. So William Weaver's death sentence for having committed a rape without killing the victim might fall within the definition of cruel and unusual punishment."

Ken Norris got up with the air of a man who realizes time is short. "It's one hell of an idea, Paul. I always said you were a better lawyer than I am." He went to the window and then came back to Paul Lowe's desk. "You realize that I'd probably end up arguing this case before the Supreme Court?"

"That's the only place it can be finally decided."

Ken Norris sat down in the chair and his stocky figure turned boneless with despondency.

"Taking it into the federal courts would mean a whole new battle. Everyman's Legal Guild simply hasn't any funds left for this sort of thing."

"That's a real problem. I can sympathize, Ken, but I don't know what to tell you to do."

Ken Norris sat up straighter in his chair. His tone altered slightly. "I want to talk to you about something else, Paul. About Eleanor."

"Is anything wrong?" he asked.

"Not exactly wrong, Paul."

"Is she all right? She's not ill or anything?"

"She's unhappy. She was at our house for dinner the other night and told us she's going to file suit for a divorce. Sheila got all watery, Eleanor broke down and . . . Oh, damn! This is actually the reason I'm here, Paul. I'm supposed to sound you out on the possibility of a reconciliation."

"I see."

"I should be more subtle, but I can't play games with you, Paul. Is there any chance?"

Paul Lowe thought, I would have stayed with Eleanor if I could. I had no desire to make her unhappy and if I could have made myself love her by an act of will I would have done it. Some things are not possible.

He said, "I don't think so, Ken."

"You ought to be damn sure before you let her go ahead with a divorce. I know that Eleanor still cares for you and is more than willing to give it another try."

On the wall between the window and the corner bookcase were several rectangular photographs in black wooden frames. One of the photographs was of Eleanor and himself with Nancy when Nancy had been about four years old. Why should anyone expect or want a marriage like ours to last? What would make for such durability? Because we were schoolmates together? Because we practiced adolescent lust in the balcony of movie theaters? We had a child and it was our duty to raise and protect her. When the child is gone, does the duty remain?

What of other young people now being drawn to each other by awakening desires? Even now, this minute, they are meeting on blind dates, being introduced at dances, accidentally finding each other in bus or train, assigned to the same class in school or working in the same office. What will they require of each other? Only that they should be of approximately the same age, same degree of attractiveness, the same race and if possible the same religion. It would also be nice if the boy were taller. That satisfies the basic requirements. But I would counsel caution. In fact, let caution be your watchword. All the instruments agree about the bad girl who is really good but if you are thinking of marriage, beware, beware the good girl who is really dull.

He said, "There isn't any use prolonging something in which neither of us can find happiness."

"You managed pretty well for a long time." Ken pulled his legs back to the chair. "Look, I'm not taking sides. I'm trying to be your friend— and Eleanor's too. You were in love with her once, Paul."

Was I? How do you know, Ken? The truth is that I was not in love with Eleanor when I married her and our years of living together did nothing to awaken love. We lived those years between habit and monotony.

"I'm afraid, Ken, that a reconciliation is out of the question."

"Well, then, is there any rush about getting a divorce?"

"Why do you ask?"

"I'm sure Eleanor would agree to a legal separation instead. That would let some of the dust settle. You might both feel differently in six months or a year."

"It wouldn't be fair to either of us. Ken, you'll have to take my word that I've thought this through. I know what has to be done—and the quicker it's done the better for Eleanor's sake as well as mine."

Ken Norris gave him a smile that came off rather oddly.

"Is there someone else?" he asked.

Paul Lowe answered slowly, "You've done the job you came for, Ken. Why don't we stop here? I appreciate what you've been trying to do."

Ken said, "Don't be offended, Paul. For you to fall in love with her, she'd have to be quite a gal." He put his hands on his knees and stood up, a short stocky blond slightly balding man. "But there is something more I'd like to say, if you promise not to take it the wrong way."

"I'll try not to."

Ken grimaced. "Proceed at my own risk, eh? All right. A friend has to speak out at certain times if he's going to be a real friend. Just keep in mind that even if you get married again it can't all be a hundred percent. You have to settle for less or you'll end up pretty disillusioned. I love Sheila but nobody has to tell me she isn't the smartest woman in the world. We get along because I don't expect marriage to be the last word in joy."

Ken's friendliness was genuine, but his motivation was impure. Ken was aware of being somehow an outsider, beyond the circle of intimacy which Paul Lowe shared only with Katherine. Ken and Sheila had a good marriage by most standards: content with each other, comfortable with each other, occupied with mutual chores involving home, career, and children. In the company of other couples like themselves they had no reason to feel that they were missing anything. All the crises that might threaten their marriage were properly provided for in the handy pocket-sized moral code that governed such matters. Unfaithfulness? Not to be forgiven, but wisely to be ignored. Apathy? To be romantically involved with each other after so many years of marriage would be regarded as faintly neurotic. A lack of interests in common? We have at least one: we have stood together at the gravesite where love now lies buried.

Eleanor and I did fit well into the pattern of this sort of marriage. Now there's been a break and with the first break the whole mutual structure is imperiled because no marriage is safe if the others begin to suspect there may be something more than is prescribed by ritual. So the first thing to renounce is joy, because if joy is to be the criterion we shall have to be compulsive about it as about every other goal in our compulsive society. We shall have to ask: am I enjoying it enough? Or: why have I failed to enjoy?

"I don't think I'm expecting too much, Ken," Paul Lowe said.

"Good. Then all I can honestly say is that I'm damn sorry it happened. And I hope both Eleanor and you will find someone else to make you happier." Ken shrugged. "I guess there just isn't any way for everyone to be happy at the same time, is there?"

Paul Lowe was struck by this sad truth.

"I guess not," he said.

The agreement drawn up by Eleanor's attorney after several conferences with Paul Lowe's attorney was a workmanlike document. All the furniture and most of the household objects in the house on Volta Place in Georgetown would go to Eleanor, also stocks and bonds in a list appended, and seven hundred dollars monthly support. Additional payments were provided for in the event of medical or dental bills, and Paul Lowe undertook to maintain payments on Blue Cross, Blue Shield, health and accident insurance, and a seventy-five-thousand-dollar life insurance policy.

Seated at the desk in his office, Paul Lowe read over the agreement.

Whereas the parties hereto are husband and wife, having been married in the city of Omaha, Nebraska, on April 13th, 1943, and . . .

On their wedding night Eleanor had prepared herself like a sultan's favorite. Perfume behind the ears. She had worn a transparent or nearly transparent pale pink nightgown. There was artful lamplight on the bed (how she must have planned it!) and the scene teetered very near the edge of a comic seduction.

Whereas unhappy differences have arisen between the said parties by reason of which they have agreed to live separate and apart . . .

In the early years she was not aware how she overdid her provocative walk, her languidness. She knew that true sex appeal demands a sort of indolence and indirection but she did not know that it also required a saving core of self-mockery—and she was incapable of that. After a while her public manners improved.

Paul Lowe read on through half-lidded eyes.

Each of the parties releases and forever discharges the other party hereto, his or her executors, administrators and assigns from every type of action and cause of action, such as, but in no way limited to, lawsuits, debts, bonds, bills, dues, accounts, promises, agreements, covenants, special assessments, damage, claims, trespasses, variances, executions, controversies and demands, whether in equity or in law, which one has against the other or which the heirs, executors, administrators and assignees of each party can, shall, or may have against the heirs, executors, administrators or assignees of the other party hereto, by reason of any matter, cause or thing whatsoever . . .

369

Lawyers suffer from a passion for overexplaining minor details that is close to an obsession. There ought to be a name for this kind of obsessional legalistics, Paul Lowe thought. *Dementia minutiae.* When you can put a name to something it doesn't bother you as much.

Nevertheless he was relieved when the door opened and Martha Scully came in to interrupt his reading.

"Mr. Justice Merriam just sent this note over by messenger."

He opened the envelope.

Paul—will you stop by for a few minutes? Something I've got to talk to you about. It concerns Charles Edmunson.

HENRY

Henry Merriam's office was around a bend of the corridor from Paul Lowe's suite.

"You can go right in, Mr. Justice," Merriam's secretary said.

Henry Merriam was standing near the window of his private office. He was a sartorial wonder in a faultless fitting light gray suit with a well-fashioned black knit tie set correctly into the starched collar of his snow-white shirt. He wore figured black onyx cufflinks.

Paul Lowe had never been able to decide whether Henry Merriam was a handsome man or a handsome production. It was the same difficulty he experienced in watching well turned out motion pictures in which the gloss was so thick it took the place of substance.

"I got your message," Paul Lowe said. "What's it about?"

Henry Merriam kept his hands clasped behind his back. His usually genial face was set in forbidding lines.

"I've just had an insulting note from Edmunson."

"I can't believe that."

"It's about my opinion in the Graziani case. Read it for yourself."

Paul Lowe read the handwriting with difficulty:

I find this rather trashy effort totally unworthy of the issue at stake—unsound in reasoning and capricious in its disregard of the central problem. I'm very disappointed, Henry. You need to do some hard thinking. I'll be glad to help you work out the proper approach.

"Well?" Henry Merriam demanded.

"I don't blame you for being annoyed. It doesn't even sound like Edmunson."

Merriam's resentment spilled over: "He thinks he's a goddamned sage who's above and beyond the rest of us. He's finally sold himself on his own legend!"

"Perhaps if you discuss it with him . . ."

"I won't climb Mount Olympus to beg a cup of wisdom from him. I'll see him damned before I will!"

370

Paul Lowe studied the note carefully. "You know, it doesn't even look like his handwriting."

"Are you trying to say he didn't write it? It was delivered by his own messenger."

"Look at it again, Henry. Tell me what you think."

Henry Merriam stared at him, then came over and stood beside him to examine the note.

The handwriting was familiar but strange. The letters were feebly formed and trailed off so that words faded to near illegibility. The bold pen stroke, once so liberal in its use of ink, was nowhere in evidence. This was the spidery and wavering ghost of Charles Edmunson's penmanship.

Merriam said faintly, "I agree with you, Paul. It's not like him at all. Do you think he's ill?"

"I don't know. Physically he seems in good fettle. He only missed a couple of days after that tooth extraction."

"Something else I've noticed. He's taken to calling me 'sonny,'" Merriam said ruefully. "And he starts a lot of sentences with things like, 'When I get to be as old and wise as you gentlemen . . .'"

"I know." Paul Lowe frowned, then went on, "Haven't you found him much more argumentative? This note is an extreme example of what I mean."

"Not particularly. Of course I don't always agree with him these days and that always bothered the Old Man."

"He used to be a master of give and take in order to arrive at a decision in common with other men of vigorous opinions. Think about it, Henry. Hasn't that changed, particularly in the last few weeks?"

Merriam said slowly, "I suppose it's true that he's had a tendency to treat his own work as sacrosanct—not to be amended. He acts as though he's already an historical figure, an equal of John Marshall and Oliver Wendell Holmes."

"That isn't the Charles Edmunson we've always known."

Henry Merriam considered this. "I put it down to his growing older, Paul," he said. "Maybe he's worried that he'll overstay his time on the Court—go the way Grier and Field and Holmes did. And he's probably tired. I'll bet he's tired a lot of the time. That's bound to make anyone irritable." Merriam's anger had disappeared. His smoothly shaven face had become a compound of kindness and concern. "What do you think, Paul?"

The silence endured long enough to create its own meaning.

Paul Lowe said, "The Chief thinks Edmunson is going downhill. It's possible he's started to slide away from us."

Henry Merriam was watching Paul Lowe with a curious intentness.

"Paul . . . Listen, I'm not angry. I just had to blow my top a little, that's all." His commanding and distinguished presence gave what he said a brief authority: "The Old Man needs a little encouragement. It always renews his vitality when someone compliments him. He needs to get back his confidence in himself."

"Do you really think that's the trouble?"

"I do," Merriam said. "Yes, I do. You've always been his favorite. If anyone can do anything for him, you can. Why don't you go to see him?"

"What can I do?"

Henry Merriam was bemused by a memory. "I remember last March he came into my office to read me one of your opinions. I had the printed opinion right in front of me but he sat there and read it to me aloud. He was like a proud father reading his favorite son's first essay. I swear at that moment his cup ran over."

Paul Lowe was more touched than he dared to show. He felt an unexpected tension in his jaw muscles. "What can I say to him?"

"Tell him he's got to take it easier. Tell him how we need him on the Court. We can have our disagreements, but he's a great man, Paul—maybe the greatest man we'll ever know."

"I'm aware of that, Henry."

"It doesn't matter if he can't do as much as he used to. . . . What would we do without him? If he left us? *That's* the important thing."

Paul Lowe nodded. "I'll go to see him tonight." He held up the note in his fingers. "But I'll talk to him about this too."

"You can forget about that," Merriam said. "Of course it may be a sign he's getting on . . . but that doesn't mean we're going to lose him. Not Edmunson."

There were tears in Henry Merriam's eyes.

Before he visited Charles Edmunson that evening Paul Lowe looked through the briefs in the Graziani case and reread Henry Merriam's opinion. The Graziani case concerned a novel of the Renaissance which had been published in Italy, banned, published in France and finally brought out in the United States. The novel by Alfredo Graziani had been widely praised by many critics and roundly condemned by many religious and civil leaders. In dealing with his central character, Pope Leo X, Alfredo Graziani had not skimped the story of papal love affairs. One critic remarked that in one sense the novel might almost have been classed as a family chronicle because it related events in the lives of so many of Pope Leo X's illegitimate children.

There was a strong erotic quality in the narrative, considered apart from its setting, and its attitude toward religion was sacrilegious and highly contemptuous.

Nevertheless the characters were vividly conceived, richly alive and treated with what would appear to a post-Freudian reader as true and original insights. During the two years of the book's exile, while it was being read abroad, Graziani's literary reputation had flourished amid violent controversy. Catholics, in particular, were outraged at the portrait of a licentious Pope, living in carnality and corruption, and dismissing Christianity as a "profitable fable."

The case that reached the Supreme Court involved the Federal Post Office, which had seized several copies of Graziani's novel that were being shipped to a Brooklyn post-office box. The lawyer for the publisher pointed out the inherent difficulty with the federal obscenity law under which the book had been seized. The law sought to punish a communication for impure sexual thoughts regarding an historically important religious figure but did not show how this was in any way related to overt antisocial conduct. Therefore the law punished thoughts rather than deeds. On the other side the counsel for the Post Office maintained that since obscenity is fundamentally repulsive to society it could be prohibited without any proof of its tendency to cause actual antisocial conduct.

At eight-thirty that evening Paul Lowe went to visit Charles Edmunson at his home. He found Edmunson in the library, seated in a huge armchair near the fireplace with a plaid blanket drawn up over his knees. Edmunson was delighted to see him.

For almost an hour they talked as they had in the old days. They talked about music, the First World War, politics. The conversation veered from topic to topic with sinuous well controlled logic. Finally they began to discuss the work on the Supreme Court. Paul Lowe congratulated Edmunson for an opinion he had just written in a water fluoridation case. Then he brought up the subject of the Graziani case and Henry Merriam's opinion.

"Have you read Merriam's opinion?" Edmunson asked.

"Yes. As a matter of fact, I have a copy of it right here in my portfolio." Paul Lowe took out the printed pages.

"I'd be interested to hear what you think of it," Edmunson said.

"I think it will rank with his very best work."

Edmunson's bushy white brows lifted.

"No reservations?" he said.

"No reservations."

"Hm. I feel strongly . . . just the other way."

"Do you? Why?"

"He completely failed to grasp the ruling principle. I wrote Henry a strong note about it. The Graziani case is important—and he simply has to measure up to it."

"I agree on its importance, Charles. It's our first chance in some time to try to find a new—and more specific—definition of what constitutes obscenity." Paul Lowe looked directly at Edmunson. "I believe Henry Merriam succeeded in doing that. He points out that the judgment of obscenity can't depend on the impurity of thought a book causes in the mind of a reader. We can't punish a book for the kind of thoughts it may cause. We can't accept that standard. If we do, we have to allow judges and juries to declare many things besides books to be obscene—including certain kinds of music, many of our finest paintings, some of our best dramas and even certain social customs such as dancing or wearing tight sweaters or even cosmetics. All these are capable of causing impure thoughts. We have to tie our judgment of obscenity to overt acts of antisocial conduct."

"He didn't go far enough."

"His position will hold the majority of the Court."

"That's not what is important, Paul." Edmunson drew the blanket further up on his knees. "I commend to you the words of the Constitution. Plain but eloquent words. 'Congress shall make no law abridging freedom of speech.' Those words mean what they say and cannot be ignored. 'Congress shall make no law . . .' That means *no law*. Henry Merriam should have said that instead of pussyfooting around the issue."

"If he tried to say there should be no legal restrictions on anything published, I can tell you that Bill Branch and the Chief would never go along with it."

"He'd have to win them over. That's what I'd have done if the opinion were assigned to me, Paul. Merriam was too timid to make the attempt."

"I can't agree it was timidity, Charles."

"What would you call it?"

"It strikes me as common sense. He was writing for the Court and trying to meet the consensus on its own ground. That's one reason Henry Merriam was assigned this touchy opinion. The verdict will be more palatable coming from a man who has a unique ability to combine boldness with grace."

"He's *compromising*."

"The position you advocate, Charles, has never won a majority of the Court. It wouldn't have a majority now."

"You don't think I'm wrong, do you?"

"I don't see how an absolute rule like the one you suggest can be fitted to the needs of a nation of two hundred million people. It's too extreme. There would be no way for society to defend itself against even hardcore pornography."

"It's more dangerous the other way. Don't you see that, Paul? If we set up obscenity as a form of impermissible communication, what's to prevent some future despot from calling everything written or spoken against him 'obscene'? That's exactly what happened in Rome under Augustus Caesar."

"This isn't ancient Rome—it's the U.S.A. under President Lamont Howard. Nothing like that could happen, Charles."

"It's our duty to *prevent* it from happening. By establishing an absolute rule that Congress can make no law, ever, abridging freedom of speech."

He saw that further argument was useless. The Old Man was adamant— more so than he had ever known him to be.

"Well, if you feel that way, Charles, I guess you can write a concurring opinion. You can agree with Merriam's verdict, but for your own reasons."

Edmunson lifted a hand in disagreement—a gesture hobbled by an arthritic slowness.

"No, no, I intend to persuade him to try it my way. He has to take a firm stand. Total freedom of the press. He must . . . he *must*."

"I'll talk to him and let him know the basis of your objections."

Edmunson's deep voice rasped, "I've already let him know what I think. Let him come to me. I'm fully capable of explaining what I expect of him."

"I don't doubt that, Charles. But I think I'd better talk to him."

"Why?"

"Well, frankly, the sharp tone of your note hurt Henry's feelings."

"Tell him not to be so concerned with his damnable pride."

"He admires you very much, Charles. But you can't treat him like your errand boy."

"If he doesn't come around, I'll write a concurring opinion that will put his to shame. But I'd sooner allow him to have the honors. I don't care about the honors any more."

What a tiresome egoist Edmunson had become! Yet in the next instant Lowe was forced to concede that Edmunson's concurring opinion *would* be a distinguished contribution to the law. He had the power to translate his particular vision of truth into language that few men could gainsay. He could illumine dark corners that others had only been staring at and in an almost theatrical new light show clearly what had been there all the time. But such an opinion, no matter how majestic its sweep, would be merely an address to posterity.

It was past time to go. He began to gather up Henry Merriam's printed opinion sheets.

"We can discuss this some other evening," he said. "It's after ten o'clock."

Edmunson's large hand gripped the chair. "When you follow principle you're on the side of the angels. Remember, Paul, that God would change things if he happened to be anywhere around." The old man's head slowly sank forward on his chest. The deep voice became a hoarse whisper: "Not that it matters. We all make the same bones in the end."

Paul Lowe stuffed the printed pages into his portfolio and quickly stood up.

"I'll say good night now, Charles."

"Good night, Paul." The voice was barely audible. "Hell is closer to us."

"What?"

"And hell has its own laws. But they serve the needs of the devil."

In the fireplace a flaked log, burnt through, broke in the middle and settled in a shower of sparks. Edmunson was now asleep.

From the doorway Paul Lowe glanced back at him. Something he heard drew his attention back.

There was a deeper note in Edmunson's stertorous breathing.

"Charles," he said anxiously.

The huge chest rose and fell evenly. One hand moved across the plaid blanket. The long fingers strayed as though looking for a hidden pin in the wool.

Paul Lowe raised his voice a little. "Charles?" When he received no answer he added, "I'm leaving now."

The fireplace hissed and crackled. Edmunson's heavy breathing hoarsely deepened.

He said more loudly, "Charles!"

Edmunson's shaggy head stirred. Then his chin settled back on his chest and a moment later a dot of spittle appeared in a corner of his mouth.

He went back into the room to touch Edmunson's shoulder. The only response was a further sag in the heavy body. When he shook him gently the massive head wagged limply.

He went quickly to the door to summon Martin Hyde. In imagination he began to live through the next five minutes. He and Martin would try again to waken Edmunson and, failing, would call the doctor. Martin Hyde would know the doctor's telephone number.

Paul Lowe's heart was beating painfully fast.

26

The first decision of the new term was delivered by a unanimous Court. Gabriel Hart read the opinion, which involved a perfectly straightforward question as to the extent of the jurisdiction of the Federal Power Commission. At twelve o'clock when they adjourned for lunch, Gabriel drifted over to Paul Lowe in the anteroom behind the bench.

"Did you speak to the doctor this morning?"

"Yes," Paul Lowe said.

"How is the patient?"

"The doctor says he is coming along as well as can be expected. The tests didn't show anything seriously wrong."

"What exactly is the trouble?"

"At Edmunson's age it isn't easy to determine. It was probably an episode—a slight stroke that left no visible impairment."

"Well, I hope he comes back to work soon. We need him. Charles Edmunson isn't only a great man. I've always considered him a great personal friend."

At lunch most of the conversation had to do with Edmunson.

Chief Justice John Hampton said, "It's pretty depressing to sit in Court with that vacant chair next to me. Certain spaces get used to a certain physical presence and they aren't occupied when that presence is missing. I felt the same way when Frank Joyce left."

Waldo Shuler giggled. "That isn't flattering to our junior justice."

Paul Lowe said, "I know exactly what the Chief means. I would feel the same way if Edmunson left. But fortunately there's a good chance he'll be back."

Nevertheless the worry remained: suppose Edmunson could not resume his duties? The day had to come. For an anxious hour after the old man's collapse in his home he was sure the day *had* come. Now things were starting to look better. There was a good chance that Edmunson would be back. . . . Still, as the Chief said, Frank Joyce had gone forever. That frail gray figure at the Chief's left had disappeared. If Edmunson was forced to resign, Waldo Shuler would move over to sit in his place of seniority and would project an entirely different image, more aggressive, brilliant in a somehow narrower and more limited way, born to administer. Andrew Cutler would take Shuler's seat—endowing it with his own special aura, remote, intense, intelligent, splinter-wide in outlook. John Hampton would be flanked by those two, Waldo Shuler and Andrew Cutler, like a prisoner in custody.

More important, there would be a new justice appointed by the President to take Edmunson's place and the balance of the Court would be altered. Waldo Shuler's group would form a majority of the Court.

Paul Lowe shivered involuntarily.

Edward McCann said, "What's the matter?"

"Nothing. I had a slight chill."

"It's that cottage cheese salad and skimmed milk you're eating. That's enough to freeze anybody's insides. Why did you order it anyway?—that's Edmunson's usual lunch."

He stared down at his plate. Only then did he realize what he had done.

As they were leaving the luncheon table at twelve-thirty, Waldo Shuler asked:

"Do you know a lawyer named Kenneth Norris?"

"Very well," Paul Lowe said. "He was my former law partner."

Waldo Shuler nodded. "I was in my office this morning when I heard the Clerk of the Court wanted to see me about something important. Then the Clerk came in with a petition from your friend Norris."

"Concerning what?"

"A stay of execution. It's the William Weaver case that's been getting so much publicity lately. Weaver is scheduled to go to the electric chair tomorrow night. Norris said he was asking for a stay because he intends as soon as possible to ask the Supreme Court to review the case."

Andrew Cutler, nearby, said, "It isn't in our jurisdiction, Waldo. There's nothing unconstitutional about electrocuting a criminal. It's a state problem—not a federal question."

Waldo Shuler said, "I'm not so sure. I agree that the problem is one the states have always handled. And personally I think they should continue to. But that doesn't mean that a federal question doesn't exist —under either the Eighth Amendment or the Fourteenth."

"What are you going to do about the stay?" Paul Lowe asked.

Waldo Shuler answered, "Grant it."

"Why?" Andrew Cutler asked.

"If I don't, William Weaver will be dead before anybody can decide anything about his case."

Paul Lowe had a sudden impulse to touch Waldo Shuler's arm, only touch it, but Waldo had already moved off in the anteroom to take his place behind the maroon curtains.

Gabriel Hart and Edward McCann lined up with Paul Lowe on the left side, waiting the signal to enter the courtroom.

"I couldn't help overhearing what you and Waldo were talking about,"

Gabriel Hart said. "I certainly would never grant a stay under those conditions."

"Why not?"

"Too flimsy an excuse. We've never granted certiorari on a case challenging capital punishment. This is just another delaying tactic by a desperate lawyer. We can't afford to encourage that sort of thing."

The Marshal began the chant from the other side of the curtains: "Oyez! Oyez! Oyez!"

William Weaver was indeed lucky, Paul Lowe thought, that his life had been placed, even if temporarily, in the custody of Waldo Shuler.

In the public conference room of the Supreme Court building Paul Lowe was making a speech.

Confronting him, in row upon row of close-packed, highbacked chairs, were almost fifty attentive men and women. They had asked to meet Nebraska's pride and joy, the Cornhusker's contribution to the Supreme Court of the United States—Paul Lincoln Lowe. This sort of request to meet a Supreme Court justice was seldom refused and the public conference room was provided for exactly such a purpose.

In the room with its impressive crystal chandeliers, Paul Lowe stood at the podium beneath a freshly burnished portrait of John Marshall. The solemn bewigged countenance of the great Chief Justice of the Supreme Court seemed to be regarding this sandy-haired, stocky, business-suited successor with a polite astonishment.

His notes were on the lectern before him.

"It is true that here on the Court all of the justices talk too much," he said. "But that helps to expose at least some of our foolishness. I believe in the adage, 'He who insists on never being wrong had better hold his tongue.'"

Predictable laughter. A running ripple of movement, legs crossed and recrossed, people glanced at each other and found new postures.

This group was soberer than most assemblies; they were from his native state of Nebraska—Ne-brath-ka—land of the shallow water, a delegation with a dry purpose, cross-grained men who had wrung success out of the land, and attractively fading cornflower women done up in their best clothes and best intentions. They had come to Washington to make another appeal direct to the President and to any influential Senators and government officials who might make the North Platte dam a reality.

On this Thursday morning Paul Lowe spoke to them on soothing subjects, a gentle stirring of familiar sentiments with no sudden jarring thrusts. . . .

"As long as we Americans can talk out our differences, our country is not in danger. It is the great virtue of our democracy that it makes room for all shades of belief—that it holds under a giant roof men of diametrically opposing views. We live harmoniously in these United States because we know there is not and never will be a monopoly on truth, a cartel on wisdom, a syndicate of virtue. Therefore we compromise, we qualify and we admit exceptions, we conciliate and adjust. This kind of continuing debate keeps a government healthy. It enables the government to make new laws by getting a consensus of opinion from the people, and in turn the people are then willing to obey the laws that are eventually passed.

"But sometimes the laws that are passed reveal the schism of ideas that preceded them: we often find two ideas embodied in one law. And when such a law arrives at this Court for us to decide its practical application in the light of our Constitution, the debate begins anew. Only this time lawyers take up the fight that the people and the legislators have abandoned. It then becomes the job of the Supreme Court to choose between these competing ideas within the law. If there were no way of doing this, of making the final judgment, our whole system would collapse. I hope you will try to remember this, and even when you think our decision is wrong, at least be charitable. Thank you."

He turned over the last page of his notes. Chairs scraped. There was a thin cracking of applause. Most of the audience was now standing.

Paul Lowe smiled, nodded. "Do you have any questions? I'll try to answer as many as I can in the time we have remaining."

The man who stood up was tall and spare and had a deprecatory manner.

"Mr. Justice, we've all read about Justice Charles Edmunson's illness. If he isn't able to be present to hear cases, that increases the chance of some tie votes at four to four. What happens in a case like that?"

"A tie vote affirms the judgment of the lower court. If there is no opinion of the Court, it has almost the same effect as a majority vote would have affirming that judgment."

"Mr. Justice . . ."

Another man was standing, small, dark, hostile.

"Mr. Justice, if Charles Edmunson retires and someone is appointed to take his seat, I say it should be a man with previous experience as a judge. Do you agree with me?"

"Not necessarily. Of course I may be prejudiced because I had no previous judicial experience myself. But that is also true of the majority of my colleagues."

"Don't you think, Mr. Justice, that before a man is appointed to the highest court in the land he ought to know a good deal about the law from a judge's point of view?"

"There are many people who feel that way. Other people don't, because they think an exclusive concern with the law is not the most important requirement for a Supreme Court justice. It puts a premium on order *within* the law and sacrifices other considerations such as a wide experience in the world of affairs and a practical knowledge of human nature. One thing I do believe. In reaching a result that will satisfy both the litigant and the needs of society, we can't use the law as our only measuring rod."

A feminine voice, a trifle high and rising with impatience. A white hat with ribbons and curved brim.

380

"Mr. Justice, a lot of people I know are upset at the decision in the Graziani case. We don't see why the Supreme Court would defend a dirty book that makes a perfectly scandalous attack on a major religious figure."

The questioner had not risen from her seat. Paul Lowe addressed his answer to the audience.

"We were not defending a particular book. The Court merely affirmed the fact that under the democratic system of government there has to be the widest possible variety of ideas and tastes. I might liken this to a great hotel where many different kinds of people, none of whom have anything in common and some of whom would actually hate each other, still manage to live together in harmony. In literature we must also live with what is repugnant to us personally, just as we obey laws that we detest or we allow ourselves to be governed by political leaders whose philosophies are contrary to our own. We must try to exercise the same democratic tolerance when confronted by a work of art."

In the rear of the audience a short angry man in a light tweed suit stood up. "Do you mean we should give up the right to protest just because somebody puts a label of Art on a dirty book?"

Paul Lowe answered mildly, "We should never abandon our right to protest—but that does not give us the right to tyrannize, to impose our will when we happen to be in a majority. We can't enforce our view of what is good on others. After all, the question of what is a good book—or a good painting or a pleasing musical composition—has been decided in different ways by different individuals all through history. At one time or another most of the great works of literature have been condemned. Apuleius and Boccaccio were forcibly removed from our bookshelves and libraries, and so were Rousseau and Rabelais, Cervantes and Shakespeare. The list is endless."

"I'll tell you this, Mr. Justice. I'm never going to stop fighting against the kind of obscenity and filth that's being passed off as literature. Garbage is garbage no matter what name anyone—even the Supreme Court—puts on it!"

The short man delivered this with the air of someone who has just played a trump card. He sat down amid scattered but vigorous applause.

"Are there any other questions?" Paul Lowe asked.

He tensed as a plump woman in a flowered white dress rose to aim herself at him.

"Mr. Justice!"

"Yes, ma'am?"

"You don't remember me, do you?"

"I'm not sure that I do, but . . ."

"Mady Druson. My husband and I met you when you were Governor."

"I'm afraid I don't recall the occasion."

"You were making a speech for the North Platte dam."

"Oh, yes."

"I just want to say that you fought hard for that, Mr. Justice. A lot harder than that nincompoop Henry Wellman we've got for Governor now. And I sure wish we had you back!"

She sat her ample person down. There were chuckles from the audience.

"Thank you, Mrs. Druson," Paul Lowe said, smiling. "I'm afraid that's all the time we have for questions from the floor. Thank you. I've enjoyed this meeting very much."

He gathered up his notes, stepped down from the podium and shook hands to the door.

As he entered his office Martha Scully was talking with Jonathan Carter, his messenger.

Martha said, "There's a phone call for you, Mr. Justice. She said it was important. I was just asking Jonathan to fetch you."

"Who is it?"

"Miss Katherine Prescott."

An involuntary quiver ran the length of his whole body.

"Is she on the phone?"

"Yes, Mr. Justice."

"I'll take it in my office."

He had to master his excitement before he picked up the telephone.

"Katherine. Is it really you?"

"It's so good to hear your voice," she said.

"I was about to say the same thing. You sound fine. Just fine. How have you been?"

She cleared her throat. "I've had Timmy in the country. It took time to clear up that bronchitis. After the bronchial pneumonia. But he's well now. He learned to ride an English saddle."

"I'm glad to hear it."

"He'll be going to school next week. I registered him in Lincoln. It didn't seem worthwhile to bring him to Washington—uproot him from his friends, including his grandfather who's mad about him."

"Where are you calling from?"

"I'm here in Washington."

"*Why didn't you say so?*"

"I thought you knew. People sound a little distorted when it's long distance. All those wires and everything."

Something between a laugh and a sob broke in his throat.

"I want to see you. Will you have lunch with me?"

"Do you think it's safe?"

"Eleanor's back in Lincoln. She's filing for a divorce. It's coming up for final decision this week."

"Then it's true," she whispered. "I saw an item in the *Capitol Tattler*. I didn't know whether it was true or not. I wanted to call you right then but I had to think about it first to find out what I would do if it turned out either way—true or false."

"What did you decide?"

"I'd love to have lunch with you, Paul," she said.

Riding along Wisconsin Avenue in the taxi, he had all he could do to keep from waving to the people passing on the sidewalks. He had known such exuberance in his youth when it was caused by a plain excess of animal spirits. But it came infrequently now.

Katherine had chosen a restaurant popular with the diplomatic set and younger socialite groups, a fairly elegant place with caricatures of well-known political figures on the walls. Not the kind of place you would take someone with whom you did not wish to be seen. Katherine pointed out that this would keep their luncheon together from starting any gossip.

A doorman in uniform came forward from the covered white archway of the restaurant and held open the door of the cab.

Paul Lowe paid the driver and jumped out.

"Isn't it a great afternoon?" he asked.

The slightly startled doorman tipped his braided cap and replied, "Yes, sir."

He entered the restaurant eagerly. The first glimpse of her seated at a table made him feel suddenly awkward. He waved off the headwaiter and started down the side aisle. She was studying the menu and he willed her not to look up. He was acutely conscious of his rolling stride. An aging shambling oaf . . . not good-looking, rather lumpish and sandy, too round and solid through the middle. He brushed his hair back with one hand—it lay lankly where he brushed it.

He hurried forward like a fighter anxious to get to the safety of close quarters.

She saw him and lifted a hand slightly in greeting.

"What day is today?" he asked, looking at her.

"The twenty-sixth. Why?"

"Good. Two and six make eight. That isn't one of your unlucky days because it doesn't add up to five. And it's the tenth month of the year. Ten and eight make eighteen and one and eight make nine so that doesn't add up to five either."

She laughed. "I didn't know you believed in numerology."

"I don't. I knew without adding that this was a lucky day. A very lucky day."

She said, "We are going to have lunch, aren't we?"

"Of course."

"Then why don't you sit down, Mr. Justice?"

Her voice faintly emphasized the last two words. He smiled, embarrassed. He had been acting exactly like a man meeting a woman he was crazy about.

When he sat down her hand lightly brushed his arm, meaning apology for having contributed to his discomfiture. The touch was exciting because it carried the physical sensation of her.

She looked more desirable than she had even in his fantasies. He had forgotten small details—or, rather, the details had been subsumed in an image that because it was without flaw lacked character. She was infinitely more appealing than he imagined her. Her plumpness, which the cut of her smart blue wool dress did not conceal, made her seem more feminine. Her face was rounder, and her eyes had wrinkles under them, and her sparkling complexion was not entirely free of one or two tiny blemishes. All this added to her reality, and that reality was so abundantly, consciously alive that everything around her was set vibrating by her presence.

"Will you have a drink?" he asked, as the waiter came to their table. "As I remember, it used to be Canadian Club manhattans."

"Still is."

Not until the waiter left did Katherine look directly at him.

"You wouldn't believe me if I told you how good it is to see you, Paul."

"I've already begun to worry about what I'll do when lunch is over."

"You might come to my place."

"Where is that?"

"The same apartment. Tom Jeffreys' friend is still wandering in the wilds of Cambodia. He won't be back for another month."

"God bless all foreign correspondents," Paul Lowe said fervently.

They were in the living room of the apartment with the shades drawn against the gray afternoon light. The tall lamp beside the sofa glowed in a small orange circle. Katherine was talking and he was fascinated with watching her. She was the only woman he had ever known who could look animated even in the most ordinary conversation.

"It was a very difficult time," she said. "Timmy and I stayed a month at this dude ranch. Except for the two of us it was all families. Husbands and wives and children. I envied them so much that I couldn't bear it. They had special recreation periods in a playground during the morning for the children and when Timmy went there I would take a horse and ride off and stay away as long as I could so I wouldn't have to be with all those married people. I kept imagining you there as my husband."

"How did I like it?"

"You hated it. It was a dreadful place really. There was no one you could have talked to. There wasn't even an intelligent dog. The only dog on the place was a beagle who was so dumb he didn't know enough to lift his hind leg when he had to pee. He just stood by a tree and dribbled all over himself."

He laughed. "Did you have any friends?"

She shook her head. "We only met as parents. I was Timmy's mother. Then there were Deborah's mother and father, Craig's mother and father, Jerry's mother and father. . . . We made parent talk. I think I would have preferred talking to the horses."

"Some horses are very interesting."

She laughed. "There was a big gentle gray horse who helped me to do double-crostics, and there was a slightly bowlegged rather stocky brown stallion that reminded me of you."

"Thank you very much."

"He was my favorite, of course." She stopped speaking and put her hand on the sofa with the palm up. He pressed the palm of his hand against hers.

"For a while everything reminded me of you until finally I decided I had to be grown up about it."

"Were you?"

"No."

"Good. That's how I feel about you."

Her soft fingers locked in his. As lightly as a feather the first pricking of desire moved across his chest and the clasp of his fingers strengthened. Lamplight was shining on her dark hair and there was faint orange luminosity on a wisp of hair that had risen a little.

Her fingers trembled slightly. "Are you going to make love to me?"

"I want to. Do you want me to?"

She bit her lower lip. "I've tried to put the thought out of my mind. These past weeks it would probably have driven me mad if I let it. I'm so terribly shameless about you. Sooner or later I *will* find a way so I won't need you as much as I do now. . . . Will you please kiss me, darling? I can't stop talking."

He moved beside her and she put her head back against his shoulder. The shape of her breast was softly against his arm. Then he felt her hands holding his head and guiding him to kiss her. He held her so tightly that he was afraid he was hurting her and said, "Katherine. Oh, Katherine."

Then the lamplight was gone and in the room there were only edges of gray light at the sides of the black window shades. He remembered the undulating curve of her with her head pressed back against the sofa bolster and her eyes almost violet in semidarkness and then he was blind to all colors and to everything except her and the nearness of her until the violent aching was gone and he was compelled back to peace. He tried to hold the pattern of a moment that was at once the consummation of all violence and the total of all quietness and calm—to understand the miraculous union of one with the other. And he knew that he never would understand.

Then he was lying at her side, his arm about her bare shoulders. The light that came through the edges of the window shade made a small area of grayness against the dark sofa behind her head.

Her eyes were tight shut, lids folded in tightly so the lashes rose up. She opened her eyes and smiled at him.

"What are you thinking?" he asked.

"That I've never known what it was until you. That there's so much more and that there will never be enough." She stretched her arms and shuddered deliciously. "That there's a great deal of contentment to be found right where I'm at."

"You do a lot of thinking for one person. Have you done any thinking about when you'd like to get married?"

"I can't bring myself to think about that, Paul. All this has caught me so unawares. I haven't allowed myself to think of it."

"I thought a quiet ceremony—sometime before Thanksgiving—and then we'll pick up Timmy over the holidays."

"Pick him up?"

"Bring him here to live with us. I know you've done your best to pretend to me that you're not a mother. But it doesn't fool me, Katherine."

She looked at him and then looked away. "I do miss Timmy. In fact, I miss him terribly. But it isn't fair to you. You've never met him and now you have to act like a father."

"I think I'm going to like that," he said.

After a moment she said, "Poor Ellen Sue."

"What?"

"This girl I knew in school when I was fifteen who ran off with a married teacher. We found out later she was pregnant."

"Oh?" He had not quite adjusted to the rapidly changing tempo of her conversation but he had faith, as in an ultramodern musical composition, that all would turn out to be part of the composer's plan.

"I remember going home the afternoon I heard about it, walking along the sidewalk and skipping all the cracks and repeating to myself, 'I won't grow up . . . and be like her.' In a jingle rhythm. 'I *won't* grow up . . . and be like her.' I wonder what's happened to Ellen Sue."

"I don't see the connection—not yet anyhow."

"She broke all the rules. Just as I have. That's why I wonder what happened to her."

"She's eminently respectable," he said. "Married and settled down with four kids. All legitimate."

"I hope she's as happy as I am right now." She reached up to put her arms around him. "I am happy, Paul, more than I can ever tell you. I know people are not supposed to know when they're happy until it's all over. But I know it now. I can feel it so I can't breathe. Isn't that sinful? To be happy for the first time in my life—*because* I've broken all the rules?"

He kissed her. "Now, about that Thanksgiving date? Would you prefer champagne and flowers so I can make a proposal on bended knee and everything?"

"I'll say yes no matter how you ask me. And Thanksgiving would be wonderful."

"Then it's a date."

"Will you promise me something?" she asked.

"Yes."

"Will you just husband your strength so you can make love to me as often as you can?"

"I'll have to do something. I don't know whether I've mentioned this, but I am forty-six and according to the very best statistical surveys rather far along a downhill slope. Or to put it another way, in order to be accurately described as middle-aged I would have to live to be ninety-two."

"Paul—don't!"

Tears sprang to her eyes.

"What's the matter, darling?"

"Don't talk about getting old or dying. I can't bear it."

He brushed the tears away. "I didn't mean to frighten you. I don't have any present plans to check off the planet."

386

"Please. I can't think of it. I wouldn't care so much if it were I. Then there wouldn't be anything else, ever. But if it happened to you, Paul . . . everything would fall away. It would all end, and what point would there be to anything?"

"Everyone has to face that problem, my darling. And none of us is conversant with what plans Someone Up There may have."

"I wish I had a religion. A real faith to believe in. That must be a consolation. Someone said the soul deserves to be immortal. It would be nice if we all got our deserts—even if only in the next world. That would be fair, wouldn't it?"

"But you don't believe it happens?"

"I don't have a high opinion of the fairness of the universe. I have a terrible suspicion the universe just *is*. No ethics to speak of and absolutely no morality."

"What about God?" he asked.

"I don't know anything about Him. I don't think the religious leaders do either. At least they never sound like they do. They all have a different picture of Him and how He operates and why."

"Perhaps each one of them has hold of a little bit of the truth."

"That's possible. I never thought of it that way."

"A man named Rufus Choate once said, 'You cannot throw to the ground the letters of the Greek alphabet and pick up the *Iliad.*' If each religion is in possession of just one letter of the alphabet, and if they all put the letters together, they still wouldn't be able to spell out His master plan."

She brooded over this. "So there isn't much we can do about it, is there?"

"Some people manage to have faith. They believe there is an *Iliad* somewhere even if men never acquire the vocabulary to read it."

"Do you want me to have faith? I'll try."

"I don't want you to be anything but what you are."

"All right." She kissed him. "I'm sure I can manage that."

Martha Scully said on the intercom: "It's Mr. Gannett—the President's appointment secretary."

"All right, Martha," Paul Lowe picked up the telephone. "Hello, Martin."

Martin Gannett's silky voice sounded as though it were maintaining its calm despite harassing pressure: "Mr. Justice, how have you been? Pretty busy, I imagine."

"I'm fine."

"Not too busy to have lunch with the President this Saturday, I hope. That's November fifth."

"Any particular reason?"

"It's an informal affair. There'll be some people you know. And the Court isn't sitting that week so you'll have more time than your usual half hour." Faint chuckle—an attempt at a human touch against the clock running. "Mr. Justice Shuler will be there, too."

"Waldo? That's fine. Anyone else I know?"

"Attorney General Keenan, Peter Daris, the Solicitor General, and a couple of Senators. Senator George Walsh. You know him?"

"All too well." He couldn't resist adding, "He fought my nomination to the Court."

"Oh, yes." The silky voice hurried on, conscious of error and of no time to redeem it. "Then we may expect you?"

"Of course."

President Lamont Howard liked to invite prominent figures in government to his informal Saturday luncheons. The luncheon table was peopled like a repertory company—with certain regular performers and a few specially invited guests. Often the luncheon was preceded by a game of volleyball on the White House lawn. The initiative for this apparently came from the White House physician, a poker-playing crony of the President, who had recommended exercise to keep his distinguished patient in good physical trim. Lamont Howard's personal preference in recreation was for martinis, straight poker and man talk in smoky rooms.

A few skeptics who knew Lamont Howard's passion for efficiency and his humorless devotion to work, thought the once-a-week volleyball games served a purpose in that they assured the availability of an inner clique on whom the President relied for advice in reaching key decisions. Lamont Howard was peculiarly dependent on advisers and friends for counsel while in the preliminary stages of making up his mind. Once he made up his mind there was nothing that could budge it.

Paul Lowe sat for a few minutes pondering the possibilities before getting back to his work. Martin Gannett had made no mention of the pre-luncheon volleyball game so he was not being invited to join what a commentator had acidly described as "Lamont Howard's volleyball cabinet." But he was sure that this was not a casual invitation. There was no clue to its meaning in the roster of guests. Waldo Shuler was not an intimate of the President, although the two men enjoyed a cordial relationship based on mutual respect and a similarity in outlook. Senator George Walsh . . . Gannett had stumbled on that name because he'd forgotten how bitterly the Senator from Virginia had fought Paul Lincoln Lowe's nomination to the Supreme Court. But there was no significance to be found in the mere presence of an important Senator. As for Attorney General Keenan and young Peter Daris, they were regulars of the volleyball cabinet, so their attendance meant nothing.

The invitation began to seem puzzling. Lamont Howard prided himself on informal get-togethers with working associates, corporation presidents, newspapermen, and diplomats. He was convinced that his man-in-the-street approach could strike common ground with every kind of human personality, from the highest to the lowest. But in all of his pleasant offhand chats—in offices and corridors, at public meetings, and even at the White House fence with awestruck sightseers—one feature never changed: Lamont Howard never spoke for the pleasure of conversation; there was always a purpose he was working toward.

What is it this time? Paul Lowe wondered.

Luncheon was a calculated informality, served in the basement dining room of the White House and consisting of large oval platters of bacon, sausages, chicken livers, and hotcakes. Lamont Howard, wearing an open sportshirt and white duck trousers, and still perspiring from the recent volleyball game, presided over the grill. There were twelve guests including the President ("just enough for a jury," Waldo Shuler whispered to Paul Lowe). Half were dressed in informal sports attire and the rest in business suits. Senator George Walsh wore a black coat with high lapels and his customary black string tie. His saturnine face forced itself into occasional smiles and he tried his best not to look discomfited when Lamont Howard clapped him on the back.

There was a good deal of joke telling, prompt laughter, mock warmth, and the kind of comradely ease that can be created in certain situations only by the most determined effort. Paul Lowe spoke with Senators Walsh and Dunbar, heard an anecdote from Peter Daris, told one to Phil Keenan, laughed with the President about some of the misadventures of the volleyball court—Dr. George Schechter had been knocked breathless charging a hard serve, and Peter Daris was hobbling because the Secretary of Defense, Harry Frame, had accidentally stepped hard on his left foot. "Could've broken his toe—but we had a doctor right there. Eh, George? Ever performed any open toe surgery?" George Schechter, a tanned lean man with dark iron graying hair and friendly manner, said he was sure there must be specialists in that field. Lamont Howard roared and clapped him on the back.

Lunch ended.

"What d'you say we adjourn to the second floor?" Lamont Howard asked.

By clear prearrangement, several guests now made their excuses and departed. "Love to stay, but business, you know."

"Government business, I hope," Lamont said.

Seven survivors made the trek to the oval study on the second floor.

Two Secret Service agents accompanied them to the door of the study and took up positions on either side of the door. Inside the oval room Lamont Howard slumped into the chair behind a huge desk and leaned backward with his hands on his abdomen.

"Whew," he said.

Phil Keenan and Peter Daris moved small canebottomed chairs toward the middle of the room. Senators Walsh and Dunbar sat with Waldo Shuler on the sofa facing the President's desk. The marble coffee table was between them and the desk. Paul Lowe sat in a wing chair to the left of the President.

Martin Gannett appeared through a side door carrying a black bottle of brandy and several goblets; he opened the bottle neatly, and poured reverently. Lamont Howard, seated sidewise at his desk, kept a fixed smile on his face until Gannett finished serving and departed.

Then the President lifted his goblet with an exaggerated flourish.

"They tell me they don't hardly make it like this any more. It's Berry

Brothers—fifty-four years old. Somebody sent it to me on my birthday."
He sipped at the rounded rim of the goblet. "Not bad." He sat back
holding the goblet between both hands. "Almost as good as one of my
martinis."

Phil Keenan laughed.

Peter Daris said, "It's really a treat."

"Let's have a toast," the President said.

Peter Daris smiled and lifted his goblet. "We've got a couple of distinguished justices with us today. How about toasting the Supreme
Court?"

Peter Daris was a vain man, confident of his ability in certain situations.
The artful flourish with which he suggested the toast was a shade too self-
satisfied. Across the room Waldo Shuler winked at Paul Lowe. They had
witnessed the opening move, pawn to the fourth king's square.

Now that a direction was given, other elements appeared to fall into
place: the presence of the Attorney General and the Solicitor General—
the government's two top-ranking lawyers—together with Senators Walsh
and Dunbar of the Senate Judiciary Committee. That meant the matter
to be dealt with definitely concerned the judiciary branch of the government and that was why the other Senators, the Secretary of Defense and
the White House physician had left directly after the luncheon was over.
Their presence had been mere camouflage.

"I'll drink to that gladly," the President said. "To the Supreme Court—
long may it wave our Constitution."

"And protect us against our enemies," Senator Dunbar said.

Senator Dunbar's long face with its deeply grooved vertical lines and
gray-rimmed eyeglasses like huge watery saucer eyes recalled to Paul Lowe
the day of his hearing before the Judiciary Committee. *Do you think that
America has a good deal to learn from Marx or Lenin? Do you believe
that Christians have something to learn from the teachings of Buddha?*
Senator Dunbar was one of those who believed that in a thousand
generations of striving, man had already freed himself of error and that
the American people in particular had somehow discovered immutable
truths which the next hundred thousand generations would not improve
upon. *Senator, we are in the first days of our infancy and the prattle we
now make will seem mindless to those who come after.*

Paul Lowe said, "And help us to know who our enemies are," and he
lifted his own goblet.

Senator Walsh answered in a deep low voice, "Some of us think we
know our enemies, Mr. Justice. All we need is a little judicial cooperation
when we finally turn over the rocks and find where the reptiles are hiding."

Lamont Howard chuckled with exactly the same effect as though he
had put a period to this phase of conversation.

He said, "Now, this is no time to air our disputes between the legislative
and judicial branches of the government. We're all on the same side in
this and we want to work it out together."

Waldo Shuler asked, "On the same side in what, Mr. President?"

Lamont Howard rubbed his chin. "Waldo, you go right to the heart of the matter. Well, since you asked . . ." he hitched himself erect in his tallbacked swivel chair, ". . . there are a couple of problems we'd like to talk about. I figure we can talk them out between us, just like friends, without having a great to-do about it, or sending letters or memorandums to each other complaining about one branch of government interfering with the other."

The President laid his heavy glance upon the others in the room.

"The first problem on our agenda is one which the Supreme Court will have to deal with in the very near future."

"What problem, Mr. President?" Waldo Shuler asked.

"How long will Charles Edmunson be able to carry on? I understand he's suffered a stroke."

Paul Lowe said, "He's feeling better, Mr. President. There's a good chance he'll be back to work soon."

"It's cruel to ask him to keep going at his age. Another year of such hard work might kill him. It's time he retired."

Waldo Shuler said quietly, "He's always managed to do his share, Mr. President. He isn't the man he was, but if he has any years of good service left we can certainly use him."

Lamont Howard waved his hand impatiently. "Well, maybe a replacement for Edmunson won't be necessary. I hope not. But you know what happens when someone gets too old for his job. The first thing he loses is flexibility." His voice became stronger. "And flexibility is what we've got to have from the Court in these dangerous times."

"I'm not sure what the word means in that context, Mr. President," Paul Lowe said.

Lamont Howard's chair swiveled about to confront Paul Lowe. "It means that the Court that was handing down decisions about Communists yesterday was acting against a different background from the one existing today. When I asked you in for a private talk I wanted to discuss the need for judges who are flexible enough to help our country meet a crisis. Well, gentlemen, that crisis is a whole lot worse now than it was when I invited you to come here. And the need for real cooperation from the Supreme Court in helping us to meet the crisis is a lot more urgent than it was a few days ago."

"What crisis are you talking about, Mr. President?" Paul Lowe asked.

"It will be on the regular news broadcasts by now. There's been a revolution in Burma."

The quiet way in which the President announced this gave the content of what he said a piercing quality that seemed to go through to the marrow. "The rebels have assassinated President U Ba Saw and set up a government in the north," the President added.

Paul Lowe felt ill. "U Ba Saw is dead?"

"That isn't all. They killed a member of our consular staff too. Caught him outside the Embassy building and impaled him. Then the mob marched around the Embassy building parading his head on a stick."

"Do you know the man's name?" Somehow, he knew what the answer would be.

"David Moss," the President said. "We're not going to take his murder lying down. I've ordered retaliatory action."

Grimly Paul Lowe recalled the gentle brown face of U Ba Saw as he said, there will be children of the act of violence and those children will have children.

"I've ordered the Seventh Fleet to steam for Rangoon," the President said. "We're sending the Marines in to guard the safety of American citizens and to reinforce and supply loyal Burmese army groups. It's possible we may be in for another—and even bloodier—Viet Nam."

Waldo Shuler said simply, "My God."

Lamont Howard said, "That brings me to the point of this meeting. If we're going to war in Burma, something has to be done about the subversives in our own country. We've got to clamp the lid down before they start with their phony peace movements and burning draft cards. This is an emergency and I'm prepared to take emergency measures. So is the Congress. And we'll need support—all-out support—from the judicial branch of government."

"I don't understand what you expect us to do, Mr. President," Paul Lowe said.

"I expect you to stand firm with the rest of the country. Specifically, if an antisubversive law passed by Congress comes up for review I don't expect you to find some technicality in the Constitution that will declare it null and void. One thing more. If any of our homegrown Communists show up before the Supreme Court yelling for their rights of free speech, I expect the Supreme Court to set an example for the rest of the country. We're going to have to deal with these vermin at home at the same time that we're fighting them overseas."

Waldo Shuler said, "Mr. President, what you seem to be asking for is an advisory opinion before the fact. That hasn't been allowed since John Jay, the first Chief Justice, turned down a similar request from George Washington."

What an unpredictable man, Paul Lowe thought admiringly. Every time he tried to fit Waldo Shuler into some sort of pigeonhole he was surprised to find a part of the man left over—like an overlooked but important document.

The President's mouth made a firm line and the heels of his palms came together as though crushing a walnut. "Now that's the sort of technicality I'm talking about. We're not going to observe all the little niceties when our country may be fighting for its life in a few more weeks or months. I'm not asking for any advisory opinion. I'm *telling* you what this country expects of the Supreme Court. One thing more. If any homegrown Commies show up before the Court yelling for their rights of free speech so they can go on sabotaging our war effort or stabbing our fighting men in the back, I expect the Supreme Court to make an example of them. We have to deal with these vermin at home in the same way that we're fighting them overseas."

What the President was announcing, Paul Lowe thought wryly, was the start of a new Crusade. Nothing is more formidable than a man armored in the certainty of being right. "God wills it!" A nine-hundred-year span between a Pope at Clermont and Lamont Howard in the White House was bridged over with righteousness.

Lamont Howard surveyed the group. His forehead was deeply furrowed and his mouth was tight. There was force in this man, a hard center beneath the folksy genial manner. As his gaze traveled the circle each man felt the impact. The circle seemed to be narrowing, the sphere constricting more and more as Lamont Howard's gaze traveled swiftly on. Paul Lowe met the President's gaze with something resembling a small physical shock.

27

Watching from the glassed-in observation wall, Paul Lowe saw the mighty silver jet streak in smoothly over the runway, hover as though reluctant to become earthbound, then settle and run and slow and wheel and taxi toward the terminal building.

Nancy was one of the first off the plane. She wore a gray-green suit and a gray fur stole about her shoulders and she carried a huge leather hand-bag by a strap.

She was looking lovely—he thought—her blonde hair in place beneath a small perky hat that clung to a high roll of hair in back. She wore long cinnamon-colored gloves.

She leaned over the aluminum railing that separated passengers from those waiting and kissed his cheek.

"It's good to see you, Dad."

"It's good to see you too, dear. You're looking beautiful."

A small dark man with a serious and preoccupied expression came toward them. He wore a lightweight blue topcoat and a blue fedora.

Nancy said, "Oh, Dad, I'd like you to meet Claude de Brussac. He's a Count, actually, but don't hold that against him. He's very sweet. Claude, my father, Mr. Justice Paul Lowe."

Claude de Brussac made an eloquent gesture of wringing Paul Lowe's hand.

"It is a very great honor," de Brussac said.

"He insisted on flying on with me," Nancy said, "when he found out he couldn't change my mind about coming."

Claude de Brussac shrugged exquisitely. "One moment here, in Paris, and then—poof—she is going to Washington in the United States. I have to make all arrangements without warning. But I wish to meet with the parent of such a delightful girl."

Nancy said, "He's French. You know how impulsive and romantic they are. He keeps insisting that he's going to make an honest woman of me. I haven't convinced him yet that I'm happy the way I am."

"Shall we get our luggage, Nancy?" Paul Lowe asked.

"*Mais certainement,*" de Brussac volunteered.

On the way through the terminal to the baggage station, de Brussac kept exclaiming at the lavishness of the décor.

"You Americans," he said. "Everything on such a grand scale. Sometimes one wonders if you try to impress yourselves or the rest of the world?"

Paul Lowe was having no trouble disliking him. He said, "Somebody must have told us once that we're a great nation so we're out to prove it."

De Brussac laughed; he had rather bad teeth. He walked beside Nancy with a prideful erectness as though he were teetering on high heels. There was more than a generation between them in age. De Brussac was older than Paul Lowe.

"One hopes America does not succeed too well in proving how great a nation it is," de Brussac said. "Who is hated more than the rich and powerful—is it not so?"

As they waited at the circular moving track where luggage went about looking for its owners, the conversation drifted into America's role in international affairs. De Brussac proved something of a surprise as the stereotype began to crack and the real man showed through. He was possessed of an almost epic bitterness—directed not only against the power and wealth of the United States but against most of the pillars of the democratic establishment. This included moderate social reform, the separation of church and state, and the principle of equality before the law. He had the anti-ethic of the outcast: he resented the disappearance of a social order which would have given his innate sense of superiority some formal recognition.

Nancy enjoyed herself as the debate continued into the taxicab. She hung on de Brussac's devastating commentaries and rewarded him with laughter. Paul Lowe understood the attraction this man had for his daughter. De Brussac was able to articulate for Nancy her unformulated but deeply felt anarchism, to give it the point and almost the coherence of a philosophy.

While they were dining at Paul Lowe's hotel he made an effort to fit this fussy older man with his nimble, fierce, destructive mind, his pathetic craving for a feudal world, into a chronology of the sort of men who had courted Nancy. At first they had all been the same—good-looking, gay, graceful youngsters from the best prep schools and the best colleges. Then there had been a succession of faceless sophisticated men in their thirties, backed by money and assurance and powered by sexual hunger. In one sense de Brussac was better than these men—his features were his own.

Over a chocolate mousse, Paul Lowe tried to compare him with Nancy's husband Arthur. De Brussac seemed stamped out of some fresher stronger mold. Although his nature was unsympathetic, de Brussac gave to his unpleasantness the hard covering of intelligence. He was apparently an omnivorous reader, incessantly, obsessively in search of raw material to buttress his personal animus against the established order. In contrast Arthur Montgomery employed his will and strength to achieve success within the established order. Arthur never questioned the confines, or was

395

even aware of them. On the other hand, de Brussac was nearly incapacitated by awareness and could not put his cynical intelligence to work within the closed circle.

At a little past eight o'clock, de Brussac made his apologies and left. He explained that he had made no hotel reservations and had to find a room that "would not be too discomfortable."

"Well, what do you think of him?" Nancy asked when he had gone.

"In some ways a brilliant man."

Nancy said, "He's the most brilliant man I ever met—except for you. I suppose that's what I like about him."

"Have you been seeing much of him?"

"I can hardly help it. We're living together."

It was Nancy's familiar attempt at shock treatment. Paul Lowe asked, "How long have you known him?"

"I met him at a party in Paris and he began telephoning me the next day. Tessie got annoyed after a while—she couldn't stand him—but he amused me. When things got impossible with Tessie, I moved to London and he followed me there. I became afraid I might take him seriously if I didn't live with him. So three or four months ago I moved into his place in Paris and I've been there since."

Paul Lowe draped an arm over the back of his chair. "What made you decide to come home, Nancy?"

"Oh, I want to talk to Arthur about the alimony payments. He's been a bit delinquent lately. I suppose he's found someone else and stopped hankering after me. And of course there's the baby. I should feed it a little mother's milk from these dried old dugs." Nancy's eyebrows shot up in that way she had when she was about to be malicious. "Actually, I wanted mostly to talk to you, Dad. Are you really getting a divorce from Mother?"

"Yes. It should be final any day now."

"Well, I can't say that you didn't give it a college try. You rate an A for effort. You and Mother will probably be a lot happier now that you don't have to pretend you're happily married."

"In any event, I hope your mother will find happiness. She certainly deserves that."

"Oh, she'll be all right. There's always Grandmother and Natalie to fall back on. They're a close-knit group. I'm more worried about you, Dad."

"About me?"

"There's no one to look after you. And you're not meant to live alone."

"I'll be all right, Nancy."

"I haven't acted much like your daughter in recent times, Dad. I've had too many of my own problems. But I do care about you, and I can't bear the thought of your being alone in some hotel room."

"I wish you wouldn't worry, Nancy."

She laughed lightly. "I don't see any good reason why we shouldn't join our miseries together. Try to make something a little better out of them."

"I'm not sure I know what you mean."

A quick flush stained her cheeks and she almost appeared to him as she had in her large colored graduation photograph, a harmony of pale forehead, blonde hair, white gown, set in a white leatherette frame with only the color in her cheeks to serve as highpoints.

"I haven't made such a wonderful success of things, Dad. I've had it with Europe. The only reason I stayed away this long is that there was nothing to come back to." She rushed on: "I'm not much of a housekeeper but I *can* keep a home of sorts together. And I think I owe you that much after all the trouble I've given you. We'll find a small apartment somewhere and . . ."

"I'm sorry, Nancy," he said.

She twisted her single strand emerald necklace. Her face was clouded with an indefinable emotion. "You don't want to."

"It isn't that. But I don't intend to live alone, Nancy."

Her color went white. "You're going to get married. Is that what you're saying?"

"Yes."

"To that woman. Katherine Prescott." Her eyes were smaller and no longer shone but gleamed like twin slivers of ice. "It's been going on all this time. It never really ended at all. Does Mother know? Have you told Mother?"

"Nancy, your mother and I have agreed to a property settlement and she's getting a divorce in a few more days. I think you can probably stir up some mischief if you want to, but not a great deal."

She rolled her eyes upward. "Mine eyes have seen the glory . . . of true love. Is that what you think? If you do, you've lost the ability to be honest with yourself."

"About what, Nancy?"

"About what you feel, for one thing. You're not in love with that woman—it's a phase, a luxury, a discovery of sensation. When the excitement has gone there won't be anything left of it. I've come out on the other side of several such affairs and I can tell you they all end the same way. In boredom."

"I suppose it's hard to believe in love, Nancy, until you've experienced it."

She began a quick and haughty dismissal but an awareness that he meant it stayed her. She laughed with a harshly grating undertone.

"You always did have a mystical streak, Dad. Part of your Welsh background that somehow never infected me. It accounts for your adolescent belief in religion—the only part of your character that ever really puzzled me."

"You may change your mind about some things in time, Nancy."

She dwelt in her own thoughts, not answering.

She said finally, "So you're going to be another middle-aging Casanova with graying hair and failing prostate glands looking for a miraculous way to recover his youth."

"It's time I took you back to your hotel. Will I see you tomorrow?"

"No," she said. "I came back because I wanted to help you, but you don't want to be helped. You want to run away and live in wonderland. Well, go ahead, Dad. I can't stop you."

"When will I see you again?"

"Not any more. Claude and I will take the first plane back to Paris tomorrow. We're going to be married."

"A rather sudden decision, isn't it?"

"You just helped me to make it."

He said, "You're disturbed and unhappy, Nancy. You'll only make things worse by doing anything so foolish as marrying Claude de Brussac. I think you know that."

"I can't afford to let him find someone else. I'd better marry him while he still has a burning desire to get me into bed. Before he finds out that I had much more fun sleeping with Tessie Samuels than I ever have with him."

Paul Lowe looked at her without showing in any way that he had heard. A pulse beat in his forehead. "You can't go on this way, Nancy. You're a beautiful woman, intelligent, with everything you need to make a constructive, useful life. It doesn't make sense to deliberately throw away all your chances."

He would never forget how she looked at this moment—instinct with the terrible vitality necessary to deny life. Some inartistic hand had retouched the graduation photograph, allowing the flawless throat and mouth to retain their lines but subtly altering the flare of the nostrils and putting almost invisible lines of tension at the cheekbones.

"Oh, I suppose when everything else fails I'll try the pill route again."

"The pill route?"

"I tried before and made an absolute mess of it. In London just before Claude found me. That's one reason I went to live with him. He was so kind and attentive and I needed someone to look after me for a while."

When he understood her, he was dazed. She had succeeded in shocking him. "In heaven's name, Nancy, why would you want to kill yourself?"

She smiled. "I was bored. Whether or not I try it again depends on whether I get bored again."

"I want you to promise me," he said, almost fiercely, "that you'll never do anything that foolish again. There's no reason for it."

Her tone turned derisive. "Are you going to play a violin tremolo? I'll need a fresh handkerchief."

"I'm your father, Nancy, and I do care about you. I know you won't believe it but it happens to be true. I want to help you in any way I can."

"Oh, I know you do," she said. "You've given me every proof of that."

"I'd like to prove it. Would you let me find you an apartment in Washington? We can live near each other. We can see each other a lot more than we've been able to do in years."

398

"That would be sweet, wouldn't it? You could always set an extra place at table for me and I could be the extra girl at your parties. Eventually, you might even find a suitable man for me. Someone who meets with your Miss Prescott's approval. No, thanks, Dad. I'd much rather arrange my own affairs." She made an impatient grimace. "Pay the check, will you? I'd like to get out of this place."

He signaled the waiter.

As he was helping her on with her coat he said, "Nancy, I beg you not to marry de Brussac. He has nothing to give you. You'll just be asking for more unhappiness."

Even in her pose as she turned to face him, one arm akimbo, one leg slightly thrust forward, there was a juvenile bravado—a daring of the lightning's power, the same willful defiance that even as a child led her to fling open a window during a thunderstorm and stretch out her hand to the silent violent strokes of light.

"I don't know how long it will last." She pushed back a strand of blonde hair from her forehead and smiled brightly. "But I imagine it'll take at least a little while before we learn to hate each other."

On Thanksgiving Eve, at a few minutes before midnight, a huge four-engined jet neared Omaha, Nebraska. There was a little snow falling and flakes frosted the window.

Paul Lowe sat beside Katherine a few rows behind the pilot's cabin. Their suitcases were in the luggage compartment somewhere in the belly of the huge plane. Katherine's were new, a set of matching luggage with new initials on their calfskin hides: KL. Katherine Lowe. He was pleased about their suitcases nestling together and he put his hand on her knee as they flew on through the night.

"What are you thinking?" he asked.

"I wouldn't dare tell you," she said. "I'd blush."

She was wearing a short pink dress with a small fur collar. She looked beautiful, but then Katherine looked beautiful in anything.

His hand tightened on her knee. Tonight they would be alone together in the hotel before going to her father's home for Thanksgiving.

"The first time isn't always the best, is it?" she asked. "I'm more excited now than I've ever been. Did you think it was a lovely wedding?"

"It couldn't have been better."

"I wish we could do it all over again. I'd like to hear you say 'I do' again to that justice of the peace. When I heard you I had such a sense of triumph. I caught myself thinking, now he's mine. Now he can't get away. You can't, can you?"

"No," he said. "I can't."

"I don't believe I've really got you. That you're really mine."

"You may not have got such a bargain. I have all sorts of annoying habits. They even annoy me sometimes."

"Then I'll adjust. Basically I'm some kind of plastic. I can mold me into any sort of person you want."

"You're the sort of person I want."

She leaned over to kiss him behind the ear. "You're sweet. But I'm afraid of you too, and that's a good thing."

"Why should you be afraid of me?"

"Because you have a better mind than I have. That's what I've always wanted in a man but now that I've found it I'm frightened of it too. I keep wondering if I'll be able to keep you interested. Of course, if it gets boring we can study Sanskrit together."

"Or read Spengler's *Decline of the West*," he said. "I've always meant to do something about that. Every time I look at it in my bookshelf it seems to stand there, ponderously accusing me."

Then they were silent. The stewardess in her light blue uniform smiled past them down the aisle.

"I'm asking an awful lot," Katherine said. "You have to get used to a whole new way of life. There's not only me—but Timmy. I hope you'll like him, Paul. He's a wonderful boy."

"We'll get along fine. Wait and see."

The sign flashed on to warn them No Smoking Please and Fasten Your Seat Belts. They were coming in for a landing at Omaha Airport.

The radio announcer said, "Today will be cold with temperature in the low twenties falling into the upper teens by evening. . . ."

He clicked off the radio in the hotel room. "And a Happy Thanksgiving Day to you," he said.

"I hate Omaha in the winter. The truth is I hate any place in the winter. Whoever invented winter in the first place made a terrible mistake."

They were on the bed in the darkened room with the shades drawn. He turned languorously, slow revolution in a well-oiled bone chamber. Without looking at her he was totally aware of her body. Her face was flushed with not quite departed passion and he remembered its hot strained look and her full bare arms holding him close. A sheet had fallen partly away from her shoulder and as he lifted it to cover her there was the rare full white melon of her breast with its dull red blossom. How deliciously her body curved at the shoulder into the curve of the back. Desire had always been for him an emotion that exhausted itself. The desperate blind urges of the flesh never passed beyond. If he could have imagined what was beyond he would have expected the next phase to be debauchery, not love.

"What time is it?" she asked.

"Almost noon."

"Oh, dear. I've lost track of time."

"So have I. I'd better start to get ready."

In the hotel bathroom he moved the whirring surface of an electric shaver over the skin of his face and lifted his chin to get at the underjaw. He thought of how it had been in his youth with Eleanor. In his relations with Eleanor he had consciously tried to play a role expected of

400

him. He had watched himself perform, rejoicing and sorrowing with the character he created, sharing his other self's emotion, partly detached yet never so detached as not to be somehow involved, mostly identifying yet never so identified that he ceased to be an observer. He was, on his own prompter's cue, ironic, demanding, remote, impatient—enacting Faust in an endless extenuation of scenes of real and imagined passion. He had understood he was playing the role of The Lover, as intensely as written by himself the dramatist, the unreal center of a real universe.

When he finished shaving, in all candidness his skin still wore a grizzled appearance. He fingered his jaw appraisingly, holding his face together. Then he ran hot water and splashed heat on his cheeks until color appeared. While he dried himself, his eyes peered out of the folds of the rough towel. He looked fierce beneath shaggy brows.

He put on a shirt and chose a light blue tie from the rack inside the closet door, tying it three times to get the full casual knot.

"You're sure you like me?" he asked Katherine.

"Yes, I'm sure," she said. She was lying on the bed wearing short yellow pajamas of a light material. Her legs were bare and she wore sandals. She was reading a magazine. "Shouldn't I like you?"

"I just don't understand why."

In the mirror he detected a small wadding of flesh beneath his chin.

"You're feeling insecure," she said.

"Not insecure exactly. Just bewildered."

"Why?"

"Because you like me."

"That's very flattering. Hold on to that feeling."

"You have absolutely no consideration."

"But I have my own kind of anxiety. I keep warning myself to develop a wonderfully interesting personality so you won't be able to get rid of me. When you start getting tired, I'll just shift over to another facet of my personality and start winning you back."

"Like a chameleon?"

She put down the magazine. "Chameleons must be insecure, come to think of it."

"Why?"

"How would you like to keep changing yourself around every time the background changes?"

"You're right. A chameleon can't work up any respect for himself. He's always selling out."

She got up and chose a white wool dress from the closet and held it before her looking in the mirror.

"Will this look respectable?"

"It'll look beautiful," he said.

She frowned at her reflection. "Never mind about beautiful. Will I look respectable?"

"Yes," he said.

She sighed. "It's a wonder. I feel so *depraved*."

He kissed the top of her head. "Take your bath and get dressed and I'll order breakfast sent up. We'll have to hurry if you want to be at your father's place in time to cook Thanksgiving dinner."

The Prescott home was a few miles outside the city of Omaha. It was a two-story, sloping-roofed frame house with an open porch, a modest lawn, a garage and a toolshed.

Jim Prescott, Katherine's father, was a tall, straight-standing, bald, serious man with careworn lines in his cheeks.

"I know several people around here who remember you when you were sharing a law office with Mr. Kenneth Norris. You handled some legal problems for them."

"I hope they were satisfied," Paul Lowe said.

"Some were. Some weren't."

The living room in which they were sitting was comfortably old-fashioned with dark chairs and just-turning-shabby fabrics. There were large oil portraits hanging from the walls, including a handsomely framed portrait of Jane Prescott, Katherine's mother, above the mantelpiece.

"A lot of folks remember your father too," Jim Prescott said. "They say he was a fine doctor and a good man. And one of the men who works in my store was a friend of your brother William."

"Is that so? What's his name?"

"Tom Van Rensselaer."

"I'm afraid I don't know him," Paul Lowe said.

"Smoke?" Jim Prescott offered a humidor of cigars to choose from.

"Thank you," Paul Lowe said, taking a cigar.

Jim Prescott bit off the end of his own cigar. "I'm sorry I didn't get to Washington for the wedding. But it happened so sudden. Seems to me almost the first thing I heard was when you were married. And when a man's got a small business on his hands . . ."

"I understand perfectly, Mr. Prescott. As a matter of fact, my secretary, Martha Scully, was only there because I needed her as a witness. The other witness was the wife of the justice of the peace and the ceremony was held in his home. Both Katherine and I wanted it to be as simple a ceremony as possible."

Jim Prescott nodded approvingly. "Good idea. Silly waste of money to have one of them big affairs."

Katherine opened the kitchen door. "Did I hear the front doorbell?"

They listened and heard a muffled jangle.

"Timmy!" Katherine wiped her hands on her apron and ran.

"You haven't met the little fellow, have you?" Jim Prescott asked.

"No, but I want to."

"He's shy with strangers. Don't be worried if you don't hit it off right away. Timmy gets along fine with fellows his own age but he's a little backward with grownups."

There was a tumult of welcome in the hallway.

Katherine came into the room hugging a small boy in a snowsuit and swinging him half off the floor. She put the boy down.

"Timmy, I want you to meet your new father."

Timmy had his mother's complexion. His smooth cheeks were bright red with cold. He looked down as Paul Lowe held out his hand.

"How do you do, sir. I'm pleased to meet you."

"I'm pleased to meet you, Tim. We're going to be good friends."

"Yes, sir." Timmy began to unzip his snowsuit. He wriggled out of his snowsuit. He wore a blue sweater and knickers with heavy woolen socks. When Katherine shook out the snowsuit crusted white patches fell from it to melt quickly on the wooden floor at the edge of the carpeting.

"Did you crawl home on your hands and knees?" she asked.

Timmy grinned without looking up. "We had a snowball fight."

"Who won?" Paul Lowe asked.

"I guess nobody."

"When we used to have a snowball fight, we had to pretend we were wounded wherever we were hit."

"Yes, sir," Timmy said.

They went into the living room. Katherine said she had to go back to the kitchen to see to the dinner. When she left Paul Lowe began to feel the anxiety of the last passenger on a sinking ship.

Jim Prescott said, "Timmy and I were in Lincoln the other day. Saw the house your father used to live in."

"Is that so?" Mr. Prescott had done a thorough job of checking him out. "I lived there when I was your age," he said to Timmy. "Would you have liked to live in a house like that?"

"No, sir," Timmy said.

Jim Prescott said, "Now, Timmy, that isn't polite."

Paul Lowe said, "It's all right. I didn't like to live there myself."

"It's a very interesting house," Jim Prescott said. "Well built. Couldn't have stood this long if it hadn't been. Family named Marvin lives there now. He's in agricultural machinery."

"I haven't been back in years," Paul Lowe said.

He turned to Timmy who was sitting on a chair with his knees dangling and his hands loosely folded in his lap.

"Are you in real school or kindergarten?" he asked.

"I started real school in September."

"Do you like it?"

"No, sir."

"I guess no one does at first. But in time you get used to . . ."

He was interrupted by a scream from the direction of the kitchen.

"*Paul!*"

He leaped up to go to Katherine. Jim Prescott was not far behind. Timmy brought up the rear.

In the kitchen Katherine was staring in horror at the open door of an oven.

"I-I opened the door to l-light the oven," she said in a shaking voice. "And a-a m-mouse jumped out!"

"A mouse?"

"One of them field mice," Jim Prescott said. "It doesn't mean anything. I don't know what's the matter with you, Katherine."

"I'll tell you what's the matter," she said. "I hate mice!"

Jim Prescott took a glance around the kitchen. "Well, he isn't around now. So there's no sense worrying about it."

"I'm not going to move a foot until somebody gets rid of him."

"Darn foolishness!" Jim Prescott snorted.

Paul Lowe said to Timmy, "What do you think? Shall we try to catch the mouse for your mother?"

Timmy's light colored eyes flickered distantly.

"If you want to, sir."

"We've got to organize this like a campaign," Paul Lowe said. "First, everyone out of the kitchen except actual combatants. That means you, darling, *and* your father."

While he held on to her hand, Katherine edged along the far wall. In the clear, she bolted out the kitchen door. Jim Prescott, with a slightly disgusted expression on his face, followed his daughter.

"Well," Paul Lowe said to Timmy, "it's up to us now. That mouse is somewhere in this kitchen."

"Yes, sir." Timmy's voice was hushed with the drama of an impending confrontation.

"How do you think we should go about this? Have you ever hunted mouse before?"

"No, sir."

"My guess is that he's either under the stove or under the sink."

Timmy eyed the suspect hiding places with grave respect.

"Yes, sir."

"We need a weapon," Paul Lowe said.

The atmosphere was becoming satisfactorily charged with tension. Zero hour.

"How about a broom?" Timmy asked.

Paul Lowe regarded him with admiration. "That's a great idea, Timmy."

Aglow with pride, Timmy brought a broom from the broom closet.

"Now, working carefully—carefully now, Timmy—you prod with the broom handle under the stove. If he's there you'll flush him out and I'll get him toward the outside door."

Timmy nodded. His eyes burned with valor. Holding the broom by its whiskered end he crouched to put the handle as far under the stove as he could reach. He moved it slowly from right to left. He had almost reached the far end of the stove when a tiny gray shape scampered toward the middle of the kitchen floor. Timmy gave a yelp and dropped the broom.

"We've got him," Paul Lowe yelled. "Cover the door. Open it when I tell you to."

404

Timmy fought down panic. He swallowed convulsively and kept a wary eye on the enemy as he moved cautiously to the outside door.

The mouse made a tentative pass toward the dark safety of the sink but retreated when met by Paul Lowe in force. The mouse drew back, circled once and settled to survey the situation. Taking up the broom handle, Paul Lowe advanced.

"Now," he shouted to Timmy.

On command Timmy flung open the door. A chill breeze swept in. Paul Lowe lunged forward.

In a quick decisive maneuver the mouse turned and fled into the out-of-doors. Timmy flung shut the door with a resounding bang.

"Well done," Paul Lowe said.

He offered his hand. Timmy wiped his palm on his sweater and clasped Lowe's hand firmly. His gaze met Paul Lowe's in the worshipful yet proud manner of a captain for his victorious general. He was grinning widely.

They re-entered the living room in a silent blare of trumpets to announce there was nothing more to fear.

The huge jet plane wheeled slowly and Capitol Hill came into view. Looking past Katherine out the window, he kept his eyes closed against the white glitter of the Capitol which seemed to throw up flakes of reflected winter sunlight. On this hill was the center of government in a land he loved. The buildings embodied American history. Seeing them again he understood the passionate desire of men to hold certain things safe from change or at least to let them change so slowly that they would give the appearance of changelessness.

Ahead of him, at the window, Timmy turned back to peer through the opening between his seat and the adjoining seat.

"Isn't that where you work, Dad?"

"No, Tim. That's where the Congress works. And there's the White House. See? Over there."

The boy's exhaled sigh of wonder reached him, "Gee."

That feeling of wonder Paul Lowe shared. He would like all these buildings to remain eternally young or else to grow old with great deliberation accepting the change as an aging body does, allowing the centuries to sink like wrinkles in the skin. Where now is Antinopolis, city drowned in the Nile? There was time before the Potomac claimed this capital. Washington was so young that only yesterday Hamilton and Madison and Mason had walked its streets. Only a hundred and forty-two years ago, hardly a wink in time, Dolly Madison was sitting at dinner and heard the British were coming. Now she was taking the butler down by candlelight to cut the portrait of George Washington out of its frame with a butcher knife. She would be pleased to know that Gilbert Stuart's painting of the first President still held a place of honor in the White House. It was not the first fraud to inhabit that gray-white mansion. For the portrait was not all done by Gilbert Stuart—it had been completed by Winstanley and even George Washington was not all George—the son-in-law of John Adams posed for the limbs and body.

A little history. We are a raw country with too few legends. One hundred and forty-two years ago, while Dolly Madison was at dinner Napoleon had not yet come to Waterloo and Europe was old, old. . . .

"I see it, Dad. Look! There!"

There? There? The boy was referring to the Supreme Court building. Paul Lowe's attention returned to the present.

"Yes, that's it, Tim."

What was he coming back to, he wondered. Charles Edmunson was still absent from the Court and without his charismatic and unifying presence, would the liberal bloc hold firm? Or would the allegiance of any of its members begin to veer? Nothing is more difficult, for judges as for other men, than to be unpopular. It is safer to take accepted maxims for granted and not try to reason from principles to conclusions that may be odious to the majority. The skeptical intelligence in its pursuit of proof must be willing to challenge the vague and equivocal beliefs which constitute public morality. But that takes the courage that comes from a total reliance on the power of the free inquiring mind. Charles Edmunson had that courage and was able to transfer some of it to men who might otherwise be too timid to follow him.

He was sure Edward McCann would not waver. As for himself he was still under Edmunson's sway, still moved by the concept of law as a Third Force, a mediator between the natural and unnatural enmities of man and man, man and government, nation and nation. It was highly dangerous to sentimentalize any human institution: there is so much possibility of error, so great unworthiness in man the creator. But there is a virtue at least in his yearning toward perfectibility, toward the ideal of justice. He was impressed by Waldo Shuler's vast knowledge but he could not help feeling that such knowledge divorced from a love of justice resembled cleverness more than wisdom.

How about John Hampton and Henry Merriam? Would they continue to be counted in Edmunson's bloc or were other pressures likely to move them in a new direction? Nothing, certainly not men, could be judged in repose: where a man stood at any given moment was never as important as the direction in which he was going. When the human pendulum began swinging it must continue irresistibly to its farthest arc.

The Supreme Court building dipped out of sight but he held the vision a moment longer. He did not want to part with it or with all that the marble palace symbolized—the patient search of reasonable men for a truth worthy to become the incandescence called law.

28

As usually happens when an abstract principle is to be embodied in human terms, *Vosburg vs. the Maryland Board of Education* was not at all the sort of confrontation that anyone expected. The conflict was not between the government of the United States and a leader of the Communist party. The government was not one of the litigants and the man whose case was being argued was not a Communist functionary on a local, state or federal level.

The man's name was Frank George Matthews. He was the author of several profound but unreadable treatises on political economy and he had been offered a teaching post at a state college in Maryland. Matthews accepted and then, with absolutely no warning, the roof fell in. Evelyn Vosburg, a housewife and a citizen of the State of Maryland, discovered that Frank George Matthews openly subscribed to the teachings of Marx and Lenin.

Mrs. Vosburg discovered this by the simple expedient of buying a book which Matthews had written that had only been published in England. She brought the book to the attention of the State Board of Education where she was told that Frank George Matthews had been signed to a teaching contract and the commitment had to be honored. She promptly went to the editor of the city newspaper with her complaint.

This was a critical time in which to bring the question of a Communist teacher to the attention of a newspaper. In that same week there had been a riot in Caracas in which four Americans were killed, a bomb had been thrown at the United States Embassy building in Ghana, the United Nations had voted to condemn American intervention in Burma, and the man in the street in his identity as an American felt as though he were in the center of a target and people all over the world were throwing darts at him.

With instinctive understanding for his readers' baffled rage, the first editor played up the Matthews case for all it was worth. Every wire service carried the story and the case was promptly seized upon by other editors of other newspapers in every major American city. Every television news broadcast featured it, and the atmosphere became more heated when Frank George Matthews in a television interview said that he was frankly hoping that the American troops now in Burma would suffer a humiliating defeat at the hands of the Communist rebels. A victory for the Communists, Matthews declared, was the only road to peace in Southeast Asia. Within a few days Frank George Matthews, whose books had never sold more than three thousand copies, became a household name in millions of homes. His physical appearance, fortyish, scrawny, with large round eyeglasses, became as well known as that of any reigning movie star.

With more than adequate financial backing the Maryland housewife, Evelyn Vosburg, took her case against the Maryland Board of Education to the courts. A trial judge held that the contract of employment was valid and Frank George Matthews could not be discharged from his job as teacher.

Then the Maryland Court of Appeals, by a vote of four to three, held that the trial judge was wrong and Frank George Matthews *could* be discharged.

Matthews' lawyers then asked the Supreme Court of the United States to review the case. The American Civil Liberties Union announced that it would file an *amicus curiae* brief in Frank Matthews' behalf and so did the Teachers Union.

In granting the petition to hear the case, the Supreme Court limited the issues to only one question: whether the statutory provision of the state Civil Service law which forbade the hiring of teachers who advocated forcible overthrow of the government was in fact unconstitutional.

On the day before *Vosburg vs. the Maryland Board of Education* was to be heard, Paul Lowe spent a late afternoon hour playing paddle tennis in the fourth-floor gymnasium of the Supreme Court building. His partner was his new law clerk, Harry Temple, and they were opposed by Gabriel Hart and his law clerk, Sy Franklin, a tall morose-looking young man with the air of a melancholy crane.

They played handball rules and it was a fairly even match. Gabriel Hart was quicker but had less power than Paul Lowe, and Hart's gangling young partner, Sy Franklin, was effective in the rear court. He had a steady backhand that offset Harry Temple's greater range in covering the court.

The lead seesawed back and forth amid the hurried sound of voices and the thumping run of feet. They were tied at eighteen all and Gabriel Hart was serving. Gabriel, wearing a bulky sweatshirt and shorts, got over a good serve and rushed the net. Harry Temple swung his wooden paddle and hammered the spongy rubber ball into a far corner. Sy Franklin made a desperate lunge for the ball, and his long arms disentangled themselves from his body barely in time to pop the ball in a futile arc.

Paul Lowe served and ran out three points and won the game.

Gabriel Hart came to the net and made a mock gesture of jumping over. He shook Paul Lowe's hand.

"We'll get you next time, Paul," he said, "or I'll have to fire Sy and get a law clerk who can cover more ground."

Sy Franklin, grinning shyly, came to the net to shake hands with Harry Temple. The two young men started off together with Paul Lowe and Gabriel Hart following behind.

"I needed this workout," Gabriel Hart said. "I've been getting more and more tensed up as the day for hearing oral argument in the Vosburg case approaches. Things are changing rapidly in this country, Paul. I think the Court is going to change along with the times. I've thought so before, but this time I know it's going to happen."

"What's going to happen, Gabriel?"

"Edmunson's coalition is going to break up. And it will mark the beginning of a change back to a proper regard for the conservative tradition of this Court."

They left the gymnasium and started down the stairs.

"In my opinion that change is long overdue," Gabriel Hart said, "although it probably won't please you too much."

"We're on different sides of the argument, Gabriel," Paul Lowe answered. "And I suppose our differences go pretty deep."

He knew what Gabriel Hart's newfound confidence was based on. With Edmunson not voting, the most likely result in a deep-cutting controversial issue like *Vosburg vs. the Maryland Board of Education* would be a tie vote of four to four. Such a vote would uphold the decision of the Maryland Court of Appeals that Frank George Matthews could be discharged. But he could not quite understand Gabriel Hart's belief that such an inconclusive result would portend a fundamental change in the Court's alignment.

On the floor below they began to walk around the bend in the corridor to the elevator.

Gabriel Hart rubbed a hand briskly through his hair. "Too bad in a way that the Old Man won't be around to help you defend this lost cause. I have a hunch even his vote wouldn't help you this time."

Paul Lowe said, "Let's wait to see what happens, Gabriel."

After a quick shower in the bathroom of his private office, Paul Lowe began to dress. He put on his underwear and began to pull on his trousers. In the mirror of the medicine cabinet he caught a partial reflection of a troubled face. The face was his own.

From the first words of the oral argument in *Vosburg vs. the Maryland Board of Education*, Paul Lowe sensed a different attitude among his colleagues on the bench. They listened with extreme courtesy and attention to Irwin Nelson, the distinguished attorney arguing the case for Mrs. Vosburg. But when Stephen Rose, the attorney for the Maryland Board of Education, started to plead his case he was interrupted by a drumfire of probing hostile questions.

The questions came not only from Waldo Shuler who took his usual delight in harassing an attorney, but also from Bill Branch and Henry Merriam. Because these two justices were usually the ones most interested in and perhaps most influenced by oral argument their aggressive questioning might have been excused. But when Stephen Rose began to fumble and stray under pressure, Chief Justice John Hampton was harsher than his custom in pointing this out to the attorney. Under the barrage Stephen

Rose began to falter, tried to recover his line of argument, failed, and began to repeat himself.

When the red light glowed on the lectern to indicate that his hour was finished, Stephen Rose looked like a man in shock, and the total effect of his argument was scarcely short of disaster.

Just before the conference began that Friday, Henry Merriam stopped by Paul Lowe's office.

"I want to warn you, Paul," he said, "that I am considering taking a different position than you'd expect on the Vosburg case. I'll wait until I hear what's said in conference today. But after reading the briefs and hearing the oral argument I've begun to wonder whether Frank George Matthews really deserves to be a teacher."

"We've decided this sort of issue before, Henry. There's a clear distinction between what a man believes and the kind of overt conduct that is punishable."

"Oh, I know. I know. There are always strong arguments for protecting our liberties. But we can't afford to be single-minded about it."

"I don't know anything I'd rather be single-minded about."

"When a strong wind's blowing you have to tack with it for a while. That's only common sense, Paul. And I can tell you in all seriousness that the mood of the people of this country right now is alarming."

Paul Lowe stirred uneasily in his chair. As chief proselytizer for the Court, Henry Merriam kept his finger tight-pressed to the public pulse. His ability as a fluent and graceful speechmaker brought him scores of invitations to Bar Associations, state conventions, Masonic breakfasts, veterans' organizations, religious groups and societies where he explained and defended the Court's decisions. Better than anyone on the Supreme Court he understood the environment of public opinion in which, at the last, all decisions of the Court must survive or perish.

Paul Lowe frowned. "If something is right we should go ahead and do it no matter how many people are upset about it. I wish you could talk with Edmunson about this, Henry."

"Oh, I know what the Old Man would say. Never back away from a fight because of the odds. Even if I could show him that a vote for Matthews would lead to certain disaster for this Court and even for the country he'd react like a leader of light cavalry at Balaklava. Forward into the guns."

"In the long run the Court has usually vindicated the Old Man's position."

"We have to try to weigh all the factors, Paul. It isn't strictly a question of law. The President is right about that."

"I see you've had the benefit of one of Lamont Howard's post-volleyball lunches."

"I haven't let that influence me," Henry Merriam said. "But he does have the security of this country in mind. You have to admit that."

Paul Lowe glanced at his watch. Only a few minutes remained before the conference was to start.

"When you've heard all the arguments, Henry, I've a feeling you'll agree that freedom of speech and thought is more important to the security of this country than whether Frank George Matthews is the right sort of teacher for a state college."

Henry Merriam nodded, a bit unhappily, Paul Lowe thought, and then they left his office and went down the corridor together.

In the conference room later that morning he felt as though he were in a familiar setting where the background had subtly been altered.

He overheard Bill Branch with Gabriel Hart. They were discussing a massive student demonstration for peace scheduled for that Sunday in Washington. Frank George Matthews was scheduled as one of the principal speakers.

Gabriel Hart said, "The damned young fools don't know what it's all about. They don't understand the seriousness of the situation. As for Matthews, he's simply thumbing his nose at us. He's an agent provocateur."

Bill Branch answered, "The leaders of this demonstration are almost certainly Communist-inspired. They know exactly what they're doing. They're trying to sabotage America's military effort."

Edward McCann said, "I would imagine there are enough pacifists in the country to make up a sizable demonstration. Not to mention all the people who honestly differ with our policy in Burma and Southeast Asia."

Andrew Cutler said, "The trouble with some people on this Court is that they can't recognize a Communist unless he's waving a red flag with a hammer and sickle on it and carrying a bomb."

Edward McCann said, "And the trouble with some others is that they have a spinster's fear of Communists hiding under their bed."

"Gentlemen," John Hampton's clear voice cut through the contention, "it's time to start the conference. Take your seats, please."

The conference proceeded smoothly until they reached *Vosburg vs. the Maryland Board of Education*. The Chief Justice gave his summation and the discussion moved down the table in order of seniority. Waldo Shuler said that the part of the state Civil Service law providing that no person should be employed who advocates the forcible overthrow of the government seemed to him both constitutional and fair.

"I for one," Shuler continued, "am willing to concede that Frank George Matthews has a perfect right to hold any belief—a perfect right to think and to speak as he wants to. But that does not give him the right to work for the State of Maryland as a teacher in a state college. Frank Matthews can't *dictate* the terms he's going to work under, in defiance of perfectly reasonable requirements by the state authorities. If he doesn't want to work under the state's terms he can go elsewhere. I fail to see how this takes the right of free speech away from him."

Andrew Cutler added icily, "What it comes down to is a question of fitness for public service. A Communist isn't fit for public service—and that's that!"

Edward McCann broke in, "Why does a man who goes into public service have to forfeit his constitutional right to freedom of speech?"

Andrew Cutler said, "When a man is considered for an important job in private industry his loyalty is weighed. Why can't the government weigh a man's loyalty before hiring him for public service?"

"There's an important difference, that's why!"

"I wish you would tell me what it is, Edward."

"A privately owned company can't enforce such a practice beyond the limits of its own business. But the government has immense power to cut off the flow of ideas into people's minds. If we allow any government, or any agency of government, to exercise that power we're taking a long step down the road to a police state!"

Bill Branch, flushed and choleric, brought his palm down with such force on the conference table that a leather container of sharpened yellow pencils jumped and rattled.

"I'd like to point out to my bleeding-heart colleagues that if the situation were reversed and Frank George Matthews were on trial in Russia or Red China he'd get mighty short shrift. He'd be lucky if he weren't shot!"

Edward McCann's plump freckled face turned an interesting shade of light pink. "That's no test for anything and I'm damned surprised to find out you think it is! If certain people in this room were brought up on morals charges at the time of the Inquisition, they'd have been burned at the stake. Does that prove that the Inquisition's methods of conducting a trial were better than ours?"

The parallel was too neatly turned, Paul Lowe thought. Bill Branch had been through two marriages, a dozen romantic intrigues, and had almost been named corespondent in an international scandal involving a famed French authoress.

Bill Branch's reaction was predictable. His jowls shook and his reply was a hardly intelligible roar of anger, ". . . no lily-livered, psalm singing . . . A monk's idea of morality . . . ought to get yourself a tonsure . . . trying to be Karl Marx in the Vatican!"

John Hampton's voice was frayed with weariness and irritability, "That's enough, gentlemen. That's enough!"

Bill Branch threw up his hands in exasperation.

"I have nothing more to say. It's no use trying to talk sense to soft-headed boobs who are still willing to stand by and let the Communists pick up all the marbles!"

Gabriel Hart passed.

Edward McCann had regained a measure of control. He said, "I happen to think our best chance of survival is to leave man's freedom to think absolutely alone. If men are free to think they'll eventually choose the best ideas. And democracy is the best idea anyone ever had on how people should govern themselves. Those who are afraid to let Frank George Matthews be a teacher simply don't have faith in the democratic system!"

When the Chief Justice called Henry Merriam, that justice appeared to be lost in reverie. He passed.

"Mr. Justice Paul Lowe?"

Paul Lowe said in a deliberate measured tone, "The issue in this case is the constitutionality of the provision in the Civil Service Law. . . ."

Silence gradually invaded the room except for the scraping of a chair leg and the rustling of paper.

". . . I would agree with Waldo Shuler's remark that Frank Matthews is entitled to think and speak as he wants to."

Edward McCann said, "Hear, hear!" in a low tone that did not carry.

Paul Lowe ignored the interruption. "I would also agree with Waldo Shuler that depriving Matthews of his right to teach in a state college is not the same thing as depriving him of the right of free speech. But it certainly would penalize him for having *exercised* his right of free speech. If men are punished for exercising a constitutional right, how can we say they have not in some degree been deprived of the right?"

He kept his query in a moderate tone. But there was an urgent message beneath his words, which was that they should treasure reliance on argument and debate because in other lands bombs were falling and men were settling their disputes in blood and terror. He wanted to suggest that while the private drama being played out in this conference room was miniscule, in the larger context of world affairs it was far from unimportant. What they were saying, doing, deciding on this day was very close to the heart of the matter. If they could express their differences without fear and without anger, they might manage to find a common ground. It is when reason fails that the rival camps must continue their argument in a different vocabulary. This was a message he had brought back from places whose names were now being writ large, Mandalay, Bharma, Mitkyina, and Rangoon.

Possibly something of what he meant did get across because when he had finished speaking the tension seemed to have completely dissipated into the air.

Chief Justice John Hampton said: "Gentlemen, we will proceed to a vote." He turned toward Paul Lowe. "Mr. Justice Lowe?"

"I would sustain the Maryland Board of Education in their decision that Frank George Matthews is entitled to keep his job."

"Mr. Justice Merriam?"

Merriam's usually sonorous voice was tight with strain. "I would uphold the decision of the Maryland Court of Appeals to dismiss Frank George Matthews from his post."

When an edifice is about to fall there is a rumbling sound, a signal that somewhere within the structure the fine and careful balance of stress and counterstress has been undermined by age or accident, erosion or the hand of time.

Paul Lowe had heard the rumbling sound before the conference began and now here was the first crack appearing, wide and jagged and undeniable.

He almost ceased to feel the chair under him. Edward McCann was voting now, but his vote would not matter.

Gabriel Hart had been right. Edmunson's coalition *was* breaking up. . . .

A few minutes later Paul Lowe opened his docket book to record the final tally. With Justice Charles Edmunson absent and with Chief Justice John Hampton and Justices Lowe and McCann dissenting, the vote was five to three against a reversal of the State Supreme Court.

Frank George Matthews had lost his job. Paul Lowe could not help wondering what the rest of them had lost.

At home, in the six-room apartment which Katherine had found on Dumbarton Street not many blocks from his former home on Volta Place, Paul Lowe worked in his study on a memorandum to the Chief Justice. It was a review of cases pending at the Christmas recess and a statement of his own position concerning each:

Memorandum to Chief Justice John Hampton:
Re: Cases Pending as of December 23rd:

Case Numbers 384, 385: *Virgison vs. United States*. Assigned to Henry Merriam. This right-to-travel case will probably draw a strong dissent from me. The ultimate issue as I see it is whether the Executive has been granted power by Congress to deny a passport for travel to a country which has a Communist form of government. I think we should interpret the statute as not having granted the power and thus leave the question to Congress for a deliberate reconsideration. We may hope that hearings will follow and a more moderate and better-drawn bill passed. It is a matter for the Congress.

Number 191: *Colorado et al vs. Wyoming et al*. This has been assigned and to you and the vote was unanimous, so you may put me down for the opinion you will write.

Numbers 411, 412: *Delaware Transportation Co. vs. United States*. Assigned to Cutler. McCann voted the other way and I was dubious. I shall not dissent unless you do—in the interests of promoting harmony.

Number 194: *New Jersey ex rel. Ostrowski vs. Eager*. Assigned to Shuler. This is an old case which we reversed a year ago. I hope it can be disposed of this time. McCann may dissent but if Shuler writes the opinion I will go along, although with some hesitation. If anyone else writes it, I may join McCann in dissent.

Number 332: *Knights of the White Star vs. United States*. Assigned to Branch. Cutler and Hart dissented. Shuler voted to affirm with a question. Branch already has an opinion prepared which I have examined and agreed to.

He stopped and put his pen down and rubbed his eyes. His memorandum had not reached some of the most important cases discussed in conference. He was tired; he was oppressed by a premonition of futility. In the broad spectrum, where a distinction could be found between the opposing factions on the Court, there was no doubt that a majority now adhered to the economic and legal viewpoint of Waldo Shuler.

414

It was possible that some success might be scored in a particular case. But the work of the Court was not limited to an individual case. In Edmunson's absence, Waldo Shuler, that fiercely brilliant little man, had begun to dominate the proceedings of the Court. Shuler had strong currents running with him, the mood of the country, the deteriorating situation of America in world affairs, but quieter and less obvious eddies were also stirring— the desire of a justice like Bill Branch for a return to old traditions of the Court, of Henry Merriam to resurrect the power of the states in a federal system, even a keener awareness by Chief Justice John Hampton of the values of judicial restraint.

The sum of these complex and unsatisfying equations had an overriding simplicity: Waldo Shuler was now in control. Paul Lowe had done his best to rally support by composing the strongest dissent of which he was capable in the Vosburg case. It had changed no one's mind, the final vote had remained five to three against him, and public sentiment in the country clearly lay with the majority of the Court. Perhaps someday there would be a reversal of the trend but that day seemed to be retreating further and further away. . . .

For the present, the prospect was so bleak that Paul Lowe could not rouse his spirits even with the thought of the Christmas season at hand.

There was a knock on the door. He said, "Come in."

Katherine entered. "I'm sorry to bother you but I knew you'd want to see this. It just arrived by messenger. It's from Charles Edmunson."

"Edmunson! Let me see it."

It was a letter, typewritten, obviously dictated.

My dear Paul: I have been, as you know, kept strictly abed by my doctors of late and forbidden emotional disturbances or excitement. However, being medical men, they are unaware of what disturbs and excites me. I saw the Vosburg vs. Board of Education decision—and was, in all truth, emotionally disturbed. The Court has overturned its own decisions almost two hundred times in its history—but never to reach a more disastrous result, at least not since Roger Taney. Only your dissent helped assuage my feelings. I am afraid the doctors would have forbidden me to read that also if they had known the excitement it would cause in me. I will only say this: you are likely to become a great justice in an old-fashioned and perhaps rapidly disappearing sense—a human being of powerful intelligence able to express himself in the law in the same way that philosophers express themselves in their metaphysical systems or mathematicians in their equations. If I were teaching constitutional law, and had to get out readings on state power versus human liberty, I could find no better illustration than the majority opinion in Vosburg and your own eloquent dissent. It strikes me as tragic that such a formal device as Shuler invented to circumvent the clear right of an American citizen to speak what he thinks should be elevated to the august level of constitutional doctrine. I do not believe that such fetters on our liberty will be allowed to endure, or long find in the Constitution their shield. They will, I suspect, furnish the historian of the future United States some interesting material on how far intelligent men can go to rationalize their timidity. Your dissent is heartening. It is important. It is devastating. Judged by morality that rises above the passions of the time, it will come to be held conclusive.—Yours in admiration, Charles Edmunson

He folded the letter and put it into the drawer of his desk.

Katherine asked, "What does Edmunson say?"

"He likes the Vosburg opinion I wrote."

"Can I read the letter?"

He gave it to her. While she read he continued to savor the contents.

She gave the letter back and her eyes were glistening. "It must be exciting to have your work praised by one of your own heroes."

"Yes," he said.

There was a timid knock on the door. Timmy entered in his pajamas.

"Now, Timmy," Katherine said. "I told you not to bother your daddy tonight."

"I wanted to say good night to him."

"Good." Paul Lowe indicated his knee.

Timmy happily came over and sat on his knee and leaned against him. There was such confiding warmth in the boy's body. He blinked round eyes as he looked up at Lowe. Everything else was complex and difficult, Paul Lowe thought, but some things were simple and made sense. Timmy made sense to him. So did Katherine.

"Will you have time to tell me a story?" Timmy asked.

"I might—if you go right to bed."

"And if he drinks his milk," Katherine said.

"And if you drink your milk."

"Okay!" Timmy slid off his knee. "Don't forget I can stay up late tomorrow. It's Christmas eve!" He scampered out of the room.

Katherine said helplessly, "He'll do anything for you. I don't understand the power you've got over him. What kind of stories do you tell, anyhow?"

"He prefers real stories. About people and things that really happened. He's not much on fairy tales or mythology. Right now, we're in our Bronko Nagurski period."

"Who is Bronko Nagurski?"

"A man who averaged seven yards from the scrimmage line. They knew he was coming through the middle of the line but there was nothing they could do about it. He went through like an armored tank."

"Football?"

He nodded. "I promised to take him to some of the Washington Redskin games next fall."

Katherine smiled. "The old saying should have been 'you haven't gained a husband—you've lost a son.'"

"You can come too, if you promise not to ask silly questions. Like how many downs are there in a quarter or why do they have a different team for when they have the ball and when they haven't?"

"All right," she said coming toward him. "I'll go brush up on Bronko

416

Nagurski. And I'll be ready in time for the first inning of the first game the Washington Redskins play."

He smiled, and returned the kiss she gave him.

Charles Edmunson returned to the Court the first week in January. He had lost a good deal of weight and seemed gaunt and weary. In the next few weeks there were two controversial civil rights cases in which a direct confrontation occurred between Charles Edmunson and Waldo Shuler.

The first important contest came in *Bailey vs. Mississippi,* and the question to be resolved was whether the petitioner's use of a peremptory challenge to exclude Negroes from a jury that had convicted a Negro at a murder trial was enough to upset the conviction. In this summation Chief Justice John Hampton pointed out that the plaintiff Thomas Bailey was not *entitled* to a jury which contained members of his race any more than a Catholic would be entitled to a jury which contains Catholics. The constitutional question was whether or not the Negroes had been excluded from the jury on the grounds of their race.

Charles Edmunson said, "There is certainly reason to believe that the exclusion in this case was deliberate. No Negro has served on a jury in Orange County for more than twenty years. It is true that eight Negroes were on the panel from which the jury was chosen, but they were all excused on peremptory challenges from the prosecutor. In effect, this use of the peremptory challenge continues the unconstitutional policy of excluding Negroes from jury service."

Waldo Shuler answered, "It isn't the same thing at all, Charles. The fact that Negroes were chosen for the panel from which jurors were picked indicates strongly that there was no policy of deliberate exclusion. As for the peremptory challenge—that has an old and honorable history in law. Any juror may be challenged without a reason. It's essential to the whole idea of the peremptory challenge that it *can* be exercised without giving a reason. There can't be any control of the use of that right."

"Do you mean there can be no control of the use of a peremptory challenge even if its use violates the equal protection clause of the Constitution?" Edmunson asked.

Waldo Shuler snapped, "Every race and every religion is subject to the same challenge without cause. That takes it out of the realm of the constitutional guarantees."

"Suppose we could prove that the peremptory challenge was used by the prosecutor in this case for the specific purpose of excluding Negroes from a jury, would that make it unconstitutional?" Edmunson inquired.

"But how can we prove that? We'd have to show that the prosecutor used his peremptory challenge against Negroes simply *because* they were Negroes. And to show that you'd have to look into the workings of the prosecutor's mind. It's obviously impossible."

Edmunson replied mildly, "The fact that no Negroes have served on a jury in Orange County for more than twenty years throws some light on the workings of the prosecutor's mind. This prosecutor is the same man who has seen to it that Negroes *don't* serve on juries. He's a leading member of a white-supremacy group and was elected to his present office by a so-called lilywhite political party. It may be true, Waldo, that we can't look into a man's mind. But we're entitled to judge his prejudices by his actions and his background."

"That will get us into a discussion of personalities," Waldo Shuler said sharply. "And that has nothing to do with the constitutional issue. Let's strip away the nonessentials. In order to throw out Thomas Bailey's conviction and order a new trial, we have to prove that the use of the peremptory challenge in this case is unconstitutional. I am perfectly willing to grant that there was discrimination in Orange County in recent years but that doesn't prove that there is discrimination now, and it certainly doesn't prove there was discrimination in this case. The fact that eight Negroes were on the panel from which jurors were chosen indicates that the climate of discrimination is changing. Against that background I don't see how we can maintain that the use of the peremptory challenge in the case before us is unconstitutional."

When the discussion moved down the table to Paul Lowe, he said, "If we don't include the peremptory challenge within the scope of our previous decisions, we'll give a weapon to those whose real purpose is to exclude Negroes. We'll be telling them it's all right to go ahead and use the peremptory challenge as a new way of avoiding the equal protection clause of the Constitution."

Waldo Shuler's view carried the day. The Chief Justice and Henry Merriam both voted with Waldo Shuler. So did Bill Branch, Andrew Cutler and Gabriel Hart.

There were only three justices in dissent—Edmunson, McCann, and Paul Lowe.

At the next Friday's conference they discussed a case that involved a test of a "benevolent quota" system. A New England state had decreed that at least one-third of the units in a public-housing project must be assigned to Negroes. In the conference, Charles Edmunson's customary eloquence was not in evidence. He seemed almost uninterested in the progress of the debate. Waldo Shuler posed a difficult question: Is it within a state's power to dictate where people must live and work? And Edward McCann tried his best to answer it.

McCann said: "If a state wants to remove the bars to integration, we'll let them do it, won't we? Now suppose that isn't enough. Suppose the state wants to go beyond the mere removal of the legal bars to make integration effective? It seems to me in that case that the state ought to be allowed to legislate a controlled amount of integration."

Waldo Shuler countered, "That would enforce a very considerable degree of unwanted unassociation on whites—especially on poorer whites who have no practical alternative to living in cheap and subsidized housing. It would seem to me a severe restriction on the freedom *not* to associate."

Paul Lowe took up the battle against Shuler. It was an issue he cared about and that he believed ought to be decided positively in favor of the state's power to induce a limited amount of association between whites and Negroes. He hoped that this issue, which for once involved defending a state's power, might win back Justice Henry Merriam to the fold.

"It isn't true that poorer white people won't have alternatives. They *can* live elsewhere. The state is merely making an effort to induce them *not* to live elsewhere. There is no coercion. The mere existence of this cheap housing, which happens to be provided for both whites and Negroes, is an inducement to these people to abandon their prejudices. But there is no attempt to compel them to do so."

"The so-called benevolent quota system is really segregation turned inside out," Waldo Shuler declared. "What will be its immediate effect? What will happen? It's true some Negroes will be allowed their freedom to associate. But the one-third rule will *deny* other Negroes their freedom to associate by keeping them out. And even those who are accepted, who are allowed to associate under the one-third rule, will be allowed to do so on the basis of a special arrangement that practically proclaims their apartness and inferiority."

It was a typical Waldo Shuler thrust, a turning of the sword into the vitals of those who wielded it. Waldo had cleverly seized upon the heart of paradox. He managed to seem plausible while making Paul Lowe appear inconsistent.

Paul Lowe hung on grimly. "Obviously, Waldo, what is hoped for in this case is that by allowing some association of races the old fears and prejudices will be removed."

"Do you think they will be?" Waldo Shuler inquired. "It seems at least as likely that this form of limited integration—or limited segregation as I prefer to call it—will open the door to prejudice in the same way as a ban on association of the races would. Under the principle of the Segregation Cases decided by this Court we have to hold a benevolent quota unconstitutional."

"We shouldn't do it until there's been more experience with it. The state's motive in trying to enforce this quota is obviously a good one. We should allow them a chance to make it work."

In his own ears his argument sounded more like ineffectual pleading. This was not how Edmunson would have mounted a challenge. He had taken up the cudgels that the Old Man seemed to have temporarily laid down but he could not wield them. *I am not Prince Hamlet nor was meant to be.* Edmunson and he wore the same black robes but a similarity in the uniform does not make a similarity in men. Comparisons are not merely odious—they are humiliating.

The final vote was five to four in favor of Waldo Shuler's position. Henry Merriam again voted with Shuler.

That afternoon, when the conference ended, Paul Lowe returned to his office.

From long experience Martha Scully was able to interpret his mood, so her face remained expressionless and she waited twenty minutes before she brought in the mail.

"Is this all, Martha?" he asked.

"I took the liberty of screening out some letters, Mr. Justice. Nothing important. Only some more people writing in about your marriage."

Since his divorce and remarriage, the mail had increased sharply both in volume and vituperation. The complaints were now more personal than political, ranging from a minister who more in sorrow than anger suggested that a divorced man had no useful place in public life, to a married woman (she signed her letter "Mother of Four") who said that his "carryings on" proved what she had suspected from the first—that "all your brains are in the seat of your pants."

"Some of these people are really crazy," Martha said. "They ought to be locked up, if you ask me."

"As bad as that today?"

Her mouth set thinly. "Worse. It gets worse all the time, Mr. Justice."

Paul Lowe sighed. "I'll look them over later. I'm not in the mood now. Were there any phone calls?"

"Your wife, Mr. Justice."

"What did she have to say?"

"She said not to worry if she wasn't home by six. She's taking Timmy over to stay at a friend's house and then she's going shopping. But she'll be back in time to make dinner."

"Fine. Anything else?"

"Just two calls—not important. I put the memos on your desk."

"Good. You can go home whenever you want to, Martha."

"Yes, Mr. Justice."

In his office Paul Lowe looked at the memorandum listing the phone calls; neither required an answer. The absence of phone calls was something he still had not gotten used to. As a lawyer his phone had been constantly busy, and as governor of Nebraska the phone had been an instrument of torture. But the telephone of a Supreme Court justice rarely rang. The work was hard and solitary and he would have welcomed an occasional friendly interruption from the outside world. It's a damn ivory tower, he thought, under siege by the lunatic fringe. All we can do is read and read, think and think, write and write. And argue. To what purpose?

He sat at his desk and put his head in his hands.

In the apartment at six o'clock, he waited for Katherine with impatient longing. Whenever he was about to see her he had the strangest sensation of something extraordinary about to happen. She was a life enhancer. She brought out in him his highest expectations.

He put down the book he had been trying to read. He was ticking like

420

a bomb that might go off at any minute. Where was she? Timmy was staying overnight at a friend's house so there was no reason to have dinner at home. He would take her out. They might even go for a drive and end up at that colonial inn in Maryland where they had gone to dinner the very first time.

With every minute he grew more restless. He began to pace the room. Some compulsive rhythm drove him. Where was she? At five minutes past seven he glanced out the window. He commanded Katherine, out there: come home now.

Finally he sat down holding both arms of the chair and tried to recall the exact shade and fleck of color of her eyes. Magnified, her eyes occupied his entire field of vision, lambent and fixed, holding him in their hazel reflection. He shook his head to clear the hallucination. My God— a schoolboy had more control of his emotions. But it had been a terrible day for him. He needed her presence to console him.

The telephone rang. He snatched it.

"Hello," he said.

"Mrs. Lowe, please." It was a woman's voice.

"She isn't at home right now."

"Would you tell her that Dr. Mulvey called and wanted to know why she didn't keep her appointment at the hospital."

"At the hospital?" The question sounded far away as though someone had asked it in a voice that was not his own.

"Will you give Mrs. Lowe that message, please?"

"What is this about?"

The woman's voice turned smooth with caution: "Ask Mrs. Lowe to call Dr. Mulvey as soon as she gets in."

"I'd like to speak to Dr. Mulvey."

"I'm sorry. The doctor is very busy just now."

"I don't care. I want . . ." He stopped. A key turned in the door lock.

Katherine entered carrying a large brown paper bag of groceries. She was breathless.

Paul Lowe put back the telephone in its cradle.

"I'm sorry, darling," she said. "I tried to get home before you but there was such a line at the supermarket and there were so many things I needed to get." She went into the kitchen and returned without the shopping bag. She began taking off her gloves. "Were you talking to someone on the telephone?"

"Yes."

"Who was it?" She took off her coat and put it on a coat hanger that she removed from the closet.

"It was Dr. Mulvey."

There was a second's hesitation before she put her coat away in the closet. "Oh."

"He wanted to know why you didn't keep your appointment."

She crossed the room to kiss his forehead. "What appointment?"

"At the hospital."

She made a tired little gesture. "All right, since you're going to start pestering me with a whole lot of silly questions I'll tell you. I'd have told you before but I didn't want you to worry. It's nothing, actually. I've been feeling a bit tired and run down. So I went to see the doctor."

"Dr. Mulvey?"

"Yes."

"And what did he say?"

"He gave me some tablets and I've been feeling much better. Really."

"That's good."

"You don't act as though you believe me."

"I don't."

"Why not?"

"You haven't said anything about the appointment at the hospital."

Katherine looked at him serenely but the words came too quickly, too warmly. "Oh, I was there. I was only a little late, that's all. My appointment was for three-thirty and I didn't get there until after four." She shook her head irritably. "They probably called Dr. Mulvey's office and then forgot to cancel it when I arrived. That's all it is. A misunderstanding."

"Why did you have to go there?"

"It's part of the treatment Dr. Mulvey recommended."

"What is?"

"I really will tell you, darling. It's just such a long boring silly thing."

"Unless you tell me the whole truth, Katherine, I'll get alarmed enough to talk to Dr. Mulvey myself. Would you prefer that?"

"You're in one of your grim investigative moods."

"I want to know what's wrong with you."

"The man of one hundred faces. This is your stern judicial one."

"Well?"

"All right, if you're going to be so stubborn. I was feeling run down and tired, and I thought I noticed something and it worried me. So I went to the doctor."

"You never mentioned it to me."

"There was no need to worry you. And I'm glad I didn't because it turned out to be nothing important."

"What was it?"

"Well, I noticed my gums were bleeding quite a bit when I brushed my teeth in the morning."

"Is that all?"

"No. I thought I saw some blood elsewhere." At his questioning look, she added, "In my urine. Not much, just a little. Dr. Mulvey says it isn't anything."

"I'd better call Dr. Mulvey and talk to him."

"You can if you want to. But I'm telling you exactly what he told me."

"And your appointment at the hospital? What was that about?"

She ran her finger down his coat lapel. "I don't suppose you'd like to change the subject."

422

"No, I wouldn't."

"Well, this is going to sound a lot worse than it is. I went to the hospital for a transfusion."

"A blood transfusion?"

"Yes."

"Why?"

"I was a bit anemic."

"Do you have to go again?"

"Yes. I might have to. But not for a while."

It isn't worth this, he thought. No matter what has been in the way of happiness, nothing is worth this terrifying moment. Everything inside him seemed to be in suspended motion.

"What did the doctor say is wrong?"

Her shoulder moved wearily. "Oh, apparently I'm not very good at making my own red blood cells at the moment. In fact, I'm something of a flop at it. So the blood runs into places it shouldn't."

"I haven't noticed any bleeding."

"I've tried to be careful. I clean off my toothbrush. And if you kiss me too hard I swallow it." She saw the expression on his face. "Isn't it terrible? I couldn't tell you that before, could I? You might not want to kiss me any more."

For an instant her composure weakened and her face seemed to crumple. He took her into his arms.

"You're not angry with me, are you?" she asked.

"Of course I'm not angry."

She looked up at him. "Paul, I've got everything I need if I have you. I'm not afraid of anything. And I really am going to be all right. Dr. Mulvey says I'll be fine. You're not to start treating me like an invalid. I'm not breakable, you know."

He held her close.

29

He gripped the felt hand strap on the side of the cab as it made a sharp turn into a side street. Life, that trickster, has so many ways to outwit you. You think you know what will come next and in what order, one, two, three, but after each numeral life intervenes with qualifying clauses and amendments. It is like doing battle with an opponent who seizes upon every phrase and construes unexpected meanings to confuse and obscure the clear purpose with which you began.

He had to keep his anxieties from running away with him. What we call premonitions, he reminded himself, are not foretellings of future events. In every situation the mind is aboil with every possibility and, whatever the outcome, we can truthfully say that the thought was in the mind before. She might not be seriously ill. There were so many signs of her vitality, of her hold on life, from her sensuality to the quick way her emotions responded; even the way she spoke, one image crowding out another, her speech bubbling with new ideas, new directions so that a single topic was often not completed but wound its way like a twisting turning torrent past any landscape that interested her. That reflected mental vigor, physical health. *Mens sana in corpore sano*. . . . It might be nothing. She tended to be faintly hypochondriac. So much of her thinking revolved about imaginary things—numerology was one example—that it would not be surprising if her illnesses were imaginary too. But that was impossible. The doctor had sent her to the hospital for a transfusion. He must take her illness seriously.

The cab pulled up before a steel and glass office building. His chaotic thinking stopped.

In the quiet anteroom a pretty woman in a crisply white nurse's uniform and cap was seated at a desk. There were three or four women in the anteroom, nervously reading magazines.

"I'd like to see Dr. Mulvey, please."

"Do you have an appointment?"

"My wife is a patient of his."

"What is her name, please?"

"Mrs. Katherine Lowe."

424

The nurse had begun to write when she suddenly looked up. "I thought I recognized you. You're Mr. Justice Lowe—of the Supreme Court."

"Yes, I am."

The tag had its effect; her manner lost its professional brusqueness.

"I'll find out if the doctor can see you."

Dr. Mulvey was a slender man, about sixty, with the lean forward-thrusting face of a greyhound. He met Paul Lowe at the door of his office to shake hands.

"This is a great pleasure, Mr. Justice. I've followed your work on the Court. My son is in law school and he tells me that his professor is now one of your admirers."

He ushered Paul Lowe into a rectangular room with a desk and chairs, a gray filing cabinet and watercolor views of Washington on the walls near his framed diplomas.

"That's very kind," Paul Lowe said. "I know you're a busy man, doctor, so I'll try not to take up too much of your time. I came to talk to you privately about my wife's condition."

Dr. Mulvey's eyes assumed a glassy glitter. "Oh, yes. Well, what can I tell you?"

"How long has she been your patient, doctor?"

Dr. Mulvey indicated a chair near his desk and Paul Lowe sat down.

"Mrs. Lowe came to see me about a year ago," he said. "She had been feeling run down, somewhat tired. I gave her a complete physical examination and she was in good health. Except that her blood count revealed a slight anemia."

Dr. Mulvey sat down behind his desk and, resting his elbows on the chair arms, clasped his hands together. "I gave her some iron pills and these seemed to help her condition somewhat. I found out later that she'd left the state and gone home to Nebraska. In any event she tells me that although she felt tired and run down for a few months she was otherwise asymptomatic."

She had never complained, but he could remember dimly now occasions on which she had created opportunities to rest—afternoons of reading in bed, evenings of lounging on the sofa, late mornings in which he surprised her by getting up, dressing, bringing back her breakfast. He had thought this a natural indolence, the necessary counterpart of her usual vitality.

"Why did she come back to you, doctor?"

"Apparently through the summer her feeling of tiredness, a lack of normal strength, had continued. She felt something had to be done about it so she came to me and I did a CBC. . . ."

"A what?"

"I'm sorry. Medical abbreviation for a complete blood count. It revealed that her anemia was persisting. The blood count was well below normal."

"Is it serious?"

"Not in itself."

"What I'm trying to ask, Dr. Mulvey, is simply whether my wife is going to be all right."

Dr. Mulvey looked toward the window blinds which were glowing with sunlight kept out of the room. "I certainly have every reason to think so, Mr. Justice." He turned back to Paul Lowe, smiling. "I've started her on a steroid treatment to stop the bleeding. And the transfusion should bring her strength back to normal. We should have the anemia under control from now on."

Paul Lowe was overwhelmed with gratitude toward him. "Well, that's good news, doctor. I feel much better about it."

Dr. Mulvey leaned back in his chair. "Recently married, aren't you?"

"Yes."

Dr. Mulvey nodded with self-satisfaction. "That explains your anxiety. It's quite normal in newlyweds. I hope you'll be very happy, Mr. Justice. Your wife is a very lovely person."

"Thank you."

"Oh, before you go, would you mind giving me your autograph? I'm sure it'll be a thrill for my son. His name is Edward if you'd care to add a personal message."

In the Supreme Court of the United States, the document began. Then there was the month of the term and the docket number followed by the name of the petitioner, William Weaver, and the name of the respondent, the state which had condemned him to death. Petition for a Writ of Certiorari.

Petitioner prays that a Writ of Certiorari issued to review the opinion and decision of the Supreme Court of the State. . . .

He turned the page and glanced through the index. On the next page was a list of Authorities Cited. The following page began the short petition, identifying the federal question involved. (Whether capital punishment as a penalty for a crime less than murder does not constitute cruel and unusual punishment within the meaning of the Eighth Amendment to the United States Constitution.) The brief then set forth arguments for the substantial character of this question, and concluded by attaching to the petition the opinions of the state courts.

Ken Norris had done a good job, he thought approvingly. Everything necessary was here, nothing extraneous, and no arguments presented in detail, only enumerated to show the constitutional areas to be covered.

He turned to the respondent's brief from the State Attorney General. It was an equally workmanlike document which set forth an impressive list of precedents to show that the federal government could not interfere with a state's administration of criminal law provided that the constitutional guarantees of due process had been met. Those guarantees of due process certainly had been fully accorded to William Weaver. The diligent efforts of Ken Norris had gotten Weaver a trial, an appeal, a rehearing and a second appeal, and now further consideration in the federal courts. The State Attorney General believed strongly that "the nation's highest tribunal should not concern itself with an individual petitioner whose only claim to uniqueness appears to be the dogged determination of his attorney."

The Attorney General also pointed out that there was no precedent for the proposition that the death penalty was a cruel and unusual punishment.

The State Attorney General was right. There was no precedent to sustain such a petition. The punishment of death was legal and was carried out regularly by most states.

. . . *and the order denying reargument and rehearing and the judgment made and entered pursuant thereto* . . .

To keep his place in the reading he moved his finger down the line.

After a while he looked up and saw Jack Broderick, gangling, shy, standing in the doorway to his office.

"You wanted to see me, Mr. Justice?"

"Yes, Jack. Come in." He waited until Broderick reached his desk. "I've been going over the petition for certiorari in the William Weaver case."

Broderick nodded and his prominent adam's apple bobbed up and down in his throat.

"You attached a quote to your cert memo." Paul Lowe picked up the typewritten sheet to read: " 'I cannot believe that any person who at all values the judicial process or distinguishes its method and philosophy from those of the political and legislative process would abandon or substantially impair the rule of *stare decisis.* . . .' "

"Robert Jackson—later Mr. Justice Jackson—said that when he was Solicitor General."

"Is there any particular reason you wanted me to see it?"

"Yes, Mr. Justice. I thought it was something you might want to keep in mind when you read the petitions."

"That's thoughtful of you, Jack. I suppose it means you don't think certiorari should be granted."

Broderick nodded. "I respect Mr. Norris' abilities as a lawyer and naturally I'm grateful to him for having recommended me for this job. But he's really gone off the deep end if he expects this Court to abolish capital punishment. It would mean overruling all previous decisions, throwing out old precedents like old garbage. A lot of people would become convinced that the Court is trying to wreck the Constitution."

Paul Lowe said, "Jack, if you look back over American history you can see the landscape strewn with wrecks of the Constitution—or what people thought the Constitution was at the time. It was unconstitutional to buy Louisiana and Florida, but we did it. It was unconstitutional to add new states to the Union from territory that didn't originally belong to it, but we did it. It was unconstitutional even to charter a bank or print paper money or make a protective tariff. We did all those things which are accepted today, and the Constitution is still looking about as shipshape as I've ever seen it."

Jack Broderick's lips tightened. "I hope you won't be offended, Mr. Justice, if I stick to my belief that a vote for certiorari in this case would be a serious mistake."

"Of course I won't be offended, Jack."

"Is there anything else, Mr. Justice?" Jack Broderick stood waiting.

"Yes, there is. Of course you know Ken Norris is my former law partner. He will probably argue the case for William Weaver if certiorari is granted. Do you think I should disqualify myself in that event?"

"Merely because you know him, Mr. Justice?"

"I'd like your honest opinion."

"I don't see any reason why you should disqualify yourself. No one would seriously believe that your opinion in a case as important as capital punishment could be influenced by the fact that your former law partner was arguing for one side. And if the issue is granted certiorari it's too important not to be settled by the whole Court."

Paul Lowe nodded. "I was thinking along the same lines."

"Is that all, Mr. Justice?"

"Yes, it is. Thanks, Jack."

Jack Broderick dipped his head in hesitant acknowledgment and left the office.

A good man, Paul Lowe thought, who would make a good lawyer someday. The bias of the young man's mind was strongly toward upholding tradition, but he had integrity and courage and it was perhaps good that he should be willing to accept traditional restraints on his private judgment. That willingness was not often found in the young, and it signified that Jack Broderick could think independently. In the end all any of us can do is think in our own vocabulary—and then try to find out why others put such a different weight on the identical words.

In March a newspaper in Madison, Wisconsin, revealed that Andrew Cutler had been a member of an organization known as the Knights of the White Star. The Knights were an ultra-rightist group with an exclusive enrollment of white, native-born American Protestants. Andrew Cutler's membership dated back to the year before his appointment to the Supreme Court bench. He had joined the Knights at a time when the junior Senator from Wisconsin, Senator Joseph McCarthy, was riding high. The announced goals of the Knights were to root out subversives from every area of American life, to defend America against the threat of Communist attack and to preserve and protect a republican form of government in the United States.

These objectives were far from blameworthy in the eyes of most Americans. But the methods used by the Knights of the White Star to attain their objectives were another matter. The Knights labeled as Communists such men as Dwight Eisenhower, General Marshall, Albert Einstein and Adlai Stevenson and they referred to Franklin Delano Roosevelt as "the late President Rosenfeld and his Jewish brain trust." They claimed the civil rights movement was "Communist inspired" and charged the most prominent white supporters of the movement were tainted with Negro blood.

Andrew Cutler refused to comment on the newspaper charges or the photostated copy of a membership application with his signature which had been put forward as proof. But the pressure mounted from liberals who had smarted in silence under the lash of recent events and now found themselves with a cause to make the most of. At last Andrew Cutler was compelled to issue a statement. He said that he had, indeed, joined the Knights of the White Star but it had been before his appointment to the Supreme Court and at a time when there was no reason to suspect the rabid nature of the organization. He had not been an active member and shortly after his appointment had written a letter of resignation from the organization. That letter, unfortunately, was no longer in the organization's files and he had failed to keep a copy of it. But he wished to assure those who did not know him (because those who did know him needed no such reassurance), that he was wholly innocent of any form of racial bias and did not approve of any of the recent virulent actions of the Knights of the White Star.

The clamor was not stilled because there was an embarrassing coincidence to be explained. The Knights of the White Star had been a plaintiff in a tax refund case before the Supreme Court. They had asked for special tax status as an educational institution and their plea was turned down but Justices Andrew Cutler and Gabriel Hart had dissented. This news broke during the height of the public furor.

In the resulting inferno of charges and countercharges, accusations and denials, it became clear that the controversy had reached beyond Andrew Cutler to involve the Supreme Court.

On a Tuesday morning in late March Chief Justice John Hampton invited Paul Lowe to his office for a private discussion.

The Chief Justice looked worried and exhausted. The fine lines in his skin were clearly marked and his eyes rested sleepily in dark sockets.

"I don't believe that Andrew Cutler personally subscribes to the principles of the Knights of the White Star, do you, Paul?"

"No, I don't."

"I'm sure he joined because it seemed at the time to be politically advantageous. It was a bad mistake, but I've talked to Andrew and he bitterly regrets what he did. Would you be willing to add your name to a statement by the justices of the Court which asserts our full confidence in Andrew Cutler's integrity?"

"Is everyone signing it?"

"I've talked to everyone except you and Edward McCann."

"How about Charles Edmunson?"

Chief Justice Hampton smiled faintly. "The statement is Edmunson's idea."

"Of course I'll sign it. I wanted to be sure that it was unanimous. If it wasn't then it would only add to the division on the Court."

The Chief Justice sighed with relief. "If such a statement is released

I can dissuade Gabriel Hart from writing an impassioned defense of Americanism and Andrew Cutler. I know that Justice Hart's motives are the best, but when he told me what he intended to do I warned that it would be taken as a highly partisan and challenging statement. At a time like this it would surely inflame feeling on both sides. It would be a most . . . injudicious performance."

In the months that Paul Lowe had been on the Supreme Court that was the strongest rebuke he had heard the Chief Justice make.

The public statement by eight justices of the Court defending Andrew Cutler's reputation and integrity was issued two days later. It breached the wall of opposition. For a short time there was dust and confusion, a few isolated and bitter cries that the Supreme Court was playing "politics." But the imprimatur of Charles Edmunson worked magic among liberals and those who worshiped his monumental integrity. Within a week all mention of the affair died out of the newspapers.

The residual effects were hard to determine. The Court had been under fire from an entirely new quarter and there was simply no way to gauge whether the incident played any part in a decision John Hampton revealed to Paul Lowe a few days later.

John Hampton and his wife, Jane, attended the formal opening of an El Greco exhibition at the National Gallery. The paintings were on loan from the Prado in Spain and were shown for the first time to important figures in the government before the public opening. The President was on hand, with most of the Cabinet. From the Supreme Court, Justices Hampton, Merriam, Shuler and Paul Lowe showed up.

Henry Merriam and Waldo Shuler left earlier to keep other engagements. John Hampton invited Paul Lowe and Katherine to an afternoon luncheon at Harvey's restaurant.

Over bowls of crab gumbo, while Katherine and Jane Hampton were discussing the El Greco exhibition, John Hampton asked, "Have you ever witnessed an execution, Paul?"

"No. And I'm grateful I haven't."

"I don't imagine any of our colleagues have witnessed one either." John Hampton's clear cool diction was as impeccable as ever but there was flickering emotion in his gray eyes. "I have."

"How did it happen?"

"I was governor at the time and despite my personal feelings in the matter, I had to refuse a clemency appeal from a man facing death in the electric chair. Later I had a phone call from the prison chaplain. I thought it was merely another last minute appeal for a commutation of sentence, and I was prepared to say no again. Instead the chaplain told me that when he brought the news to the prisoner that there was to be no commutation, the prisoner said he would not allow a chaplain to be with him when he went to his death. He asked instead for me to be present."

"It was an odd request, John."

"Of course it was. But the chaplain told me that in his opinion this man

—his name was Harry Lightner—would badly need someone to be with him in his last hour. The psychiatric report listed him as psychoneurotic and emotionally unstable. He had killed a woman in a drunken rage. The chaplain said that so far Lightner had accepted with dignity the fact that he was going to die, and bore no hatred or resentment toward anyone, certainly not to me. But Lightner wanted me to be present to see what it was like. He thought it might have some influence the next time I had to decide whether a man would live or die."

The conversation between Katherine and Jane had stopped. Both women were now listening. Katherine leaned back against her chair with her arm across the back of Paul Lowe's chair. He felt the touch of her fingers lightly against his back.

John Hampton continued: "The chaplain felt that if it was possible for me to be there I should come. Harry Lightner was hanging on by a thread and needed someone with him but he would allow no one to be present but me. It was only an hour's drive from the prison. Jane didn't want me to go, of course . . ."

His wife did not react to the mention of her name. Her high-boned handsome haughty face was soft and melancholy.

". . . but I thought it was my duty. I made only one condition. No publicity, no mention at all of the fact that I would be Harry Lightner's sole companion on the last night of his life. As my car pulled up in front of the prison it was snowing heavily. I remember it clearly. I didn't want to go into the prison with snow on my clothing. Somehow that seemed a needless affront to Lightner, reminding him of weather in the outside world. The warden and the chaplain met me and took me down a narrow passageway to the holding-room area. I remember a death-watch guard on duty who was listening to a transistor radio.

"Harry Lightner was lying on his back on a cot in a small cell. There was a toilet in his cell, and the cell was brightly lit. The warden said, 'Hello, Harry. Here's the man you were looking for.' Harry Lightner sat up and looked at me and said very casually, 'Hello, Governor. I'm glad you could make it.'

"I pulled up a stool and sat down beside his cot. 'I thought it was the least I could do,' I told him. I had never felt more foolish or helpless in my life. Then I said, 'I hope you understand I had no choice except to do what I did. It wasn't a personal decision. I was acting as governor of the state.' Harry Lightner smiled at me. 'You don't have to apologize, Governor. It's all right. I killed that woman.' Did I tell you that he had an IQ of 134—very superior intelligence?"

"No, you didn't mention it." Paul Lowe would have liked to stop him from going on but could not think of a way to do it.

John Hampton seemed to be caught up in a compulsion to speak: "I don't remember all of our conversation during that terrible hour. I asked him whether he believed in God, and he said he wasn't sure but he didn't have to worry about it because he'd know soon enough. I asked him whether he'd gotten any sleep, and he said he hadn't slept for two nights. They had offered him anything he wanted to eat and he had ordered supper but hadn't touched any of it. 'I guess I'm just not very hungry,' he told me. At one time he mentioned that he had bequeathed his eyes to an eye bank. 'I hope that jolt of electricity won't ruin them,' he said. I tried to change the topic of conversation and we talked about the kind of jobs he'd had. He had wanted to be an engineer but he never finished high school so he had to work at different trades, mostly as a handyman. As the time drew near I saw he was getting tense but I tried to keep him talking. And I kept talking to him. At least I hoped to show him that in his last moments he was not completely alone. Then we heard an announcer on the guard's transistor radio. The announcer said that everyone should tune in for the latest news at eleven o'clock. Harry Lightner and I tried not to look at each other but I knew he was thinking the same thought I was. When the eleven o'clock news broadcast came on Harry Lightner would be dead. Then I heard him ask, 'What time is it, Governor?' I told him there were twelve minutes to go. 'Would you like a cup of coffee?' I asked him. He shook his head and said, 'I couldn't keep it down.' Then the warden and the doctor came in with two guards to prepare him for the execution. I stood up and asked, 'Are you all right, Harry?' He said, 'I'm all right. They're going to give me a clean white shirt so I'll look good for the people in the witness room. I'll see you there, Governor.' I nodded and said 'Goodbye, Harry,' and left. When I next saw him he was entering the death room. He glanced at the witnesses watching from behind the glass partition. When he saw me there he waved to me. Then he sat down and they began tightening the electrodes. He complained that one of the straps was too tight on his wrist and they loosened it for him. Then the guards stepped back, the warden nodded, and the switch was thrown . . . I couldn't see Harry Lightner's face behind the mask that covered it. But I saw his body lunge against the strap, and I saw the small curls of smoke, and . . . and the odor of burning—"

A small gasp escaped Katherine.

John Hampton said quickly, "I'm sorry. I shouldn't talk about these things. But it is something I have never forgotten." He looked around at the others at the table and then his glance focused on Paul Lowe. "Are you a religious man, Paul?"

"I suppose I am."

"Isn't that a beautiful passage in the New Testament where Jesus says 'Inasmuch as ye did it to one of the least of these My brethren, ye did it to Me'?"

"Yes, it is," Paul Lowe said.

He was certain now there would be the necessary four votes for certiorari in the William Weaver case.

As he put the key into the lock he heard running feet on the other side of the door. He barely crossed the threshold when Timmy latched onto him. He half carried and half dragged the boy into the foyer and closed the door.

"How's my boy?" he asked.

Timmy looked up at him with shy pride. "I got all the words right in the spelling bee," he said, "except one."

"What was that?"

"Remedy."

"With an *i*?"

"No. Two *m*'s."

"Oh, well, it's a pretty advanced word for a first-grade spelling bee."

"What is a remedy?"

"Something that cures something."

"Like a sickness?"

"Like a sickness, that's right."

"Like a pill like Mommy takes?"

"That's one kind. Where is Mommy?"

"She's in the back room working."

He heard the clacking of her typewriter, rapid and hurried as though racing time.

"Let's go see her."

"Okay," Timmy said.

Paul Lowe offered Timmy his hand and the boy took it. He liked the feeling of the boy's small hand trustfully in his own. Having Timmy in the apartment made it easier for him to believe Katherine and he were really man and wife, for the boy had never known a real father and from the first meeting had offered, in the generous and uncritical and unquestioning way of children, all his pent-up affection to Paul Lowe.

Katherine was squinting at the typewriter as though it were a strange form of crustacean life. She wore her new eyeglasses and when she heard him enter the room she quickly took them off. She was convinced that she looked like a fading schoolmarm in eyeglasses, although, in truth, she was rather comically appealing and seemed at least ten years younger.

"Paul, darling."

She got up to kiss him.

"I wanted to bother you," he said. "I heard your typewriter going."

"You monster."

"You've been working too hard. I don't approve of it."

"Would you watch a Superman cartoon with me?" Timmy asked. "It's going on in a minute."

"You go ahead and watch it, Timmy. I may join you in a few minutes."

"Don't come too late or you won't be able to guess the end."

This was a game they played when they watched any of Timmy's shows on television. Paul Lowe would try to foretell how the action would come out while the show was on. The boy's amazement at Lowe's ability to predict what would happen had been growing week by week.

"This time I'll try to guess the end without even seeing the beginning."

Timmy's eyes grew round with wonder. "Could you?"

"I can't swear to it. But I'll try."

"Okay!" Timmy went off delighted to tune in the television set in his bedroom.

Katherine said, smiling: "Are you sure you haven't overreached yourself?"

"I can always fall back on kryptonite. It's a pretty safe bet that Superman's going to come up against that strange green metal somewhere or other before the story ends."

He put his arm about her as they strolled into the living room.

He sat down heavily in the club chair that flanked the sofa.

"Is something the matter, darling?" she asked.

"Not a thing. Why?"

"I think that what you need is a drink. How about a Jack Daniels with a splash of soda?"

"How about without the splash of soda?"

"Coming up. On the rocks."

She went to the bar in the living room, a cherrywood affair with a fold-up top that was in a new position in the living room.

"You've been moving furniture again," he said.

"I wondered when you would notice. Like it this way? I think I do, but I'm not sure. We really ought to have a piano to fill in that corner, but then I don't really play the piano and I would never have the time for lessons. That's something I always wanted, though. Didn't you tell me that Charles Edmunson was a very talented . . ." She stopped, holding the glass partly filled with bourbon. "*There*—I saw it in your eyes. It has something to do with him."

"What has?"

"That look I saw before. You're worried about Charles Edmunson."

Her intuitions were uncanny—antennae that picked up the faintest signals. Even when she could not tell the exact nature of the object hidden from view she sensed its presence.

Paul Lowe shrugged as he accepted the drink she brought him. "The Old Man had a rough day today. It was a long conference that had to do with some important matters. Including a grant of certiorari in the William Weaver case. Edmunson was showing signs of fatigue before it was over."

"Tell me about it."

"It's hard to explain. I think I noticed it first during the discussion of the Weaver case. Henry Merriam had some objections to granting certiorari and while Edmunson was trying to answer him he suddenly stopped. He had lost touch with the point he was making and he couldn't seem to pick up the thread of the argument again."

"That must happen to everyone at one time or another."

"Yes, I know. But it was more than that. After a while he seemed to lose interest in the entire proceeding. He sat there like a huge Buddha contemplating everything that was going on but without any real participation—only that godlike watchful contemplation."

"That can be pretty formidable in itself sometimes."

He nodded. "In a sort of alien and superior way. But in the end he got just the four votes he needed for certiorari—Edmunson, McCann, the

434

Chief Justice and I voted for it. Henry Merriam voted against and I can't help wondering if his vote might have been different if some of the answers Edmunson gave him . . . well, they weren't quite to the point. They weren't wrong exactly, but . . ."

As he kept trying to explain, his uneasiness mounted because he was not telling her the whole truth about Edmunson's performance in the conference room that day. He was merely relating events as straight narrative when what was needed to make the description significant were the shadings, the nuances, the reactions of the other justices. He was deliberately avoiding placing the episode in a context that would reveal its meaning.

He would have been more truthful if he had been able to say, "I've noticed signs of Edmunson's deterioration before this. He isn't the man he was before he suffered that minor stroke. What I'm telling you about the conference today doesn't seem significant because the mere narration doesn't begin to convey my feeling, my alarm, that this may be how a superbly logical intelligence like Edmunson's begins to fail. It doesn't happen all at once because there is simply too much power there to dissipate in a day, so there is meaning in what he says, often well expressed, but there are also bits and pieces of the connective tissue missing. He isn't able to tune his thought—the instrument is still a fine one but it is starting to give off discordant harmonies."

He did not want to give that much precision and clarity to his fears. It was obvious that his bare account of the events at the conference did not really disturb her.

"Well, it's only a few more months to the end of the term," she said. "If he can stand the pace until then, a summer's vacation will help him to recover his strength."

He finished the last of the bourbon and put the glass down. "Come here."

"Are you going to kiss me?"

"That's my intention."

"Good."

She laughed and came to him and everything was better when he held her in his arms. When they parted there was a moist salt taste on his lips and he touched his index finger to it. The tip of his finger came away stained with red.

"What's this?"

She stood up quickly.

"Has it started again?" he asked.

"It's nothing to worry about. I'll wash my mouth out."

He followed her to the bathroom and stood in the doorway. She filled a glass with water and swirled liquid in her mouth. When she spat it out the water was a deep pink color.

"How long has it been going on?" he asked quietly.

"I noticed it the past week or so. Usually when I brush my teeth too hard."

"Have you told Dr. Mulvey?"

"He doesn't think it's anything. It's one of the symptoms of the anemia. But I'm fine. I'm not even as tired as I was. I feel marvelous."

"Isn't the doctor doing anything about it?"

"He said he'd take a repeat blood count. And if my anemia isn't any better he might give me another transfusion."

"I don't like his casual air about the whole thing. I may insist that you go to another doctor."

"Darling, don't act so solemn. I'll do whatever you want as long as you promise you won't go up in the air about it. Dr. Mulvey is a very fine doctor. Everyone says so. And he said I'm basically a very healthy person." She put her arms about his shoulders. "Will you do something for me? Something really special?"

"Anything."

"Take me out to dinner. I'll order calf's liver or rare roast beef or something that's supposed to be good for me."

"How about Timmy?"

"I'd like to have dinner alone with you tonight. I can give Timmy his dinner at home, and we'll get a babysitter. There's a service right in the building."

"All right," he said.

Timmy appeared in the doorway of his bedroom. "Superman just disappeared into another dimension," he announced.

"I'll bet you don't know what's going to happen now," Paul Lowe said.

Timmy's eyes dilated and his small face stiffened with a dreadful anticipation. "What?"

"He's going to find kryptonite there," Paul Lowe said.

He put his arm about Katherine, and went with Timmy into the bedroom to find out if his prediction would come true.

30

At forty minutes past the hour of ten o'clock on the first Tuesday in April, the courtroom was packed with spectators. One or two chairs were placed in the aisles. The seats in the section reserved for friends of the justices were also filled. The opening ceremonies and the admissions of lawyers to practice before the Court had been completed.

The first case on the day's agenda was oral argument in the William Weaver case.

Ken Norris was standing at the counsel table consulting with other attorneys. At the counsel table on the right side of the lectern the Louisiana Attorney General, Walter Riegel, was seated with his assistants.

Walter Riegel was a nervous uncomfortable-looking man with narrow shoulders, a hawk nose and high temples. He had elected to wear the morning coat and striped trousers that were required of government attorneys but optional for anyone else. Walter Riegel had never argued a case before the Supreme Court and he had come prepared for a solemn and historic occasion.

Chief Justice Hampton announced, "The orders of the Court have been filed with the Clerk and will not be orally delivered this morning."

As two soberly dressed young pages moved quickly about the courtroom handing out the printed copies of the orders, the Chief Justice said quietly:

"William Weaver versus the State of Louisiana."

Ken Norris stood up from the counsel table on the left and went to the lectern. He arranged his notes and put on his eyeglasses for reading.

Walter Riegel, the attorney general, was seated closest to the lectern. He folded his arms to give his full attention to Ken Norris.

Ken Norris began in a very low voice.

Justice Gabriel Hart said, "Would you mind speaking a bit louder? I can't hear you."

Ken Norris nodded. "If it please the Court . . ." he said in a louder tone, "in considering whether William Weaver is to die we are going to deal with some new and some old legal arguments. The new arguments are necessary because we are moving up to a frontier of law where the borders are not clearly marked and where familiar landmarks no longer serve as guides. But I would like to deal with the old arguments first so

437

that we may proceed from what is generally accepted to the question: How shall we interpret the Eighth Amendment to bring it up to date with the dramatic changes taking place in our ideas of crime and punishment and with the new values and new standards being formed in our advancing society . . ."

The attention of everyone in the chamber seemed to center on Ken Norris' stocky solid figure at the lectern. Paul Lowe made notes on the pad in the light of the tiny lamp. He wanted to hear how Ken sounded without the distraction of watching his friend speak.

"William Weaver is charged with rape," Ken was saying, "and I maintain that to punish him with death is too severe and falls within the prohibition of the Eighth Amendment against cruel and unusual punishment.

"It is not necessary in this case to stretch the Constitution to include a sanction against the death penalty itself; the Eighth Amendment can be directed against all punishments which are disproportionate to the offense." Then he cited previous decisions of the Court beginning with *Wilkerson vs. Utah* which had established this precedent.

He went on to argue that the case of William Weaver did not necessarily involve the issue of federalism in the sense of any new invasion of the right to interfere with a state's criminal procedures.

After a few minutes Paul Lowe began to feel a disappointment that flowed out of him and mingled with a general disappointment in the audience.

At the table Attorney General Walter Riegel kept his head down over a paper he was reading but the fingers of his free hand were lightly tapping the table. He was impatient. In the public section beyond him there were outward signs of diminishing attention—a man whispering to the woman beside him, another woman on the aisle trying to get the attention of the guard on duty. Most of the spectators had strained, politely blank expressions. They were impressed by the importance of the occasion but fighting off an increasing conviction that it was all not going to be very interesting.

Ken Norris plowed ahead. He made the point that different methods of sentencing for capital crimes in different states resulted in criminals not being accorded equal justice.

"In Alabama and Missouri, robbery is held to be an offense that is punishable by death. In North Carolina and Virginia arson is held to be a capital crime. In Kentucky a man who commits assault with intent to rob may be sentenced to death. But in other states not even the crime of murder can merit the death penalty."

Henry Merriam interrupted with a drawling query, "Mr. Norris, I agree that a criminal's right to live is often subject to a mere matter of geography. But what is the alternative? Can we enforce a uniform penal code on all the states?"

"No, Mr. Justice, we cannot," Ken Norris answered. "But the issue of uniformity is of crucial importance in capital punishment cases. These are the cases in which a miscarriage of justice can never be corrected. I'd like to give an example of what I mean. It happened in the year 1940. This Supreme Court granted a stay of execution to a man under sentence of death. Half an hour before the execution, the deputy clerk of this Court telephoned the warden to inform him of the stay. But the warden simply refused to take orders from anyone but the state's governor or the state's attorney general. . . ."

Paul Lowe sensed the instant that it happened, that magnetic moment in which a chance phrase, a sudden revelation, a colorful incident or expressive gesture captures the onlookers as though they were watching a stage play, and they begin to live the events, to will the destinies, of what is transpiring. It was happening now.

Ken Norris continued, ". . . the warden insisted that he could not accept an order from a strange voice over the telephone. The deputy clerk tried to reach the governor, who was in transit between his office and his home and not available by phone. Then he tried the attorney general's home. The line was busy. He finally got the telephone operator to break in and he gave the attorney general the message. The attorney general called the prison warden with less than one minute left before the execution." Ken Norris paused while the clock ticked off fifteen seconds. "Later this man's case was heard—and his conviction reversed—by this very Court." He quietly surveyed the justices before him. "That innocent man would have been legally murdered because he happened to live in a state which inflicts the death penalty. Make no mistake. It was the death penalty *per se* that would have been to blame for his death, not the legal procedures which led to his conviction. *Any* legal procedure is capable of making a mistake. The death penalty makes such a mistake irretrievable."

Bill Branch leaned forward in his black swivel chair. "Mr. Norris, isn't that why we have additional safeguards where the death penalty is involved? I understand that the average time between an arrest and an execution is now three years. That would seem to allow plenty of time for every precaution to be taken against a miscarriage of justice."

Ken Norris turned to face Bill Branch on the right side of the bench. "No amount of time is enough to guard against this kind of error. We all have read of cases where men have been mistakenly imprisoned for ten or even twenty years. Those mistakes, terrible as they are, can be at least partially redeemed. But suppose those men had been executed? There would not have been even the partial remedy of an eventual pardon and exoneration. The miscarriage of justice would have been confirmed for all time by the victim's death.

"And far more important even than this, Mr. Justice Branch, is the fact that the delay you mention between arrest and execution is in itself a form of almost medieval torture. A famed lawyer has said that 'the cruelty of an execution after respite is equal to many deaths.' Almost every one of the approximately fifty persons executed in this country every year has been granted respite after respite. But what does this mean? It means they have been allowed to live for months under the imminent threat of death, given hope with each new reprieve, driven to desperation by each new setback. I can't imagine any greater horror than living all these months with the knowledge that your life will be taken, not in a blaze of passion or by misadventure, but coldly, deliberately, at an appointed time and place—by a society which calls itself humane."

Ken Norris paused, waiting for some further inquiry. But Bill Branch sat back in his chair to indicate he had no other question to ask.

At the counsel table near the lectern Walter Riegel, the attorney general, held his pen poised over a memorandum he was writing. For a second he seemed to be searching for an idea, then he began to write swiftly.

Ken Norris got through to the halfway point in his argument without serious challenge from any of the justices. They were listening intently or taking notes.

Chief Justice Hampton intervened at that point to inquire, "Mr. Norris, why can't we leave the entire problem to the discretion of the states? Many states are now considering doing away with the death penalty; some have already done so. Why ask this Court to interfere with a state's criminal procedure to declare it unconstitutional if the same end is being accomplished by other means?"

"Mr. Chief Justice, only a dozen states have so far abolished the penalty. If this practice is unconstitutional, as I believe it to be, how can we allow it to continue in the other states?"

The Chief Justice nodded and asked no further questions.

Ken Norris resumed his argument and as he was saying, ". . . the most disturbing aspect of capital punishment is that it is almost entirely reserved for the poor," he was interrupted by the glacial tones of Mr. Justice Andrew Cutler.

"Mr. Norris, you are not going to stand there and tell us that all murderers are poor."

"No, Mr. Justice, but in a survey recently taken—which you find quoted in an *amicus curiae* brief filed by the Association against the Death Penalty—you will find that every person now under a sentence of death in this country was represented at his trial by a court-appointed attorney. All the men on Death Row are obviously so poor they could not afford to hire a lawyer. Naturally a court-appointed lawyer will not have the benefit of the kind of expensive private investigation which is so helpful to any defense. Nor is he likely to persevere, after conviction, through state *coram nobis*, federal *habeas corpus*, and the other proceedings which often mean the difference between life and death."

Ken Norris looked directly at Justice Andrew Cutler as he said earnestly, "On the façade of this building are engraved the words 'Equal Justice Under Law.' That ideal becomes a mockery if the decision as to whether murderers live or die is to be made not on the basis of whether they are guilty but on whether they are poor."

Andrew Cutler replied, "We cannot in this case, Mr. Norris, or in any other case magically achieve complete equality in the administration of criminal justice. That ideal won't be reached in either of our lifetimes."

440

"On the other hand, Mr. Justice, we can take a long step toward realizing that ideal if we remove this special form of punishment which is administered only to the poor."

They are probably both right, Paul Lowe reflected. The answer to great and fundamental questions is never a complete answer and even the partial answers do not come swiftly. The partial answers are good only for a time and they are the result of the continuing dialogue between the political institutions and the needs of society. In that dialogue the great question is shaped and reduced until it appears as one man, William Weaver, rapist, under sentence of death.

What had brought the question into this room of velvet and marble at this time, and never before? Preceding events must have taken place in state legislatures which discussed and sometimes passed statutes outlawing the death penalty, in church pulpits where the name of God and His mighty commandment "Thou Shalt Not Kill" was invoked by His ministers against a state's man-made law of vengeance, in public forums where debaters contended, and in newspaper editorials, books, pamphlets, and in the many-sided activities of numerous organizations. Preceding events must also have taken place in the conscience of a generation shocked by the Second World War and the limited wars that had followed it—a generation taught that life was sacred yet seeing it sacrificed in struggles beyond their comprehension, seeing it obliterated in a millisecond in the horrendous flash of a bomb. Hiroshima lived in the conscience of a generation which was now turned to deal with the problem of saving individual human lives from the vengeance of the state.

His thoughts were interrupted by Gabriel Hart's husky whisper.

"Mr. Norris, if we enforce on the states a uniform penal code regarding criminals who have committed what at least up to now has always been treated as a capital offense, won't we be guilty of dispensing unequal justice? We'd be discriminating against all other kinds of criminals, who don't have such a uniform penal code because they have committed *lesser* crimes."

It was the kind of question that might be expected from a former president of the American Bar Association. Gabriel Hart's knowledge of the law was sufficiently profound, Paul Lowe thought sourly, to enable him to disregard human values and avoid the simple facts.

Ken Norris dealt with Gabriel Hart's question in casual fashion, both answering and dismissing it: "The problem, it seems to me, Mr. Justice, is how we should deal with inequities from *society's* point of view, not from the criminal's. I am not proposing that a man who commits a capital crime should be excused from punishment—merely that his punishment should be limited to life imprisonment. I can't see how putting such a man in jail for the rest of his life discriminates unfairly against other criminals who are sentenced to shorter terms."

Ken Norris then proceeded to a legalism of his own: the question of *necessity*. He observed that the *necessity* of the death penalty, particularly in relation to the crime of rape, had never been established before any court.

"The traditional humanity of the Anglo-Saxon law forbids the infliction of unnecessary pain. Therefore if the death penalty is not *necessary* in this case, it constitutes cruelty within the meaning of the Eighth Amendment."

He seemed prepared to go on in this vein for some time, thereby incurring the danger of losing his acquired momentum and allowing the argument to diminish and fade like smoke in the air. Paul Lowe was trying to think of a way to get Ken back on the main line of his argument when Edmunson's deep voice reverberated.

"Aren't you saying, Mr. Norris, that punishment can be achieved just as effectively if we punish rape less severely than by death?"

"Yes, Mr. Justice Edmunson."

"Let us suppose that this Court decides that your client is entitled to a new trial because the penalty of death *is* too severe in a rape case. Would that satisfy you?"

"Mr. Justice, it would save the life of my client. But I would also like this Court to consider whether the death penalty itself is not inherently cruel and therefore forbidden as a punishment for any crime."

How effortlessly Charles Edmunson had underlined the fact that William Weaver's fate might be decided on narrow limits while he directed the argument back to the larger question. Now he moved on to indicate where further arguments should be developed:

"I believe certiorari was granted to discuss this question of capital punishment. I would like to know why you believe the death penalty does not meet the permissible objectives of punishment."

Ken Norris nodded. "If you like, I'll attempt to deal with that now, Mr. Justice."

The air around Paul Lowe seemed to have become lighter and easier to breathe. Charles Edmunson might have sat silent amid his rusty thunderbolts but in this short exchange he had forked a little lightning. In a case of this importance it was useful to have Charles Edmunson at his best.

Ken Norris began to develop his argument along the new line. "What are the objectives of capital punishment?" he asked. "There is, first, the desire to give expression to the condemnation of the community, to make an example of the criminal. Wouldn't we accomplish the same condemnation better by putting him behind bars? A man in prison is able to feel, insofar as his nature is able to feel, the full reproach of his fellow men. But an executed criminal cannot feel anything. In a second he pays his full share of guilt and forever ends his awareness of how his fellow men feel about him.

"There is a second objective of capital punishment—the removal of the criminal as an unsocial animal. The criminal is removed by death from the sphere of the society to which he has proven himself an enemy. . . . But would not imprisoning him be a more discriminating, more compassionate way of achieving the same end? Imprisonment, too, isolates the criminal—but for as long as may be necessary. It differs from capital punishment in this: there is hope of his eventual return to play a useful role again among his fellow men. Imprisonment measures out the meaning of his crime in years and so has a scale of values to match the gravity of the crime. A punishment which is scaled to match the crime satisfies our instinct for what is just and proper and accords with what we have learned about criminal psychology. Capital punishment has no such scale of values."

Walter Riegel put down the pen with which he had been writing. He laid it carefully crosswise on his notes. An assistant leaned toward him to whisper something. Walter Riegel listened with an impassive face but his attention remained fixed on Ken Norris at the lectern.

Gabriel Hart leaned forward. "Mr. Norris, you are saying, it seems to me, that if we frighten the criminal with a more serious punishment—a longer jail term—for committing a more serious crime we may restrain his brutality. Doesn't that argument apply if we frighten him with the prospect of the most severe punishment—death—in order to keep him from committing a murder?"

"The argument for deterrence, Mr. Justice, is the strongest argument put forward by those who favor capital punishment," Ken Norris conceded. "But that argument raises a new and a legitimate question. Is capital punishment an *effective* deterrent? And we happen to have the answer. For the statistics from every nation in the world, and from every state in our Union that has abolished the death penalty, show that crimes of murder actually decrease."

"I can't see any reason for that to happen, Mr. Norris."

"It seems clear that the very existence of the death penalty often causes the crime it is supposed to deter. If a man has killed once, why not kill again? The criminal has nothing more to lose. His life can't be *twice* forfeit. Why not even kill the police official who is sent to capture him? In fact, statistics also show that the number of police officers killed in the execution of their duty in states where capital punishment is in effect is much higher than the number killed in those states where capital punishment has been abolished."

"So in your opinion, Mr. Norris, the best way to stop murders from happening is to give the criminal assurance that he won't be executed for committing a murder. Somehow that doesn't seem to me to be a very practical way to go about it."

"It isn't the severity but the certainty of being punished, Mr. Justice, that stops a criminal from committing a crime. Any prosecutor in any criminal court will tell you how much harder it is to get a conviction in a case where the punishment may be death. Juries are much more reluctant to convict a man if they think that by so doing they may send him to his death. Where a man's life is *not* involved, juries often convict on the very same evidence on which they would acquit if the penalty is death. So the threat of death *reduces* the certainty of punishment."

Andrew Cutler asked, "Mr. Norris, shouldn't the law allow society to take revenge for an injury done? That applies to individuals. Why not to society as a whole?"

"Mr. Justice, revenge—retribution, if you prefer—is certainly one of the objectives of punishment. But capital punishment is the most extreme form of revenge—the most primitive and most bloodthirsty. It is the law of the jungle, the law of the talon. Does such a law belong in a modern society? Must we adopt the caveman's ethic as ours? We might fairly ask if executing the criminal will restore the moral order that his crime disturbed? It cannot. It cannot because taking a life for a life does not cancel out the crime—it merely multiplies the brutality. And where brutality is condoned, where it is made a part of official government policy, civilization itself suffers. All men who live in such a land are brutalized."

On Paul Lowe's left an attendant was working the controls of the sound recording equipment. Everything spoken in the courtroom was being transcribed. The panel before the attendant glowed and winked with lights. As he watched, a curious fancy struck Paul Lowe. Suppose the lights on the panel did not record variations in pitch and sound levels but registered connections between what Ken Norris was saying and his auditors, brief but significant discharges that might cause alterations in the nervous system and the electrical wisdom of the brain. Then one could trace the illuminating current through sterile circuits of familiar prejudices to the point of contact where a dazzling blinding flash might demonstrate a new way of looking at things.

Edmunson asked, "Isn't it true, Mr. Norris, that the one objective of punishment which most people agree is the most moral, most Christian, most unarguable objective is rehabilitation?"

"Yes, Mr. Justice, and it is precisely the objective of rehabilitation which is made impossible by capital punishment. No one has ever encountered a successfully rehabilitated corpse. Many of us have heard the grimly humorous remark '"This will be a good lesson to me"—as the man said when he sat down in the electric chair.' That remark conveys an elementary understanding that we all share, for we all know that dead men *never* learn a lesson."

Walter Riegel, the attorney general, shifted in his chair like a man with a painful sunburn.

Frowning, Waldo Shuler had been staring at the desk before him.

"Mr. Norris . . ."

Now Waldo's head came up and he craned his neck in a familiar belligerent pose. He continued dryly, "I applaud your humanitarianism and your rhetoric. I would add that, as an individual, I am opposed to capital punishment. But I am here, and so are my brother justices, to decide whether there is a *constitutional* prohibition against killing a man—in this present case, for rape, or by your extension, for any other crime. In your impressive exposition I have so far heard very little about the death penalty as a cruel and unusual punishment within the meaning of the Eighth Amendment to the Constitution."

In the spare irony, the deliberate understatement, there was the un-

444

mistakable ring of assurance and authority. Waldo Shuler seemed almost to be saying, now the decks have been cleared, the preliminaries done with, and *we* can begin the battle in earnest.

Ken Norris said, "I believe, Mr. Justice Shuler, that the arguments I have advanced all bear upon that purpose. If I can show that the death penalty is not achieving a useful purpose, then the penalty must automatically become a cruel one."

"Nothing happens automatically in this Court. As far as I can see, there are no established legal standards by which we can decide what is cruel and inhuman punishment."

"That is why we are here today, Mr. Justice. This Court must accept the final responsibility for setting such a standard."

"You're asking us to decide a very delicate question in federal and state relationships, Mr. Norris, and you have nothing to go on but a phrase— 'cruel and unusual'—which is susceptible of a good many meanings to a good many different people."

"Mr. Justice Shuler, the Eighth Amendment's prohibition—at a minimum—of inhuman and barbarous punishment has already been recognized."

"Where?"

"In Wilkerson versus Utah . . ."

"As I recall, it was said quite plainly there that it is difficult to determine the meaning of the term 'cruel and unusual punishment.'"

"But the Court *did* define it, Mr. Justice—as a punishment exceeding the severity of the offense. And in that same case it was acknowledged by the Court that the death penalty might be unconstitutionally cruel."

"Only if it were administered in a way involving torture, lingering death or unnecessary pain."

"I have submitted with my brief, Mr. Justice, many books and pamphlets which show that execution as practiced in this country—whether by gas chamber or firing squad, hangman's rope or the electric chair—is brutal to a degree that can be called 'the deliberate inflicting of pain or torture.'"

Waldo Shuler's sharply downward-angling nose seemed to be sniffing a heady scent. Waldo had been a prominent trial lawyer before he came to the bench, and still took delight in the adversary method of arriving at judicial truth. He was capable of reaching a decision by weighing and pondering but his instinct was for the give and take of verbal warfare. He relished a battle with a worthy antagonist.

His high voice was thin with the repressed joy of combat.

"You have *not* shown that there is any purpose to inflict such pain or torture," he said. "None of your documents establish that. There are some sensational accounts of executions—but I found no proof that executions are not carried out in the most painless possible manner."

"There is proof that executions have resulted in torture. Whether or not that was the purpose, Mr. Justice, that was the result."

"Would you call that kind of evidence sufficient to bring into question the constitutionality of the death penalty?"

"Yes, Mr. Justice. This Court itself held, in *Ex parte Kemmler*, that such forms of punishment as burning at the stake, crucifixion, or breaking on the wheel would be unconstitutionally forbidden because they were extreme and caused unusual suffering."

"In *Ex parte Kemmler* this Court also held that the electric chair was a *permissible* form of execution—because it is the most ingenious and humane available."

"That opinion is more than three-quarters of a century behind us, Mr. Justice. Just as it was unthinkable for civilized men at that time to countenance the sort of cruelty that was freely practiced in previous times, so now I believe it is unthinkable for us to countenance the cruelty that was practiced in our own past."

"It is being practiced today, Mr. Norris."

"I find that equally unthinkable."

Waldo Shuler pursed his lips and small dimples appeared at the mouth corners.

"It may be unthinkable, Mr. Norris. The question, however, is whether it is unconstitutional."

There was a slight but audible exhalation of breath from the spectators in the courtroom.

"In applying the Constitution, Mr. Justice, I don't think we can use only the standards of what has been . . . but what should be. The concept of cruelty is a changing one."

"Even if you establish that there was unnecessary pain in the *method* of carrying out the death penalty, that would not make the death penalty itself a violation of the Constitution. It would merely prohibit that particular method."

"It isn't a far leap, Mr. Justice, from a finding that there is a constitutional flaw in the *method* to a finding that there is a constitutional flaw in the *prescription* of punishment."

"It may not be a far leap for you, Mr. Norris—but the justices of this Court are rather aged and infirm. We can't go bounding about with quite your legal ability."

There was some laughter in the courtroom. Paul Lowe looked anxiously to the clock at the far end of the courtroom. It showed that no time remained of Ken Norris' appointed hour.

Waldo Shuler sat back, with a small satisfied quirk on his lips. Ken Norris was smiling too. Paul Lowe could guess the reason for Ken's smile. They had often discussed Waldo Shuler's technique of harassing an attorney with a quick barrage of questions and now Ken had experienced it for the first time.

The light glowed on the lectern. Ken Norris nodded to the bench, said, "I thank the honorable members of this Court for their courtesy," and stepped down.

446

Walter Riegel moved to the lectern, elegant in cutaway coat and striped trousers. Watching him gather his papers before him on the lectern, Paul Lowe wondered what Walter Riegel really thought. As a man he might be horrified at the fact that officials of his state were presiding over legally sanctioned murder in which two thousand volts of electric current were sent through moistened electrodes fastened to a man's leg and to a shaved spot on the back of his head in order to paralyze and destroy the brain. But as an advocate, and the attorney general of his state, Walter Riegel had no choice except to plead that they be allowed to do so.

His voice was well cultivated and pleasant to listen to: "My distinguished opponent has, in effect, urged a new and wider definition of what constitutes cruel and unusual punishment. But how can any definition be wide enough to include an instantaneous and painless method of causing death? And if the method is not cruel, how can the prescription of death by that method be found so? If we are to weigh only the psychological aspects, is it not equally cruel to shut a man away for the rest of his life, without women, without constructive work to do, among depraved companions, and without any hope for a future? That might conceivably be more cruel and unusual a punishment than the death penalty. Shall we then declare life imprisonment to be unconstitutional? Or, how shall we describe a long term of imprisonment which turns a man out into the world too old to make a new start in life, friendless and penniless? Isn't *that* cruelty? Is *that* also unconstitutional? Where shall we call a halt?

"And why should we direct our attack against capital punishment? There has been an attempt to link capital punishment with such social evils as segregation, racketeering and drug and liquor traffic. But the difference is that those activities are antisocial while capital punishment has been instituted for the *benefit* of society. Any of us may have a strong compulsion to find within our Constitution some means to prohibit a type of behavior which is clearly against the public good. But there is no such compulsion in this case."

Edward McCann pinched the temple bars of his eyeglasses. "Mr. Riegel, your opposing attorney quoted figures to show that the abolition of the death penalty does not result in an increased murder rate. If that is true, how can you defend the proposition that capital punishment is of benefit to society?"

"Disraeli's well-known remark is appropriate here," Walter Riegel said. "Disraeli said there are three kinds of lies—plain lies, damned lies and statistics. Most fair-minded men would agree that the statistics which show how many murders occur in certain states are influenced by an incalculable range of human, social and economic factors. Some states will therefore continue to have an enviably low murder rate even after the death penalty is removed because the other basic factors are more important. In other states a study of the statistics will lead different people to different conclusions—a clear indication that the statistics in themselves are not reliable guides on this point."

In a contentious world, Paul Lowe thought, how loud is the voice of sweet reason. Edward McCann, beside him, looked down at his notes and nodded slightly to show he had no further question.

As Walter Riegel proceeded with his argument, he continued to demonstrate that he was a formidable antagonist. He spoke for a viewpoint that was balanced, sincere, undoctrinaire.

"I will not take the time of this Court by referring to many expert opinions which hold that the death penalty is a major deterrent to crime. They are mentioned in my brief, and in several *amicus curiae* briefs. However, I will try to sum up these statements by leading authorities, by men with hard experience in the business of fighting crime.

"All of them agree that the only effective deterrents to crime are certain detection, quick apprehension, and adequate punishment. Each of these is a necessary part of the whole—subtract one and the whole collapses. Opponents of capital punishment tell us that the death penalty is not a deterrent. But how do they know? The threat of punishment by death is like a policeman's gun in a holster—or a burglar alarm in a store. It is a warning. We hear about the occasions in which this warning is defied, but how can we know the number of times that the warning is heeded?

"In a democracy our concern must be with the greatest good of the greatest number. To ensure the safety of the great majority of law-abiding people, we *need* policemen and we *need* burglar alarms. We have a varied arsenal of weapons with which to combat criminals. Capital punishment is one of our weapons and we should not lightly bind ourselves never to use it."

The clock on the far wall read one minute to twelve o'clock. Chief Justice Hampton glanced at the Marshal, who promptly rose.

The Marshal's voice rang out, "This honorable Court stands in recess until twelve-thirty this afternoon."

The gavel sounded. Paul Lowe and the other justices rose from their seats behind the bench, and turned to leave. With Edward McCann and Gabriel Hart, Paul Lowe went through the red velvet curtains.

Gabriel Hart said, "I'm impressed with this fellow Riegel. He's got good arguments. I think he's getting over. What do you think, Paul?"

"It's an effective presentation," Paul Lowe said. "I'll reserve judgment until I've heard what else he's got to say."

Gabriel Hart nodded. "That's the spirit. Keep an open mind."

"You do the same," Edward McCann answered quickly.

Gabriel Hart moved ahead to speak to the Chief Justice.

McCann growled, "He'll glow all through lunch about his new fair-haired boy."

"Talk baseball back to him," Paul Lowe advised. "It's only half an hour. And you have to finish your chopped steak."

"Veal cutlet."

Paul Lowe made a face. "I ordered it yesterday. I should have warned you."

"No matter what I eat today," McCann said gloomily, "I'll probably get indigestion."

448

Promptly at twelve-thirty the Court convened. Walter Riegel again took his place at the lectern.

"Mr. Chief Justice, may it please the Court . . ."

The cultivated voice, eminently reasonable, began its mellifluous assault on another key point.

"Let me try to deal with the argument that the death penalty is reserved exclusively for the poor. It is a serious charge—all inequality before the law must be considered an offense. Furthermore, I think this charge rests on fact. The death penalty is *not* applied equally to the rich or powerful—and they *do* generally escape from it. But also in fairness it should be pointed out that this statement applies to all other forms of punishment, not to the death penalty alone. The rich get better medical care, wear better clothes, drive better cars, live in better homes—and get better legal advice. As a consequence, they are not often punished as severely for their crimes. Is the law to blame for this—or the faulty administration of the law?

"If we abolish the death penalty because it operates most heavily against the poor, then we should abolish the entire criminal code. We will then be saying in effect that if justice does not always triumph, we must do away with justice! And by the same reasoning, let us do away with the Ten Commandments! Those ideals of human conduct are no more honored than our own laws.

"I believe that all men should be treated equally at the bar of justice. But I know this ideal is not likely to be attained—because the law has to operate through men, and men are fallible. If this Court finds that capital punishment must be struck down because it discriminates against a certain class of men, then this Court must proceed to strike down all criminal law which so discriminates. And I predict that we would then be left with no law at all!

"Let me propose another ideal instead. As men should stand equal before the law, laws should stand equal before the Constitution. If the Supreme Court singles out the death penalty for oblivion on constitutional grounds, it will be dispensing unequal justice because it will have singled out this one law among many, on the ground that it is discriminatory, and will have allowed other and equally offensive laws to stand."

An ingenious argument, Paul Lowe thought admiringly, with a calculated appeal to the loyalties of men trained to believe there was nothing more important than the structure of law. But Walter Riegel had subtly changed the issue, from whether justice should be done to whether the mechanism of obtaining justice should be tampered with.

Walter Riegel was saying now, "We have been told how crime rates do not rise in those states of the Union which have abolished capital punishment. But I heard no mention made of the fact that eight states in the Union have *restored* capital punishment after having abandoned it. Why did those eight states do so—if not from an unhappy experience?"

Paul Lowe asked, "Mr. Riegel, do you have the figures on the crime rate in those eight states?"

449

"No, Mr. Justice."

"Then how can you assume why they did it?"

"Mr. Justice, it is a natural assumption that they would not reinstate the death penalty unless experience proved it was needed. Those eight states would not have changed back if they hadn't discovered that capital punishment was an effective deterrent to crime."

"Mr. Riegel, is it true that Maine, the state with the lowest murder rate in this country, has abolished capital punishment?"

"There is no proof that the murder rate would have been higher if they had kept it."

"I agree, Mr. Riegel. And there is equally no proof that states which have reinstated capital punishment have done so because of an *increase* in the murder rate."

Gabriel Hart muttered irritably under his breath. Paul Lowe heard Edward McCann's whisper:

"Good going, Paul."

Walter Riegel began again, with slightly less assurance, on a new tack. He defended the right of Louisiana to punish duly convicted criminals without interference from the federal government. The right of a state to fix the punishment for crimes, he said, went back in a clear line to the Framers and was virtually sacrosanct.

"As Justice Oliver Wendell Holmes said, 'the first requirement of a sound law is that it should correspond with the actual feelings and demands of the community, whether right or wrong.' This statute providing for capital punishment has been on the books for eighty years—and there has never been a serious attempt to have it repealed. There has never been a serious community effort to have it modified. Only a minority of voices have been raised against it from the pulpit or from newspapers. No candidate has run for office on a platform that proposed the repeal of this law. I can say therefore with certainty that this statute fully meets Oliver Wendell Holmes' test of a sound law—it corresponds with the actual feelings and demands of the community."

In an interval of silence between words spoken and words to come, Paul Lowe glanced along the bench. Just beyond the Chief Justice was Charles Edmunson's commanding figure in black robes. Would Edmunson speak? Erect and towering over the others on the bench, a bushy halo of white hair crowning his lion's head, he gave no sign that he intended to interrupt with a question.

As Walter Riegel turned a page of his notes and prepared to go on, Paul Lowe asked:

"Mr. Riegel, suppose that your state had a law which provided for the state militia to be quartered in private homes without the owner's consent. Suppose that this law corresponded with the actual feelings and demands of the community. Should such a law be allowed to stand merely because the community wished it to?"

"No, Mr. Justice."

"Why not?"

"Because it would be in clear violation of the Third Amendment to the Constitution."

"And therefore the Constitution and *not* the feeling of a community about a particular law is what would be decisive. Am I correct?"

"The difference, Mr. Justice, is that the words of the Third Amendment are plain. The words 'cruel and unusual punishment' as set forth in the Eighth Amendment are not so clear. No one knows what those words mean."

"That determination is about to be made, Mr. Riegel. Once that determination is made by this Court the feelings and demands of the community in relation to this law may not be relevant. The law itself may be unconstitutional." Paul Lowe smiled. "Unless of course you intend to challenge the jurisdiction of this Court."

"I have no intention of doing that, Your Honor."

Paul Lowe's smile widened. "I'm sure we all appreciate that, Mr. Riegel."

Walter Riegel touched the side of his temple as though a vein had begun to throb.

"If it please the Court, I will continue. . . ."

"Please do," the Chief Justice said.

Edmunson reached for a glass of water on the desk before him and drank it steadily. Palest blue shimmer in glass holding colorless water . . .

In not many more weeks this session of the Court would end and there would be the entire summer. Last night, with Timmy seated between them on the living room sofa, they had been looking through travel brochures. Katherine favored Mexico City and he liked the Pacific Northwest, perhaps British Columbia. Timmy immediately spoke up for the Pacific Northwest. Katherine, laughing, said she would consult a lawyer about how to sue your husband for alienating the affections of your child. Timmy asked what it was like in the Pacific Northwest and listened, wide-eyed, entranced, while Paul Lowe described to him waterfalls that spilled from incredible heights in streams that were like water poured from a high bucket.

Edmunson put down his water glass and Paul Lowe's attention damply returned to the business at hand.

Walter Riegel was now examining the history of the Court's decisions in previous cases, particularly citing the decision in *Resweber* and in the Caryl Chessman case in which the Court declined to say that executing a man who had survived a previous execution, or whose execution had been delayed for eleven years, was cruel and unusual punishment.

"It is clear from these decisions that there is nothing that violates the Constitution *per se*, for even when the method of execution has been much increased in severity by outside factors, the Court has held that no issue of cruel and inhu . . ."

"Irreversibility," rumbled a deep voice. "That is the point you're overlooking."

One by one the justices on the bench turned to Edmunson. Every eye in the courtroom was centered on the majestic figure seated beside the Chief Justice.

Walter Riegel answered in a slightly puzzled tone, "Irreversibility, Mr. Justice?"

"The death penalty, sir, is irreversible. If a man is convicted and then found innocent, we can set him free. But if he has been executed we can only express our posthumous regrets."

"Mr. Justice Edmunson, I know you agree with me that a law cannot be found unconstitutional simply because it is capable of making a mistake."

"A mistake which takes a man's life is not a simple mistake. Not at all."

"But the constitutional question . . ."

"You have heard of the Fourteenth Amendment, I presume. No one may be deprived of life, liberty, or property without due process of law."

Walter Riegel answered a shade crisply, "There has been no claim, Mr. Justice, that William Weaver was deprived of due process. His conviction was upheld on appeal. There have been many opportunities for a full hearing of the evidence against him."

"Do you think that weight of the evidence, no matter how conclusive, has the same finality as a man's death?"

Edmunson's tone, deep and peremptory, almost supplied a relevance that the question lacked. Walter Riegel hesitated before answering, reacting with the instinctive respect that a listener pays to a superior mind by assuming that there is a reason for a statement which on its face seems to lack significance. In that moment's deliberation his intelligence was hard at work checking through the separate words of the question, dissecting them for hidden traps or pertinences, and finally deciding that incredible as it seemed no real challenge had been posed.

"Mr. Justice, my personal opinion hardly matters. Neither do my personal convictions on the question of capital punishment. If you are asking whether William Weaver had a fair trial which fully met the requirements of due process . . ."

Edmunson shook his head. His erect posture seemed to have broken slightly near the shoulders but he was pulled up stiffly by a force not part of his body, the stick backbone of a scarecrow.

"I am asking, sir, whether you think that any evidence can wipe out the fact that a man has to die and that when he dies it is an irreversible fact which no amount of evidence can undo."

Walter Riegel answered patiently, "I don't believe there is any evidence that can reverse the fact of death, Mr. Justice Edmunson, but I don't see how . . ."

Edmunson moved restlessly. "We must recognize, sir, that human beings are complex. They operate from complex motives. Sometimes they cannot help what they do. Should they be sent to death because they are prisoners of their personality? Shouldn't society try to help them instead of killing them?"

452

Walter Riegel's usual quick readiness was thwarted by the unexpectedness of the query.

He said slowly, "Mr. Justice, it is not our business to inquire into the psychoanalytic nature of crime. We can't define murder out of existence by saying that murderers' motives are complex—any more than we can do away with crime by admitting that most criminals are mentally disturbed and need a psychiatrist. Our concern must be with establishing proper safeguards for society to protect itself."

"Would you accept safeguards for society other than killing? It seems to me, sir, that if we want to continue to be called civilized we have to defend and not destroy the sacredness of human life."

Paul Lowe felt as though a weight had rolled on to his chest. There was nothing wrong with the approach Edmunson was taking—*if* it had been adopted on a lecture platform by some orotund orator. But in a Court sitting to decide a constitutional question, during the fleeting moments allowed for oral argument, its irrelevancy bordered on insult.

Walter Riegel replied with more sharpness, "Mr. Justice, the issue here is whether capital punishment *in toto,* and in particular capital punishment for a convicted rapist, is forbidden by the Eighth Amendment to the Constitution. I hope we will not be led astray into a discussion of our relative positions concerning the sanctity of human life."

"George Bernard Shaw," Edmunson said, his deep voice faintly whistling through his dentures, "said that hanging the wrong man could deter as well as hanging the right one. Would you call that an effective deterrent—hanging the wrong man?"

The tall erect figure on the bench still had great dignity but the impressive demeanor began to seem all illusion. He was like a figure in a tableau.

Walter Riegel looked puzzled and helpless as he opened his hands in an admission that he could not cope with this sort of questioning.

Edmunson's deep voice grew loud. "It's a matter of principle! Can't you understand that taking a human life offends the decency of human beings living together?"

Paul Lowe stared dumbly into space, afraid to look and afraid to hear.

Walter Riegel turned quietly to Chief Justice Hampton. "Mr. Chief Justice, may it please the Court, I would like to continue with my previous line of argument."

Edmunson's voice cracked with the first signs of temper. "I have not finished, sir. I have another question!"

Chief Justice Hampton rubbed his index finger along the side of his nose. "Mr. Justice Edmunson, please ask your question. But remember that we have only a few minutes left for oral argument."

Edmunson nodded, satisfied, but for the space of ten seconds he did not speak. His forehead knotted with the effort to concentrate.

Then he asked, "When we lose our respect for human life, don't we sink lower in the scale, sir? Isn't that what happens when we close our consciences to the tragedy and the shame involved when the state commits a brutal murder?"

Walter Riegel answered with cool hostility. "It would be better to say, Mr. Justice, that the state is defending the vast majority of its citizens against the brutality of criminals."

Edmunson's rumble filled the courtroom. "Shall we use the Constitution to defend a practice that cheapens our humanity? The more severe and terrible the punishment, the more backward the society that practices it. Isn't that proved by history, sir?"

Walter Riegel said shortly, "In the time that remains to me I would rather not trade speeches with the eminent justice of the Supreme Court."

"Answer the question!" Edmunson thundered.

Walter Riegel remained unruffled. "I believe the question is rhetorical in nature and incapable of being properly answered."

Edmunson shook his white hair like an angry halo.

"What is being challenged here, sir, is not merely the act of a state legislature. It is the dignity of man! Of man! The weapon of challenge is the Constitution—and it is our duty to wield that weapon! Would you tell me how this case differs from Territory versus Ketchum?"

Walter Riegel allowed himself a tolerant smile. "The death penalty was *sustained* by that decision. Am I to hope, Mr. Justice, that you are now arguing for a similar decision here?"

The courtroom echoed faintly with a flare of laughter, hushed and daring, irreverent and frightened of its temerity. There was derision in the laughter and yet a fundamental awe; it was the tentative scorn of skeptics for a god in whose powers they still maintained a superstitious faith.

Edmunson's complexion became dark and mottled and his eyes were piercing beneath shaggy brows.

"In that decision a state supreme court in its review of a death sentence took note of the condition of the territory. The condition of the territory! You are capable of understanding that, are you not, sir? If it can be established that the condition of the territory—meaning the state and its people—are such that they may do away with the death penalty, then this Court should strike it down. Should strike it off the statute books forever!"

"Subject to a factual test for cruelty," Walter Riegel interjected. "No such case has been presented here."

Edmunson's anger was spent. "Off the statute books," he said. "Strike it down!" He sat back wearily and his shoulders drooped. He added in a weak voice, "That's the only way to handle it. Reverence for life. A proper reverence for life."

Walter Riegel merely stared at him.

The red light glowed on the lectern.

"I thank the justices of the Court for their courtesy," Riegel said, gathered his notes, and stepped down.

At the counsel table Ken Norris' face was blanched white. He met

454

Paul Lowe's gaze with the stunned unbelieving look of a man who had just asked a question and received an unbelievable answer.

As a tension seemed to mount in the courtroom, Paul Lowe concentrated on the memo pad before him on which he had scribbled notes.

From the courtroom he heard drifting whispers. The lawyers for both sides rose from the counsel tables in a scrape of chairs. The aisles began to fill with departing spectators.

Before Paul Lowe's eyes the paper blurred. *What a fall was there, my countrymen. Then you fell and I fell and all Rome . . .* There was so much noise that he hardly heard the Chief Justice call the next case.

When he raised his eyes he saw that beside him Edward McCann was leaning forward, with his elbows on the counter. McCann briefly covered his face with his hands.

Stillness returned to the courtroom. A new set of lawyers took their places at the counsel tables.

From a seat on the high bench, Charles Edmunson looked down at them with terrible eyes.

31

Katherine was seated on the sofa, reading, when he wearily put down the telephone in the living room at six o'clock that evening.

She laid her book on the table beside her. "Why did John Hampton call you?"

"He's worried about Edmunson. We all are. He talked with Edmunson shortly after Court recessed today and the Old Man was almost incoherent. His law clerk got him safely home, and he's been resting ever since."

"What do you think will happen?"

"He needs a rest, Katherine. A long rest."

"Will he take one?"

"I'm not sure he'll be willing to. He's a proud stubborn old man and his work means everything to him. The Chief says he tried to bring up the subject by suggesting that Edmunson take as much time as he needs to recuperate, but Edmunson wouldn't hear of it. He said he'd be back in Court in a day or so."

"Do you think he'll be able to come back?"

He sat down heavily next to her on the sofa.

"Katherine, if you saw what happened in the courtroom . . . I don't see how he can even remain on the Court any longer."

She said softly, "You mean he'll have to resign?"

"I'm afraid so."

She removed her eyeglasses and folded them thoughtfully. "What a terrible thing to happen," she said. "I can hardly imagine the Court without Charles Edmunson. In a way he *is* the Supreme Court like Capitol Hill is the Congress and the White House is the Presidency. He's a part of our history."

"That's how I feel."

Another thought displaced that one in her mind. "A Supreme Court justice is appointed by the President for life, isn't he? Suppose Edmunson doesn't want to resign. What happens then?"

"We've never had a situation quite like that. Justice Grier and Justice Fields both overstayed their time and had to be pushed along a little. But they finally saw the handwriting on the wall."

456

"Perhaps Charles Edmunson wouldn't. You said his work is everything to him."

"We can't sit through a repetition of what happened in the courtroom today."

"Suppose Edmunson isn't aware of what's happened to him? In that case, he wouldn't feel that he had to resign. Is there a way he could be forced to leave?"

"Yes. The Chief could call a special meeting of the other justices and ask for unanimous consent to Edmunson's removal."

Without looking at him she put her eyeglasses on the table beside her book. "Would you vote for his removal if it became necessary?"

He could not answer directly: "If I were in the Chief's place, I'd feel I had to preserve the integrity of the Court. But John Hampton would have to be very sure of his ground before he asked for anything like that."

"Would you vote for Edmunson's removal?" she asked again.

"It's only a few more weeks to the end of the term. He might stick it out that long and then retire. It seems to me that we owe him that much consideration."

"Suppose Edmunson makes it clear that he doesn't intend to retire at the end of the session. In that case, what would you do, Paul?"

Her insistence finally forced him to consider the answer without equivocation.

He put his head down and studied the pattern in the rug that islanded them in a corner of the living room. He was reminded of past loyalties. Against the human values that appealed so strongly to him—his reverence for Edmunson's greatness, charity toward old age and infirmity, simple kindness, the pull of loyalty and long friendship—what was there to weigh in the balance? The continued efficiency of the Court's operation, keeping the docket clear, enforcing a proper contribution from each of nine men charged with carrying out duties levied upon them by the Constitution. These were bloodless considerations. It was so much easier to commit oneself to people than to principles. He wished he could quickly ignite some certainty in himself that would reveal a right course of action to follow.

"I couldn't possibly be a part of an execution squad," he said slowly. "If I voted to remove Charles Edmunson from the Supreme Court I'd feel like a traitor. Along with Judas and Benedict Arnold."

Her eyes dropped slightly and she touched the rim of the book cover beside her.

"Then what would you do, Paul?"

"I don't know," he said. He was struck by the terrible solitude in which moral questions must be decided. "I don't know."

All the mysterious power of the Court's prestige, all the unimpeachable purity of its status as a national symbol, was needed to back up its decisions. If he allowed personal loyalties to sway his decision in a matter as important as whether a colleague was fit to serve on the Court, how could he then expect the Court to win the popular consent necessary to give any sort of permanence to what the Court ruled?

His voice rasped with irritability at his dilemma. "Edmunson himself must realize that he can't carry on any longer. The Court has to survive its great men."

"It might help if someone he trusted would talk over the decision with him," Katherine said, gently. "Someone he knew was his friend."

"You mean that I should go to him?"

Katherine nodded. "I'll give Timmy his dinner. We can have ours when you get back."

He gave her an accusing look. "You had this in mind all the time, didn't you?"

Her shoulders seemed to draw together and she raised a hand to shield her eyes against the lamplight. "I just thought it was the answer you'd finally come to, darling," she told him.

Martin Hyde met him at the door of Charles Edmunson's home.

"How is he, Martin?" Paul Lowe asked.

"Feeling better, Mr. Justice. He spent most of the afternoon resting."

Martin Hyde took Paul Lowe's hat and topcoat and hung them in the closet.

"He'll be pleased to see you, Mr. Justice. The doctor was here about an hour ago and said he's suffering from exhaustion mostly. The doctor wanted him to go to bed but he's sitting up at his desk. You won't stay very long, will you?"

"Just a little while."

Martin ushered him into the library. Charles Edmunson was seated behind his desk. He wore a tweed jacket and a black tie and his green eyeshade dangled on a projecting knob of the desk lamp.

"Paul. Forgive me for not getting up. It's good of you to come to see me."

"How are you, Charles?"

"Oh, I'm better tonight." He indicated pages on his desk that he had filled with writing. "I've even been doing a little work."

"Is that wise, Charles? You shouldn't try to force yourself."

The dark blue eyes centered on Paul Lowe, fuzzily, then with sharpening focus. His unnaturally large pupils almost seemed to have pinpoints of light in their centers that contracted to find the proper range.

"I have to get back into the rhythm of things, Paul. Work is good for me."

Paul Lowe's voice had no particular inflection. "The burden gets heavier for all of us every year, Charles. You've held up magnificently. But we're all worried that you may be trying to do more than your strength permits." He took a chair near the desk. Edmunson was wearing a quilted robe over the lower part of his body. "I was talking about that with the Chief earlier this evening."

458

"I wish everyone wouldn't be concerned about me every time I'm slightly indisposed."

"It's been a long demanding year. You have to conserve your strength, Charles."

"I know that."

"It's hard for any of us to know when we are trying to do too much. For example, you were pretty tired today in the courtroom during argument in the William Weaver case."

Edmunson nodded. "Yes, I was. But I'm feeling better now. I've always been able to rebound quickly. Did you know, Paul, that I have the best record for attendance of any justice that ever sat on the bench? There are very few days I've had to miss."

"That was certainly true until this year."

Edmunson moved in his chair and the quilted robe slipped to the floor. "Oh, I won't deny that there are discouraging days. One has to expect that as one grows older. There are some mornings in which I feel fit for absolutely nothing except to lie in bed, when I'm reconciled to being a healthy invalid. There have even been times when I've been ready to look up the applicable statute and write my resignation."

Paul Lowe picked up the quilted robe from the floor and helped to adjust it over Edmunson's lap.

"When was the last time you felt like that, Charles?"

"Not recently, Paul." Edmunson's expression became brooding. "You know, a man only has meaning to himself while he's negotiating with the world. If a halt is called—the negotiations broken off by death or retirement—there is nothing left of importance."

"Have you talked with Frank Joyce recently?"

"No, I haven't."

"I don't believe he feels that way. He seems to have a great many interests."

"Oh, I think he must be quite submerged and unhappy. That's what happens when you have nothing to keep your mind active."

He was not sure how much further to pursue the topic. There was the danger of dealing an irreparable injury to Charles Edmunson's pride.

"I don't think you'd be unhappy, Charles. You're not the type to decay in a parlor with his secretary reading to him."

"You can't tell, Paul." Edmunson winced slightly as his old shoulder injury seemed to bother him. "It's really a tragedy about Frank Joyce, though. Such a beautiful spirit. We used to go for long walks by the old barge canal. It rained so hard the mud came up over our rubber boots."

He could see exhaustion taking a new toll. Edmunson's huge frame was absorbing the shock as it had once absorbed the shock of the bullet now lodged somewhere near his shoulder blade.

The voice remained sonorous: "I've always flattered myself that when the time comes for me to go, Paul, I will recognize it first and no one will have to tell me."

Paul Lowe was overcome with a craving to have done with it. "Charles,

459

you have to remember that you have not only a duty to yourself—but to the Court. When the time comes that you can't do your best, you ought to consider retirement."

Edmunson appeared to shrink inside his tweed coat until it hung loosely on his gaunt torso. His hand drifted over a paper on his desk. "I must do my work as long as I'm capable of it. It may be harder for me to push my pen across paper than it used to be but I still manage. And when my strength improves, my brain begins to chatter with ideas again. At such times I feel that I can still touch the peaks."

Paul Lowe felt a spasm of pity. There aren't enough peaks left, he thought. There may even be none.

Edmunson's dark blue eyes focused with almost hypnotic force. "There's another reason I feel I must stay. When I go, the President will appoint someone who agrees with Waldo Shuler's philosophy. That will put Waldo in control of the Court."

"That consideration mustn't weigh against preserving the ability of the Court to function, Charles."

"Of course not." Edmunson shook his head and the bushy white hair at his temples rose and fell like cat's fur. "If I didn't feel capable of doing the work, I'd resign at once." He chuckled. "But I can still be as valuable as some of the antedeluvian specimens we've got there. They're younger than I am by the calendar but their thinking is a lot older." He chuckled again and his head kept nodding. Finally he shifted in his chair with awkward effort; he did not appear to notice when the quilted robe slipped partly off his lap again. There was a distinct tremor in the left hand that rested on the desk top.

"You need rest," Paul Lowe said. "At your age you have to be careful about going beyond your strength."

It was exquisite cruelty to witness how swiftly weariness was hollowing Charles Edmunson out. His chest began to cave in slightly. The face, long, powerful, with large jaw and straggly brows, now had the tentative inquiring look of a face seen in an old photograph.

"Oh, I may take a day or two off," Edmunson said. "But I'll be back for the conference on Friday."

"Friday! It's only a few days away."

"I'll be well rested by then."

There was petulance in the old man's tone. He had been surprised by Paul Lowe's surprise.

Paul Lowe said quickly, "I only meant that if you don't feel up to it you shouldn't force yourself to come back so soon."

"I wouldn't miss Friday's conference, Paul. That's when we'll consider the William Weaver case. We have a good chance to win that, and I can make a contribution." Edmunson's gaze had become opalescent and fixed and he seemed to be staring inward. "It will be an exciting challenge. Capital punishment. My, Frank Joyce would have been pleased."

"I wish Joyce could have been on the Court to see it happen."

"Yes, it would have been the capstone to his career. His last testament."

460

Edmunson's interest flagged; he lapsed into rumination. "Joyce deserved to have something to be remembered for . . . instead of a little incidental wisdom . . . a few aphorisms . . . some opinions that have lost the redeeming power of contemporary meaning. . . . He should have finished with something more important . . . something to show that he had passed this way . . ."

Paul Lowe understood that Charles Edmunson's thoughts were also about himself. Appraising the old man's condition he was sure that Charles Edmunson would not be at the conference on Friday. It was doubtful whether he would have the strength to leave the house.

In the softly lit library the small desk lamp glowed with a hard intense glare.

"I'll say good night, Charles."

There was no need to worry about Edmunson's resignation. That was inevitable; the issue would be resolved in a very little time. Perhaps when Edmunson found himself unable to attend Friday's conference he would realize that he had played out his string.

"I'll see you to the door, Paul."

"That isn't necessary."

Edmunson rose with a painfully slow lunging motion as though fighting free of tentacles that held him down. "No, I want to."

Paul Lowe offered him his arm and the old man put his hand on it; his weight bore down heavily.

As they went toward the library door Edmunson was muttering, "Not much rain this spring . . . so there won't be flooding. I can't remember a more . . . laborious spring. All drudgery . . ."

Martin Hyde was waiting at the library door.

"Mr. Justice Edmunson is tired, Martin," Paul Lowe said.

Martin Hyde nodded silently and put his arm beneath Edmunson's shoulder.

Edmunson smiled a vague apology. "I think I will go to bed, Paul. I have to rest to be ready for our Friday conference. It can be such . . . a great day for us all."

He started slowly up the stairs with Martin Hyde supporting him. Then he paused, clinging with his left hand to the banister.

"Paul."

"Yes."

Edmunson gripped the banister. "We have to go forward. Oliver Wendell Holmes said, 'If you believe in great things you may make other people believe in them.' That's what we must try to do. To believe in great things."

"You always have, Charles," Paul Lowe said.

Edmunson resumed his slow climb. His black polished shoes, ill fitting at the ankles, lifted and came down ponderously on each new stair level.

Late on Thursday afternoon, Paul Lowe was working at his desk on an opinion he had been assigned. The case involved a floor-waxing concern which claimed its product made linoleum shine exactly like glass. On television the advertising commercials showed a woman removing wads of chewing gum that tightly adhered to the linoleum surface by using the floor waxer. The gum wads dissolved as neatly as brown sugar melting in a liquid. The reason the gum dissolved so neatly was that the so-called gum wads actually were brown sugar. A prop or mock-up had been used to simulate the less photogenic and more obstinate chewing gum wads.

The Federal Trade Commission found advertisements of this type misleading and entered a cease-and-desist order, forbidding the company to use any more commercials which employed this deceptive practice. The Court of Appeals had reversed the Commission, and its decision had been appealed to the Supreme Court.

Paul Lowe's thoughts kept wandering from the problem of floor waxers and brown sugar and chewing gum. When Martha Scully showed up in the doorway, wearing a new hat—a cannon-shaped affair that projected belligerently from her head—he was grateful for something new on which to focus his attention.

"I like your new hat, Martha," he told her.

She flushed. "Oh, thank you, Mr. Justice. I'll be going home now if you don't need me any longer."

"No, I don't need you. Good night, Martha."

"Have you heard any more about Mr. Justice Edmunson?"

"I called his house this morning. Martin Hyde said he was still in bed and he didn't want to disturb him."

"If you do talk to him, will you tell him I send my love and best wishes for a quick recovery?"

"Yes, I will, Martha. Good night."

The door closed.

He pushed the papers on which he had been working away from him and leaned with his elbows on the desk, his fingers near his ears to shut off the hearing of memory. John Hampton with one hand lightly resting on his protruding abdomen had said—Let's hope you're right, Paul, and Edmunson will resign. But I can't shirk my responsibility as Chief much longer. No matter how painful it may be, I will simply have to ask for his resignation.

There was the implicit threat: if his resignation is not offered, it will be compelled by unanimous consent of all the other justices. They would all have to go along—even himself, even Edward McCann—because the fact of Edmunson's incapacity was too apparent to be ignored.

Paul Lowe started slightly as the telephone rang on the desk beside him.

"Hello," he said.

"Is that you, darling?" Katherine asked. Her voice had an odd note of strain. "I was afraid you might have gone home already."

"Where are you calling from?"

"I had an appointment with Dr. Mulvey today."

"Are you still in his office? I'll pick you up there."

"Well, no, as a matter of fact I'm home. But that's the reason I called. Dr. Mulvey wants me to take some further tests."

"What kind of tests?" He heard his voice harsh with alarm.

"Oh, nothing unusual. He told me it's strictly routine. But they can only be done at the hospital. So he's gotten me a room for tonight."

"Which hospital?" he asked, and when she told him, "I'll meet you at home and take you there."

"Now, darling, you mustn't be upset. It's only for tonight and I can arrange for Timmy to have dinner at his friend's house and . . ."

"I'll be home in twenty minutes," he said.

In the taxi with Katherine going to the hospital he was hardly conscious of the route or the buildings passing by. Her small overnight bag was on the floor before him. It was part of the luggage she had bought with the initials KL. Katherine Lowe.

"Do you have anything to read?" he asked.

"I won't need anything. I'll be getting the tests and everything. And they have magazines in the hospital."

"I'll get you something frivolous. Art Buchwald or Jules Feiffer."

"They're not frivolous. They say perfectly serious things in a frivolous way."

"I suppose you'd prefer one of those heavy Germanic thinkers who say funny things in a perfectly serious way."

She put her hand on his knee. "Really, darling, I'm fine. There's no reason for me to be in a hospital at all except it's the only place where they can give these tests."

Anxiety lay like sediment in the bottom of his stomach. "Are you sure you can go home tomorrow?"

"In the morning. Dr. Mulvey promised."

The taxi pulled into the driveway of the hospital and when he looked up at the somber tan building with its narrow windows the sharp edge of fear cut him.

Off the corridor on the fourteenth floor there was a lounge with chromium chairs colored in green and pink and covered in vinyl. The lounge was a passageway between two corridors and at the left a starched woman in a white uniform and cap was seated at a desk with a wheeled card index before her.

"Mrs. Paul Lowe? Room one-four-oh-five."

As he started to go with her the nurse stopped him.

"You'll have to wait here, Mr. Lowe. I'll let you know when you can see your wife."

"Can't I go with her?"

"I'm afraid not. But it will only be a few minutes."

He gave Katherine her overnight case and watched her go off down the corridor.

In the lounge a woman was seated, wearing a protective apron over her head and shoulders. She was young—in her twenties—and there was something about the way she sat, constantly uneasily shifting in little spasms of irritability, that was disturbing to a brittle-looking, pretty, blonde woman in her forties who sat beside her, trying to brush her hair.

"Will you sit still?" the blonde woman asked the young girl. "Will you please please *please* sit still?"

There was a slackness to the young girl's mouth and a baffled empty expression in her eyes. Then he realized her spasms were involuntary—she was a spastic. A drool of spittle ran down a corner of her mouth and the blonde woman wiped it away with a handkerchief. Small brown dabs of argyrol stained the young woman's nostrils.

The nurse's phone rang and she picked it up.

"You can see your wife now, Mr. Lowe," she said.

He went through the connecting lounge to a farther corridor and followed the arrows that indicated where to find the rooms numbered from fourteen hundred to fourteen hundred and twenty.

Katherine was wearing a high-necked gray hospital gown and slippers and was seated near the window of her room. He crossed the room and she looked up and held out her hands but he leaned over to kiss her check. Her warmth was reassuring.

"What was that about? Why couldn't I come in with you?"

"I had to change clothes and they took one of those blood samples. In the morning I'm to get another transfusion and some other tests. Have you ever had a transfusion, darling?"

"No."

"There's no pain but it's so weird lying there and having someone else's blood run into you. It makes me feel inhabited."

The conversation made him anxious again.

"I wonder why Dr. Mulvey wants to take new tests."

"It's nothing serious, darling. He'll keep testing me until I'm exhausted in order to find out why I get tired so easily." She sighed. "I don't mind anything except that I won't sleep at home with you tonight."

His whole body seemed to form into a wave that rolled irresistibly toward her but he was warned by a side shift of her eyes that they were being observed. Conscious of another presence in the room, he turned.

"Oh, Dr. Mulvey," Katherine said. "I'm glad you got here so early. You know my husband, don't you?"

Dr. Mulvey held out his hand. "Of course. Nice to see you again, Mr. Justice."

They shook hands briskly.

"Well, how is our patient?" Dr. Mulvey asked Katherine. "Comfortable, I hope. Is there anything I can get for you?"

Katherine said, "All I want to know, doctor, is what time I can go home tomorrow."

Dr. Mulvey's smile did not waver. "Did I say tomorrow?"

"You most certainly did."

"I'm afraid that won't be enough time to take all the tests. Tomorrow is going to be a busy day for you, young lady." Dr. Mulvey took Katherine's wrist and arched two fingers over her pulse. "Very good. A nice strong heartbeat."

"How long will she have to be here, doctor?" Paul Lowe asked.

"Not long. Not long at all. Perhaps two or three days. No more than that."

"Two or three days!" Katherine exclaimed.

"We want to get your strength up," Dr. Mulvey said. "I've put you on a special diet that'll soon have you feeling much stronger."

"I'll get fat," Katherine said. "I'm not used to eating three meals a day."

"What sort of tests do you want to take, doctor?" Paul Lowe asked.

"Routine. I just think it's time we had a more thorough diagnostic evaluation."

Paul Lowe said to Katherine, "It's all right. I'll come every day and tell you interesting inside stories about what's happening at the Court."

Dr. Mulvey said, "If Mrs. Lowe tells me them later I can pass them along to my son in law school."

Katherine fluffed a pillow behind her head. "I hate to be stuck in a hospital. I can't work and I don't know what to do about Timmy. There's no one to look after him."

Paul Lowe said, "We'll get by. Timmy can stay at his friend's house tonight, and tomorrow by day there's Elfie." Elfie was their cleaning woman who came several times a week. "I can be with him over the weekend. We'll have our meals out and the rest of the time we'll be here with you." He touched her cheek. "Everything is going to be fine. You concentrate on getting well."

"I'm not sick. That's what's annoying. I wish I were pregnant or something. Then I wouldn't feel so useless just sitting here."

"I'll be back to see you tomorrow morning," Dr. Mulvey said.

Paul Lowe walked out with him to the corridor.

"What is the trouble, doctor? You're worried about something, aren't you?"

"No, nothing as strong as that. But I am a little puzzled."

Dr. Mulvey's habitually assured manner could be annoying.

"Why, doctor?"

"This last blood study we made revealed a pancytopenia—a decrease in all the formed elements of the blood. That's why I brought her here for a more thorough diagnosis of her condition. Tomorrow we'll perform a bone-marrow aspiration. That should give us a better clinical picture."

"What do you think the trouble is, doctor?"

"Hard to say. There are a number of possibilities. I'll want to check them all out."

"I want everything possible done for her, doctor. As a matter of fact, I'd like you to call in someone else for a consultation."

"There's no need for that. As soon as we locate what the trouble is we'll have it under control in jig time."

"It can't do any harm to get another opinion."

Dr. Mulvey said stiffly, "Of course, if you feel that one is necessary."

"I want the very best medical help available for my wife."

"Very well, Mr. Justice," Dr. Mulvey said.

When he returned to the room Katherine was in bed. Her eyes were drooping with weariness.

She asked sleepily, "What did the doctor say about me?"

"He said you were charming."

"You know what I mean. Please tell me."

"He repeated exactly what he told you. He needs time to make these tests. Doctors never like to admit they don't know anything until they've taken all the tests they can think of to prove they really don't know anything."

"He doesn't think I have something wrong, does he?"

"He says you're going to be absolutely all right and there's nothing to worry about."

"I don't know you well enough yet to be able to tell when you're lying."

He bent over the bed and kissed her. "I'll see to it that you never know me that well."

Her eyes closed. She murmured, "I'm going to sleep now, darling," and in a minute she was asleep. He sat by her bed, watching the peaceful expression on her face and thinking: this is all I want forever. Just this face to look at for the rest of my life. At the thought that anything might happen to her he felt as though someone had cut him in two right down to the roots.

He had not believed in such all-embracing tenderness or, at best, had believed in it as astronomers believe in the existence of a planet that cannot be seen on their telescopes—by its influence on neighboring bodies. Now he had only the familiar words to give expression to it: "I love you." He did not actually speak the words—they formed in his brain and on his tongue and on the roof of his mouth.

Yet somehow she heard. She turned slightly and her lips smiled even while her eyes remained closed. The hairs on his wrist tingled as though her fingertips had glided over the back of his hand. All his senses were alert to her.

On the way out he passed through the lounge. The young spastic girl was sitting there with the blonde woman who was apparently her mother.

The blonde woman was smoking. The girl sat nodding her head as though it were on a stick that had somehow worked loose. Then she opened her mouth and made gaping silent breaths like a fish and suddenly began to cough and sputter. The blonde woman got up nervously and tried to stop her by shaking her shoulder but the coughing grew worse. Suddenly a dribble of blood appeared in a nostril. The thin scarlet stream ran down the girl's face while she made gasping sounds like someone strangling. The blonde woman, holding her daughter's shoulder, looked helplessly at Paul Lowe.

"I'll get the nurse," he said.

He found a nurse in the corridor and summoned her. When they re-

466

turned to the lounge the young girl was gargling and snuffling and blood was dripping steadily on the protective apron. When she leaned forward, blood stained her dress. All the while she made the terrible *arrgghhh* sound and her hands described vague meaningless patterns of movement in the air.

Her mother, the blonde woman, watched her with an expression of dazed horror. The nurse worked at the young girl. Finally the mother gave a small shudder and turned away. She walked past Paul Lowe unseeingly to the sand urn and ground out the butt of her cigarette. Her face was black with anger and loathing. She kept saying over and over, without even being aware that she spoke, "Enough. Isn't it enough?" Her daughter began to spew up vomit.

There was nothing Paul Lowe could do, so he left.

"Death," said Chief Justice John Hampton, "is not in itself a cruel and inhuman punishment. Nor has it been proven that the method to be employed in this instance—that of electrocution—is anything but instantaneous and painless."

He looked down the conference table. All the justices were in their seats and listening attentively. Only the seat at John Hampton's right was vacant. Charles Edmunson had failed to appear at the conference.

John Hampton cleared his throat. "Therefore, despite my strong personal bias against capital punishment, it seems to me that we would be stretching the Eighth Amendment too far to make it apply to any so-called cruelty in the method.

"Now as for the crime classified by the Louisiana statute as punishable by death—the crime of rape—it is a more serious crime than many held by other states of the Union to merit the death penalty. I need only refer to the fact that in seventeen states of this Union it is currently a capital crime to kill someone in a duel, or that in Arkansas the death penalty may be inflicted for selling wood alcohol or for causing a boat to ram another boat. I would conclude that this Court has no reason to invoke the Eighth Amendment against Louisiana's right to decide its own method of punishment."

John Hampton's brisk authoritative review moved on to cite several previous decisions of the Court which he believed supported his conviction.

Paul Lowe gazed out the windows at the far end of the room to the drab uninspiring view of low-lying, middle-class residential districts. John Hampton, obeying his own scrupulous dictates of fairness, had come down on the side of capital punishment. It was not too surprising. John Hampton had voted for certiorari in the William Weaver case because he felt the issue deserved fuller discussion, but his impartiality now led him to define sharply the limits of where he believed the Court had a right to intervene.

The choice must have been difficult for the Chief, however. No man's desire to be impartial entirely overrides the commandments of his personal conscience. Although John Hampton had firmly stated his position he might have arrived at it only after close and troubled deliberation. There were weighty questions to be resolved. Was there a greater purpose to be served by departing from a strict interpretation of the Eighth Amendment? That was not the kind of question John Hampton would dismiss as a trifle. He must have fought with phantoms of himself in order to square justice with law and to weigh the relative claims of logic and of the attainment of a just result. He surely must have been troubled by the cloudy area in which the lines of division blurred and intermingled. In looking for the presence of a general rule, some inclusive answer in which logic would interact with justice, sentiment with reason, which would contain its own sufficient method yet conform to precedent and provide a basis for future judgments, John Hampton had at last decided not to move forward into unexplored legal territory but to fall back upon other men's interpretations of the Constitution. A forgivable frailty. It was the sort of vacillation on which Charles Edmunson—the Edmunson of a year ago— could work a most powerful influence, washing away legalisms as a tide washes away sand sculpture on a beach.

"Justice Shuler?" Chief Justice John Hampton said.

There was a knock at the door. It was an unexpected interruption. There had been no requests for information from any of the justices. John Hampton glanced toward Paul Lowe, who pushed back his chair and got up and went to the door.

As he opened the door he stood absolutely still with astonishment. A sea-surge beat in his brain, his pulse.

"I'm sorry to be late," Charles Edmunson said. His tall figure moved majestically into the room.

John Hampton rose from his chair. "Charles. I didn't expect you here today."

"I told Paul I'd be here," Edmunson said. "I wouldn't miss it for anything. But I'm afraid I overslept. I left word to be awakened but my man-servant apparently forgot."

Chief Justice Hampton shook hands with him, and then Waldo Shuler did and soon the others were crowding around to shake his hand. Charles Edmunson wore a dark blue suit with a crisp white shirt and a maroon tie with a stickpin. He was freshly barbered and there was a pinkness in his cheeks. When he shook Paul Lowe's hand his handclasp was firm and strong. Was this the same man who had been faltering up the staircase in his own home, the sallow-faced, sunken man whose body had grown so old and lost its sinew? It hardly seemed possible. The chemistry of age had left almost no mark on this tall-standing magisterial man. There was only one explanation. Amazing as it seemed, Edmunson's great resiliency was showing itself once again, and the former power was back.

"Did I interrupt anyone?" Charles Edmunson asked.

"I had just summed up my opinion about the William Weaver case," Chief Justice Hampton said. "If no one objects, I can repeat it. It won't be necessary to go into the facts of the case. I'm sure you know them quite well, Charles."

468

"I've done a little boning up for the conference today," Charles Edmunson said with a smile.

He took his place at the conference table, and listened impassively as Chief Justice Hampton repeated the reasons for his opinion in the William Weaver case. Behind Edmunson's restraint, the silent authority of his manner, there lay a deepening power felt in the room more strongly than his physical presence. John Hampton's crisp assurance was somewhat undermined by it. Hampton spoke now with a hint of defensiveness, almost of apology, and the fine tiny lines in his cheeks seemed to spread a web of uncertainty across his countenance.

"And therefore I find no constitutional flaw in the Louisiana statute under which William Weaver was condemned to death." The Chief Justice finished, and turned to Charles Edmunson on his right.

"Justice Edmunson?"

Edmunson's long hands were folded together on the table and his long fingers entwined like strands of rope.

He began speaking in a deep slow voice: "It strikes me that most of the arguments about this case, both pro and con, are merely efforts toward the framing of the ultimate question—which is the moral standing of the death penalty. Within that ultimate question are contained all the other questions. When we ask whether the death penalty is cruel we are asking fundamentally whether such a penalty violates the conscience of men today—whether it accords with our present concepts of humanity and the dignity of human life."

Waldo Shuler's forehead wrinkled with a scowl. With his opening words Charles Edmunson was serving notice that he intended to strike beyond the boundaries that Waldo Shuler set for himself to a larger issue. Waldo disapproved because his conception of the Constitution could not be separated from his conception of a judge's function in applying it. In his view, Charles Edmunson was already going too far.

Edmunson said, "In discussing this basic question I will not appeal to what men *ought* to feel. I will discuss how men—contemporary men—in fact do react to legal murder by the state.

"Let us first examine the euphemisms with which men try to disguise from themselves the ugly reality. If you pick up your morning newspaper on the day after an execution you will read there how a criminal has 'walked the last mile,' how he has 'paid for his crime,' or 'paid his debt to society.' You may even read that 'justice was done.' If the man died by electrocution, you will find a description of how the lights flickered or the switch was thrown. If he was hanged, you will learn that a trap door was sprung. You will not read of the death—how the man's brains were fried, or his neck broken from the spinal column, or his lungs filled with poison gas. . . . Yet, why not? Is this a concern only for the delicate sensibilities of newspaper readers? Hardly. In the same newspaper you will find the most horrifying accounts of train wrecks, airplane crashes, automobile accidents, shootings, knifings. These are told in gruesome detail. But the account of the legal execution is told practically in whispers. What is the reason? Is it because if the details become known to people who have been willing to close their eyes, if they should be made to *see*, the suddenly aroused conscience of the whole community would condemn this practice once and for all?

"I think that is the reason. Because the proof of how modern men regard capital punishment—if they allow their imaginations to work—is not only shown in the too-careful reports we get of executions. It is shown most clearly in the very conditions under which the punishment is carried out. The chief claim for capital punishment is, as we have heard, deterrence. In former times this claim might appear to have some validity. Executions were carried out in public—and the populace turned out for a hanging as for any entertaining spectacle. And they witnessed for themselves the horror that awaited them if they broke the law. But today executions are carried out under conditions of the utmost secrecy—with only a few witnesses. Why, if we are not ashamed of the deed? If we wish to deter people from becoming murderers we ought to make clear what they face. We ought to give the widest possible publicity to executions. Interviews with the condemned man should be published widely, there should be scarifying accounts of his mental torment. The terror and agony of his last moments should be set forth to the very last convulsive twitch of his body. The largest audience possible should be made familiar with the penalty that faces murderers. We should put the electric chair, the gas chamber, the scaffold on television and thereby instruct millions in the intimacy of horror. *That* is the proper way to make use of capital punishment as a deterrent. But we don't consider doing this for a moment. Again, why not? Because the facts—the facts shielded from us, altered by euphemistic reporting—would so offend our consciences that even one such example would rouse people to do away with capital punishment forever."

Edward McCann took off his eyeglasses and wiped them. Chief Justice Hampton's mouth was touched at the corners by a faint smile that softened his stern features. Somewhere inside John Hampton's meticulously fair, delicately balanced judgment, the deep organ note of Edmunson was being heard.

Gabriel Hart was holding a pencil tipped against his teeth and chewing at the eraser.

Edmunson said, "Let me now discuss if there is a way by which we *can* legally dispense with capital punishment. I will not deny that the State has the power to punish. But the Eighth Amendment stands as a wall between a State's power to punish—and the limit of punishment. That amendment must set the proper limits of civilized morality. Is the language of the Eighth Amendment too unclear to serve such a purpose? Behind and beneath the mere language of our Constitution, undefined but clear to those with insight, lies a body of precepts from which all new law must be derived.

"This is a higher law even than our Constitution—or rather we cherish the Constitution as one of the best attempts ever made to interpret that higher law. Why is it one of the best? Because the Constitution allows for the constant influence of the higher law to play beneficently over the common practices of the day. It is by this compass that we must continually correct our course. For we are all, being men, embarked on the same great adventure, and the destination of our voyage is harmony and order—the penetrating of chaos and the making sense of the ungraspable material universe. This is the great challenge we must meet—to find a regulating power which will expand our humanity, control it and set it free."

A slight breeze stirred the curtains of the three windows of the conference room. Glancing up, Paul Lowe met John Marshall's somber appraising eyes in the portrait above the mantelpiece. You should be here today, he thought. You and Edmunson.

Charles Edmunson paused; his fingers strayed to his forehead as though to locate the position of the next thought.

"In the long view of history we all know that capital punishment will not be countenanced. Then why should we not forbid it now? Does not the Constitution allow us to exercise the power of our conscience? The Constitution was set up, this Supreme Court was established, for no other purpose than to give us such freedom to act. Surely no one will claim that simply because a law exists it is justified—that because the state has been taking men's lives for centuries we are justified in maintaining the practice. By that kind of reasoning, we should still be cutting criminals into quarters or burning them at the stake. Those practices have been done away with because men decided they were cruel and unusual punishments. Man's conscience is steadily evolving. We are in the dawn of the human mind and hardly awake to the call of morality. Let our generation be chosen among all others to make one more small but significant step forward."

Across the table Henry Merriam's silver-haired handsome head was still. He stared ahead, blinking solemnly, misty-eyed with gentle astonishment. As he saw Paul Lowe watching him his lips gradually widened in a smile.

Andrew Cutler's face had congealed into a remote disdainful expression. Gabriel Hart was leaning forward, holding his pencil poised over a memo pad but writing nothing. Waldo Shuler's restless gaze searched the length of the table and he touched the knuckle of his index finger to the bridge of his nose in the gesture of a fighter who has been dealt a stinging blow.

Paul Lowe looked up; he heard Edward McCann cough.

Edmunson was in the same position as before, his arm resting on the table and the long fingers touching his forehead. But the arm now seemed to be supporting his weight and the fingers had splayed out to hold the head erect. Too long, Paul Lowe thought suddenly, this silence. Why doesn't he speak? Why doesn't he conclude his argument?

Edmunson gave a slight start. His hand came away from his forehead and the chin lifted. When he began to speak his voice gradually lowered to a sepulchral mumble.

"We should adopt the ancient principle of Anglo-Saxon law: the burden of proof rests upon those who favor the death penalty. It is not for those who favor abolition to prove that the taking of a human life is cruel and unusual—it is for those who would take life to prove it is not." Edmunson fell silent but his jaw worked as though he were still speaking. Then the sounds began to come in unexpected spurts as though a needle were playing in grooves from which meaningful impressions had vanished: ". . . decide if long-term imprisonment will deter as well as a punishment of death . . . one would think that this was sufficiently proven by those acquainted with the horrible apparatus at first hand . . . the man who built the gas chamber at San Quentin ended up as one of its victims. And the builder of Ohio's electric chair died in it. . . ."

What relevance did that have?

Charles Edmunson moved silver-rimmed spectacles forward on his nose and began to read from a paper he held before him. It was a table showing the homicide rate in states that had abolished capital punishment. Monotonous sentences unfolded one after another in numbing unaccented cadences.

At the conference table there was a shifting of position. Bill Branch gave the Chief Justice a look that plainly requested a halt to be called.

Edmunson put down the paper but continued speaking. His voice could scarcely be heard. The phrases which became audible added up to a cumulative incoherence.

"Old Testament justified capital punishment . . . but also bans bearing wool and linen . . . and requires a brother to have children by his brother's widow. Deuteronomy twenty-five, line five . . ."

The inaudible droning went on until the first reaction, delayed out of shock or pity or lingering respect, came in an abrupt interruption.

"Mr. Chief Justice!"

Gabriel Hart impatiently tapped the pencil he was holding against the edge of the table.

"I suggest it's time we got on with the discussion."

Edmunson continued with his murmured monologue a moment longer. Then he slipped his silver-rimmed glasses up on his forehead and tilted his head to one side with an expression of annoyance. Gabriel Hart was impaled on that formidable glance like a specimen on a pin.

"I believe the Justice is out of order," Edmunson said. "I haven't finished."

Gabriel Hart answered defiantly because he had been a little intimidated, "It's a charade. No one can understand a single word you've been saying."

"Do you wish me to speak louder?"

"I'd like you to yield to Mr. Justice Shuler!"

Voices instantly mingled in controversy. All semblance of decorum vanished. Paul Lowe heard McCann shout, "*He's* out of order!"

Waldo Shuler held up a hand. "Mr. Chief Justice, it does appear that Mr. Justice Edmunson is indisposed. Perhaps if he has time to rest, he can continue with his statement after everyone else has been heard."

"Is that satisfactory?" the Chief asked Edmunson.

The old man took a handkerchief from his breast pocket and patted his cheek.

"It is *not* satisfactory, Mr. Chief Justice," he said firmly. "I intend to finish making a statement. If the others wish me to speak more clearly, then I'll try to oblige them. But I intend to finish."

The Chief nodded. "You may proceed."

Edmunson began again in a fairly audible tone. He had a gentle look, melancholy and dreaming, and his hand trembled as he turned the page of a new report. What he was reading was a summary of innocent persons who had been executed in the United States. He then launched into reading a survey of prison officials which established that admitted errors in execution had taken place. In the middle of this recital his voice faltered. Perspiration stood out from his forehead in large drops, squeezed out by the fierceness of his effort to concentrate. He stopped, smiled faintly and touched his cheek, the fingers like softly brushing feathers against his quivering mouth.

"I believe that is all. Yes, I believe that is all."

Henry Merriam got up, went over to Edmunson, and bent to speak to him. Paul Lowe could not hear what Merriam said but Edmunson's reply was clear.

"I'm all right, Henry. I'll just sit here if you don't mind. You mustn't concern yourself about me."

In a dead silence Merriam returned to his seat at the conference table.

When Chief Justice Hampton finally spoke, his usually cool precise voice sounded blurred.

"Justice Shuler."

Waldo Shuler signified that he had heard by a nod of his head. His lips were thrust out, and there was a strange expression in his liquid brown eyes.

"Mr. Chief Justice," he began, as though he were going to continue with a statement of his position. Then he seemed to change his mind midway. "Mr. Chief Justice, this has been a long and wearing day. I suggest that we take half an hour's recess before resuming."

"That's a good idea," Chief Justice Hampton answered. He looked about the table for some sign of disagreement but there was none. "We will take half an hour."

As the Chief Justice rose the others rose; Charles Edmunson remained seated.

Paul Lowe went to him and took his arm. The bicep muscles seemed curiously flabby to the touch. Edmunson raised his massive head slowly. His mouth was drawn in serious lines, and a wattle of flesh bobbed at a corner of his jaw. He seemed stunned, dimly aware of being trapped in a flaccid and decaying prison. Paul Lowe supported his arm as they slowly left the room.

The other justices stood in their places, near their chairs and the two-tiered carts. The Chief Justice's head was slightly bowed.

473

32

The vote in conference on the William Weaver case was four to three in favor of upholding the Louisiana statute. Justices Shuler, Cutler, Branch and Hart voted together to form the majority. Only Edward McCann and Paul Lowe voted to invalidate the Louisiana statute on the ground that capital punishment was forbidden as cruel and unusual within the meaning of the Eighth Amendment. Chief Justice Hampton concurred on the limited ground that sentencing a man to death for rape was excessively severe.

In Charles Edmunson's absence, Henry Merriam's failure to vote gave the majority to Waldo Shuler's position.

That afternoon Henry Merriam seemed depressed and preoccupied. He anxiously fingered his silver-headed tiepin. "I wish I could have gone along with Edmunson on the William Weaver case," he told Paul Lowe.

"I'm a little surprised you didn't, Henry."

Henry Merriam sat back in his swivel chair. "I can tell you why I couldn't vote for Edmunson's position. There was one clinching argument for me that never even came up in the conference room."

"That's interesting, Henry. What was it?"

"The *amicus curiae* briefs," Merriam said.

Paul Lowe could not help being puzzled. The *amicus curiae*—literally "friend of the court"—was by definition not directly affected by the case and was allowed to be heard only because the resolution of the legal problem might eventually have an effect on him or because the *amicus* is an organization trying to promote a worthwhile social aim that would be affected by the judicial decision.

"The only reason for permitting the filing of *amicus curiae* briefs," Paul Lowe said, "is that they might develop a line of argument which would otherwise have been ignored. I'm wondering which argument had such an influence on you."

"It wasn't anything that the briefs said," Henry Merriam answered. "It was the fact that they were submitted by *all* the attorneys general of states which have capital punishment statutes. Those states obviously don't want the capital punishment statutes changed."

474

"In the past, Henry, when a state law came up against the Constitution you've never hesitated to strike down the state law."

Henry Merriam regarded him soberly. "Of course, the difference is that this particular state law doesn't clearly come into conflict with the Constitution."

Nevertheless, Paul Lowe's observation registered. Henry Merriam swung about in his swivel chair, picked up a pen and tapped the metal casing of the pen against the desk top. Paul Lowe had reminded Merriam that his reputation as a justice had been established by a willingness to abandon the State's Rights position he had rigidly upheld as a Southern Senator.

Paul Lowe wondered whether Henry Merriam's decision not to support Charles Edmunson's position really had deep roots. No matter how logical a line of reasoning seemed it often was no more than an ordered marshaling of facts to bolster a conclusion arrived at deep in the emotions. That deeper choice was made first and then the brain, that subtle sophist, summoned up history, sociology, philosophy, economics and law to make the choice appear objective and impartial.

Similarly, the fact that Henry Merriam had chosen a neutral course might reflect not a reasoned analysis but an emotional state that was in supple readiness to move either way.

"I had a curious letter this morning," Paul Lowe said. "It was from a minister who suggested that all members of the Court should witness the execution of a criminal—see the horror of it—before deciding whether capital punishment is cruel."

"I don't agree with that, Paul. That would be rendering judgment by the degree of shock we felt. There are stronger ethical arguments than that on both sides. We went into all of them pretty carefully."

"Still, the Chief Justice is the only one of us who ever witnessed an execution. And he ended up voting to knock down the Louisiana statute."

"Only on the narrow ground that rape doesn't merit the death penalty."

"Yes—but he found a constitutional prohibition. Charles Edmunson always said we should adapt the Constitution to modern concepts. And in the long run history has agreed with him. The Constitution is vague enough to be adaptable to any new set of conditions. That's one reason it's survived this long."

"I'm in no mood to renew the debate, Paul. I just want to explain why I didn't vote. I didn't agree with Edmunson. But with his empty chair staring me in the face, I couldn't bring myself to vote against him."

Paul Lowe hunched slightly forward. "Henry, how many of those *amicus* briefs you mentioned were from states which punish rape as a capital crime?"

"I don't know exactly. Not many."

"The Chief Justice's opinion would only affect states which do punish rape as a capital crime."

"Yes, that's true."

"Then you can't oppose too strongly the Chief Justice's position in the William Weaver case."

Henry Merriam held the arms of his chair as though they were a support curving him into the padded security of leather and wood.

"Well, no, I don't," he answered hesitantly. "Except that the principle is the same, of course, even if only one state is affected."

"But the interest of one state in defending its criminal procedures can't weigh equally with protecting and extending the individual rights guaranteed by the Constitution. To protect and extend those rights was Charles Edmunson's guiding star. It's a pretty good guide for us to follow."

"What are you saying I should do? Join in the Chief's opinion?"

"I wouldn't presume to tell you what to do, Henry. But if you did agree with the Chief that rape should not be punishable by death, your vote would cause a deadlock at four to four."

Henry Merriam returned his look steadily. "And Charles Edmunson's vote would decide the issue."

"Yes, it would." Paul Lowe sighed and put his hands on his knees. "I can't help wishing that the Old Man could leave us on a note of triumph. This particular defeat will be bitter for him."

"I've always felt that Charles Edmunson was so sure of his private vision that even a defeat was almost irrelevant to him."

"That might have been true when he was still on the Court and could work toward changing defeat into an eventual victory. But that isn't so any longer. Charles Edmunson will never take part in deciding another case."

Henry Merriam said sadly, "I know." His chest seemed to fill out as though straining against invisible bonds. "I'd do almost anything for the Old Man, but I can't change my vote as a tribute to him."

"You wouldn't be changing your vote, Henry. You haven't cast it."

"I can't turn over my conscience either—not even to Charles Edmunson."

"Charles Edmunson would never expect that of you, Henry."

"But the only honest decision I can make is one that is based on conscience."

"Henry, I'll wager that you have as much conscience about capital punishment as about State's Rights."

Henry Merriam stiffened like a man who has felt the first fusillade of a firing squad. "There are a great many factors that have to be considered, Paul."

"There certainly are."

"This is too important a matter to let any minor considerations sway my decision."

"I agree."

"As I say, it's a matter of conscience."

"But it is also a chance—a last chance—to pay something on a debt we all owe to a great man. There couldn't be a better valedictory for Charles Edmunson than to win his last and most important case."

A tiny spasm of muscle in one cheek was Merriam's only reaction.

"I'll think about it, Paul. That's all I can promise."

"That's all anyone can ask, Henry."

476

Merriam was silent for a long moment. Then he looked up and smiled at Paul Lowe.

"You know what I was just thinking?"

"What?"

"It's barely possible that Charles Edmunson's leaving the Court won't make as much difference as we all thought it would."

"Why not?"

Henry Merriam's smile widened. "It occurred to me that you may turn out to be a match for that fox Waldo Shuler."

On Saturday Paul Lowe had a quiet talk with Chief Justice Hampton in the comfortable sitting room atmosphere of the library reserved for the use of justices of the Supreme Court.

They were seated on a sofa to the right of the entrance. The hour was shortly past noon and they were alone. Charles Edmunson's collapse in the conference room was more than twenty-four hours in the past but reverberations were present in their conversation like the diminishing echoes of an explosion.

"I spoke to Martin Hyde this morning," John Hampton said. "Edmunson told him he intends to compose a letter of resignation to the President as soon as he's well enough."

"Somehow I haven't fully accepted the fact that Edmunson won't be here with us any more," Paul Lowe said. "It feels like the end of everything. This morning, as I was coming here through the corridors of the building, I had the eerie sensation that I was moving through a sepulcher in which a great man now lies buried."

"We all need more time to adjust ourselves to the idea that Charles Edmunson won't be around. Fortunately, I don't think the President will try to fill the vacancy on the Court until after the summer."

"Good."

John Hampton linked his hands, turning the palms inward and staring down at them. "I had a telephone call from Henry Merriam this morning."

"What did he have to say?"

"He's decided to join me in striking down the Louisiana statute on the narrow ground."

Paul Lowe said in a tone measured carefully to conceal his satisfaction. "That will deadlock the vote in the William Weaver case at four to four."

"The deadlock will last only until Charles Edmunson casts his vote. There's no doubt Edmunson will put a majority of the Court in favor of invalidating the Louisiana statute."

"I think that's good news."

William Weaver's life will be saved, Paul Lowe thought, and the lives of all the William Weavers to come who might have been put to death for a crime such as rape. A vagina rudely forced would no longer exact its price in human life. That was only fair in a world where standards of chivalry have changed and she works beside us in the marketplace and demands uncorseted rights. She survives seduction, easy nights in motels with *prix compris* breakfast and even the accusing morning mirror to show up cheery-faced for work in the office.

"Of course there won't be a majority for abolishing capital punishment," the Chief Justice went on. "But either Henry Merriam or I will write for the Court on the narrow ground. The others can concur on the broad ground that capital punishment itself should be abolished."

"Charles Edmunson should write that concurring opinion. It will be his last great effort."

John Hampton stared off down the long corridor that led off from the center of the private library room. The corridor was lined with stacks of bookshelves.

He said wearily, "Edmunson can't do it, Paul. We both know it."

"He deserves the chance."

John Hampton shook his head. "I don't believe he'll even want to attempt it. He can't make the sustained effort needed to write such an important opinion."

A vision flashed through Paul Lowe's mind of Charles Edmunson staring down with dark-rimmed eyes from the high bench and seated, broken and slumped, at the conference table. That vision brought him restless to his feet. He wheeled slowly about the room before he returned to the Chief Justice seated on the sofa.

"You may be right, John," he said.

John Hampton sighed. "Paul, when Edmunson tenders his resignation it will mark the end of an era. I believe it has been a great era in the history of the Court."

"So do I. It's been Edmunson's era."

"Yes, and I would like it to end in a manner worthy of what Charles Edmunson has meant in the life of this country." The Chief Justice looked at Paul Lowe intently before he averted his face. "Paul, I want you to write the concurring opinion—and sum up how Edmunson and you and McCann feel about this."

Paul Lowe felt a congestion in his chest, followed by a foreboding weight. "It's a great responsibility, John."

"If any man on the Court is equal to it, you are. I hope someday they'll study your opinion in the schools," John Hampton's smile became wistful, "and probably everyone will wonder why it wasn't written for a unanimous Court."

Paul Lowe said, "Thank you, John."

A few minutes later he left the library with John Hampton. They descended in the elevator into the underground caverns of the garage beneath the Supreme Court building. Everything became concrete and plaster with odors of gasoline and exhaust fumes.

Chief Justice Hampton shook hands briefly.

"Good luck, Paul. I'm counting on you to do the sort of job we can all be proud of."

Chief Justice Hampton walked off to his waiting car and chauffeur. Jonathan Carter was waiting beside Paul Lowe's Chrysler sedan. He opened the door.

In the vast underground vault, sealed in a concrete membrane, Paul Lowe felt quite suddenly abandoned, as though something vital had been taken away from him.

As the car door clicked to behind him he sank into deep gray upholstery. The ascending runway was gray with afternoon light. There was a grayness in everything. The fact that he was to write the concurring opinion underlined for him the reality of Edmunson's disappearance from the Court.

What a task had descended into his hand. *The end of worldly life awaits us all. Let him who may, gain honor ere death.* Old brave Norse words returned to him in the quiet interior of the car. Other men had struggled in the dark mists, amid clangor of swords, to slay dragons. The setting had changed but the challenge was the same. He was being granted a chance to put one more dragon's corpse in the records.

Charles Edmunson would have composed an opinion that clearly and eloquently would have established a new legal concept of the sanctity of human life. But Edmunson was gone.

The ascending car bumped over a worn fracture in the driveway.

He had to beware of counting Charles Edmunson's loss in might-have-beens or in the brutally cut connections between Edmunson and those on whom he might still have had an incalculable impact.

Paul Lowe had to establish his own connections with the sensibilities of numberless other people. Their minds were pulsing just beyond his nerve ends. How could he reach them?

Jonathan Carter sat erect in the driver's seat. His dark neck showed above the stiff collar and his hair began at the collar line and climbed the small vertebra valley until it became thick and crinkly on the back of his head.

"Jonathan," he said.

"Yes, Mr. Justice."

"What is your wife's name?"

"Alice, sir."

"How many children do you have?"

"Seven. Five boys. Two girls."

"Seven children." How long had he known Jonathan Carter? How little he had learned about him. Actually, he was almost newborn in this business of relating to others—an infant to whom only one voice had become entirely real. Katherine's. Unlike him, Katherine had a natural ability to love, a gift that was like speech or hearing; he could acquire it only with an ultimate effort. She could help him to extend the range of his communication. She was the whiteness against which he would project some new message of himself. How lucky anyone was to adventure into the soul of even one other person. How incredibly lucky he was that it should have been Katherine.

On Sunday he decided with Timmy that they would surprise Katherine when she came home. They would announce a change of plan. They were not going to spend the summer in British Columbia, after all, but in Mexico City as she wanted.

Before he went to visit her in the hospital, he spent an hour with Timmy reading to him a conversational guide to Spanish. Timmy struggled with the unfamiliar Spanish phonetics. They practiced useful phrases (the conversational guide *said* they were useful) to each other:

"What do you say at the dentist, Timmy?"

Timmy replied in Spanish: "*Me duele ese diente.*"

"And when it's too late and the dentist has pulled the wrong tooth already?"

The guide proved a useful Spanish substitute for "ouch." "*Aieee!*" said Timmy, and Paul Lowe laughed with him at the absurdity of it.

He taught Timmy to memorize the names of the volcanoes. Popocatepetl, Xinantecatl, Iztaccihuatl.

"Good," he said finally. "I want you to be the one to announce it, Timmy. When Mother comes home you just say, 'Mom I've decided I'd rather visit Popocatepetl, Xinantecatl, and Iztaccihuatl.'"

Timmy grinned. "Okay, Dad."

As he made the turn from the elevator on the fourteenth floor of the hospital the nurse saw him approaching. She got up hurriedly and came over.

"We've been trying to reach you at home on the telephone. It's your wife, Mr. Justice."

His heart beat with a painful pulse. "Is anything wrong?"

Her face was masklike. "About half an hour ago she began to complain of a severe headache. One of the staff doctors gave her something to quiet her. A few minutes ago she became unconscious."

He fought down an impulse to tear away and go to Katherine at once. "Where is Dr. Mulvey?"

"We're trying to reach him. Dr. Standish from the hospital staff is with her now."

When he entered the hospital room he saw Katherine lying still on the bed. She seemed rather small, perhaps because her body was hidden by the sheet drawn up almost to her neck. Her face was flushed yet wan—a tint of pink on gray.

A tall, earnest-looking young man in a white doctor's smock was at her bedside. He had close-cropped dark hair and dark eyeglasses. He was taking her pulse.

He put Katherine's limp wrist down and nodded to Paul Lowe.

"I'm Dr. Standish. Dr. Donald Standish. Are you her husband?"

"Yes. What happened? She was fine when I saw her last night."

"It may be an intracranial hemorrhage."

Paul Lowe was unable to meet the doctor's gaze. "Is she in danger?"

Dr. Standish said, "It isn't an unusual development in an illness like hers."

"I didn't realize anemia could have such serious complications, doctor," he managed to say quietly.

"It's not a simple anemia, of course," Dr. Standish said. "Aplastic anemia is quite a different matter. She must have a really strong constitution to have lasted this long."

The moment between the doctor's speaking and Paul Lowe's understanding might as well have been an eternity.

"Lasted this long?" he asked. He felt a retching in the back of his throat. He had not missed the sense of the remark, only its application to Katherine.

"There have been cases where remission took place for a considerable period but she hasn't had much luck in that way. The disease has been making a steady advance."

He had an unreasoning, insane fury against he knew not what, nor whom.

"Dr. Mulvey never said anything."

Dr. Standish nodded. "He wouldn't have been sure until the tests were completed."

His skin was stretched tight over the bones of a Piltdown man. "He must have known something. If she was this ill, he must at least have suspected."

Dr. Standish said, "I don't believe there's been any delay in the treatment. She's had cortisone and she was getting transfusions. We've begun giving her platelets—a clotting element in the blood. We intend to do everything possible to save her."

To save her! Paul Lowe was confused and angry. Doctors could minister to Katherine in the cold gleaming light of science but Katherine was not a statistic. *Her* life was not something to be discussed as a thing which might be lost. *Her* life was a lantern that kept the light of her senses alive.

"There's always hope." Dr. Standish had the benevolent skeptic air of the young scientist who truly did not believe in hope unless subject to verification.

"She isn't going to die," Paul Lowe told him. "I want the best man in the country. What's his name?"

"You'll have to speak to Dr. Mulvey about . . ."

"Hang Dr. Mulvey," Paul Lowe exclaimed. He would have liked to explode in maniacal anger, to spring upon the doctor in a bound and drive his head against the wall. "What's the name of the best man you know? I want him here immediately."

Some of the repressed fury simmering below the surface of his request made itself apparent to Dr. Standish.

The young man's answer was an attempt at exorcism. "Well, I suppose Dr. Harvey Peters is as good as any in this field. He's associated with this hospital."

"How can I reach him?"

"I can give you his home telephone number. I used to study with Dr. Peters and I know him quite well."

When Dr. Standish gave him the number, Paul Lowe went outside and retraced his steps to the lounge.

"Is there a telephone?" he asked the nurse at the desk.

She nodded and indicated where he could find it.

He entered a booth set into a wall of the corridor.

"Dr. Peters," he said when he got him on the telephone, "I'm calling from the hospital. A Dr. Standish recommended you to me. My wife is very ill—they think it's aplastic anemia—and she's suffered a hemorrhage. I'd like you to come here as quickly as you can."

"Isn't she being treated by her own doctor?"

"Yes. Dr. Mulvey."

"He's a good man. I'm sure Dr. Mulvey will do everything I would under the circumstances."

"I want you, Dr. Peters. Will you please come? I'll pay anything you want, but . . . *please come.*" Around his eyes the frayed nerve centers began to twitch.

Dr. Peters' voice became slightly unctuous: "My wife and I are expecting guests tonight."

His voice roughened. "Dr. Peters, you have to do something. Dr. Mulvey isn't here. They can't reach him."

"All right. I'll try to get there as soon as I can."

When Paul Lowe hung up, he was faintly ill with relief. After a moment's consideration he dialed Race Hardman's home.

When Race Hardman came on the phone he said, "It's good to hear from you, Paul."

"Race, I'm calling with bad news. Katherine is ill. The doctor says it's serious. I'm at the hospital now."

Race Hardman answered in a slightly high-pitched voice, "My God, Paul. Is there anything I can do?"

"There may be. Her son Timmy is at home. I don't want to leave but I can't leave the boy there. There's just the cleaning woman and she has to leave at six o'clock. Would you take care of him for me? Just until I find out what's going to happen."

"I'll send for him right away. No, better. I'll go over myself. I'll take the boy back with me. He'll be in good hands, Paul. You won't have to worry about him."

Paul Lowe was too depressed, too preoccupied with anxieties to thank him properly. "I'll call home and try to prepare him for what's happening. He won't understand it, but I'll try."

He called the house and told Elfie what had happened.

"Please don't alarm the boy," he asked. "Let me speak to him."

"I've been practicing the names, Daddy," Timmy said when he came on the phone. "I can say them perfectly. Listen. Popocatepetl, Xinantecatl, Iztaccihuatl . . . When can I see Mommy?"

"Timmy, I'm going to ask a favor of you."

"Sure, Dad."

"Your mother is asleep. She may be asleep for quite a long while. I'd like to stay here until she wakes up so I can talk to her."

"That's okay," Timmy said promptly.

"But you need your dinner and you have to be in bed by nine o'clock. Your mother may sleep later than that."

"I can stay up. I'm not sleepy." Timmy's voice was unworried. "I'm not hungry either."

The interactions between himself and the boy were complex and delicate, resembling one of those mobiles in which a push can change all the relations of every part.

"That's why I have to ask you a favor," he told Timmy. "I know your mother would worry if she knew you were staying up late or going without your dinner, or if you had no one to stay with you. We can't afford to worry her with anything like that when she isn't well. So I want you to have dinner at a friend of mine's house and stay there tonight. He has two lovely daughters not much older than you are, and you'll feel at home there."

"Do I have to go?" Timmy's voice quivered.

"You don't have to do anything you don't want to, Timmy. I'm asking it as a favor. It will make everything a lot easier for me and for your mother too."

"When will I be able to try out my Spanish on her?"

"We can do that soon."

"You won't tell her about Mexico City when she wakes up?"

"I promise."

"Well, I'd rather not," Timmy said. "But if it's a favor . . ."

"It's a very big favor," Paul Lowe said.

He stayed on the telephone long enough to tell Elfie to leave Timmy with a Mr. Hardman when he called for him.

On his way back to the room there was a bustle of activity in the corridor. Someone went past in the opposite direction wheeling an instrument cart, and a group of four people, two men and two women, were checking room numbers looking for the name of a patient they had come to see.

A woman in a faded blue nightgown walked slowly along the wall. Her slippers made scuffing noises on the linoleum. Her hand shuddered out from her body, never quite touching the wall. She saw Paul Lowe and straightened, aware that she was performing before a witness. She wore no makeup and her face was ravaged. Her eyes were dark holes in her face. She brushed back her graying dark hair with one hand as she went past him.

In the patient's lounge a Negro nurse and a woman patient were watching a television soap opera. The setting was a hospital. Oblivious of where they were, they watched with fascination a miniaturized reproduction of their surroundings.

In her room Katherine was lying quietly on the bed. Dr. Standish was gone and a nurse was in the room with her.

"It's all right," Paul Lowe told the nurse. "I'll stay with her now."

"Just push the buzzer if you need me," she said.

He took a chair quietly and sat near the bed, not moving from his position and not trying to read. Katherine looked as though she were merely asleep. He could imagine the hazel eyes beneath her closed lids—clear and sparkling eyes with that inexplicable vitality. One arm was now outside the sheet and there on the inside of her elbow he saw a small purplish spot. He touched it experimentally with his finger. Then he realized it was a sign of the creeping blight that was hidden in her. The little purplish spot was from bleeding beneath the skin.

He forced himself to look away from her. The view from the large window in the room was of a roof opposite where in the late afternoon a man wearing a sweater and very brief shorts was sunbathing on a blanket. Farther down, a painter's scaffold was being lowered down the side of the building. Leisure and work went on outside the hospital with no interruption. Everyone outside was in a gigantic conspiracy to avoid the reality of death. That's why they were able to pass, unbelieving, funeral chapels and mortuaries. That's why they could accept the inevitability of death in the same way they accepted the existence of other galaxies—as a mathematical certainty of no present interest.

He watched the sun sink through the sky until it vanished in a fiery explosion among a bank of low-lying black clouds. How much longer he sat he did not know. Once, there was a light from the hall as the nurse entered, this time with a tall stooped Negro man whose gray hair clung to his scalp as though it were damp.

"I'm Dr. Peters," he said. "Are you Mr. Justice Lowe?"

"Yes, doctor." Paul Lowe stood up and shook hands. "Thank you very much for coming."

Dr. Peters said, "I've looked at your wife's chart. You'd better wait outside while I examine her."

Paul Lowe waited outside the room while Dr. Peters made an examination with the assistance of the nurse.

Dr. Peters came out to meet him. "There's bleeding inside the mouth and in the urine and seeping into the skin. There are also strong indications of intracranial hemorrhage. How severe that is we can't tell yet."

"What's your prognosis, doctor?"

"Her condition is dangerous, of course. But she seems to be coming out of the coma. If she is strong enough we may try something new. Removal of the spleen. It can cut down the rate at which blood elements are being destroyed. It's had good results in some experiments."

"I don't want you to take unnecessary risks."

"I won't." Dr. Peters shrugged in a gesture that appeared to say there was nothing much to lose. "We'll do our very best for her, Mr. Justice."

Paul Lowe would not accept Katherine as the kind of abstraction called a patient. She was Katherine. But there *was* a part of her shared with everything mortal—a part which could become ill, respond to a remedy,

484

find health again through the narrow egress of suffering. That part of Katherine he had to leave in the care of doctors.

"I realize that, Dr. Peters. I'm sorry."

After Dr. Peters left, he let the nurse go to dinner and he remained with Katherine. He caught a glimpse of his reflection in a mirror. He had a slightly flushed, wild expression. He sat, waiting.

Much later he heard a whisper somewhere in the dark room.

"How is she?"

Race Hardman was in the doorway.

Paul Lowe put a finger to his lips and went to him.

"She's still unconscious. When did you arrive?"

"A few minutes ago. The nurse let me look into the room but she was asleep and you didn't notice me." Race Hardman looked at him suspiciously. "Have you had anything to eat?"

He shook his head.

"There's a cafeteria in the hospital. Let's go."

"I can't. I have to be here when she wakes up."

"That might not be for hours." Race Hardman took his arm firmly. "Come on. I insist."

Paul Lowe gently pulled his arm away. "I don't want anything, Race. How is Timmy?"

"Fine. He had supper with our family a couple of hours ago. My girls are mad about him and they're spoiling him outrageously."

"I'll see him as soon as I can. As soon as I know about Katherine."

"How is she? What did the doctor say?"

"It's very serious, Race, but she's going to be all right." He would not consider any other possibility. "The doctor said she's coming out of her coma."

"Are you sure I can't bring you something to eat?"

"Yes, I'm sure."

He was reminded of that scene in the Odyssey when Ulysses and his fellow voyagers watched six of their company devoured alive by the ravening monster Scylla and, narrowly escaping with their own lives, sat afterward on the beach and had a fine supper before mourning their lost comrades.

Race Hardman stayed with him for a while, and finally left. He was hardly aware of the fact that Race Hardman was gone, and he was unaware of the times the nurse came and went from the room. All his concentration was centered on the quiet figure in the bed.

He looked down at his clasped hands. He said a short silent prayer. "Hello, darling."

Katherine was looking toward him.

He went quickly to her. He touched her hand on the sheet.

"I don't want you to worry," she said.

Her breath going in and out over the lower edges of white teeth seemed visible. So still and motionless she lay. Her tumbled black hair was spread out in tangles held together by damp perspiration.

"Don't try to talk," he said. "Just rest."

A husky murmur: "Will you stay?"

"I'll stay."

There was another lapse of time and Dr. Mulvey arrived. He was wearing a black topcoat over a tuxedo.

"I was in New Haven attending a father-son banquet," he explained. "They didn't reach me until early this evening. I came without bothering to change."

Paul Lowe went outside while Dr. Mulvey made his examination.

He came out looking rather worried and rumpled.

"She's resting quietly now. She's out of the coma."

"You never told me her condition was this serious, doctor."

Dr. Mulvey lifted his head and peered at him. "We were never quite certain of that. And I don't believe in alarming people unnecessarily."

"I wish I had known. We might have had someone in earlier as a consultant."

"Earlier?"

"I've asked Dr. Peters to be a consulting physician on the case."

"I see." Dr. Mulvey's slender body quivered. "Well, of course that's your decision." Dr. Mulvey nodded his head, turned, and walked rapidly off down the corridor.

At nine-thirty the warning signal flashed outside the door while he was in Katherine's room. The light made a pale green reflection in the darkness.

A few minutes later the nurse entered.

"All visitors must leave," she told him.

"Not just yet."

"It's regulations."

"I'll stay here until she wakes up," he said. "I want her to see me when she does."

The nurse was a middle-aged woman with a wrinkled smiling face which she made an effort to keep looking stern. "It's really against regulations," she said, but she went out and closed the door.

At twelve o'clock the night nurse came on duty. She was a heavy-set, competent woman.

She came in to find him sitting near the bed.

"I'm sorry," she said firmly.

He said, "I know it's regulations. But I have to be here when she wakens."

"I'll call the doctor."

"All right. I'll wait here for you to get back."

Shortly after the nurse left, Katherine began to move and to mutter slightly. He went to her bedside. It was dark in the room but a rectangle of light came in from the partly open door to the hall. The lower half of her bed was in the light and she was in shadow. Nevertheless he saw her eyes open. She looked up, then her glance shifted and she saw him.

She smiled, "Hello, darling."

486

"Hello."

"What time is it?"

"A little past midnight."

"Have I been asleep long?"

"Not very long."

"I feel much better. Has the dog stopped barking?"

He stared at her uncertainly. "The dog?"

"It was such a lovely day at the beach. I wish we could stay here forever."

"Katherine!"

Her eyes drooped, closed again. Her chest rose and fell evenly. He went into the corridor to summon the nurse. She was already approaching with Dr. Standish.

"Something's wrong," Paul Lowe said. "She woke up and she was talking out of her head. Then she dropped off again."

Dr. Standish and the nurse returned to the room where Katherine was sleeping. The nurse turned on the room lights and Dr. Standish rolled up Katherine's right eyelid and searched the pupil with a pencil of light. The nurse was standing near and blocked Paul Lowe's view.

"Better call Dr. Peters," Dr. Standish said.

The nurse hurried out. Paul Lowe waited for a moment when the doctor was not busy with the examination to ask, "What is it, doctor?"

Dr. Standish looked up with mild surprise.

"You'd better wait outside," he said.

"What's the matter?"

"Not now," Dr. Standish finished checking Katherine's pulse and respiration. Then he flexed her knee, and then another. She stirred restlessly. When he saw Paul Lowe still in the room he spoke more sharply, "Outside, please. You're in the way here."

Paul Lowe stared at him. After a minute he left the room and went into the corridor. When the nurse returned she went into the room and closed the door behind her. He saw the reflection of light beneath the door. Not long afterward Dr. Peters came down the corridor hurrying and seeming abstracted. Paul Lowe moved toward him but Dr. Peters looked at him blankly, opened the door, and went in.

The hospital corridor was dark except for small glowing panel lights in the floorboards and a bright island at the nurse's desk down the hall. Two nurses went on duty and they went on with their tasks without appearing to notice Paul Lowe's presence.

It was five o'clock in the morning. He looked at his watch so often that he had the illusion he could see its magnified slow ticking. Then the door opened and the nurse came out and without a glance at him went off down the hall to the nurse's desk. He was about to follow her when the door opened again and Dr. Peters emerged. He was perspiring.

He said, "She's slipped back into a coma. Her blood pressure is way, way down. We're trying everything. But I don't know." He shook his head. "I simply don't know."

Paul Lowe tried to speak but no sound came. His throat had closed.

Finally he managed, "What are the chances, doctor?"

"A lot depends on how long the coma lasts. It's the result of the inter-cranial hemorrhage. How long she's unconscious will be an indication of how big the hemorrhage is." Dr. Peters paused, aware that he had evaded the question. "Not better than one in ten," he said gently.

"I'll stay. I won't bother anyone. I just want to be here."

Dr. Peters seemed very tired and sad. "Suit yourself."

At six o'clock in the morning, Katherine began to roll and twist in the bed. The nurse got up to attend to her. Paul Lowe stood at the foot of the bed. He had been praying for hours and had exhausted his faith. He was almost calm. He watched Katherine struggle like a sleeper in the grip of a nightmare, swaddled in incommunicable fear. One chance in ten. Fight, Katherine, my darling, if I could I would go where you are. We would fight our way back together through whatever darkness surrounds. Together we are invincible. He willed his strength to flow into her, his blood to run powerfully in her veins; they would live joined, or perish. He concentrated upon making the link so he could pour strength into her. Her restlessness moderated—her body hung quietly, listening. He walked in her darkness, shared her unconscious world. All else was apart; he had overcome a final wall of resistance and they would never again be separate. She was in him and he in her, fully sharing.

The nurse said, "She's coming to."

Her eyelids fluttered, a hand flung out as though to tear away some invisible frail veil. At the same instant he saw through blackness a beckoning light and hurried with her toward it. Out of a far country they emerged together.

Her eyes opened. She saw him without surprise. She knew that he had been with her.

"Dearest." Her voice was very faint—as though speaking from a long distance.

"Yes."

"I don't want to die."

A deep roll of silence pealed over him.

"I won't let you," he said.

The nurse waited, pallid at the side of the bed. The nurse did not matter. This was between himself and Katherine.

"I thought I was dying, a little while ago. It wasn't unpleasant drifting away, knowing I could never come back. I wasn't even afraid—until I thought of you. Then I had to see you." She stopped speaking. Her chest heaved two or three times. Her hand moved toward him on the coverlet. He reached to take it; she was clammy and cold.

"I love you, Katherine. You mustn't leave me."

"It isn't fair. I hate you to be alone."

"Don't say that."

488

"I hate that more than anything. If I never know anything else, I think I'll always know when you're alone."

Stay, stay, he pleaded. Now, when my fear is greatest, God, take pity. Demand what sacrifice You will, only let her rise from this. If that is too much, let me not be different or solitary; let me share with her whatever fate you have decreed.

"Would you like something to drink?" the nurse asked Katherine.

Katherine nodded, smiling a little. He stood by her, holding her hand. Now, now, my prayer will be answered. Let it be now while we are here together—this time beyond question—while the universe itself does not exist—while nothing exists that is not the two of us.

The nurse returned.

"Here you are; drink this."

She gave her a glass of orange juice with a straw. She propped Katherine's head on the pillow so Katherine could drink it.

"Isn't that good?" the nurse asked.

Katherine's face lit with a pleasure that made her seem girlish. She was a young child indulging a slightly wicked whim—wearing braids, at a counter, laughing with other girls over a chocolate malt or a candy bar—irrepressible in her youth.

Katherine said, "It's very good. It's the best thing I've had."

He said to the nurse in a shaky voice, "She's better. If you want to step outside for a cigarette, I'll stay with her." He was so greedy to be alone with her.

When he turned back, Katherine's head had fallen back on the pillow. Her mouth was open and she was breathing with great sobbing gasps. The orange juice glass had fallen from her hand and a pulpy stream of golden yellow inched its way along a fold of the coverlet.

"Nurse," he cried, and then sharply, "*Nurse!*"

The nurse said, "I'll get the doctor."

Dr. Peters went in, and then someone brought a portable oxygen cylinder. Paul Lowe waited painfully in the corridor outside her room. Nurses came and went several times. When the door opened he could see that an oxygen tent had been drawn over her bed. When he called her in his mind there was no answer. No queer, wonderful sensation of making contact. He was entirely nonexistent, yet naked on all sides. Other people's faces were a torture to him.

The door opened again and the heavy-set nurse came out. She came toward him.

"The doctor asked me to tell you it doesn't look good. He is doing everything he can but it doesn't look good."

"I understand." There was nothing else to say. Each minute passed with incredible slowness but there were gaps in time; he did not know how much time had gone by when at last Dr. Peters came out of the room. He walked slowly and brushed the palm of his hand on his jacket.

"We did our best," he said. "I'm afraid she's gone."

The seventh seal opened and the universe moved past the crack of doom.

"May I see her?" Paul Lowe asked.

Dr. Peters shook his head, then quickly touched Paul Lowe's arm in apology.

"I could use a drink," he said. "You look as though you could use one too."

"I want to see her."

"It won't change anything."

He shook off the doctor's hand. "I know that." Dr. Peters made only a partial attempt to block him. That was as well.

They were folding back the screen that had been around her bed. They were lifting off the transparent oxygen tent.

He said, "I need a minute with her."

The heavy-set nurse looked to the doorway. Someone, perhaps Dr. Peters, gave her an order. She and the other nurse and young Dr. Standish—had he been here?—left the room.

She looked very well, he thought. Very pretty. Her mouth was closed, her eyelids shut, and struggle had gone out of her. He touched her hand and it felt warm. Where was she? He heard nothing, experienced nothing. It was impossible that she was gone. Even now she might be retreating from him in a succession of mirror images. He might see her again if he tried. He raised his head to look about the room. If she were somewhere near, there would be a signal. If she were anywhere, she would tell him so. He felt chilly. He held his elbows with the palms of his hands to contain himself.

She was so peaceful. He touched her hair, and tucked a strand in place. On impulse, he bent and kissed her lips. It was then he knew with certainty that she was dead.

He stood a moment, filling his memory with her.

He said, "I will miss you, Katherine."

When he left the room there was nowhere to go. The drizzle had become a steady fine rain, bitterly penetrating. As he walked on, the streets around him emerged into the gray wet light of morning.

L'ENVOI

All days merged into a series of quick impressions, too fast for him to distinguish clearly.

The day of the chapel was a cloudy day. Cars were parked all down the block. On the bulletin board downstairs her name was listed. She was in one of the rooms numbered with griefs. There was a constant traffic of mourners in the elevators and on the stairs. . . .

The day of the funeral was bright and sunny and the ground was muddy from rain. The sky was clear pale blue with white clouds. He was glad of that. Katherine loved days like this.

The minister was a white-haired old man who was bothered by the sun in his eyes. His stiff white collar wilted. At the cemetery everyone seemed to have bright faces with hard black reflections swaying on the ground behind them.

At the gravesite this minister closed his Bible with a sigh. In the bright sunlight the headstones all around were like an army marching upon oblivion.

He saw Race and Brenda Hardman. Brenda wore black fetchingly; it set off the delicacy of her beauty. Her wide black straw hat allowed sunlight to stream through so her face resembled that of a woman in a French impressionist painting.

Paul Lowe thought: her loveliness will change. Katherine will remain forever beyond the possibility of change.

Mourners threw their sprigs of flowers onto the coffin in its deep resting place.

When it was Timmy's turn he wouldn't throw his sprig of flowers.

"If I do," he said, "will Mommy ever come back?"

He held the boy's head tightly into his side. . . .

There was a day when he was seated in an armchair by a window watching the sun come up out of the east in a silent explosion. The great round red rim bulged on the horizon, swelling to a round-roofed temple.

Katherine's father, Jim Prescott, came to see him that day.

"Paul, I want to talk to you about Timmy," Jim Prescott said.

"What about him?"

"He doesn't belong here now. Without his mother this isn't home for him. Of course I know how you feel but you have nothing to give the boy right now, Paul. And it's mighty depressing for a youngster."

"What do you think I should do?"

"I'm the boy's grandfather and he's lived with me most of his life. I'd like to take him back to Omaha with me."

"That's up to Timmy. Whatever he decides."

"The boy is very fond of you, Paul. But he needs a real home. If you'd just tell him you think it's best, he'd come with me. You can talk him into anything."

"I don't know," Paul Lowe said. "I'll do what I can."

Jim Prescott held him by the elbow in a tight grip.

"Paul, it ought to be some comfort to know that you made her very happy."

He did not remember exactly when Timmy left. After the first death there is no other. That first parting is sharp as a guillotine and afterward one feels nothing. . . .

On another day the rain was slashing at the windowpanes when the telephone rang.

"Paul?"

"Who is this?"

"It's Eleanor."

He should have known her voice but it was sealed off—it came to him through a protective layer that had formed around a scar.

"How are you?" he asked.

"Paul, didn't you get my messages? I wrote as soon as I heard. And I've been calling."

"That's nice of you, Eleanor."

"Paul dear, I can't feel any bitterness to that woman. I only feel sorry for her—and you. I know what a shock it must have been. I can't stand the way you must be feeling at this moment."

"I really would rather not talk about it now."

"Do you want me to come? I can be there if you need me."

"I'll be all right."

"Mother and Natalie send their love. Have you heard from Nancy?"

"No," he said.

Put the genie back into the bottle with the stopper on. That spirit will never be heard from again. In fables a genie will not stay bottled up forever—but fables are kinder than real life.

"I had a short letter some time ago," Eleanor said. "She seems happy with de Brussac. I'm beginning to hope they may be right for each other. Don't you think so?"

"Eleanor, it's hard for me to think straight about things just now."

"It's only natural. I just want you to know that you aren't alone—that there are people who love you."

"Thank you," he said.

492

"There are wonderful times ahead, Paul. You mustn't allow this to break you."

The years break us, Eleanor—nothing else. We are broken and trampled under the tread of a great black wheel. And the wheel rolls on.

"Thank you," he said.

He walked night streets where globes of street lamps made avenues of light.

He was seated on a bench and dark tree branches drooped around him.

He was crossing the street.

"What's the matter with you, mister? Look where you're going. You could've been killed!"

There are so many tags by which a man is identified. Let him be struck by a car and there is no question of who was hit. There are tags representing social security, driver's license, car ownership, surgical-medical plan, private club memberships, insurance, charge accounts, library card, museum membership . . . the number grows until even the poorest of us is no longer anonymous.

"Justice Paul Lincoln Lowe. I thought I recognized you. You had a real close call. I hope you know that."

"It was my fault."

"Okay, next time be careful, Mr. Justice. Lucky I got good brakes. . . ."

Far below the airplane the domed center of Washington moved into a new perspective.

From the picture window he saw the capital city fall behind. In the sunlight the buildings seemed dressed in white and the moving dots were cars and buses.

He pushed the stick forward and suddenly from the level ground the mountains stood out sharp and clear with the sheer wall coated with ice rising on his left and distant summits beyond. There was the narrow canyon with tangled underbrush black in the moonlight and the still blacker shape of the wreckage of his P-38.

So easy to find a place there.

The rest is silence.

—No, Katherine said.

As he pulled slowly back on the aluminum stick the plane leveled off from its steep dive.

—I think I will always know when you are alone, she said.

Before him on the instrument panel the needle swung to indicate he had made the proper correction. Ancient aid to navigation, second oldest after the map, the needle guided him as it had guided the Phoenician sailor. The needle warned of error. Man guessing the currents of his world, guessing wrong, needed to be warned of error.

He strained his eyes eastward and south in a slanting angle against the dazzle of sun. On this summer's day, high in a soundless blue vault of sky, his single engine *thrummed*.

And if there are no answers? he asked. Do I serve a cause if I just survive? Will that introduce order into chaos?

To believe that would be humility on the grand scale—an aggrandizement of self to fill the vacuum. In the scheme of things we are too small to matter. It is so hard to comprehend, this thinking that takes place in an atom, in a particle of energy, in a meaningless flash in a void.

Newton, Descartes, Leibniz, those high priests of the celibate intellect, took off the universe layer by layer. What did they discover that was more than man? More than the mystery of the inviolable soul?

Alone, we pit the supremacy of our will against the authority of evil. Helpless creatures caught in a great tide, we preserve our kind even as the freezing cold of outer space creeps in. Are we a hypothesis or a kind of proof?

What does it matter, as long as we have work to occupy us to the moment of final disaster? Each of us can bring his ant-load to the place where something—we know not what—is being built.

He stirred in his curved metal seat. The leather cushion was creased and made sitting uncomfortable.

Everything we know is in process from one state to another and there is no intrinsic enduring value except the search for what is true.

That was a concluding line from Charles Edmunson's letter of resignation. Edmunson believed in work as a sort of footbridge over catastrophe. Perhaps he was right. Perhaps work is not merely the cross to which we are nailed, but our salvation.

Perhaps.

Below him now was the white magnificence of the Capitol Dome. Beneath the dome there was a hollow immensity where one might climb narrow twisting stairs to a dizzy height to look down at people in the bottom of a huge bowl. Within the ninety-six-foot-wide rotunda the statues of great men stood lonely on their pedestals, deified for having done what they had to do.

Directly before him was the aluminum stick with its corrugated rubber cap. He gripped it, enjoying the contact with reality. The stick obeyed his hand and the rudders responded to the pressure of his feet.

Amid reports of victories in Burma, new riots in Latin America, continuing unrest and continuing boom in the United States, the session of the Supreme Court neared its end. In the last few weeks of the term decisions were rendered on complex questions and fundamental issues took shape in quietly read opinions.

"One of the landmark opinions, Paul. It will be the cornerstone of a great career."

How embarrassed Ken Norris sounded, stroking his scanty blond hair.

"Actually, Ken, I borrowed a good deal from your own arguments."

"I supplied some of the bricks. You built the wall. Charles Edmunson himself couldn't have built it any higher."

Now the wall itself was a barrier between them. Ken Norris admired the achievement and could no longer completely understand the man who had written it. There was this new element of strangeness in their friendship.

Homo sum; humani nil a me alienum est. . . . Terence, how untrue. I am a man and all things human seem alien to me.

We all dwell as separate equal monads in a void where communication has ceased.

There is simply no one I care about.

Suddenly he was seized by a powerful astonishing thought so palpable he could put his hands on it and hold it. There could be communion with a precise other person, equally strange, equally solitary. Katherine had shown him the way. What was needed to make the communion possible was nothing more, but nothing less, than emotion which exalted and made free, which put a finger to lips that asked questions and made the questioner mute and satisfied; at rest. He had to reach out toward someone again—expecting nothing and offering whatever he had to give.

He felt a painful throbbing in his fingers holding the telephone.

"Timmy?"

"Is that you, Daddy?"

The familiar voice forced his spirit to rise from despondency, lightened the burden of all that had aged him. He had been carrying an insupportable load for too long a distance.

"What are you doing, Timmy?"

"I'm watching a Superman cartoon. But it's all right, Daddy. It's one I saw before."

His throat was parched.

"I've missed you, Timmy. Have you missed me?"

"Oh, boy!"

"Would you like to come home? I can hire a woman to look after the house. Would you like to live with me again?"

There was an incredulous crack in the high voice. "*When?*"

"As soon as you can. Are you sure you'd like that, Timmy? Because I'd like it very much."

Timmy was crying a little. "Golly."

"Let me speak to your grandfather."

There were no guarantees. The boy would remind him too much of Katherine. And he could never fill the emptiness for Timmy where she had been. But no one arrives at a destination merely by thinking ahead to it. The only proper end to thinking is in doing.

Hand in hand, they passed the Capitol and the Congressional Library.

"That's it, Timmy. Just beyond the library."

He never saw the white façade of the Supreme Court building without recalling the first day he had mounted those steps between the gigantic stone figures. Now it seemed to open like a great white flower blooming in the daylight—wilting in sudden shadow.

"It's pretty big, isn't it?"

Familiarity had undone none of his own awe; the excitement remained.

"It is pretty big, Timmy."

"There must be a lot of people making laws, huh?"

"I guess there are."

Something in the building's purity of white marble, its delicate strength, spoke out against the nameless formless enemies that threatened all this building stood for. This must be how the Greeks regarded their Acropolis. And on the day the victorious Roman legions marched into the Acropolis, in the long shadow of conquest, they must have experienced this feeling of a splendor beyond the force of arms.

"Can we go inside?" Timmy asked.

"Of course we can."

Timmy's hand clutched his tightly in confiding warmth. They started up the steps together.